JOSEPH ANDREWS

JOSEPH ANDREWS

Henry Fielding

edited by Paul A. Scanlon

broadview literary texts

National Library of Canada cataloguing in publication data

Fielding, Henry, 1707-1754
Joseph Andrews

(Broadview literary texts)
Includes bibliographical references.
ISBN 1-55111-220-5

I. Scanlon, Paul A. II. Title. III. Series.

PR3454.J6 2001 823'.5 C00-933174-3

Broadview Press Ltd., is an independent, international publishing house, incorporated in 1985.

North America:
P.O. Box 1243, Peterborough, Ontario, Canada K9J 7H5
3576 California Road, Orchard Park, NY 14127
TEL: (705) 743-8990; FAX: (705) 743-8353;
E-MAIL: customerservice@broadviewpress.com

United Kingdom:
Turpin Distribution Services Ltd.,
Blackhorse Rd., Letchworth, Hertfordshire SG6 1HN
TEL: (1462) 672555; FAX (1462) 480947; E-MAIL: turpin@rsc.org

Australia:
St. Clair Press, P.O. Box 287, Rozelle, NSW 2039
TEL: (02) 818-1942; FAX: (02) 418-1923

www.broadviewpress.com

Broadview Press gratefully acknowledges the financial support of the Book Publishing Industry Development Program, Ministry of Canadian Heritage, Government of Canada.

Broadview Press is grateful to Professor Eugene Benson for advice on editorial matters for the Broadview Literary Texts series.

Text design and composition by George Kirkpatrick

PRINTED IN CANADA

Gravé d'après Reynolds par Cazenave

Henry Fielding by Cazenave after Reynolds (undated)
(courtesy of the Department of Prints and Drawings, The British Museum)

Contents

Acknowledgements

It is a pleasure to be able to thank those who have, in different ways, helped in the preparation of the present volume. Various colleagues and friends, including Kazuya Okada, Neil McEwan, and John Wilks, have offered valuable advice and of their time. As well, the library staff at Okayama University, Japan, has been of great assistance in providing pertinent material, often from well beyond the physical resources of the university.

Eugene Benson, as both friend and adviser, has given much guidance to the project. And lastly, it is with love and gratitude that I acknowledge the contribution made by my wife Marit, whose patience and active support are inestimable.

Introduction

In various ways, as has been noted by other critics, the history of *Joseph Andrews* begins with the passage of the Licensing Act. From 1730 to the early summer of 1737, when the bill was enacted, Fielding had been pleasing the town and scandalizing the government with his "theatrical entertainments." Much of his satire, commonly in the form of parody or farce, was directed at literary affectation, carrying on (or so he believed) Pope's war on dunces. Booksellers, critics, dramatists, actors, the editors of Shakespeare and the writers of biography—anyone in the literary domain who he thought contributed to its disorder—became fair game. However, "In revealing literary aberration," Irwin rightly remarks, "Fielding could not dissociate the republic of letters from human society as a whole.... The same laws govern both and the same privileges and obligations obtain in both."[1] Accordingly, polite society as well was often Fielding's target; and with his return to the Little Theatre in the Haymarket in 1736, Sir Robert Walpole and his government became the primary object of his scathing satire. Over the following year came a flurry of "irregular" plays, including *Pasquin* and *The Historical Register for the Year 1736*. They were tumultuously acclaimed, but eventually succeeded in bringing Fielding's stage career to a fairly abrupt end. Clearly there were a number of factors involved which led to the Theatrical Licensing Act of 1737, including a series of playhouse riots by footmen which occurred in the spring of the same year. But Fielding's portrayal in *The Historical Register* of Walpole as the fiddler Quidam, bribing the Patriots (the opposition party) who danced to his tune, finally spurred the government into action. It was, in fact, precisely the opportunity Walpole wanted: a play which would cause Parliament to place the theatres under restraint. This Act, which was Parliament's last piece of business of the spring session, not only limited the number of theatres to those with official patents, but also required all new plays to be

1 W.R. Irwin, "Satire and Comedy in the Works of Henry Fielding," *ELH* 13 (1946): 170.

licensed by the Lord Chamberlain. Fielding's "scandal-shop," as Eliza Haywood termed it, was now shut down.[1]

Indeed, with the closing of the Little Theatre on 24 June, Fielding was forced to seek a living elsewhere in order to support his wife and young family. Deprived of the lucrative business of writing for the stage he now suddenly found himself in considerable financial difficulty, a condition which only worsened over the following years. Casting about for work and a new direction, he entered the Middle Temple in November and applied himself with such energy and determination that by June 1740 he was called to the bar. But despite certain helpful family connections and his diligence as a barrister in assize courts, travelling the Western Circuit (Cornwall, Devon, Somerset, Dorset, and Hampshire), he had few briefs and little in the way of profit.

In order to supplement his income both during the period of his law studies and then afterwards as a member of the profession, Fielding resumed his labours in greater earnest as a Grub Street hack-writer, especially toiling on behalf of the Patriot cause. In *The Champion*, a newspaper launched in November 1739 in collaboration with James Ralph, he planned to write almost exclusively on social and literary topics, only to realize (particularly through decreasing sales figures) the public's insatiable interest in politics. Moreover, over the same terrible winter, somewhat reminiscent of Mr. Wilson's plight in *Joseph Andrews*, he agreed to translate from French the three-volume *Military History of Charles XII. King of Sweden*. Nothing, however, seemed to interrupt the steady decline of Fielding's fortunes, and in late 1740 his creditors gathered. Unable to meet their demands, he was eventually detained in a sponging-house, only a step away from debtor's prison. While there, during the fortnight before he was released on bail, drawing together many of the themes from *The Champion* and dramatic features of his plays, he wrote *An Apology for the Life of Mrs. Shamela Andrews*.

Three books in particular, all of them published within the previous year, prompted Fielding to write this work. He thought Conyers Middleton's *The History of the Life of Marcus*

1 See Jenny Uglow, *Henry Fielding* (Plymouth, UK: Northcote House, 1995) 15.

Tullius Cicero (February 1741) was simply awful and its obsequious Dedication to the effeminate Lord Hervey, minion of Walpole, outrageously funny. He was also amused and irritated by the self-congratulatory autobiography of the Poet Laureate, *An Apology for the Life of Mr. Colley Cibber, Comedian, and Late Patentee of the Theatre-Royal. Written by Himself* (April 1740). But it was Samuel Richardson's *Pamela: or, Virtue Rewarded* that especially irked him.[1] Published on 6 November, it was an immediate sensation, with five authoritative editions being called for in under twelve months. No book in English had ever received such an enthusiastic reception as this fictional account of the beleaguered maid servant. The clergy, the literary establishment, the general reading public—all were enthralled by the "virtue," courage and triumph of Richardson's young heroine. Accordingly, what Fielding endeavoured to do in his brilliant little parody, beyond having a good joke, was to expose the fundamental falseness of *Pamela*, ridiculing both its spirit and its method. That is to say, he saw it as an example of bad morality and bad writing, and hoped (in the approved tradition of Pope) to laugh the public into good sense. As one would expect, however, *Shamela* met with mixed success, although enough to warrant a second edition later in the year. Yet "From our vantage point two and a half centuries later," reflects Battestin, "this little book marked a turning point in the development of the modern novel: for as Fielding's initial response to Richardson's *Pamela: or, Virtue Rewarded*, it prepared the way for *Joseph Andrews* and that rival tradition of comic fiction evolving through Smollett to Thackeray and Dickens."[2]

* * *

Interestingly, Fielding never acknowledged authoring *Shamela*, though it was immediately recognized as his. Nor in dashing it off did he know who had written *Pamela*. With its appearance, nevertheless, two things can be said with almost equal cer-

1 See Appendix B for excerpts from both *Pamela* and *Shamela*.

2 Martin C. Battestin with Ruthe R. Battestin, *Henry Fielding: A Life* (London: Routledge, 1989) 302.

tainty: while *Shamela* earned him the lifelong enmity of Richardson, he profited little from it in financial terms. But whatever the sum, as the year 1741 drew to a close, with the death of his father in the summer and the first signs of his own health failing, he and his family were on the brink of calamity. In the Preface to *Miscellanies* (1743), Fielding was to recall these grim times:

> Indeed when I look a year or two backwards, and survey the accidents which have befallen me, and the distresses I have waded through whilst I have been engaged in these works, I could almost challenge some philosophy to myself, for having been able to finish them as I have …
>
> … While I was last winter [i.e., 1741-42] laid up in the gout, with a favourite child dying in one bed, and my wife in a condition very little better, on another, attended with other circumstances, which served as very proper decorations to such a scene …

Yet it was during these months, roughly between September and December 1741, that most of *Joseph Andrews* was written. Certain internal evidence strongly suggests that Fielding was no more than halfway through the novel by late autumn. Moreover, he interrupted his work in early December in order to write an extraordinary political pamphlet, *The Opposition: A Vision*, in which he flays his former Patriot friends and lauds Walpole, whom he had until then regularly denounced for bribery and corruption. At any rate, sometime before the end of the year the manuscript was in the hands of the bookseller Andrew Millar, who published the work anonymously in two volumes on 22 February 1742.[1] Particularly when one bears in mind the terrible conditions under which Fielding laboured during these months, *Joseph Andrews* stands as a testament to his irrepressible humour and the "philosophical" temper to which he repeatedly makes reference in his writings.

If *Shamela* provides a parodic antidote to Richardson's epis-

---

1 For further details, see Appendix E.

tolary romance, *Joseph Andrews* offers an alternative approach to both life and art. In its Preface, most probably composed upon completing the narrative, Fielding endeavours to explain himself to "the mere English reader."[1] Surprisingly enough, however, after all the subsequent years of criticism and commentary, there is still considerable disagreement over some of the most fundamental issues discussed here. This is partly due, it must be said, to Fielding's use of key literary terminology, which is not always consistent and sometimes differs from contemporary meaning. Moreover, in establishing principles governing a "species of writing ... hitherto unattempted in our language" based on a variety of literary theories, a certain incoherence is almost bound to occur.

Fielding begins the Preface by stating that the "reader may have a different idea of romance with the author of these little volumes." His work, he affirms, is to be "a comic romance," which is the same as "a comic epic-poem in prose." Furthermore, he wants it clearly understood that his new genre is not in any way to be connected with the immense French prose romances of the previous century, composed by such figures as Madeleine de Scudéry and Honoré d'Urfé, about which he says later in *Joseph Andrews*, "without any assistance from nature or history, record persons who never were, or will be, and facts which never did nor possibly can happen" (III, 1). And finally, along with these older works in translation, Fielding dissociates himself from "the modern novel and *Atalantis* writers" (III, 1), all of which formed an important part of popular contemporary reading. In fact, if we are to believe Francis Coventry, in his *Essay* of 1751, such foreign imports and English imitations had at the time "overflow'd the Press."

> Nothing was receiv'd with any kind of Applause, that did not appear under the Title of a Romance, or Novel; and

1 All quotations from *Joseph Andrews* are according to the present edition. Those without further information, cited parenthetically in the text, are from the Preface. Other references to Fielding's writings are from *The Complete works of Henry Fielding, Esq.*, ed. William Ernest Henley, 16 vols. (1903; New York: Barnes and Noble, 1967).

> Common Sense was kick'd out of Doors to make Room for marvellous Dullness. The Stile in all these Performances was to be equal to the Subject—amazing: And may be call'd with great Propriety, "Prose run mad."[1]

Consequently, Fielding in his Preface and elsewhere was attempting to distinguish his new species of writing not only from "those voluminous works commonly called romances" but from all such "amazing" fiction. This, however, begs the question: if the term romance carried such implications, what was Fielding's different understanding of it? Quite certainly he was using both terms, romance and epic, in the broader, generic sense, as can be found in Samuel Johnson's *Dictionary* (1755)—that is, as extended narrative. Hence he is able to conclude that "a comic romance is a comic epic-poem in prose," the former being traditionally in prose and the latter in verse.

Nevertheless, while it was important for Fielding to distance himself from various kinds of prose narrative which contained "very little instruction or entertainment," he did not seriously intend to compose a modern *Odyssey* or *Aeneid* in comic terms, as is sometimes argued. Nor is there any indication his contemporary readers understood that he had done so. It was not of course that he was unfamiliar with the more specific meaning of the term epic, which was then in usage; but in referring to Aristotle and Homer in the opening paragraphs of the Preface, and to the lost *Margites*, he was attempting little more than to give his work, as one critic puts it, "a literary pedigree,"[2] just as the French writers of heroic romance had done before him. Such classical references, Baker confirms, "ally him with great literature and serious purpose: they form a large category of extended narrative literature in which he is placing his 'Idea of Romance' ..."[3] On several other occasions,

1 "An Essay on the New Species of Writing founded by Mr. Fielding." For further details, see Appendix F, pp. 515-16.

2 Homer Goldberg, "Comic Prose Epic or Comic Romance: The Argument of the Preface to *Joseph Andrews*," *Philological Quarterly* 43 (1964): 198.

3 Sheridan Baker, "Fielding's Comic Epic-in-Prose Romances Again," *Philological Quarterly* 58 (1979): 64.

it is true, Fielding briefly took up the same basic ideas, but it was only to leave them again in much the same condition as he had found them.

This is not to imply that Fielding's debt to various classical writers is insignificant. In like manner, however, we find him acknowledging his literary obligations to Ben Jonson, Samuel Butler, Jonathan Swift, and Alexander Pope, all of whom in different ways greatly contributed to his writing. The point is that, with *Joseph Andrews* (as with his other novels), he was attempting something quite new in English, which is reflected in his choice of subtitle: "Written in Imitation of the Manner of Cervantes, Author of Don Quixote." It was this Spanish novel of the early seventeenth century, along with other related Continental works of the past and present, that particularly inspired Fielding and provided him with new narrative material and techniques and, perhaps above all, a sympathetic "comic" vision of life. While separating himself from the heroic romances and modern novels in the early pages of the third book of *Joseph Andrews*, he praises Cervantes and aligns himself with such fiction as Scarron's *Le Roman comique* (the source of the "comic romance" term), Le Sage's *Gil Blas* and Marivaux's *Le Paysan parvenu*. "The epic had been done," states Baker. Rather, his aim was to make "Cervantic comedy out of realism and romance in native English terms."[1]

* * *

In reading through the Preface, therefore, it is not surprising to discover that Fielding devoted most of it to clarifying and expounding on the term comic, which lies at the very heart of his argument. Largely derived from Aristotelian literary principles, he begins by distinguishing between comic narrative (whether epic or romance) and comic drama, emphasizing the varied and comprehensive nature of the former; then he contrasts the main elements of comic and serious narrative, the comic exhibiting features of both the "low" and the ludicrous.

---

1 Baker 68.

> Now a comic romance is a comic epic-poem in prose; differing from comedy, as the serious epic from tragedy: its action being more extended and comprehensive; containing a much larger circle of incidents, and introducing a greater variety of characters. It differs from the serious romance in its fable and action [i.e., plot], in this; that as in the one these are grave and solemn, so in the other they are light and ridiculous: it differs in its characters, by introducing persons of inferiour rank, and consequently of inferiour manners, whereas the grave romance, sets the highest before us; lastly in its sentiments and diction, by preserving the ludicrous instead of the sublime.

Having thus set forth the nature of the major elements of his comic romance, again in conformity with classical thinking, Fielding turns his attention to its moral function through satire, or what he calls "the true ridiculous," whose source is to be found in affectation as manifested in vanity and hypocrisy. "Great vices," he states, "are the proper objects of our detestation, smaller faults of our pity: but affectation appears to me the only true source of the ridiculous." While vanity is more "of the nature of ostentation," hypocrisy is the opposite of what it pretends to be, and hence is of the character of villainy. He admits there is sometimes difficulty in distinguishing between them; yet as their motivation is quite distinct, they express themselves in equally different ways. Finally in this regard, in an attempt to forestall the charge that "great vices" have been introduced into the work, his answer is that they are not of a primary nature, rather the objects of detestation than of ridicule, and in any event are unavoidable.

Thus Fielding is able to say that "From the discovery of this affectation arises the ridiculous—which always strikes the reader with surprize and pleasure; and that in a higher and stronger degree when the affectation arises from hypocrisy, than when from vanity." Rather than developing a series of actions leading to suspense, that is, Fielding more often relies upon the unexpected, closely linking the level of surprise and pleasure with that of the ridiculous. This, observes Battestin, is the other part of his theory of comedy, "the doctrine of 'the Benefit of Laughing,'"[1] offering a comic (as opposed to Aristotle's tragic) *catharsis* as one of the form's primary functions. Although this doctrine receives relatively little attention in the pages of the Preface in relation to his remarks on comedy, it is surely borne out by the great wit and humour apparent throughout the narrative itself.

It is interesting to note, though, that while Fielding goes to considerable lengths to exclude burlesque from his theory of comedy, admitting it only occasionally in the diction of his comic romance, he praises its ability to raise simple laughter, with all of its beneficial effects.

> ... it [i.e., burlesque] contributes more to exquisite mirth and laughter than any other; and these are probably more wholesome physic for the mind, and conduce better to purge away spleen, melancholy and ill affections, than is generally imagined. Nay, I will appeal to common observation, whether the same companies are not found more full of good-humour and benevolence, after they have been sweeten'd for two or three hours with entertainments of this kind, than when soured by a tragedy or a grave lecture.

Yet for all that, he agrees with Lord Shaftesbury's claims to have found no such writing among the ancients. Indeed, Fielding goes so far as to say that comedy and burlesque are not only entirely different species but polar opposites,

> for as the latter is ever the exhibition of what is monstrous and unnatural, and where our delight, if we examine it, arises from the surprizing absurdity, as in appropriating the manners of the highest to the lowest, or *è converso*; so in the former, we should ever confine ourselves strictly to nature from the just imitation of which, will

1 Battestin 328.

> flow all the pleasure we can this way convey to a sensible reader.

The distinction here is somewhat reminiscent of the one which Addison had made in the *Spectator*. But while *Don Quixote*, *Hudibras*, and Lucian are cited there as examples of burlesque, Fielding claims that the first two are of the comic kind. Scarron's *Le Roman comique*, as well, was almost certainly a work which he thought was sometimes mistakenly categorized. What becomes increasingly obvious is that, in placing *Joseph Andrews* within the classical literary canon, Fielding felt obliged not only to distance himself from popular fiction but also from the contemporary stage, where he admits to having "had some little success." Hence with an eye to a readership somewhat more literate than the audiences of the Little Theatre, Fielding is at pains in the Preface to clarify his position in relation to burlesque, banishing it (other than in diction) from his new literary species. Nonetheless, his backward glance (above) is telling, and his warm words of tribute to the form are perhaps just as apt in describing the comic genre. Lastly, as he himself surely realized, it was more easily said in establishing the literary principles than in actually making the work. For much of Fielding's satire, like that of Lucian and Swift, is of the Menippean tradition, portraying a world of sharp contrasts and inversions, one in which such polarities as mirth and gravity, high and low, sublimity and dullness are confused and finally fused. While strongly supporting the social order, with its squires and parsons and attorneys as the only conceivable state of things, he was also aware of the brutal realities of life. As he writes in "An Essay on the Knowledge of the Characters of Men,"

> Thus while the crafty and designing part of mankind, consulting only their own separate advantage, endeavour to maintain one constant imposition on others, the whole world becomes a vast masquerade, where the greatest part appear disguised under false vizors and habits; a very few

only showing their own faces, who become, by so doing, the astonishment and ridicule of all the rest.[1]

* * *

The reversal of expectations, therefore, of both readers and characters, becomes a basic tactic in *Joseph Andrews*, beginning with the inversion of *Pamela*.[2] Instead of Mr. B—'s assault on Pamela's virtue at one or other of his country estates, it is her brother Joseph who is threatened by Lady Booby upon moving to her London residence. Pamela is virtually a prisoner during most of the struggle, which results in her conquering and reforming the master, while Joseph and Fanny confront and overcome many obstacles together as they journey homewards along the western road. And in the end each weds according to his or her principles, the sister gaining a high marriage (and social position) and the brother choosing a "low" one to Fanny.

In this important way, Fielding was able to move well beyond the stricter form of *Shamela's* parody, which is largely dependent upon the host for its existence. Whether he was fully aware of his overall intentions at the onset of the work is questionable, especially in light of his initial treatment of Joseph and his virtue. But once the titular hero sets out from London in search of Fanny, a new thematic course is clearly struck. And then with the introduction of Parson Adams soon after, towards the end of Book I, the parodic comedy of *Pamela* soon gives way to a world in which different forms of idealism conflict with bruising reality.

Joseph's first serious encounter, before joining up with Parson Adams and Fanny, takes place on the very night he is dismissed from Lady Booby's service. Alone on the road, he is suddenly attacked by two highwaymen who, after robbing and beating him, leave him for dead. A little later a stagecoach passes along; but once Joseph's plight is understood, all but the lowly postillion ("a lad who hath been since transported for

---

1 This quotation is part of a longer passage in Appendix D, pp. 494-97.

2 See Uglow 35.

robbing a hen-roost") urge the coachman to hurry by. Based on the biblical parable of the Good Samaritan, it is not the vicious assault on Joseph which is central to the story but the different responses of the people involved. Collectively, they are meant to offer a microcosm of contemporary society.

> The postillion hearing a man's groans, stopt his horses, and told the coachman, "he was certain there was a *dead* man lying in the ditch, for he heard him groan." "Go on, sirrah," says the coachman, "we are confounded late, and have no time to look after dead men." A lady, who heard what the postillion said, and likewise heard the groan, called eagerly to the coachman, "to stop and see what was the matter." Upon which he bid the postillion "alight, and look into the ditch." He did so, and returned, "that there was a man sitting upright as naked as ever he was born."—"O *J-sus*," cry'd the lady, "A naked man! Dear coachman, drive on and leave him." Upon this the gentlemen got out of the coach; and Joseph begged them, "to have mercy upon him: for that he had been robbed, and almost beaten to death." "Robbed," cries an old gentleman; "let us make all the haste imaginable, or we shall be robbed too." (I, 12)

This scene, with its strong moral implications, recurs in various forms and from different perspectives throughout the narrative, and serves as an introduction for the reader as to what is to follow.

With the appearance of Parson Adams, however, on his way to London to sell his sermons, the focus of the story largely shifts from Joseph to him. And as it does, the parodic spirit in the next two books becomes essentially of the Quixotic kind, with the clerical knight errant, accompanied by the two lovers, jousting valiantly in the pragmatic world. As these figures journey back to Booby-Hall, and so to their home, they are tested in different ways by the people whom they meet, whether in inns or coaches, or on open grasslands or country estates. While Joseph and Fanny preserve their chastity against all odds, and Parson Adams unfailingly offers universal kindness and friendship, other qualities including courage, love and loyalty are also proven. But it is particularly the active virtue of charity, as embodied in Adams, which lies at the moral centre of the work. Certainly other views besides his are voiced on the subject, such as the one of Mrs. Tow-wouse, the boisterous innkeeper's wife: "'Common charity, a f—t!' says she, 'common charity teaches us to provide for ourselves, and our families'" (I, 12). Nor does Peter Pounce, Lady Booby's steward, much like the word, finding that it has "a mean parsonlike quality" (III, 13). But in Adams' quick rebuttal, Fielding's own understanding of the term is undoubtedly expressed: "'Sir,'" says he, "'my definition of charity is a generous disposition to relieve the distressed.'" This doctrine of benevolence, which is referred to throughout as "good-nature," forms the cornerstone of Fielding's moral and religious thought and is seen by Battestin as "in all respects consonant with the Low Church latitudinarianism of the day."[1]

As the unlikely trio make their way home, however, with scant means of providing for their food or lodging, they are forced in turn to seek the charity of those around them. Quite unashamedly, after confessing to his impecunious condition, Adams invariably approaches his host for a loan, believing that it is better to give than receive. With this conviction firmly in mind, he visits the clergyman Trulliber and, after a cup of ale and some breakfast, and due discussion on "the dignity of the cloth," attempts to borrow fourteen shillings from him, concluding that it will be returned, "but if not, I am convinced you will joyfully embrace such an opportunity of laying up a treasure in a better place than any this world affords" (II, 14). Trulliber's response, although more vociferous and threatening than most, simply confirms the general impression of mankind gained from Joseph's earlier experience in the episode of the highwaymen.

Along with the dramatization of kindness, benevolence, good nature (call it what you will), therefore, the ridicule of

---

1 Battestin 332. For further information, see Appendix A, pp. 426-27.

affectation in its different forms is a major concern of *Joseph Andrews*. But the real triumph of the work, it should be remembered, is owing to its rich and sympathetic humour. The comic spirit here is a genial and sociable one, quite capable of overcoming much of the awfulness of life. The behaviour of Lady Booby and the Trullibers, Slipslop (that "mighty affecter of hard words") and the parsimonious Pounce, are all subjected to Fielding's wit and irony, leaving no doubt as to the seriousness of their social and moral offences. And yet as we judge them, we cannot help but share his surprise at and delight in this comedy of mankind.

* * *

It is the Cervantic incidents of *Joseph Andrews*, then, especially in the central books, which carry much of the satire and humour, with Adams rescuing damsels and assaulting inns, crabstick in hand. Idealistic, learned, ignorant of the world and yet fearless of it, he is both the English version of the Spanish don and, as indicated by his name, the primal fallen man in God's image. However, if Adams serves as the centre of the Cervantic mode, Joseph is not only the clerical knight's Sancho Panza but also the hero of the romantic plot. With the revelation of Joseph's love for Fanny, just as he is about to set out from London late in Book I, idealistic love is introduced into the narrative. And with it, Fielding's attitude to Joseph's chastity essentially changes from the parodic to the sympathetic, which now begins to take on far greater significance. Following one of his encounters with Lady Booby in her bedchamber not long before his departure, Joseph writes to Pamela of the incident and of Adams' teaching on the subject, which stresses that chastity before marriage "is as great a virtue in a man as in a woman" (I, 10). This principle, however, becomes less abstract as he journeys homeward with Fanny, marriage now being the primary goal and integrally a part of his relationship with her. It is also much in keeping with the romance tradition, beginning with such ancient pastoral stories as Longus' *Daphnis and Chloe*. So too is the similarity in appearance of the young couple, almost like twin foundlings, with the male in particular sharing features of feminine beauty with his beloved. This is the image of Joseph as he appeared before Lady Booby in the previous scene.

> Mr. Joseph Andrews was now in the one and twentieth year of his age. He was of the highest degree of middle stature. His limbs were put together with great elegance and no less strength. His legs and thighs were formed in the exactest proportion.... His hair was of a nut-brown colour, and was displayed in wanton ringlets down his back. His forehead was high, his eyes dark, and as full of sweetness as of fire. His nose a little inclined to the Roman. His teeth white and even. His lips full, red, and soft. (I, 8)

Many other elements of romance, in addition, which would have been familiar to the contemporary reader, begin to appear and give greater shape to the story as they merge with the more open Cervantic structure. The abrupt separations and surprising reunions of the couple, abductions and battles, passionate and introspective soliloquies, amorous poems and courtly rhetoric—even the employment of interpolated tales—are all part and parcel of the extended tradition of romance. Finally in Book IV, as the relevant characters of the story converge on Booby-Hall, the different strands of the work are brought together in a grand ensemble scene worthy of Heliodorus himself, the reputed master of Greek romance. Through accident or design, birthmarks are produced, secrets uncovered, identities revealed, and families and lovers reunited, all to the great amazement of participants and onlookers alike, permitting marriage to follow and general peace and happiness to reign.

Moreover, with the arrival at Booby-Hall of Pamela and her husband, whose nuptials are still virtually unknown to the gathering, Fielding returns to the parody of the first book with renewed vigour and wit, leaving it largely up to the couple themselves to reveal their various frailties. Upon learning of

Joseph's impending marriage, Pamela takes the first opportunity to chide Fanny "for her assurance, in aiming at such a match as her brother" (IV, 11). She also speaks in a similar vein to Joseph, with the full support of her husband, when he professes his love for Fanny.

> "... It would become you better, brother, to pray for the assistance of grace against such a passion, than to indulge it."—"Sure, sister, you are not in earnest; I am sure she is your equal at least."—"She was my equal," answered Pamela, "but I am no longer Pamela Andrews, I am now this gentleman's lady, and as such am above her—I hope I shall never behave with an unbecoming pride; but at the same time I shall endeavour to know myself, and question not the assistance of grace to that purpose." (IV, 7)

In the end, however, once it is understood that the two young women are sisters, Mr. Booby "saluted Fanny, called her sister, and introduced her as such to Pamela, who behaved with great decency on the occasion" (IV, 16). In Fanny's presence, with her gentle modesty and natural beauty, Pamela's affectations are all the more glaring, and serve as a foil to the former's virtues throughout the final book. Sisters by birth they may be, but just as Fanny and Joseph are naturally paired, the true sisters of Pamela are to be found in Lady Booby and the indomitable Slipslop.

Similar to the Pamela part of the narrative, the Cervantic comedy here becomes more vivid and direct, with various humorous and satirical features brought into greater prominence as the characters continue to assemble at Booby-Hall. Certainly Lady Booby is seen in a much more ruthless light from the moment she rides in coach and six into her parish, having impoverished many of its inhabitants through her absence. Her contempt for Adams and his clerical responsibilities soon becomes evident as she seeks to prevent the marriage banns between Joseph and Fanny from being published. As well, she tramples on civil law in her attempt to have Fanny removed from the parish, using privilege and power to accomplish her ends. Accordingly, she employs the services of Lawyer Scout, who tells her that he will do his utmost "to prevent the law's taking effect" (IV, 3); and the local justice of the peace, a squire and neighbour, confides in Mr. Booby that he would have been more lenient in his judgment but for the wishes of his aunt. Even in the countryside, therefore, where Mr. Wilson and his family—and later Joseph and Fanny—are able to find happiness and contentment, ignorance, greed, and cruelty would seem to prevail, the poor being systematically stripped of their rights and livelihood by those in positions of authority. Fielding's social satire is probably at its most indignant here, at times employing elements of the absurd in order to gain greater effect. "'Jesu!' said the squire," upon reading Lawyer Scout's deposition against Joseph and Fanny, "'would you commit two persons to Bridewell for a twig?' 'Yes,' said the lawyer, 'and with great lenity too; for if we had called it a young tree they would have been both hanged'" (IV, 5).

Nevertheless, in this world of social corruption, class snobbery and self-interest, noble acts are done and principles of virtue upheld. And always accompanying this comic ridicule, even at its severest, is Fielding's great good humour, which allows the reader to enjoy the characters while at the same time censoring them. The scheming between Lady Booby and Slipslop to bring about Joseph's and Fanny's separation is reminiscent of several scenes in the first book, as the two continue to spar with each other over a number of social and moral issues; but there is now a greater sense of urgency about the matter at hand, and with it a heightened passion and rhetoric. Of a decidedly different nature is the comedy of errors resulting from Adams' gallant attempt while at Booby-Hall to rescue yet another damsel in distress. This time, though, there is some confusion concerning the sex of the person requiring assistance, which leads to one of the most uproarious sequences in the novel. The mistake begins when Beau Didapper enters Slipslop's bedchamber, believing it to be Fanny's, provoking screams for help from the one and abject whimpering from the other.

> ... Parson Adams ... jumped out of bed, and without staying to put a rag of clothes on, hastened into the apartment whence the cries proceeded. He made directly to the bed in the dark, where laying hold of the beau's skin (for Slipslop had torn his shirt almost off) and finding his skin extremely soft, and hearing him in a low voice begging Slipslop to let him go, he no longer doubted but this was the young woman in danger of ravishing, and immediately falling on the bed, and laying hold on Slipslop's chin, where he found a rough beard, his belief was confirmed; he therefore rescued the beau, who presently made his escape, and then turning towards Slipslop, receiv'd such a cuff on his chops, that his wrath kindling immediately ... (IV, 14)

Much of the farce here has been transported from Fielding's earlier stage career; but with Adams and Slipslop pummelling each other in the dark, unaware of the other's identity, we are back once again in the inn with Don Quixote and the mule carrier.

* * *

The grand ensemble scene, therefore, prepared for as far back as the pedlar's appearance late in Book II, resolves the plot and restores a sense of social and moral order and well being. But lying behind this wonderfully orchestrated comic-romance conclusion are many unanswered questions related to the work as a whole. In the end Providence quite firmly rules, but along the way numerous incidents would appear to happen by chance or accident, including the surprise meeting of Joseph and Adams at the inn early in the journey and Adams' rescue of Fanny in the woods a while later. It might be argued that such coincidences are little more than romance conventions, or that Fortune lies within the larger framework of Providence. Undoubtedly Adams would agree with the latter view, telling Joseph in his misery at Fanny's abduction "that no accident happens to us without the Divine permission" (III, 11). And yet in his autobiographical account, Mr. Wilson, whose moral authority in the novel is considerable, speaks of his lottery prize as "a trick of Fortune" and himself as "one whom Fortune could not save, if she would" (III, 3).

Such conflicting attitudes as this, then, are not uncommon in *Joseph Andrews* and in fact reflect a basic feature of the work. Fielding's presentation of women, for example, contains certain stereotypical views of the day while at the same time challenging a good number of them. Generally speaking, the female sex is either attacked as women or praised as women in a way that does not happen with the male characters. While Mrs. Towwouse is witchlike in appearance and Slipslop's ugliness is in part dependent upon her deformed breasts, Fanny is perceived as the embodiment of rustic feminine beauty and modesty. Moreover, in explaining why Lady Booby "loved" Joseph long before she knew it, Fielding takes the opportunity to outline the instruction given by mothers to their daughters regarding "the master," which is essentially an education in deception. It is in sharp contrast to the training received by the Wilson girls, whose mother inculcates in them her own moral and domestic virtues. In this she is strongly supported by her husband, who describes to Adams his most unusual relationship with his family.

> ... for I am neither ashamed of conversing with my wife, nor of playing with my children: to say the truth, I do not perceive that inferiority of understanding which the levity of rakes, the dulness of men of business, or the austerity of the learned would persuade us of in women. As for my woman, I declare I have found none of my own sex capable of making juster observations on life, or of delivering them more agreeably; nor do I believe any one possessed of a faithfuller or braver friend. (III, 4)

Sometimes as here, the real and ideal are set in some kind of juxtaposition. But in other instances, with Adams often serving as catalyst, current ideas and issues spark much argument and debate. Trulliber and Adams end up almost at blows over the question of faith versus good works; the innkeeper and Adams (again) violently disagree on the relative merits of reading and actual experience in the attainment of knowledge; and the poet and player, in agreement at first, fall out over matters relating to the stage. One of the most notable points of dispute concerns education, specifically educational theory and character development. In reviewing the background of the characters in the novel, it is apparent that they have been raised in very different ways, from the illiterate Fanny to the learned Parson Adams. While Joseph (rather incongruously) argues in favour of public schools, Adams supports private education; Leonora's aunt, in "The Unfortunate Jilt," prefers "a fine gentleman" to "a sneaking fellow, who hath been bred at a university" (II, 4); and the "roasting" squire's mother sends her son on the traditional Grand Tour in order to round out his dismal home education. One of Mr. Wilson's main regrets, in reflecting upon his wasted youth, is that he did not have a proper guide, a point already stressed in regard to Leonora's sad fate. Other than for this, Kropf insists, "The novel demonstrates that no theory of education, no matter how finely argued, is worth anything more than the quality of the results it produces." Furthermore, he concludes, "In this sense, educational theory receives the same treatment accorded the other major ideas of the novel. The poet may have all his dramatic theories in order, but it is the player who must face the audience."[1]

One of the key roles of the narrator, in fact, is to give greater order and coherence to such clashes and contradictions as these. Rather than referring to the work as "a comic romance" or "comic epic-poem in prose," as appears in the Preface, the terms biography or history are now regularly used, emphasizing the essential truth of the fiction. "I have writ little more than I have seen," he declares at the beginning of Book III, occasionally reminding the reader that he is actually a participant of sorts in this ongoing tale. But it is not this feature of his narrative so much as its universality that is the real issue here.

---

1 C.R. Kropf, "Educational Theory and Human Nature in Fielding's Works," *PMLA* 89 (1974): 116.

> The lawyer is not only alive, but hath been so these 4000 years.... He hath not indeed confined himself to one profession, one religion, or one country; but when the first mean selfish creature appeared on the human stage ... then was our lawyer born; and whilst such a person as I have described, exists on earth, so long shall he remain upon it. (III, 1)

It is a "true history," therefore, in quite different senses of the word, and we are invited to participate in it, as a shared experience with the story-teller, in these different ways. The nature of this narrative transaction is made more explicit at the beginning of Book II through the coaching metaphor, a favourite of Fielding in the past and one that he further developed in *Tom Jones*. The reader here is seen as a passenger on a stagecoach (in *Tom Jones* engaged in conversation with the narrating voice), stopping along the way at various inns much as readers might do between chapters and books, and taking into account the gate inscriptions as one would the books' chapter headings. This of course means that our attention must be not only on the narrative itself but also on the self-conscious narrator, who as Booth points out, "intrudes into his novel to comment on himself as a writer, and on his book, not simply as a series of events with moral implications, but as a created literary product."[1]

It is in such ways that the narrator is able to establish his authority over the work—and in a sense over the reader as well. At one moment he confides in us that certain relevant information is simply unobtainable, then in the next he is tweaking us for our ignorance of country matters or limited knowledge of Latin. More often his role is to transport us from one incident to another, guiding our feelings and moral judgment, and serving as ringmaster for his multitude of characters, who come and go with great regularity. Usually his tone is at once good-humoured and ironic, but he is quite capable of suddenly shifting register, sometimes mainly for comic effect

---

1 Wayne C. Booth, "The Self-Conscious Narrator in Comic Fiction Before *Tristram Shandy*," *PMLA* 67 (1952): 165.

(e.g., assuming the mock-heroic style) and at other times for satiric purposes, as he does in order to ridicule the ignorance and corruption of Lawyer Scout and all his breed. "They are the pests of society, and a scandal to a profession, to which indeed they do not belong; and which owes to such kind of rascallions the ill-will which weak persons bear towards it" (IV, 3). Unmistakably, the mask has slipped here, if only for a moment, and we hear the author's own voice speaking to us.

To suggest, though, that all the conflicting and discordant elements in *Joseph Andrews* have in some way or another been largely reconciled is to miss a most important point. With the dual qualities of selfishness and selflessness forming the novel's moral polarities, a lively panorama of mid-Georgian England is played out against a backdrop more timeless in nature, presented by a narrator who is at once sympathetic and ironically ambivalent. It is this satiric debate, presided over with great wit and gusto—and perhaps above all, a tolerant understanding of the human condition—that is one of Fielding's most remarkable accomplishments in this, his first masterpiece of comic fiction.

Henry Fielding: A Brief Chronology

1707 April 22: Henry Fielding born at Sharpham Park, near Glastonbury, Somerset, son of Colonel Edmund Fielding and Sarah Fielding (née Gould).

1709-19 Boyhood spent on farm at East Stour, Dorset (his mother dies in 1718).

1719-24 Attends Eton College, a public school for boys (his father remarries in early 1719).

1724-28 Man-about-London.

1728 30 January: his first work published, *The Masquerade*, a satiric poem.
16 February: his first play, *Love in Several Masques*, performed at Drury Lane.
16 March: registers as student of literature, University of Leyden, Holland.

1729 By the end of April, discontinues his studies at Leyden and returns to London.

1730-37 Career as a dramatist, writing popular comedies and burlesques including *The Author's Farce* (1730), *Tom Thumb* (1730), *Rape Upon Rape* (1730), *The Lottery* (1732), *The Modern Husband* (1732), *The Miser* (1733), *Don Quixote in England* (1734), *Pasquin* (1736), *The Historical Register for the Year 1736* (1737).

1734 28 November: elopes with and marries Charlotte Cradock.

1735 Spends several months at East Stour, Dorset.

1736 27 April: their first child, Charlotte, is born. As the year advances, he more actively supports the Opposition against Sir Robert Walpole and his government.

1737 21 June: the Theatrical Licensing Act is passed, ending his career as a playwright.
1 November: admitted as a student of law at the Middle Temple, London.

1739 15 November (- June 1741): edits *The Champion*, a social and cultural journal supporting the Opposition (ends writing for it probably sometime in December 1740).

1740 20 June: called to the bar at the Middle Temple.

1741 2 April: *Shamela* published.
Death of his father, buried 25 June.
15 December: *The Opposition* published, satirizing his former party and praising Walpole.

1741-42 Only son of first marriage, Henry, is born (exact date unknown).

1742 22 February: *Joseph Andrews* published.
Death of daughter Charlotte, buried 9 March.

1743 7 April: *Miscellanies* published, including *A Journey from This World to the Next* and *Jonathan Wild*, together with poems, essays, and two plays.
Second daughter, Henrietta ("Harriet"), is born (exact date unknown).

1744 13 July: publication of the second edition of his sister Sarah's *David Simple*, to which he contributes the Preface.
Death of Charlotte Cradock Fielding, buried 14 November.

1745 5 November (-17 June 1746): edits *The True Patriot*, supporting the Hanoverian cause against the Young Pretender, Charles Stuart ("Bonny Prince Charlie").

1747 27 November: marries Mary Daniel, his housekeeper.
5 December (-5 November 1748): edits *The Jacobite's Journal*, again supporting the Hanoverian government.

1748 15 October: writes a letter of congratulation to Richardson on *Clarissa*.
25 October: commissioned as justice of the peace for the district of Westminster, London.

1749 January: commissioned as magistrate for County of Middlesex.
c. 3 February: *Tom Jones* published.

1750 Death of son Henry, buried 3 August.

1751 19 January: *An Enquiry into the Causes of the Late*

Increase of Robbers published.
19 December: *Amelia* published.

1752 4 January (–25 November): edits *The Covent-Garden Journal.*
13 April: *Examples of the Interposition of Providence in the Detection and Punishment of Murder* published.

1753 29 January: *A Proposal for Making an Effectual Provision for the Poor* published.

1754 April: illness leads to resignation from magistracy.
26 June–7 August: in failing health he travels to Lisbon, during which *The Journal of a Voyage to Lisbon* is written (published posthumously in early 1755).
8 October: Fielding dies at Junqueria, near Lisbon.

Fielding's Times: A Brief Chronology

1705 Blenheim Palace, built for the Duke of Marlborough as a monument to his victories over the French (completed 1725).

1707 The Act of Union passed, formally uniting the governments of Scotland and England.
Farquhar, *The Beaux' Stratagem*; Farquhar dies.

1708 Whigs gain majority in new British Parliament.

1709 Defoe, *History of the Union of Great Britain*; Swift, *Project for the Advancement of Religion*; Manley, *The New Atalantis*; Steele begins *The Tatler.*

1710 Parliament dissolved; subsequent election gives Tories a majority.
Berkeley, *Principles of Human Knowledge.*

1711 Pope, *Essay on Criticism*; Steele and Addison begin *The Spectator.*
St. Paul's Cathedral completed.

1712 Pope, *The Rape of the Lock.*

1713 Treaty of Utrecht ends War of Spanish Succession.
Formation of Scriblerus Club.
Addison, *Cato.*

1714 Death of Queen Anne; accession of George I.

1715 First Jacobite Rebellion, led by James Stuart, the Old Pretender.
Pope, *Iliad* (trans., completed 1720).
Le Sage, *Gil Blas* (completed 1735).

1719 Defoe, *Robinson Crusoe.*
Addison dies.

1720 South Sea Bubble scandal.
Walpole forms a new government and is soon known as "prime minister."
Clarendon, *History of the Rebellion in Ireland.*

1722 Defoe, *Journal of the Plague Year* and *Moll Flanders*; Steele, *The Conscious Lovers.*

1724 Defoe, *Roxana* and *Tour Through the Whole Island of Great Britain* (completed 1726).

1725 Jonathan Wild, the most famous criminal of the time, is hanged at Tyburn.
Pope, *Odyssey* (trans., completed 1726).

1726 John Wesley becomes a Fellow of Lincoln College, Oxford, and joins a group known as the Oxford Methodists.
Swift, *Gulliver's Travels*; Thomson, *The Seasons* (completed 1730).
Rob Roy imprisoned in Newgate.

1727 George I dies; accession of George II.

1728 Cibber, *The Provoked Husband*; Pope, *The Dunciad*; Gay, *The Beggar's Opera*.

1729 An Act passed for the better regulation of attorneys and solicitors.
Swift, *A Modest Proposal*.
Steele and Congreve die.

1730 Cibber becomes Poet Laureate.
Goldsmith born.

1731 Treaty of Vienna ends Anglo-French alliance.
Marivaux, *Marianne* (final part 1741); Lillo, *The London Merchant*.
Hogarth, *A Harlot's Progress* (completed 1732).

1732 Whigs reimpose salt tax.

1733 Pope, *Essay on Man* (completed 1734); Voltaire, *Letters Concerning the English Nation* (trans.).
Hogarth, *A Rake's Progress* (completed 1735).

1734 Marivaux, *Le Paysan parvenu* (final part 1736).

1735 Pope, *An Epistle to Dr. Arbuthnot*.

1737 Theatrical Licensing Act passed.

1739 War of Jenkin's Ear (ends 1748).

1740 War in Europe over the Austrian succession.
Cibber, *An Apology for the Life of Mr. Colley Cibber*; Richardson, *Pamela*; Hume, *A Treatise of Human Nature*; Middleton, *Life of Cicero*.

1741 First performance of Handel's *Messiah*.
Hume, *Essays Moral and Political*; Arbuthnot, Gay, etc., *Memoirs of Scriblerus*.

Thomas Osborne founds The Society of Booksellers for Promoting Learning.
Irish famine.

1742 Walpole resigns.

1743 Final version of Pope's *The Dunciad*.
Hogarth, *Marriage à la Mode* (completed 1745).

1744 Sarah Fielding, *David Simple*.
Pope dies.

1745 Second Jacobite Rebellion, led by Charles Stuart, the Young Pretender.
Swift dies.

1746 Battle of Culloden.

1747 Richardson, *Clarissa* (completed 1748).

1748 Treaty of Aix-la-Chapelle ends War of the Austrian Succession.
Hume, *Philosophical Essays concerning Human Understanding*; Smollett, *Roderick Random*.

1751 Gray, *Elegy Written in a Country Churchyard*; Smollett, *Peregrine Pickle*.
Sheridan born.
Clive defeats French at Arcot, India.
An Act passed greatly increasing the duty on spirits and restricting its sale.

1753 Hardwicke's *Marriage Act* passed.
Richardson, *Sir Charles Grandison* (completed 1754).

1754 Chippendale, *The Gentleman and Cabinet Maker's Director*.

1755 Johnson, *Dictionary of the English Language*.

A Note on the Text

The present text of *Joseph Andrews* follows Martin C. Battestin's "Wesleyan" edition, first published in 1967 by the Wesleyan University Press and then jointly with Clarendon Press. Based on a critical analysis of the four authorial editions, though relying principally on the first two, it is indisputably the best representation available of Fielding's final intentions for the novel.

In the interest of the modern reader, however, capitalization and italicization have been normalized. A number of minor alterations have also been silently made. All else remains virtually as it was for the reader of Fielding's times.

The History of the Adventures of

JOSEPH ANDREWS,

and of his Friend Mr. Abraham Adams

PREFACE

As it is possible the mere English reader[1] may have a different idea of romance with the author of these little volumes;[2] and may consequently expect a kind of entertainment, not to be found, nor which was even intended, in the following pages; it may not be improper to premise a few words concerning this kind of writing, which I do not remember to have seen hitherto attempted in our language.

The epic as well as the drama is divided into tragedy and comedy. Homer, who was the father of this species of poetry, gave us a pattern of both these, tho' that of the latter kind is entirely lost; which Aristotle tells us, bore the same relation to comedy which his *Iliad* bears to tragedy.[3] And perhaps, that we have no more instances of it among the writers of antiquity, is owing to the loss of this great pattern, which, had it survived, would have found its imitators equally with the other poems of this great original.

And farther, as this poetry may be tragic or comic, I will not scruple to say it may be likewise either in verse or prose: for tho' it wants one particular, which the critic enumerates in the constituent parts of an epic poem, namely metre; yet, when any kind of writing contains all its other parts, such as fable, action, characters, sentiments, and diction,[4] and is deficient in metre only; it seems, I think, reasonable to refer it to the epic; at least, as no critic hath thought proper to range it under any other head, nor to assign it a particular name to itself.

Thus the *Telemachus*[5] of the Arch-Bishop of Cambray appears to me of the epic kind, as well as the *Odyssey* of Homer; indeed, it is much fairer and more reasonable to give it

---

1 That is, one who reads only English.

2 Joseph Andrews was originally published in two duodecimo volumes. See Appendix E.

3 Aristotle attributes a lost satirical epic, the *Margites*, to Homer (*Poetics* 4).

4 In *Poetics* 24, Aristotle lists the major parts for the epic as: plot (Fielding's *fable* and *action*), character, diction, and thought (Fielding's *sentiments*).

5 *Les Avantures de Télémaque fils d'Ulysse* (1699), a lengthy allegorical work concerned with the moral education of a prince, by François de Salignac de la Mothe-Fénelon.

a name common with that species from which it differs only in a single instance, than to confound it with those which it resembles in no other. Such are those voluminous works commonly called *romances*, namely, *Clelia*, *Cleopatra*, *Astræa*, *Cassandra*, the *Grand Cyrus*,[1] and innumerable others which contain, as I apprehend, very little instruction or entertainment.

Now a comic romance is a comic epic-poem in prose; differing from comedy, as the serious epic from tragedy: its action being more extended and comprehensive; containing a much larger circle of incidents, and introducing a greater variety of characters. It differs from the serious romance in its fable and action, in this; that as in the one these are grave and solemn, so in the other they are light and ridiculous: it differs in its characters, by introducing persons of inferiour rank, and consequently of inferiour manners, whereas the grave romance, sets the highest before us; lastly in its sentiments and diction, by preserving the ludicrous instead of the sublime. In the diction I think, burlesque itself may be sometimes admitted; of which many instances will occur in this work, as in the descriptions of the battles, and some other places, not necessary to be pointed out to the classical reader; for whose entertainment those parodies or burlesque imitations are chiefly calculated.

But tho' we have sometimes admitted this in our diction, we have carefully excluded it from our sentiments and characters: for there it is never properly introduced, unless in writings of the burlesque kind, which this is not intended to be. Indeed, no two species of writing can differ more widely than the comic and the burlesque: for as the latter is ever the exhibition of what is monstrous and unnatural, and where our delight, if we examine it, arises from the suprizing absurdity, as in appropriating the manners of the highest to the lowest, or *è converso*;[2] so in the former, we should ever confine ourselves strictly to nature from the just imitation of which, will flow all the pleasure we

---

1 Huge aristocratic and improbable French romances of the seventeenth century by Madeleine de Scudéry (*Clélie*, 1654-60; *Artamène, ou le Grand Cyrus*, 1649-53), Gauthier de Costes de la Calprenède (*Cassandre*, 1644-50; *Cléopâtre*, 1647-56), and Honoré d'Urfé (*Astrée*, 1607-28). They remained popular in England through their translations well into the eighteenth century.

2 "Vice versa."

can this way convey to a sensible reader. And perhaps, there is one reason, why a comic writer should of all others be the least excused for deviating from nature, since it may not be always so easy for a serious poet to meet with the great and the admirable; but life every where furnishes an accurate observer with the ridiculous.

I have hinted this little, concerning burlesque; because, I have often heard that name given to performances, which have been truly of the comic kind, from the author's having sometimes admitted it in his diction only; which as it is the dress of poetry, doth like the dress of men establish characters, (the one of the whole poem, and the other of the whole man,) in vulgar opinion, beyond any of their greater excellencies: but surely, a certain drollery in style, where the characters and sentiments are perfectly natural, no more constitutes the burlesque, than an empty pomp and dignity of words, where every thing else is mean and low, can entitle any performance to the appellation of the true sublime.

And I apprehend, my Lord Shaftesbury's opinion of mere burlesque agrees with mine, when he asserts, 'There is no such thing to be found in the writings of the antients.'[1] But perhaps, I have less abhorrence than he professes for it: and that not because I have had some little success on the stage this way;[2] but rather, as it contributes more to exquisite mirth and laughter than any other; and these are probably more wholesome physic for the mind, and conduce better to purge away spleen, melancholy and ill affections, than is generally imagined. Nay, I will appeal to common observation, whether the same companies are not found more full of good-humour and benevolence, after they have been sweeten'd for two or three hours with entertainments of this kind, than when soured by a tragedy or a grave lecture.

But to illustrate all this by another science, in which, perhaps, we shall see the distinction more clearly and plainly: let us examine the works of a comic history-painter, with those per-

---

1 Anthony Ashley Cooper, third Earl of Shaftesbury, makes a statement to this effect in his *Sensus Communis; An Essay on the Freedom of Wit and Humour* (1709) 1.5.

2 Fielding's most popular theatrical burlesque, *Tom Thumb* (1730), expanded to *The Tragedy of Tragedies* (1731), had an opening run of more than forty nights.

formances which the Italians call *caricatura*; where we shall find the true excellence of the former, to consist in the exactest copying of nature; insomuch, that a judicious eye instantly rejects any thing *outré*; any liberty which the painter hath taken with the features of that *alma mater.*—Whereas in the *caricatura* we allow all licence. Its aim is to exhibit monsters, not men; and all distortions and exaggerations whatever are within its proper province.

Now what *caricatura* is in painting, burlesque is in writing; and in the same manner the comic writer and painter correlate to each other. And here I shall observe, that as in the former, the painter seems to have the advantage; so it is in the latter infinitely on the side of the writer: for the *monstrous* is much easier to paint than describe, and the *ridiculous* to describe than paint.

And tho' perhaps this latter species doth not in either science so strongly affect and agitate the muscles as the other; yet it will be owned, I believe, that a more rational and useful pleasure arises to us from it. He who should call the ingenious Hogarth[1] a burlesque painter, would, in my opinion, do him very little honour: for sure it is much easier, much less the subject of admiration, to paint a man with a nose, or any other feature of a preposterous size, or to expose him in some absurd or monstrous attitude, than to express the affections of men on canvas. It hath been thought a vast commendation of a painter, to say his figures *seem to breathe*; but surely, it is a much greater and nobler applause, that *they appear to think*.

But to return—the ridiculous only, as I have before said, falls within my province in the present work.—Nor will some explanation of this word be thought impertinent by the reader, if he considers how wonderfully[2] it hath been mistaken, even by writers who have profess'd it: for to what but such a mistake, can we attribute the many attempts to ridicule the blackest vil-

---

1 William Hogarth, the "comic history-painter" referred to above, was a friend of Fielding, who repeatedly expresses admiration for him. He is best known for his satirical portrayals of moral subjects such as *A Harlot's Progress* (1731-32) and *Marriage* à la *Mode* (1743-45).

2 Astonishingly.

lanies; and what is yet worse, the most dreadful calamities? What could exceed the absurdity of an author, who should write *the Comedy of Nero, with the merry incident of ripping up his mother's belly*;[1] or what would give a greater shock to humanity, than an attempt to expose the miseries of poverty and distress to ridicule? And yet, the reader will not want much learning to suggest such instances to himself.

Besides, it may seem remarkable, that Aristotle, who is so fond and free of definitions, hath not thought proper to define the ridiculous. Indeed, where he tells us it is proper to comedy, he hath remarked that villany is not its object:[2] but he hath not, as I remember, positively asserted what is. Nor doth the Abbé Bellegarde,[3] who hath writ a treatise on this subject, tho' he shews us many species of it, once trace it to its fountain.

The only source of the true ridiculous (as it appears to me) is affectation. But tho' it arises from one spring only, when we consider the infinite streams into which this one branches, we shall presently cease to admire[4] at the copious field it affords to an observer. Now affectation proceeds from one of these two causes, vanity, or hypocrisy: for as vanity puts us on affecting false characters, in order to purchase applause; so hypocrisy sets us on an endeavour to avoid censure by concealing our vices under an appearance of their opposite virtues. And tho' these two causes are often confounded, (for there is some difficulty in distinguishing them) yet, as they proceed from very different motives, so they are as clearly distinct in their operations: for indeed, the affectation which arises from vanity is nearer to truth than the other; as it hath not that violent repugnancy of nature to struggle with, which that of the hypocrite hath. It may be likewise noted, that affectation doth not imply an absolute negation of those qualities which are affected: and

---

1 The Roman emperor Nero had his mother, Agrippina, murdered in AD 59. Symbolically, she urged the assassin to stab her in the womb.

2 "The Ridiculous may be defined as a mistake or deformity not productive of pain or harm to others ..." (*Poetics* 5).

3 Jean Baptiste Morvan Bellegarde wrote *Reflexions sur le ridicule* (1696), which was translated into English in 1706.

4 To wonder.

therefore, tho', when it proceeds from hypocrisy, it be nearly allied to deceit; yet when it comes from vanity only, it partakes of the nature of ostentation: for instance, the affectation of liberality in a vain man, differs visibly from the same affectation in the avaricious; for tho' the vain man is not what he would appear, or hath not the virtue he affects, to the degree he would be thought to have it; yet it sits less aukwardly on him than on the avaricious man, who *is* the very reverse of what he would *seem* to be.

From the discovery of this affectation arises the ridiculous—which always strikes the reader with surprize and pleasure; and that in a higher and stronger degree when the affectation arises from hypocrisy, than when from vanity: for to discover any one to be the exact reverse of what he affects, is more surprizing, and consequently more ridiculous, than to find him a little deficient in the quality he desires the reputation of. I might observe that our Ben Johnson,[1] who of all men understood the *ridiculous* the best, hath chiefly used the hypocritical affectation.

Now from affectation only, the misfortunes and calamities of life, or the imperfections of nature, may become the objects of ridicule. Surely he hath a very ill-framed mind, who can look on ugliness, infirmity, or poverty, as ridiculous in themselves: nor do I believe any man living who meets a dirty fellow riding through the streets in a cart, is struck with an idea of the ridiculous from it; but if he should see the same figure descend from his coach and six, or bolt from his chair[2] with his hat under his arm, he would then begin to laugh, and with justice. In the same manner, were we to enter a poor house, and behold a wretched family shivering with cold and languishing with hunger, it would not incline us to laughter, (at least we must have very diabolical natures, if it would:) but should we discover there a grate, instead of coals, adorned with flowers, empty plate or china dishes on the side-board, or any other affectation of riches and finery either on their persons or in their furni-

---

1 Ben Jonson exposed pretensions in such satiric comedies as *Volpone* (1606) and *The Alchemist* (1610).

2 Sedan chair, an enclosed conveyance for one person which was carried between poles by two men.

ture; we might then indeed be excused, for ridiculing so fantastical an appearance. Much less are natural imperfections the objects of derision: but when ugliness aims at the applause of beauty, or lameness endeavours to display agility; it is then that these unfortunate circumstances, which at first moved our compassion, tend only to raise our mirth.

The poet carries this very far;

> None are for being what they are in fault,
> But for not being what they would be thought.[1]

Where if the metre would suffer the word *ridiculous* to close the first line, the thought would be rather more proper. Great vices are the proper objects of our detestation, smaller faults of our pity: but affectation appears to me the only true source of the ridiculous.

But perhaps it may be objected to me, that I have against my own rules introduced vices, and of a very black kind into this work. To which I shall answer: first, that it is very difficult to pursue a series of human actions and keep clear from them. Secondly, that the vices to be found here, are rather the accidental consequences of some human frailty, or foible, than causes habitually existing in the mind. Thirdly, that they are never set forth as the objects of ridicule but detestation. Fourthly, that they are never the principal figure at that time on the scene; and lastly, they never produce the intended evil.

Having thus distinguished *Joseph Andrews* from the productions of romance writers on the one hand, and burlesque writers on the other, and given some few very short hints (for I intended no more) of this species of writing, which I have affirmed to be hitherto unattempted in our language; I shall leave to my good-natur'd reader to apply my piece to my observations, and will detain him no longer than with a word concerning the characters in this work.

And here I solemnly protest, I have no intention to vilify or asperse any one: for tho' every thing is copied from the book of

---

1 William Congreve (1670-1729), from his poem "Of Pleasing," ll. 63-64.

nature, and scarce a character or action produced which I have not taken from my own observations and experience, yet I have used the utmost care to obscure the persons by such different circumstances, degrees,[1] and colours,[2] that it will be impossible to guess at them with any degree of certainty; and if it ever happens otherwise, it is only where the failure characterized is so minute, that it is a foible only which the party himself may laugh at as well as any other.

As to the character of Adams, as it is the most glaring[3] in the whole, so I conceive it is not to be found in any book now extant. It is designed a character of perfect simplicity; and as the goodness of his heart will recommend him to the good-natur'd; so I hope it will excuse me to the gentlemen of his cloth; for whom, while they are worthy of their sacred order, no man can possibly have a greater respect. They will therefore excuse me, notwithstanding the low adventures in which he is engaged, that I have made him a clergyman; since no other office could have given him so many opportunities of displaying his worthy inclinations.

1 Ranks, classes.
2 Appearances, hues.
3 Conspicuous.

CONTENTS

BOOK I

BOOK II

BOOK III

BOOK IV

BOOK I

CHAPTER I

Of writing Lives in general, and particularly of Pamela; *with a word by the bye of Colley Cibber and others.*

IT is a trite but true observation, that examples work more forcibly on the mind than precepts: and if this be just in what is odious and blameable, it is more strongly so in what is amiable and praise-worthy. Here emulation most effectually operates upon us, and inspires our imitation in an irresistible manner. A good man therefore is a standing lesson to all his acquaintance, and of far greater use in that narrow circle than a good book.

But as it often happens that the best men are but little known, and consequently cannot extend the usefulness of their examples a great way; the writer may be called in aid to spread their history farther, and to present the amiable pictures to those who have not the happiness of knowing the originals; and so, by communicating such valuable patterns to the world, he may perhaps do a more extensive service to mankind than the person whose life originally afforded the pattern.

In this light I have always regarded those biographers who have recorded the actions of great and worthy persons of both sexes. Not to mention those antient writers which of late days are little read, being written in obsolete, and, as they are generally thought, unintelligible languages; such as Plutarch, Nepos,[1] and others which I heard of in my youth; our own language affords many of excellent use and instruction, finely calculated to sow the seeds of virtue in youth, and very easy to be comprehended by persons of moderate capacity. Such are the history of John the Great, who, by his brave and heroic actions against men of large and athletic bodies, obtained the glorious appellation of the Giant-killer; that of an Earl of Warwick, whose Christian name was Guy; the lives of Argalus and Parthenia, and above all, the history of those seven worthy per-

1 Two of the most famous historians of antiquity: the Greek Plutarch (c. AD 46-c. 120), famous for his lives of Greek and Roman statesmen, and the Roman Cornelius Nepos (c. 99-c. 25 BC), biographer of *De Viris Illustribus*.

sonages, the Champions of Christendom.[1] In all these, delight is mixed with instruction, and the reader is almost as much improved as entertained.

But I pass by these and many others, to mention two books lately published, which represent an admirable pattern of the amiable in either sex. The former of these which deals in male-virtue, was written by the great person himself, who lived the life he hath recorded, and is by many thought to have lived such a life only in order to write it. The other is communicated to us by an historian who borrows his lights, as the common method is, from authentic papers and records.[2] The reader, I believe, already conjectures, I mean, the lives of Mr. Colley Cibber,[3] and of Mrs.[4] Pamela Andrews. How artfully doth the former, by insinuating that he *escaped* being promoted to the highest stations in Church and State, teach us a contempt of worldly grandeur! how strongly doth he inculcate an absolute submission to our superiors! Lastly, how completely doth he arm us against so uneasy, so wretched a passion as the fear of shame; how clearly doth he expose the emptiness and vanity of that fantom, reputation!

What the female readers are taught by the memoirs of Mrs. Andrews, is so well set forth in the excellent essays or letters prefixed to the second and subsequent editions of that work, that it would be here a needless repetition. The authentic history with which I now present the public, is an instance of the great good that book is likely to do, and of the prevalence of example which I have just observed: since it will appear that it was by keeping the excellent pattern of his sister's virtues before his eyes, that Mr. Joseph Andrews was chiefly enabled to preserve his purity in the midst of such great temptations; I

---

1 These were some of the popular penny romances and folktales that were hawked about by chapmen down through the years.

2 *Pamela: or, Virtue Rewarded* (1740) is professedly edited from Pamela's private correspondence.

3 *An Apology for the Life of Mr. Colley Cibber, Comedian, and Late Patentee of The Theatre-Royal. Written by Himself* (1740). Cibber's autobiography was a favourite target of Fielding's satire. See Introduction, p. 11.

4 Mistress, a title which could apply to unmarried as well as married women, suggesting some position of authority.

shall only add, that this character of male-chastity, tho' doubtless as desirable and becoming in one part of the human species, as in the other, is almost the only virtue which the great apologist[1] hath not given himself for the sake of giving the example to his readers.

CHAPTER II

Of Mr. Joseph Andrews his birth, parentage, education, and great endowments, with a word or two concerning ancestors.

Mr. Joseph Andrews, the hero of our ensuing history, was esteemed to be the only son of Gaffar and Gammer[2] Andrews, and brother to the illustrious Pamela, whose virtue is at present so famous. As to his ancestors, we have searched with great diligence, but little success: being unable to trace them farther than his great grandfather, who, as an elderly person in the parish remembers to have heard his father say, was an excellent cudgel-player.[3] Whether he had any ancestors before this, we must leave to the opinion of our curious reader, finding nothing of sufficient certainty to relie on. However, we cannot omit inserting an epitaph which an ingenious friend of ours hath communicated.

> Stay traveller, for underneath this pew
> Lies fast asleep that merry man *Andrew*;
> When the last day's great sun shall gild the skies,
> Then he shall from his tomb get up and rise.
> Be merry while thou can'st: for surely thou
> Shall shortly be as sad as he is now.

The words are almost out of the stone with antiquity. But it is needless to observe, that Andrew here is writ without an *s*, and is besides a Christian name. My friend moreover conjectures

1 That is, Colley Cibber.
2 Terms of respect applied to older people of low rank, especially in the country.
3 A popular sporting contest, played with short thick sticks.

this to have been the founder of that sect of laughing philosophers, since called *Merry Andrews.*[1]

To wave therefore a circumstance, which, tho' mentioned in conformity to the exact rules of biography, is not greatly material; I proceed to things of more consequence. Indeed it is sufficiently certain, that he had as many ancestors, as the best man living; and perhaps, if we look five or six hundred years backwards, might be related to some persons of very great figure at present, whose ancestors within half the last century are buried in as great obscurity. But suppose for argument's sake we should admit that he had no ancestors at all, but had sprung up, according to the modern phrase, out of a dunghill, as the Athenians pretended they themselves did from the earth,[2] would not this **autokopros* have been justly entitled to all the praise arising from his own virtues? Would it not be hard, that a man who hath no ancestors should therefore be render'd incapable of acquiring honour, when we see so many who have no virtues, enjoying the honour of their forefathers? At ten years old (by which time his education was advanced to writing and reading) he was bound an apprentice, according to the statute,[3] to Sir Thomas Booby, an uncle of Mr. Booby's by the father's side. Sir Thomas having then an estate in his own hands, the young Andrews was at first employed in what in the country they call *keeping birds.* His office was to perform the part the antients assigned to the god Priapus,[4] which deity the moderns call by the name of Jack-o'-Lent:[5] but his voice being so extremely musical, that it rather allured the birds than terrified them, he

* In English, sprung from a dunghil [Fielding's note].

1 Buffoons, clowns.

2 The ancient Athenians claimed ("pretended") to be autocthones (sprung from the earth), believing their ancestors to be the legendary Cecrops and Erichthonius, who were mothered by Earth.

3 The Statute of Artificers (1563) made a seven-year apprenticeship obligatory in the learning of a craft.

4 The Greco-Roman god of fertility and guardian of agriculture, usually depicted as an ugly little figure with a huge phallus. Statues of Priapus were set up in orchards and gardens to act as scarecrows.

5 A figure usually associated with Ash Wednesday. But here apparently it simply means a scarecrow.

was soon transplanted from the fields into the dog-kennel, where he was placed under the huntsman, and made what sportsmen term a *whipper-in*.[1] For this place likewise the sweetness of his voice disqualified him: the dogs preferring the melody of his chiding to all the alluring notes of the huntsman, who soon became so incensed at it, that he desired Sir Thomas to provide otherwise for him; and constantly laid every fault the dogs were at, to the account of the poor boy, who was now transplanted to the stable. Here he soon gave proofs of strength and agility, beyond his years, and constantly rode the most spirited and vicious horses to water with an intrepidity which surprized every one. While he was in this station, he rode several races for Sir Thomas, and this with such expertness and success, that the neighbouring gentlemen frequently solicited the knight, to permit little Joey (for so he was called) to ride their matches. The best gamesters, before they laid their money, always enquired which horse little Joey was to ride, and the betts were rather proportioned by the rider than by the horse himself; especially after he had scornfully refused a considerable bribe to play booty[2] on such an occasion. This extremely raised his character,[3] and so pleased the Lady Booby, that she desired to have him (being now seventeen years of age) for her own foot-boy.

Joey was now preferred from the stable to attend on his lady; to go on her errands, stand behind her chair, wait at her tea-table, and carry her prayer-book to church; at which place, his voice gave him an opportunity of distinguishing himself by singing psalms: he behaved likewise in every other respect so well at divine service, that it recommended him to the notice of Mr. Abraham Adams the curate; who took an opportunity one day, as he was drinking a cup of ale in Sir Thomas's kitchin, to ask the young man several questions concerning religion; with his answers to which he was wonderfully pleased.

---

1 A huntsman's assistant, who keeps the hounds from straying.

2 To lose deliberately.

3 Reputation.

CHAPTER III

Of Mr. Abraham Adams the curate, Mrs. Slipslop the chambermaid, and others.

MR. Abraham Adams was an excellent scholar. He was a perfect master of the Greek and Latin languages; to which he added a great share of knowledge in the oriental tongues, and could read and translate French, Italian and Spanish. He had applied many years to the most severe study, and had treasured up a fund of learning rarely to be met with in a university. He was besides a man of good sense, good parts,[1] and good nature; but was at the same time as entirely ignorant of the ways of this world, as an infant just entered into it could possibly be. As he had never any intention to deceive, so he never suspected such a design in others. He was generous, friendly and brave to an excess; but simplicity was his characteristic:[2] he did, no more than Mr. Colley Cibber, apprehend any such passions as malice and envy to exist in mankind,[3] which was indeed less remarkable in a country parson than in a gentleman who hath past his life behind the scenes, a place which hath been seldom thought the school of innocence; and where a very little observation would have convinced the great apologist, that those passions have a real existence in the human mind.

His virtue and his other qualifications, as they rendered him equal to his office, so they made him an agreeable and valuable companion, and had so much endeared and well recommended him to a bishop, that at the age of fifty, he was provided with a handsome income of twenty-three pounds a year;[4] which however, he could not make any great figure with: because he lived in a dear country, and was a little incumbered with a wife and six children.

---

1 Endowments, natural abilities.

2 Essential trait.

3 In the first chapter of the *Apology*, Cibber writes: "My Ignorance, and want of Jealousy [suspicion] of Mankind has been so strong, that it is with Reluctance I even yet believe any Person, I am acquainted with, can be capable of Envy, Malice, or Ingratitude ..."

4 A licensed curate qualified on first appointment for a stipend of between £20 and £50, so Adams' was very low for his age.

It was this gentleman, who, having, as I have said, observed the singular devotion of young Andrews, had found means to question him, concerning several particulars; as how many books there were in the New Testament? which were they? how many chapters they contained? and such like; to all which Mr. Adams privately said, he answer'd much better than Sir Thomas, or two other neighbouring justices of the peace could probably have done.

Mr. Adams was wonderfully sollicitous to know at what time, and by what opportunity the youth became acquainted with these matters: Joey told him, that he had very early learnt to read and write by the goodness of his father, who, though he had not interest enough to get him into a charity school,[1] because a cousin of his father's landlord did not vote on the right side for a church-warden in a borough town, yet had been himself at the expence of sixpence a week for his learning. He told him likewise, that ever since he was in Sir Thomas's family, he had employed all his hours of leisure in reading good books; that he had read the Bible, the *Whole Duty of Man*, and *Thomas à Kempis*; and that as often as he could, without being perceived, he had studied a great good book which lay open in the hall window, where he had read, *as how the Devil carried away half a church in sermon-time, without hurting one of the congregation; and as how a field of corn ran away down a hill with all the trees upon it, and covered another man's meadow.* This sufficiently assured Mr. Adams, that the good book meant could be no other than Baker's Chronicle.[2]

The curate, surprized to find such instances of industry and application in a young man, who had never met with the least encouragement, asked him, if he did not extremely regret the

---

1 From the beginning of the eighteenth century, charity schools offered free instruction in reading, writing, arithmetic, and some vocational training. Organized by the Society for the Promotion of Christian Knowledge, a strong emphasis was placed on religion and morality.

2 *The Whole Duty of Man* (1658), probably written by Richard Allestree, one of the most popular devotional works of the period and an important early influence on Fielding; Thomas à Kempis, Augustinian monk and supposed author of the widely read *De Imitatio Christi* (1441); and *A Chronicle of the Kings of England* (1643), by Richard Baker, somewhat inaccurately represented by Joseph.

want of a liberal education, and the not having been born of parents, who might have indulged his talents and desire of knowledge? To which he answered, 'he hoped he had profited somewhat better from the books he had read, than to lament his condition in this world. That for his part, he was perfectly content with the state to which he was called, that he should endeavour to improve his talent,[1] which was all required of him, but not repine at his own lot, nor envy those of his betters.' 'Well said, my lad,' reply'd the curate, 'and I wish some who have read many more good books, nay and some who have written good books themselves, had profited so much by them.'

Adams had no nearer access to Sir Thomas, or my lady, than through the waiting-gentlewoman: for Sir Thomas was too apt to estimate men merely by their dress, or fortune; and my lady was a woman of gaiety, who had been bless'd with a town-education, and never spoke of any of her country neighbours, by any other appellation than that of *the brutes*. They both regarded the curate as a kind of domestic only, belonging to the parson of the parish,[2] who was at this time at variance with the knight; for the parson had for many years lived in a constant state of civil war, or, which is perhaps as bad, of civil law, with Sir Thomas himself and the tenants of his manor. The foundation of this quarrel was a modus,[3] by setting which aside, an advantage of several shillings *per annum* would have accrued to the rector: but he had not yet been able to accomplish his purpose; and had reaped hitherto nothing better from the suits than the pleasure (which he used indeed frequently to say was no small one) of reflecting that he had utterly undone many of the poor tenants, tho' he had at the same time greatly impoverish'd himself.

Mrs. Slipslop the waiting-gentlewoman, being herself the daughter of a curate, preserved some respect for Adams; she professed great regard for his learning, and would frequently

---

1 See the parable of the talents (Matthew 25:14–30). The sanctimonious tone parodies *Pamela*.

2 Although appointed by the bishop, Adams would be paid by the rector who owned the benefice, or living, and could be dismissed by him at any time.

3 A *modus decimandi* was a fixed money payment in lieu of tithe that parishioners were expected to pay to the Church.

dispute with him on points of theology; but always insisted on a deference to be paid to her understanding, as she had been frequently at London, and knew more of the world than a country parson could pretend to.

She had in these disputes a particular advantage over Adams: for she was a mighty affecter of hard words, which she used in such a manner, that the parson, who durst not offend her, by calling her words in question, was frequently at some loss to guess her meaning, and would have been much less puzzled by an Arabian manuscript.

Adams therefore took an opportunity one day, after a pretty long discourse with her on the *essence*, (or, as she pleased to term it, the *incense*) of matter, to mention the case of young Andrews; desiring her to recommend him to her lady as a youth very susceptible of learning, and one, whose instruction in Latin he would himself undertake; by which means he might be qualified for higher station than that of a footman: and added, she knew it was in his master's power easily to provide for him in a better manner. He therefore desired, that the boy might be left behind under his care.

'La Mr. Adams,' said Mrs. Slipslop, 'do you think my lady will suffer any *preambles* about any such matter? She is going to London very *concisely*, and I am *confidous* would not leave Joey behind her on any account; for he is one of the genteelest young fellows you may see in a summer's day, and I am *confidous* she would as soon think of parting with a pair of her grey-mares: for she values herself as much on one as the other.' Adams would have interrupted, but she proceeded: 'And why is Latin more *necessitous* for a footman than a gentleman? It is very proper that you clargymen must learn it, because you can't preach without it: but I have heard gentlemen say in London, that it is fit for no body else. I am *confidous* my lady would be angry with me for mentioning it, and I shall draw myself into no such *delemy*.' At which words her lady's bell rung, and Mr. Adams was forced to retire; nor could he gain a second opportunity with her before their London journey, which happened a few days afterwards. However, Andrews behaved very thankfully and gratefully to him for his intended kindness, which he told him he never would forget, and at the same time received from the good man many admonitions concerning the regulation of his future conduct, and his perseverance in innocence and industry.

CHAPTER IV

What happened after their journey to London.

No sooner was young Andrews arrived at London, than he began to scrape an acquaintance with his party-colour'd brethren,[1] who endeavour'd to make him despise his former course of life. His hair was cut after the newest fashion, and became his chief care. He went abroad with it all the morning in papers, and drest it out in the afternoon; they could not however teach him to game, swear, drink, nor any other genteel vice the town abounded with. He applied most of his leisure hours to music, in which he greatly improved himself, and became so perfect a connoisseur in that art, that he led the opinion of all the other footmen at an opera, and they never condemned or applauded a single song contrary to his approbation or dislike. He was a little too forward in riots[2] at the play-houses and assemblies;[3] and when he attended his lady at church (which was but seldom) he behaved with less seeming devotion than formerly: however, if he was outwardly a pretty fellow,[4] his morals remained entirely uncorrupted, tho' he was at the same time smarter and genteeler, than any of the beaus in town, either in or out of livery.

His lady, who had often said of him that Joey was the handsomest and genteelest footman in the kingdom, but that it was pity he wanted spirit, began now to find that fault no longer; on the contrary, she was frequently heard to cry out, *Aye, there is some life in this fellow*. She plainly saw the effects which town-air

1 Variegated liveries were worn by footmen.

2 Revelry.

3 Social gatherings of polite society, with footmen in attendance.

4 An ironical term for a fop.

hath on the soberest constitutions. She would now walk out with him into Hyde-Park in a morning, and when tired, which happened almost every minute, would lean on his arm, and converse with him in great familiarity. Whenever she stept out of her coach she would take him by the hand, and sometimes, for fear of stumbling, press it very hard; she admitted him to deliver messages at her bed-side in a morning, leered at him at table, and indulged him in all those innocent freedoms which women of figure may permit without the least sully of their virtue.

But tho' their virtue remains unsullied, yet now and then some small arrows will glance on the shadow of it, their reputation; and so it fell out to Lady Booby, who happened to be walking arm in arm with Joey one morning in Hyde-Park, when Lady Tittle and Lady Tattle came accidentally by in their coach. *Bless me*, says Lady Tittle, *can I believe my eyes? Is that Lady Booby? Surely*, says Tattle. *But what makes you surprized? Why is not that her footman?* reply'd Tittle. At which Tattle laughed and cryed, *An old business, I assure you, is it possible you should not have heard it? The whole town hath known it this half year.* The consequence of this interview was a whisper through a hundred visits, which were separately performed by the two ladies* the same afternoon, and might have had a mischievous effect, had it not been stopt by two fresh reputations which were published[1] the day afterwards, and engrossed the whole talk of the town.

But whatever opinion or suspicion the scandalous inclination of defamers might entertain of Lady Booby's innocent freedoms, it is certain they made no impression on young Andrews, who never offered to encroach beyond the liberties which his lady allowed him. A behaviour which she imputed to the violent respect he preserved for her, and which served

---

* It may seem an absurdity that Tattle should visit, as she actually did, to spread a known scandal: but the reader may reconcile this, by supposing with me, that, notwithstanding what she says, this was her first acquaintance with it [Fielding's note].

---

1 Exposed to public scrutiny.

only to heighten a something she began to conceive, and which the next chapter will open a little farther.

CHAPTER V

The death of Sir Thomas Booby, with the affectionate and mournful behaviour of his widow, and the great purity of Joseph Andrews.

AT this time, an accident happened which put a stop to these agreeable walks, which probably would have soon puffed up the cheeks of Fame,[1] and caused her to blow her brazen trumpet through the town, and this was no other than the death of Sir Thomas Booby, who departing this life, left his disconsolate lady confined to her house as closely as if she herself had been attacked by some violent disease. During the first six days the poor lady admitted none but Mrs. Slipslop and three female friends who made a party at cards: but on the seventh she ordered Joey, whom for a good reason we shall hereafter call JOSEPH,[2] to bring up her tea-kettle. The lady being in bed, called Joseph to her, bad him sit down, and having accidentally laid her hand on his, she asked him, *if he had never been in love?* Joseph answered, with some confusion, 'it was time enough for one so young as himself to think on such things.' 'As young as you are,' reply'd the lady, 'I am convinced you are no stranger to that passion; come Joey,' says she, 'tell me truly, who is the happy girl whose eyes have made a conquest of you?' Joseph returned, 'that all women he had ever seen were equally indifferent to him.' 'O then,' said the lady, 'you are a general lover. Indeed you handsome fellows, like handsome women, are very long and difficult in fixing: but yet you shall never persuade me that your heart is so insusceptible of affection; I rather impute what you say to your secrecy, a very commendable quality, and what I am far from being angry with you for. Nothing can be more

---

1 Probably an allusion to the goddess Fama (rumour) in the *Aeneid* 4.173-97, spreading news of the love affair between Dido and Aeneas.

2 An allusion to the chastity of the biblical Joseph, who resisted the advances of Potiphar's wife (Genesis 39:7-20).

unworthy in a young man than to betray any intimacies with the ladies.' *Ladies! Madam*, said Joseph, *I am sure I never had the impudence to think of any that deserve that name*. 'Don't pretend to too much modesty,' said she, 'for that sometimes may be impertinent: but pray, answer me this question, suppose a lady should happen to like you, suppose she should prefer you to all your sex, and admit you to the same familiarities as you might have hoped for, if you had been born her equal, are you certain that no vanity could tempt you to discover her? Answer me honestly, Joseph, have you so much more sense and so much more virtue than you handsome young fellows generally have, who make no scruple of sacrificing our dear reputation to your pride, without considering the great obligation we lay on you, by our condescension and confidence? Can you keep a secret, my Joey?' 'Madam,' says he, 'I hope your ladyship can't tax me with ever betraying the secrets of the family, and I hope, if you was to turn me away, I might have that character[1] of you.' 'I don't intend to turn you away, Joey,' said she, and sighed, 'I am afraid it is not in my power.' She then raised herself a little in her bed, and discovered one of the whitest necks that ever was seen; at which Joseph blushed. 'La!' says she, in an affected surprize, 'what am I doing? I have trusted myself with a man alone, naked in bed; suppose you should have any wicked intentions upon my honour, how should I defend myself?' Joseph protested that he never had the least evil design against her. 'No,' says she, 'perhaps you may not call your designs wicked, and perhaps they are not so.'—He swore they were not. 'You misunderstand me,' says she, 'I mean if they were against my honour, they may not be wicked, but the world calls them so. But then, say you, the world will never know any thing of the matter, yet would not that be trusting to your secrecy? Must not my reputation be then in your power? Would you not then be my master?' Joseph begged her ladyship to be comforted, for that he would never imagine the least wicked thing against her, and that he had rather die a thousand deaths than give her any reason to suspect him. 'Yes,' said she, 'I

1 A character reference, testimonial.

must have reason to suspect you. Are you not a man? and without vanity I may pretend to some charms. But perhaps you may fear I should prosecute you; indeed I hope you do, and yet heaven knows I should never have the confidence to appear before a court of justice, and you know, Joey, I am of a forgiving temper. Tell me Joey, don't you think I should forgive you?' 'Indeed madam,' says Joseph, 'I will never do any thing to disoblige your ladyship.' 'How,' says she, 'do you think it would not disoblige me then? Do you think I would willingly suffer you?' 'I don't understand you, madam,' says Joseph. 'Don't you?' said she, 'then you are either a fool or pretend to be so, I find I was mistaken in you, so get you down stairs, and never let me see your face again: your pretended innocence cannot impose on me.' 'Madam,' said Joseph, 'I would not have your ladyship think any evil of me. I have always endeavoured to be a dutiful servant both to you and my master.' 'O thou villain,' answered my lady, 'why did'st thou mention the name of that dear man, unless to torment me, to bring his precious memory to my mind, (*and then she burst into a fit of tears.*) Get thee from my sight, I shall never endure thee more.' At which words she turned away from him, and Joseph retreated from the room in a most disconsolate condition, and writ that letter which the reader will find in the next chapter.

CHAPTER VI

How Joseph Andrews writ a letter to his sister Pamela.

To Mrs. Pamela Andrews, living with Squire Booby.

'Dear Sister,

'Since I received your letter of your good lady's death, we have had a misfortune of the same kind in our family. My worthy master, Sir Thomas, died about four days ago,[1] and what is

---

1 In the previous chapter, it was seven days after the death of Sir Thomas that Joseph was summoned to Lady Booby's bedside. Similarly, Pamela's troubles began when her mistress died, putting her in the power of her lady's son. In various ways, Joseph's letter mimics those written by his sister.

worse, my poor lady is certainly gone distracted. None of the servants expected her to take it so to heart, because they quarrelled almost every day of their lives: but no more of that, because you know, Pamela, I never loved to tell the secrets of my master's family; but to be sure you must have known they never loved one another, and I have heard her ladyship wish his honour dead above a thousand times: but no body knows what it is to lose a friend till they have lost him.

'Don't tell any body what I write, because I should not care to have folks say I discover[1] what passes in our family: but if it had not been so great a lady, I should have thought she had had a mind to me. Dear Pamela, don't tell any body: but she ordered me to sit down by her bed-side, when she was in naked bed; and she held my hand, and talked exactly as a lady does to her sweetheart in a stage-play, which I have seen in Covent-Garden, while she wanted him to be no better than he should be.

'If madam be mad, I shall not care for staying long in the family; so I heartily wish you could get me a place either at the squire's, or some other neighbouring gentleman's, unless it be true that you are going to be married to Parson Williams, as folks talk, and then I should be very willing to be his clerk: for which you know I am qualified, being able to read, and to set a psalm.

'I fancy, I shall be discharged very soon; and the moment I am, unless I hear from you, I shall return to my old master's country seat, if it be only to see Parson Adams, who is the best man in the world. London is a bad place, and there is so little good fellowship, that next-door neighbours don't know one another. Pray give my service[2] to all friends that enquire for me; so I rest

Your loving brother,
Joseph Andrews.'

As soon as Joseph had sealed and directed this letter, he walked down stairs, where he met Mrs. Slipslop, with whom

1 Reveal, disclose.
2 Respects, regards.

we shall take this opportunity to bring the reader a little better acquainted. She was a maiden gentlewoman of about forty-five years of age, who having made a small slip in her youth had continued a good maid ever since. She was not at this time remarkably handsome; being very short, and rather too corpulent in body, and somewhat red, with the addition of pimples in the face. Her nose was likewise rather too large, and her eyes too little; nor did she resemble a cow so much in her breath, as in two brown globes which she carried before her; one of her legs was also a little shorter than the other, which occasioned her to limp as she walked. This fair creature had long cast the eyes of affection on Joseph, in which she had not met with quite so good success as she probably wished, tho' besides the allurements of her native charms, she had given him tea, sweetmeats, wine, and many other delicacies, of which by keeping the keys, she had the absolute command. Joseph however, had not returned the least gratitude to all these favours, not even so much as a kiss; tho' I would not insinuate she was so easily to be satisfied: for surely then he would have been highly blameable. The truth is, she was arrived at an age when she thought she might indulge herself in any liberties with a man, without the danger of bringing a third person into the world to betray them. She imagined, that by so long a self-denial, she had not only made amends for the small slip of her youth above hinted at: but had likewise laid up a quantity of merit to excuse any future failings. In a word, she resolved to give a loose to her amorous inclinations, and pay off the debt of pleasure which she found she owed herself, as fast as possible.

With these charms of person, and in this disposition of mind, she encountered poor Joseph at the bottom of the stairs, and asked him if he would drink a glass of something good this morning. Joseph, whose spirits were not a little cast down, very readily and thankfully accepted the offer; and together they went into a closet, where having delivered him a full glass of ratifia,[1] and desired him to sit down, Mrs. Slipslop thus began:

---

1 A cordial or liqueur flavoured with certain fruits or their kernels, usually almonds, peaches, or apricots. (Also *ratafia*.)

'Sure nothing can be a more simple *contract* in a woman, than to place her affections on a boy. If I had ever thought it would have been my fate, I should have wished to die a thousand deaths rather than live to see that day. If we like a man, the lightest hint *sophisticates*. Whereas a boy *proposes* upon us to break through all the *regulations* of modesty, before we can make any *oppression* upon him.' Joseph, who did not understand a word she said, answered, '*Yes madam*;—' 'Yes madam!' reply'd Mrs. Slipslop with some warmth, 'do you intend to *result* my passion? Is it not enough, ungrateful as you are, to make no return to all the favours I have done you: but you must treat me with *ironing*? Barbarous monster! how have I deserved that my passion should be *resulted* and treated with *ironing*?' 'Madam,' answered Joseph, 'I don't understand your hard words: but I am certain, you have no occasion to call me ungrateful: for so far from intending you any wrong, I have always loved you as well as if you had been my own mother.' 'How, sirrah!' says Mrs. Slipslop in a rage: 'your own mother! Do you *assinuate* that I am old enough to be your mother? I don't know what a stripling may think: but I believe a man would *refer* me to any green-sickness[1] silly girl *whatsomdever*: but I ought to despise you rather than be angry with you, for *referring* the conversation of girls to that of a woman of sense.' 'Madam,' says Joseph, 'I am sure I have always valued the honour you did me by your conversation; for I know you are a woman of learning.' 'Yes but, Joseph,' said she a little softened by the compliment to her learning, 'if you had a value for me, you certainly would have found some method of shewing it me; for I am *convicted* you must see the value I have for you. Yes, Joseph, my eyes whether I would or no, must have declared a passion I cannot conquer.—Oh! Joseph!—'

As when a hungry tygress,[2] who long had traversed the woods in fruitless search, sees within the reach of her claws a lamb, she prepares to leap on her prey; or as a voracious pike, of immense size, surveys through the liquid element a roach or gudgeon which cannot escape her jaws, opens them wide to

---

1 A kind of anemia that sometimes affects young girls at puberty.

2 A parody of Homeric similes.

swallow the little fish: so did Mrs. Slipslop prepare to lay her violent amorous hands on the poor Joseph, when luckily her mistress's bell rung, and delivered the intended martyr from her clutches. She was obliged to leave him abruptly, and defer the execution of her purpose to some other time. We shall therefore return to the Lady Booby, and give our reader some account of her behaviour, after she was left by Joseph in a temper of mind not greatly different from that of the inflamed Slipslop.

CHAPTER VII

Sayings of wise men. A dialogue between the lady and her maid, and a panegyric or rather satire on the passion of love, in the sublime style.

IT is the observation of some antient sage, whose name I have forgot, that passions operate differently on the human mind, as diseases on the body, in proportion to the strength or weakness, soundness or rottenness of the one and the other.

We hope therefore, a judicious reader will give himself some pains to observe, what we have so greatly laboured to describe, the different operations of this passion of love in the gentle and cultivated mind of the Lady Booby, from those which it effected in the less polished and coarser disposition of Mrs. Slipslop.

Another philosopher, whose name also at present escapes my memory, hath somewhere said, that resolutions taken in the absence of the beloved object are very apt to vanish in its presence; on both which wise sayings the following chapter may serve as a comment.

No sooner had Joseph left the room in the manner we have before related, than the lady, enraged at her disappointment, began to reflect with severity on her conduct. Her love was now changed to disdain, which pride assisted to torment her. She despised herself for the meanness[1] of her passion, and Joseph for its ill success. However, she had now got the better

---

1 Baseness.

of it in her own opinion, and determined immediately to dismiss the object. After much tossing and turning in her bed, and many soliloquies, which, if we had no better matter for our reader, we would give him; she at last rung the bell as abovementioned, and was presently attended by Mrs. Slipslop, who was not much better pleased with Joseph, than the lady herself.

Slipslop, said Lady Booby, *when did you see Joseph?* The poor woman was so surprized at the unexpected sound of his name, at so critical a time, that she had the greatest difficulty to conceal the confusion she was under from her mistress, whom she answered nevertheless, with pretty good confidence, though not entirely void of fear of suspicion, that she had not seen him that morning. 'I am afraid,' said Lady Booby, 'he is a wild young fellow.' 'That he is,' said Slipslop, 'and a wicked one too. To my knowledge he games, drinks, swears and fights eternally: besides he is horribly *indicted* to wenching.' 'Ay!' said the lady, 'I never heard that of him.' 'O madam,' answered the other, 'he is so lewd a rascal that if your ladyship keeps him much longer, you will not have one virgin in your house except myself. And yet I can't conceive what the wenches see in him, to be so foolishly fond as they are; in my eyes he is as ugly a scarecrow as I ever *upheld*.' 'Nay,' said the lady, 'the boy is well enough.'—'La ma'am,' cries Slipslop, 'I think him the *ragmaticallest* fellow in the family.' 'Sure, Slipslop,' says she, 'you are mistaken: but which of the women do you most suspect?' 'Madam,' says Slipslop, 'there is Betty[1] the chamber-maid, I am almost *convicted*, is with child by him.' 'Ay!' says the lady, 'then pray pay her her wages instantly. I will keep no such sluts in my family. And as for Joseph, you may discard him too.' 'Would your ladyship have him paid off immediately?' cries Slipslop, 'for perhaps, when Betty is gone, he may mend; and really the boy is a good servant, and a strong healthy *luscious* boy enough.' 'This morning,' answered the lady with some vehemence. 'I wish madam,' cries Slipslop, 'your ladyship would be so good as to try him a little longer.' 'I will not have my commands disputed,' said the lady, 'sure you are not fond of him yourself.' 'I madam?' cries Slip-

---

1 A generic name for chambermaids at the time.

slop, reddening, if not blushing, 'I should be sorry to think your ladyship had any reason to *respect* me of fondness for a fellow; and if it be your pleasure, I shall fulfill it with as much *reluctance* as possible.' 'As little, I suppose you mean,' said the lady; 'and so about it instantly.' Mrs. Slipslop went out, and the lady had scarce taken two turns before she fell to knocking and ringing with great violence. Slipslop, who did not travel post-haste, soon returned, and was countermanded as to Joseph, but ordered to send Betty about her business without delay. She went out a second time with much greater alacrity than before; when the lady began immediately to accuse herself of want of resolution, and to apprehend the return of her affection with its pernicious consequences: she therefore applied herself again to the bell, and resummoned Mrs. Slipslop into her presence; who again returned, and was told by her mistress, that she had consider'd better of the matter, and was absolutely resolved to turn away Joseph; which she ordered her to do immediately. Slipslop, who knew the violence of her lady's temper, and would not venture her place for any Adonis or Hercules in the universe, left her a third time; which she had no sooner done, than the little god Cupid, fearing he had not yet done the lady's business, took a fresh arrow with the sharpest point out of his quiver, and shot it directly into her heart: in other and plainer language, the lady's passion got the better of her reason. She called back Slipslop once more, and told her, she had resolved to see the boy, and examine him herself; therefore bid her send him up. This wavering in her mistress's temper probably put something into the waiting-gentlewoman's head, not necessary to mention to the sagacious reader.

Lady Booby was going to call her back again, but could not prevail with herself. The next consideration therefore was, how she should behave to Joseph when he came in. She resolved to preserve all the dignity of the woman of fashion to her servant, and to indulge herself in this last view of Joseph (for that she was most certainly resolved it should be) at his own expence, by first insulting, and then discarding him.

O Love, what monstrous tricks dost thou play with thy votaries of both sexes! How dost thou deceive them, and make them deceive themselves! Their follies are thy delight! Their sighs make thee laugh, and their pangs are thy merriment!

Not the great Rich,[1] who turns men into monkeys, wheel-barrows, and whatever else best humours his fancy, hath so strangely metamorphosed the human shape; nor the great Cibber, who confounds all number, gender, and breaks through every rule of grammar at his will, hath so distorted the English language, as thou dost metamorphose and distort the human senses.

Thou puttest out our eyes, stoppest up our ears, and takest away the power of our nostrils; so that we can neither see the largest object, hear the loudest noise, nor smell the most poignant perfume. Again, when thou pleasest, thou can'st make a mole-hill appear as a mountain; a jew's-harp sound like a trumpet; and a dazy smell like a violet. Thou can'st make cowardice brave, avarice generous, pride humble, and cruelty tender-hearted. In short, thou turnest the heart of man inside-out, as a juggler[2] doth a petticoat, and bringest whatsoever pleaseth thee out from it. If there be any one who doubts all this, let him read the next chapter.

CHAPTER VIII

In which, after some very fine writing, the history goes on, and relates the interview between the lady and Joseph; where the latter hath set an example, which we despair of seeing followed by *his sex, in this vicious age.*

Now the rake Hesperus[3] had called for his breeches, and having well rubbed his drowsy eyes, prepared to dress himself for all night; by whose example his brother rakes on earth likewise

1 John Rich, theatrical manager at Lincoln's Inn Fields from 1714 and of a new theatre in Covent Garden from 1732. At both he produced pantomimes and entertainments. He was satirized by such writers as Fielding and Pope for debasing and vulgarizing theatre.

2 A magician.

3 The evening star.

leave those beds, in which they had slept away the day. Now Thetis the good housewife began to put on the pot in order to regale the good man Phœbus,[1] after his daily labours were over. In vulgar language, it was in the evening when Joseph attended his lady's orders.

But as it becomes us to preserve the character of this lady, who is the heroine of our tale; and as we have naturally a wonderful tenderness for that beautiful part of the human species, called the fair sex; before we discover too much of her frailty to our reader, it will be proper to give him a lively idea of that vast temptation, which overcame all the efforts of a modest and virtuous mind; and then we humbly hope his good-nature will rather pity than condemn the imperfection of human virtue.

Nay, the ladies themselves will, we hope, be induced, by considering the uncommon variety of charms, which united in this young man's person, to bridle their rampant passion for chastity, and be at least, as mild as their violent modesty and virtue will permit them, in censuring the conduct of a woman, who, perhaps, was in her own disposition as chaste as those pure and sanctified virgins, who, after a life innocently spent in the gaieties of the town, begin about fifty to attend twice *per diem*, at the polite churches and chapels, to return thanks for the grace which preserved them formerly amongst beaus from temptations, perhaps less powerful than what now attacked the Lady Booby.

Mr. Joseph Andrews was now in the one and twentieth year of his age. He was of the highest degree of middle stature. His limbs were put together with great elegance and no less strength. His legs and thighs were formed in the exactest proportion. His shoulders were broad and brawny, but yet his arms hung so easily, that he had all the symptoms of strength without the least clumsiness. His hair was of a nut-brown colour, and was displayed in wanton ringlets down his back. His forehead was high, his eyes dark, and as full of sweetness as of fire. His nose a little inclined to the Roman. His teeth white and even. His lips full, red, and soft. His beard was only rough on his chin

1 Thetis is a Nereid (or divinity) of the sea, where the sun in classical literature rose and set; and Phoebus (or Apollo) is god of the sun.

and upper lip; but his cheeks, in which his blood glowed, were overspread with a thick down. His countenance had a tenderness joined with a sensibility[1] inexpressible. Add to this the most perfect neatness in his dress, and an air, which to those who have not seen many noblemen, would give an idea of nobility.

Such was the person who now appeared before the lady. She viewed him some time in silence, and twice or thrice before she spake, changed her mind as to the manner in which she should begin. At length, she said to him, 'Joseph, I am sorry to hear such complaints against you; I am told you behave so rudely to the maids, that they cannot do their business in quiet; I mean those who are not wicked enough to hearken to your solicitations. As to others, they may not, perhaps, call you rude: for there are wicked sluts who make one ashamed of one's own sex; and are as ready to admit any nauseous familiarity as fellows to offer it; nay, there are such in my family: but they shall not stay in it; that impudent trollop, who is with child by you, is discharged by this time.'

As a person who is struck through the heart with a thunderbolt, looks extremely surprised, nay, and perhaps is so too.— Thus the poor Joseph received the false accusation of his mistress; he blushed and looked confounded, which she misinterpreted to be symptoms of his guilt, and thus went on.

'Come hither, Joseph: another mistress might discard you for these offences; but I have a compassion for your youth, and if I could be certain you would be no more guilty—Consider, child, (*laying her hand carelessly upon his*) you are a handsome young fellow, and might do better; you might make your fortune—.' 'Madam,' said Joseph, 'I do assure your ladyship, I don't know whether any maid in the house is man or woman —.' 'Oh fie! Joseph,' answer'd the lady, 'don't commit another crime in denying the truth. I could pardon the first; but I hate a lyar.' 'Madam,' cries Joseph, 'I hope your ladyship will not be offended at my asserting my innocence: for by all that is sacred, I have never offered more than kissing.' 'Kissing!' said the lady, with

1 Sensitivity.

great discomposure of countenance, and more redness in her cheeks, than anger in her eyes, 'do you call that no crime? Kissing, Joseph, is as a prologue to a play. Can I believe a young fellow of your age and complexion will be content with kissing? No, Joseph, there is no woman who grants that but will grant more, and I am deceived greatly in you, if you would not put her closely to it. What would you think, Joseph, if I admitted you to kiss me?' Joseph reply'd, 'he would sooner die than have any such thought.' 'And yet, Joseph,' returned she, 'ladies have admitted their footmen to such familiarities; and footmen, I confess to you, much less deserving them; fellows without half your charms: for such might almost excuse the crime. Tell me, therefore, Joseph, if I should admit you to such freedom, what would you think of me?—tell me freely.' 'Madam,' said Joseph, 'I should think your ladyship condescended a great deal below yourself.' 'Pugh!' said she, 'that I am to answer to myself: but would not you insist on more? Would you be contented with a kiss? Would not your inclinations be all on fire rather by such a favour?' 'Madam,' said Joseph, 'if they were, I hope I should be able to controll them, without suffering them to get the better of my virtue.'—You have heard, reader, poets talk of the statue of Surprize;[1] you have heard likewise, or else you have heard very little, how Surprize made one of the sons of Crœsus speak tho' he was dumb.[2] You have seen the faces, in the eighteen-penny gallery, when through the trap-door, to soft or no musick, Mr. Bridgewater, Mr. William Mills,[3] or some other of ghostly appearance, hath ascended with a face all pale with powder, and a shirt all bloody with ribbons; but from none of these, nor from Phidias, or Praxiteles,[4] if they should return to

---

1 A fairly common poetical image, found for example in Ovid's *Metamorphoses* (3.418–19) and Shakespeare's *Richard III* (3.7.25–26). Contemporary acting manuals also advised actors to study statues, prints etc. for poses of different passions.

2 The mute son of Croesus, king of Lydia, was shocked into uttering his first words when he saw an enemy soldier approaching his father: "Fellow, slay not Croesus" (Herodotus 1.85).

3 Two actors who performed in Fielding's plays. Roger Bridgewater (d. 1754) also regularly appeared as the ghost in *Hamlet* and William Mills (d. 1750) as Banquo in *Macbeth*.

4 Phidias and Praxiteles were Athenian sculptors of the 5th and 4th centuries BC respectively.

life—no, not from the inimitable pencil of my friend Hogarth,[1] could you receive such an idea of surprize, as would have entered in at your eyes, had they beheld the Lady Booby, when those last words issued out from the lips of Joseph.—'Your virtue! (said the lady recovering after a silence of two minutes) I shall never survive it. Your virtue! Intolerable confidence! Have you the assurance to pretend, that when a lady demeans herself to throw aside the rules of decency, in order to honour you with the highest favour in her power, your virtue should resist her inclination? That when she had conquer'd her own virtue, she should find an obstruction in yours?' 'Madam,' said Joseph, 'I can't see why her having no virtue should be a reason against my having any. Or why, because I am a man, or because I am poor, my virtue must be subservient to her pleasures.' 'I am out of patience,' cries the lady: 'did ever mortal hear of a man's virtue! Did ever the greatest, or the gravest men pretend to any of this kind! Will magistrates who punish lewdness, or parsons, who preach against it, make any scruple of committing it? And can a boy, a stripling, have the confidence to talk of his virtue?' 'Madam,' says Joseph, 'that boy is the brother of Pamela, and would be ashamed, that the chastity of his family, which is preserved in her, should be stained in him. If there are such men as your ladyship mentions, I am sorry for it, and I wish they had an opportunity of reading over those letters, which my father hath sent me of my sister Pamela's, nor do I doubt that such an example would amend them.' 'You impudent villain,' cries the lady in a rage, 'do you insult me with the follies of my relation, who hath exposed himself all over the country upon your sister's account? a little vixen, whom I have always wondered my late Lady John Booby ever kept in her house. Sirrah! get out of my sight, and prepare to set out this night, for I will order you your wages immediately, and you shall be stripped and turned away.—' 'Madam,' says Joseph, 'I am sorry I have offended your ladyship, I am sure I never intended it.' 'Yes, sirrah,' cries she, 'you have had the vanity to misconstrue the little innocent freedom I took in order to try, whether what I

---

1 See above, p. 44, n. 1.

had heard was true. O' my conscience, you have had the assurance to imagine, I was fond of you myself.' Joseph answered, he had only spoke out of tenderness for his virtue; at which words she flew into a violent passion, and refusing to hear more, ordered him instantly to leave the room.

He was no sooner gone, than she burst forth into the following exclamation: 'Whither doth this violent passion hurry us? What meannesses do we submit to from its impulse? Wisely we resist its first and least approaches; for it is then only we can assure ourselves the victory. No woman could ever safely say, *so far only will I go*. Have I not exposed myself to the refusal of my footman? I cannot bear the reflection.' Upon which she applied herself to the bell, and rung it with infinite more violence than was necessary; the faithful Slipslop attending near at hand: to say the truth, she had conceived a suspicion at her last interview with her mistress; and had waited ever since in the antichamber, having carefully applied her ears to the key-hole during the whole time, that the preceeding conversation passed between Joseph and the lady.

CHAPTER IX

What passed between the lady and Mrs. Slipslop, in which we prophesy there are some strokes which every one will not truly comprehend at the first reading.

'SLIPSLOP,' said the lady, 'I find too much reason to believe all thou hast told me of this wicked Joseph; I have determined to part with him instantly; so go you to the steward, and bid him pay him his wages.' Slipslop, who had preserved hitherto a distance to her lady, rather out of necessity than inclination, and who thought the knowledge of this secret had thrown down all distinction between them, answered her mistress very pertly, 'she wished she knew her own mind; and that she was certain she would call her back again, before she was got half way down stairs.' The lady replied, 'she had taken a resolution, and was resolved to keep it.' 'I am sorry for it,' cries Slipslop; 'and if I had known you would have punished the poor lad so severely, you should never have heard a *particle* of the matter. Here's a fuss indeed, about nothing.' 'Nothing!' returned my lady; 'do you think I will countenance lewdness in my house?' 'If you will turn away every footman,' said Slipslop, 'that is a lover of the sport, you must soon open the coach-door yourself, or get a sett of *mophrodites*[1] to wait upon you; and I am sure I hated the sight of them even singing in an opera.' 'Do as I bid you,' says my lady, 'and don't shock my ears with your beastly language.' 'Marry-come-up,' cries Slipslop, 'people's ears are sometimes the nicest[2] part about them.'

The lady, who began to admire the new style in which her waiting-gentlewoman delivered herself, and by the conclusion of her speech, suspected somewhat the truth, called her back, and desired to know what she meant by that extraordinary degree of freedom in which she thought proper to indulge her tongue. 'Freedom!' says Slipslop, 'I don't know what you call freedom, madam; servants have tongues as well as their mistresses.' 'Yes, and saucy ones too,' answered the lady: 'but I assure you I shall bear no such impertinence.' 'Impertinence! I don't know that I am impertinent,' says Slipslop. 'Yes indeed you are,' cries my lady; 'and unless you mend your manners, this house is no place for you.' 'Manners!' cries Slipslop, 'I never was thought to want manners *nor modesty neither*; and for places, there are more places than one; and I know what I know.' 'What do you know, mistress?' answered the lady. 'I am not obliged to tell that to every body,' says Slipslop, 'any more than I am obliged to keep it a secret.' 'I desire you would provide yourself,'[3] answered the lady. 'With all my heart,' replied the waiting-gentlewoman; and so departed in a passion, and slapped the door after her.

The lady too plainly perceived that her waiting-gentlewoman knew more than she would willingly have had her acquainted with; and this she imputed to Joseph's having dis-

---

1 Hermaphrodites. Slipslop is referring to the *castrati* (male sopranos) of Italian opera, which was very popular in London during the first half of the century but also the object of much criticism.

2 Most fastidious or "particular."

3 That is, make preparations to leave Lady Booby's service.

covered to her what past at the first interview. This therefore blew up her rage against him, and confirmed her in a resolution of parting with him.

But the dismissing Mrs. Slipslop was a point not so easily to be resolved upon: she had the utmost tenderness for her reputation, as she knew on that depended many of the most valuable blessings of life; particularly cards, making court'sies in public places, and above all, the pleasure of demolishing the reputations of others, in which innocent amusement she had an extraordinary delight. She therefore determined to submit to any insult from a servant, rather than run a risque of losing the title to so many great privileges.

She therefore sent for her steward, Mr. Peter Pounce; and ordered him to pay Joseph his wages, to strip off his livery and turn him out of the house that evening.

She then called Slipslop up, and after refreshing her spirits with a small cordial which she kept in her closet, she began in the following manner:

'Slipslop, why will you, who know my passionate temper, attempt to provoke me by your answers? I am convinced you are an honest servant, and should be very unwilling to part with you. I believe likewise, you have found me an indulgent mistress on many occasions, and have as little reason on your side to desire a change. I can't help being surprized therefore, that you will take the surest method to offend me. I mean repeating my words, which you know I have always detested.'

The prudent waiting-gentlewoman, had duly weighed the whole matter, and found on mature deliberation, that a good place in possession was better than one in expectation; as she found her mistress therefore inclined to relent, she thought proper also to put on some small condescension;[1] which was as readily accepted: and so the affair was reconciled, all offences forgiven, and a present of a gown and petticoat made her as an instance of her lady's future favour.

She offered once or twice to speak in favour of Joseph: but

1 Sense of submission.

found her lady's heart so obdurate, that she prudently dropt all such efforts. She considered there were more footmen in the house, and some as stout fellows, tho' not quite so handsome as Joseph: besides, the reader hath already seen her tender advances had not met with the encouragement she might have reasonably expected. She thought she had thrown away a great deal of sack and sweet-meats[1] on an ungrateful rascal; and being a little inclined to the opinion of that female sect, who hold one lusty young fellow to be near as good as another lusty young fellow, she at last gave up Joseph and his cause, and with a triumph over her passion highly commendable, walked off with her present, and with great tranquility paid a visit to a stone-bottle,[2] which is of sovereign use to a philosophical temper.

She left not her mistress so easy. The poor lady could not reflect, without agony, that her dear reputation was in the power of her servants. All her comfort, as to Joseph was, that she hoped he did not understand her meaning; at least, she could say for herself, she had not plainly express'd any thing to him; and as to Mrs. Slipslop, she imagined she could bribe her to secrecy.

But what hurt her most was, that in reality she had not so entirely conquered her passion; the little god lay lurking in her heart, tho' anger and disdain so hoodwinked her, that she could not see him. She was a thousand times on the very brink of revoking the sentence she had passed against the poor youth. Love became his advocate, and whispered many things in his favour. Honour likewise endeavoured to vindicate his crime, and Pity to mitigate his punishment; on the other side, Pride and Revenge spoke as loudly against him: and thus the poor lady was tortured with perplexity; opposite passions distracting and tearing her mind different ways.

So have I seen, in the Hall of Westminster; where Serjeant Bramble hath been retained on the right side, and Serjeant Puzzle on the left; the balance of opinion (so equal were their

---

1 White wine and sugared cakes, etc.

2 Stoneware liquor bottle.

fees) alternately incline to either scale.[1] Now Bramble throws in an argument, and Puzzle's scale strikes the beam; again, Bramble shares the like fate, overpowered by the weight of Puzzle. Here Bramble hits, there Puzzle strikes; here one has you, there t'other has you; 'till at last all becomes one scene of confusion in the tortured minds of the hearers; equal wagers are laid on the success, and neither judge nor jury can possibly make any thing of the matter; all things are so enveloped by the careful serjeants in doubt and obscurity.

Or as it happens in the conscience, where honour and honesty pull one way, and a bribe and necessity another.—If it was only our present business to make similies, we could produce many more to this purpose: but a similie (as well as a word) to the wise. We shall therefore see a little after our hero, for whom the reader is doubtless in some pain.

CHAPTER X

Joseph writes another letter: his transactions with Mr. Peter Pounce, &c. with his departure from Lady Booby.

THE disconsolate Joseph, would not have had an understanding sufficient for the principal subject of such a book as this, if he had any longer misunderstood the drift of his mistress; and indeed that he did not discern it sooner, the reader will be pleased to apply to an unwillingness in him to discover what he must condemn in her as a fault. Having therefore quitted her presence, he retired into his own garret, and entered himself into an ejaculation on the numberless calamities which attended beauty, and the misfortune it was to be handsomer than one's neighbours.

He then sat down and addressed himself to his sister Pamela, in the following words:

---

1 The Hall of Westminster was the principal court of justice; serjeants (or sergeants) were lawyers of high rank; and scales are the traditional emblems of justice.

'Dear Sister Pamela,

'Hoping you are well, what news have I to tell you! O Pamela my mistress is fallen in love with me—that is, what great folks call falling in love, she has a mind to ruin me; but I hope, I shall have more resolution and more grace[1] than to part with my virtue to any lady upon earth.

'Mr. Adams hath often told me, that chastity is as great a virtue in a man as in a woman. He says he never knew any more than his wife, and I shall endeavour to follow his example. Indeed, it is owing entirely to his excellent sermons and advice, together with your letters, that I have been able to resist a temptation, which he says no man complies with, but he repents in this world, or is damned for it in the next; and why should I trust to repentance on my death-bed, since I may die in my sleep? What fine things are good advice and good examples! But I am glad she turned me out of the chamber as she did: for I had once almost forgotten every word Parson Adams had ever said to me.

'I don't doubt, dear sister, but you will have grace to preserve your virtue against all trials; and I beg you earnestly to pray, I may be enabled to preserve mine: for truly, it is very severely attacked by more than one: but, I hope I shall copy your example, and that of Joseph, my name's-sake;[2] and maintain my virtue against all temptations.'

Joseph had not finished his letter, when he was summoned down stairs by Mr. Peter Pounce, to receive his wages: for, besides that out of eight pounds a year, he allowed his father and mother four, he had been obliged, in order to furnish himself with musical instruments, to apply to the generosity of the aforesaid Peter, who, on urgent occasions, used to advance the servants their wages: not before they were due, but before they were payable; that is, perhaps, half a year after they were due, and this at the moderate premiums of fifty per cent, or a little more; by which charitable methods, together with lending

---

1 Divine favour and influence. Pamela makes similar appeals in her letters, and in similar language.

2 See above, p. 70, n. 2.

money to other people, and even to his own master and mistress, the honest man had, from nothing, in a few years amassed a small sum of twenty thousand pounds or thereabouts.[1]

Joseph having received his little remainder of wages, and having stript off his livery, was forced to borrow a frock and breeches of one of the servants: (for he was so beloved in the family, that they would all have lent him any thing) and being told by Peter, that he must not stay a moment longer in the house, than was necessary to pack up his linnen,[2] which he easily did in a very narrow compass; he took a melancholy leave of his fellow-servants, and set out at seven in the evening.

He had proceeded the length of two or three streets, before he absolutely determined with himself, whether he should leave the town that night, or procuring a lodging, wait 'till the morning. At last, the moon, shining very bright, helped him to come to a resolution of beginning his journey immediately, to which likewise he had some other inducements which the reader, without being a conjurer,[3] cannot possibly guess; 'till we have given him those hints, which it may be now proper to open.

CHAPTER XI

Of several new matters not expected.

It is an observation sometimes made, that to indicate our idea of a simple fellow, we say, *He is easily to be seen through*: nor do I believe it a more improper denotation of a simple book. Instead of applying this to any particular performance, we chuse rather to remark the contrary in this history, where the scene opens itself by small degrees, and he is a sagacious reader who can see two chapters before him.

---

1 The model for Peter Pounce was Peter Walter (1664?-1746), a landowner near the Fielding family estates. While steward to the Duke of Newcastle, he amassed a fortune lending money to his "betters" at exorbitant rates.

2 Underclothes, etc.

3 A person with special powers, a gifted person.

For this reason, we have not hitherto hinted a matter which now seems necessary to be explained; since it may be wondered at, first, that Joseph made such extraordinary haste out of town, which hath been already shewn; and secondly, which will be now shewn, that instead of proceeding to the habitation of his father and mother, or to his beloved sister Pamela, he chose rather to set out full speed to the Lady Booby's country seat, which he had left on his journey to London.

Be it known then, that in the same parish where this seat stood, there lived a young girl whom Joseph (tho' the best of sons and brothers) longed more impatiently to see than his parents or his sister. She was a poor girl, who had been formerly bred up in Sir John's[1] family; whence a little before the journey to London, she had been discarded by Mrs. Slipslop on account of her extraordinary beauty: for I never could find any other reason.

This young creature (who now lived with a farmer in the parish) had been always beloved by Joseph, and returned his affection. She was two years only younger than our hero. They had been acquainted from their infancy, and had conceived a very early liking for each other, which had grown to such a degree of affection, that Mr. Adams had with much ado prevented them from marrying; and persuaded them to wait, 'till a few years service and thrift had a little improved their experience, and enabled them to live comfortably together.

They followed this good man's advice; as indeed his word was little less than a law in his parish; for as he had shewn his parishioners by a uniform behaviour of thirty-five years duration, that he had their good entirely at heart; so they consulted him on every occasion, and very seldom acted contrary to his opinion.

Nothing can be imagined more tender than was the parting between these two lovers. A thousand sighs heaved the bosom of Joseph; a thousand tears distilled from the lovely eyes of Fanny, (for that was her name.) Tho' her modesty would only suffer her to admit his eager kisses, her violent love made her

---

1 Fielding means "Sir Thomas's."

more than passive in his embraces; and she often pulled him to her breast with a soft pressure, which, tho' perhaps it would not have squeezed an insect to death, caused more emotion in the heart of Joseph, than the closest Cornish hug[1] could have done.

The reader may perhaps wonder, that so fond a pair should during a twelve-month's absence never converse with one another; indeed there was but one reason which did, or could have prevented them; and this was, that poor Fanny could neither write nor read, nor could she be prevailed upon to transmit the delicacies of her tender and chaste passion, by the hands of an amanuensis.

They contented themselves therefore with frequent enquiries after each other's health; with a mutual confidence in each other's fidelity, and the prospect of their future happiness.

Having explained these matters to our reader, and, as far as possible, satisfied all his doubts, we return to honest Joseph, whom we left just set out on his travels by the light of the moon.

Those who have read any romance or poetry antient or modern, must have been informed, that love hath wings; by which they are not to understand, as some young ladies by mistake have done, that a lover can fly: the writers, by this ingenious allegory, intending to insinuate no more, than that lovers do not march like horse-guards;[2] in short, that they put the best leg foremost, which our lusty youth, who could walk with any man, did so heartily on this occasion, that within four hours, he reached a famous house of hospitality well known to the western traveller. It presents you a lion on the sign-post: and the master, who was christened Timotheus, is commonly called plain Tim.[3] Some have conceived that he hath particularly chosen the lion for his sign, as he doth in countenance greatly resemble that magnanimous beast, tho' his disposition savours more of the sweetness of the lamb. He is a person well received

---

1 The wrestlers of Cornwall were famous, and used a stranglehold called the Cornish hug.

2 The cavalry brigade of the household troops of the British royal family, who marched in stately fashion.

3 Probably Timothy Harris, the innkeeper of "The Red Lion" at Egham, Surrey.

among all sorts of men, being qualified to render himself agreeable to any; as he is well versed in history and politicks, hath a smattering in law and divinity, cracks a good jest, and plays wonderfully well on the French horn.

A violent storm of hail forced Joseph to take shelter in this inn, where he remembered Sir Thomas had dined in his way to town. Joseph had no sooner seated himself by the kitchin-fire, than Timotheus, observing his livery,[1] began to condole[2] the loss of his late master; who was, he said, his very particular and intimate acquaintance, with whom he had cracked many a merry bottle, aye many a dozen in his time. He then remarked that all those things were over now, all past, and just as if they had never been; and concluded with an excellent observation on the certainty of death, which his wife said was indeed very true. A fellow now arrived at the same inn with two horses, one of which he was leading farther down into the country to meet his master; these he put into the stable, and came and took his place by Joseph's side, who immediately knew him to be the servant of a neighbouring gentleman, who used to visit at their house.

This fellow was likewise forced in by the storm; for he had orders to go twenty miles farther[3] that evening, and luckily on the same road which Joseph himself intended to take. He therefore embraced this opportunity of complimenting his friend with his master's horses, (notwithstanding he had received express commands to the contrary) which was readily accepted: and so after they had drank a loving pot, and the storm was over, they set out together.

1 Fielding seems to have forgotten that in the previous chapter Joseph had been stripped of his livery.

2 Lament.

3 Probably Hartfordbridge, 35 miles from London, a stage for Salisbury.

CHAPTER XII

Containing many surprizing adventures, which Joseph Andrews met with on the road, scarce credible to those who have never travelled in a stage-coach.

NOTHING remarkable happened on the road, 'till their arrival at the inn, to which the horses were ordered; whither they came about two in the morning. The moon then shone very bright, and Joseph making his friend a present of a pint of wine, and thanking him for the favour of his horse, notwithstanding all entreaties to the contrary, proceeded on his journey on foot.

He had not gone above two miles, charmed with the hopes of shortly seeing his beloved Fanny, when he was met by two fellows in a narrow lane, and ordered to stand and deliver.[1] He readily gave them all the money he had, which was somewhat less than two pounds; and told them he hoped they would be so generous as to return him a few shillings, to defray his charges on his way home.

One of the ruffians answered with an oath, *Yes, we'll give you something presently: but first strip and be d—n'd to you.—Strip*, cry'd the other, *or I'll blow your brains to the devil.* Joseph, remembring that he had borrowed his coat and breeches of a friend; and that he should be ashamed of making any excuse for not returning them, reply'd, he hoped they would not insist on his clothes, which were not worth much; but consider the coldness of the night. *You are cold, are you, you rascal!* says one of the robbers, *I'll warm you with a vengeance*; and damning his eyes, snapt a pistol[2] at his head: which he had no sooner done, than the other levelled a blow at him with his stick, which Joseph, who was expert at cudgel-playing, caught with his, and returned the favour so successfully on his adversary, that he laid him sprawling at his feet, and at the same instant received a blow from behind, with the butt-end of a pistol from the other villain, which felled him to the ground, and totally deprived him of his senses.

---

1 This episode is based on the parable of the Good Samaritan, Luke 10:30-37.

2 Pulled the trigger, but the flintlock failed to fire.

The thief, who had been knocked down, had now recovered himself; and both together fell to be-labouring poor Joseph with their sticks, till they were convinced they had put an end to his miserable being: they then stript him entirely naked, threw him into a ditch, and departed with their booty.

The poor wretch, who lay motionless a long time, just began to recover his senses as a stage-coach came by. The postillion hearing a man's groans, stopt his horses, and told the coachman, 'he was certain there was a *dead* man lying in the ditch, for he heard him groan.' 'Go on, sirrah,' says the coachman, 'we are confounded late, and have no time to look after dead men.' A lady, who heard what the postillion said, and likewise heard the groan, called eagerly to the coachman, 'to stop and see what was the matter.' Upon which he bid the postillion 'alight, and look into the ditch.' He did so, and returned, 'that there was a man sitting upright as naked as ever he was born.'—'O *J-sus*,' cry'd the lady, 'A naked man! Dear coachman, drive on and leave him.' Upon this the gentlemen got out of the coach; and Joseph begged them, 'to have mercy upon him: for that he had been robbed, and almost beaten to death.' 'Robbed,' cries an old gentleman; 'let us make all the haste imaginable, or we shall be robbed too.' A young man, who belonged to the law answered, 'he wished they had past by without taking any notice: but that now they might be proved to have been *last in his company*; if he should die, they might be called to some account for his murther. He therefore thought it adviseable to save the poor creature's life, for their own sakes, if possible; at least, if he died, to prevent the jury's finding *that they fled for it*.[1] He was therefore *of opinion*, to take the man into the coach, and carry him to the next inn.' The lady insisted, 'that he should not come into the coach. That if they lifted him in, she would herself alight: for she had rather stay in that place to all eternity, than ride with a naked man.' The coachman objected, 'that he could not suffer him to be taken in, unless some body would pay a shilling for his carriage the four miles.' Which the two gentlemen refused to do; but the lawyer, who was afraid of some mischief happen-

---

1 Fleeing the scene of a capital crime, even if innocent, was an offence punishable by forfeiture of one's goods.

ing to himself if the wretch was left behind in that condition, saying, 'no man could be too cautious in these matters, and that he remembred very extraordinary cases in the books,' threatned the coachman, and bid him deny taking him up at his peril; 'for that if he died, he should be indicted for his murther, and if he lived, and brought an action against him, he would willingly take a brief in it.' These words had a sensible effect on the coachman, who was well acquainted with the person who spoke them; and the old gentleman abovementioned, thinking the naked man would afford him frequent opportunities of shewing his wit to the lady, offered to join with the company in giving a mug of beer for his fare; till partly alarmed by the threats of the one, and partly by the promises of the other, and being perhaps *a little* moved with compassion at the poor creature's condition, who stood bleeding and shivering with the cold, he at length agreed; and Joseph was now advancing to the coach, where seeing the lady, who held the sticks of her fan before her eyes, he absolutely refused, miserable as he was, to enter, unless he was furnished with sufficient covering, to prevent giving the least offence to decency. So perfectly modest was this young man; such mighty effects had the spotless example of the amiable Pamela, and the excellent sermons of Mr. Adams wrought upon him.

Though there were several great coats about the coach, it was not easy to get over this difficulty which Joseph had started. The two gentlemen complained they were cold, and could not spare a rag; the man of wit saying, with a laugh, *that charity began at home*; and the coachman, who had two great coats spread under him, refused to lend either, lest they should be made bloody; the lady's footman desired to be excused for the same reason, which the lady herself, notwithstanding her abhorence of a naked man, approved: and it is more probable, poor Joseph, who obstinately adhered to his modest resolution, must have perished, unless the postillion, (a lad who hath been since transported for robbing a hen-roost) had voluntarily stript off a great coat, his only garment, at the same time swearing a great oath, (for which he was rebuked by the passengers) 'that he would rather ride in his shirt all his life, than suffer a fellow-creature to lie in so miserable a condition.'

Joseph, having put on the great coat, was lifted into the coach, which now proceeded on its journey. He declared himself almost dead with the cold, which gave the man of wit an occasion to ask the lady, if she could not accommodate him with a dram.[1] She answered with some resentment, 'she wondered at his asking her such a question;' but assured him, 'she never tasted any such thing.'

The lawyer was enquiring into the circumstances of the robbery, when the coach stopt, and one of the ruffians, putting a pistol in, demanded their money of the passengers; who readily gave it them; and the lady, in her fright, delivered up a little silver bottle, of about a half-pint size, which the rogue clapping it to his mouth, and drinking her health, declared held some of the best Nantes[2] he had ever tasted; this the lady afterwards assured the company was the mistake of her maid, for that she had ordered her to fill the bottle with Hungary water.[3]

As soon as the fellows were departed, the lawyer, who had, it seems, a case of pistols in the seat of the coach, informed the company, that if it had been day-light, and he could have come at his pistols, he would not have submitted to the robbery; he likewise set forth, that he had often met highwaymen when he travelled on horseback, but none ever durst attack him; concluding, that if he had not been more afraid for the lady than for himself, he should not have now parted with his money so easily.

As wit is generally observed to love to reside in empty pockets; so the gentleman, whose ingenuity we have above remark'd, as soon as he had parted with his money, began to grow wonderfully facetious. He made frequent allusions to Adam and Eve, and said many excellent things on figs and fig-leaves; which perhaps gave more offence to Joseph than to any other in the company. The lawyer likewise made several very pretty jests, without departing from his profession. He said, 'if Joseph and the lady were alone, he would be the more capable of making a *conveyance* to her, as his *affairs* were not *fettered* with

1 A small quantity of alcoholic drink.

2 Brandy, from Nantes, France.

3 A medicinal liquor made of rosemary flowers and spirit of wine.

any *incumbrance*; he'd warrant, he soon suffered a *recovery* by a writ of *entry*, which was the proper way to create *heirs in tail*; that for his own part, he would engage to make so *firm a settlement* in a coach, that there should be no danger of an ejectment;'[1] with an inundation of the like gibbrish, which he continued to vent till the coach arrived at an inn, where one servant-maid only was up in readiness to attend the coachman, and furnish him with cold meat and a dram. Joseph desired to alight, and that he might have a bed prepared for him, which the maid readily promised to perform; and being a good-natur'd wench, and not so squeamish as the lady had been, she clapt a large faggot on the fire, and furnishing Joseph with a great coat belonging to one of the hostlers, desired him to sit down and warm himself, whilst she made his bed. The coachman, in the mean time, took an opportunity to call up a surgeon, who lived within a few doors: after which, he reminded his passengers how late they were, and after they had taken leave of Joseph, hurried them off as fast as he could.

The wench soon got Joseph to bed, and promised to use her interest[2] to borrow him a shirt; but imagined, as she afterwards said, by his being so bloody, that he must be a dead man: she ran with all speed to hasten the surgeon, who was more than half drest, apprehending that the coach had been overturned and some gentleman or lady hurt. As soon as the wench had informed him at his window, that it was a poor foot passenger who had been stripped of all he had, and almost murdered; he chid her for disturbing him so early, slipped off his clothes again, and very quietly returned to bed and to sleep.

Aurora now began to shew her blooming cheeks over the hills, whilst ten millions of feathered songsters, in jocund chorus, repeated odes a thousand times sweeter than those of our Laureate, and sung both *the day and the song*;[3] when the master of the inn, Mr. Tow-wouse, arose, and learning from his maid

---

1 The lawyer's ribald double-entendres are drawn from the language of property law.

2 Influence.

3 Colley Cibber had been Poet Laureate since 1730, composing poetry for certain public occasions which had long become standing jokes. The allusion here is to one of the official New Year odes ("Then sing the day, / And sing the song").

an account of the robbery, and the situation of his poor naked guest, he shook his head, and cried, *Good-lack-a-day*! and then ordered the girl to carry him one of his own shirts.

Mrs. Tow-wouse was just awake, and had stretched out her arms in vain to fold her departed husband, when the maid entered the room. 'Who's there? Betty?' 'Yes madam.' 'Where's your master?' 'He's without, madam; he hath sent me for a shirt to lend a poor naked man, who hath been robbed and murdered.' 'Touch one, if you dare, you slut,' said Mrs. Tow-wouse, 'your master is a pretty sort of a man to take in naked vagabonds, and clothe them with his own clothes. I shall have no such doings.—If you offer to touch any thing, I will throw the chamber-pot at your head. Go, send your master to me.' 'Yes madam,' answered Betty. As soon as he came in, she thus began: 'What the devil do you mean by this, Mr. Tow-wouse? Am I to buy shirts to lend to a sett of scabby rascals?' 'My dear,' said Mr. Tow-wouse, 'this is a poor wretch.' 'Yes,' says she, 'I know it is a poor wretch, but what the devil have we to do with poor wretches? The law makes us provide for too many already. We shall have thirty or forty poor wretches in red coats shortly.'[1] 'My dear,' cries Tow-wouse, 'this man hath been robbed of all he hath.' 'Well then,' says she, 'where's his money to pay his reckoning? Why doth not such a fellow go to an alehouse?[2] I shall send him packing as soon as I am up, I assure you.' 'My dear,' said he, 'common charity won't suffer you to do that.' 'Common charity, a f—t!' says she, 'common charity teaches us to provide for ourselves, and our families; and I and mine won't be ruined by your charity, I assure you.' 'Well,' says he, 'my dear, do as you will when you are up, you know I never contradict you.' 'No,' says she, 'if the Devil was to contradict me, I would make the house too hot to hold him.'

With such like discourses they consumed near half an hour, whilst Betty provided a shirt from the hostler, who was one of her sweethearts, and put it on poor Joseph. The surgeon had

---

1 Because of the shortage of barracks, innkeepers were compelled to billet soldiers for a pittance.

2 Whereas inns were set up to lodge and feed travellers, alehouses (the humblest form of hostelry) were primarily places for drinking.

likewise at last visited him, had washed and drest his wounds, and was now come to acquaint Mr. Tow-wouse, that his guest was in such extreme danger of his life, that he scarce saw any hopes of his recovery.—'Here's a pretty kettle of fish,' cries Mrs. Tow-wouse, 'you have brought upon us! We are like to have a funeral at our own expence.' Tow-wouse, (who notwithstanding his charity, would have given his vote as freely as he ever did at an election, that any other house in the kingdom, should have had quiet possession of his guest) answered, 'My dear, I am not to blame: he was brought hither by the stage-coach; and Betty had put him to bed before I was stirring.' 'I'll *Betty* her,' says she—At which, with half her garments on, the other half under her arm, she sallied out in quest of the unfortunate Betty, whilst Tow-wouse and the surgeon went to pay a visit to poor Joseph, and enquire into the circumstance of this melancholy affair.

CHAPTER XIII

What happened to Joseph during his sickness at the inn, with the curious discourse between him and Mr. Barnabas the parson of the parish.

As soon as Joseph had communicated a particular history of the robbery, together with a short account of himself, and his intended journey, he asked the surgeon 'if he apprehended him to be in any danger:' to which the surgeon very honestly answered, 'he feared he was; for that his pulse was very exalted and feverish, and if his fever should prove more than *symptomatick*,[1] it would be impossible to save him.' Joseph, fetching a deep sigh, cried, '*Poor Fanny, I would I could have lived to see thee! but G—'s will be done.*'

The surgeon then advised him, 'if he had any worldly affairs to settle, that he would do it as soon as possible; for though he hoped he might recover, yet he thought himself obliged to

1 Not simply an indication of the injury, but a primary illness in itself.

acquaint him he was in great danger, and if the malign concoction of his humours[1] should cause a suscitation[2] of his fever, he might soon grow delirious, and incapable to make his will.' Joseph answered, 'that it was impossible for any creature in the universe to be in a poorer condition than himself: for since the robbery he had not one thing of any kind whatever, which he could call his own.' *I had*, said he, *a poor little piece of gold which they took away, that would have been a comfort to me in all my afflictions, but surely, Fanny, I want nothing to remind me of thee. I have thy dear image in my heart, and no villain can ever tear it thence.*

Joseph desired paper and pens to write a letter, but they were refused him; and he was advised to use all his endeavours to compose himself. They then left him; and Mr. Tow-wouse sent to a clergyman, to come and administer his good offices to the soul of poor Joseph, since the surgeon despaired of making any successful applications to his body.

Mr. Barnabas (for that was the clergyman's name)[3] came as soon as sent for, and having first drank a dish of tea with the landlady, and afterwards a bowl of punch with the landlord, he walked up to the room where Joseph lay: but, finding him asleep, returned to take the other sneaker,[4] which when he had finished, he again crept softly up to the chamber-door, and, having opened it, heard the sick man talking to himself in the following manner:

'O most adorable Pamela! most virtuous sister, whose example could alone enable me to withstand all the temptations of riches and beauty, and to preserve my virtue pure and chaste, for the arms of my dear Fanny, if it had pleased Heaven that I should ever have come unto them. What riches, or honours, or pleasures can make us amends for the loss of innocence? Doth

---

1 According to the doctrine of the Greek physician Hippocrates (c. 460–c. 357 BC), credited with founding medical science, complete health could prevail only if the four cardinal humours—blood, yellow bile, black bile, and phlegm—were perfectly proportioned. By Fielding's time, however, this theory had been somewhat discredited.

2 A rousing or quickening.

3 Ironically named, for the biblical Barnabas gives the apostles all his wealth (Acts 4:36).

4 A small bowl of punch.

not that alone afford us more consolation, than all worldly acquisitions? What but innocence and virtue could give any comfort to such a miserable wretch as I am? Yet these can make me prefer this sick and painful bed to all the pleasures I should have found in my lady's. These can make me face death without fear; and though I love my Fanny more than ever man loved a woman; these can teach me to resign myself to the Divine will without repining. O thou delightful charming creature, if Heaven had indulged thee to my arms, the poorest, humblest state would have been a paradise; I could have lived with thee in the lowest cottage, without envying the palaces, the dainties, or the riches of any man breathing. But I must leave thee, leave thee for ever, my dearest angel, I must think of another world, and I heartily pray thou may'st meet comfort in this.'—Barnabas thought he had heard enough; so down stairs he went, and told Tow-wouse he could do his guest no service: for that he was very light-headed, and had uttered nothing but a rhapsody of nonsense all the time he stayed in the room.

The surgeon returned in the afternoon, and found his patient in a higher fever, as he said, than when he left him, though not delirious: for notwithstanding Mr. Barnabas's opinion, he had not been once out of his senses since his arrival at the inn.

Mr. Barnabas was again sent for, and with much difficulty prevailed on to make another visit. As soon as he entered the room, he told Joseph, 'he was come to pray by him, and to prepare him for another world: in the first place therefore, he hoped he had repented of all his sins?' Joseph answered, 'he hoped he had: but there was one thing which he knew not whether he should call a sin; if it was, he feared he should die in the commission of it, and that was the regret of parting with a young woman, whom he loved as tenderly as he did his heart-strings?' Barnabas bad him be assured, 'that any repining at the Divine will, was one of the greatest sins he could commit; that he ought to forget all carnal affections, and think of better things.' Joseph said, 'that neither in this world nor the next, he could forget his Fanny, and that the thought however grievous, of parting from her for ever, was not half so tormenting, as the fear of what she would suffer when she knew his misfortune.' Barnabas said, 'that such fears argued a diffidence[1] and despondence very criminal; that he must divest himself of all human passion, and fix his heart above.' Joseph answered, 'that was what he desired to do, and should be obliged to him, if he would enable him to accomplish it.' Barnabas replied, 'That must be done by grace.' Joseph besought him to discover how he might attain it. Barnabas answered, 'By prayer and faith.' He then questioned him concerning his forgiveness of the thieves. Joseph answered, 'he feared, that was more than he could do: for nothing would give him more pleasure than to hear they were taken.' 'That,' cries Barnabas, 'is for the sake of justice.' 'Yes,' said Joseph, 'but if I was to meet them again, I am afraid I should attack them, and kill them too, if I could.' 'Doubtless,' answered Barnabas, 'it is lawful to kill a thief: but can you say, you forgive them as a Christian ought?' Joseph desired to know what that forgiveness was. 'That is,' answered Barnabas, 'to forgive them as—as—it is to forgive them as—in short, it is to forgive them as a Christian.' Joseph reply'd, 'he forgave them as much as he could.' 'Well, well,' said Barnabas, 'that will do.' He then demanded of him, 'if he remembered any more sins unrepented of; and if he did, he desired him to make haste and repent of them as fast as he could: that they might repeat over a few prayers together.' Joseph answered, 'he could not recollect any great crimes he had been guilty of, and that those he had committed, he was sincerely sorry for.' Barnabas said that was enough, and then proceeded to prayer with all the expedition he was master of: some company then waiting for him below in the parlour, where the ingredients for punch were all in readiness; but no one would squeeze the oranges till he came.

Joseph complained he was dry, and desired a little tea; which Barnabas reported to Mrs. Tow-wouse, who answered, 'she had just done drinking it, and could not be slopping[2] all day;' but ordered Betty to carry him up some small beer.

Betty obeyed her mistress's commands; but Joseph, as soon as he had tasted it, said, he feared it would encrease his fever, and

---

1 A lack of faith.

2 Steeping tea.

that he longed very much for tea: to which the good-natured Betty answered, he should have tea, if there was any in the land; she accordingly went and bought him some herself, and attended him with it; where we will leave her and Joseph together for some time, to entertain the reader with other matters.

CHAPTER XIV

Being very full of adventures, which succeeded each other at the inn.

It was now the dusk of the evening, when a grave person rode into the inn, and committing his horse to the hostler, went directly into the kitchin, and having called for a pipe of tobacco, took his place by the fire-side; where several other persons were likewise assembled.

The discourse ran altogether on the robbery which was committed the night before, and on the poor wretch, who lay above in the dreadful condition, in which we have already seen him. Mrs. Tow-wouse said, 'she wondered what the devil Tom Whipwell meant by bringing such guests to her house, when there were so many ale-houses on the road proper for their reception? But she assured him, if he died, the parish should be at the expence of the funeral.' She added, 'nothing would serve the fellow's turn but tea, she would assure him.' Betty, who was just returned from her charitable office, answered, she believed he was a gentleman: for she never saw a finer skin in her life. 'Pox on his skin,' replied Mrs. Tow-wouse, 'I suppose, that is all we are like to have for the reckoning. I desire no such gentlemen should ever call at the Dragon;' (which it seems was the sign of the inn.)[1]

The gentleman lately arrived discovered a great deal of emotion at the distress of this poor creature, whom he observed not to be fallen into the most compassionate hands. And indeed, if Mrs. Tow-wouse had given no utterance to the sweetness of her temper, nature had taken such pains in her

1 Although a popular sign of inns, the dragon was traditionally an emblem of avarice.

countenance, that Hogarth himself never gave more expression to a picture.

Her person was short, thin, and crooked. Her forehead projected in the middle, and thence descended in a declivity to the top of her nose, which was sharp and red, and would have hung over her lips, had not nature turned up the end of it. Her lips were two bits of skin, which, whenever she spoke, she drew together in a purse. Her chin was peeked, and at the upper end of that skin, which composed her cheeks, stood two bones, that almost hid a pair of small red eyes. Add to this, a voice most wonderfully adapted to the sentiments it was to convey, being both loud and hoarse.

It is not easy to say, whether the gentleman had conceived a greater dislike for his landlady, or compassion for her unhappy guest. He enquired very earnestly of the surgeon, who was now come into the kitchin, 'whether he had any hopes of his recovery?' He begged him, to use all possible means towards it, telling him, 'it was the duty of men of all professions, to apply their skill *gratis* for the relief of the poor and necessitous.' The surgeon answered, 'he should take proper care: but he defied all the surgeons in London to do him any good.' 'Pray, sir,' said the gentleman, 'what are his wounds?'—'Why, do you know any thing of wounds?' says the surgeon, (winking upon Mrs. Towwouse.) 'Sir, I have a small smattering in surgery,' answered the gentleman. 'A smattering—ho, ho, ho!' said the surgeon, 'I believe it is a smattering indeed.'

The company were all attentive, expecting to hear the doctor, who was what they call a dry fellow, expose the gentleman.

He began therefore with an air of triumph: 'I suppose, sir, you have travelled.' 'No really, sir,' said the gentleman. 'Ho! then you have practised in the hospitals, perhaps.'—'No, sir.' 'Hum! not that neither? Whence, sir, then, if I may be so bold to enquire, have you got your knowledge in surgery?' 'Sir,' answered the gentleman, 'I do not pretend to much; but, the little I know I have from books.' 'Books!' cries the doctor.—'What, I suppose you have read Galen and Hippocrates!'[1] 'No,

1 Galen, most celebrated Greek physician (c. AD 130–c. 200); for Hippocrates, see above, p. 101, n. 1.

sir,' said the gentlman. 'How! you understand surgery,' answers the doctor, 'and not read Galen and Hippocrates!' 'Sir,' cries the other, 'I believe there are many surgeons who have never read these authors.' 'I believe so too,' says the doctor, 'more shame for them: but thanks to my education: I have them by heart, and very seldom go without them both in my pocket.' 'They are pretty large books,' said the gentleman. 'Aye,' said the doctor, 'I believe I know how large they are better than you,' (at which he fell a winking, and the whole company burst into a laugh.)

The doctor pursuing his triumph, asked the gentleman, 'if he did not understand physick as well as surgery.' 'Rather better,' answered the gentleman. 'Aye, like enough,' cries the doctor, with a wink. 'Why, I know a little of physick too.' 'I wish I knew half so much,' said Tow-wouse, 'I'd never wear an apron again.' 'Why, I believe, landlord,' cries the doctor, 'there are few men, tho' I say it, within twelve miles of the place, that handle a fever better.—*Veniente occurrite morbo*:[1] that is my method.—I suppose brother, you understand Latin?' 'A little,' says the gentleman. 'Aye, and Greek now I'll warrant you: *Ton dapomibominos poluflosboio thalasses*.[2] But I have almost forgot these things, I could have repeated Homer by heart once.'—'Efags![3] the gentleman has caught a *traytor*,'[4] says Mrs. Tow-wouse; at which they all fell a laughing.

The gentleman, who had not the least affection for joking, very contentedly suffered the doctor to enjoy his victory; which he did with no small satisfaction: and having sufficiently sounded his depth, told him, 'he was thoroughly convinced of his great learning and abilities; and that he would be obliged to him, if he would let him know his opinion of his patient's case above stairs.' 'Sir,' says the doctor, 'his case is that of a dead man.—The contusion on his head has *perforated* the *internal membrane* of the *occiput*, and *divellicated* that *radical* small *minute*

---

1 "Oppose the disease at its onset" (Persius, *Satires* 3.64). It is a misquotation.

2 Two unconnected phrases from the *Iliad*, resulting in a line of high-flown nonsense: *Ton dapomibominos* ("answering him") and *poluflosboio thalasses* ("of the loud sounding sea").

3 In faith, by my faith. (Also *ifaukins*.)

4 Mrs. Tow-wouse probably means "caught a tartar," that is, "to tackle one who unexpectedly proves to be too formidable" (*OED*).

invisible *nerve*, which *coheres* to the *pericranium*; and this was attended with a fever at first *symptomatick*, then *pneumatick*, and he is at length *grown deliruus*, or delirious, as the vulgar express it.'[1]

He was proceeding in this learned manner, when a mighty noise interrupted him. Some young fellows in the neighbourhood had taken one of the thieves, and were bringing him into the inn. Betty ran up stairs with this news to Joseph; who begged they might search for a little piece of broken gold, which had a ribband tied to it, and which he could swear to amongst all the hoards of the richest men in the universe.

Notwithstanding the fellow's persisting in his innocence, the mob were very busy in searching him, and presently, among other things, pulled out the piece of gold just mentioned; which Betty no sooner saw, than she laid violent hands on it, and conveyed it up to Joseph, who received it with raptures of joy, and hugging it in his bosom declared, *he could now die contented.*

Within a few minutes afterwards, came in some other fellows, with a bundle which they had found in a ditch; and which was indeed the clothes which had been stripped off from Joseph, and the other things they had taken from him.

The gentleman no sooner saw the coat, than he declared he knew the livery;[2] and if it had been taken from the poor creature above stairs, desired he might see him: for that he was very well acquainted with the family to whom that livery belonged.

He was accordingly conducted up by Betty: but what, reader, was the surprize on both sides, when he saw Joseph was the person in bed; and when Joseph discovered the face of his good friend Mr. Abraham Adams.

It would be impertinent to insert a discourse which chiefly turned on the relation of matters already well known to the reader: for as soon as the curate had satisfied Joseph concerning

---

1 The doctor's jargon-ridden diagnosis of Joseph's condition, including such terms as "occiput" (the back of the skull), "pericranium" (the membrane covering the skull), and "divellicated" (torn apart), is a further example of his medical incompetence.

2 Again Fielding forgets that in leaving Lady Booby's service, Joseph's livery had been replaced by a fellow-servant's frock and breeches.

the perfect health of his Fanny, he was on his side very inquisitive into all the particulars which had produced this unfortunate accident.

To return therefore to the kitchin, where a great variety of company were now assembled from all the rooms of the house, as well as the neighbourhood: so much delight do men take in contemplating the countenance of a thief.

Mr. Tow-wouse began to rub his hands with pleasure, at seeing so large an assembly; who would, he hoped, shortly adjourn into several apartments, in order to discourse over the robbery; and drink a health to all honest men: but Mrs. Tow-wouse, whose misfortune it was commonly to see things a little perversly, began to rail at those who brought the fellow into her house; telling her husband, 'they were very likely to thrive, who kept a house of entertainment for beggars and thieves.'

The mob had now finished their search; and could find nothing about the captive likely to prove any evidence: for as to the clothes, tho' the mob were very well satisfied with that proof; yet, as the surgeon observed, they could not convict him, because they were not found in his custody; to which Barnabas agreed: and added, that these were *bona waviata*,[1] and belonged to the lord of the manor.

'How,' says the surgeon, 'do you say these goods belong to the lord of the manor?' 'I do,' cried Barnabas. 'Then I deny it,' says the surgeon. 'What can the lord of the manor have to do in the case? Will any one attempt to persuade me that what a man finds is not his own?' 'I have heard, (says an old fellow in the corner) Justice Wise-one say, that if every man had his right, whatever is found belongs to the king of London.' 'That may be true,' says Barnabas, 'in some sense: for the law makes a difference between things stolen, and things found: for a thing may be stolen that never is found; and a thing may be found that never was stolen. Now goods that are both stolen and found are *waviata*, and they belong to the lord of the manor.' 'So the

---

1 This is the legal term for goods stolen and waived (or discarded) by a thief in flight. There is considerable confusion here concerning the forfeiture of the goods either to the king or the lord of the manor as a punishment to the owner for not making pursuit.

lord of the manor is the receiver of stolen goods:' (says the doctor) at which there was a universal laugh, being first begun by himself.

While the prisoner, by persisting in his innocence, had almost (as there was no evidence against him) brought over Barnabas, the surgeon, Tow-wouse, and several others to his side; Betty informed them, that they had over-looked a little piece of gold, which she had carried up to the man in bed; and which he offered to swear to amongst a million, aye, amongst ten thousand. This immediately turned the scale against the prisoner; and every one now concluded him guilty. It was resolved therefore, to keep him secured that night, and early in the morning to carry him before a justice.

CHAPTER XV

Shewing how Mrs. Tow-wouse was a little mollified; and how officious Mr. Barnabas and the surgeon were to prosecute the thief: with a dissertation accounting for their zeal; and that of many other persons not mentioned in this history.

BETTY told her mistress, she believed the man in bed was a greater man than they took him for: for besides the extreme whiteness of his skin, and the softness of his hands; she observed a very great familiarity between the gentleman and him; and added, she was certain they were intimate acquaintance, if not relations.

This somewhat abated the severity of Mrs. Tow-wouse's countenance. She said, 'God forbid she should not discharge the duty of a Christian, since the poor gentleman was brought to her house. She had a natural antipathy to vagabonds: but could pity the misfortunes of a Christian as soon as another.' Tow-wouse said, 'If the traveller be a gentleman, tho' he hath no money about him now, we shall most likely be paid hereafter; so you may begin to score[1] whenever you will.' Mrs.

1 To keep an account of the charges incurred.

Tow-wouse answered, 'Hold your simple tongue, and don't instruct me in my business. I am sorry for the gentleman's misfortune with all my heart, and I hope the villain who hath used him so barbarously will be hanged. Betty, go, see what he wants. G— forbid he should want any thing in my house.'

Barnabas, and the surgeon went up to Joseph, to satisfy themselves concerning the piece of gold. Joseph was with difficulty prevailed upon to shew it them; but would by no entreaties be brought to deliver it out of his own possession. He, however, attested this to be the same which had been taken from him; and Betty was ready to swear to the finding it on the thief.

The only difficulty that remained, was how to produce this gold before the justice: for as to carrying Joseph himself, it seemed impossible; nor was there any greater likelihood of obtaining it from him: for he had fastened it with a ribband to his arm, and solemnly vowed, that nothing but irresistible force should ever separate them; in which resolution, Mr. Adams, clenching a fist rather less than the knuckle of an ox, declared he would support him.

A dispute arose on this occasion concerning evidence, not very necessary to be related here; after which the surgeon dress'd Mr. Joseph's head; still persisting in the imminent danger in which his patient lay: but concluding with a very important look, 'that he began to have some hopes; that he should send him a *sanative soporiferous* draught,[1] and would see him in the morning.' After which Barnabas and he departed, and left Mr. Joseph and Mr. Adams together.

Adams informed Joseph of the occasion of this journey which he was making to London, namely to publish three volumes of sermons;[2] being encouraged, he said, by an advertisement lately set forth by a society of booksellers, who proposed to purchase any copies offered to them at a price to be settled by two persons:[3] but tho' he imagined he should get a consid-

---

1 A healing and sleep-inducing potion.

2 In chapter 16 and thereafter, they become nine volumes.

3 The Society of Booksellers for Promoting Learning was founded by Thomas Osborne in 1741. It proposed that the acceptance of works for publication and the nature of payment would be determined by "two Persons of Judgment."

erable sum of money on this occasion, which his family were in urgent need of; he protested, 'he would not leave Joseph in his present condition:' finally, he told him, 'he had nine shillings and three-pence-halfpenny in his pocket,[1] which he was welcome to use as he pleased.'

This goodness of Parson Adams brought tears into Joseph's eyes; he declared 'he had now a second reason to desire life, that he might shew his gratitude to such a friend.' Adams bad him 'be chearful, for that he plainly saw the surgeon, besides his ignorance, desired to make a merit of curing him, tho' the wounds in his head, he perceived, were by no means dangerous; that he was convinced he had no fever, and doubted not but he would be able to travel in a day or two.'

These words infused a spirit into Joseph; he said, 'he found himself very sore from the bruises, but had no reason to think any of his bones injured, or that he had received any harm in his inside; unless that he felt something very odd in his stomach: but he knew not whether that might arise from not having eaten one morsel for above twenty-four hours.' Being then asked, if he had any inclination to eat, he answered in the affirmative; then Parson Adams desired him to name what he had the greatest fancy for; whether a poached egg, or chicken-broth: he answered, 'he could eat both very well; but that he seemed to have the greatest appetite for a piece of boiled beef and cabbage.'

Adams was pleased with so perfect a confirmation that he had not the least fever: but advised him to a lighter diet, for that evening. He accordingly eat either a rabbit or a fowl, I never could with any tolerable certainty discover which; after this he was by Mrs. Tow-wouse's order conveyed into a better bed, and equipped with one of her husband's shirts.

In the morning early, Barnabas and the surgeon came to the inn, in order to see the thief conveyed before the justice. They had consumed the whole night in debating what measures they should take to produce the piece of gold in evidence against him: for they were both extremely zealous in the business, tho'

---

1 That is, roughly the equivalent of one week of Adams' annual income.

neither of them were in the least interested in[1] the prosecution; neither of them had ever received any private injury from the fellow, nor had either of them ever been suspected of loving the publick well enough, to give them a sermon or a dose of physick for nothing.

To help our reader therefore as much as possible to account for this zeal, we must inform him, that as this parish was so unfortunate as to have no lawyer in it; there had been a constant contention between the two doctors, spiritual and physical, concerning their abilities in a science, in which, as neither of them professed it,[2] they had equal pretensions to dispute each other's opinions. These disputes were carried on with great contempt on both sides, and had almost divided the parish; Mr. Tow-wouse and one half of the neighbours inclining to the surgeon, and Mrs. Tow-wouse with the other half to the parson. The surgeon drew his knowledge from those inestimable fountains, called the *Attorney's Pocket-Companion*, and *Mr. Jacob's Law-Tables*; Barnabas trusted entirely to *Wood's Institutes*.[3] It happened on this occasion, as was pretty frequently the case, that these two learned men differed about the sufficiency of evidence: the doctor being of opinion, that the maid's oath[4] would convict the prisoner without producing the gold; the parson, *è contra, totis viribus*.[5] To display their parts therefore before the justice and the parish was the sole motive, which we can discover, to this zeal, which both of them pretended to be for publick justice.

O Vanity! How little is thy force acknowledged, or thy operations discerned? How wantonly dost thou deceive mankind under different disguises? Sometimes thou dost wear the face of pity, sometimes of generosity: nay, thou hast the assurance even to put on those glorious ornaments which belong only to

---

1 Would profit from.

2 That is, it was neither of their professions.

3 Three contemporary legal handbooks: *The Attorney's Pocket Companion* (1733) by John Mallory; *The Statute-Law Common-plac'd* (1719) by Giles Jacob; and *An Institute of the Laws of England* (1720) by Thomas Wood.

4 Whereas treason required two witnesses, the testimony of one witness was sufficient for other crimes.

5 "Strongly of the opposite opinion."

heroick virtue. Thou odious, deformed monster! whom priests have railed at, philosophers despised, and poets ridiculed: is there a wretch so abandoned as to own thee for an acquaintance in publick? yet, how few will refuse to enjoy thee in private? nay, thou art the pursuit of most men through their lives. The greatest villanies are daily practised to please thee: nor is the meanest thief below, or the greatest hero above thy notice. Thy embraces are often the sole aim and sole reward of the private robbery, and the plundered province. It is, to pamper up thee, thou harlot, that we attempt to withdraw from others what we do not want,[1] or to with-hold from them what they do. All our passions are thy slaves. Avarice itself is often no more than thy hand-maid, and even Lust thy pimp. The bully Fear like a coward, flies before thee, and Joy and Grief hide their heads in thy presence.

I know thou wilt think, that whilst I abuse thee, I court thee; and that thy love hath inspired me to write this sarcastical panegyrick on thee: but thou art deceived, I value thee not of a farthing; nor will it give me any pain, if thou should'st prevail on the reader to censure this digression as errant nonsense: for know to thy confusion, that I have introduced thee for no other purpose than to lengthen out a short chapter; and so I return to my history.

CHAPTER XVI

The escape of the thief. Mr. Adams's disappointment. The arrival of two very extraordinary personages, and the introduction of Parson Adams to Parson Barnabas.

BARNABAS and the surgeon being returned, as we have said, to the inn, in order to convey the thief before the justice, were greatly concerned to find a small accident had happened which somewhat disconcerted them; and this was no other than the thief's escape, who had modestly withdrawn himself by night,

1 Need.

declining all ostentation, and not chusing, in imitation of some great men, to distinguish himself at the expence of being pointed at.

When the company had retired the evening before, the thief was detained in a room where the constable, and one of the young fellows who took him, were planted as his guard. About the second watch, a general complaint of drowth was made both by the prisoner and his keepers. Among whom it was at last agreed, that the constable should remain on duty, and the young fellow call up the tapster; in which disposition the latter apprehended not the least danger, as the constable was well armed, and could besides easily summon him back to his assistance, if the prisoner made the least attempt to gain his liberty.

The young fellow had not long left the room, before it came into the constable's head, that the prisoner might leap on him by surprize, and thereby, preventing him of the use of his weapons, especially the long staff in which he chiefly confided, might reduce the success of a struggle to an equal chance. He wisely therefore, to prevent this inconvenience, slipt out of the room himself and locked the door, waiting without with his staff in his hand, ready lifted to fell the unhappy prisoner, if by ill fortune he should attempt to break out.

But human life, as hath been discovered by some great man or other, (for I would by no means be understood to affect the honour of making any such discovery) very much resembles a game at chess: for, as in the latter, while a gamester is too attentive to secure himself very strongly on one side of the board, he is apt to leave an unguarded opening on the other; so doth it often happen in life; and so did it happen on this occasion: for whilst the cautious constable with such wonderful sagacity had possessed himself of the door, he most unhappily forgot the window.

The thief who played on the other side, no sooner perceived this opening, than he began to move that way; and finding the passage easy, he took with him the young fellow's hat; and without any ceremony, stepped into the street, and made the best of his way.

The young fellow returning with a double mug of strong

beer was a little surprized to find the constable at the door: but much more so, when, the door being opened, he perceived the prisoner had made his escape, and which way: he threw down the beer, and without uttering any thing to the constable, except a hearty curse or two, he nimbly leapt out at the window, and went again in pursuit of his prey: being very unwilling to lose the reward which he had assured himself of.

The constable hath not been discharged of suspicion on this account: it hath been said, that not being concerned in the taking the thief, he could not have been entitled to any part of the reward, if he had been convicted. That the thief had several guineas in his pocket; that it was very unlikely he should have been guilty of such an oversight. That his pretence for leaving the room was absurd: that it was his constant maxim, that a wise man never refused money on any conditions: that at every election, he always had sold his vote to both parties, &c.

But notwithstanding these and many other allegations, I am sufficiently convinced of his innocence; having been positively assured of it, by those who received their informations from his own mouth; which, in the opinion of some moderns, is the best and indeed only evidence.

All the family were now up, and with many others assembled in the kitchin, where Mr. Tow-wouse was in some tribulation; the surgeon having declared, that by law, he was liable to be indicted for the thief's escape, as it was out of his house: he was a little comforted however by Mr. Barnabas's opinion, that as the escape was by night, the indictment would not lie.[1]

Mrs. Tow-wouse delivered herself in the following words: 'Sure never was such a fool as my husband! would any other person living have left a man in the custody of such a drunken, drowsy blockhead as Tom Suckbribe?' (which was the constable's name) 'and if he could be indicted without any harm to his wife and children, I should be glad of it.' (Then the bell rung in Joseph's room.) 'Why Betty, John Chamberlain, where the devil are you all? Have you no ears, or no conscience, not

1 Since the thief was held in Mr. Tow-wouse's house, he was legally responsible for him. However, he could not be charged with negligence for failing to pursue the escaped criminal at night.

to tend the sick better?—See what the gentleman wants; why don't you go yourself, Mr. Tow-wouse? but any one may die for you; you have no more feeling than a deal-board.[1] If a man lived a fortnight in your house without spending a penny, you would never put him in mind of it. See whether he drinks tea or coffee for breakfast.' 'Yes, my dear,' cry'd Tow-wouse. She then asked the doctor and Mr. Barnabas what morning's draught they chose, who answered, they had a pot of syder-and,[2] at the fire; which we will leave them merry over, and return to Joseph.

He had rose pretty early this morning: but tho' his wounds were far from threatning any danger, he was so sore with the bruises, that it was impossible for him to think of undertaking a journey yet; Mr. Adams therefore, whose stock was visibly decreased with the expences of supper and breakfast, and which could not survive that day's scoring, began to consider how it was possible to recruit it. At last he cry'd, 'he had luckily hit on a sure method, and though it would oblige him to return himself home together with Joseph, it mattered not much.' He then sent for Tow-wouse, and taking him into another room, told him, 'he wanted to borrow three guineas, for which he would put ample security into his hands.' Tow-wouse who expected a watch, or ring, or something of double the value, answered, 'he believed he could furnish him.' Upon which Adams pointing to his saddle-bag told him with a face and voice full of solemnity, 'that there were in that bag no less than nine volumes of manuscript sermons, as well worth a hundred pound as a shilling was worth twelve pence, and that he would deposite one of the volumes in his hands by way of pledge; not doubting but that he would have the honesty to return it on his repayment of the money: for otherwise he must be a very great loser, seeing that every volume would at least bring him ten pounds, as he had been informed by a neighbouring clergyman in the country: for, (said he) as to my own part, having never yet dealt in printing, I do not pretend to ascertain the exact value of such things.'

---

1 A piece of wood, a plank.

2 A hot drink made of cider, spirits, sugar, and spices.

Tow-wouse, who was a little surprized at the pawn, said (and not without some truth) 'that he was no judge of the price of such kind of goods; and as for money, he really was very short.' Adams answered, 'certainly he would not scruple to lend him three guineas, on what was undoubtedly worth at least ten.' The landlord replied, 'he did not believe he had so much money in the house, and besides he was to make up a sum.[1] He was very confident the books were of much higher value, and heartily sorry it did not suit him.' He then cry'd out, *Coming sir*! though no body called, and ran down stairs without any fear of breaking his neck.

Poor Adams was extremely dejected at this disappointment, nor knew he what farther stratagem to try. He immediately apply'd to his pipe, his constant friend and comfort in his afflictions; and leaning over the rails, he devoted himself to meditation, assisted by the inspiring fumes of tobacco.

He had on a night-cap drawn over his wig, and a short great coat, which half covered his cassock;[2] a dress, which added to something comical enough in his countenance, composed a figure likely to attract the eyes of those who were not overgiven to observation.

Whilst he was smoaking his pipe in this posture, a coach and six, with a numerous attendance, drove into the inn. There alighted from the coach a young fellow, and a brace of pointers,[3] after which another young fellow leapt from the box, and shook the former by the hand, and both together with the dogs were instantly conducted by Mr. Tow-wouse into an apartment; whither as they passed, they entertained themselves with the following short facetious dialogue.

'You are a pretty fellow for a coachman, Jack!' says he from the coach, 'you had almost overturned us just now.' 'Pox take you,' says the coachman, 'if I had only broke your neck, it would have been saving somebody else the trouble: but I

---

1 That is, he must pay a debt by a certain date.

2 A long garment, usually black in colour, reaching to the feet and worn by Anglican clergymen.

3 A breed of hunting dog that, on scenting game, stands rigidly with its nose pointed towards the prey.

should have been sorry for the pointers.' 'Why, you son of a b—,' answered the other, 'if no body could shoot better than you, the pointers would be of no use.' 'D—n me,' says the coachman, 'I will shoot with you, five guineas a shot.' 'You be hang'd,' says the other, 'for five guineas you shall shoot at my a—.' 'Done,' says the coachman, 'I'll pepper you better than ever you was peppered[1] by Jenny Bouncer.' 'Pepper your grandmother,' says the other, 'here's Tow-wouse will let you shoot at him for a shilling a time.' 'I know his honour better,' cries Tow-wouse, 'I never saw a surer shot at a partridge. Every man misses now and then; but if I could shoot half as well as his honour, I would desire no better livelihood than I could get by my gun.' 'Pox on you,' said the coachman, 'you demolish more game now than your head's worth. There's a bitch, Tow-wouse, by G— she never *blinked*[*] a bird in her life.' 'I have a puppy, not a year old, shall hunt with her for a hundred,' cries the other gentleman. 'Done,' says the coachman, 'but you will be pox'd before you make the bett. If you have a mind for a bett,' cries the coachman, 'I will match my spotted dog with your white bitch for a hundred, play or pay.' 'Done,' says the other, 'and I'll run Baldface against Slouch with you for another.' 'No,' cries he from the box, 'but I'll venture Miss Jenny against Baldface, or Hannibal either.' 'Go to the devil,' cries he from the coach, 'I will make every bett your own way, to be sure! I will match Hannibal with Slouch for a thousand, if you dare, and I say done first.'

They were now arrived, and the reader will be very contented to leave them, and repair to the kitchin, where Barnabas, the surgeon, and an exciseman[2] were smoaking their pipes over some syderand, and where the servants, who attended the two noble gentlemen we have just seen alight, were now arrived.

'Tom,' cries one of the footmen, 'there's Parson Adams

---

* To blink is a term used to signify the dog's passing by a bird without pointing at it [Fielding's note].

---

1 Infected with venereal disease.

2 Many hostelries brewed for themselves, and hospitality to excisemen (a type of tax collector) was common.

smoaking his pipe in the gallery.' 'Yes,' says Tom, 'I pulled off my hat to him, and the parson spoke to me.'

'Is the gentleman a clergyman then?' says Barnabas, (for his cassock had been tied up when first he arrived.) 'Yes, sir,' answered the footman, 'and one there be but a few like.' 'Ay,' said Barnabas, 'if I had known it sooner, I should have desired his company; I would always shew a proper respect for the cloth; but what say you, doctor, shall we adjourn into a room, and invite him to take part of a bowl of punch?'

This proposal was immediately agreed to, and executed; and Parson Adams accepting the invitation; much civility passed between the two clergymen, who both declared the great honour they had for the cloth. They had not been long together before they entered into a discourse on small tithes, which continued a full hour, without the doctor or the exciseman's having one opportunity to offer a word.

It was then proposed to begin a general conversation, and the exciseman opened on foreign affairs: but a word unluckily dropping from one of them introduced a dissertation on the hardships suffered by the inferiour clergy;[1] which, after a long duration, concluded with bringing the nine volumes of sermons on the carpet.

Barnabas greatly discouraged poor Adams; he said, 'The age was so wicked, that no body read sermons: would you think it, Mr. Adams, (said he) I once intended to print a volume of sermons myself, and they had the approbation of two or three bishops: but what do you think a bookseller offered me?' 'Twelve guineas perhaps (cried Adams.)' 'Not twelve pence, I assure you,' answered Barnabas, 'nay the dog refused me a concordance in exchange.—At last, I offered to give him the printing them, for the sake of dedicating them to that very gentleman who just now drove his own coach into the inn, and I assure you, he had the impudence to refuse my offer: by which means I lost a good living,[2] that was afterwards given away in

---

1 The regular parsons or priests, as distinct from bishops and archbishops. Fielding wrote on clerical distress in *The Champion*, March–April 1740.

2 While the practice of writing laudatory dedications in exchange for patronage still continued at this time, its meaning and value had been considerably eroded.

exchange for a pointer, to one who—but I will not say any thing against the cloth. So you may guess, Mr. Adams, what you are to expect; for if sermons would have gone down,[1] I believe—I will not be vain: but to be concise with you, three bishops said, they were the best that ever were writ: but indeed there are a pretty moderate number printed already, and not all sold yet.'—'Pray, sir,' said Adams, 'to what do you think the numbers may amount?' 'Sir,' answered Barnabas, 'a bookseller[2] told me he believed five thousand volumes at least.' 'Five thousand!' quoth the surgeon, 'what can they be writ upon? I remember, when I was a boy, I used to read one Tillotson's sermons;[3] and I am sure, if a man practised half so much as is in one of those sermons, he will go to Heaven.' 'Doctor,' cried Barnabas, 'you have a profane way of talking, for which I must reprove you. A man can never have his duty too frequently inculcated into him. And as for Tillotson, to be sure he was a good writer, and said things very well: but comparisons are odious, another man may write as well as he—I believe there are some of my sermons,'—and then he apply'd the candle to his pipe.—'And I believe there are some of my discourses,' cries Adams, 'which the bishops would not think totally unworthy of being printed; and I have been informed, I might procure a very large sum (indeed an immense one) on them.' 'I doubt that;' answered Barnabas: 'however, if you desire to make some money of them, perhaps you may sell them by advertising *the manuscript sermons of a clergyman lately deceased, all warranted originals, and never printed.* And now I think of it, I should be obliged to you, if there be ever a funeral one among them, to lend it me: for I am this very day to preach a funeral sermon, for which I have not penned a line, though I am to have a double price.' Adams answered, 'he had but one, which he feared would not serve his purpose, being sacred to the memory of a magistrate, who had exerted himself very singularly in the preserva-

1 Met with acceptance.

2 Booksellers were generally publishers as well.

3 John Tillotson (1630–94), Archbishop of Canterbury and latitudinarian divine, was popular for his "natural, easy" manner of preaching and his moderate, optimistic theology.

tion of the morality of his neighbours, insomuch that he had neither ale-house, nor lewd woman in the parish where he lived.'—'No,' replied Barnabas, 'that will not do quite so well; for the deceased, upon whose virtues I am to harangue, was a little too much addicted to liquor, and publickly kept a mistress.—I believe I must take a common sermon, and trust to my memory to introduce something handsome on him.'—'To your invention rather, (said the doctor) your memory will be apter to put you out: for no man living remembers any thing good of him.'

With such kind of spiritual discourse, they emptied the bowl of punch, paid their reckoning, and separated: Adams and the doctor went up to Joseph; Parson Barnabas departed to celebrate the aforesaid deceased, and the exciseman descended into the cellar to gage the vessels.

Joseph was now ready to sit down to a loin of mutton, and waited for Mr. Adams, when he and the doctor came in. The doctor having felt his pulse, and examined his wounds, declared him much better, which he imputed to *that sanative soporiferous draught*, a medicine, 'whose virtues,' he said, 'were never to be sufficiently extolled:' and great indeed they must be, if Joseph was so much indebted to them as the doctor imagined, since nothing more than those effluvia, which escaped the cork, could have contributed to his recovery: for the medicine had stood untouched in the window ever since its arrival.

Joseph passed that day and the three following with his friend Adams, in which nothing so remarkable happened as the swift progress of his recovery. As he had an excellent habit of body,[1] his wounds were now almost healed, and his bruises gave him so little uneasiness, that he pressed Mr. Adams to let him depart, told him he should never be able to return sufficient thanks for all his favours; but begged that he might no longer delay his journey to London.

Adams, notwithstanding the ignorance, as he conceived it, of Mr. Tow-wouse, and the envy (for such he thought it) of Mr. Barnabas, had great expectations from his sermons: seeing

---

1 Physical constitution.

therefore Joseph in so good a way, he told him he would agree to his setting out the next morning in the stage-coach, that he believed he should have sufficient after the reckoning paid, to procure him one day's conveyance in it, and afterwards he would be able to get on, on foot, or might be favoured with a lift in some neighbour's waggon, especially as there was then to be a fair in the town whither the coach would carry him, to which numbers from his parish resorted.—And as to himself, he agreed to proceed to the great city.

They were now walking in the inn yard, when a fat, fair, short person rode in, and alighting from his horse went directly up to Barnabas, who was smoaking his pipe on a bench. The parson and the stranger shook one another very lovingly by the hand, and went into a room together.

The evening now coming on, Joseph retired to his chamber, whither the good Adams accompanied him; and took this opportunity to expatiate on the great mercies God had lately shewn him, of which he ought not only to have the deepest inward sense; but likewise to express outward thankfulness for them. They therefore fell both on their knees, and spent a considerable time in prayer and thanksgiving.

They had just finished, when Betty came in and told Mr. Adams, Mr. Barnabas desired to speak to him on some business of consequence below stairs. Joseph desired, if it was likely to detain him long, he would let him know it, that he might go to bed, which Adams promised, and in that case, they wished one another good night.

CHAPTER XVII

A pleasant discourse between the two parsons and the bookseller, which was broke off by an unlucky accident happening in the inn, which produced a dialogue between Mrs. Tow-wouse and her maid of no gentle kind.

As soon as Adams came into the room, Mr. Barnabas introduced him to the stranger, who was, he told him, a bookseller, and would be as likely to deal with him for his sermons as any man whatever. Adams, saluting the stranger, answered Barnabas, that he was very much obliged to him, that nothing could be more convenient, for he had no other business to the great city, and was heartily desirous of returning with the young man who was just recovered of his misfortune. He then snapt his fingers (as was usual with him) and took two or three turns about the room in an extasy.—And to induce the bookseller to be as expeditious as possible, as likewise to offer him a better price for his commodity, he assured him, their meeting was extremely lucky to himself: for that he had the most pressing occasion for money at that time, his own being almost spent, and having a friend then in the same inn who was just recovered from some wounds he had received from robbers, and was in a most indigent condition. 'So that nothing,' says he, 'could be so opportune, for the supplying both our necessities, as my making an immediate bargain with you.'

As soon as he had seated himself, the stranger began in these words, 'Sir, I do not care absolutely to deny engaging in what my friend Mr. Barnabas recommends: but sermons are mere drugs. The trade is so vastly stocked with them, that really unless they come out with the name of Whitfield or Westley,[1] or some other such great man, as a bishop, or those sort of people, I don't care to touch, unless it was a sermon preached on

---

1 George Whitefield and John Wesley began the evangelical movement within the Church of England in the 1730s which became known as Methodism. It was Whitefield's strong Calvinistic leanings, placing emphasis on faith or grace rather than good works, which eventually led to a break with Wesley and was the main cause of Fielding's attacks on him.

the *30th of January*,[1] or we could say in the title page, published at the *earnest request* of the congregation, or the inhabitants: but truly for a dry piece of sermons, I had rather be excused; especially as my hands are so full at present. However, sir, as Mr. Barnabas mentioned them to me, I will, if you please, take the manuscript with me to town, and send you my opinion of it in a very short time.'

'O,' said Adams, 'if you desire it, I will read two or three discourses as a specimen.' This Barnabas, who loved sermons no better than a grocer doth figs, immediately objected to, and advised Adams to let the bookseller have his sermons; telling him, if he gave him a direction,[2] he might be certain of a speedy answer: adding, he need not scruple trusting them in his possession. 'No,' said the bookseller, 'if it was a play that had been acted twenty nights together, I believe it would be safe.'

Adams did not at all relish the last expression; he said, he was sorry to hear sermons compared to plays. 'Not by me, I assure you,' cry'd the bookseller, 'though I don't know whether the Licensing Act[3] may not shortly bring them to the same footing: but I have formerly known a hundred guineas given for a play —.' 'More shame for those who gave it,' cry'd Barnabas. 'Why so?' said the bookseller, 'for they got hundreds by it.' 'But is there no difference between conveying good or ill instructions to mankind?' said Adams; 'would not an honest mind rather lose money by the one, than gain it by the other?' 'If you can find any such, I will not be their hinderance,' answered the bookseller, 'but I think those persons who get by preaching sermons, are the properest to lose by printing them: for my part, the copy that sells best, will be always the best copy in my opinion; I am no enemy to sermons but because they don't sell: for I would as soon print one of Whitfield's, as any farce whatever.'

'Whoever prints such heterodox stuff, ought to be hanged,' says Barnabas. 'Sir,' said he, turning to Adams, 'this fellow's writ-

---

1 Sermons delivered on the anniversary of the execution of Charles I (in 1649) were often political.

2 An address.

3 The Theatrical Licensing Act, provoked largely by Fielding's political satires, was passed 21 June 1737. See Introduction, p. 9.

ings (I know not whether you have seen them) are levelled at the clergy. He would reduce us to the example of the primitive ages forsooth! and would insinuate to the people, that a clergyman ought to be always preaching and praying. He pretends[1] to understand the Scripture literally, and would make mankind believe, that the poverty and low estate, which was recommended to the Church in its infancy, and was only temporary doctrine adapted to her under persecution, was to be preserved in her flourishing and established state. Sir, the principles of Toland, Woolston,[2] and all the free-thinkers, are not calculated to do half the mischief, as those professed by this fellow and his followers.'

'Sir,' answered Adams, 'if Mr. Whitfield had carried his doctrine no farther than you mention, I should have remained, as I once was, his well-wisher. I am myself as great an enemy to the luxury and splendour of the clergy as he can be. I do not, more than he, by the flourishing estate of the Church, understand the palaces, equipages, dress, furniture, rich dainties, and vast fortunes of her ministers. Surely those things, which savour so strongly of this world, become not the servants of one who professed His kingdom was not of it: but when he began to call nonsense and enthusiam[3] to his aid, and to set up the detestable doctrine of faith against good works, I was his friend no longer; for surely, that doctrine was coined in Hell, and one would think none but the Devil himself could have the confidence to preach it. For can any thing be more derogatory to the honour of God, than for men to imagine that the all-wise Being will hereafter say to the good and virtuous, *Notwithstanding the purity of thy life, notwithstanding that constant rule of virtue and goodness in which you walked upon earth, still as thou did'st not believe every thing in the true orthodox manner, thy want of faith shall condemn thee*? Or on the other side, can any doctrine have a more pernicious influence on society than a persuasion, that it will be a

---

1 Claims, professes.

2 John Toland (1670-1722) and Thomas Woolston (1670-1733) were Deists, who challenged the accepted doctrines of the Church and advocated "the light of reason" and "the Religion of Nature."

3 Excessive religious emotion; a false sense of divine inspiration.

good plea for the villain at the last day; *Lord, it is true I never obeyed one of thy commandments, yet punish me not, for I believe them all*? 'I suppose, sir,' said the bookseller, 'your sermons are of a different kind.' 'Ay, sir,' said Adams, 'the contrary, I thank Heaven, is inculcated in almost every page, or I should belye my own opinion, which hath always been, that a virtuous and good Turk, or heathen, are more acceptable in the sight of their Creator, than a vicious and wicked Christian, tho' his faith was as perfectly orthodox as St. Paul's himself.'—'I wish you success,' says the bookseller, 'but must beg to be excused, as my hands are so very full at present; and indeed I am afraid, you will find a backwardness in the trade, to engage in a book which the clergy would be certain to cry down.' 'God forbid,' says Adams, 'any books should be propagated which the clergy would cry down: but if you mean by the clergy, some few designing factious men, who have it at heart to establish some favourite schemes at the price of the liberty of mankind, and the very essence of religion, it is not in the power of such persons to decry any book they please; witness that excellent book called, *A Plain Account of the Nature and End of the Sacrament*; a book written (if I may venture on the expression) with the pen of an angel,[1] and calculated to restore the true use of Christianity, and of that sacred institution: for what could tend more to the noble purposes of religion, than frequent cheerful meetings among the members of a society, in which they should in the presence of one another, and in the service of the Supreme Being, make promises of being good, friendly and benevolent to each other? Now this excellent book was attacked by a party, but unsuccessfully.' At these words Barnabas fell a ringing with all the violence imaginable, upon which a servant attending, he bid him 'bring a bill immediately: for that he was in company, for aught he knew, with the Devil himself; and he expected to hear the Alcoran, the *Leviathan*, or Woolston[2] commended, if

1 Fielding greatly admired this work by Benjamin Hoadly (1676-1761), the latitudinarian Bishop of Winchester. Its account of the Lord's Supper aroused much controversy.

2 The Koran, holy book of Islam; *The Leviathan* (1651) by the English philosopher Thomas Hobbes; for Woolston, see above, p. 125, n. 2.

he staid a few minutes longer.' Adams desired, 'as he was so much moved at his mentioning a book, which he did without apprehending any possibility of offence, that he would be so kind to propose any objections he had to it, which he would endeavour to answer.' 'I propose objections!' said Barnabas, 'I never read a syllable in any such wicked book; I never saw it in my life, I assure you.'—Adams was going to answer, when a most hideous uproar began in the inn. Mrs. Tow-wouse, Mr. Tow-wouse, and Betty, all lifting up their voices together: but Mrs. Tow-wouse's voice, like a bass viol in a concert, was clearly and distinctly distinguished among the rest, and was heard to articulate the following sounds.—'O you damn'd villain, is this the return to all the care I have taken of your family? This is the reward of my virtue?[1] Is this the manner in which you behave to one who brought you a fortune, and preferred you to so many matches, all your betters? To abuse my bed, my own bed, with my own servant: but I'll maul the slut, I'll tear her nasty eyes out; was ever such a pitiful dog, to take up with such a mean trollop? If she had been a gentlewoman like my self, it had been some excuse, but a beggarly saucy dirty servant-maid. Get you out of my house, you whore.' To which, she added another name, which we do not care to stain our paper with.—It was a monosyllable, beginning with a b—, and indeed was the same, as if she had pronounced the words, she-dog. Which term, we shall, to avoid offence, use on this occasion, tho' indeed both the mistress and maid uttered the above-mentioned b—, a word extremely disgustful to females of the lower sort. Betty had borne all hitherto with patience, and had uttered only lamentations: but the last appellation stung her to the quick, 'I am a woman as well as yourself,' she roared out, 'and no she-dog, and if I have been a little naughty, I am not the first; if I have been no better than I should be,' cries she sobbing, 'that's no reason you should call me out of my name; my be—betters are wo—worse than me.' 'Huzzy, huzzy,' says Mrs. Tow-wouse, 'have you the impudence to answer me? Did I not catch you, you saucy—' and then again repeated the terri-

1 The subtitle of *Pamela* is "Virtue Rewarded."

ble word so odious to female ears. 'I can't bear that name,' answered Betty, 'if I have been wicked, I am to answer for it myself in the other world, but I have done nothing that's unnatural, and I will go out of your house this moment: for I will never be called she-dog, by any mistress in England.' Mrs. Tow-wouse then armed herself with the spit: but was prevented from executing any dreadful purpose by Mr. Adams, who confined her arms with the strength of a wrist, which Hercules would not have been ashamed of. Mr. Tow-wouse being caught, as our lawyers express it, with the manner,[1] and having no defence to make, very prudently withdrew himself, and Betty committed herself to the protection of the hostler, who, though she could not conceive him pleased with what had happened, was in her opinion rather a gentler beast than her mistress.

Mrs. Tow-wouse, at the intercession of Mr. Adams, and finding the enemy vanished, began to compose herself, and at length recovered the usual serenity of her temper, in which we will leave her, to open to the reader the steps which led to a catastrophe, common enough, and comical enough too, perhaps in modern history, yet often fatal to the repose and well-being of families, and the subject of many tragedies, both in life and on the stage.

CHAPTER XVIII

The history of Betty the chambermaid, and an account of what occasioned the violent scene in the preceding chapter.

BETTY, who was the occasion of all this hurry,[2] had some good qualities. She had good-nature, generosity and compassion, but unfortunately her constitution was composed of those warm ingredients, which, though the purity of courts or nunneries might have happily controuled them, were by no means able to endure the ticklish situation of a chamber-maid at an inn, who

1 With the stolen goods.

2 Fuss, disturbance.

is daily liable to the solicitations of lovers of all complexions, to the dangerous addresses of fine gentlemen of the army, who sometimes are obliged to reside with them a whole year together, and above all are exposed to the caresses of footmen, stage-coachmen, and drawers;[1] all of whom employ the whole artillery of kissing, flattering, bribing and every other weapon which is to be found in the whole armory of love, against them.

Betty, who was but one and twenty, had now lived three years in this dangerous situation, during which she had escaped pretty well. An ensign of foot was the first person who made any impression on her heart; he did indeed raise a flame in her,[2] which required the care of a surgeon to cool.

While she burnt for him, several others burnt for her. Officers of the army, young gentlemen travelling the Western Circuit,[3] inoffensive squires, and some of graver character were set afire by her charms!

At length, having perfectly recovered the effects of her first unhappy passion, she seemed to have vowed a state of perpetual chastity. She was long deaf to all the sufferings of her lovers, till one day at a neighbouring fair, the rhetorick of John the hostler, with a new straw hat, and a pint of wine, made a second conquest over her.

She did not however feel any of those flames on this occasion, which had been the consequence of her former amour; nor indeed those other ill effects, which prudent young women very justly apprehend from too absolute an indulgence to the pressing endearments of their lovers. This latter, perhaps, was a little owing to her not being entirely constant to John, with whom she permitted Tom Whipwell the stage-coachman, and now and then a handsome young traveller, to share her favours.

Mr. Tow-wouse had for some time cast the languishing eyes of affection on this young maiden. He had laid hold on every opportunity of saying tender things to her, squeezing her by

---

1 Tapsters, bartenders.

2 That is, infected her with a venereal disease.

3 A region in southwestern England visited semiannually by judges and barristers (including Fielding) for the trial of cases. See Introduction, p. 10.

the hand, and sometimes of kissing her lips: for as the violence of his passion had considerably abated to Mrs. Tow-wouse; so like water, which is stopt from its usual current in one place, it naturally sought a vent in another. Mrs. Tow-wouse is thought to have perceived this abatement, and probably it added very little to the natural sweetness of her temper: for tho' she was as true to her husband, as the dial to the sun, she was rather more desirous of being shone on, as being more capable of feeling his warmth.

Ever since Joseph's arrival, Betty had conceived an extraordinary liking to him, which discovered itself more and more, as he grew better and better; till that fatal evening, when, as she was warming his bed, her passion grew to such a height, and so perfectly mastered both her modesty and her reason, that after many fruitless hints, and sly insinuations, she at last threw down the warming-pan, and embracing him with great eagerness, swore he was the handsomest creature she had ever seen.

Joseph in great confusion leapt from her, and told her, he was sorry to see a young woman cast off all regard to modesty: but she had gone too far to recede, and grew so very indecent, that Joseph was obliged, contrary to his inclination, to use some violence to her, and taking her in his arms, he shut her out of the room, and locked the door.

How ought man to rejoice, that his chastity is always in his own power, that if he hath sufficient strength of mind, he hath always a competent strength of body to defend himself: and cannot, like a poor weak woman, be ravished against his will.

Betty was in the most violent agitation at this disappointment. Rage and Lust pulled her heart, as with two strings, two different ways; one moment she thought of stabbing Joseph, the next, of taking him in her arms, and devouring him with kisses; but the latter passion was far more prevalent. Then she thought of revenging his refusal on herself: but whilst she was engaged in this meditation, happily Death presented himself to her in so many shapes of drowning, hanging, poisoning, &c. that her distracted mind could resolve on none. In this perturbation of spirit, it accidentally occurred to her memory, that her master's bed was not made, she therefore went directly to his room;

where he happened at that time to be engaged at his bureau. As soon as she saw him, she attempted to retire: but he called her back, and taking her by the hand, squeezed her so tenderly, at the same time whispering so many soft things into her ears, and, then pressed her so closely with his kisses, that the vanquished fair-one, whose passions were already raised, and which were not so whimsically capricious that one man only could lay them, though perhaps, she would have rather preferred that one: the vanquished fair-one quietly submitted, I say, to her master's will, who had just attained the accomplishment of his bliss, when Mrs. Tow-wouse unexpectedly entered the room, and caused all that confusion which we have before seen, and which it is not necessary at present to take any farther notice of: since without the assistance of a single hint from us, every reader of any speculation,[1] or experience, though not married himself, may easily conjecture, that it concluded with the discharge of Betty, the submission of Mr. Tow-wouse, with some things to be performed on his side by way of gratitude for his wife's goodness in being reconciled to him, with many hearty promises never to offend any more in the like manner: and lastly, his quietly and contentedly bearing to be reminded of his transgressions, as a kind of penance, once or twice a day, during the residue of his life.

---

1 Comprehension.

BOOK II

CHAPTER I

Of divisions in authors.

THERE are certain mysteries or secrets in all trades from the highest to the lowest, from that of *prime ministring* to this of *authoring*, which are seldom discovered, unless to members of the same calling. Among those used by us gentlemen of the latter occupation, I take this of dividing our works into books and chapters to be none of the least considerable. Now for want of being truly acquainted with this secret, common readers imagine, that by this art of dividing, we mean only to swell our works to a much larger bulk than they would otherwise be extended to. These several places therefore in our paper, which are filled with our books and chapters, are understood as so much buckram, stays, and stay-tape in a taylor's bill, serving only to make up the sum total, commonly found at the bottom of our first page, and of his last.

But in reality the case is otherwise, and in this, as well as all other instances, we consult the advantage of our reader, not our own; and indeed many notable uses arise to him from this method: for first, those little spaces between our chapters may be looked upon as an inn or resting-place, where he may stop and take a glass, or any other refreshment, as it pleases him. Nay, our fine[1] readers will, perhaps, be scarce able to travel farther than through one of them in a day. As to those vacant pages which are placed between our books, they are to be regarded as those stages, where, in long journeys, the traveller stays some time to repose himself, and consider of what he hath seen in the parts he hath already past through; a consideration which I take the liberty to recommend a little to the reader: for however swift his capacity may be, I would not advise him to travel through these pages too fast: for if he doth, he may probably miss the seeing some curious productions of nature which will be observed by the slower and more accurate reader. A volume without any such places of rest resembles the opening

---

1 Delicate.

of wilds or seas, which tires the eye and fatigues the spirit when entered upon.

Secondly, what are the contents prefixed to every chapter, but so many inscriptions over the gates of inns (to continue the same metaphor,) informing the reader what entertainment he is to expect, which if he likes not, he may travel on to the next: for in biography, as we are not tied down to an exact concatenation equally with other historians; so a chapter or two (for instance this I am now writing) may be often pass'd over without any injury to the whole. And in these inscriptions I have been as faithful as possible, not imitating the celebrated Montagne, who promises you one thing and gives you another;[1] nor some title-page authors, who promise a great deal, and produce nothing at all.

There are, besides these more obvious benefits, several others which our readers enjoy from this art of dividing; tho' perhaps most of them too mysterious to be presently understood, by any who are not initiated into the science of authoring. To mention therefore but one which is most obvious, it prevents spoiling the beauty of a book by turning down its leaves, a method otherwise necessary to those readers, who, (tho' they read with great improvement and advantage) are apt, when they return to their study, after half an hour's absence, to forget where they left off.

These divisions have the sanction of great antiquity. Homer not only divided his great work into twenty-four books, (in compliment perhaps to the twenty-four letters[2] to which he had very particular obligations) but, according to the opinion of some very sagacious critics, hawked them all separately,[3] delivering only one book at a time, (probably by subscription).[4]

---

1 The *Essais* of Michel Eyquem de Montaigne, first published in 1580, have frequent digressions from the subjects announced.

2 That is, of the Greek alphabet.

3 Fielding alludes here to an ancient theory which had gained considerable attention in more recent times, that Homer's epics were originally scattered poems and songs assembled into their present form in the sixth century BC at the direction of Pisistratus of Athens.

4 An increasing number of works, including Pope's *Iliad* (1715-20) and *Odyssey* (1725-26) were published by subscription.

He was the first inventor of the art which hath so long lain dormant, of publishing by numbers,[1] an art now brought to such perfection, that even dictionaries are divided and exhibited piece-meal to the public; nay, one bookseller hath (*to encourage learning and ease the public*) contrived to give them a dictionary in this divided manner for only fifteen shillings more than it would have cost entire.[2]

Virgil hath given us his poem in twelve books,[3] an argument of his modesty; for by that doubtless he would insinuate that he pretends to no more than half the merit of the Greek: for the same reason, our Milton went originally no farther than ten; 'till being puffed up by the praise of his friends, he put himself on the same footing with the Roman poet.[4]

I shall not however enter so deep into this matter as some very learned criticks have done; who have with infinite labour and acute discernment discovered what books are proper for embellishment,[5] and what require simplicity only, particularly with regard to similies, which I think are now generally agreed to become any book but the first.

I will dismiss this chapter with the following observation: that it becomes an author generally to divide a book, as it doth a butcher to joint his meat, for such assistance is of great help to both the reader and the carver. And now having indulged myself a little, I will endeavour the curiosity of my reader, who is no doubt impatient to know what he will find in the subsequent chapters of this book.

---

1 That is, in a series of weekly or monthly parts.

2 The bookseller Thomas Osborne released Robert James' *Medicinal Dictionary* (1742) by numbers at a particularly high price.

3 The *Aeneid*.

4 The first edition of *Paradise Lost* (1667) appeared in ten books, the second one of 1674 was expanded to twelve.

5 In accordance with a precept of Aristotle (*Poetics* 22 and 24).

CHAPTER II

A surprizing instance of Mr. Adams's short memory, with the unfortunate consequences which it brought on Joseph.

MR. ADAMS and Joseph were now ready to depart different ways, when an accident determined the former to return with his friend, which Tow-wouse, Barnabas, and the bookseller had not been able to do. This accident was, that those sermons, which the parson was travelling to London to publish, were, O my good reader, left behind; what he had mistaken for them in the saddlebags being no other than three shirts, a pair of shoes, and some other necessaries, which Mrs. Adams, who thought her husband would want shirts more than sermons on his journey, had carefully provided him.

This discovery was now luckily owing to the presence of Joseph at the opening the saddlebags; who having heard his friend say, he carried with him nine volumes of sermons, and not being of that sect of philosophers, who can reduce all the matter of the world into a nut-shell, seeing there was no room for them in the bags, where the parson had said they were deposited, had the curiosity to cry out, 'Bless me, sir, where are your sermons?' The parson answer'd 'There, there, child, there they are, under my shirts.' Now it happened that he had taken forth his last shirt, and the vehicle remained visibly empty. 'Sure, sir,' says Joseph, 'there is nothing in the bags.' Upon which Adams starting, and testifying some surprize, cry'd 'Hey! fie, fie upon it; they are not here sure enough. Ay, they are certainly left behind.'

Joseph was greatly concerned at the uneasiness which he apprehended his friend must feel from this disappointment: he begged him to pursue his journey, and promised he would himself return with the books to him, with the utmost expedition. 'No, thank you, child,' answered Adams, 'it shall not be so. What would it avail me, to tarry in the great city, unless I had my discourses with me, which are, *ut ita dicam*, the sole cause, the *aitia monotate* of my peregrination.[1] No, child, as this acci-

1 The first phrase is in Latin ("so to speak") and the second one in Greek ("sole cause").

dent hath happened, I am resolved to return back to my cure, together with you; which indeed my inclination sufficiently leads me to. This disappointment may, perhaps, be intended for my good.' He concluded with a verse out of Theocritus, which signifies no more than, *that sometimes it rains and sometimes the sun shines.*[1]

Joseph bowed with obedience, and thankfulness for the inclination which the parson express'd of returning with him; and now the bill was called for, which, on examination, amounted within a shilling to the sum Mr. Adams had in his pocket. Perhaps the reader may wonder how he was able to produce a sufficient sum for so many days: that he may not be surprized, therefore, it cannot be unnecessary to acquaint him, that he had borrowed a guinea of a servant belonging to the coach and six, who had been formerly one of his parishioners, and whose master, the owner of the coach, then lived within three miles of him: for so good was the credit of Mr. Adams, that even Mr. Peter the Lady Booby's steward, would have lent him a guinea with very little security.

Mr. Adams discharged the bill, and they were both setting out, having agreed *to ride and tie*: a method of travelling much used by persons who have but one horse between them, and is thus performed. The two travellers set out together, one on horseback, the other on foot: now as it generally happens that he on horseback out-goes him on foot, the custom is, that when he arrives at the distance agreed on, he is to dismount, tie the horse to some gate, tree, post, or other thing, and then proceed on foot; when the other comes up to the horse, he unties him, mounts and gallops on, 'till having passed by his fellow-traveller, he likewise arrives at the place of tying. And this is that method of travelling so much in use among our prudent ancestors, who knew that horses had mouths as well as legs, and that they could not use the latter, without being at the expence of suffering the beasts themselves to use the former. This was the method in use in those days: when, instead of a coach and six, a member of parliament's lady used to mount a pillion behind her husband; and a grave serjeant at law condescended

1 *Idylls* 4.41-43

to amble to Westminster on an easy pad,[1] with his clerk kicking his heels[2] behind him.

Adams was now gone some minutes, having insisted on Joseph's beginning the journey on horseback, and Joseph had his foot in the stirrup, when the hostler presented him a bill for the horse's board during his residence at the inn. Joseph said Mr. Adams had paid all; but this matter being referred to Mr. Tow-wouse was by him decided in favour of the hostler, and indeed with truth and justice: for this was a fresh instance of that shortness of memory which did not arise from want of parts, but that continual hurry in which Parson Adams was always involved.

Joseph was now reduced to a dilemma which extremely puzzled him. The sum due for horse-meat[3] was twelve shillings, (for Adams who had borrowed the beast of his clerk, had ordered him to be fed as well as they could feed him) and the cash in his pocket amounted to sixpence, (for Adams had divided the last shilling with him). Now, tho' there have been some ingenious persons who have contrived to pay twelve shillings with sixpence, Joseph was not one of them. He had never contracted a debt in his life, and was consequently the less ready at an expedient to extricate himself. Tow-wouse was willing to give him credit 'till next time, to which Mrs. Tow-wouse would probably have consented (for such was Joseph's beauty, that it had made some impression even on that piece of flint which that good woman wore in her bosom by way of heart.) Joseph would have found therefore, very likely, the passage free, had he not, when he honestly discovered the nakedness of his pockets, pulled out that little piece of gold which we have mentioned before. This caused Mrs. Tow-wouse's eyes to water; she told Joseph, she did not conceive a man could want money whilst he had gold in his pocket. Joseph answered, he had such a value for that little piece of gold, that he would not part with it for a hundred times the riches which the greatest esquire in the county was worth. 'A pretty way indeed,' said

---

1 A slow-paced horse.

2 Walking.

3 Feed for the horse, fodder.

Mrs. Tow-wouse, 'to run in debt, and then refuse to part with your money, because you have a value for it. I never knew any piece of gold of more value than as many shillings as it would change for.' 'Not to preserve my life from starving, nor to redeem it from a robber, would I part with this dear piece,' answered Joseph. 'What (says Mrs. Tow-wouse) I suppose, it was given you by some vile trollop, some miss[1] or other; if it had been the present of a virtuous woman, you would not have had such a value for it. My husband is a fool if he parts with the horse, without being paid for him.' 'No, no, I can't part with the horse indeed, till I have the money,' cried Tow-wouse. A resolution highly commended by a lawyer then in the yard, who declared Mr. Tow-wouse might justify the detainer.[2]

As we cannot therefore at present get Mr. Joseph out of the inn, we shall leave him in it, and carry our reader on after Parson Adams, who, his mind being perfectly at ease, fell into a contemplation on a passage in Æschylus,[3] which entertained him for three miles together, without suffering him once to reflect on his fellow-traveller.

At length having spun out this thread, and being now at the summit of a hill, he cast his eyes backwards, and wondered that he could not see any sign of Joseph. As he left him ready to mount the horse, he could not apprehend any mischief had happened, neither could he suspect that he had miss'd his way, it being so broad and plain: the only reason which presented itself to him, was that he had met with an acquaintance who had prevailed with him to delay some time in discourse.

He therefore resolved to proceed slowly forwards, not doubting but that he should be shortly overtaken, and soon came to a large water, which filling the whole road, he saw no method of passing unless by wading through, which he accordingly did up to his middle; but was no sooner got to the other side, than he perceived, if he had looked over the hedge, he would have found a foot-path capable of conducting him without wetting his shoes.

---

1 Kept mistress, whore.

2 A legal term for withholding the possessions of another.

3 Aeschylus (c. 525-456 BC) was the first and grandest of the great Greek tragedians.

His surprize at Joseph's not coming up grew now very troublesome: he began to fear he knew not what, and as he determined, to move no farther; and, if he did not shortly overtake him, to return back; he wished to find a house of publick entertainment where he might dry his clothes and refresh himself with a pint: but seeing no such (for no other reason than because he did not cast his eyes a hundred yards forwards) he sat himself down on a stile, and pulled out his Æschylus.

A fellow passing presently by, Adams asked him, if he could direct him to an alehouse. The fellow who had just left it, and perceived the house and sign to be within sight, thinking he had jeered him, and being of a morose temper, bad him *follow his nose and be d—n'd.* Adams told him he was a saucy jackanapes; upon which the fellow turned about angrily: but perceiving Adams clench his fist he thought proper to go on without taking any farther notice.

A horseman following immediately after, and being asked the same question, answered, 'Friend, there is one within a stone's-throw; I believe you may see it before you.' Adams lifting up his eyes, cry'd, 'I protest and so there is;' and thanking his informer proceeded directly to it.

CHAPTER III

The opinion of two lawyers concerning the same gentleman, with Mr. Adams's enquiry into the religion of his host.

HE had just entered the house, had called for his pint and seated himself, when two horsemen came to the door, and fastening their horses to the rails, alighted. They said there was a violent shower of rain coming on, which they intended to weather there, and went into a little room by themselves, not perceiving Mr. Adams.

One of these immediately asked the other, if he had seen a more comical adventure a great while? Upon which the other said, 'he doubted whether by law, the landlord could justify detaining the horse for his corn and hay.' But the former answered, 'Undoubtedly he can: it is an adjudged case, and I have known it tried.'

Adams, who tho' he was, as the reader may suspect, a little inclined to forgetfulness, never wanted more than a hint to remind him, over-hearing their discourse, immediately suggested to himself that this was his own horse, and that he had forgot to pay for him, which upon enquiry, he was certified of[1] by the gentlemen; who added, that the horse was likely to have more rest than food, unless he was paid for.

The poor parson resolved to return presently to the inn, tho' he knew no more than Joseph, how to procure his horse his liberty: he was however prevailed on to stay under covert, 'till the shower which was now very violent, was over.

The three travellers then sat down together over a mug of good beer; when Adams, who had observed a gentleman's house as he passed along the road, enquired to whom it belonged: one of the horsemen had no sooner mentioned the owner's name, than the other began to revile him in the most opprobrious terms. The English language scarce affords a single reproachful word, which he did not vent on this occasion. He charged him likewise with many particular facts.[2] He said,— 'he no more regarded a field of wheat when he was hunting, than he did the high-way; that he had injured several poor farmers by trampling their corn[3] under his horse's heels; and if any of them begged him with the utmost submission to refrain, his horse-whip was always ready to do them justice.' He said, 'that he was the greatest tyrant to the neighbours in every other instance, and would not suffer a farmer to keep a gun, tho' he might justify it by law; and in his own family so cruel a master, that he never kept a servant a twelve-month. In his capacity as a justice,' continued he, 'he behaves so partially, that he commits or acquits just as he is in the humour, without any regard to truth or evidence: the Devil may carry any one before him for me; I would rather be tried before some judges than be a prosecutor before him: if I had an estate in the neigh-

1 Informed with certainty.

2 Acts, specifically of a criminal nature.

3 Grain crop.

bourhood, I would sell it for half the value, rather than live near him.' Adams shook his head, and said, 'he was sorry such men were suffered to proceed with impunity, and that riches could set any man above law.' The reviler a little after retiring into the yard, the gentleman, who had first mentioned his name to Adams, began to assure him, 'that his companion was a prejudiced person. It is true,' says he, 'perhaps, that he may have sometimes pursued his game over a field of corn, but he hath always made the party ample satisfaction; that so far from tyrannizing over his neighbours, or taking away their guns, he himself knew several farmers not qualified, who not only kept guns, but killed game with them. That he was the best of masters to his servants, and several of them had grown old in his service. That he was the best justice of peace in the kingdom, and to his certain knowledge had decided many difficult points, which were referred to him, with the greatest equity, and the highest wisdom. And he verily believed, several persons would give a year's purchase[1] more for an estate near him, than under the wings of any other great man.' He had just finished his encomium, when his companion returned and acquainted him the storm was over. Upon which, they presently mounted their horses and departed.

Adams, who was in the utmost anxiety at those different characters of the same person, asked his host if he knew the gentleman: for he began to imagine they had by mistake been speaking of two several gentlemen. 'No, no, master!' answered the host, a shrewd cunning fellow, 'I know the gentleman very well of whom they have been speaking, as I do the gentlemen who spoke of him. As for riding over other men's corn, to my knowledge he hath not been on horseback these two years. I never heard he did any injury of that kind; and as to making reparation, he is not so free of his money as that comes to neither. Nor did I ever hear of his taking away any man's gun; nay, I know several who have guns in their houses: but as for killing game with them, no man is stricter; and I believe he would ruin any who did. You heard one of the gentlemen say, he was

1 That is, the annual return or rent from land.

the worst master in the world, and the other that he is the best: but as for my own part, I know all his servants, and never heard from any of them that he was either one or the other.—' 'Aye, aye,' says Adams, 'and how doth he behave as a justice, pray?' 'Faith, friend,' answered the host, 'I question whether he is in the commission: the only cause I have heard he hath decided a great while, was one between those very two persons who just went out of this house; and I am sure he determined that justly, for I heard the whole matter.' 'Which did he decide it in favour of?' quoth Adams. 'I think I need not answer that question,' cried the host, 'after the different characters you have heard of him. It is not my business to contradict gentlemen, while they are drinking in my house: but I knew neither of them spoke a syllable of truth.' 'God forbid! (said Adams,) that men should arrive at such a pitch of wickedness, to be-lye the character of their neighbour from a little private affection,[1] or what is infinitely worse, a private spite. I rather believe we have mistaken them, and they mean two other persons: for there are many houses on the road.' 'Why prithee, friend,' cries the host, 'dost thou pretend never to have told a lye in thy life?' 'Never a malicious one, I am certain,' answered Adams; 'nor with a design to injure the reputation of any man living.' 'Pugh, malicious! no, no,' replied the host; 'not malicious with a design to hang a man, or bring him into trouble: but surely out of love to one's self, one must speak better of a friend than an enemy.' 'Out of love to your self, you should confine yourself to truth,' says Adams, 'for by doing otherwise, you injure the noblest part of yourself, your immortal soul. I can hardly believe any man such an idiot to risque the loss of that by any trifling gain, and the greatest gain in this world is but dirt in comparison of what shall be revealed hereafter.' Upon which the host taking up the cup, with a smile drank a health to hereafter: adding, 'he was for something present.' 'Why,' says Adams very gravely, 'do not you believe another world?' To which the host answered, 'yes, he was no atheist.' 'And you believe you have an immortal soul?' cries Adams: he answered, 'God forbid he should not.' 'And

1 Feeling or emotion.

Heaven and Hell?' said the parson. The host then bid him 'not to prophane: for those were things not to be mentioned nor thought of but in church.' Adams asked him, 'why he went to church, if what he learned there had no influence on his conduct in life?' 'I go to church,' answered the host, 'to say my prayers and behave godly.' 'And dost not thou,' cry'd Adams, 'believe what thou hearest at church?' 'Most part of it, master,' returned the host. 'And dost not thou then tremble,' cries Adams, 'at the thought of eternal punishment?' 'As for that, master,' said he, 'I never once thought about it: but what signifies talking about matters so far off? The mug is out,[1] shall I draw another?'

Whilst he was gone for that purpose, a stage-coach drove up to the door. The coachman coming into the house, was asked by the mistress, what passengers he had in his coach? 'A parcel of squinny-gut[2] b—s, (says he) I have a good mind to overturn them; you won't prevail upon them to drink any thing I assure you.' Adams asked him, if he had not seen a young man on horse-back on the road, (describing Joseph). 'Aye,' said the coachman, 'a gentlewoman in my coach that is his acquaintance redeemed him and his horse; he would have been here before this time, had not the storm driven him to shelter.' 'God bless her,' said Adams in a rapture; nor could he delay walking out to satisfy himself who this charitable woman was; but what was his surprize, when he saw his old acquaintance, Madam Slipslop? Her's indeed was not so great, because she had been informed by Joseph, that he was on the road. Very civil were the salutations on both sides; and Mrs. Slipslop rebuked the hostess for denying the gentleman to be there when she asked for him: but indeed the poor woman had not erred designedly: for Mrs. Slipslop asked for a clergyman; and she had unhappily mistaken Adams for a person travelling to a neighbouring fair with the thimble and button,[3] or some other such operation: for he

---

1 Empty.

2 Scrawny.

3 An earlier version of the shell game, in which the participant is called upon by a trickster (a "thimblerigger") to guess under which of three thimbles the button is to be found.

marched in a swinging great, but short, white coat with black buttons, a short wig, and a hat, which so far from having a black hatband, had nothing black about it.[1]

Joseph was now come up, and Mrs. Slipslop would have had him quit his horse to the parson, and come himself into the coach: but he absolutely refused, saying he thanked Heaven he was well enough recovered to be very able to ride, and added, he hoped he knew his duty better than to ride in a coach while Mr. Adams was on horseback.

Mrs. Slipslop would have persisted longer, had not a lady in the coach put a short end to the dispute, by refusing to suffer a fellow in a livery to ride in the same coach with herself: so it was at length agreed that Adams should fill the vacant place in the coach, and Joseph should proceed on horseback.

They had not proceeded far before Mrs. Slipslop, addressing herself to the parson, spoke thus: 'There hath been a strange alteration in our family, Mr. Adams, since Sir Thomas's death.' 'A strange alteration indeed!' says Adams, 'as I gather from some hints which have dropped from Joseph.' 'Aye,' says she, 'I could never have believed it, but the longer one lives in the world, the more one sees. So Joseph hath given you hints.'—'But of what nature, will always remain a perfect secret with me,' cries the parson; 'he forced me to promise before he would communicate any thing. I am indeed concerned to find her ladyship behave in so unbecoming a manner. I always thought her in the main, a good lady, and should never have suspected her of thoughts so unworthy a Christian, and with a young lad her own servant.' 'These things are no secrets to me, I assure you,' cries Slipslop; 'and I believe, they will be none any where shortly: for ever since the boy's departure she hath behaved more like a mad woman than any thing else.' 'Truly, I am heartily concerned,' says Adams, 'for she was a good sort of a lady; indeed I have often wished she had attended a little more constantly at the service, but she hath done a great deal of good in the parish.' 'O Mr. Adams!' says Slipslop, 'people that don't see all, often know nothing. Many things have been given away

---

1 Generally clergymen wore long frock coats and were dressed largely in black.

in our family, I do assure you, without her knowledge. I have heard you say in the pulpit, we ought not to brag: but indeed I can't avoid saying, if she had kept the keys herself, the poor would have wanted many a cordial which I have let them have. As for my late master, he was as worthy a man as ever lived, and would have done infinite good if he had not been controlled: but he loved a quiet life, Heavens rest his soul! I am confident he is there, and enjoys a quiet life, which some folks would not allow him here.' Adams answered, 'he had never heard this before, and was mistaken, if she herself,' (for he remembered she used to commend her mistress and blame her master,) 'had not formerly been of another opinion.' 'I don't know, (replied she,) what I might once think: but now I am *confidous* matters are as I tell you: the world will shortly see who hath been deceived; for my part I say nothing, but that it is *wondersome* how some people can carry all things with a grave face.'

Thus Mr. Adams and she discoursed: 'till they came opposite to a great house which stood at some distance from the road; a lady in the coach spying it, cry'd, 'Yonder lives the unfortunate Leonora, if one can justly call a woman unfortunate, whom we must own at the same time guilty, and the author of her own calamity.' This was abundantly sufficient to awaken the curiosity of Mr. Adams, as indeed it did that of the whole company, who jointly solicited the lady to acquaint them with Leonora's history, since it seemed, by what she had said, to contain something remarkable.

The lady, who was perfectly well bred, did not require many entreaties, and having only wished their entertainment might make amends for the company's attention, she began in the following manner.

CHAPTER IV

The History of Leonora, or the Unfortunate Jilt.

LEONORA was the daughter of a gentleman of fortune; she was tall and well-shaped, with a sprightliness in her countenance, which often attracts beyond more regular features joined with an insipid air; nor is this kind of beauty less apt to deceive than allure; the good-humour which it indicates, being often mistaken for good-nature, and the vivacity for true understanding.

Leonora, who was now at the age of eighteen, lived with an aunt of her's in a town in the north of England. She was an extreme lover of gaiety, and very rarely missed a ball or any other publick assembly; where she had frequent opportunities of satisfying a greedy appetite of vanity with the preference which was given her by the men to almost every other woman present.

Among many young fellows who were particular in their gallantries towards her, Horatio soon distinguished himself in her eyes beyond all his competitors; she danced with more than ordinary gaiety when he happened to be her partner; neither the fairness of the evening nor the musick of the nightingale, could lengthen her walk like his company. She affected no longer to understand the civilities of others: whilst she inclined so attentive an ear to every compliment of Horatio, that she often smiled even when it was too delicate for her comprehension.

'Pray, madam,' says Adams, 'who was this squire Horatio?'

Horatio, says the lady, was a young gentleman of a good family, bred to the law, and had been some few years called to the degree of a barrister.[1] His face and person were such as the generality allowed handsome: but he had a dignity in his air very rarely to be seen. His temper was of the saturnine complexion,[2] but without the least taint of moroseness. He had wit

1 A lawyer who has the right to plead cases in the higher courts of law.

2 In astrological terms, the temperament of a person born under the sign of Saturn was thought to be gloomy and taciturn.

and humour with an inclination to satire, which he indulged rather too much.

This gentleman, who had contracted the most violent passion for Leonora, was the last person who perceived the probability of its success. The whole town had made the match for him, before he himself had drawn a confidence from her actions sufficient to mention his passion to her; for it was his opinion, (and perhaps he was there in the right) that it is highly impolitick to talk seriously of love to a woman before you have made such a progress in her affections, that she herself expects and desires to hear it.

But whatever diffidence the fears of a lover may create, which are apt to magnify every favour conferred on a rival, and to see the little advances towards themselves through the other end of the perspective;[1] it was impossible that Horatio's passion should so blind his discernment, as to prevent his conceiving hopes from the behaviour of Leonora; whose fondness for him was now as visible to an indifferent person in their company, as his for her.

'I never knew any of these forward sluts come to good, (says the lady, who refused Joseph's entrance into the coach,) nor shall I wonder at any thing she doth in the sequel.'

The lady proceeded in her story thus: It was in the midst of a gay conversation in the walks one evening, when Horatio whispered Leonora, 'that he was desirous to take a turn or two with her in private; for that he had something to communicate to her of great consequence.' 'Are you sure it is of consequence?' said she, smiling.—'I hope,' answered he, 'you will think so too, since the whole future happiness of my life must depend on the event.'[2]

Leonora, who very much suspected what was coming, would have deferred it 'till another time: but Horatio, who had more than half conquered the difficulty of speaking by the first motion, was so very importunate, that she at last yielded, and leaving the rest of the company, they turned aside into an unfrequented walk.

---

1 That is, through the other end of the telescope, hence diminishing them.

2 Result, outcome.

They had retired far out of the sight of the company, both maintaining a strict silence. At last Horatio made a full stop, and taking Leonora, who stood pale and trembling, gently by the hand, he fetched a deep sigh, and then looking on her eyes with all the tenderness imaginable, he cried out in a faltering accent; 'O Leonora! is it necessary for me to declare to you on what the future happiness of my life must be founded! Must I say, there is something belonging to you which is a bar to my happiness, and which unless you will part with, I must be miserable?' 'What can that be?' replied Leonora.—'No wonder,' said he, 'you are surprized, that I should make an objection to any thing which is yours, yet sure you may guess, since it is the only one which the riches of the world, if they were mine, should purchase of me.—O it is that which you must part with, to bestow all the rest! Can Leonora, or rather will she doubt longer?—Let me then whisper it in her ears,—It is your name, madam. It is by parting with that, by your condescension to be for ever mine, which must at once prevent me from being the most miserable, and will render me the happiest of mankind.' Leonora, covered with blushes, and with as angry a look as she could possibly put on, told him, 'that had she suspected what his declaration would have been, he should not have decoyed her from her company; that he had so surprized and frighted her, that she begged him to convey her back as quick as possible;' which he, trembling very near as much as herself, did.

'More fool he,' cried Slipslop, 'it is a sign he knew very little of our *sect*.' 'Truly, madam,' said Adams, 'I think you are in the right, I should have insisted to know a piece of her mind, when I had carried matters so far.' But Mrs. Grave-airs desired the lady to omit all such fulsome stuff in her story: for that it made her sick.

Well then, madam, to be as concise as possible, said the lady, many weeks had not past after this interview, before Horatio and Leonora were what they call on a good footing together. All ceremonies except the last were now over; the writings were now drawn, and every thing was in the utmost forwardness preparative to the putting Horatio in possession of all his wishes. I will if you please repeat you a letter from each of them which I have got by heart, and which will give you no small idea of their passion on both sides.

Mrs. Grave-airs objected to hearing these letters: but being put to the vote, it was carried against her by all the rest in the coach; Parson Adams contending for it with the utmost vehemence.

Horatio to Leonora

How vain, most adorable creature, is the pursuit of pleasure in the absence of an object to which the mind is entirely devoted, unless it have some relation to that object! I was last night condemned to the society of men of wit and learning, which, however agreeable it might have formerly been to me, now only gave me a suspicion that they imputed my absence in conversation to the true cause. For which reason, when your engagements forbid me the extatic happiness of seeing you, I am always desirous to be alone; since my sentiments for Leonora are so delicate, that I cannot bear the apprehension of another's prying into those delightful endearments with which the warm imagination of a lover will sometimes indulge him, and which I suspect my eyes then betray. To fear this discovery of our thoughts, may perhaps appear too ridiculous a nicety to minds, not susceptible of all the tendernesses of this delicate passion. And surely we shall suspect there are few such, when we consider that it requires every human virtue to exert itself in its full extent. Since the beloved whose happiness it ultimately respects, may give us charming opportunities of being brave in her defence, generous to her wants, compassionate to her afflictions, grateful to her kindness, and, in the same manner, of exercising every other virtue, which he who would not do to any degree, and that with the utmost rapture, can never deserve the name of a lover: it is therefore with a view to the delicate modesty of your mind that I cultivate it so purely in my own, and it is that which will sufficiently suggest to you the uneasiness I bear from those liberties which men to whom the world allow politeness will sometimes give themselves on these occasions.

Can I tell you with what eagerness I expect the arrival of that blest day, when I shall experience the falshood of a common assertion that the greatest human happiness consists in hope? A doctrine which no person had ever stronger reason to believe than myself at present, since none ever tasted such bliss as fires my bosom with the thoughts of spending my future days with such a companion, and that every action of my life will have the glorious satisfacion of conducing to your happiness.

*LEONORA to HORATIO

The refinement of your mind has been so evidently proved, by every word and action ever since I had first the pleasure of knowing you, that I thought it impossible my good opinion of Horatio could have been heightened by any additional proof of merit. This very thought was my amusement when I received your last letter, which, when I opened, I confess I was surprized to find the delicate sentiments expressed there, so far exceeded what I thought could come even from you, (altho' I know all the generous principles human nature is capable of, are centered in your breast) that words cannot paint what I feel on the reflection, that my happiness shall be the ultimate end of all your actions.

Oh Horatio! What a life that must be, where the meanest domestick cares are sweetened by the pleasing consideration that the man on earth who best deserves, and to whom you are most inclined to give your affections, is to reap either profit or pleasure from all you do! In such a case, toils must be turned into diversions, and nothing but the unavoidable inconveniences of life can make us remember that we are mortal.

If the solitary turn of your thoughts, and the desire of keeping them undiscovered, makes even the conversation of men of wit and learning tedious to you, what anxious hours must I

---

* This letter was written by a young lady on reading the former [Fielding's note].[1]

---

1 This note, probably referring to Fielding's sister Sarah, was added to the second edition. See Appendix D, pp. 499-500.

spend who am condemn'd by custom to the conversation of women, whose natural curiosity leads them to pry into all my thoughts, and whose envy can never suffer Horatio's heart to be possessed by any one without forcing them into malicious designs, against the person who is so happy as to possess it: but indeed, if ever envy can possibly have any excuse, or even alleviation, it is in this case, where the good is so great, that it must be equally natural to all to wish it for themselves, nor am I ashamed to own it: and to your merit, Horatio, I am obliged, that prevents my being in that most uneasy of all the situations I can figure in my imagination, of being led by inclination to love the person whom my own judgment forces me to condemn.

Matters were in so great forwardness between this fond couple, that the day was fixed for their marriage, and was now within a fortnight, when the sessions[1] chanced to be held for that county in a town about twenty miles distance from that which is the scene of our story. It seems, it is usual for the young gentlemen of the bar to repair to these sessions, not so much for the sake of profit, as to shew their parts and learn the law of the justices of peace: for which purpose one of the wisest and gravest of all the justices is appointed speaker or chairman, as they modestly call it, and he reads them a lecture, and instructs them in the true knowledge of the law.

'You are here guilty of a little mistake,' says Adams, 'which if you please I will correct; I have attended at one of these quarter sessions, where I observed the counsel taught the justices, instead of learning any thing of them.'

It is not very material, said the lady: hither repaired Horatio, who as he hoped by his profession to advance his fortune, which was not at present very large, for the sake of his dear Leonora, he resolved to spare no pains, nor lose any opportunity of improving or advancing himself in it.

The same afternoon in which he left the town, as Leonora stood at her window, a coach and six passed by: which she declared to be the completest, genteelest, prettiest equipage she

1 The Court of Quarter Sessions, composed of the county's justices of the peace, met four times a year.

ever saw; adding these remarkable words, *O I am in love with that equipage!* which, tho' her friend Florella at that time did not greatly regard, she hath since remembered.

In the evening an assembly was held, which Leonora honoured with her company: but intended to pay her dear Horatio the compliment of refusing to dance in his absence.

O why have not women as good resolution to maintain their vows, as they have often good inclinations in making them!

The gentleman who owned the coach and six, came to the assembly. His clothes were as remarkably fine as his equipage could be. He soon attracted the eyes of the company; all the smarts,[1] all the silk waistcoats with silver and gold edgings, were eclipsed in an instant.

'Madam', said Adams, 'if it be not impertinent, I should be glad to know how this gentleman was drest.'

Sir, answered the lady, I have been told he had on a cut-velvet coat of a cinnamon colour, lined with a pink satten, embroidered all over with gold; his waistcoat, which was cloth of silver, was embroidered with gold likewise. I cannot be particular as to the rest of his dress: but it was all in the French fashion, for Bellarmine, (that was his name) was just arrived from Paris.

This fine figure did not more entirely engage the eyes of every lady in the assembly, than Leonora did his. He had scarce beheld her, but he stood motionless and fixed as a statue, or at least would have done so, if good-breeding had permitted him. However, he carried it so far before he had power to correct himself, that every person in the room easily discovered where his admiration was settled. The other ladies began to single out their former partners, all perceiving who would be Bellarmine's choice; which they however endeavoured, by all possible means, to prevent: many of them saying to Leonora, 'O madam, I suppose we shan't have the pleasure of seeing you dance to-night;' and then crying out in Bellarmine's hearing, 'O Leonora will not dance, I assure you; her partner is not

1 Gay sparks, beaus.

here.' One maliciously attempted to prevent her, by sending a disagreeable fellow to ask her, that so she might be obliged either to dance with him, or sit down: but this scheme proved abortive.

Leonora saw herself admired by the fine stranger, and envied by every woman present. Her little heart began to flutter within her, and her head was agitated with a convulsive motion; she seemed as if she would speak to several of her acquaintance, but had nothing to say: for as she would not mention her present triumph, so she could not disengage her thoughts one moment from the contemplation of it: she had never tasted any thing like this happiness. She had before known what it was to torment a single woman; but to be hated and secretly cursed by a whole assembly, was a joy reserved for this blessed moment. As this vast profusion of ecstasy had confounded her understanding, so there was nothing so foolish as her behaviour; she played a thousand childish tricks, distorted her person into several shapes, and her face into several laughs, without any reason. In a word, her carriage was as absurd as her desires, which were to affect an insensibility of the stranger's admiration, and at the same time a triumph from that admiration over every woman in the room.

In this temper of mind, Bellarmine, having enquired who she was, advanced to her, and with a low bow, begged the honour of dancing with her, which she with as low a curt'sy immediately granted. She danced with him all night, and enjoyed perhaps the highest pleasure, which she was capable of feeling.

At these words, Adams fetched a deep groan, which frighted the ladies, who told him, 'they hoped he was not ill.' He answered, 'he groaned only for the folly of Leonora.'

Leonora retired, (continued the lady) about six in the morning, but not to rest. She tumbled and tossed in her bed, with very short intervals of sleep, and those entirely filled with dreams of the equipage and fine clothes she had seen, and the balls, operas and ridotto's,[1] which had been the subject of their conversation.

---

1 Entertainments or social assemblies featuring dancing and music, introduced from Italy and fashionable during the period.

In the afternoon Bellarmine, in the dear coach and six, came to wait on her. He was indeed charmed with her person, and was, on enquiry, so well pleased with the circumstances of her father, (for he himself, notwithstanding all his finery, was not quite so rich as a Crœsus or an Attālus.)[1] 'Attălus,' says Mr. Adams, 'but pray how came you acquainted with these names?'[2] The lady smiled at the question, and proceeded—He was so pleased, I say, that he resolved to make his addresses to her directly. He did so accordingly, and that with so much warmth and briskness, that he quickly baffled her weak repulses, and obliged the lady to refer him to her father, who, she knew, would quickly declare in favour of a coach and six.

Thus, what Horatio had by sighs and tears, love and tenderness, been so long obtaining, the French-English Bellarmine with gaiety and gallantry possessed himself of in an instant. In other words, what modesty had employed a full year in raising, impudence demolished in twenty-four hours.

Here Adams groaned a second time, but the ladies, who began to smoke him,[3] took no notice.

From the opening of the assembly 'till the end of Bellarmine's visit, Leonora had scarce once thought of Horatio: but he now began, tho' an unwelcome guest, to enter into her mind. She wished she had seen the charming Bellarmine and his charming equipage before matters had gone so far. 'Yet, why (says she) should I wish to have seen him before, or what signifies it that I have seen him now? Is not Horatio my lover? almost my husband? Is he not as handsome, nay handsomer than Bellarmine? Aye, but Bellarmine is the genteeler and the finer man; yes, that he must be allowed. Yes, yes, he is that certainly. But did not I no longer ago than yesterday love Horatio more than all the world? aye, but yesterday I had not seen Bellarmine. But doth not Horatio doat on me, and may he not in despair break his heart if I abandon him? Well, and hath not

---

1 The wealth of Croesus, king of Lydia in the sixth century BC, and of the Attalids, rulers of the Hellenistic city of Pergamon (269-133 BC), was proverbial.

2 Adams' surprise here is due to the fact that women were not usually educated in the classics.

3 To make him out, size him up.

Bellarmine a heart to break too? Yes, but I promised Horatio first; but that was poor Bellarmine's misfortune, if I had seen him first, I should certainly have preferred him. Did not the dear creature prefer me to every woman in the assembly, when every she was laying out for him? When was it in Horatio's power to give me such an instance of affection? Can he give me an equipage or any of those things which Bellarmine will make me mistress of? How vast is the difference between being the wife of a poor counsellor, and the wife of one of Bellarmine's fortune! If I marry Horatio, I shall triumph over no more than one rival: but by marrying Bellarmine, I shall be the envy of all my acquaintance. What happiness!—But can I suffer Horatio to die? for he hath sworn he cannot survive my loss: but perhaps he may not die; if he should, can I prevent it? Must I sacrifice my self to him? besides, Bellarmine may be as miserable for me too.' She was thus arguing with herself, when some young ladies called her to the walks, and a little relieved her anxiety for the present.

The next morning Bellarmine breakfasted with her in presence of her aunt, whom he sufficiently informed of his passion for Leonora; he was no sooner withdrawn, than the old lady began to advise her niece on this occasion.—'You see, child, (says she) what Fortune hath thrown in your way, and I hope you will not withstand your own preferments.' Leonora sighing, 'begged her not to mention any such thing, when she knew her engagements to Horatio.' 'Engagements to a fig,' cry'd the aunt, 'you should thank Heaven on your knees that you have it yet in your power to break them. Will any woman hesitate a moment, whether she shall ride in a coach or walk on foot all the days of her life?—But Bellarmine drives six, and Horatio not even a pair.' 'Yes, but, madam, what will the world say?' answered Leonora; 'will not they condemn me?' 'The world is always on the side of prudence,' cries the aunt, 'and would surely condemn you if you sacrificed your interest to any motive whatever. O, I know the world very well, and you shew your own ignorance, my dear, by your objection. O' my conscience the world is wiser. I have lived longer in it than you, and I assure you there is not any thing worth our regard besides money: nor did I ever know one person who married from other considerations, who did not afterwards heartily repent it. Besides, if we examine the two men, can you prefer a sneaking[1] fellow, who hath been bred at a university, to a fine gentleman just come from his travels?—All the world must allow Bellarmine to be a fine gentleman, positively a fine gentleman, and a handsome man.—' 'Perhaps, madam, I should not doubt, if I knew how to be handsomely off with the other.' 'O leave that to me,' says the aunt. 'You know your father hath not been acquainted with the affair.[2] Indeed, for my part, I thought it might do well enough, not dreaming of such an offer: but I'll disengage you, leave me to give the fellow an answer. I warrant you shall have no farther trouble.'

Leonora was at length satisfied with her aunt's reasoning; and Bellarmine supping with her that evening, it was agreed he should the next morning go to her father and propose the match, which she consented should be consummated at his return.

The aunt retired soon after supper, and the lovers being left together, Bellarmine began in the following manner: 'Yes, madam, this coat I assure you was made at Paris, and I defy the best English taylor even to imitate it. There is not one of them can cut, madam, they can't cut. If you observe how this skirt is turned, and this sleeve, a clumsy English rascal can do nothing like it.—Pray how do you like my liveries?' Leonora answered, 'she thought them very pretty.' 'All French,' says he, 'I assure you, except the great coats; I never trust any thing more than a great coat to an Englishman; you know one must encourage our own people what one can, especially as, before I had a place, I was in the country interest,[3] he, he, he! but for myself, I would see the dirty island at the bottom of the sea, rather than

---

1 Servile, mean.

2 Earlier in the chapter, however, it is stated that "All ceremonies except the last were now over; the writings were now drawn, and everything was in the utmost forwardness . . ."

3 The Country Party or Patriots opposed the Walpole administration, claiming to rise above factionalism for the good of the country as a whole. Fielding added this passage to the revised second edition, having previously supported the Patriots. See Introduction, pp. 9-12.

wear a single rag of English work about me, and I am sure after you have made one tour to Paris, you will be of the same opinion with regard to your own clothes. You can't conceive what an addition a French dress would be to your beauty; I positively assure you, at the first opera I saw since I came over, I mistook the English ladies for chambermaids, he, he, he!'

With such sort of polite discourse did the gay Bellarmine entertain his beloved Leonora, when the door opened on a sudden, and Horatio entered the room. Here 'tis impossible to express the surprize of Leonora.

'Poor woman,' says Mrs. Slipslop, 'what a terrible *quandary*[1] she must be in!' 'Not at all,' says Miss Grave-airs, 'such sluts can never be confounded.' 'She must have then more than Corinthian assurance,' said Adams; 'ay, more than Lais herself.'[2]

A long silence, continued the lady, prevailed in the whole company: if the familiar entrance of Horatio struck the greatest astonishment into Bellarmine, the unexpected presence of Bellarmine no less surprized Horatio. At length Leonora collecting all the spirits she was mistress of, addressed herself to the latter, and pretended to wonder at the reason of so late a visit. 'I should, indeed,' answered he, 'have made some apology for disturbing you at this hour, had not my finding you in company assured me I do not break in on your repose.' Bellarmine rose from his chair, traversed the room in a minuet step, and humm'd an opera tune, while Horatio advancing to Leonora ask'd her in a whisper, if that gentleman was not a relation of her's; to which she answered with a smile, or rather sneer, 'No, he is no relation of mine yet;' adding, 'she could not guess the meaning of his question.' Horatio told her softly, 'it did not arise from jealousy.' 'Jealousy!' cries she, 'I assure you;—it would be very strange in a common acquaintance to give himself any of those airs.' These words a little surprized Horatio, but before he had time to answer, Bellarmine danced up to the lady, and told her, 'he feared he interrupted some business between her and the

---

1 Although in use since the sixteenth century, Johnson's *Dictionary* refers to it as a "low word."

2 Lais was one of the most famous courtesans of ancient Corinth, a city notorious for its profligacy.

gentleman.' 'I can have no business,' said she, 'with the gentleman, nor any other, which need be any secret to you.'

'You'll pardon me,' said Horatio, 'if I desire to know who this gentleman is, who is to be intrusted with all our secrets.' 'You'll know soon enough,' cries Leonora, 'but I can't guess what secrets can ever pass between us of such mighty consequence.' 'No madam!' cries Horatio, 'I'm sure you would not have me understand you in earnest.' ''Tis indifferent to me,' says she, 'how you understand me; but I think so unseasonable a visit is difficult to be understood at all, at least when people find one engaged, though one's servants do not deny one, one may expect a well-bred person should soon take the hint.' 'Madam,' said Horatio, 'I did not imagine any engagement with a stranger, as it seems this gentleman is, would have made my visit impertinent, or that any such ceremonies were to be preserved between persons in our situation.' 'Sure you are in a dream,' says she, 'or would persuade me that I am in one. I know no pretensions a common acquaintance can have to lay aside the ceremonies of good breeding.' 'Sure,' said he, 'I am in a dream; for it is impossible I should be really esteemed a common acquaintance by Leonora, after what has passed between us!' 'Passed between us! Do you intend to affront me before this gentleman?' 'D—n me, affront the lady,' says Bellarmine, cocking his hat and strutting up to Horatio, 'does any man dare affront this lady before me, d—n me?' 'Harkee, sir,' says Horatio, 'I would advise you to lay aside that fierce air; for I am mightily deceived, if this lady has not a violent desire to get your worship a good drubbing.' 'Sir,' said Bellarmine,' I have the honour to be her protector, and d—n me, if I understand your meaning.' 'Sir,' answered Horatio, 'she is rather your protectress: but give yourself no more airs, for you see I am prepared for you,' (shaking his whip at him.) 'Oh!' *Serviteur tres humble,*' says Bellarmine, '*Je vous entend parfaitement bien.*'[1] At which time the aunt, who had heard of Horatio's visit, entered the room and soon satisfied all his doubts. She convinced him that he was never more awake in his life, and that nothing more extraordi-

1 "Your very humble servant. I understand you perfectly."

nary had happened in his three days absence, than a small alteration in the affections of Leonora: who now burst into tears, and wondered what reason she had given him to use her in so barbarous a manner. Horatio desired Bellarmine to withdraw with him: but the ladies prevented it by laying violent hands on the latter; upon which, the former took his leave without any great ceremony, and departed, leaving the lady with his rival to consult for his safety, which Leonora feared her indiscretion might have endangered: but the aunt comforted her with assurances, that Horatio would not venture his person against so accomplished a cavalier as Bellarmine, and that being a lawyer, he would seek revenge in his own way, and the most they had to apprehend from him was an action.[1]

They at length therefore agreed to permit Bellarmine to retire to his lodgings, having first settled all matters relating to the journey which he was to undertake in the morning, and their preparations for the nuptials at his return.

But alas! as wise men have observed, the seat of valour is not the countenance, and many a grave and plain man, will, on a just provocation, betake himself to that mischievous metal, cold iron; while men of a fiercer brow, and sometimes with that emblem of courage, a cockade,[2] will more prudently decline it.

Leonora was waked in the morning, from a visionary coach and six, with the dismal account, that Bellarmine was run through the body by Horatio, that he lay languishing at an inn, and the surgeons had declared the wound mortal. She immediately leap'd out of the bed, danced about the room in a frantic manner, tore her hair and beat her breast in all the agonies of despair; in which sad condition her aunt, who likewise arose at the news, found her. The good old lady applied her utmost art to comfort her niece. She told her, 'while there was life, there was hope: but that if he should die, her affliction would be of no service to Bellarmine, and would only expose herself, which might probably keep her some time without any future offer; that as matters had happened, her wisest way would be to think no more of Bellarmine, but to endeavour to regain the affec-

---

1 A lawsuit.

2 An ornament worn on hats by soldiers, etc.

tions of Horatio.' 'Speak not to me,' cry'd the disconsolate Leonora, 'is it not owing to me, that poor Bellarmine has lost his life? have not these cursed charms' (at which words she looked stedfastly in the glass,) 'been the ruin of the most charming man of this age? Can I ever bear to comtemplate my own face again?' (with her eyes still fixed on the glass.) 'Am I not the murderess of the finest gentleman? No other woman in the town could have made any impression on him.' 'Never think of things passed.' cries the aunt, 'think of regaining the affections of Horatio.' 'What reason,' said the niece, 'have I to hope he would forgive me? no, I have lost him as well as the other, and it was your wicked advice which was the occasion of all; you seduced me, contrary to my inclinations, to abandon poor Horatio,' at which words she burst into tears; 'you prevailed upon me, whether I would or no, to give up my affections for him; had it not been for you, Bellarmine never would have entered into my thoughts; had not his addresses been backed by your persuasions, they never would have made any impression on me; I should have defied all the fortune and equipage in the world: but it was you, it was you, who got the better of my youth and simplicity, and forced me to lose my dear Horatio for ever.'

The aunt was almost borne down with this torrent of words, she however rallied all the strength she could, and drawing her mouth up in a purse, began: 'I am not surprized, niece, at this ingratitude. Those who advise young women for their interest, must always expect such a return: I am convinced my brother will thank me for breaking off your match with Horatio at any rate.' 'That may not be in your power yet,' answered Leonora; 'tho' it is very ungrateful in you to desire or attempt it, after the presents you have received from him.' (For indeed true it is, that many presents, and some pretty valuable ones, had passed from Horatio to the old lady: but as true it is, that Bellarmine when he breakfasted with her and her niece, had complimented her with a brilliant[1] from his finger, of much greater value than all she had touched of the other.)

---

1 A precious gem, especially a diamond finely cut.

The aunt's gall was on float to reply, when a servant brought a letter into the room; which Leonora hearing it came from Bellarmine, with great eagerness opened, and read as follows:

'Most Divine Creaure,

The wound which I fear you have heard I received from my rival, is not like to be so fatal as those shot into my heart, which have been fired from your eyes, *tout-brilliant.* Those are the only cannons by which I am to fall: for my surgeon gives me hopes of being soon able to attend your *ruelle*;[1] 'till when, unless you would do me an honour which I have scarce the *hardiesse* to think of, your absence will be the greatest anguish which can be felt by,

MADAM,
Avec tout le respecte in the world,
Your most obedient, most absolute
Devoté,
Bellarmine'

As soon as Leonora perceived such hopes of Bellarmine's recovery, and that the gossip Fame had, according to custom, so enlarged his danger, she presently abandoned all farther thoughts of Horatio, and was soon reconciled to her aunt, who received her again into favour, with a more Christian forgiveness than we generally meet with. Indeed it is possible she might be a little alarmed at the hints which her niece had given her concerning the presents. She might apprehend such rumours, should they get abroad, might injure a reputation, which by frequenting church twice a day, and preserving the utmost rigour and strictness in her countenance and behaviour for many years, she had established.

Leonora's passion returned now for Bellarmine with greater force after its small relaxation than ever. She proposed to her aunt to make him a visit in his confinement, which the old lady, with great and commendable prudence advised her to

1 A morning reception held by ladies of fashion in their bedchambers.

decline: 'For,' says she, 'should any accident intervene to prevent your intended match, too forward a behaviour with this lover may injure you in the eyes of others. Every woman 'till she is married ought to consider of and provide against the possibility of the affair's breaking off.' Leonora said, 'she should be indifferent to whatever might happen in such a case: for she had now so absolutely placed her affections on this dear man (so she called him) that, if it was her misfortune to lose him, she should for ever abandon all thoughts of mankind.' She therefore resolved to visit him, notwithstanding all the prudent advice of her aunt to the contrary, and that very afternoon executed her resolution.

The lady was proceeding in her story, when the coach drove into the inn where the company were to dine, sorely to the dissatisfaction of Mr. Adams, whose ears were the most hungry part about him; he being, as the reader may perhaps guess, of an insatiable curiosity, and heartily desirous of hearing the end of this amour, tho' he professed he could scarce wish success to a lady of so inconstant a disposition.

CHAPTER V

A dreadful quarrel which happened at the inn where the company dined, with its bloody consequences to Mr. Adams.

As soon as the passengers had alighted from the coach, Mr. Adams, as was his custom, made directly to the kitchin, where he found Joseph sitting by the fire and the hostess anointing his leg: for the horse which Mr. Adams had borrowed of his clerk, had so violent a propensity to kneeling, that one would have thought it had been his trade as well as his master's: nor would he always give any notice of such his intention; he was often found on his knees, when the rider least expected it. This foible however was of no great inconvenience to the parson, who was accustomed to it, and as his legs almost touched the ground when he bestrode the beast, had but a little way to fall, and threw himself forward on such occasions with so much dexterity, that he never received any mischief; the horse and he frequently rolling many paces distance, and afterwards both getting up and meeting as good friends as ever.

Poor Joseph, who had not been used to such kind of cattle, tho' an excellent horseman, did not so happily disengage himself: but falling with his leg under the beast, received a violent contusion, to which the good woman was, as we have said, applying a warm hand with some camphirated spirits just at the time when the parson entered the kitchin.

He had scarce express'd his concern for Joseph's misfortune, before the host likewise entered. He was by no means of Mr. Tow-wouse's gentle disposition, and was indeed perfect master of his house and every thing in it but his guests.

This surly fellow, who always proportioned his respect to the appearance of a traveller, from *God bless your honour*, down to plain *Coming presently*, observing his wife on her knees to a footman, cried out, without considering his circumstances, 'What a pox is the woman about? why don't you mind the company in the coach? Go and ask them what they will have for dinner?' 'My dear,' says she, 'you know they can have nothing but what is at the fire, which will be ready presently; and really the poor young man's leg is very much bruised.' At which words, she fell to chafing more violently than before: the bell then happening to ring, he damn'd his wife, and bid her go in to the company, and not stand rubbing there all day: for he did not believe the young fellow's leg was so bad as he pretended; and if it was, within twenty miles he would find a surgeon to cut it off. Upon these words, Adams fetched two strides across the room; and snapping his fingers over his head muttered aloud, 'he would excommunicate such a wretch for a farthing: for he believed the Devil had more humanity.' These words occasioned a dialogue between Adams and the host, in which there were two or three sharp replies, 'till Joseph bad the latter know how to behave himself to his betters. At which the host, (having first strictly surveyed Adams) scornfully repeating the word *betters*, flew into a rage, and telling Joseph he was as able to walk out of his house as he had been to walk into it, offered to lay violent hands on him; which perceiving, Adams dealt him so sound a compliment over his face with his fist, that the blood immediately gushed out of his nose in a stream. The host being unwilling to be outdone in courtesy, especially by a person of Adams's figure, returned the favour with so much gratitude, that the parson's nostrils likewise began to look a little redder than usual. Upon which he again assailed his antagonist, and with another stroke laid him sprawling on the floor.

The hostess, who was a better wife than so surly a husband deserved, seeing her husband all bloody and stretched along, hastened presently to his assistance, or rather to revenge the blow which to all appearance was the last he would ever receive; when, lo! a pan full of hog's-blood,[1] which unluckily stood on the dresser, presented itself first to her hands. She seized it in her fury, and without any reflection discharged it into the parson's face, and with so good an aim, that much the greater part first saluted his countenance, and trickled thence in so large a current down his beard, and over his garments, that a more horrible spectacle was hardly to be seen or even imagined. All which was perceived by Mrs. Slipslop, who entered the kitchin at that instant. This good gentlewoman, not being of a temper so extremely cool and patient as perhaps was required to ask many questions on this occasion; flew with great impetuosity at the hostess's cap, which, together with some of her hair, she plucked from her head in a moment, giving her at the same time several hearty cuffs in the face, which by frequent practice on the inferiour servants, she had learned an excellent knack of delivering with a good grace. Poor Joseph could hardly rise from his chair; the parson was employed in wiping the blood from his eyes, which had intirely blinded him, and the landlord was but just beginning to stir, whilst Mrs. Slipslop holding down the landlady's face with her left hand, made so dextrous a use of her right, that the poor woman began to roar in a key, which alarmed all the company in the inn.

There happened to be in the inn at this time, besides the ladies who arrived in the stage-coach, the two gentlemen who

---

1 The basic ingredient of blood pudding, a sausagelike preparation.

were present at Mr. Tow-wouse's when Joseph was detained for his horse's-meat, and whom we have before mentioned to have stopt at the alehouse with Adams. There was likewise a gentleman just returned from his travels to Italy; all whom the horrid outcry of murther, presently brought into the kitchin, where the several combatants were found in the postures already described.

It was now no difficulty to put an end to the fray, the conquerors being satisfied with the vengeance they had taken, and the conquered having no appetite to renew the fight. The principal figure, and which engaged the eyes of all was Adams, who was all over covered with blood, which the whole company concluded to be his own; and consequently imagined him no longer for this world. But the host, who had now recovered from his blow, and was risen from the ground, soon delivered them from this apprehension, by damning his wife, for wasting the hog's puddings, and telling her all would have been very well if she had not intermeddled like a b— as she was; adding, he was very glad the gentlewoman had paid her, tho' not half what she deserved. The poor woman had indeed fared much the worst, having, besides the unmerciful cuffs received, lost a quantity of hair which Mrs. Slipslop in triumph held in her left hand.

The traveller, addressing himself to Miss Grave-airs, desired her not to be frightened: for here had been only a little boxing, which he said to their *disgracia* the English were *accustomata* to; adding, it must be however a sight somewhat strange to him, who was just come from Italy, the Italians not being addicted to the *cuffardo*, but *bastonza,* says he. He then went up to Adams, and telling him he looked liked the ghost of Othello, bid him *not shake his gory locks at him, for he could not say he did it.*[1] Adams very innocently answered, *Sir, I am far from accusing you*. He then returned to the lady, and cried, 'I find the bloody gentleman is *uno insipido del nullo senso. Damnata di me*, if I have seen such a *spectaculo* in my way from Viterbo.'[2]

---

1 Macbeth addresses the ghost of Banquo with the following words: "Thou canst not say I did it. Never shake / Thy gory locks at me" (*Macbeth* 3.4.50–51).

2 Italianized English words and phrases, as specious as the gentleman's knowledge of Shakespeare.

One of the gentlemen having learnt from the host the occasion of this bustle, and being assured by him that Adams had struck the first blow, whispered in his ear: 'he'd warrant he would *recover*.' 'Recover! master,' said the host, smiling: 'Yes, yes, I am not afraid of dying with a blow or two neither; I am not such a chicken as that.' 'Pugh!' said the gentleman, 'I mean you will recover damages, in that action which undoubtedly you intend to bring, as soon as a writ can be returned from London;[1] for you look like a man of too much spirit and courage to suffer any one to beat you without bringing your action against him: he must be a scandalous fellow indeed, who would put up a drubbing whilst the law is open to revenge it; besides, he hath drawn blood from you and spoiled your coat, and the jury will give damages for that too. An excellent new coat upon my word, and now not worth a shilling!

'I don't care,' continued he, 'to intermeddle in these cases: but you have a right to my evidence; and if I am sworn, I must speak the truth. I saw you sprawling on the floor, and the blood gushing from your nostrils. You may take your own opinion; but was I in your circumstances, every drop of my blood should convey an ounce of gold into my pocket: remember I don't advise you to go to law, but if your jury were Christians, they must give swinging[2] damages, that's all.' 'Master,' cry'd the host, scratching his head, 'I have no stomach to law, I thank you. I have seen enough of that in the parish, where two of my neighbours have been at law about a house, 'till they have both lawed themselves into a goal.' At which words he turned about, and began to enquire again after his hog's puddings, nor would it probably have been a sufficient excuse for his wife that she spilt them in his defence, had not some awe of the company, especially of the Italian traveller, who was a person of great dignity, with-held his rage. Whilst one of the above-mentioned gentlemen was employed, as we have seen him, on the behalf of the landlord, the other was no less hearty on the side of Mr. Adams, whom he advised to bring his action immediately. He

1 To initiate a lawsuit, a writ had to be obtained from the Court of Chancery, London.

2 Huge.

said the assault of the wife was in law the assault of the husband; for they were but one person; and he was liable to pay damages, which he said must be considerable, where so bloody a disposition appeared. Adams answered, if it was true that they were but one person he had assaulted the wife; for he was sorry to own he had struck the husband the first blow. 'I am sorry you own it too,' cries the gentleman; 'for it could not possibly appear to the court: for here was no evidence present but the lame man in the chair, whom I suppose to be your friend, and would consequently say nothing but what made for you.' 'How, sir,' says Adams, 'do you take me for a villain, who would prosecute revenge in cold blood, and use unjustifiable means to obtain it? If you knew me and my order, I should think you affronted both.' At the word order, the gentleman stared, (for he was too bloody to be of any modern order of knights,) and turning hastily about, said, every man knew his own business.

Matters being now composed, the company retired to their several apartments, the two gentlemen congratulating each other on the success of their good offices, in procuring a perfect reconciliation between the contending parties; and the traveller went to his repast, crying, as the Italian poet says,

> '*Je voi* very well, *que tutta e pace*,
> So send up dinner, good Boniface.'[1]

The coachman began now to grow importunate with his passengers, whose entrance into the coach was retarded by Miss Grave-airs insisting, against the remonstrances of all the rest, that she would not admit a footman into the coach: for poor Joseph was too lame to mount a horse. A young lady, who was, as it seems, an earl's grand daughter, begged it with almost tears in her eyes; Mr. Adams prayed, and Mrs. Slipslop scolded, but all to no purpose. She said, 'she would not demean herself to ride with a footman: that there were waggons on the road: that if the master of the coach desired it, she would pay for two

---

1 The jovial innkeeper in George Farquhar's *The Beaux' Stratagem* (1707), whose name soon applied to innkeepers generally.

places: but would suffer no such fellow to come in.' 'Madam,' says Slipslop, 'I am sure no one can refuse another coming into a stage-coach.' 'I don't know, madam,' says the lady, 'I am not much used to stage-coaches, I seldom travel in them.' 'That may be, madam,' replied Slipslop, 'very good people do, and some people's betters, for aught I know.' Miss Grave-airs said, 'some folks, might sometimes give their tongues a liberty, to some people that were their betters, which did not become them: for her part, she was not used to converse with servants.' Slipslop returned, 'some people kept no servants to converse with: for her part, she thanked Heaven, she lived in a family where there were a great many; and had more under her own command, than any paultry little gentlewoman in the kingdom.' Miss Grave-airs cry'd, 'she believed, her mistress would not encourage such sauciness to her betters.' 'My betters,' says Slipslop, 'who is my betters, pray?' 'I am your betters,' answered Miss Grave-airs, 'and I'll acquaint your mistress.'—At which Mrs. Slipslop laughed aloud, and told her, 'her lady was one of the great gentry, and such little paultry gentlewomen, as some folks who travelled in stage-coaches, would not easily come at her.'

This smart dialogue between some people, and some folks, was going on at the coach-door, when a solemn person riding into the inn, and seeing Miss Grave-airs, immediately accosted her with, 'Dear child, how do you?' She presently answered, 'O! papa, I am glad you have overtaken me.' 'So am I,' answered he: 'for one of our coaches is just at hand; and there being room for you in it, you shall go no farther in the stage, unless you desire it.' 'How can you imagine I should desire it?' says she; so bidding Slipslop, 'ride with her fellow, if she pleased;' she took her father by the hand, who was just alighted, and walked with him into a room.

Adams instantly asked the coachman in a whisper, if he knew who the gentleman was? The coachman answered, he was now a gentleman, and kept his horse and man: 'but times are altered, master,' said he, 'I remember, when he was no better born than myself.' 'Aye, aye,' says Adams. 'My father drove the squire's coach,' answered he, 'when that very man rode postilion; but he is now his steward, and a great gentleman.' Adams then snapped his fingers, and cry'd, he thought *she was some such trollop*.

Adams made haste to acquaint Mrs. Slipslop with this good news, as he imagined it; but it found a reception different from what he expected. That prudent gentlewoman, who despised the anger of Miss Grave-airs, whilst she conceived her the daughter of a gentleman of small fortune, now she heard her alliance with the upper servants of a great family in her neighbourhood, began to fear her interest with the mistress. She wished she had not carried the dispute so far, and began to think of endeavouring to reconcile herself to the young lady before she left the inn; when luckily, the scene at London, which the reader can scarce have forgotten, presented itself to her mind, and comforted her with such assurance, that she no longer apprehended any enemy with her mistress.

Every thing being now adjusted, the company entered the coach, which was just on its departure, when one lady recollected she had left her fan, a second her gloves, a third a snuff-box, and a fourth a smelling-bottle behind her; to find all which, occasioned some delay, and much swearing of the coachman.

As soon as the coach had left the inn, the women all together fell to the character of Miss Grave-airs, whom one of them declared she had suspected to be some low creature from the beginning of their journey; and another affirmed had not even the looks of a gentlewoman; a third warranted she was no better than she should be, and turning to the lady who had related the story in the coach, said, 'Did you ever hear, madam, any thing so prudish as her remarks? Well, deliver me from the censoriousness of such a prude.' The fourth added, 'O madam! all these creatures are censorious: but for my part, I wonder where the wretch was bred; indeed I must own I have seldom conversed with these mean kind of people, so that it may appear stranger to me; but to refuse the general desire of a whole company, hath something in it so astonishing, that, for my part, I own I should hardly believe it, if my own ears had not been witnesses to it.' 'Yes, and so handsome a young fellow,' cries

Slipslop, 'the woman must have no compassion[1] in her, I believe she is more of a Turk than a Christian; I am certain if she had any Christian woman's blood in her veins, the sight of such a young fellow must have warm'd it. Indeed there are some wretched, miserable old objects that turn one's stomach, I should not wonder if she had refused such a one; I am as nice[2] as herself, and should have cared no more than herself for the company of stinking old fellows: but hold up thy head, Joseph, thou are none of those and she who hath no *compulsion* for thee is a *Myhummetman*,[3] and I will maintain it.' This conversation made Joseph uneasy, as well as the ladies; who perceiving the spirits which Mrs. Slipslop was in, (for indeed she was not a cup too low) began to fear the consequence; one of them therefore desired the lady to conclude the story—'Ay madam,' said Slipslop, 'I beg your ladyship to give us that story you *commencated* in the morning,' which request that well-bred woman immediately complied with.

CHAPTER VI

Conclusion of the Unfortunate Jilt.

LEONORA having once broke through the bounds which custom and modesty impose on her sex, soon gave an unbridled indulgence to her passion. Her visits to Bellarmine were more constant, as well as longer, than his surgeon's; in a word, she became absolutely his nurse, made his water-gruel, administred him his medicines, and, notwithstanding the prudent advice of her aunt to the contrary, almost intirely resided in her wounded lover's apartment.

The ladies of the town began to take her conduct under consideration; it was the chief topick of discourse at their tea-

---

1 Changed to *compulsion* in the 1762 edition, making it consistent with Slipslop's malapropism a little later in the passage.

2 Fastidious.

3 Slipslop of course means "Mohammedan," the Turks probably being the most well known of these "infidels."

tables, and was very severely censured by the most part; especially by Lindamira, a lady whose discreet and starch carriage, together with a constant attendance at church three times a day, had utterly defeated many malicious attacks on her own reputation: for such was the envy that Lindamira's virtue had attracted, that notwithstanding her own strict behaviour and strict enquiry into the lives of others, she had not been able to escape being the mark of some arrows herself, which however did her no injury; a blessing perhaps owed by her to the clergy, who were her chief male companions, and with two or three of whom she had been barbarously and unjustly calumniated.

'Not so unjustly neither perhaps,' says Slipslop, 'for the clergy are men as well as other folks.'

The extreme delicacy of Lindamira's virtue was cruelly hurt by these freedoms which Leonora allowed herself; she said, 'it was an affront to her sex, that she did not imagine it consistent with any woman's honour to speak to the creature, or to be seen in her company; and that, for her part, she should always refuse to dance at an assembly with her, for fear of contamination, by taking her by the hand.'

But to return to my story: As soon as Bellarmine was recovered, which was somewhat within a month from his receiving the wound, he set out, according to agreement, for Leonora's father's, in order to propose the match and settle all matters with him touching settlements, and the like.

A little before his arrival, the old gentleman had received an intimation of the affair by the following letter; which I can repeat *verbatim*, and which they say was written neither by Leonora nor her aunt, tho' it was in a woman's hand. The letter was in these words:

'Sir,

I am sorry to acquaint you that your daughter Leonora hath acted one of the basest, as well as most simple[1] parts with a young gentleman to whom she had engaged herself, and whom she hath (pardon the word) jilted for another of inferiour for-

1 Foolish, silly.

tune, notwithstanding his superiour figure. You may take what measures you please on this occasion; I have performed what I thought my duty, as I have, tho' unknown to you, a very great respect for your family.'

The old gentleman did not give himself the trouble to answer this kind epistle, nor did he take any notice of it after he had read it, 'till he saw Bellarmine. He was, to say the truth, one of those fathers who look on children as an unhappy consequence of their youthful pleasures; which as he would have been delighted not to have had attended them, so was he no less pleased with any opportunity to rid himself of the incumbrance. He pass'd in the world's language as an exceeding good father, being not only so rapacious as to rob and plunder all mankind to the utmost of his power, but even to deny himself the conveniences and almost necessaries of life; which his neighbours attributed to a desire of raising immense fortunes for his children: but in fact it was not so, he heaped up money for its own sake only, and looked on his children as his rivals, who were to enjoy his beloved mistress, when he was incapable of possessing her, and which he would have been much more charmed with the power of carrying along with him: nor had his children any other security of being his heirs, than that the law would constitute them such without a will, and that he had not affection enough for any one living to take the trouble of writing one.

To this gentleman came Bellarmine on the errand I have mentioned. His person, his equipage, his family and his estate seemed to the father to make him an advantageous match for his daughter; he therefore very readily accepted his proposals: but when Bellarmine imagined the principal affair concluded, and began to open the incidental matters of fortune; the old gentleman presently changed his countenance, saying, 'he resolved never to marry his daughter on a Smithfield match;[1] that whoever had love for her to take her, would, when he died, find her share of his fortune in his coffers: but he had seen

1 A marriage for money (as if purchased at Smithfield cattle market).

such examples of undutifulness happen from the too early generosity of parents, that he had made a vow never to part with a shilling whilst he lived.' He commended the saying of Solomon, *he that spareth the rod, spoileth the child*:[1] but added, 'he might have likewise asserted, that *he that spareth the purse, saveth the child*.' He then ran into a discourse on the extravagance of the youth of the age; whence he launched into a dissertation on horses, and came at length to commend those Bellarmine drove. That fine gentleman, who at another season would have been well enough pleased to dwell a little on that subject, was now very eager to resume the circumstance of fortune. He said, 'he had a very high value for the young lady, and would receive her with less than he would any other whatever; but that even his love to her made some regard to worldly matters necessary; for it would be a most distracting sight for him to see her, when he had the honour to be her husband, in less that a coach and six.' The old gentleman answer'd, 'Four will do, four will do;' and then took a turn from horses to extravagance, and from extravagance to horses, till he came round to the equipage again, whither he was no sooner arrived, than Bellarmine brought him back to the point; but all to no purpose, he made his escape from that subject in a minute, till at last the lover declared, 'that in the present situation of his affairs it was impossible for him, though he loved Leonora more than *tout le monde*; to marry her without any fortune.' To which the father answered, 'he was sorry then his daughter must lose so valuable a match; that if he had an inclination at present, it was not in his power to advance a shilling: that he had had great losses and been at great expences on projects, which, though he had great expectation from them, had yet produced him nothing: that he did not know what might happen hereafter, as on the birth of a son, or such accident, but he would make no promise, or enter into any article: for he would not break his vow for all the daughters in the world.'

In short, ladies, to keep you no longer in suspense, Bellarmine having tried every argument and persuasion which he

---

1 Proverbs 13:24.

could invent,[1] and finding them all ineffectual, at length took his leave, but not in order to return to Leonora; he proceeded directly to his own seat, whence after a few days stay, he returned to Paris, to the great delight of the French, and the honour of the English nation.

But as soon as he arrived at his home, he presently dispatched a messenger, with the following epistle to Leonora.

'*Adorable* and *charmante*,

I am sorry to have the honour to tell you I am not the *heureux* person destined for your divine arms. Your papa hath told me so with a *politesse* not often seen on this side Paris. You may perhaps guess his manner of refusing me—*Ah mon Dieu!* You will certainly believe me, madam, incapable of my self delivering this *triste* message: which I intend to try the French air to cure the consequences of—*Ah jamais! Cœur! Ange!*—*Ah Diable!*—If your papa obliges you to a marriage, I hope we shall see you at Paris, till when the wind that flows from thence will be the warmest *dans le monde*: for it will consist almost entirely of my sighs. *Adieu, ma princesse! Ah l'amour!*

Bellarmine'

I shall not attempt ladies, to describe Leonora's condition when she received this letter. It is a picture of horrour, which I should have as little pleasure in drawing as you in beholding. She immediately left the place, where she was the subject of conversation and ridicule, and retired to that house I shewed you when I began the story, where she hath ever since led a disconsolate life, and deserves perhaps pity for her misfortunes more than our censure, for a behaviour to which the artifices of her aunt very probably contributed, and to which very young women are often rendered too liable, by that blameable levity in the education of our sex.

'If I was inclined to pity her,' said a young lady in the coach, 'it would be for the loss of Horatio; for I cannot discern any misfortune in her missing such a husband as Bellarmine.'

---

1 Think of.

'Why I must own,' says Slipslop, 'the gentleman was a little false-hearted: but *howsumever* it was hard to have two lovers, and get never a husband at all—But pray, madam, what became of *Ourasho*?'

He remains, said the lady, still unmarried, and hath applied himself so strictly to his business, that he hath raised I hear a very considerable fortune. And what is remarkable, they say, he never hears the name of Leonora without a sigh, nor hath ever uttered one syllable to charge her with her ill conduct towards him.

CHAPTER VII

A very short chapter, in which Parson Adams went a great way.

THE lady having finished her story received the thanks of the company, and now Joseph putting his head out of the coach, cried out, 'Never believe me, if yonder be not our Parson Adams walking along without his horse.' 'On my word, and so he is,' says Slipslop; 'and as sure as two-pence, he hath left him behind at the inn.' Indeed, true it is, the parson had exhibited a fresh instance of his absence of mind: for he was so pleased with having got Joseph into the coach, that he never once thought of the beast in the stable; and finding his legs as nimble as he desired, he sallied out brandishing a crabstick, and had kept on before the coach, mending and slackening his pace occasionally, so that he had never been much more or less than a quarter of a mile distant from it.

Mrs. Slipslop desired the coachman to overtake him, which he attempted, but in vain: for the faster he drove, the faster ran the parson, often crying out, *Aye, aye, catch me if you can*: 'till at length the coachman swore he would as soon attempt to drive after a greyhound; and giving the parson two or three hearty curses, he cry'd, 'Softly, softly boys,' to his horses, which the civil beasts immediately obeyed.

But we will be more courteous to our reader than he was to Mrs. Slipslop, and leaving the coach and its company to pursue their journey, we will carry our reader on after Parson Adams, who stretched forwards without once looking behind him, 'till having left the coach full three miles in his rear, he came to a place, where by keeping the extremest track to the right, it was just barely possible for a human creature to miss his way. This track however did he keep, as indeed he had a wonderful capacity at these kinds of bare possibilities; and travelling in it about three miles over the plain, he arrived at the summit of a hill, whence looking a great way backwards, and perceiving no coach in sight, he sat himself down on the turf, and pulling out his Æschylus determined to wait here for its arrival.

He had not sat long here, before a gun going off very near, a little startled him; he looked up, and saw a gentleman within a hundred paces taking up a partridge, which he had just shot.

Adams stood up, and presented a figure to the gentleman which would have moved laughter in many: for his cassock had just again fallen down below his great coat, that is to say, it reached his knees; whereas, the skirts of his great coat descended no lower than half way down his thighs: but the gentleman's mirth gave way to his surprize, at beholding such a personage in such a place.

Adams advancing to the gentleman told him he hoped he had good sport; to which the other answered, 'Very little.' 'I see, sir,' says Adams, 'you have *smote* one partridge:' to which the sportsman made no reply, but proceeded to charge his piece.

Whilst the gun was charging, Adams remained in silence, which he at last broke, by observing that it was a delightful evening. The gentleman, who had at first sight conceived a very distasteful opinion of the parson, began, on perceiving a book in his hand, and smoking[1] likewise the information of the cassock, to change his thoughts, and made a small advance to conversation on his side, by saying, *Sir, I suppose you are not one of these parts?*

Adams immediately told him, No; that he was a traveller, and invited by the beauty of the evening and the place to repose a little, and amuse himself with reading. 'I may as well repose

---

1 Making out, sizing up.

myself too,' said the sportsman; 'for I have been out this whole afternoon, and the devil a bird have I seen 'till I came hither.'

'Perhaps then the game is not very plenty hereabouts,' cries Adams. 'No, sir,' said the gentleman, 'the soldiers, who are quartered in the neighbourhood, have killed it all.'[1] 'It is very probable,' cries Adams, 'for shooting is their profession.' 'Ay, shooting the game,' answered the other, 'but I don't see they are so forward to shoot our enemies. I don't like that affair of Carthagena;[2] if I had been there, I believe I should have done other-guess things, d—n me; what's a man's life when his country demands it; a man who won't sacrifice his life for his country deserves to be hanged, d—n me.' Which words he spoke with so violent a gesture, so loud a voice, so strong an accent, and so fierce a countenance, that he might have frightned a captain of trained-bands[3] at the head of his company; but Mr. Adams was not greatly subject to fear, he told him intrepidly that he very much approved his virtue, but disliked his swearing, and begged him not to addict himself to so bad a custom, without which he said he might fight as bravely as Achilles did. Indeed he was charm'd with this discourse, he told the gentleman he would willingly have gone many miles to have met a man of his generous way of thinking; that if he pleased to sit down, he should be greatly delighted to commune with him: for tho' he was a clergyman, he would himself be ready, if thereto called, to lay down his life for his country.

The gentleman sat down and Adams by him, and then the latter began, as in the following chapter, a discourse which we have placed by itself, as it is not only the most curious in this, but perhaps in any other book.

---

1 Soldiers who hunted game without permission of the landowner were liable to a fine of £5 for each partridge killed.

2 In the spring of 1741, a British expedition of troops and warships unsuccessfully attacked the Spanish stronghold of Cartagena in the West Indies. The Opposition capitalized on the disaster, blaming Walpole for his handling of the affair.

3 A trained company of citizen soldiers.

CHAPTER VIII

A notable dissertation, by Mr. Abraham Adams; wherein that gentleman appears in a political light.

'I DO assure you, sir,' says he, taking the gentleman by the hand, 'I am heartily glad to meet with a man of your kidney: for tho' I am a poor parson, I will be bold to say, I am an honest man, and would not do an ill thing to be made a bishop: nay, tho' it hath not fallen in my way to offer so noble a sacrifice, I have not been without opportunities of suffering for the sake of my conscience, I thank Heaven for them: for I have had relations, tho' I say it, who made some figure in the world; particularly a nephew, who was a shopkeeper, and an alderman of a corporation.[1] He was a good lad, and was under my care when a boy, and I believe would do what I bad him to his dying day. Indeed, it looks like extreme vanity in me, to affect being a man of such consequence, as to have so great an interest in[2] an alderman; but others have thought so too, as manifestly appeared by the rector, whose curate I formerly was, sending for me on the approach of an election, and telling me if I expected to continue in his cure, that I must bring my nephew to vote for one Colonel Courtly, a gentleman whom I had never heard tidings of 'till that instant. I told the rector, I had no power over my nephew's vote, (God forgive me for such prevarication!) that I supposed he would give it according to his conscience, that I would by no means endeavour to influence him to give it otherwise. He told me it was in vain to equivocate: that he knew I had already spoke to him in favour of Esquire Fickle my neighbour, and indeed it was true I had: for it was at a season when the *Church was in danger*,[3] and when all good men expected they knew not what would happen to us all. I then answered boldly, if he thought I had given my promise, he affronted me, in proposing any breach of it. Not to

---

1 The civic authorities of a town or borough.

2 Influence on.

3 A slogan generally heard from High Churchmen against nonconformists and dissenters.

be too prolix: I persevered, and so did my nephew, in the esquire's interest, who was chose chiefly through his means, and so I lost my curacy. Well, sir, but do you think the esquire ever mentioned a word of the Church? *Ne verbum quidem, ut ita dicam;*[1] within two years he got a place,[2] and hath ever since lived in London; where I have been informed, (but G— forbid I should believe that) that he never so much as goeth to church. I remained, sir, a considerable time without any cure, and lived a full month on one funeral sermon, which I preached in the indisposition of a clergyman: but this by the bye. At last, when Mr. Fickle got his place, Colonel Courtly stood again; and who should make interest for him, but Mr. Fickle himself: that very identical Mr. Fickle, who had formerly told me, the colonel was an enemy to both the Church and State, had the confidence to sollicite my nephew for him, and the colonel himself offered me to make me chaplain to his regiment, which I refused in favour of Sir Oliver Hearty, who told us, he would sacrifice every thing to his country; and I believe he would, except his hunting, which he stuck so close to, that in five years together, he went but twice up to parliament; and one of those times, I have been told, never was within sight of the House. However, he was a worthy man, and the best friend I ever had: for by his interest with a bishop, he got me replaced into my curacy, and gave me eight pounds out of his own pocket to buy me a gown and cassock, and furnish my house. He had our interest while he lived, which was not many years. On his death, I had fresh applications made to me; for all the world knew the interest I had in my good nephew, who now was a leading man in the corporation; and Sir Thomas Booby, buying the estate which had been Sir Oliver's, proposed himself a candidate. He was then a young gentleman just come from his travels; and it did me good to hear him discourse on affairs, which for my part I knew nothing of. If I had been master of a thousand votes, he should have had them all. I engaged my nephew in his interest, and he was elected, and a very fine parliament-man he was. They tell me he made speeches of an

1 "Not so much as a word, so to say."

2 Government appointment.

hour long; and I have been told very fine ones: but he could never persuade the parliament to be of his opinion.—*Non omnia possumus omnes.*[1] He promised me a living, poor man; and I believe I should have had it, but an accident happened; which was, that my lady had promised it before unknown to him. This indeed I never heard 'till afterwards: for my nephew, who died about a month before the incumbent, always told me I might be assured of it. Since that time, Sir Thomas, poor man, had always so much business, that he never could find leisure to see me. I believe it was partly my lady's fault too: who did not think my dress good enough for the gentry at her table. However, I must do him the justice to say, he never was ungrateful; and I have always found his kitchin, and his cellar too, open to me; many a time after service on a Sunday, for I preach at four churches, have I recruited my spirits with a glass of his ale. Since my nephew's death, the corporation is in other hands; and I am not a man of that consequence I was formerly. I have now no longer any talents to lay out[2] in the service of my country; and to whom nothing is given, of him can nothing be required. However, on all proper seasons, such as the approach of an election, I throw a suitable dash or two into my sermons; which I have the pleasure to hear is not disagreeable to Sir Thomas, and the other honest gentlemen my neighbours, who have all promised me these five years, to procure an ordination for a son of mine, who is now near thirty, hath an infinite stock of learning, and is, I thank Heaven, of an unexceptionable life; tho', as he was never at an university, the bishop refuses to ordain him. Too much care cannot indeed be taken in admitting any to the sacred office; tho' I hope he will never act so as to be a disgrace to any order: but will serve his God and his country to the utmost of his power, as I have endeavoured to do before him; nay, and will lay down his life whenever called to that purpose. I am sure I have educated him in those principles; so that I have acquitted my duty, and shall have nothing to answer for on that account: but I do not distrust him; for he is a

1 "We cannot all do everything" (Virgil, *Eclogues* 8.63).

2 An allusion to the parable of the talents (Matthew 25:14-30), and the parable of the wise steward (Luke 12:41-48).

good boy; and if Providence should throw it in his way, to be of as much consequence in a public light, as his father once was, I can answer for him, he will use his talents as honestly as I have done.'

CHAPTER IX

In which the gentleman descants on bravery and heroic virtue, 'till an unlucky accident puts an end to the discourse.

THE gentleman highly commended Mr. Adams for his good resolutions, and told him, 'he hoped his son would tread in his steps;' adding, 'that if he would not die for his country, he would not be worthy to live in it; I'd make no more of shooting a man that would not die for his country, than —

'Sir,' said he, 'I have disinherited a nephew who is in the army, because he would not exchange his commission, and go to the West-Indies. I believe the rascal is a coward, tho' he pretends to be in love forsooth. I would have all such fellows hanged, sir, I would have them hanged.' Adams answered, 'that would be too severe: that men did not make themselves; and if fear had too much ascendance in the mind, the man was rather to be pitied than abhorred: that reason and time might teach him to subdue it.' He said, 'a man might be a coward at one time, and brave at another. Homer,' says he, 'who so well understood and copied nature, hath taught us this lesson: for Paris fights, and Hector runs away:[1] nay, we have a mighty instance of this in the history of later ages, no longer ago, than the 705th year of Rome, when the great Pompey, who had won so many battles, and been honoured with so many triumphs, and of whose valour, several authors, especially Cicero and Paterculus, have formed such elogiums;[2] this very Pompey left the battle of Pharsalia before he had lost it, and retreated to his tent, where

1 Paris dreads combat, but later fights Diomedes; and Hector, bravest of the Trojans, flees Achilles (*Iliad* 11 and 22 respectively).

2 Eulogies. See Cicero's speech for the Lex Manilia (66 BC), and Velleius Paterculus' *Roman History* 2.19.

he sat like the most pusillanimous rascal in a fit of despair, and yielded a victory, which was to determine the empire of the world, to Cæsar.[1] I am not much travelled in the history of modern times, that is to say, these last thousand years: but those who are, can, I make no question, furnish you with parallel instances.' He concluded therefore, that had he taken any such hasty resolutions against his nephew, he hoped he would consider better and retract them. The gentleman answered with great warmth, and talked much of courage and his country, 'till perceiving it grew late, he asked Adams, 'what place he intended for that night?' He told him, 'he waited there for the stage-coach.' 'The stage-coach! Sir,' said the gentleman, 'they are all past by long ago. You may see the last yourself, almost three miles before us.' 'I protest and so they are,' cries Adams, 'then I must make haste and follow them.' The gentleman told him, 'he would hardly be able to overtake them; and that if he did not know his way, he would be in danger of losing himself on the downs; for it would be presently dark; and he might ramble about all night, and perhaps, find himself farther from his journey's end in the morning than he was now. He advised him therefore to accompany him to his house, which was very little out of his way,' assuring him, 'that he would find some country-fellow in his parish, who would conduct him for sixpence to the city, where he was going.' Adams accepted this proposal, and on they travelled, the gentleman renewing his discourse on courage, and the infamy of not being ready at all times to sacrifice our lives to our country. Night overtook them much about the same time as they arrived near some bushes: whence, on a sudden, they heard the most violent shrieks imaginable in a female voice. Adams offered[2] to snatch the gun out of his companion's hand. 'What are you doing?' said he. 'Doing!' says Adams, 'I am hastening to the assistance of the poor creature whom some villains are murdering.' 'You are not mad enough, I hope,' says the gentleman, trembling: 'do you consider this gun is only charged with shot, and that the robbers are most

1 Pompey retired to his tent in shame and despair after being routed by Caesar's forces at the battle of Pharsalia (48 BC). See Plutarch's *Life of Pompey*.

2 Attempted.

probably furnished with pistols loaded with bullets? This is no business of ours; let us make as much haste as possible out of the way, or we may fall into their hands ourselves.' The shrieks now encreasing, Adams made no answer, but snapt his fingers, and brandishing his crabstick, made directly to the place whence the voice issued; and the man of courage made as much expedition towards his own home, whither he escaped in a very short time without once looking behind him: where we will leave him, to contemplate his own bravery, and to censure the want of it in others; and return to the good Adams, who, on coming up to the place whence the noise proceeded, found a woman struggling with a man, who had thrown her on the ground, and had almost overpowered her. The great abilities of Mr. Adams were not necessary to have formed a right judgment of this affair, on the first sight. He did not therefore want the entreaties of the poor wretch to assist her, but lifting up his crabstick, he immediately levelled a blow at that part of the ravisher's head, where, according to the opinion of the ancients, the brains of some persons are deposited, and which he had undoubtedly let forth, had not nature, (who, as wise men have observed, equips all creatures with what is most expedient for them;) taken a provident care, (as she always doth with those she intends for encounters) to make this part of the head three times as thick as those of ordinary men, who are designed to exercise talents which are vulgarly called rational, and for whom, as brains are necessary, she is obliged to leave some room for them in the cavity of the skull: whereas, those ingredients being entirely useless to persons of the heroic calling, she hath an opportunity of thickening the bone, so as to make it less subject to any impression or liable to be cracked or broken; and indeed, in some who are predestined to the command of armies and empires, she is supposed sometimes to make that part perfectly solid.

As a game-cock when engaged in amorous toying with a hen, if perchance he espies another cock at hand, immediately quits his female, and opposes himself to his rival; so did the ravisher, on the information of the crabstick, immediately leap from the woman, and hasten to assail the man. He had no weapons but what nature had furnished him with. However, he clenched his fist, and presently darted it at that part of Adams's breast where the heart is lodged. Adams staggered at the violence of the blow, when throwing away his staff, he likewise clenched that fist which we have before commemorated, and would have discharged it full in the breast of his antagonist, had he not dexterously caught it with his left hand, at the same time darting his head, (which some modern heroes, of the lower class, use like the battering-ram of the ancients, for a weapon of offence; another reason to admire the cunningness of nature, in composing it of those impenetrable materials) dashing his head, I say, into the stomach of Adams, he tumbled him on his back, and not having any regard to the laws of heroism, which would have restrained him from any farther attack on his enemy, 'till he was again on his legs, he threw himself upon him, and laying hold on the ground with his left hand, he with his right belaboured the body of Adams 'till he was weary, and indeed, 'till he concluded (to use the language of fighting) *that he had done his business*; or, in the language of poetry, *that he had sent him to the shades below*; in plain English, *that he was dead*.

But Adams, who was no chicken,[1] and could bear a drubbing as well as any boxing champion in the universe, lay still only to watch his opportunity; and now perceiving his antagonist to pant with his labours, he exerted his utmost force at once, and with such success, that he overturned him and became his superiour; when fixing one of his knees in his breast, he cried out in an exulting voice, *It is my turn now*: and after a few minutes constant application, he gave him so dextrous a blow just under his chin, that the fellow no longer retained any motion, and Adams began to fear he had struck him once too often; for he often asserted, 'he should be concerned to have the blood of even the wicked upon him.'

Adams got up, and called aloud to the young woman,—'Be of good cheer, damsel,' said he, 'you are no longer in danger of your ravisher, who, I am terribly afraid, lies dead at my feet; but G— forgive me what I have done in defence of innocence.'

1 Coward.

The poor wretch, who had been some time in recovering strength enough to rise, and had afterwards, during the engagement, stood trembling, being disabled by fear, even from running away, hearing her champion was victorious, came up to him, but not without apprehensions, even of her deliverer; which, however, she was soon relieved from, by his courteous behaviour and gentle words. They were both standing by the body, which lay motionless on the ground, and which Adams wished to see stir much more than the woman did, when he earnestly begged her to tell him 'by what misfortune she came, at such a time of night, into so lonely a place?' She acquainted him, 'she was travelling towards London, and had accidentally met with the person from whom he had delivered her, who told her he was likewise on his journey to the same place, and would keep her company; an offer which, suspecting no harm, she had accepted; that he told her, they were at a small distance from an inn where she might take up her lodging that evening, and he would show her a nearer way to it than by following the road. That if she had suspected him, (which she did not, he spoke so kindly to her,) being alone on these downs in the dark, she had no human means to avoid him; that therefore she put her whole trust in Providence, and walk'd on, expecting every moment to arrive at the inn; when, on a sudden, being come to those bushes, he desired her to stop, and after some rude kisses, which she resisted, and some entreaties, which she rejected, he laid violent hands on her, and was attempting to execute his wicked will, when, she thanked G—, he timely came up and prevented him.' Adams encouraged her for saying, she had put her whole trust in Providence, and told her 'he doubted not but Providence had sent him to her deliverance, as a reward for that trust. He wished indeed he had not deprived the wicked wretch of life, but G—'s will be done;' he said, 'he hoped the goodness of his intention would excuse him in the next world, and he trusted in her evidence to acquit him in this.' He was then silent, and began to consider with himself, whether it would be properer to make his escape, or to deliver himself into the hands of justice; which meditation ended, as the reader will see in the next chapter.

CHAPTER X

Giving an account of the strange catastrophe of the preceding adventure, which drew poor Adams into fresh calamities; and who the woman was who owed the preservation of her chastity to his victorious arm.

THE silence of Adams, added to the darkness of the night, and loneliness of the place, struck dreadful apprehensions into the poor woman's mind: she began to fear as great an enemy in her deliverer, as he had delivered her from; and as she had not light enough to discover the age of Adams, and the benevolence visible in his countenance, she suspected he had used her as some very honest men have used their country;[1] and had rescued her out of the hands of one rifler, in order to rifle her himself. Such were the suspicions she drew from his silence: but indeed they were ill-grounded. He stood over his vanquished enemy, wisely weighing in his mind the objections which might be made to either of the two methods of proceeding mentioned in the last chapter, his judgment sometimes inclining to the one and sometimes to the other; for both seemed to him so equally adviseable, and so equally dangerous, that probably he would have ended his days, at least two or three of them, on that very spot, before he had taken any resolution: at length he lifted up his eyes, and spied a light at a distance, to which he instantly addressed himself with *Heus tu, traveller, heus tu!*[2] He presently heard several voices, and perceived the light approaching toward him. The persons who attended the light began some to laugh, others to sing, and others to hollow, at which the woman testified some fear, (for she had concealed her suspicions of the parson himself,) but Adams said, 'Be of good cheer, damsel, and repose thy trust in the same Providence, which hath hitherto protected thee, and never will forsake the innocent.' These people who now approached were no other, read-

---

1 This passage, which was added to the second edition, refers to Fielding's disillusionment with the behaviour of the Patriots after Walpole's fall from power in February 1742.

2 "Ho there!"

er, than a set of young fellows, who came to these bushes in pursuit of a diversion which they call *bird-batting*. This, if thou art ignorant of it (as perhaps if thou hast never travelled beyond Kensington, Islington, Hackney, or the Borough,[1] thou mayst be) I will inform thee, is performed by holding a large clap-net[2] before a lanthorn, and at the same time, beating the bushes: for the birds, when they are disturbed from their places of rest, or roost, immediately make to the light, and so are enticed within the net. Adams immediately told them, what had happened, and desired them, 'to hold the lanthorn to the face of the man on the ground, for he feared he had *smote* him fatally.' But indeed his fears were frivolous, for the fellow, though he had been stunned by the last blow he received, had long since recovered his senses, and finding himself quit of Adams, had listened attentively to the discourse between him and the young woman; for whose departure he had patiently waited, that he might likewise withdraw himself, having no longer hopes of succeeding in his desires, which were moreover almost as well cooled by Mr. Adams, as they could have been by the young woman herself, had he obtained his utmost wish. This fellow, who had a readiness at improving any accident, thought he might now play a better part than that of a dead man; and accordingly, the moment the candle was held to his face, he leapt up, and laying hold on Adams, cried out, 'No, villain, I am not dead, though you and your wicked whore might well think me so, after the barbarous cruelties you have exercised on me. Gentlemen,' said he, 'you are luckily come to the assistance of a poor traveller, who would otherwise have been robbed and murdered by this vile man and woman, who led me hither out of my way from the high-road, and both falling on me have used me as you see.' Adams was going to answer, when one of the young fellows, cry'd, 'D—n them, let's carry them both before the justice.' The poor woman began to tremble, and Adams lifted up his voice, but in vain. Three or four of them

1 Suburbs of London at the time. They were fashionable places, other than for the Borough of Southwark, on the south side of the Thames, which was the site of a popular fair.

2 A net that can be suddenly closed by pulling a string.

laid hands on him, and one holding the lanthorn to his face, they all agreed, *he had the most villainous countenance* they ever beheld, and an attorney's clerk who was of the company declared, *he was sure he had remembered him at the bar.* As to the woman, her hair was dishevelled in the struggle, and her nose had bled, so that they could not perceive whether she was handsome or ugly: but they said her fright plainly discovered her guilt. And searching her pockets, as they did those of Adams for money, which the fellow said he had lost, they found in her pocket a purse with some gold in it, which abundantly convinced them, especially as the fellow offered to swear to it. Mr. Adams was found to have no more than one halfpenny about him. This the clerk said, 'was a great presumption that he was an old offender, by cunningly giving all the booty to the woman.' To which all the rest readily assented.

This accident promising them better sport, than what they had proposed, they quitted their intention of catching birds, and unanimously resolved to proceed to the justice with the offenders. Being informed what a desperate fellow Adams was, they tied his hands behind him, and having hid their nets among the bushes, and the lanthorn being carried before them, they placed the two prisoners in their front, and then began their march: Adams not only submitting patiently to his own fate, but comforting and encouraging his companion under her sufferings.

Whilst they were on their way, the clerk informed the rest, that this adventure would prove a very beneficial one: for that they would be all entitled to their proportions of 80*l.*[1] for apprehending the robbers. This occasion'd a contention concerning the parts which they had severally born in taking them; one insisting, 'he ought to have the greatest share, for he had first laid his hands on Adams;' another claiming a superiour part for having first held the lanthorn to the man's face, on the ground, by which, he said 'the whole was discovered.' The clerk claimed four fifths of the reward, for having proposed to search the prisoners; and likewise the carrying them before the justice:

---

1 Forty pounds was the reward for capturing and prosecuting a highwayman.

he said indeed, 'in strict justice he ought to have the whole.' These claims however they at last consented to refer to a future decision, but seem'd all to agree that the clerk was intitled to a moiety.[1] They then debated what money should be allotted to the young fellow, who had been employed only in holding the nets. He very modestly said, 'that he did not apprehend any large proportion would fall to his share; but hoped they would allow him something: he desired them to consider, that they had assigned their nets to his care, which prevented him from being as forward as any in laying hold of the robbers, (for so these innocent people were called;) that if he had not occupied the nets, some other must; concluding however that he should be contented with the smallest share imaginable, and should think that rather their bounty than his merit.' But they were all unanimous in excluding him from any part whatever, the clerk particularly swearing, 'if they gave him a shilling, they might do what they pleased with the rest; for he would not concern himself with the affair.' This contention was so hot, and so totally engaged the attention of all the parties, that a dextrous nimble thief, had he been in Mr. Adams's situation, would have taken care to have given the justice no trouble that evening. Indeed it required not the art of a Shepherd[2] to escape, especially as the darkness of the night would have so much befriended him: but Adams trusted rather to his innocence than his heels, and without thinking of flight, which was easy, or resistance (which was impossible, as there were six lusty young fellows, besides the villain himself, present) he walked with perfect resignation the way they thought proper to conduct him.

Adams frequently vented himself in ejaculations during their journey; at last poor Joseph Andrews occurring to his mind, he could not refrain sighing forth his name, which being heard by his companion in affliction, she cried, with some vehemence, 'Sure I should know that voice, you cannot certainly, sir, be Mr. Abraham Adams?' 'Indeed damsel,' says he, 'that is my name; there is something also in your voice, which persuades me I

---

1 Half of the amount.

2 Jack Sheppard, highwayman and popular hero, escaped repeatedly from prison in 1724, only to be executed at Tyburn later the same year.

have heard it before.' 'La, sir,' says she, 'don't you remember poor Fanny?' 'How Fanny!' answered Adams, 'indeed I very well remember you; what can have brought you hither?' 'I have told you sir,' replied she, 'I was travelling towards London; but I thought you mentioned Joseph Andrews, pray what is become of him?' 'I left him, child, this afternoon,' said Adams, 'in the stage-coach, in his way towards our parish, whither he is going to see you.' 'To see me? La, sir,' answered Fanny, 'sure you jeer me; what should he be going to see me for?' 'Can you ask that?' replied Adams. 'I hope Fanny you are not inconstant; I assure you he deserves much better of you.' 'La! Mr. Adams,' said she, 'what is Mr. Joseph to me? I am sure I never had any thing to say to him, but as one fellow-servant might to another.' 'I am sorry to hear this,' said Adams, 'a vertuous passion for a young man, is what no woman need be ashamed of. You either do not tell me truth, or you are false to a very worthy man.' Adams then told her what had happened at the inn, to which she listened very attentively; and a sigh often escaped from her, notwithstanding her utmost endeavours to the contrary, nor could she prevent herself from asking a thousand questions, which would have assured any one but Adams, who never saw farther into people than they desired to let him, of the truth of a passion she endeavoured to conceal. Indeed the fact was, that this poor girl having heard of Joseph's misfortune by some of the servants belonging to the coach, which we have formerly mentioned to have stopped at the inn while the poor youth was confined to his bed, that instant abandoned the cow she was milking, and taking with her a little bundle of clothes under her arm, and all the money she was worth in her own purse, without consulting any one, immediately set forward, in pursuit of one, whom, notwithstanding her shyness to the parson, she loved with inexpressible violence, though with the purest and most delicate passion. This shyness therefore, as we trust it will recommend her character to all our female readers, and not greatly surprize such of our males as are well acquainted with the younger part of the other sex, we shall not give our selves any trouble to vindicate.

CHAPTER XI

What happened to them while before the justice. A chapter very full of learning.

THEIR fellow-travellers were so engaged in the hot dispute concerning the division of the reward for apprehending these innocent people, that they attended very little to their discourse. They were now arrived at the justice's house, and sent one of his servants in to acquaint his worship, that they had taken two robbers, and brought them before him. The justice, who was just returned from a fox-chace, and had not yet finished his dinner, ordered them to carry the prisoners into the stable, whither they were attended by all the servants in the house, and all the people of the neighbourhood, who flock'd together to see them with as much curiosity as if there was something uncommon to be seen, or that a rogue did not look like other people.

The justice being now in the height of his mirth and his cups, bethought himself of the prisoners, and telling his company he believed they should have good sport in their examination, he ordered them into his presence. They had no sooner entered the room, than he began to revile them, saying, 'that robberies on the highway were now grown so frequent, that people could not sleep safely in their beds, and assured them they both should be made examples of at the ensuing assizes.' After he had gone on some time in this manner, he was reminded by his clerk, 'that it would be proper to take the deposition of the witnesses against them.' Which he bid him do, and he would light his pipe in the mean time. Whilst the clerk was employed in writing down the depositions of the fellow who had pretended to be robbed, the justice employed himself in cracking jests on poor Fanny, in which he was seconded by all the company at table. One asked, 'whether she was to be indicted for a *highwayman*?' Another whispered in her ear, 'if she had not provided herself a great belly,[1] he was at her

1 A pregnant woman condemned to death could "plead her belly" in the hope of having the sentence delayed or commuted.

service.' A third said, 'he warranted she was a relation of Turpin.'[1] To which one of the company, a great wit, shaking his head and then his sides, answered, 'he believed she was nearer related to Turpis;'[2] at which there was an universal laugh. They were proceeding thus with the poor girl, when somebody smoaking the cassock, peeping forth from under the great coat of Adams, cried out, 'What have we here, a parson?' 'How, sirrah,' says the justice, 'do you go a robbing in the dress of a clergyman? let me tell you, your habit will not entitle you to the *benefit of the clergy*.'[3] 'Yes,' said the witty fellow, 'he will have one benefit of clergy, he will be exalted above the heads of the people,' at which there was a second laugh. And now the witty spark, seeing his jokes take, began to rise in spirits; and turning to Adams, challenged him to *cap* verses,[4] and provoking him by giving the first blow, he repeated,

Molle meum levibus cord est vilebile telis.[5]

Upon which Adams, with a look full of ineffable contempt, told him, he deserved scourging for his pronuntiation. The witty fellow answered, 'What do you deserve, doctor, for not being able to answer the first time? Why, I'll give you one you blockhead—with an S?

Si licet, ut fulvum spectatur in igdibus haurum.[6]

'What can'st not with an M neither? Thou are a pretty fellow for a parson—. Why did'st not steal some of the parson's Latin as well as his gown?' Another at the table then answered, 'If he

---

1 Dick Turpin was hanged in 1739 for murder and horse stealing.

2 Latin for "shameful" or "base."

3 The exemption of clergy from trial by civil law. By the eighteenth century, however, this right had been withdrawn from many offences, including highway robbery.

4 A game in which verses are exchanged, each beginning with the last letter of the preceding one.

5 A garbled line from Ovid's *Heroides* 15.79: "Tender is my heart and easily injured by swift darts." This quotation and the subsequent ones occur in a Latin grammar used at the time at Eton College.

6 Another misquotation, this time from Ovid's *Tristia* 1.5.25: "Truly, as yellow gold is tested in fire."

had, you would have been too hard for him; I remember you at the college a very devil at this sport, I have seen you catch a fresh man: for no body that knew you, would engage with you.' 'I have forgot those things now,' cried the wit, 'I believe I could have done pretty well formerly.—Let's see, what did I end with—an M again—ay—

Mars, Bacchus, Apollo, virorum.[1]

I could have done it once.'—'Ah! evil betide you, and so you can now,' said the other, 'no body in the county will undertake you.' Adams could hold no longer; 'Friend,' said he, 'I have a boy not above eight years old, who would instruct thee, that the last verse runs thus:

Ut sunt Divorum, Mars, Bacchus, Apollo, virorum.'

'I'll hold thee a guinea of that,' said the wit, throwing the money on the table.—'And I'll go your halves,' cries the other. 'Done,' answered Adams, but upon applying to his pocket, he was forced to retract, and own he had no money about him; which set them all a laughing, and confirmed the triumph of his adversary, which was not moderate, any more than the approbation he met with from the whole company, who told Adams he must go a little longer to school, before he attempted to attack that gentleman in Latin.

The clerk having finished the depositions, as well of the fellow himself, as of those who apprehended the prisoners, delivered them to the justice; who having sworn the several witnesses, without reading a syllable, ordered his clerk to make the *mittimus.*[2]

Adams then said, 'he hoped he should not be condemned unheard.' 'No, no,' cries the justice, 'you will be asked what you have to say for your self, when you come on your trial, we are

---

1 Adams quotes the formula correctly a few lines further along, which is from the chapter on noun gender in the Eton Latin grammar: "As are [those] of the Gods—Mars, Bacchus, Apollo—[and] of men."

2 A writ from a justice of the peace committing a suspect to prison.

not trying you now; I shall only commit you to goal: if you can prove your innocence at *size* , you will be found *ignoramus*,[1] and so no harm done.' 'Is it no punishment, sir, for an innocent man to lie several months in goal?' cries Adams: 'I beg you would at least hear me before you sign the *mittimus*.' 'What signifies all you can say?' says the justice, 'is it not here in black and white against you? I must tell you, you are a very impertinent fellow, to take up so much of my time.—So make haste with his *mittimus*.'

The clerk now acquainted the justice, that among other suspicious things, as a penknife, &c. found in Adams's pocket, they had discovered a book written, as he apprehended, in ciphers: for no one could read a word in it. 'Ay,' says the justice, 'this fellow may be more that a common robber, he may be in a plot against the government.—Produce the book.' Upon which the poor manuscript of Æschylus, which Adams had transcribed with his own hand, was brought forth; and the justice looking at it, shook his head, and turning to the prisoner, asked the meaning of those ciphers. 'Ciphers!' answer'd Adams, 'it is a manuscript of Æschylus.' 'Who? who?' said the justice. Adams repeated, 'Æschylus.' 'That is an outlandish[2] name,' cried the clerk. 'A fictitious name rather, I believe,' said the justice. One of the company declared it looked very much like Greek. 'Greek!' said the justice, 'why 'tis all writing.' 'Nay,' says the other, 'I don't positively say it is so: for it is a very long time since I have seen any Greek. There's one,' says he, turning to the parson of the parish, who was present, 'will tell us immediately.' The parson taking up the book, and putting on his spectacles and gravity together, muttered some words to himself, and then pronounced aloud—'Ay indeed it is a Greek manuscript, a very fine piece of antiquity. I make no doubt but it was stolen from the same clergyman from whom the rogue took the cassock.' 'What did the rascal mean by his Æschylus?' says

1 The term used by a grand jury (literally "we do not know") when they found the evidence against a person insufficient to warrant prosecution. "Size" is a colloquial term for assizes, the court sessions held in the counties for the trial of civil or criminal cases (see above, p. 154, n. 1).

2 Foreign, strange.

the justice. 'Pooh!' answered the doctor with a contemptuous grin, 'do you think that fellow knows any thing of this book? Æschylus! ho! ho! ho! I see now what it is.—A manuscript of one of the Fathers.[1] I know a nobleman who would give a great deal of money for such a piece of antiquity.—Ay, ay, question and answer. The beginning is the catechism in Greek.—Ay,—Ay,—*Pollaki toi*[2]—What's your name?'—'Ay, what's your name?' says the justice to Adams, who answered, 'It is Æschylus, and I will maintain it.'—'O it is,' says the justice; 'make Mr. Æschylus his *mittimus*. I will teach you to banter me with a false name.'

One of the company having looked stedfastly at Adams, asked him, 'if he did not know Lady Booby?' Upon which Adams presently calling him to mind, answered in a rapture, 'O squire, are you there? I believe you will inform his worship I am innocent.' 'I can indeed say,' replied the squire, 'that I am very much surprized to see you in this situation;' and then addressing himself to the justice, he said, 'Sir, I assure you Mr. Adams is a clergyman as he appears, and a gentleman of a very good character. I wish you would enquire a little farther into this affair: for I am convinced of his innocence.' 'Nay,' says the justice, 'if he is a gentleman, and you are sure he is innocent, I don't desire to commit him, not I; I will commit the woman by herself, and take your bail for the gentleman; look into the book, clerk, and see how it is to take bail; come—and make the *mittimus* for the woman as fast as you can.' 'Sir', cries Adams, 'I assure you she is as innocent as myself.' 'Perhaps,' said the squire, 'there may be some mistake; pray let us hear Mr. Adams's relation.' 'With all my heart,' answered the justice, 'and give the gentleman a glass to whet his whistle before he begins. I know how to behave myself to gentlemen as well as another. No body can say I have committed a gentleman since I have been in the commission.' Adams then began the narrative, in which, though he was very prolix, he was uninterrupted, unless by several *hums* and *ha's* of the justice, and his desire to repeat those

1 Fathers of the Church, the early Christian teachers and writers.

2 "Often." The parson would seem to be misreading a phrase from Aeschylus' *Seven Against Thebes* l. 227.

parts which seemed to him most material. When he had finished; the justice, who, on what the squire had said, believed every syllable of his story on his bare affirmation, notwithstanding the depositions on oath to the contrary, began to let loose several *rogues and rascals* against the witness, whom he ordered to stand forth, but in vain: the said witness, long since finding what turn matters were like to take, had privily withdrawn, without attending the issue. The justice now flew into a violent passion, and was hardly prevailed with not to commit the innocent fellows, who had been imposed on as well as himself. He swore, 'they had best find out the fellow who was guilty of perjury, and bring him before him within two days; or he would bind them all over to their good behaviour.' They all promised to use their best endeavours to that purpose, and were dismissed. Then the justice insisted, that Mr. Adams should sit down and take a glass with him; and the parson of the parish delivered him back the manuscript without saying a word; nor would Adams, who plainly discerned his ignorance, expose it. As for Fanny, she was, at her own request, recommended to the care of a maid-servant of the house, who helped her to new dress, and clean herself.

The company in the parlour had not been long seated, before they were alarmed with a horrible uproar from without, where the persons who had apprehended Adams and Fanny, had been regaling, according to the custom of the house, with the justice's strong beer. These were all fallen together by the ears, and were cuffing each other without any mercy. The justice himself sallied out, and with the dignity of his presence, soon put an end to the fray. On his return into the parlour, he reported, 'that the occasion of the quarrel, was no other than a dispute, to whom, if Adams had been convicted, the greater share of the reward for apprehending him had belonged.' All the company laughed at this, except Adams, who taking his pipe from his mouth fetched a deep groan, and said, he was concerned to see so litigious a temper in men. That he remembered a story something like it in one of the parishes where his cure lay: 'There was,' continued he, 'a competition between three young fellows, for the place of the clerk, which I disposed of, to the best of my abilities, according to merit: that is, I gave it to him who had the happiest knack at setting a psalm. The clerk was no sooner established in his place, than a contention began between the two disappointed candidates, concerning their excellence, each contending, on whom, had they two been the only competitors, my election would have fallen. This dispute frequently disturbed the congregation, and introduced a discord into the psalmody, 'till I was forced to silence them both. But alas, the litigious spirit could not be stifled; and being no longer able to vent itself in singing, it now broke forth in fighting. It produced many battles, (for they were very near a match;) and, I believe, would have ended fatally, had not the death of the clerk given me an opportunity to promote one of them to his place; which presently put an end to the dispute, and entirely reconciled the contending parties.' Adams then proceeded to make some philosophical observations on the folly of growing warm in disputes, in which neither party is interested. He then applied himself vigorously to smoaking; and a long silence ensued, which was at length broken by the justice; who began to sing forth his own praises, and to value himself exceedingly on his nice discernment in the cause, which had lately been before him. He was quickly interrupted by Mr. Adams, between whom and his worship a dispute now arose, whether he ought not, in strictness of law, to have committed him, the said Adams; in which the latter maintained he ought to have been committed, and the justice as vehemently held he ought not. This had most probably produced a quarrel, (for both were very violent and positive in their opinions) had not Fanny accidentally heard, that a young fellow was going from the justice's house, to the very inn where the stage-coach in which Joseph was, put up. Upon this news, she immediately sent for the parson out of the parlour. Adams, when he found her resolute to go, (tho' she would not own the reason, but pretended she could not bear to see the faces of those who had suspected her of such a crime,) was as fully determined to go with her; he accordingly took leave of the justice and company, and so ended a dispute, in which the law seemed shamefully to intend to set a magistrate and a divine together by the ears.

CHAPTER XII

A very delightful adventure, as well to the persons concerned as to the good-natur'd reader.

ADAMS, Fanny, and the guide set out together, about one in the morning, the moon then just being risen. They had not gone above a mile, before a most violent storm of rain obliged them to take shelter in an inn, or rather alehouse; where Adams immediately procured himself a good fire, a toast and ale,[1] and a pipe, and began to smoke with great content, utterly forgetting every thing that had happened.

Fanny sat likewise down by the fire; but was much more impatient at the storm. She presently engaged the eyes of the host, his wife, the maid of the house, and the young fellow who was their guide; they all conceived they had never seen any thing half so handsome; and indeed, reader, if thou art of an amorous hue, I advise thee to skip over the next paragraph; which to render our history perfect, we are obliged to set down, humbly hoping, that we may escape the fate of Pygmalion:[2] for if it should happen to us or to thee to be struck with this picture, we should be perhaps in as helpless a condition as Narcissus;[3] and might say to ourselves, *Quod petis est nusquam.*[4] Or if the finest features in it should set Lady ——'s image before our eyes, we should be still in as bad situation, and might say to our desires, *Cœlum ipsum petimus stultitia.*[5]

Fanny was now in the nineteenth year of her age; she was tall and delicately shaped; but not one of those slender young women, who seem rather intended to hang up in the hall of an anatomist, than for any other purpose. On the contrary, she was so plump, that she seemed bursting through her tight stays,

---

1 Toast was often put into beverages.

2 A legendary king of Cyprus, who fell hopelessly in love with an ivory statue of a maiden he had created (Ovid, *Metamorphoses* 10.243-97).

3 A beautiful youth, who fell in love with his own image in a fountain and died of longing (Ovid, *Metamorphoses* 3.339-510).

4 "What you seek is nowhere"—Ovid's comment on Narcissus (*Metamorphoses* 3.433).

5 "In our folly we seek the heavens themselves" (Horace, *Odes* 1.3.38).

especially in the part which confined her swelling breasts. Nor did her hips want the assistance of a hoop to extend them. The exact shape of her arms, denoted the form of those limbs which she concealed; and tho' they were a little redden'd by her labour, yet if her sleeve slipt above her elbow, or her handkerchief discovered any part of her neck, a whiteness appeared which the finest Italian paint would be unable to reach. Her hair was of a chestnut brown, and nature had been extremely lavish to her of it, which she had cut, and on Sundays used to curl down her neck in the modern fashion. Her forehead was high, her eye-brows arched, and rather full than otherwise. Her eyes black and sparkling; her nose, just inclining to the Roman; her lips red and moist, and her under-lip, according to the opinion of the ladies, too pouting. Her teeth were white, but not exactly even. The small-pox had left one only mark on her chin, which was so large, it might have been mistaken for a dimple, had not her left cheek produced one so near a neighbour to it, that the former served only for a foil to the latter. Her complexion was fair, a little injured by the sun, but overspread with such a bloom, that the finest ladies would have exchanged all their white for it: add to these, a countenance in which tho' she was extremely bashful, a sensibility appeared almost incredible; and a sweetness, whenever she smiled, beyond either imitation or description. To conclude all, she had a natural gentility, superior to the acquisition of art, and which surprized all who beheld her.

This lovely creature was sitting by the fire with Adams, when her attention was suddenly engaged by a voice from an inner room, which sung the following song:

THE SONG

SAY, *Chloe*, where must the swain stray
Who is by thy beauties undone,
To wash their remembrance away,
To what distant *Lethe*[1] must run?

---

1 The river of oblivion in Hades.

The wretch who is sentenc'd to die,
  May escape and leave justice behind;
From his country perhaps he may fly,
  But O can he fly from his mind!

O rapture! unthought of before,
  To be thus of *Chloe* possest;
Nor she, nor no tyrant's hard power,
  Her image can tear from my breast.
But felt not *Narcissus* more joy,
  With his eyes he beheld his lov'd charms?
Yet what he beheld, the fond boy
  More eagerly wish'd in his arms.

How can it thy dear image be,
  Which fills thus my bosom with woe?
Can aught bear resemblance to thee,
  Which grief and not joy can bestow?
This counterfeit[1] snatch from my heart,
  Ye pow'rs, tho' with torment I rave,
Tho' mortal will prove the fell smart,
  I then shall find rest in my grave.

Ah! see, the dear nymph o'er the plain,
  Comes smiling and tripping along,
A thousand loves dance in her train,
  The Graces around her all throng.
To meet her soft *Zephyrus* flies,
  And wafts all the sweets from the flow'rs;
Ah rogue! whilst he kisses her eyes,
  More sweets from her breath he devours.

My soul, whilst I gaze, is on fire,
  But her looks were so tender and kind,
My hope almost reach'd my desire,
  And left lame despair far behind.

---

1 Portrait.

Transported with madness I flew
   And eagerly seiz'd on my bliss;
Her bosom but half she withdrew,
   But half she refus'd my fond kiss.

Advances like these made me bold,
   I whisper'd her, *Love,—we're alone*,
The rest let immortals unfold,
   No language can tell but their own.
Ah! *Chloe*, expiring, I cry'd,
   How long I thy cruelty bore?
Ah! *Strephon*, she blushing reply'd,
   You ne'er was so pressing before.

Adams had been ruminating all this time on a passage in Æschylus, without attending in the least to the voice, tho' one of the most melodious that ever was heard; when casting his eyes on Fanny, he cried out, 'Bless us, you look extremely pale.' 'Pale! Mr. Adams,' says she, 'O Jesus!' and fell backwards in her chair. Adams jumped up, flung his Æschylus into the fire, and fell a roaring to the people of the house for help. He soon summoned every one into the room, and the songster among the rest: but, O reader, when this nightingale, who was no other than Joseph Andrews himself, saw his beloved Fanny in the situation we have described her, can'st thou conceive the agitations of his mind? If thou can'st not, wave that meditation to behold his happiness, when clasping her in his arms, he found life and blood returning into her cheeks; when he saw her open her beloved eyes, and heard her with the softest accent whisper, 'Are you Joseph Andrews?' 'Art thou my Fanny?' he answered eagerly, and pulling her to his heart, he imprinted numberless kisses on her lips, without considering who were present.

If prudes are offended at the lusciousness of this picture, they may take their eyes off from it, and survey Parson Adams dancing about the room in a rapture of joy. Some philosophers may perhaps doubt, whether he was not the happiest of the three; for the goodness of his heart enjoyed the blessings which were exulting in the breasts of both the other two, together with his own. But we shall leave such disquisitions as too deep for us, to those who are building some favourite hypotheses, which they will refuse no metaphysical rubbish to erect, and support: for our part, we give it clearly on the side of Joseph, whose happiness was not only greater than the parson's, but of longer duration: for as soon as the first tumults of Adams's rapture were over, he cast his eyes towards the fire, where Æschylus lay expiring; and immediately rescued the poor remains, to-wit, the sheepskin covering of his dear friend, which was the work of his own hands, and had been his inseparable companion for upwards of thirty years.

Fanny had no sooner perfectly recovered herself, than she began to restrain the impetuosity of her transports; and reflecting on what she had done and suffered in the presence of so many, she was immediately covered with confusion; and pushing Joseph gently from her, she begged him to be quiet: nor would admit of either kiss or embrace any longer. Then seeing Mrs. Slipslop she curt'sied, and offered to advance to her; but that high woman would not return her curt'sies; but casting her eyes another way, immediately withdrew into another room, muttering as she went, she wondered *who the creature was*.

CHAPTER XIII

A dissertation concerning high people and low people, with Mrs. Slipslop's departure in no very good temper of mind, and the evil plight in which she left Adams and his company.

It will doubtless seem extremely odd to many readers, that Mrs. Slipslop, who had lived several years in the same house with Fanny, should in a short separation utterly forget her. And indeed the truth is, that she remembered her very well. As we would not willingly therefore, that any thing should appear unnatural in this our history, we will endeavour to explain the reasons of her conduct; nor do we doubt being able to satisfy the most curious reader, that Mrs. Slipslop did not in the least deviate from the common road in this behaviour; and indeed, had she done otherwise, she must have descended below herself, and would have very justly been liable to censure.

Be it known then, that the human species are divided into two sorts of people, to-wit, *high* people and *low* people. As by high people, I would not be understood to mean persons literally born higher in their dimensions than the rest of the species, nor metaphorically those of exalted characters or abilities; so by low people I cannot be construed to intend the reverse. High people signify no other than people of fashion, and low people those of no fashion. Now this word *fashion*, hath by long use lost its original meaning, from which at present it gives us a very different idea: for I am deceived, if by persons of fashion, we do not generally include a conception of birth and accomplishments superior to the herd of mankind; whereas in reality, nothing more was originally meant by a person of fashion, than a person who drest himself in the fashion of the times; and the word really and truly signifies no more at this day. Now the world being thus divided into people of fashion, and people of no fashion, a fierce contention arose between them, nor would those of one party, to avoid suspicion, be seen publickly to speak to those of the other; tho' they often held a very good correspondence in private. In this contention, it is difficult to say which party succeeded: for whilst the people of fashion seized several places to their own use, such as courts, assemblies, operas, balls, &c. the people of no fashion, besides one royal place called his Majesty's Bear-Garden,[1] have been in constant possession of all hops,[2] fairs, revels, &c. Two places have been agreed to be divided between them, namely the church and the play-house; where they segregate themselves from each other in a remarkable manner: for as the people of fashion exalt themselves at church over the heads of the people of no fashion; so in the play-house they abase themselves in the same degree under their feet.[3] This distinction I have never met with

1 The Bear Garden at Hockley-in-the-Hole, on the north side of London, was famous for bearbaiting, cudgel-playing, dogfights, etc.

2 Popular dancing parties (named after an informal dance of the time).

3 Whereas persons of quality regularly sat in enclosed pews raised above the church floor, the pit and the boxes at the theatre, which they particularly favoured, were below the galleries occupied by the apprentices and footmen.

any one able to account for; it is sufficient, that so far from looking on each other as brethren in the Christian language, they seem scarce to regard each other as of the same species. This the terms *strange persons*, *people one does not know*, *the creature*, *wretches*, *beasts*, *brutes*, and many other appellations evidently demonstrate; which Mrs. Slipslop having often heard her mistress use, thought she had also a right to use in her turn: and perhaps she was not mistaken; for these two parties, especially those bordering nearly on each other, to-wit the lowest of the high, and the highest of the low, often change their parties according to place and time; for those who are people of fashion in one place, are often people of no fashion in another: and with regard to time, it may not be unpleasant to survey the picture of dependance like a kind of ladder; as for instance, early in the morning arises the postillion, or some other boy which great families no more than great ships are without, and falls to brushing the clothes, and cleaning the shoes of John the footman, who being drest himself, applies his hands to the same labours for Mr. Second-hand the squire's gentleman; the gentleman in the like manner, a little later in the day, attends the squire; the squire is no sooner equipped, than he attends the levee[1] of my lord; which is no sooner over, than my lord himself is seen at the levee of the favourite, who after his hour of homage is at an end, appears himself to pay homage to the levee of his sovereign. Nor is there perhaps, in this whole ladder of dependance, any one step at a greater distance from the other, than the first from the second: so that to a philosopher the question might only seem whether you would chuse to be a great man at six in the morning, or at two in the afternoon. And yet there are scarce two of these, who do not think the least familiarity with the persons below them a condescension, and if they were to go one step farther, a degradation.

And now, reader, I hope thou wilt pardon this long digression, which seemed to me necessary to vindicate the great character of Mrs. Slipslop, from what low people, who have never seen high people, might think an absurdity: but we who

---

1 Morning reception by a man of quality.

know them, must have daily found very high persons know us in one place and not in another, to-day, and not to-morrow; all which, it is difficult to account for, otherwise than I have here endeavour'd; and perhaps, if the gods, according to the opinion of some, made men only to laugh at them, there is no part of our behaviour which answers the end of our creation better than this.

But to return to our history: Adams, who knew no more of all this than the cat which sat on the table, imagining Mrs. Slipslop's memory had been much worse than it really was, followed her into the next room, crying out, 'Madam Slipslop, here is one of your old acquaintance: do but see what a fine woman she is grown since she left Lady Booby's service.' 'I think I *reflect* something of her,' answered she with great dignity, 'but I can't remember all the inferior servants in our family.' She then proceeded to satisfy Adams's curiosity, by telling him, 'when she arrived at the inn, she found a chaise ready for her; that her lady being expected very shortly in the country, she was obliged to make the utmost haste, and in *commensuration* of Joseph's lameness, she had taken him with her;' and lastly, 'that the excessive *virulence* of the storm had driven them into the house where he found them.' After which, she acquainted Adams with his having left his horse, and exprest some wonder at his having strayed so far out of his way, and at meeting him, as she said, 'in the company of that wench, who she feared was no better than she should be.'

The horse was no sooner put into Adams's head, but he was immediately driven out by this reflection on the character of Fanny. He protested, 'he believed there was not a chaster damsel in the universe. I heartily wish, I heartily wish,' cry'd he, (snapping his fingers) 'that all her betters were as good.' He then proceeded to inform her of the accident of their meeting; but when he came to mention the circumstance of delivering her from the rape, she said, 'she thought him properer for the army than the clergy: that it did not become a clergyman to lay violent hands on any one, that he should have rather prayed that she might be strengthened.' Adams said, 'he was very far from being ashamed of what he had done;' she replied, 'want of shame was not the *currycuristick* of a clergyman.' This dialogue might have probably grown warmer, had not Joseph opportunely entered the room, to ask leave of Madam Slipslop to introduce Fanny: but she positively refused to admit any such trollops; and told him, 'she would have been burnt before she would have suffered him to get into a chaise with her; if she had once *respected* him of having his sluts way-laid on the road for him,' adding, 'that Mr. Adams acted a very pretty part, and she did not doubt but to see him a bishop.' He made the best bow he could, and cried out, 'I thank you, madam, for that right reverend appellation, which I shall take all honest means to deserve.' 'Very honest means,' returned she with a sneer, 'to bring good people together.' At these words, Adams took two or three strides a-cross the room, when the coachman came to inform Mrs. Slipslop, 'that the storm was over, and the moon shone very bright.' She then sent for Joseph, who was sitting without with his Fanny; and would have had him gone with her: but he peremptorily refused to leave Fanny behind; which threw the good woman into a violent rage. She said, 'she would inform her lady what doings were carrying on, and did not doubt, but she would rid the parish of all such people;' and concluded a long speech full of bitterness and very hard words, with some reflections on the clergy, not decent to repeat: at last finding Joseph unmoveable, she flung herself into the chaise, casting a look at Fanny as she went, not unlike that which Cleopatra gives Octavia in the play.[1] To say the truth, she was disagreeably disappointed by the presence of Fanny; she had from her first seeing Joseph at the inn, conceived hopes of something which might have been accomplished at an alehouse as well as a palace; indeed it is probable, Mr. Adams had rescued more than Fanny from the danger of a rape that evening.

When the chaise had carried off the enraged Slipslop; Adams, Joseph, and Fanny assembled over the fire; where they had a great deal of innocent chat, pretty enough; but as possibly, it would not be very entertaining to the reader, we shall hasten

1 This takes place at the end of the third act of John Dryden's *All for Love* (1678), but it is actually Octavia who stares at Cleopatra and leaves in indignation.

to the morning; only observing that none of them went to bed that night. Adams, when he had smoked three pipes, took a comfortable nap in a great chair, and left the lovers, whose eyes were too well employed to permit any desire of shutting them, to enjoy by themselves during some hours, an happiness which none of my readers, who have never been in love, are capable of the least conception of, tho' we had as many tongues as Homer desired[1] to describe it with, and which all true lovers will represent to their own minds without the least assistance from us.

Let it suffice then to say, that Fanny after a thousand entreaties at last gave up her whole soul to Joseph, and almost fainting in his arms, with a sigh infinitely softer and sweeter too, than any Arabian breeze, she whispered to his lips, which were then close to hers, 'O Joseph, you have won me; I will be yours for ever.' Joseph, having thanked her on his knees, and embraced her with an eagerness, which she now almost returned, leapt up in a rapture, and awakened the parson, earnestly begging him, 'that he would that instant join their hands together.' Adams rebuked him for his request, and told him, 'he would by no means consent to any thing contrary to the forms of the Church, that he had no licence, nor indeed would he advise him to obtain one. That the Church had prescribed a form, namely the publication of banns,[2] with which all good Christians ought to comply, and to the omission of which, he attributed the many miseries which befel great folks in marriage; concluding, *As many as are joined together otherwise than* G—'s *word doth allow, are not joined together by* G—, *neither is their matrimony lawful*.'[3] Fanny agreed with the parson, saying to Joseph with a blush, 'she assured him she would not consent to any such thing, and that she wondred at his offering it.' In which resolution she was comforted, and commended by Adams; and Joseph was obliged to wait patiently till after the

---

1 In the *Iliad* 2.489, Homer wishes for ten tongues and ten mouths.

2 The established marriage procedure within the Church was the proclamation of the banns three times in the parish church or churches of the betrothed. Alternatively, the bishop could issue a licence, although this practice was largely reserved for the upper classes. Outside of the Church, however, any contract made before witnesses was still deemed legally valid.

3 Taken from the marriage ceremony in the Book of Common Prayer.

third publication of the banns, which however, he obtained the consent of Fanny in the presence of Adams to put in at their arrival.

The sun had been now risen some hours, when Joseph finding his leg surprisingly recovered, proposed to walk forwards; but when they were all ready to set out, an accident a little retarded them. This was no other than the reckoning which amounted to seven shillings; no great sum, if we consider the immense quantity of ale which Mr. Adams poured in. Indeed they had no objection to the reasonableness of the bill, but many to the probability of paying it; for the fellow who had taken poor Fanny's purse, had unluckily forgot to return it. So that the account stood thus:

Mr. Adams and Company Dr.[1]	0	7	0
In Mr. Adams's Pocket, ————	0	0	6½
In Mr. Joseph's, ————	0	0	0
In Mrs. Fanny's, ————	0	0	0
Balance ————	0	6	5½

They stood silent some few minutes, staring at each other, when Adams whipt out on his toes, and asked the hostess 'if there was no clergyman in that parish?' She answered, 'there was.' 'Is he wealthy?' replied he, to which she likewise answered in the affirmative. Adams then snapping his fingers returned overjoyed to his companions, crying out, '*Eureka*, *Eureka*;'[2] which not being understood, he told them in plain English 'they need give themselves no trouble; for he had a brother in the parish, who would defray the reckoning, and that he would just step to his house and fetch the money, and return to them instantly.'

1 "Debtor," indicating the debit side of the account. Adams seems to have six pence more than he was previously thought to have (see p.191), reducing the debt to six shillings five and a half pence.

2 "I have found it"—Archimedes' supposed exclamation when he discovered the principle of specific gravity.

CHAPTER XIV

An interview between Parson Adams and Parson Trulliber.[1]

PARSON Adams came to the house of Parson Trulliber, whom he found stript into his waistcoat, with an apron on, and a pail in his hand, just come from serving his hogs; for Mr. Trulliber was a parson on Sundays, but all the other six might more properly be called a farmer.[2] He occupied a small piece of land of his own, besides which he rented a considerable deal more. His wife milked his cows, managed his dairy, and followed the markets with butter and eggs. The hogs fell chiefly to his care, which he carefully waited on at home, and attended to fairs; on which occasion he was liable to many jokes, his own size being with much ale rendered little inferiour to that of the beasts he sold. He was indeed one of the largest men you should see, and could have acted the part of Sir John Falstaff without stuffing. Add to this, that the rotundity of his belly was considerably increased by the shortness of his stature, his shadow ascending very near as far in height when he lay on his back, as when he stood on his legs. His voice was loud and hoarse, and his accents extremely broad; to complete the whole, he had a stateliness in his gate, when he walked, not unlike that of a goose, only he stalked slower.

Mr. Trulliber being informed that somebody wanted to speak with him, immediately slipt off his apron, and clothed himself in an old night-gown,[3] being the dress in which he always saw his company at home. His wife who informed him of Mr. Adams's arrival, had made a small mistake; for she had told her husband, 'she believed here was a man come for some of his hogs.' This supposition made Mr. Trulliber hasten with the utmost expedition to attend his guest; he no sooner saw Adams, than not in the least doubting the cause of his errand to

---

1 The name is probably derived from the words *trullibub* (entrails; a fat man) and *trolubber* (a farm labourer).

2 In *The Champion*, 12 April 1740, Fielding had already pointed out that it was illegal for clergymen to take lands to farm or to buy and sell such produce for profit.

3 A dressing gown.

be what his wife had imagined, he told him, 'he was come in very good time; that he expected a dealer that very afternoon;' and added, 'they were all pure and fat, and upwards of twenty score a piece.'[1] Adams answered, 'he believed he did not know him.' 'Yes, yes,' cry'd Trulliber, 'I have seen you often at fair; why, we have dealt before now mun, I warrant you; yes, yes,' cries he, 'I remember thy face very well, but won't mention a word more till you have seen them, tho' I have never sold thee a flitch[2] of such bacon as is now in the stye.' Upon which he laid violent hands on Adams, and dragged him into the hogs-stye, which was indeed but two steps from his parlour window. They were no sooner arrived there than he cry'd out, 'Do but handle them, step in, friend, art welcome to handle them whether dost buy or no.' At which words opening the gate, he pushed Adams into the pig-stye, insisting on it, that he should handle them, before he would talk one word with him. Adams, whose natural complacence was beyond any artificial, was obliged to comply before he was suffered to explain himself, and laying hold on one of their tails, the unruly beast gave such a sudden spring, that he threw poor Adams all along in the mire. Trulliber instead of assisting him to get up, burst into a laughter, and entring the stye, said to Adams with some contempt, *Why, dost not know how to handle a hog?* and was going to lay hold of one himself; but Adams, who thought he had carried his complacence far enough, was no sooner on his legs, than he escaped out of the reach of the animals, and cry'd out, *nihil habeo cum porcis:*[3] 'I am a clergyman, sir, and am not come to buy hogs.' Trulliber answered, 'he was sorry for the mistake; but that he must blame his wife;' adding, 'she was a fool, and always committed blunders.' He then desired him to walk in and clean himself, that he would only fasten up the stye and follow him. Adams desired leave to dry his great coat, wig, and hat by the fire, which Trulliber granted. Mrs. Trulliber would have brought him a bason of water to wash his face, but her husband bid her be quiet like a fool as she was, or she would

---

1 That is, more than four hundred pounds each.

2 A side of a pig preserved in salt.

3 "I have nothing to do with pigs."

commit more blunders, and then directed Adams to the pump. While Adams was thus employed, Trulliber conceiving no great respect for the appearance of his guest, fastened the parlour-door, and now conducted him into the kitchin; telling him, he believed a cup of drink would do him no harm, and whispered his wife to draw a little of the worst ale. After a short silence, Adams said, 'I fancy, sir, you already perceive me to be a clergyman.' 'Ay, ay,' cries Trulliber grinning; 'I perceive you have some cassock; I will not venture to *caale* it a whole one.' Adams answered, 'it was indeed none of the best; but he had the misfortune to tear it about ten years ago in passing over a stile.' Mrs. Trulliber returning with the drink, told her husband 'she fancied the gentleman was a traveller, and that he would be glad to eat a bit.' Trulliber bid her 'hold her impertinent tongue;' and asked her 'if parsons used to travel without horses?' adding, 'he supposed the gentleman had none by his having no boots on.' 'Yes, sir, yes,' says Adams, 'I have a horse, but I have left him behind me.' 'I am glad to hear you have one,' says Trulliber; 'for I assure you, I don't love to see clergymen on foot; it is not seemly nor suiting the dignity of the cloth.' Here Trulliber made a long oration on the dignity of the cloth (or rather gown) not much worth relating, till his wife had spread the table and set a mess[1] of porridge on it for his breakfast. He then said to Adams, 'I don't know, friend, how you came to *caale* on me; however, as you are here, if you think proper to eat a morsel, you may.' Adams accepted the invitation, and the two parsons sat down together, Mrs. Trulliber waiting behind her husband's chair, as was, it seems, her custom. Trulliber eat heartily, but scarce put any thing in his mouth without finding fault with his wife's cookery. All which the poor woman bore patiently. Indeed she was so absolute an admirer of her husband's greatness and importance, of which she had frequent hints from his own mouth, that she almost carried her adoration to an opinion of his infallibility. To say the truth, the parson had exercised her more ways than one; and the pious woman had so well edified by her husband's sermons, that she

---

1 A dish.

had resolved to receive the good things of this world together with the bad. She had indeed been at first a little contentious; but he had long since got the better, partly by her love for *this*, partly by her fear of *that*, partly by her religion, partly by the respect he paid himself, and partly by that which he received from the parish: she had, in short, absolutely submitted, and now worshipped her husband as Sarah did Abraham, calling him (not lord but) master.[1] Whilst they were at table, her husband gave her a fresh example of his greatness; for as she had just delivered a cup of ale to Adams, he snatched it out of his hand, and crying out, *I caal'd vurst*, swallowed down the ale. Adams denied it, and it was referred to the wife, who tho' her conscience was on the side of Adams, durst not give it against her husband. Upon which he said, 'No, sir, no, I should not have been so rude to have taken it from you, if you had *caal'd vurst*; but I'd have you know I'm a better man than to suffer the best he in the kingdom to drink before me in my own house, when I *caale vurst*.'

As soon as their breakfast was ended, Adams began in the following manner: 'I think, sir, it is high time to inform you of the business of my embassy. I am a traveller, and am passing this way in company with two young people, a lad and a damsel, my parishioners, towards my own cure: we stopt at a house of hospitality in the parish, where they directed me to you, as having the cure.'—'Tho' I am but a curate,' says Trulliber, 'I believe I am as warm[2] as the vicar himself, or perhaps the rector of the next parish too; I believe I could buy them both.' 'Sir,' cries Adams, 'I rejoice thereat. Now, sir, my business is, that we are by various accidents stript of our money, and are not able to pay our reckoning, being seven shillings. I therefore request you to assist me with the loan of those seven shillings, and also seven shillings more, which peradventure I shall return to you; but if not, I am convinced you will joyfully embrace such an opportunity of laying up a treasure in a better place than any this world affords.'[3]

---

1 "Even as Sarah obeyed Abraham, calling him Lord" (I Peter 3:6).

2 Well-to-do, comfortably off.

3 See Matthew 6:19-21.

Suppose a stranger, who entered the chambers of a lawyer, being imagined a client, when the lawyer was preparing his palm for the fee, should pull out a writ against him. Suppose an apothecary, at the door of a chariot containing some great doctor of eminent skill, should, instead of directions to a patient, present him with a potion for himself. Suppose a minister should, instead of a good round sum, treat my Lord —— or Sir —— or Esq; —— with a good broomstick. Suppose a civil companion, or a led captain[1] should, instead of virtue, and honour, and beauty, and parts, and admiration, thunder vice and infamy, and ugliness, and folly, and contempt, in his patron's ears. Suppose when a tradesman first carries in his bill, the man of fashion should pay it; or suppose, if he did so, the tradesman should abate what he had overcharged on the supposition of waiting. In short—suppose what you will, you never can nor will suppose anything equal to the astonishment which seiz'd on Trulliber, as soon as Adams had ended his speech. A while he rolled his eyes in silence, some times surveying Adams, then his wife, then casting them on the ground, then lifting them to heaven. At last, he burst forth in the following accents. 'Sir, I believe I know where to lay my little treasure up as well as another; I thank G— if I am not so warm as some, I am content; that is a blessing greater than riches; and he to whom that is given need ask no more. To be content with a little is greater than to possess the world, which a man may possess without being so. Lay up my treasure! what matters where a man's treasure is, whose heart is in the Scriptures?[2] there is the treasure of a Christian.' At these words the water ran from Adams's eyes; and catching Trulliber by the hand, in a rapture, 'Brother,' says he, 'Heavens bless the accident by which I came to see you; I would have walked many a mile to have communed with you, and, believe me, I will shortly pay you a second visit: but my friends, I fancy, by this time, wonder at my stay, so let me have the money immediately.' Trulliber then put on a stern look, and cry'd out, 'Thou dost not intend to rob me?' At which the wife, bursting into tears, fell on her knees and roared out, 'O dear sir,

1 A hanger-on.

2 See Matthew 6:12; Luke 6:45; and Proverbs 15:16.

for Heaven's sake don't rob my master, we are but poor people.' 'Get up for a fool as thou art, and go about thy business,' said Trulliber, 'dost think the man will venture his life? he is a beggar and no robber.' 'Very true indeed,' answered Adams. 'I wish, with all my heart, the tithing-man[1] was here,' cries Trulliber, 'I would have thee punished as a vagabond for thy impudence. Fourteen shillings indeed! I won't give thee a farthing. I believe thou art no more a clergyman than the woman there, (pointing to his wife) but if thou art, dost deserve to have thy gown stript over thy shoulders, for running about the country in such a manner.' 'I forgive your suspicions,' says Adams, 'but suppose I am not a clergyman, I am nevertheless thy brother, and thou, as a Christian, much more as a clergyman, art obliged to relieve my distress.' 'Dost preach to me,' replied Trulliber, 'dost pretend to instruct me in my duty?' 'Ifacks, a good story,' cries Mrs. Trulliber, 'to preach to my master.' 'Silence, woman,' cries Trulliber; 'I would have thee know, friend, (addressing himself to Adams,) I shall not learn my duty from such as thee; I know what charity is, better than to give to vagabonds.' 'Besides, if we were inclined, the poors rate[2] obliges us to give so much charity,' (cries the wife.) 'Pugh! thou art a fool. Poors reate! hold thy nonsense,' answered Trulliber, and then turning to Adams, he told him, 'he would give him nothing.' 'I am sorry,' answered Adams, 'that you do know what charity is, since you practise it no better; I must tell you, if you trust to your knowledge for your justification, you will find yourself deceived, tho' you should add faith to it without good works.' 'Fellow,' cries Trulliber, 'dost thou speak against faith in my house? Get out of my doors, I will no longer remain under the same roof with a wretch who speaks wantonly of faith and the Scriptures.' 'Name not the Scriptures,' says Adams. 'How, not name the Scriptures! Do you disbelieve the Scriptures?' cries Trulliber. 'No, but you do,' answered Adams, 'if I may reason from your practice: for their commands are so explicite, and their rewards and punishments so immense, that it is impossible a man should stedfastly believe without obeying. Now, there is no command

---

1 The parish constable.
2 A parish tax for supporting the poor.

more express, no duty more frequently enjoined than charity. Whoever therefore is void of charity, I make no scruple of pronouncing that he is no Christian.'[1] 'I would not advise thee, (says Trulliber) to say that I am no Christian. I won't take it of you: for I believe I am as good a man as thyself;' (and indeed, tho' he was now rather too corpulent for athletic exercises, he had in his youth been one of the best boxers and cudgel-players in the county.) His wife seeing him clench his fist, interposed, and begged him not to fight, but shew himself a true Christian, and take the law of him. As nothing could provoke Adams to strike, but an absolute assault on himself or his friend; he smiled at the angry look and gestures of Trulliber; and telling him, he was sorry to see such men in orders, departed without farther ceremony.

CHAPTER XV

An adventure, the consequence of a new instance which Parson Adams gave of his forgetfulness.

WHEN he came back to the inn, he found Joseph and Fanny sitting together. They were so far from thinking his absence long, as he had feared they would, that they never once miss'd or thought of him. Indeed, I have been often assured by both, that they spent these hours in a most delightful conversation: but as I never could prevail on either to relate it, so I cannot communicate it to the reader.

Adams acquainted the lovers with the ill success of his enterprize. They were all greatly confounded, none being able to propose any method of departing, 'till Joseph at last advised calling in the hostess, and desiring her to trust them; which Fanny said she despaired of her doing, as she was one of the sourest-fac'd women she had ever beheld.

But she was agreeably disappointed; for the hostess was no sooner asked the question than she readily agreed; and with a

---

1 See I Corinthians 13:2.

curt'sy and smile, wished them a good journey. However, lest Fanny's skill in physiognomy should be called in question, we will venture to assign one reason, which might probably incline her to this confidence and good-humour. When Adams said he was going to visit his brother, he had unwittingly imposed[1] on Joseph and Fanny; who both believed he had meant his natural brother, and not his brother in divinity; and had so informed the hostess on her enquiry after him. Now Mr. Trulliber had by his professions of piety, by his gravity, austerity, reserve, and the opinion of his great wealth, so great an authority in his parish, that they all lived in the utmost fear and apprehension of him. It was therefore no wonder that the hostess, who knew it was in his option whether she should ever sell another mug of drink, did not dare to affront his supposed brother by denying him credit.

They were now just on their departure, when Adams recollected he had left his great coat and hat at Mr. Trulliber's. As he was not desirous of renewing his visit, the hostess herself, having no servant at home, offered to fetch it.

This was an unfortunate expedient: for the hostess was soon undeceived in the opinion she had entertained of Adams, whom Trulliber abused in the grossest terms, especially when he heard he had had the assurance to pretend to be his near relation.

At her return therefore, she entirely changed her note. She said, 'Folks might be ashamed of travelling about and pretending to be what they were not. That taxes were high, and for her part, she was obliged to pay for what she had; she could not therefore possibly, nor would she trust any body, no not her own father. That money was never scarcer, and she wanted to make up a sum. That she expected therefore they should pay their reckoning before they left the house.'

Adams was now greatly perplexed: but as he knew that he could easily have borrowed such a sum in his own parish, and as he knew he would have lent it himself to any mortal in distress; so he took fresh courage, and sallied out all round the

---

1 Misled.

parish, but to no purpose; he returned as pennyless as he went, groaning and lamenting, that it was possible in a country professing Christianity, for a wretch to starve in the midst of his fellow-creatures who abounded.

Whilst he was gone, the hostess who stayed as a sort of guard with Joseph and Fanny entertained them with the goodness of Parson Trulliber; and indeed he had not only a very good character, as to other qualities, in the neighbourhood, but was reputed a man of great charity: for tho' he never gave a farthing, he had always that word in his mouth.

Adams was no sooner returned the second time, than the storm grew exceeding high, the hostess declaring among other things, that if they offered to stir without paying her, she would soon overtake them with a warrant.

Plato or Aristotle, or some body else hath said, THAT WHEN THE MOST EXQUISITE CUNNING FAILS, CHANCE OFTEN HITS THE MARK, AND THAT BY MEANS THE LEAST EXPECTED. Virgil expresses this very boldly:

> *Turne quod optanti divûm promittere nemo*
> *Auderet, volvenda dies en attulit ultro.*[1]

I would quote more great men if I could: but my memory not permitting me, I will proceed to exemplify these observations by the following instance.

There chanced (for Adams had not cunning enough to contrive it) to be at that time in the alehouse, a fellow, who had been formerly a drummer in an Irish regiment, and now travelled the country as a pedlar. This man having attentively listened to the discourse of the hostess, at last took Adams aside, and asked him what the sum was for which they were detained. As soon as he was informed, he sighed and said, 'he was sorry it was so much: for that he had no more than six shillings and sixpence in his pocket, which he would lend them with all his heart.' Adams gave a caper, and cry'd out, 'it would do: for that he had sixpence himself.' And thus these poor people, who

1 "Turnus, what none of the gods would have dared promise to your prayers, lo! rolling time has brought unasked" (*Aeneid* 9.6-7).

could not engage the compassion of riches and piety, were at length delivered out of their distress by the charity of a poor pedlar.

I shall refer it to my reader, to make what observations he pleases on this incident: it is sufficient for me to inform him, that after Adams and his companions had returned him a thousand thanks, and told him where he might call to be repaid, they all sallied out of the house without any complements from their hostess, or indeed without paying her any; Adams declaring, he would take particular care never to call there again, and she on her side assuring them she wanted no such guests.

CHAPTER XVI

A very curious adventure, in which Mr. Adams gave a much greater instance of the honest simplicity of his heart than of his experience in the ways of this world.

OUR travellers had walked about two miles from that inn, which they had more reason to have mistaken for a castle, than Don Quixote ever had any of those in which he sojourned;[1] seeing they had met with such difficulty in escaping out of its walls; when they came to a parish, and beheld a sign of invitation hanging out. A gentleman sat smoaking a pipe at the door; of whom Adams enquired the road, and received so courteous and obliging an answer, accompanied with so smiling a countenance, that the good parson, whose heart was naturally disposed to love and affection, began to ask several other questions; particularly the name of the parish, and who was the owner of a large house whose front they then had in prospect. The gentleman answered as obligingly as before; and as to the house, acquainted him it was his own. He then proceeded in the following manner: 'Sir, I presume by your habit you are a clergyman: and as you are travelling on foot, I suppose a glass of good beer will not be disagreeable to you; and I can recom-

1 For much of the first part of *Don Quixote*, the knight mistakes an inn for a castle. See Appendix C, pp. 464-69.

mend my landlord's within, as some of the best in all this county. What say you, will you halt a little and let us take a pipe together: there is no better tobacco in the kingdom?' This proposal was not displeasing to Adams, who had allayed his thirst that day, with no better liquor than what Mrs. Trulliber's cellar had produced; and which was indeed little superior either in richness or flavour to that which distilled from those grains her generous husband bestowed on his hogs. Having therefore abundantly thanked the gentleman for his kind invitation, and bid Joseph and Fanny follow him, he entered the ale-house, where a large loaf and cheese and a pitcher of beer, which truly answered the character given of it, being set before them, the three travellers fell to eating with appetites infinitely more voracious than are to be found at the most exquisite eating-houses in the parish of St. James's.[1]

The gentleman expressed great delight in the hearty and chearful behaviour of Adams; and particularly in the familiarity with which he conversed with Joseph and Fanny, whom he often called his children, a term, he explained to mean no more than his parishioners; saying, he looked on all those whom God had entrusted to his cure, to stand to him in that relation. The gentleman shaking him by the hand highly applauded those sentiments. 'They are indeed,' says he, 'the true principles of a Christian divine; and I heartily wish they were universal: but on the contrary, I am sorry to say the parson of our parish instead of esteeming his poor parishioners as a part of his family, seems rather to consider them as not of the same species with himself. He seldom speaks to any unless some few of the richest of us; nay indeed, he will not move his hat to the others. I often laugh when I behold him on Sundays strutting along the church-yard, like a turky-cock, through rows of his parishioners; who bow to him with as much submission and are as unregarded as a sett of servile courtiers by the proudest prince in Christendom. But if such temporal pride is ridiculous, surely the spiritual is odious and detestable: if such a puffed up empty

---

1 An especially fashionable area of London, noted for its taverns, clubs, chocolate houses, and dining places.

human bladder strutting in princely robes, justly moves one's derision; surely in the habit of a priest it must raise our scorn.'

'Doubtless,' answered Adams, 'your opinion is right; but I hope such examples are rare. The clergy whom I have the honour to know, maintain a different behaviour; and you will allow me, sir, that the readiness, which too many of the laity show to contemn the order, may be one reason of their avoiding too much humility.' 'Very true indeed,' says the gentleman; 'I find, sir, you are a man of excellent sense, and am happy in this opportunity of knowing you: perhaps, our accidental meeting may not be disadvantageous to you neither. At present, I shall only say to you, that the incumbent of this living is old and infirm; and that it is in my gift. Doctor, give me your hand; and assure yourself of it at his decease.' Adams told him, 'he was never more confounded in his life, than at his utter incapacity to make any return to such noble and unmerited generosity.' 'A mere trifle, sir,' cries the gentleman, 'scarce worth your acceptance; a little more than three hundred a year. I wish it was double the value for your sake.' Adams bowed, and cried from the emotions of his gratitude; when the other asked him, 'if he was married, or had any children, besides those in the spiritual sense he had mentioned.' 'Sir,' replied the parson, 'I have a wife and six at your service.' 'That is unlucky,' says the gentleman; 'for I would otherwise have taken you into my own house as my chaplain: however, I have another in the parish, (for the parsonage house is not good enough) which I will furnish for you. Pray does your wife understand a dairy?' 'I can't profess she does,' says Adams. 'I am sorry for it,' quoth the gentleman; 'I would have given you half a dozen cows, and very good grounds to have maintained them.' 'Sir,' says Adams, in an ecstacy, 'you are too liberal; indeed you are.' 'Not at all,' cries the gentleman, 'I esteem riches only as they give me an opportunity of doing good; and I never saw one whom I had a greater inclination to serve.' At which words he shook him heartily by the hand, and told him he had sufficient room in his house to entertain him and his friends. Adams begged he might give him no such trouble, that they could be very well accommodated in the house where they were; forgetting they had not a sixpenny piece among them. The gentleman would not be denied; and informing himself how far they were travelling, he said it was too long a journey to take on foot, and begged that they would favour him, by suffering him to lend them a servant and horses; adding withal, that if they would do him the pleasure of their company only two days, he would furnish them with his coach and six. Adams turning to Joseph, said, 'How lucky is this gentleman's goodness to you, who I am afraid would be scarce able to hold out on your lame leg,' and then addressing the person who made him these liberal promises, after much bowing, he cried out, 'Blessed be the hour which first introduced me to a man of your charity: you are indeed a Christian of the true primitive kind, and an honour to the country wherein you live. I would willingly have taken a pilgrimage to the Holy Land to have beheld you: for the advantages which we draw from your goodness, give me little pleasure, in comparison of what I enjoy for your own sake; when I consider the treasures you are by these means laying up for your self in a country that passeth not away. We will therefore, most generous sir, accept your goodness, as well the entertainment you have so kindly offered us at your house this evening, as the accommodation of your horses to-morrow morning.' He then began to search for his hat, as did Joseph for his; and both they and Fanny were in order of departure, when the gentleman stopping short, and seeming to meditate by himself for the space of about a minute, exclaimed thus: 'Sure never any thing was so unlucky; I have forgot that my house-keeper was gone abroad, and hath locked up all my rooms; indeed I would break them open for you, but shall not be able to furnish you with a bed; for she hath likewise put away all my linnen. I am glad it entered into my head before I had given you the trouble of walking there; besides, I believe you will find better accommodations here than you expect. Landlord, you can provide good beds for these people, can't you?' 'Yes and please your worship,' cries the host, 'and such as no lord or justice of the peace in the kingdom need be ashamed to lie in.' 'I am heartily sorry,' says the gentleman, 'for this disappointment. I am resolved I will never suffer her to carry away the keys again.'

'Pray, sir, let it not make you uneasy,' cries Adams, 'we shall do very well here; and the loan of your horses is a favour, we shall be incapable of making any return to.' 'Ay!' said the squire, 'the horses shall attend you here at what hour in the morning you please.' And now after many civilities too tedious to enumerate, many squeezes by the hand, with most affectionate looks and smiles on each other, and after appointing the horses at seven the next morning, the gentleman took his leave of them, and departed to his own house. Adams and his companions returned to the table, where the parson smoaked another pipe, and then they all retired to rest.

Mr. Adams rose very early and called Joseph out of his bed, between whom a very fierce dispute ensued, whether Fanny should ride behind Joseph, or behind the gentleman's servant; Joseph insisting on it, that he was perfectly recovered, and was as capable of taking care of Fanny, as any other person could be. But Adams would not agree to it, and declared he would not trust her behind him; for that he was weaker than he imagined himself to be.

This dispute continued a long time, and had begun to be very hot, when a servant arrived from their good friend, to acquaint them that he was unfortunately prevented from lending them any horses; for that his groom had, unknown to him, put his whole stable under a course of physick.

This advice presently struck the two disputants dumb; Adams cried out, 'Was ever any thing so unlucky as this poor gentleman? I protest I am more sorry on his account, than my own. You see, Joseph, how this good-natur'd man is treated by his servants; one locks up his linen, another physicks his horses; and I suppose by his being at this house last night, the butler had locked up his cellar. Bless us! how good-nature is used in this world! I protest I am more concerned on his account than my own.' 'So am not I,' cries Joseph; 'not that I am much troubled about walking on foot; all my concern is, how we shall get out of the house; unless God sends another pedlar to redeem us. But certainly, this gentleman has such an affection for you, that he would lend you a larger sum than we owe here; which is not above four or five shillings.' 'Very true, child,' answered

Adams; 'I will write a letter to him, and will even venture to sollicit him for three half-crowns; there will be no harm in having two or three shillings in our pockets: as we have full forty miles to travel, we may possibly have occasion for them.'

Fanny being now risen, Joseph paid her a visit, and left Adams to write his letter; which having finished, he dispatched a boy with it to the gentleman, and then seated himself by the door, lighted his pipe, and betook himself to meditation.

The boy staying longer than seemed to be necessary, Joseph who with Fanny was now returned to the parson, expressed some apprehensions, that the gentleman's steward had locked up his purse too. To which Adams answered, 'It might very possibly be; and he should wonder at no liberties which the Devil might put into the head of a wicked servant to take with so worthy a master:' but added, 'that as the sum was so small, so noble a gentleman would be easily able to procure it in the parish; tho' he had it not in his own pocket. Indeed,' says he, 'if it was four or five guineas, or any such large quantity of money, it might be a different matter.'

They were now sat down to breakfast over some toast and ale, when the boy returned; and informed them, that the gentleman was not at home. 'Very well,' cries Adams; 'but why, child, did you not stay 'till his return? Go back again, my good boy, and wait for his coming home: he cannot be gone far, as his horses are all sick; and besides, he had no intention to go abroad; for he invited us to spend this day and to-morrow at his house. Therefore, go back, child, and tarry 'till his return home.' The messenger departed, and was back again with great expedition; bringing an account, that the gentleman was gone a long journey, and would not be at home again this month. At these words, Adams seemed greatly confounded, saying, 'This must be a sudden accident, as the sickness or death of a relation, or some such unforeseen misfortune;' and then turning to Joseph, cried, 'I wish you had reminded me to have borrowed this money last night.' Joseph smiling, answered, 'he was very much deceived, if the gentleman would not have found some excuse to avoid lending it. I own,' says he, 'I was never much pleased with his professing so much kindness for you at first sight: for I have heard the gentlemen of our cloth in London tell many such stories of their masters. But when the boy brought the message back of his not being at home, I presently knew what would follow; for whenever a man of fashion doth not care to fulfil his promises, the custom is, to order his servants that he will never be at home to the person so promised. In London they call it *denying him.* I have my self denied Sir Thomas Booby above a hundred times; and when the man hath danced attendance for about a month, or sometimes longer, he is acquainted in the end, that the gentleman is gone out of town, and could do nothing in the business.' 'Good Lord!' says Adams; 'what wickedness is there in the Christian world? I profess, almost equal to what I have read of the heathens. But surely, Joseph, your suspicions of this gentleman must be unjust; for, what a silly fellow must he be, who would do the Devil's work for nothing? and can'st thou tell me any interest[1] he could possibly propose to himself by deceiving us in his professions?' 'It is not for me,' answered Joseph, 'to give reasons for what men do, to a gentleman of your learning.' 'You say right,' quoth Adams; 'knowledge of men is only to be learnt from books, Plato and Seneca[2] for that; and those are authors, I am afraid child, you never read.' 'Not I, sir, truly,' answered Joseph; 'all I know is, it is a maxim among the gentlemen of our cloth, that those masters who promise the most perform the least; and I have often heard them say, they have found the largest vailes[3] in those families, where they were not promised any. But, sir, instead of considering any farther these matters, it would be our wisest way to contrive some method of getting out of this house: for the generous gentleman, instead of doing us any service, hath left us the whole reckoning to pay.' Adams was going to answer, when their host came in; and with a kind of jeering-smile said, 'Well, masters! the squire hath not sent his horses for you yet. Laud help me! how easily some folks make

1 Benefit.

2 Lucius Annaeus Seneca (c. 4 BC–AD 65), Roman statesman, Stoic philosopher, and tragedian.

3 Gratuities or tips, often forming a major part of a servant's income.

promises!' 'How!' says Adams, 'have you ever known him do any thing of this kind before?' 'Aye marry have I,' answered the host; 'it is no business of mine, you know, sir, to say any thing to a gentleman to his face: but now he is not here, I will assure you, he hath not his fellow within the three next market-towns. I own, I could not help laughing, when I heard him offer you the living; for thereby hangs a good jest. I thought he would have offered you my house next; for one is no more his to dispose of than the other.' At these words, Adams blessing himself, declared, 'he had never read of such a monster; but what vexes me most,' says he, 'is that he hath decoyed us into running up a long debt with you, which we are not able to pay; for we have no money about us; and what is worse, live at such a distance, that if you should trust us, I am afraid you would lose your money, for want of our finding any conveniency of sending it.' 'Trust you, master!' says the host, 'that I will with all my heart; I honour the clergy too much to deny trusting one of them for such a trifle; besides, I like your fear of never paying me. I have lost many a debt in my lifetime; but was promised to be paid them all in a very short time. I will score this reckoning for the novelty of it. It is the first I do assure you of its kind. But what say you, master, shall we have t'other pot before we part? It will waste but a little chalk more; and if you never pay me a shilling, the loss will not ruin me.' Adams liked the invitation very well; especially as it was delivered with so hearty an accent.—He shook his host by the hand, and thanking him, said, 'he would tarry another pot, rather for the pleasure of such worthy company than for the liquor;' adding, 'he was glad to find some Christians left in the kingdom; for that he almost began to suspect that he was sojourning in a country inhabited only by Jews and Turks.'

The kind host produced the liquor, and Joseph with Fanny retired into the garden; where while they solaced themselves with amorous discourse, Adams sat down with his host; and both filling their glasses and lighting their pipes, they began that dialogue, which the reader will find in the next chapter.

CHAPTER XVII

A dialogue between Mr. Abraham Adams and his host, which, by the disagreement in their opinions seemed to threaten an unlucky catastrophe, had it not been timely prevented by the return of the lovers.

'SIR,' said the host, 'I assure you, you are not the first to whom our squire hath promised more than he hath performed. He is so famous for this practice, that his word will not be taken for much by those who know him. I remember a young fellow whom he promised his parents to make an exciseman. The poor people, who could ill afford it, bred their son to writing and accounts, and other learning, to qualify him for the place; and the boy held up his head above his condition with these hopes; nor would he go to plough, nor do any other kind of work; and went constantly drest as fine as could be, with two clean Holland[1] shirts a week, and this for several years; 'till at last he followed the squire up to London, thinking there to mind him of his promises: but he could never get sight of him. So that being out of money and business, he fell into evil company, and wicked courses; and in the end came to a sentence of transportation, the news of which broke the mother's heart. I will tell you another true story of him: there was a neighbour of mine, a farmer, who had two sons whom he bred up to the business. Pretty lads they were; nothing would serve the squire, but that the youngest must be made a parson. Upon which, he persuaded the father to send him to school, promising, that he would afterwards maintain him at the university; and when he was of a proper age, give him a living. But after the lad had been seven years at school, and his father brought him to the squire with a letter from his master, that he was fit for the university; the squire, instead of minding his promise, or sending him thither at his expence, only told his father, that the young man was a fine scholar; and it was pity he could not afford to keep him at Oxford for four or five years more, by which time,

1 Fine linen from Holland.

if he could get him a curacy, he might have him ordained.' The farmer said, 'he was not a man sufficient to do any such thing.' 'Why then,' answered the squire; 'I am very sorry you have given him so much learning; for if he cannot get his living by that, it will rather spoil him for any thing else; and your other son who can hardly write his name, will do more at plowing and sowing, and is in a better condition than he: and indeed so it proved; for the poor lad not finding friends to maintain him in his learning, as he had expected; and being unwilling to work, fell to drinking, though he was a very sober lad before; and in a short time, partly with grief, and partly with good liquor, fell into a consumption and died. Nay, I can tell you more still: there was another, a young woman, and the handsomest in all this neighbourhood, whom he enticed up to London, promising to make her a gentlewoman to one of your women of quality: but instead of keeping his word, we have since heard, after having a child by her himself, she became a common whore; then kept a coffee-house in Covent-Garden, and a little after died of the French distemper[1] in a goal. I could tell you many more stories: but how do you imagine he served me myself? You must know, sir, I was bred a sea-faring man, and have been many voyages; 'till at last I came to be master of a ship myself, and was in a fair way of making a fortune, when I was attacked by one of those cursed *guarda-costas*, who took our ships before the beginning of the war;[2] and after a fight wherein I lost the greater part of my crew, my rigging being all demolished, and two shots received between wind and water, I was forced to strike.[3] The villains carried off my ship, a brigantine of 150 tons, a pretty creature she was, and put me, a man, and a boy, into a little bad pink,[4] in which with much ado, we at last made Falmouth; tho' I believe the Spaniards did not imagine she could possibly live a day at sea. Upon my return

---

1 One of the many such names given by the English to venereal disease. Covent Garden was a district in London well known for its brothels.

2 The war with Spain (1739-48), following years of hostility between the two countries over West Indian trade etc. *Guarda-costas* were Spanish coastguard ships.

3 To lower the ship's flag or sail as a sign of surrender.

4 A sailing vessel with a flat bottom and narrow stern.

hither, where my wife who was of this country then lived, the squire told me, he was so pleased with the defence I had made against the enemy, that he did not fear getting me promoted to a lieutenancy of a man of war, if I would accept of it, which I thankfully assured him I would. Well, sir, two or three years past, during which, I had many repeated promises, not only from the squire, but (as he told me) from the Lords of the Admiralty.[1] He never returned from London, but I was assured I might be satisfied now, for I was certain of the first vacancy; and what surprizes me still, when I reflect on it, these assurances were given me with no less confidence, after so many disappointments, than at first. At last, sir, growing weary and somewhat suspicious after so much delay, I wrote to a friend in London, who I knew had some acquaintance at the best house in the Admiralty; and desired him to back the squire's interest: for indeed, I feared he had sollicited the affair with more coldness than he pretended.—And what answer do you think my friend sent me?—Truly, sir, he acquainted me, that the squire had never mentioned my name at the Admiralty in his life; and unless I had much faithfuller interest, advised me to give over my pretensions, which I immediately did; and with the concurrence of my wife, resolved to set up an alehouse, where you are heartily welcome: and so my service to you; and may the squire, and all such sneaking rascals go to the devil together.' 'Oh fie!' says Adams; 'Oh fie! He is indeed a wicked man; but G— will, I hope, turn his heart to repentance. Nay, if he could but once see the meanness of this detestable vice; would he but once reflect that he is one of the most scandalous as well as pernicious lyars; sure he must despise himself to so intolerable a degree, that it would be impossible for him to continue a moment in such a course. And to confess the truth, notwithstanding the baseness of this character, which he hath too well deserved, he hath in his countenance sufficient symptoms of that *bona indoles*,[2] that sweetness of disposition which furnishes out a good Christian.' 'Ah! master, master, (says the host,) if you had travelled as far as I have, and conversed with the many

1 Presumably the Admiralty Board, having control over British naval affairs.
2 "Good nature."

nations where I have traded, you would not give any credit to a man's countenance. Symptoms in his countenance, quotha! I would look there perhaps to see whether a man had had the small-pox, but for nothing else!' He spoke this with so little regard to the parson's observation, that it a good deal nettled him; and taking the pipe hastily from his mouth, he thus answered:—'Master of mine, perhaps I have travelled a great deal farther than you without the assistance of a ship. Do you imagine sailing by different cities or countries is travelling? No.

Cœlum non animum mutant qui trans mare currunt.[1]

I can go farther in an afternoon, than you in a twelve-month. What, I suppose you have seen the Pillars of Hercules, and perhaps the walls of Carthage. Nay, you may have heard Scylla, and seen Charybdis;[2] you may have entered the closet where Archimedes was found at the taking Syracuse.[3] I suppose you have sailed among the Cyclades,[4] and passed the famous streights which take their name from the unfortunate Helle, whose fate is sweetly described by Apollonius Rhodius;[5] you have past the very spot, I conceive, where Dædalus fell into that sea,[6] his waxen wings being melted by the sun; you have traversed the Euxine Sea, I make no doubt; nay, you may have been on the banks of the Caspian, and called at Colchis, to see if there is ever another golden fleece.'—'Not I truly, master,' answered the host, 'I never touched at any of these places.' 'But I

---

1 "Those who cross the sea change climate but not their character" (Horace, *Epistles* 1.11.27).

2 Adams uses classical names for places in this passage, which otherwise would likely be known to the innkeeper: the Pillars of Hercules are the peaks flanking the Straits of Gibraltar; Carthage was a Phoenician city on the Gulf of Tunis in North Africa; and Scylla and Charybdis were the monsters that hindered Odysseus' progress homeward.

3 Archimedes, the great mathematician and inventor, was killed by Roman soldiers at the capture of Syracuse in 212 BC.

4 Islands in the Aegean Sea, off the coast of Peloponnesus.

5 Apollonius Rhodius (b. c. 235 BC), in his *Argonautica*, tells the story of the expedition led by Jason to recover the golden fleece from Colchis.

6 In fact it was Daedalus' son, Icarus, who fell into the Aegean Sea and drowned (Ovid, *Metamorphoses* 8.183-235).

have been at all these,' replied Adams. 'Then I suppose,' cries the host, 'you have been at the East Indies, for there are no such, I will be sworn, either in the West or the Levant.' 'Pray where's the Levant?' quoth Adams, 'that should be in the East Indies by right.'[1]—'O ho! you are a pretty traveller,' cries the host, 'and not know the Levant. My service to you, master; you must not talk of these things with me! you must not tip us[2] the traveller; it won't go here.' 'Since thou art so dull to misunderstand me still,' quoth Adams, 'I will inform thee; the travelling I mean is in books, the only way of travelling by which any knowledge is to be acquired. From them I learn what I asserted just now, that nature generally imprints such a portraiture of the mind in the countenance, that a skilful physiognomist will rarely be deceived. I presume you have never read the story of Socrates to this purpose, and therefore I will tell it you. A certain physiognomist asserted of Socrates, that he plainly discovered by his features that he was a rogue in his nature. A character so contrary to the tenour of all this great man's actions, and the generally received opinion concerning him, incensed the boys of Athens so that they threw stones at the physiognomist, and would have demolished him for his ignorance, had not Socrates himself prevented them by confessing the truth of his observations, and acknowledging that tho' he corrected his disposition by philosophy, he was indeed naturally as inclined to vice as had been predicated of him.[3] Now, pray resolve me,— How should a man know this story, if he had not read it?' 'Well master,' said the host, 'and what signifies it whether a man knows it or no? He who goes abroad as I have done, will always have opportunities enough of knowing the world, without troubling his head with Socrates, or any such fellows.'— 'Friend,' cries Adams, 'if a man would sail round the world, and anchor in every harbour of it, without learning, he would return home as ignorant as he went out.' 'Lord help you,' answered the host, 'there was my boatswain, poor fellow! he

1 The eastern part of the Mediterranean was called the Levant, but Adams confuses it with the root meaning of the word.

2 Present the character of.

3 See Cicero's *Tusculan Disputations* 4.37.80, where the story is cited.

could scarce either write or read, and yet he would navigate a ship with any master of a man of war; and a very pretty knowledge of trade he had too.' 'Trade,' answered Adams, 'as Aristotle proves in his first chapter of *Politics*,[1] is below a philosopher, and unnatural as it is managed now.' The host look'd stedfastly at Adams, and after a minute's silence asked him 'if he was one of the writers of the *Gazetteers*?[2] for I have heard,' says he, 'they are writ by parsons.' '*Gazetteers*!' answer'd Adams 'What is that?' 'It is a dirty news-paper,' replied the host, 'which hath been given away all over the nation for these many years to abuse trade and honest men, which I would not suffer to lie on my table, tho' it hath been offered me for nothing.' 'Not I truly,' said Adams, 'I never write any thing but sermons, and I assure you I am no enemy to trade, whilst it is consistent with honesty; nay, I have always looked on the tradesman, as a very valuable member of society, and perhaps inferior to none but the man of learning.' 'No, I believe he is not, nor to him neither,' answered the host. 'Of what use would learning be in a country without trade? What would all you parsons do to clothe your backs and feed your bellies? Who fetches you your silks and your linens, and your wines, and all the other necessaries of life? I speak chiefly with regard to the sailors.' 'You should say the extravagancies of life,' replied the parson, 'but admit they were the necessaries, there is something more necessary than life it self, which is provided by learning; I mean the learning of the clergy. Who clothes you with piety, meekness, humility, charity, patience, and all the other Christian virtues? Who feeds your souls with the milk of brotherly love, and diets them with all the dainty food of holiness, which at once cleanses them of all impure carnal affections, and fattens them with the truly rich spirit of grace?—Who doth this?' 'Ay, who indeed!' cries the host; 'for I do not remember ever to have seen any such clothing or such feeding. And so in the mean time, master, my service to you.' Adams was going to answer with some severity, when Joseph

---

1 *Politics* 1.3.23 and 4.5.

2 The *Daily Gazetteer* was founded in 1735 and published by Samuel Richardson until 1746. It was Walpole's main propaganda paper and many copies were distributed free.

and Fanny returned, and pressed his departure so eagerly, that he would not refuse them; and so grasping his crabstick, he took leave of his host, (neither of them being so well pleased with each other as they had been at their first sitting down together) and with Joseph and Fanny, who both exprest much impatience, departed; and now all together renewed their journey.

BOOK III

CHAPTER I

Matter prefatory in praise of biography.

NOTWITHSTANDING the preference which may be vulgarly given to the authority of those romance-writers, who intitle their books, the History of England, the History of France, of Spain, &c. it is most certain, that truth is only to be found in the works of those who celebrate the lives of great men, and are commonly called biographers, as the others should indeed be termed topographers or chorographers:[1] words which might well mark the distinction between them; it being the business of the latter chiefly to describe countries and cities, which, with the assistance of maps, they do pretty justly, and may be depended upon: but as to the actions and characters of men, their writings are not quite so authentic, of which there needs no other proof than those eternal contradictions, occurring between two topographers who undertake the history of the same country: for instance, between my Lord Clarendon and Mr. Whitlock, between Mr. Echard and Rapin, and many others;[2] where facts being set forth in a different light, every reader believes as he pleases, and indeed the more judicious and suspicious very justly esteem the whole as no other than a romance, in which the writer hath indulged a happy and fertile invention. But tho' these widely differ in the narrative of facts; some ascribing victory to the one, and others to the other party: some representing the same man as a rogue, to whom others give a great and honest character, yet all agree in the scene where the fact is supposed to have happened; and where the person, who is both a rogue, and an honest man, lived. Now with us biographers the case is different, the facts we deliver may be relied on, tho' we often mistake the age and country wherein they happened: for tho' it may be worth the examination of critics, whether the shepherd Chrysostom,

1 Local geographers.

2 Whereas Edward Hyde, Earl of Clarendon (1609–74), and Laurence Echard (1670?–1730) favoured the Royalist side in their histories, Bulstode Whitelocke (1605–75) and Paul de Rapin de Thoyras (1661–1725) wrote in defence of the Puritans.

who, as Cervantes informs us, died for love of the fair Marcella, who hated him, was ever in Spain, will any one doubt but that such a silly fellow hath really existed? Is there in the world such a sceptic as to disbelieve the madness of Cardenio, the perfidy of Ferdinand, the impertinent curiosity of Anselmo, the weakness of Camilla, the irresolute friendship of Lothario;[1] tho' perhaps as to the time and place where those several persons lived, that good historian may be deplorably deficient: but the most known instance of this kind is in the true history of Gil-Blas,[2] where the inimitable biographer hath made a notorious blunder in the country of Dr. Sangrado, who used his patients as a vintner doth his wine-vessels, by letting out their blood, and filling them up with water. Doth not every one, who is the least versed in physical[3] history, know that Spain was not the country in which this doctor lived? The same writer hath likewise erred in the country of his arch-bishop, as well as that of those great personages whose understandings were too sublime to taste any thing but tragedy, and in many others. The same mistakes may likewise be observed in Scarron,[4] the *Arabian Nights*, the *History of Marianne* and *Le Paisan Parvenu*,[5] and perhaps some few other writers of this class, whom I have not read, or do not at present recollect; for I would by no means be thought to comprehend those persons of surprising genius, the authors of immense romances, or the modern novel and *Atalantis* writers;[6] who without any assistance from nature or history, record persons who never were, or will be, and facts which

1 See *Don Quixote* 1.2.4-6, 1.3.9-13, and 1.4.6-8.

2 *L'Histoire de Gil Blas de Santillane*, a popular picaresque novel by Alain René Le Sage, appeared in 1715-35. A translation by Tobias Smollett was published in 1749. In the following passage, Fielding refers to Dr. Sangrado, whose two curative principles were copious bleedings and a diet of warm water (2.3-5); the Archbishop of Granada (7.2-4); and the "great personages" who frequent the literary salon of the Marchioness de Chaves (4.8).

3 Medical.

4 Paul Scarron, author of the comic romance *Le Roman comique* (1651-57).

5 *La Vie de Marianne* (1731-42) and *Le Paysan parvenu* (1734-36), novels by Pierre Carlet de Chamblain de Marivaux.

6 Mrs. Mary de la Rivière Manley wrote a scandalous roman à clef called *Secret Memoirs and Manners of Several Persons of Quality, of both Sexes. From the New Atalantis* (1709) exposing the Whig ministry.

never did nor possibly can happen: whose heroes are of their own creation, and their brains the chaos whence all their materials are collected. Not that such writers deserve no honour; so far otherwise, that perhaps they merit the highest: for what can be nobler than to be as an example of the wonderful extent of human genius. One may apply to them what Balzac says of Aristotle, that they are *a second nature*;[1] for they have no communication with the first; by which authors of an inferiour class, who can not stand alone, are obliged to support themselves as with crutches; but these of whom I am now speaking, seem to be possessed of *those stilts*, which the excellent Voltaire tells us in his letters *carry the genius far off, but with an irregular pace*.[2] Indeed far out of the sight of the reader,

> Beyond the realm of Chaos and old Night.[3]

But, to return to the former class, who are contented to copy nature, instead of forming originals from the confused heap of matter in their own brains; is not such a book as that which records the atchievements of the renowned Don Quixotte, more worthy the name of a history than even Mariana's;[4] for whereas the latter is confined to a particular period of time, and to a particular nation; the former is the history of the world in general, at least that part which is polished by laws, arts and sciences; and of that from the time it was first polished to this day; nay and forwards, as long as it shall so remain.

I shall now proceed to apply these observations to the work before us; for indeed I have set them down principally to obviate some constructions, which the good-nature of mankind, who are always forward to see their friends' virtues recorded,

---

1 Jean-Louis Guez de Balzac, in the second of *Deux Discours envoyez à Rome* (1627).

2 Voltaire's reference, in Letter 18 of his *Letters Concerning the English Nation*, trans. J. Lockman (1733), is to the faults and virtues of the figurative style of English tragedy.

3 A reworking of Milton's *Paradise Lost* 1.542-43: "A shout that tore Hell's concave, and beyond / Frighted the reign of Chaos and old Night."

4 *Historiae de Rebus Hispaniae* (1592), by Juan de Mariana. Fielding owned a copy of the 1699 English translation by John Stevens.

may put to particular parts. I question not but several of my readers will know the lawyer in the stage-coach, the moment they hear his voice. It is likewise odds, but the wit and the prude meet with some of their acquaintance, as well as all the rest of my characters. To prevent therefore any such malicious applications, I declare here once for all, I describe not men, but manners; not an individual, but a species. Perhaps it will be answered, Are not the characters then taken from life? To which I answer in the affirmative; nay, I believe I might aver, that I have writ little more than I have seen. The lawyer is not only alive, but hath been so these 4000 years, and I hope G— will indulge his life as many yet to come. He hath not indeed confined himself to one profession, one religion, or one country; but when the first mean selfish creature appeared on the human stage, who made self the centre of the whole creation; would give himself no pain, incur no danger, advance no money to assist, or preserve his fellow-creatures; then was our lawyer born; and whilst such a person as I have described, exists on earth, so long shall he remain upon it. It is therefore doing him little honour, to imagine he endeavours to mimick some little obscure fellow, because he happens to resemble him in one particular feature, or perhaps in his profession; whereas his appearance in the world is calculated for much more general and noble purposes; not to expose one pitiful wretch, to the small and contemptible circle of his acquaintance; but to hold the glass to thousands in their closets, that they may contemplate their deformity, and endeavour to reduce it, and thus by suffering private mortification may avoid public shame. This places the boundary between, and distinguishes the satirist from the libeller; for the former privately corrects the fault for the benefit of the person, like a parent; the latter publickly exposes the person himself, as an example to others, like an executioner.

There are besides little circumstances to be considered, as the drapery of a picture, which tho' fashion varies at different times, the resemblance of the countenance is not by those means diminished. Thus, I believe, we may venture to say, Mrs. Tow-wouse is coeval with our lawyer, and tho' perhaps during the changes, which so long an existence must have passed through, she may in her turn have stood behind the bar at an inn, I will not scruple to affirm, she hath likewise in the revolution of ages sat on a throne. In short where extreme turbulency of temper, avarice, and an insensibility of human misery, with a degree of hypocrisy, have united in a female composition, Mrs. Tow-wouse was that woman; and where a good inclination eclipsed by a poverty of spirit and understanding, hath glimmer'd forth in a man, that man hath been no other than her sneaking husband.

I shall detain my reader no longer than to give him one caution more of an opposite kind: for as in most of our particular characters we mean not to lash individuals, but all of the like sort; so in our general descriptions, we mean not universals, but would be understood with many exceptions: for instance, in our description of high people, we cannot be intended to include such, as whilst they are an honour to their high rank, by a well-guided condescension, make their superiority as easy as possible, to those whom fortune chiefly hath placed below them. Of this number I could name a peer[1] no less elevated by nature than by fortune, who whilst he wears the noblest ensigns of honour on his person, bears the truest stamp of dignity on his mind, adorned with greatness, enriched with knowledge, and embelished with genius. I have seen this man relieve with generosity, while he hath conversed with freedom, and be to the same person a patron and a companion. I could name a commoner[2] raised higher above the multitude by superiour talents, than is in the power of his prince to exalt him; whose behaviour to those he hath obliged is more amiable than the obligation itself, and who is so great a master of affability, that if he could divest himself of an inherent greatness in his manner, would often make the lowest of his acquaintance forget who was the master of that palace, in which they are so courteously entertained. These are pictures which must be, I

---

1 Probably Philip Dormer Stanhope, fourth Earl of Chesterfield (1694-1773), who had earlier been Fielding's patron and at the time was a leading figure against Walpole.

2 Ralph Allen (1693-1764), founder of the British postal service, philanthropist, patron, and one of the models for Squire Allworthy of *Tom Jones*.

believe, known: I declare they are taken from the life, and not intended to exceed it. By those high people therefore whom I have described, I mean a set of wretches, who while they are a disgrace to their ancestors, whose honours and fortunes they inherit, (or perhaps a greater to their mother, for such degeneracy is scarce credible) have the insolence to treat those with disregard, who are at least equal to the founders of their own splendor. It is, I fancy, impossible to conceive a spectacle more worthy of our indignation, than that of a fellow who is not only a blot in the escutcheon of a great family, but a scandal to the human species, maintaining a supercilious behaviour to men who are an honour to their nature, and a disgrace to their fortune.

And now, reader, taking these hints along with you, you may, if you please, proceed to the sequel of this our true history.

CHAPTER II

A night-scene, wherein several wonderful adventures befel Adams and his fellow-travellers.

It was so late when our travellers left the inn or ale-house, (for it might be called either) that they had not travelled many miles before night overtook them, or met them, which you please. The reader must excuse me if I am not particular as to the way they took; for as we are now drawing near the seat of the Boobies; and as that is a ticklish name, which malicious persons may apply according to their evil inclinations to several worthy country squires, a race of men whom we look upon as entirely inoffensive, and for whom we have an adequate regard, we shall lend no assistance to any such malicious purposes.

Darkness had now overspread the hemisphere, when Fanny whispered Joseph, 'that she begged to rest herself a little, for that she was so tired, she could walk no farther.' Joseph immediately prevailed with Parson Adams, who was as brisk as a bee, to stop. He had no sooner seated himself, than he lamented the loss of his dear Æschylus; but was a little comforted, when reminded, that if he had it in his possession, he could not see to read.

The sky was so clouded, that not a star appeared. It was indeed, according to Milton, darkness visible.[1] This was a circumstance however very favourable to Joseph; for Fanny, not suspicious of being[2] overseen by Adams, gave a loose to her passion, which she had never done before; and reclining her head on his bosom, threw her arm carelesly round him, and suffered him to lay his cheek close to hers. All this infused such happiness into Joseph, that he would not have changed his turf for the finest down in the finest palace in the universe.

Adams sat at some distance from the lovers, and being unwilling to disturb them, applied himself to meditation; in which he had not spent much time, before he discovered a light at some distance, that seemed approaching towards him. He immediately hailed it, but to his sorrow and surprize it stopped for a moment and then disappeared. He then called to Joseph, asking him, 'if he had not seen the light.' Joseph answered, 'he had.' 'And did you not mark how it vanished? (returned he) tho' I am not afraid of ghosts, I do not absolutely disbelieve them.'

He then entered into a meditation on those unsubstantial beings, which was soon interrupted, by several voices which he thought almost at his elbow, tho' in fact they were not so extremely near. However, he could distinctly hear them agree on the murther of any one they met. And a little after heard one of them say, 'he had killed a dozen since that day fortnight.'

Adams now fell on his knees, and committed himself to the care of Providence; and poor Fanny, who likewise heard those terrible words, embraced Joseph so closely, that had not he, whose ears were also open, been apprehensive on her account, he would have thought no danger which threatned only himself too dear a price for such embraces.

Joseph now drew forth his penknife, and Adams having finished his ejaculations, grasped his crabstick, his only weapon, and coming up to Joseph would have had him quit Fanny, and place her in their rear: but his advice was fruitless, she clung closer to him, not at all regarding the presence of Adams, and in

---

1 *Paradise Lost* 1.63.

2 Not expecting to be.

a soothing voice declared, 'she would die in his arms.' Joseph clasping her with inexpressible eagerness, whispered her, 'that he preferred death in hers, to life out of them.' Adams brandishing his crabstick, said, 'he despised death as much as any man,' and then repeated aloud,

> '*Est hic, est animus lucis contemptor, et illum,*
> *Qui vita bene credat emi quo tendis, honorem.*'[1]

Upon this the voices ceased for a moment, and then one of them called out, 'D—n you, who is there?' To which Adams was prudent enough to make no reply; and of a sudden he observed half a dozen lights, which seemed to rise all at once from the ground, and advance briskly towards him. This he immediately concluded to be an apparition, and now beginning to conceive that the voices were of the same kind, he called out, 'In the name of the L—d what would'st thou have?' He had no sooner spoke, than he heard one of the voices cry out, 'D—n them, here they come;' and soon after heard several hearty blows, as if a number of men had been engaged at quarterstaff. He was just advancing towards the place of combat, when Joseph catching him by the skirts, begged him that they might take the opportunity of the dark, to convey away Fanny from the danger which threatned her. He presently[2] complied, and Joseph lifting up Fanny, they all three made the best of their way, and without looking behind them or being overtaken, they had travelled full two miles, poor Fanny not once complaining of being tired; when they saw far off several lights scattered at a small distance from each other, and at the same time found themselves on the descent of a very steep hill. Adams's foot slipping, he instantly disappeared, which greatly frightned both Joseph and Fanny; indeed, if the light had permitted them to see it, they would scarce have refrained laughing to see the parson rolling down the hill, which he did from top to bottom, without receiving any harm. He then

1 "Here is a spirit that scorns the light [life], and believes the honour which you seek to be well bought with a life" (Virgil, *Aeneid* 9.205-06).

2 Immediately, at once.

hollowed as loud as he could, to inform them of his safety, and relieve them from the fears which they had conceived for him. Joseph and Fanny halted some time, considering what to do; at last they advanced a few paces, where the declivity seemed least steep; and then Joseph taking his Fanny in his arms, walked firmly down the hill, without making a false step, and at length landed her at the bottom, where Adams soon came to them.

Learn hence, my fair countrywomen, to consider your own weakness, and the many occasions on which the strength of a man may be useful to you; and duly weighing this, take care, that you match not yourselves with the spindle-shanked beaus and *petit maîtres*[1] of the age, who instead of being able like Joseph Andrews, to carry you in lusty arms through the rugged ways and downhill steeps of life, will rather want to support their feeble limbs with your strength and assistance.

Our travellers now moved forwards, whither the nearest light presented itself, and having crossed a common field, they came to a meadow, whence they seemed to be at a very little distance from the light, when, to their grief, they arrived at the banks of a river. Adams here made a full stop, and declared he could swim, but doubted how it was possible to get Fanny over; to which Joseph answered, 'if they walked along its banks they might be certain of soon finding a bridge, especially as by the number of lights they might be assured a parish was near.' 'Odso, that's true indeed,' said Adams, 'I did not think of that.' Accordingly Joseph's advice being taken, they passed over two meadows, and came to a little orchard, which led them to a house. Fanny begged of Joseph to knock at the door, assuring him, 'she was so weary that she could hardly stand on her feet.' Adams who was foremost performed this ceremony, and the door being immediately opened, a plain kind of a man appeared at it; Adams acquainted him, 'that they had a young woman with them, who was so tired with her journey, that he should be much obliged to him, if he would suffer her to come in and rest herself.' The man, who saw Fanny by the light of the candle which he held in his hand, perceiving her innocent and

---

1 "Fops."

modest look, and having no apprehensions from the civil behaviour of Adams, presently answered, that the young woman was very welcome to rest herself in his house, and so were her company. He then ushered them into a very decent room, where his wife was sitting at a table; she immediately rose up, and assisted them in setting forth chairs, and desired them to sit down, which they had no sooner done, than the man of the house asked them if they would have any thing to refresh themselves with? Adams thanked him, and answered, he should be obliged to him for a cup of his ale, which was likewise chosen by Joseph and Fanny. Whilst he was gone to fill a very large jugg with this liquor, his wife told Fanny she seemed greatly fatigued, and desired her to take something stronger than ale; but she refused, with many thanks, saying it was true, she was very much tired, but a little rest she hoped would restore her. As soon as the company were all seated, Mr. Adams, who had filled himself with ale, and by publick permission had lighted his pipe; turned to the master of the house, asking him, 'if evil spirits did not use to walk in that neighbourhood?' To which receiving no answer, he began to inform him of the adventure which they had met with on the downs; nor had he proceeded far in his story, when somebody knocked very hard at the door. The company expressed some amazement, and Fanny and the good woman turned pale; her husband went forth, and whilst he was absent, which was some time, they all remained silent looking at one another, and heard several voices discoursing pretty loudly. Adams was fully persuaded that spirits were abroad, and began to meditate some exorcisms; Joseph a little inclined to the same opinion: Fanny was more afraid of men, and the good woman herself began to suspect her guests, and imagined those without were rogues belonging to their gang. At length the master of the house returned, and laughing, told Adams he had discovered his apparition; that the murderers were sheep-stealers, and the twelve persons murdered were no other than twelve sheep. Adding that the shepherds had got the better of them, had secured two, and were proceeding with them to a justice of peace. This account greatly relieved the fears of the whole company; but Adams muttered to himself, 'he was convinced of the truth of apparitions for all that.'

They now sat chearfully round the fire, 'till the master of the house having surveyed his guests, and conceiving that the cassock, which having fallen down, appeared under Adams's great-coat, and the shabby livery on Joseph Andrews, did not well suit with familiarity between them, began to entertain some suspicions, not much to their advantage: addressing himself therefore to Adams, he said, 'he preceived he was a clergyman by his dress, and supposed that honest man was his footman.' 'Sir,' answered Adams, 'I am a clergyman at your service; but as to that young man, whom you have rightly termed honest, he is at present in no body's service, he never lived in any other family than that of Lady Booby, from whence he was discharged, I assure you, for no crime.' Joseph said, 'he did not wonder the gentleman was surprised to see one of Mr. Adams's character condescend to so much goodness with a poor man.' 'Child,' said Adams, 'I should be ashamed of my cloth, if I thought a poor man, who is honest, below my notice or my familiarity. I know not how those who think otherwise, can profess themselves followers and servants of Him who made no distinction, unless, peradventure, by preferring the poor to the rich. Sir,' said he, addressing himself to the gentleman, 'these two poor young people are my parishioners, and I look on them and love them as my children. There is something singular enough in their history, but I have not now time to recount it.' The master of the house, notwithstanding the simplicity which discovered itself in Adams, knew too much of the world to give a hasty belief to professions. He was not yet quite certain that Adams had any more of the clergyman in him than his cassock. To try him therefore further, he asked him, 'if Mr. Pope had lately published any thing new?' Adams answered, 'he had heard great commendations of that poet, but that he had never read, nor knew any of his works.' 'Ho! ho!' says the gentleman to himself, 'have I caught you?' 'What,' said he, 'have you never seen his Homer?'[1] Adams answered, 'he had never read

1 Pope's celebrated translation of the *Iliad* appeared in 1715-20, the *Odyssey* (in collaboration with William Broome and Elijah Fenton) in 1725-26.

any translation of the classicks.' 'Why truly,' reply'd the gentleman, 'there is a dignity in the Greek language which I think no modern tongue can reach.' 'Do you understand Greek, sir?' said Adams hastily. 'A little, sir,' answered the gentleman. 'Do you know, sir,' cry'd Adams, 'where I can buy an Æschylus? an unlucky misfortune lately happened to mine.' Æschylus was beyond the gentleman, tho' he knew him very well by name; he therefore returning back to Homer, asked Adams 'what part of the *Iliad* he thought most excellent.' Adams return'd, 'his question would be properer, what kind of beauty was the chief in poetry, for that Homer was equally excellent in them all.

'And indeed,' continued he, 'what Cicero says of a complete orator, may well be applied to a great poet; *He ought to comprehend all perfections.*[1] Homer did this in the most excellent degree; it is not without reason therefore that the philosopher, in the 22d chapter of his *Poeticks*, mentions him by no other appellation than that of *the poet*:[2] He was the father of the drama, as well as the epic: not of tragedy only, but of comedy also; for his *Margites*, which is deplorably lost, bore, says Aristotle, the same analogy to comedy, as his *Odyssey* and *Iliad* to tragedy.[3] To him therefore we owe Aristophanes, as well Euripides, Sophocles, and my poor Æschylus. But if you please we will confine ourselves (at least for the present) to the *Iliad*, his noblest work; tho' neither Aristotle, nor Horace give it the preference, as I remember, to the *Odyssey*. First then as to his subject, can any thing be more simple, and at the same time more noble? He is rightly praised by the first of those judicious critics, for not chusing the whole war,[4] which, tho' he says, it hath a compleat beginning and end, would have been too great for the understanding to comprehend at one view. I have therefore often wondered why so correct a writer as Horace should in his epistle to Lollius call him the *Trojani belli scrip-*

1 *De Oratore* 1.6.

2 In the *Poetics* 22.9, Aristotle refers to Homer as "the poet."

3 *Poetics* 4. Compare the opening remarks in Fielding's Preface.

4 *Poetics* 23. In his discourse, Adams' order of topics is derived from Aristotle's arrangement of tragedy into the following parts: plot, character, diction, thought, melody, and spectacle.

torem.[1] Secondly, his action, termed by Aristotle *pragmaton systasis*;[2] is it possible for the mind of man to conceive an idea of such perfect unity, and at the same time so replete with greatness? And here I must observe what I do not remember to have seen noted by any, the *harmotton*,[3] that agreement of his action to his subject: for as the subject is anger, how agreeable is his action, which is war? from which every incident arises, and to which every episode immediately relates. Thirdly, his manners,[4] which Aristotle places second in his description of the several parts of tragedy, and which he says are included in the action; I am at a loss whether I should rather admire the exactness of his judgment in the nice[5] distinction, or the immensity of his imagination in their variety. For, as to the former of these, how accurately is the sedate, injured resentment of Achilles distinguished from the hot insulting passion of Agamemnon? How widely doth the brutal courage of Ajax differ from the amiable bravery of Diomedes; and the wisdom of Nestor, which is the result of long reflection and experience, from the cunning of Ulysses, the effect of art and subtilty only? If we consider their variety, we may cry out with Aristotle in his 24th chapter,[6] that no part of this divine poem is destitute of manners. Indeed I might affirm, that there is scarce a character in human nature untouched in some part or other. And as there is no passion which he is not able to describe, so is there none in his reader which he cannot raise. If he hath any superior excellence to the rest, I have been inclined to fancy it is in the pathetick. I am sure I never read with dry eyes, the two episodes, where Andromache is introduced,[7] in the former lamenting the danger, and in the latter the death of Hector. The images are so extremely tender in these, that I am convinced, the poet had the worthiest and best heart imaginable. Nor can I help observing how short Sophocles falls of the beauties of the orig-

---

1 "Writer of the Trojan War" (*Epistles* 1.2.1).
2 "Arrangement of the incidents" (*Poetics* 6).
3 "Appropriateness" or "propriety" (*Poetics* 15 and 22).
4 That is, the study of "character" (*Poetics* 6).
5 Subtle.
6 *Poetics* 24.
7 *Iliad* 6.407–39 and 24.723–45.

inal, in that imitation of the dissuasive speech of Andromache, which he hath put into the mouth of Tecmessa.[1] And yet Sophocles was the greatest genius who ever wrote tragedy, nor have any of his successors in that art, that is to say, neither Euripides nor Seneca the tragedian been able to come near him. As to his sentiments and diction, I need say nothing; the former are particularly remarkable for the utmost perfection on that head, namely propriety; and as to the latter, Aristotle, whom doubtless you have read over and over, is very diffuse.[2] I shall mention but one thing more, which that great critic in his division of tragedy calls *opsis*,[3] or the scenery, and which is as proper to the epic as to the drama, with this difference, that in the former it falls to the share of the poet, and in the latter to that of the painter. But did ever painter imagine a scene like that in the 13th and 14th *Iliads*? where the reader sees at one view the prospect of Troy, with the army drawn up before it; the Grecian army, camp, and fleet, Jupiter sitting on Mount Ida, with his head wrapt in a cloud, and a thunderbolt in his hand looking towards Thrace; Neptune driving through the sea, which divides on each side to permit his passage, and then seating himself on Mount Samos: the heavens opened, and the deities all seated on their thrones. This is sublime! This is poetry!' Adams then rapt out a hundred Greek verses, and with such a voice, emphasis and action, that he almost frighten'd the women; and as for the gentleman, he was so far from entertaining any further suspicion of Adams, that he now doubted whether he had not a bishop in his house. He ran into the most extravagant encomiums on his learning, and the goodness of his heart began to dilate to all the strangers. He said he had great compassion for the poor young woman, who looked pale and faint with her journey; and in truth he conceived a much higher opinion of her quality than it deserved. He said, he was sorry he could not accommodate them all: but if they were contented with his fire-side, he would sit up with the men, and the young woman might, if she pleased, partake his wife's bed,

---

1 *Ajax* 2.485-524.

2 *Poetics* 19.

3 *Poetics* 6. Usually translated as "spectacle."

which he advis'd her to; for that they must walk upwards of a mile to any house of entertainment, and that not very good neither. Adams, who liked his seat, his ale, his tobacco and his company, persuaded Fanny to accept this kind proposal, in which sollicitation he was seconded by Joseph. Nor was she very difficultly prevailed on; for she had slept little the last night, and not at all the preceding, so that love itself was scarce able to keep her eyes open any longer. The offer therefore being kindly accepted, the good woman produced every thing eatable in her house on the table, and the guests being heartily invited, as heartily regaled themselves, especially Parson Adams. As to the other two, they were examples of the truth of the physical[1] observation, that love, like other sweet things, is no whetter of the stomach.

Supper was no sooner ended, than Fanny at her own request retired, and the good woman bore her company. The man of the house, Adams and Joseph, who would modestly have withdrawn, had not the gentleman insisted on the contrary, drew round the fire-side, where Adams, (to use his own words) replenished his pipe, and the gentleman produced a bottle of excellent beer, being the best liquor in his house.

The modest behaviour of Joseph, with the gracefulness of his person, the character which Adams gave of him,and the friendship he seemed to entertain for him, began to work on the gentleman's affections, and raised in him a curiosity to know the singularity which Adams had mentioned in his history. This curiosity Adams was no sooner informed of, than with Joseph's consent, he agreed to gratify it, and accordingly related all he knew, with as much tenderness as was possible for the character of Lady Booby; and concluded with the long, faithful and mutual passion between him and Fanny, not concealing the meanness of her birth and education. These latter circumstances entirely cured a jealousy[2] which had lately risen in the gentleman's mind, that Fanny was the daughter of some person of fashion, and that Joseph had run away with her, and Adams was concerned in the plot. He was now enamour'd of his

1 Medical.
2 Suspicion.

guests, drank their healths with great cheerfulness, and return'd many thanks to Adams, who had spent much breath; for he was a circumstantial teller of a story.

Adams told him it was now in his power to return that favour; for his extraordinary goodness, as well as that fund of literature he was master of*, which he did not expect to find under such a roof, had raised in him more curiosity than he had ever known. 'Therefore,' said he, 'if it be not too toublesome, sir, your history, if you please.'

The gentleman answered, he could not refuse him what he had so much right to insist on; and after some of the common apologies, which are the usual preface to a story, he thus began.

CHAPTER III

In which the gentleman relates the history of his life.

SIR, I am descended of a good family, and was born a gentleman. My education was liberal, and at a public school, in which I proceeded so far as to become master of the Latin, and to be tolerably versed in the Greek language. My father died when I

---

* The author hath by some been represented to have made a blunder here: for Adams had indeed shewn some learning, (say they) perhaps all the author had; but the gentleman hath shewn none, unless his approbation of Mr. Adams be such: but surely it would be preposterous in him to call it so. I have however, notwithstanding this criticism which I am told came from the mouth of a great orator,[1] in a public coffee-house, left this blunder as it stood in the first edition. I will not have the vanity to apply to any thing in this work, the observation which M. Dacier makes in her preface to her *Aristophanes: Je tiens pour une maxime constante qu'une beauté médiocre plait plus generalement qu'une beauté sans défaut.*[2] Mr. Congreve hath made such another blunder in his *Love for Love*, where Tattle tells Miss Prue, *She should admire him as much for the beauty he commends in her, as if he himself was possest* of it[3] [Fielding's note].

---

1 Perhaps John "Orator" Henley (see below, p. 289, n. 3).

2 "It is my invariable maxim that a middling beauty is more generally pleasing than a faultless one," from the preface to *Le Plutus et les Nuées d'Aristophanes* (Paris, 1684), translated by Mme. Anne Lefèvre.

3 William Congreve, *Love for Love* (1695) 2.2. Fielding added this note to the second edition.

was sixteen, and left me master of myself. He bequeathed me a moderate fortune, which he intended I should not receive till I attained the age of twenty-five: for he constantly asserted that was full early enough to give up any man entirely to the guidance of his own discretion. However, as this intention was so obscurely worded in his will, that the lawyers advised me to contest the point with my trustees, I own I paid so little regard to the inclinations of my dead father, which were sufficiently certain to me, that I followed their advice, and soon succeeded: for the trustees did not contest the matter very obstinately on their side. 'Sir,' said Adams, 'may I crave the favour of your name?' The gentleman answer'd, 'his name was Wilson,' and then proceeded.

I stay'd a very little while at school after his death; for being a forward youth, I was extremely impatient to be in the world: for which I thought my parts, knowledge, and manhood thoroughly qualified me. And to this early introduction into life, without a guide, I impute all my future misfortunes; for besides the obvious mischiefs which attend this, there is one which hath not been so generally observed. The first impression which mankind receives of you, will be very difficult to eradicate. How unhappy, therefore, must it be to fix your character in life, before you can possibly know its value, or weigh the consequences of those actions which are to establish your future reputation?

A little under seventeen I left my school and went to London, with no more than six pounds in my pocket. A great sum as I then conceived; and which I was afterwards surprized to find so soon consumed.

The character I was ambitious of attaining, was that of a fine gentleman; the first requisites to which, I apprehended were to be supplied by a taylor, a periwig-maker, and some few more tradesmen, who deal in furnishing out the human body. Notwithstanding the lowness of my purse, I found credit with them more easily than I expected, and was soon equipped to my wish. This I own then agreeably surprized me; but I have since learn'd, that it is a maxim among many tradesmen at the polite end of the town to deal as largely[1] as they can, reckon as high as they can, and arrest as soon as they can.

The next qualifications, namely dancing, fencing, riding the great horse,[2] and musick, came into my head; but as they required expence and time, I comforted myself, with regard to dancing, that I had learned a little in my youth, and could walk a minuet genteelly enough; as to fencing, I thought my good-humour would preserve me from the danger of a quarrel; as to the horse, I hoped it would not be thought of; and for musick, I imagined I could easily acquire the reputation of it; for I had heard some of my school-fellows pretend to knowledge in operas, without being able to sing or play on the fiddle.

Knowledge of the town seemed another ingredient; this I thought I should arrive at by frequenting publick places. Accordingly I paid constant attendance to them all; by which means I was soon master of the fashionable phrases, learn'd to cry up the fashionable diversions, and knew the names and faces of the most fashionable men and women.

Nothing now seemed to remain but an intrigue, which I was resolved to have immediately; I mean the reputation of it; and indeed I was so successful, that in a very short time I had half a dozen with the finest women in town.

At these words Adams fetched a deep groan, and then blessing himself, cry'd out, *Good Lord! What wicked times these are?*

Not so wicked as you imagine, continued the gentleman; for I assure you, they were all vestal virgins for any thing which I knew to the contrary. The reputation of intriguing with them was all I sought, and was what I arriv'd at: and perhaps I only flattered myself even in that; for very probably the persons to whom I shewed their billets, knew as well as I, that they were counterfeits, and that I had written them to myself.

'WRITE *letters to yourself!*' said Adams staring!

O sir, answered the gentleman, *It is the very error of the times.*[3]

---

1 Freely.

2 The art of horsemanship in conformity with certain principles and rules.

3 Among other plays, Congreve's *Way of the World* (1700) and Fielding's *The Old Debauchees* (1732) include such letters. It has also been suggested that Fielding is playfully recalling an anecdote of this nature about the Reverend William Young, generally accepted as the original of Parson Adams.

Half our modern plays have one of these characters in them. It is incredible the pains I have taken, and the absurd methods I employed to traduce the character of women of distinction. When another had spoken in raptures of any one, I have answered, 'D—n her, she! We shall have her at H—d's[1] very soon.' When he hath reply'd, 'he thought her virtuous,' I have answered, 'Ay, thou wilt always think a woman virtuous, till she is in the streets, but you and I, Jack or Tom, (turning to another in company) know better.' At which I have drawn a paper out of my pocket, perhaps a taylor's bill, and kissed it, crying at the same time, *By Gad I was once fond of her.*

'Proceed, if you please, but do not swear any more,' said Adams.

Sir, said the gentleman, I ask your pardon. Well, sir, in this course of life I continued full three years,—'What course of life?' answered Adams; 'I do not remember you have yet mentioned any.' —Your remark is just, said the gentleman smiling, I should rather have said, in this course of doing nothing. I remember some time afterwards I wrote the journal of one day, which would serve, I believe, as well for any other, during the whole time; I will endeavour to repeat it to you.

In the morning I arose, took my great stick, and walked out in my green frock with my hair in papers, (*a groan from Adams*) and sauntered about till ten.

Went to the auction; told Lady —— she had a dirty face; laughed heartily at something Captain —— said; I can't remember what, for I did not very well hear it; whispered Lord ——; bowed to the Duke of ——; and was going to bid for a snuff-box; but did not, for fear I should have had it.

From	2	to	4,	drest myself.	A groan.
	4	to	6,	dined.	A groan.
	6	to	8,	coffee-house.	
	8	to	9,	Drury-Lane play-house.	
	9	to	10,	Lincoln's-Inn-Fields.[2]	
	10	to	12,	drawing-room.	A great groan.

1 Mother Haywood's brothel in Covent Garden.

2 The site of another theatre.

At all which places nothing happened worth remark. At which Adams said with some vehemence, 'Sir, this is below the life of an animal, hardly above vegetation; and I am surprized what could lead a man of your sense into it.' What leads us into more follies than you imagine, doctor, answered the gentleman; vanity: for as contemptible a creature as I was, and I assure you, yourself cannot have more contempt for such a wretch than I now have, I then admir'd myself, and should have despised a person of your present appearance (you will pardon me) with all your learning, and those excellent qualities which I have remarked in you. Adams bowed, and begged him to proceed. After I had continued two years in this course of life, said the gentleman, an accident happened which obliged me to change the scene. As I was one day at St. James's coffee-house,[1] making very free with the character of a young lady of quality, an officer of the guards who was present, thought proper to give me the lye. I answered, I might possibly be mistaken; but I intended to tell no more than the truth. To which he made no reply, but by a scornful sneer. After this I observed a strange coldness in all my acquaintance; none of them spoke to me first, and very few returned me even the civility of a bow. The company I used to dine with, left me out, and within a week I found myself in as much solitude at St. James's, as if I had been in a desart. An honest elderly man, with a great hat and long sword, at last told me, he had a compassion for my youth, and therefore advised me to shew the world I was not such a rascal as they thought me to be. I did not at first understand him: but he explained himself, and ended with telling me, if I would write a challenge to the captain, he would out of pure charity go to him with it. 'A very charitable person truly!' cried Adams. I desired till the next day, continued the gentleman, to consider on it, and retiring to my lodgings, I weighed the consequences on both sides as fairly as I could. On the one, I saw the risk of this alternative, either losing my own life, or having on my hands the blood of a man with whom I was not in the least angry. I soon determined that the good which appeared

1 A favourite meeting place for Whigs and Guards officers near St. James's Palace.

on the other, was not worth this hazard. I therefore resolved to quit the scene, and presently retired to the Temple,[1] where I took chambers. Here I soon got a fresh set of acquaintance, who knew nothing of what had happened to me. Indeed they were not greatly to my approbation; for the beaus of the Temple are only the shadows of the others. They are the affectation of affectation. The vanity of these is still more ridiculous, if possible, than of the others. Here I met with smart fellows who drank with lords they did not know, and intrigued with women they never saw. Covent-Garden was now the farthest stretch of my ambition, where I shone forth in the balconies at the play-houses, visited whores, made love to orange-wenches, and damned plays. This career was soon put a stop to by my surgeon, who convinced me of the necessity of confining myself to my room for a month. At the end of which, having had leisure to reflect, I resolved to quit all further conversation with beaus and smarts of every kind, and to avoid, if possible, any occasion of returning to this place of confinement. 'I think,' said Adams, 'the advice of a month's retirement and reflection was very proper; but I should rather have expected it from a divine than a surgeon.' The gentleman smiled at Adams's simplicity, and without explaining himself farther on such an odious subject went on thus: I was no sooner perfectly restored to health, than I found my passion for women, which I was afraid to satisfy as I had done, made me very uneasy; I determined therefore to keep a mistress. Nor was I long before I fixed my choice on a young woman, who had before been kept by two gentlemen, and to whom I was recommended by a celebrated bawd. I took her home to my chambers, and made her a settlement, during cohabitation. This would perhaps have been very ill paid: however, she did not suffer me to be perplexed on that account; for before quarter-day,[2] I found her at my chambers in too familiar conversation with a young fellow

1 A complex of buildings in the old City of London housing the Inner and Middle Temple, two of the four legal societies of the Inns of Court. Fielding studied law at the Middle Temple from 1737 to 1739.

2 One of four days of the year fixed by custom for the quarterly payment of rent, etc.

who was drest like an officer, but was indeed a City[1] apprentice. Instead of excusing her inconstancy, she rapped out half a dozen oaths, and snapping her fingers at me, swore she scorned to confine herself to the best man in England. Upon this we parted, and the same bawd presently provided her another keeper. I was not so much concerned at our separation, as I found within a day or two I had reason to be for our meeting: for I was obliged to pay a second visit to my surgeon. I was now forced to do penance for some weeks, during which time I contracted an acquaintance with a beautiful young girl, the daughter of a gentleman, who after having been forty years in the army, and in all the campaigns under the Duke of Marlborough,[2] died a lieutenant on half-pay; and had left a widow with this only child, in very distrest circumstances: they had only a small pension from the government, with what little the daughter could add to it by her work; for she had great excellence at her needle. This girl was, at my first acquaintance with her, sollicited in marriage by a young fellow in good circumstances. He was apprentice to a linen-draper, and had a little fortune sufficient to set up his trade. The mother was greatly pleased with this match, as indeed she had sufficient reason. However, I soon prevented it. I represented him in so low a light to his mistress, and made so good an use of flattery, promises, and presents, that, not to dwell longer on this subject than is necessary, I prevailed with the poor girl, and convey'd her away from her mother! In a word, I debauched her.—(At which words, Adams started up, fetch'd three strides cross the room, and then replaced himself in his chair.) You are not more affected with this part of my story than myself: I assure you it will never be sufficiently repented of in my own opinion: but if you already detest it, how much more will your indignation be raised when you hear the fatal consequences of this barbarous, this villainous action? If you please therefore, I will here desist.—'By no means,' cries Adams, 'go on, I beseech you, and

1 The financial and commercial centre of London, situated within its ancient boundaries.

2 John Churchill, first Duke of Marlborough (1650-1722), under whom Fielding's father had served against the French.

Heaven grant you may sincerely repent of this and many other things you have related.'—I was now, continued the gentleman, as happy as the possession of a fine young creature, who had a good education, and was endued with many agreeable qualities, could make me. We liv'd some months with vast fondness together, without any company or conversation more than we found in one another: but this could not continue always; and tho' I still preserved a great affection for her, I began more and more to want the relief of other company, and consequently to leave her by degrees, at last, whole days to herself. She failed not to testify some uneasiness on these occasions, and complained of the melancholy life she led; to remedy which, I introduced her into the acquaintance of some other kept mistresses, with whom she used to play at cards, and frequent plays and other diversions. She had not liv'd long in this intimacy, before I perceived a visible alteration in her behaviour; all her modesty and innocence vanished by degrees, till her mind became thoroughly tainted. She affected the company of rakes, gave herself all manner of airs, was never easy but abroad, or when she had a party at my chambers. She was rapacious of money, extravagant to excess, loose in her conversation; and if ever I demurred to any of her demands, oaths, tears, and fits, were the immediate consequences. As the first raptures of fondness were long since over, this behaviour soon estranged my affections from her; I began to reflect with pleasure that she was not my wife, and to conceive an intention of parting with her, of which having given her a hint, she took care to prevent me the pains of turning her out of doors, and accordingly departed herself, having first broken open my escrutore,[1] and taken with her all she could find, to the amount of about 200 *l.* In the first heat of my resentment, I resolved to pursue her with all the vengeance of the law: but as she had the good luck to escape me during that ferment, my passion afterwards cooled, and having reflected that I had been the first aggressor, and had done her an injury for which I could make her no reparation, by robbing her of the innocence of her mind; and

1 A small writing-desk.

hearing at the same time that the poor old woman her mother had broke her heart, on her daughter's elopement from her, I, concluding myself her murderer ('As you very well might,' cries Adams, with a groan;) was pleased that God Almighty had taken this method of punishing me, and resolved quietly to submit to the loss. Indeed I could wish I had never heard more of the poor creature, who became in the end an abandoned profligate; and after being some years a common prostitute, at last ended her miserable life in Newgate.[1]—Here the gentleman fetch'd a deep sigh, which Mr. Adams echo'd very loudly, and both continued silent looking on each other for some minutes. At last the gentleman proceeded thus: I had been perfectly constant to this girl, during the whole time I kept her: but she had scarce departed before I discovered more marks of her infidelity to me, than the loss of my money. In short, I was forced to make a third visit to my surgeon, out of whose hands I did not get a hasty discharge.

I now forswore all future dealings with the sex, complained loudly that the pleasure did not compensate the pain, and railed at the beautiful creatures, in as gross language as Juvenal himself formerly reviled them in.[2] I looked on all the town-harlots with a detestation not easy to be conceived, their persons appeared to me as painted palaces inhabited by disease and death: nor could their beauty make them more desirable objects in my eyes, than gilding could make me covet a pill, or golden plates a coffin. But tho' I was no longer the absolute slave, I found some reasons to own myself still the subject of love. My hatred for women decreased daily; and I am not positive but time might have betrayed me again to some common harlot, had I not been secured by a passion for the charming Saphira; which having once entered upon, made a violent progress in my heart. Saphira was wife to a man of fashion and gallantry, and one who seemed, I own, every way worthy of her affections, which however he had not the reputation of having. She was indeed a *coquette achevée*.[3] 'Pray sir,' says Adams, 'what is

---

1 The main prison of London.

2 The Roman satirist Juvenal (AD 60?–140?), in his *Sixth Satire*, fiercely attacks women.

3 " An accomplished flirt."

a coquette? I have met with the word in French authors, but never could assign any idea to it. I believe it is the same with *une sotte*, Anglicé *a fool*.' Sir, answer'd the gentleman, perhaps you are not much mistaken: but as it is a particular kind of folly, I will endeavour to describe it. Were all creatures to be ranked in the order of creation, according to their usefulness, I know few animals that would not take place of a coquette; nor indeed hath this creature much pretence to any thing beyond instinct: for tho' sometimes we might imagine it was animated by the passion of vanity, yet far the greater part of its actions fall beneath even that low motive; for instance, several absurd gestures and tricks, infinitely more foolish than what can be observed in the most ridiculous birds and beasts, and which would persuade the beholder that the silly wretch was aiming at our contempt. Indeed its characteristick is affectation, and this led and governed by whim only: for as beauty, wisdom, wit, good-nature, politeness and health are sometimes affected by this creature; so are ugliness, folly, nonsense, ill-nature, ill-breeding and sickness likewise put on by it in their turn. Its life is one constant lye, and the only rule by which you can form any judgment of them is, that they are never what they seem. If it was possible for a coquette to love (as it is not, for if ever it attains this passion, the coquette ceases instantly) it would wear the face of indifference if not of hatred to the beloved object; you may therefore be assured, when they endeavour to persuade you of their liking, that they are indifferent to you at least. And indeed this was the case of my Saphira, who no sooner saw me in the number of her admirers, than she gave me what is commonly called encouragement; she would often look at me, and when she perceived me meet her eyes, would instantly take them off, discovering at the same time as much surprize and emotion as possible. These arts failed not of the success she intended; and as I grew more particular to her than the rest of her admirers, she advanced in proportion more directly to me than to the others. She affected the low voice, whisper, lisp, sigh, start, laugh, and many other indications of passion, which daily deceive thousands. When I play'd at whisk[1] with her, she would look earnestly at me, and at the same time lose deal or revoke; then burst into a ridiculous laugh, and cry, 'La! I can't imagine what I was thinking of.' To detain you no longer, after I had gone through a sufficient course of gallantry, as I thought, and was thoroughly convinced I had raised a violent passion in my mistress; I sought an opportunity of coming to an *eclaircissement*[2] with her. She avoided this as much as possible, however great assiduity at length presented me one. I will not describe all the particulars of this interview; let it suffice, that when she could no longer pretend not to see my drift, she first affected a violent surprize, and immediately after as violent a passion: she wondered what I had seen in her conduct, which could induce me to affront her in this manner: and breaking from me the first moment she could, told me, I had no other way to escape the consequence of her resentment, than by never seeing, or at least speaking to her more. I was not contented with this answer; I still pursued her, but to no purpose, and was at length convinced that her husband had the sole possession of her person, and that neither he nor any other had made any impression on her heart. I was taken off from following this *ignis fatuus*[3] by some advances which were made me by the wife of a citizen, who tho' neither very young nor handsome, was yet too agreeable to be rejected by my amorous constitution. I accordingly soon satisfy'd her, that she had not cast away her hints on a barren or cold soil; on the contrary, they instantly produced her an eager and desiring lover. Nor did she give me any reason to complain; she met the warmth she had raised with equal ardour. I had no longer a coquette to deal with, but one who was wiser than to prostitute the noble passion of love to the ridiculous lust of vanity. We presently understood one another; and as the pleasures we sought lay in a mutual gratification, we soon found and enjoyed them. I thought myself at first greatly happy in the possession of this new mistress, whose fondness would have quickly surfeited a more sickly appetite, but it had a different effect on

1 The earlier name for whist, a game of cards.
2 A fashionable word for a mutual understanding, especially between lovers.
3 "Will-o'-the-wisp."

mine; she carried my passion higher by it than youth or beauty had been able: but my happiness could not long continue uninterrupted. The apprehensions we lay under from the jealousy of her husband, gave us great uneasiness. 'Poor wretch! I pity him,' cry'd Adams. He did indeed deserve it, said the gentleman, for he loved his wife with great tenderness, and I assure you it is a great satisfaction to me that I was not the man who first seduced her affections from him. These apprehensions appeared also too well grounded; for in the end he discovered us, and procur'd witnesses of our caresses. He then prosecuted me at law, and recovered 3000 *l.* damages, which much distressed my fortune to pay: and what was worse, his wife being divorced, came upon my hands. I led a very uneasy life with her; for besides that my passion was now much abated, her excessive jealousy was very troublesome. At length death delivered me from an inconvenience, which the consideration of my having been the author of her misfortunes, would never suffer me to take any other method of discarding.

I now bad adieu to love, and resolved to pursue other less dangerous and expensive pleasures. I fell into the acquaintance of a set of jolly companions, who slept all day and drank all night: fellows who might rather be said to consume time than to live. Their best conversation was nothing but noise: singing, hollowing, wrangling, drinking, toasting, sp—wing,[1] smoking, were the chief ingredients of our entertainment. And yet bad as these were, they were more tolerable than our graver scenes, which were either excessive tedious narratives of dull common matters of fact, or hot disputes about trifling matters, which commonly ended in a wager. This way of life the first serious reflection put a period to, and I became member of a club frequented by young men of great abilities.[2] The bottle was now only called in to the assistance of our conversation, which rolled on the deepest points of philosophy. These gentlemen

---

1 Spewing (vomiting).

2 Fielding seems to be satirizing the so-called freethinkers, whose contradictory principles included Deistic views (the "Rule of Right") and the moral relativism of the seventeenth-century English philosopher Thomas Hobbes ("there was nothing absolutely good or evil in itself").

were engaged in a search after truth, in the pursuit of which they threw aside all the prejudices of education, and governed themselves only by the infallible guide of human reason. This great guide, after having shewn them the falshood of that very antient but simple[1] tenet, that there is such a being as a Deity in the universe, helped them to establish in his stead a certain *Rule of Right*, by adhering to which they all arrived at the utmost purity of morals. Reflection made me as much delighted with this society, as it had taught me to despise and detest the former. I began now to esteem myself a being of a higher order than I had ever before conceived, and was the more charmed with this *Rule of Right*, as I really found in my own nature nothing repugnant to it. I held in utter contempt all persons who wanted any other inducement to virtue besides her intrinsick beauty and excellence; and had so high an opinion of my present companions, with regard to their morality, that I would have trusted them with whatever was nearest and dearest to me. Whilst I was engaged in this delightful dream, two or three accidents happen'd successively, which at first much surprized me. For, one of our greatest philosophers, or *Rule of Right-men* withdrew himself from us, taking with him the wife of one of his most intimate friends. Secondly, another of the same society left the club without remembring to take leave of his bail.[2] A third having borrowed a sum of money of me, for which I received no security, when I asked him to repay it, absolutely denied the loan. These several practices, so inconsistent with our golden rule, made me begin to suspect its infallibility; but when I communicated my thoughts to one of the club, he said 'there was nothing absolutely good or evil in itself; that actions were denominated good or bad by the circumstances of the agent. That possibly the man who ran away with his neighbour's wife might be one of very good inclinations, but over-prevailed on by the violence of an unruly passion, and in other particulars might be a very worthy member of society: that if the beauty of any woman created in him an uneasiness, he had

---

1 Naive.

2 Another member had apparently provided financial surety for his friend concerning club responsibilities.

a right from nature to relieve himself;' with many other things, which I then detested so much, that I took leave of the society that very evening, and never returned to it again. Being now reduced to a state of solitude, which I did not like, I became a great frequenter of the play-houses, which indeed was always my favourite diversion, and most evenings past away two or three hours behind the scenes, where I met with several poets,[1] with whom I made engagements at the taverns. Some of the players were likewise of our parties. At these meetings we were generally entertain'd by the poets with reading their performances, and by the players with repeating their parts: upon which occasions, I observed the gentleman who furnished our entertainment, was commonly the best pleased of the company; who, tho' they were pretty civil to him to his face, seldom failed to take the first opportunity of his absence to ridicule him. Now I made some remarks, which probably are too obvious to be worth relating. 'Sir,' says Adams, 'your remarks if you please.' First then, says he, I concluded that the general observation, that wits are most inclined to vanity, is not true. Men are equally vain of riches, strength, beauty, honours, &c. But, these appear of themselves to the eyes of the beholders, whereas the poor wit is obliged to produce his performance to shew you his perfection, and on his readiness to do this that vulgar opinion I have before mentioned is grounded: but doth not the person who expends vast sums in the furniture of his house, or the ornaments of his person, who consumes much time, and employs great pains in dressing himself, or who thinks himself paid for self-denial, labour, or even villany by a title or a ribbon, sacrifice as much to vanity as the poor wit, who is desirous to read you his poem or his play? My second remark was, that vanity is the worst of passions, and more apt to contaminate the mind than any other: for as selfishness is much more general than we please to allow it, so it is natural to hate and envy those who stand between us and the good we desire. Now in lust and ambition these are few; and even in avarice we find many who are no obstacles to our pursuits; but the vain man seeks pre-

1 Playwrights.

eminence; and every thing which is excellent or praise-worthy in another, renders him the mark of his antipathy. Adams now began to fumble in his pockets, and soon cried out, 'O la! I have it not about me.'—Upon this the gentleman asking him what he was searching for, he said he searched after a sermon, which he thought his master-piece, against vanity. 'Fie upon it, fie upon it,' cries he, 'why do I ever leave that sermon out of my pocket? I wish it was within five miles, I would willingly fetch it, to read it to you.' The gentleman answered, that there was no need, for he was cured of the passion. 'And for that very reason,' quoth Adams, 'I would read it, for I am confident you would admire it: indeed, I have never been a greater enemy to any passion than that silly one of vanity.' The gentleman smiled, and proceeded—From this society I easily past to that of the gamesters, where nothing remarkable happened, but the finishing my fortune, which those gentlemen soon helped me to the end of. This opened scenes of life hitherto unknown; poverty and distress with their horrid train of duns, attorneys, bailiffs, haunted me day and night. My clothes grew shabby, my credit bad, my friends and acquaintance of all kinds cold. In this situation the strangest thought imaginable came into my head; and what was this, but to write a play? for I had sufficient leisure; fear of bailiffs confined me every day to my room; and having always had a little inclination and something of a genius that way, I set myself to work, and within few months produced a piece of five acts, which was accepted of at the theatre. I remembred to have formerly taken tickets of other poets for their benefits long before the appearance of their performances, and resolving to follow a precedent, which was so well suited to my present circumstances; I immediately provided myself with a large number of little papers.[1] Happy indeed would be the state of poetry, would these tickets pass current at the bakehouse, the ale-house, and the chandler's-shop: but alas! far otherwise; no taylor will take them in payment for buckram, stays, stay-tape; nor no bailiff for civility-money.[2] They are

1 As a playwright had to guarantee the theatre's expenses for the first night of the performance, he would often personally sell tickets in advance of the production.

2 A tip to a jailer to ensure good treatment while under arrest.

indeed no more than a passport to beg with, a certificate that the owner wants five shillings, which induces well-disposed Christians to charity. I now experienced what is worse than poverty, or rather what is the worst consequence of poverty, I mean attendance and dependance on the great. Many a morning have I waited hours in the cold parlours of men of quality, where after seeing the lowest rascals in lace and embroidery, the pimps and buffoons in fashion admitted, I have been sometimes told on sending in my name, that my lord could not possibly see me this morning: a sufficient assurance that I should never more get entrance into that house. Sometimes I have been at last admitted, and the great man hath thought proper to excuse himself, by telling me he was *tied up*. '*Tied up*,' says Adams, 'pray what's that?' Sir, says the gentleman, the profit which booksellers allowed authors for the best works, was so very small, that certain men of birth and fortune some years ago, who were the patrons of wit and learning, thought fit to encourage them farther, by entring into voluntary subscriptions for their encouragement. Thus Prior, Rowe, Pope, and some other men of genius, received large sums for their labours from the public.[1] This seemed so easy a method of getting money, that many of the lowest scriblers of the times ventured to publish their works in the same way; and many had the assurance to take in subscriptions for what was not writ, nor ever intended. Subscriptions in this manner growing infinite, and a kind of tax on the public; some persons finding it not so easy a task to discern good from bad authors, or to know what genius was worthy encouragement, and what was not, to prevent the expence of subscribing to so many, invented a method to excuse themselves from all subscriptions whatever; and this was to receive a small sum of money in consideration of giving a large one if ever they subscribed; which many have done, and many more have pretended to have done, in order to silence all sollicitation. The same method was likewise taken with playhouse

1 Nicholas Rowe's *Tragedy of Jane Shore* (1714) was published by subscription, as was Matthew Prior's *Poems on Several Occasions* (1719) and Alexander Pope's *Iliad* (1715-20) and *Odyssey* (1725-26). Pope received about £9,000 for his Homer translations, which gave him financial independence.

tickets, which were no less a public grievance; and this is what they call being *tied up* from subscribing. 'I can't say but the term is apt enough, and somewhat typical,' said Adams; 'for a man of large fortune, who ties himself up, as you call it, from the encouragement of men of merit, ought to be tied up in reality.' Well, sir, says the gentleman, to return to my story. Sometimes I have received a guinea from a man of quality, given with as ill a grace as alms are generally to the meanest beggar, and purchased too with as much time spent in attendance, as, if it had been spent in honest industry, might have brought me more profit with infinitely more satisfaction. After about two months spent in this disagreeable way with the utmost mortification, when I was pluming my hopes on the prospect of a plentiful harvest from my play, upon applying to the prompter to know when it came into rehearsal, he informed me he had received orders from the managers to return me the play again; for that they could not possibly act it that season; but if I would take it and revise it against the next, they would be glad to see it again. I snatch'd it from him with great indignation, and retired to my room, where I threw myself on the bed in a fit of despair— 'You should rather have thrown yourself on your knees,' says Adams; 'for despair is sinful.' As soon, continued the gentleman, as I had indulged the first tumult of my passion, I began to consider coolly what course I should take, in a situation without friends, money, credit or reputation of any kind. After revolving many things in my mind, I could see no other possibility of furnishing myself with the miserable necessaries of life than to retire to a garret near the Temple, and commence hackney-writer to the lawyers; for which I was well qualify'd, being an excellent penman. This purpose I resolved on, and immediately put it in execution. I had an acquaintance with an attorney who had formerly transacted affairs for me, and to him I applied: but instead of furnishing me with any business, he laugh'd at my undertaking, and told me 'he was afraid I should turn his deeds into plays, and he should expect to see them on the stage.' Not to tire you with instances of this kind from others, I found that Plato himself did not hold poets in greater abhorrence[1] than these men of business do. Whenever I durst venture to a coffee-house, which was on Sundays only,[2] a whisper ran round the room, which was constantly attended with a sneer—*That's poet Wilson*: for I know not whether you have observed it, but there is a malignity in the nature of man, which when not weeded out, or at least covered by a good education and politeness, delights in making another uneasy or dissatisfied with himself. This abundantly appears in all assemblies, except those which are filled by people of fashion, and especially among the younger people of both sexes, whose birth and fortunes place them just without the polite circles; I mean the lower class of the gentry, and the higher of the mercantile world, who are in reality the worst bred part of mankind. Well, sir, whilst I continued in this miserable state, with scarce sufficient business to keep me from starving, the reputation of a poet being my bane, I accidentally became acquainted with a bookseller, who told me 'it was a pity a man of my learning and genius should be obliged to such a method of getting his livelihood; that he had a compassion for me, and if I would engage with him, he would undertake to provide handsomely for me.' A man in my circumstances, as he very well knew, had no choice. I accordingly accepted his proposal with his conditions, which were none of the most favourable, and fell to translating with all my might. I had no longer reason to lament the want of business; for he furnished me with so much, that in half a year I almost writ myself blind. I likewise contracted a distemper by my sedentary life, in which no part of my body was exercised but my right arm, which rendered me incapable of writing for a long time. This unluckily happening to delay the publication of a work, and my last performance not having sold well, the bookseller declined any further engagement, and aspersed me to his brethren as a careless, idle fellow. I had however, by having half-work'd and half-starv'd myself to death during the time I was in his service, saved a few guineas, with which I bought a lottery-ticket,[3] resolving to throw myself into

---

1 *The Republic* 2, 3, and 10.

2 Arrests for debt could not legally take place on Sunday.

3 Fielding ridiculed this form of gambling, run by the government to fund public works, in his farce *The Lottery* (1732).

Fortune's lap, and try if she would make me amends for the injuries she had done me at the gaming-table. This purchase being made left me almost pennyless; when, as if I had not been sufficiently miserable, a bailiff in woman's clothes got admittance to my chamber, whither he was directed by the bookseller. He arrested me at my taylor's suit, for thirty-five pounds; a sum for which I could not procure bail, and was therefore conveyed to his house, where I was locked up in an upper chamber. I had now neither health (for I was scarce recovered from my indispositon) liberty, money, or friends; and had abandoned all hopes, and even the desire of life. 'But this could not last long,' said Adams, 'for doubtless the taylor released you the moment he was truly acquainted with your affairs; and knew that your circumstances would not permit you to pay him.' Oh, sir, answered the gentleman, he knew that before he arrested me; nay, he knew that nothing but incapacity could prevent me paying my debts; for I had been his customer many years, had spent vast sums of money with him, and had always paid most punctually in my prosperous days: but when I reminded him of this, with assurances that if he would not molest my endeavours, I would pay him all the money I could, by my utmost labour and industry, procure, reserving only what was sufficient to preserve me alive: he answered, his patience was worn out; that I had put him off from time to time; that he wanted the money; that he had put it into a lawyer's hands; and if I did not pay him immediately, or find security, I must lie in goal and expect no mercy. 'He may expect mercy,' cries Adams starting from his chair, 'where he will find none. How can such a wretch repeat the Lord's Prayer, where the word which is translated, I know not for what reason, *trespasses*, is in the original *debts*?[1] And as surely as we do not forgive others their debts when they are unable to pay them; so surely shall we ourselves be unforgiven, when we are in no condition of paying.' He ceased, and the gentleman proceeded. While I was in this deplorable situation a former acquaintance, to whom I had communicated my lottery-ticket, found me out, and making

1 Adams notes a discrepancy between two versions of the prayer, one in the *Book of Common Prayer* and the other in the gospels' version (Matthew 6:12 and Luke 11:4).

me a visit with great delight in his countenance, shook me heartily by the hand, and wished me joy of my good fortune: 'For,' says he, 'your ticket is come up a prize of 3000 *l.*' Adams snapt his fingers at these words in an ecstasy of joy; which however did not continue long: for the gentleman thus proceeded. Alas! sir, this was only a trick of Fortune to sink me the deeper: for I had disposed of this lottery-ticket two days before to a relation, who refused lending me a shilling without it, in order to procure myself bread.[1] As soon as my friend was acquainted with my unfortunate sale, he began to revile me, and remind me of all the ill conduct and miscarriages of my life. He said, 'I was one whom Fortune could not save, if she would; that I was now ruined without any hopes of retrieval, nor must expect any pity from my friends; that it would be extreme weakness to compassionate the misfortunes of a man who ran headlong to his own destruction.' He then painted to me in as lively colours as he was able, the happiness I should have now enjoyed, had I not foolishly disposed of my ticket. I urg'd the plea of necesssity: but he made no answer to that, and began again to revile me, till I could bear it no longer, and desired him to finish his visit. I soon exchanged the bailiff's house for a prison; where, as I had not money sufficient to procure me a separate apartment, I was crouded in with a great number of miserable wretches, in common with whom I was destitute of every convenience of life, even that which all the brutes enjoy, wholesome air. In these dreadful circumstances I applied by letter to several of my old acquaintance, and such to whom I had formerly lent money without any great prospect of its being returned, for their assistance; but in vain. An excuse instead of a denial was the gentlest answer I received.—Whilst I languished in a condition too horrible to be described, and which in a land of humanity, and, what is much more Christianity, seems a strange punishment for a little inadvertency and indiscretion. Whilst I was in this condition, a fellow came into the prison, and enquiring me out deliver'd me the following letter:

1 Imprisoned debtors were legally entitled to basic subsistence, but there was no obligation on the part of jailors to feed them.

Sir,

My father, to whom you sold your ticket in the last lottery, died the same day in which it came up a prize, as you have possibly heard, and left me sole heiress of all his fortune. I am so much touched with your present circumstances, and the uneasiness you must feel at having been driven to dispose of what might have made you happy, that I must desire your acceptance of the inclosed, and am

Your humble servant,
Harriet Hearty

And what do you think was inclosed? 'I don't know,' cried Adams: 'not less than a guinea, I hope.'—Sir, it was a bank-note for 200 *l.*—'200 *l.*!' says Adams, in a rapture.—No less, I assure you, answered the gentleman; a sum I was not half so delighted with, as with the dear name of the generous girl that sent it me; and who was not only the best, but the handsomest creature in the universe; and for whom I had long had a passion, which I never durst disclose to her. I kiss'd her name a thousand times, my eyes overflowing with tenderness and gratitude, I repeated—. But not to detain you with these raptures, I immediately acquired my liberty, and having paid all my debts, departed with upwards of fifty pounds in my pocket, to thank my kind deliverer. She happened to be then out of town, a circumstance which, upon reflection, pleased me; for by that means I had an opportunity to appear before her in a more decent dress. At her return to town within a day or two, I threw myself at her feet with the most ardent acknowledgments, which she rejected with an unfeigned greatness of mind, and told me, I could not oblige her more than by never mentioning, or if possible, thinking on a circumstance which must bring to my mind an accident that might be grievous to me to think on. She proceeded thus: 'What I have done is in my own eyes a trifle, and perhaps infinitely less than would have become me to do. And if you think of engaging in any business, where a larger sum may be serviceable to you, I shall not be over-rigid, either as to the security or interest.' I endeavoured to express all the gratitude in my power to this profusion of goodness, tho' perhaps it was my enemy, and began to afflict my mind with more agonies, than all the miseries I had underwent; it affected me with severer reflections than poverty, distress, and prisons united had been able to make me feel: for, sir, these acts and professions of kindness, which were sufficient to have raised in a good heart the most violent passion of friendship to one of the same, or to age and ugliness in a different sex, came to me from a woman, a young and beautiful woman, one whose perfections I had long known; and for whom I had long conceived a violent passion, tho' with a despair, which made me endeavour rather to curb and conceal, than to nourish or acquaint her with it. In short, they came upon me united with beauty, softness, and tenderness, such bewitching smiles.—O Mr. Adams, in that moment, I lost myself, and forgetting our different situations, nor considering what return I was making to her goodness, by desiring her who had given me so much, to bestow her all, I laid gently hold on her hand, and conveying it to my lips, I prest it with inconceivable ardour; then lifting up my swimming eyes, I saw her face and neck overspread with one blush; she offered to withdraw her hand, yet not so as to deliver it from mine, tho' I held it with the gentlest force. We both stood trembling, her eyes cast on the ground, and mine stedfastly fixed on her. Good G—, what was then the condition of my soul! burning with love, desire, admiration, gratitude, and every tender passion, all bent on one charming object. Passion at last got the better of both reason and respect, and softly letting go her hand, I offered madly to clasp her in my arms; when a little recovering herself, she started from me, asking me with some shew of anger, 'if she had any reason to expect this treatment from me.' I then fell prostrate before her, and told her, 'if I had offended, my life was absolutely in her power, which I would in any manner lose for her sake. Nay, madam, (said I) you shall not be so ready to punish me, as I to suffer. I own my guilt. I detest the reflection that I would have sacrificed your happiness to mine. Believe me, I sincerely repent my ingratitude, yet believe me too, it was my passion, my unbounded passion for you, which hurried me so far; I have loved you long and tenderly; and the goodness you have shewn me, hath innocently weighed down a wretch undone before. Acquit me of all mean mercenary views, and before I take my leave of you for ever, which I am resolved instantly to do, believe me, that Fortune could have raised me to no height to which I could not have gladly lifted you. O curst be Fortune.'—'Do not,' says she, interrupting me with the sweetest voice, 'do not curse Fortune, since she hath made me happy, and if she hath put your happiness in my power, I have told you, you shall ask nothing in reason which I will refuse.' 'Madam,' said I, 'you mistake me if you imagine, as you seem, my happiness is in the power of Fortune now. You have obliged me too much already; if I have any wish, it is for some blest accident, by which I may contribute with my life to the least augmentation of your felicity. As for my self, the only happiness I can ever have, will be hearing of your's; and if Fortune will make that complete, I will forgive her all her wrongs to me.' 'You may, indeed,' answered she, smiling, 'for your own happiness must be included in mine. I have long known your worth; nay, I must confess,' said she, blushing, 'I have long discovered that passion for me you profess, notwithstanding those endeavours which I am convinced were unaffected, to conceal it; and if all I can give with reason will not suffice,—take reason away,—and now I believe you cannot ask me what I will deny.'—She uttered these words with a sweetness not to be imagined. I immediately started, my blood which lay freezing at my heart, rushed tumultuously through every vein. I stood for a moment silent, then flying to her, I caught her in my arms, no longer resisting,—and softly told her, she must give me then herself.—O sir,—can I describe her look? She remained silent and almost motionless several minutes. At last, recovering herself a little, she insisted on my leaving her, and in such a manner that I instantly obeyed: you may imagine, however, I soon saw her again.—But I ask pardon, I fear I have detained you too long in relating the particulars of the former interview. 'So far otherwise,' said Adams, licking his lips, 'that I could willingly hear it over again.' Well, sir, continued the gentleman, to be as concise as possible, within a week she consented to make me the happiest of mankind. We were married shortly after; and when I came to examine the circumstances of my wife's fortune; (which I do assure you I was not presently at leisure enough to do) I found it amounted to about six thousand pounds, most part of which lay in effects; for her father had been a wine-merchant, and she seemed willing, if I liked it, that I should carry on the same trade. I readily and too inconsiderately undertook it: for not having been bred up to the secrets of the business, and endeavouring to deal with the utmost honesty and uprightness, I soon found our fortune in a declining way, and my trade decreasing by little and little: for my wines which I never adulterated after their importation, and were sold as neat as they came over, were universally decried by the vintners,[1] to whom I could not allow them quite as cheap as those who gained double the profit by a less price. I soon began to despair of improving our fortune by these means; nor was I at all easy at the visits and familiarity of many who had been my acquaintance in my prosperity, but denied, and shunned me in my adversity, and now very forwardly renewed their acquaintance with me. In short, I had sufficiently seen, that the pleasures of the world are chiefly folly, and the business of it mostly knavery; and both, nothing better than vanity: the men of pleasure tearing one another to pieces, from the emulation of spending money, and the men of business from envy in getting it. My happiness consisted entirely in my wife, whom I loved with an inexpressible fondness, which was perfectly returned; and my prospects were no other than to provide for our growing family; for she was now big of her second child; I therefore took an opportunity to ask her opinion of entering into a retired life, which after hearing my reasons, and perceiving my affection for it, she readily embraced. We soon put our small fortune, now reduced under three thousand pounds, into money, with part of which we purchased this little place, whither we retired soon after her delivery, from a world full of bustle, noise, hatred, envy, and ingratitude, to ease, quiet, and love. We have here liv'd almost twenty years, with little other conversation than our own, most of the neighbourhood taking us for very strange people; the squire of the parish repre-

---

1 Innkeepers. It was common practice to dilute wine with water or cider.

senting me as a madman, and the parson as a Presbyterian; because I will not hunt with the one, nor drink with the other.[1] 'Sir,' says Adams, 'Fortune hath I think paid you all her debts in this sweet retirement.' Sir, replied the gentleman, I am thankful to the great Author of all things for the blessings I here enjoy. I have the best of wives, and three pretty children, for whom I have the true tenderness of a parent; but no blessings are pure in this world. Within three years of my arrival here I lost my eldest son. (*Here he sighed bitterly.*) 'Sir,' says Adams, 'we must submit to Providence, and consider death is common to all.' We must submit, indeed, answered the gentleman; and if he had died, I could have borne the loss with patience: but alas! sir, he was stolen away from my door by some wicked travelling people whom they call *gipsies*, nor could I ever with the most diligent search recover him. Poor child! he had the sweetest look, the exact picture of his mother; at which some tears unwittingly dropt from his eyes, as did likewise from those of Adams, who always sympathized with his friends on those occasions. Thus, sir, said the gentleman, I have finished my story, in which if I have been too particular, I ask your pardon; and now, if you please, I will fetch you another bottle; which proposal the parson thankfully accepted.

CHAPTER IV

A description of Mr. Wilson's way of living. The tragical adventure of the dog, and other grave matters.

THE gentleman returned with the bottle, and Adams and he sat some time silent, when the former started up and cried, '*No, that won't do.*' The gentleman enquired into his meaning; he answered, 'he had been considering that it was possible the late famous King Theodore[2] might have been that very son whom

---

1 Like most dissenters, Presbyterians were strongly opposed to drunkenness.

2 Theodor Stephen, Baron von Neuhof, a German adventurer and spendthrift. He was proclaimed Theodore I of Corsica in 1736, but was expelled by the Genoese a few years later, and spent the last part of his life in England.

he lost;' but added, 'that his age could not answer that imagination. However,' says he, 'G— disposes all things for the best, and very probably he may be some great man, or duke, and may one day or other revisit you in that capacity.' The gentleman answered, he should know him amongst ten thousand, for he had a mark on his left breast, of a strawberry, which his mother had given him by longing for that fruit.

That beautiful young lady, the Morning, now rose from her bed, and with a countenance blooming with fresh youth and sprightliness, like Miss *——, with soft dews hanging on her pouting lips, began to take her early walk over the eastern hills; and presently after, that gallant person the Sun stole softly from his wife's chamber to pay his addresses to her; when the gentleman ask'd his guest if he would walk forth and survey his little garden, which he readily agreed to, and Joseph at the same time awaking from a sleep in which he had been two hours buried, went with them. No parterres,[1] no fountains, no statues embellished this little garden. Its only ornament was a short walk, shaded on each side by a filbert hedge, with a small alcove at one end, whither in hot weather the gentleman and his wife used to retire and divert themselves with their children, who played in the walk before them: but tho' vanity had no votary in this little spot, here was variety of fruit, and every thing useful for the kitchin, which was abundantly sufficient to catch the admiration of Adams, who told the gentleman he had certainly a good gardener. Sir, answered he, that gardener is now before you; whatever you see here, is the work solely of my own hands. Whilst I am providing necessaries for my table, I likewise procure myself an appetite for them. In fair seasons I seldom pass less than six hours of the twenty-four in this place, where I am not idle, and by these means I have been able to preserve my health ever since my arrival here without assistance from physick. Hither I generally repair at the dawn, and exercise myself whilst my wife dresses her children, and pre-

* Whoever the reader pleases [Fielding's note].

1 An ornamental arrangement of flower beds of different shapes and sizes.

pares our breakfast, after which we are seldom asunder during the residue of the day; for when the weather will not permit them to accompany me here I am usually within with them; for I am neither ashamed of conversing with my wife, nor of playing with my children: to say the truth, I do not perceive that inferiority of understanding which the levity of rakes, the dulness of men of business, or the austerity of the learned would persuade us of in women. As for my woman, I declare I have found none of my own sex capable of making juster observations on life, or of delivering them more agreeably; nor do I believe any one possessed of a faithfuller or braver friend. And sure as this friendship is sweetened with more delicacy and tenderness, so is it confirmed by dearer pledges than can attend the closest male alliance: for what union can be so fast, as our common interest in the fruits of our embraces? Perhaps, sir, you are not yourself a father; if you are not, be assured you cannot conceive the delight I have in my little-ones. Would you not despise me, if you saw me stretched on the ground, and my children playing round me? 'I should reverence the sight,' quoth Adams, 'I myself am now the father of six, and have been of eleven, and I can say I never scourged a child of my own, unless as his school-master, and then have felt every stroke on my own posteriors. And as to what you say concerning women, I have often lamented my own wife did not understand Greek.'—The gentleman smiled, and answered, he would not be apprehended to insinuate that his own had an understanding above the care of her family, on the contrary, says he, my Harriet I assure you is a notable housewife, and the house-keepers of few gentlemen understand cookery or confectionary better; but these are arts which she hath no great occasion for now: however, the wine you commended so much last night at supper, was of her own making, as is indeed all the liquor in my house, except my beer, which falls to my province. ('And I assure you it is as excellent,' quoth Adams, 'as ever I tasted.') We formerly kept a maid-servant, but since my girls have been growing up, she is unwilling to indulge them in idleness; for as the fortunes I shall give them will be very small, we intend not to breed[1] them above the rank

1 Raise, train.

they are likely to fill hereafter, nor to teach them to despise or ruin a plain husband. Indeed I could wish a man of my own temper, and a retired life, might fall to their lot: for I have experienced that calm serene happiness which is seated in content, is inconsistent with the hurry and bustle of the world. He was proceeding thus, when the little things, being just risen, ran eagerly towards him, and asked him blessing: they were shy to the strangers, but the eldest acquainted her father that her mother and the young gentlewoman were up, and that breakfast was ready. They all went in, where the gentleman was surprized at the beauty of Fanny, who had now recovered herself from her fatigue, and was entirely clean drest; for the rogues who had taken away her purse, had left her her bundle. But if he was so much amazed at the beauty of this young creature, his guests were no less charmed at the tenderness which appeared in the behaviour of husband and wife to each other, and to their children, and at the dutiful and affectionate behaviour of these to their parents. These instances pleased the well-disposed mind of Adams equally with the readiness which they exprest to oblige their guests, and their forwardness to offer them the best of every thing in their house; and what delighted him still more, was an instance or two of their charity: for whilst they were at breakfast, the good woman was called forth to assist her sick neighbour, which she did with some cordials made for the public use; and the good man went into his garden at the same time, to supply another with something which he wanted thence, for they had nothing which those who wanted it were not welcome to. These good people were in the utmost cheerfulness, when they heard the report of a gun, and immediately afterwards a little dog, the favourite of the eldest daughter, came limping in all bloody, and laid himself at his mistress's feet: the poor girl, who was about eleven years old,[1] burst into tears at the sight, and presently one of the neighbours came in and informed them, that the young squire, the son of the lord of the manor, had shot him as he past by, swearing at the same time he would prosecute the master of

1 The age of this daughter appears to be inconsistent with information given earlier by Mr. Wilson near the end of his narrative.

him for keeping a spaniel; for that he had given notice he would not suffer one in the parish.[1] The dog, whom his mistress had taken into her lap, died in a few minutes, licking her hand. She exprest great agony at his loss, and the other children began to cry for their sister's misfortune, nor could Fanny herself refrain. Whilst the father and mother attempted to comfort her, Adams grasped his crab stick, and would have sallied out after the squire, had not Joseph with-held him. He could not however bridle his tongue—He pronounced the word *rascal* with great emphasis, said he deserved to be hanged more than a highwayman, and wish'd he had the scourging him. The mother took her child, lamenting and carrying the dead favourite in her arms out of the room, when the gentleman said, this was the second time this squire had endeavoured to kill the little wretch, and had wounded him smartly once before, adding, he could have no motive but ill-nature; for the little thing, which was not near as big as one's fist, had never been twenty yards from the house in the six years his daughter had had it. He said he had done nothing to deserve this usage: but his father had too great a fortune to contend with. That he was as absolute as any tyrant in the universe, and had killed all the dogs, and taken away all the guns in the neighbourhood, and not only that, but he trampled down hedges, and rode over corn and gardens, with no more regard than if they were the highway. 'I wish I could catch him in my garden,' said Adams; 'tho' I would rather forgive him riding through my house than such an ill-natur'd act as this.'

The cheerfulness of their conversation being interrupted by this accident, in which the guests could be of no service to their kind entertainer, and as the mother was taken up in administring consolation to the poor girl, whose disposition was too good hastily to forget the sudden loss of her little favourite, which had been fondling with her a few minutes before; and as Joseph and Fanny were impatient to get home and begin those previous ceremonies to their happiness which

---

1 For Fielding's views on cruelty to animals, see Appendix D, pp. 484-86.

Adams had insisted on, they now offered to take their leave. The gentleman importuned them much to stay dinner: but when he found their eagerness to depart, he summoned his wife, and accordingly having performed all the usual ceremonies of bows and curtsies, more pleasant to be seen than to be related, they took their leave, the gentleman and his wife heartily wishing them a good journey, and they as heartily thanking them for their kind entertainment. They then departed, Adams declaring that this was the manner in which the people had lived in the Golden Age.

CHAPTER V

A disputation on schools, held on the road between Mr. Abraham Adams and Joseph; and a discovery not unwelcome to them both.

OUR travellers having well refreshed themselves at the gentleman's house, Joseph and Fanny with sleep, and Mr. Abraham Adams with ale and tobacco, renewed their journey with great alacrity; and, pursuing the road in which they were directed, travelled many miles before they met with any adventure worth relating. In this interval, we shall present our readers with a very curious discourse, as we apprehend it, concerning public schools, which pass'd between Mr. Joseph Andrews and Mr. Abraham Adams.

They had not gone far, before Adams calling to Joseph, asked him if he had attended to the gentleman's story; he answered, 'to all the former part.' 'And don't you think,' says he, 'he was a very unhappy man in his youth?' 'A very unhappy man indeed,' answered the other. 'Joseph,' cries Adams, screwing up his mouth, 'I have found it; I have discovered the cause of all the misfortunes which befel him. A public school, Joseph, was the cause of all the calamities which he afterwards suffered. Public schools are the nurseries of all vice and immorality. All the wicked fellows whom I remember at the university were bred at them.—Ah Lord! I can remember as well as if it was but yesterday, a knot of them; they called them King's scholars,[1] I forget why—very wicked fellows! Joseph, you may thank the Lord you were not bred at a public school, you would never have preserved your virtue as you have. The first care I always take, is of a boy's morals, I had rather he should be a blockhead than an atheist or a Presbyterian. What is all the learning of the world compared to his immortal soul? What shall a man take in exchange for his soul? But the masters of great schools trouble themselves about no such thing. I have known a lad of eighteen at the university, who hath not been able to say his catechism; but for my own part, I always scourged a lad sooner for missing that than any other lesson. Believe me, child, all that gentleman's misfortunes arose from his being educated at a public school.'

'It doth not become me,' answer'd Joseph, 'to dispute any thing, sir, with you, especially a matter of this kind; for to be sure you must be allowed by all the world to be the best teacher of a school in all our county.' 'Yes, that,' says Adams, 'I believe, is granted me; that I may without much vanity pretend to—nay I believe I may go to the next county too—but *gloriari non est meum*.'[2]—'However, sir, as you are pleased to bid me speak,' says Joseph, 'you know, my late master, Sir Thomas Booby, was bred at a public school, and he was the finest gentleman in all the neighbourhood. And I have often heard him say, if he had a hundred boys he would breed them all at the same place. It was his opinion, and I have often heard him deliver it, that a boy taken from a public school, and carried into the world, will learn more in one year there, than one of a private education will in five. He used to say, the school itself initiated him a great way, (I remember that was his very expression) for great schools are little societies, where a boy of any observation may see in epitome what he will afterwards find in the world at large.' '*Hinc illæ lachrymæ*;[3] for that very reason,' quoth Adams, 'I prefer a private school, where boys may be kept in innocence and

1 Scholars supported by the foundation of a public school established by royal charter or funded by royal endowment.

2 "It is not for me to boast."

3 "Hence those tears" (Horace, *Epistles* 1.19.41).

ignorance: for, according to that fine passage in the play of *Cato*, the only English tragedy I ever read,

> If knowledge of the world must make men villains,
> May *Juba* ever live in ignorance.[1]

Who would not rather preserve the purity of his child, than wish him to attain the whole circle of arts and sciences; which, by the bye, he may learn in the classes of a private school? for I would not be vain, but I esteem myself to be second to none, *nulli secundum*, in teaching these things; so that a lad may have as much learning in a private as in a public education.' 'And with submission,' answered Joseph, 'he may get as much vice, witness several country gentlemen, who were educated within five miles of their own houses, and are as wicked as if they had known the world from their infancy. I remember when I was in the stable, if a young horse was vicious in his nature, no correction would make him otherwise; I take it to be equally the same among men: if a boy be of a mischievous wicked inclination, no school, tho' ever so private, will ever make him good; on the contrary, if he be of a righteous temper, you may trust him to London, or whereever else you please, he will be in no danger of being corrupted. Besides, I have often heard my master say, that the discipline practised in public schools was much better than that in private.'—'You talk like a jackanapes,' says Adams, 'and so did your master. Discipline indeed! Because one man scourges twenty or thirty boys more in a morning than another, is he therefore a better disciplinarian? I do presume to confer in this point with all who have taught from Chiron's[2] time to this day; and, if I was master of six boys only, I would preserve as good discipline amongst them as the master of the greatest school in the world. I say nothing, young man; remember, I say nothing; but if Sir Thomas himself had been educated nearer home, and under the tuition of somebody, remember, I name nobody, it might have been better for him—but his

---

1 Joseph Addison, *Cato* (1713) 2.5. Adams slightly alters the quotation.

2 Chiron, the wisest of the centaurs, instructed such Greek heroes as Hercules and Achilles.

father must institute him in the knowledge of the world. *Nemo mortalium omnibus horis sapit*.'[1] Joseph seeing him run on in this manner asked pardon many times, assuring him he had no intention to offend. 'I believe you had not, child,' said he, 'and I am not angry with you: but for maintaining good discipline in a school; for this,—' And then he ran on as before, named all the masters who are recorded in old books, and preferred himself to them all. Indeed if this good man had an enthusiasm, or what the vulgar call a blind-side, it was this: he thought a schoolmaster the greatest character in the world, and himself the greatest of all schoolmasters, neither of which points he would have given up to Alexander the Great at the head of his army.

Adams continued his subject till they came to one of the beautifullest spots of ground in the universe. It was a kind of natural amphitheatre, formed by the winding of a small rivulet, which was planted with thick woods, and the trees rose gradually above each other by the natural ascent of the ground they stood on; which ascent, as they hid with their boughs, they seemed to have been disposed by the design of the most skillful planter. The soil was spread with a verdure which no paint could imitate, and the whole place might have raised romantic ideas in elder minds than those of Joseph and Fanny, without the assistance of love.

Here they arrived about noon, and Joseph proposed to Adams that they should rest a while in this delightful place, and refresh themselves with some provisions which the good-nature of Mrs. Wilson had provided them with. Adams made no objection to the proposal, so down they sat, and pulling out a cold fowl, and a bottle of wine, they made a repast with a cheerfulness which might have attracted the envy of more splendid tables. I should not omit, that they found among their provision a little paper, containing a piece of gold, which Adams imagining had been put there by mistake, would have returned back, to restore it; but he was at last convinced by Joseph, that Mr. Wilson had taken this handsome way of fur-

1 "No mortal is wise all the time" (Pliny, *Natural History* 7.40.131).

nishing them with a supply for their journey, on his having related the distress which they had been in, when they were relieved by the generosity of the pedlar. Adams said, he was glad to see such an instance of goodness, not so much for the conveniency which it brought them, as for the sake of the doer, whose reward would be great in Heaven. He likewise comforted himself with a reflection, that he should shortly have an opportunity of returning it him; for the gentleman was within a week to make a journey into Somersetshire, to pass through Adams's parish, and had faithfully promised to call on him: a circumstance which we thought too immaterial to mention before; but which those who have as great an affection for that gentleman as ourselves will rejoice at, as it may give them hopes of seeing him again. Then Joseph made a speech on charity, which the reader, if he is so disposed, may see in the next chapter; for we scorn to betray him into any such reading, without first giving him warning.

CHAPTER VI

Moral reflections by Joseph Andrews, with the hunting adventure, and Parson Adams's miraculous escape.

'I HAVE often wondered, sir,' said Joseph, 'to observe so few instances of charity among mankind; for tho' the goodness of a man's heart did not incline him to relieve the distresses of his fellow-creatures, methinks the desire of honour should move him to it. What inspires a man to build fine houses, to purchase fine furniture, pictures, clothes, and other things at a great expence, but an ambition to be respected more than other people? Now would not one great act of charity, one instance of redeeming a poor family from all the miseries of poverty, restoring an unfortunate tradesman by a sum of money to the means of procuring a livelihood by his industry, discharging an undone debtor from his debts or a goal, or any such like example of goodness, create a man more honour and respect than he could acquire by the finest house, furniture, pictures or clothes that were ever beheld? For not only the object himself, who was thus relieved, but all who heard the name of such a person must, I imagine, reverence him infinitely more than the possessor of all those other things: which when we so admire, we rather praise the builder, the workman, the painter, the laceman, the taylor, and the rest, by whose ingenuity they are produced, than the person who by his money makes them his own. For my own part, when I have waited behind my lady in a room hung with fine pictures, while I have been looking at them I have never once thought of their owner, nor hath any one else, as I ever observed; for when it hath been asked whose picture that was, it was never once answered, the master's of the house, but Ammyconni, Paul Varnish, Hannibal Scratchi, or Hogarthi,[1] which I suppose were the names of the painters: but if it was asked, who redeemed such a one out of prison? who lent such a ruined tradesman money to set up? who cloathed that family of poor small children? it is very plain, what must be the answer. And besides, these great folks are mistaken, if they imagine they get any honour at all by these means; for I do not remember I ever was with my lady at any house where she commended the house or furniture, but I have heard her at her return home make sport and jeer at whatever she had before commended: and I have been told by other gentlemen in livery, that it is the same in their families: but I defy the wisest man in the world to turn a true good action into ridicule. I defy him to do it. He who should endeavour it, would be laughed at himself, instead of making others laugh. Nobody scarce doth any good, yet they all agree in praising those who do. Indeed it is strange that all men should consent in commending goodness, and no man endeavour to deserve that commendation; whilst, on the contrary, all rail at wickedness, and all are as eager to be what they abuse. This I know not the reason of, but it is as plain as daylight to those who converse in the world, as I have done these three years.' 'Are all the great folks wicked

1 Joseph is referring in a confused fashion to the Italian painters Jacopo Amigoni (1675–1752), Paolo Veronese (1528–88), and Annibale Carracci (1560–1609). Fielding pays a further compliment to his friend Hogarth by associating him with these illustrious names.

then?' says Fanny. 'To be sure there are some exceptions,' answered Joseph. 'Some gentlemen of our cloth report charitable actions done by their lords and masters, and I have heard Squire Pope, the great poet, at my lady's table, tell stories of a man that lived at a place called Ross,[1] and another at the Bath, one Al— Al— I forget his name, but it is in the book of verses.[2] This gentleman hath built up a stately house too, which the squire likes very well; but his charity is seen farther than his house, tho' it stands on a hill, ay, and brings him more honour too. It was his charity that put him in the book, where the squire says he puts all those who deserve it; and to be sure, as he lives among all the great people, if there were any such, he would know them.'—This was all of Mr. Joseph Andrews's speech which I could get him to recollect, which I have delivered as near as was possible in his own words, with a very small embellishment. But I believe the reader hath not been a little surprized at the long silence of Parson Adams, especially as so many occasions offer'd themselves to exert his curiosity and observation. The truth is, he was fast asleep, and had so been from the beginning of the preceding narrative: and indeed if the reader considers that so many hours had past since he had closed his eyes, he will not wonder at his repose, tho' even Henley himself, or as great an orator (if any such be) had been in his rostrum or tub before him.[3]

Joseph, who, whilst he was speaking, had continued in one attitude, with his head reclining on one side, and his eyes cast on the ground, no sooner perceived, on looking up, the position of Adams, who was stretched on his back, and snored louder than the usual braying of the animal with long ears; than he turned towards Fanny, and taking her by the hand, began a dalliance, which, tho' consistent with the purest innocence and decency, neither he would have attempted, nor she permitted

---

1 John Kyrle (1634?-1724), better known as the "the Man of Ross" (Herefordshire), celebrated in Pope's *Epistle to Bathurst* 250-90.

2 Ralph Allen (see above, p. 243, n. 2), whom Pope compliments in his *Epilogue to the Satires*, Dialogue 1.135-36.

3 John "Orator" Henley (1692-1756), an eccentric and nonconformist preacher, who set up his "tub," or pulpit, in Newport market and later in Lincoln's Inn Fields.

before any witness. Whilst they amused themselves in this harmless and delightful manner, they heard a pack of hounds approaching in full cry towards them, and presently afterwards saw a hare pop forth from the wood, and crossing the water, land within a few yards of them in the meadows. The hare was no sooner on shore, than it seated itself on its hinder legs, and listened to the sound of the pursuers. Fanny was wonderfully pleased with the little wretch, and eagerly longed to have it in her arms, that she might preserve it from the dangers which seemed to threaten it: but the rational part of the creation do not always aptly distinguish their friends from their foes; what wonder then if this silly creature, the moment it beheld her, fled from the friend who would have protected it, and traversing the meadows again, past the little rivulet on the opposite side. It was however so spent and weak, that it fell down twice or thrice in its way. This affected the tender heart of Fanny, who exclaimed with tears in her eyes against the barbarity of worrying a poor innocent defenceless animal out of its life, and putting it to the extremest torture for diversion. She had not much time to make reflections of this kind, for on a sudden the hounds rushed through the wood, which resounded with their throats, and the throats of their retinue, who attended on them on horseback. The dogs now past the rivulet, and pursued the footsteps of the hare; five horsemen attempted to leap over, three of whom succeeded, and two were in the attempt thrown from their saddles into the water; their companions and their own horses too proceeded after their sport, and left their friends and riders to invoke the assistance of Fortune, or employ the more active means of strength and agility for their deliverance. Joseph however was not so unconcerned on this occasion; he left Fanny for a moment to herself, and ran to the gentlemen, who were immediately on their legs, shaking their ears, and easily with the help of his hand attained the bank, (for the rivulet was not at all deep) and without staying to thank their kind assister, ran dripping across the meadow, calling to their brother sportsmen to stop their horses: but they heard them not.

The hounds were now very little behind their poor reeling, staggering prey, which fainting almost at every step, crawled through the wood, and had almost got round to the place where Fanny stood, when it was overtaken by its enemies; and being driven out of the covert was caught, and instantly tore to pieces before Fanny's face, who was unable to assist it with any aid more powerful than pity; nor could she prevail on Joseph, who had been himself a sportsman in his youth, to attempt any thing contrary to the laws of hunting, in favour of the hare, which he said was killed fairly.

The hare was caught within a yard or two of Adams, who lay asleep at some distance from the lovers, and the hounds in devouring it, and pulling it backwards and forwards, had drawn it so close to him, that some of them (by mistake perhaps for the hare's skin) laid hold of the skirts of his cassock; others at the same time applying their teeth to his wig, which he had with a handkerchief fastened to his head, they began to pull him about; and had not the motion of his body had more effect on him than seemed to be wrought by the noise, they must certainly have tasted his flesh, which delicious flavour might have been fatal to him: but being roused by these tuggings, he instantly awaked, and with a jerk delivering his head from his wig, he with most admirable dexterity recovered his legs, which now seemed the only members he could entrust his safety to. Having therefore escaped likewise from at least a third part of his cassock, which he willingly left as his *exuviæ* or spoils to the enemy, he fled with the utmost speed he could summon to his assistance. Nor let this be any detraction from the bravery of his character; let the number of the enemies, and the surprize in which he was taken, be considered; and if there be any modern so outragiously brave, that he cannot admit of flight in any circumstance whatever, I say (but I whisper that softly, and I solemnly declare, without any intention of giving offence to any brave man in the nation) I say, or rather I whisper that he is an ignorant fellow, and hath never read Homer nor Virgil, nor knows he any thing of Hector or Turnus;[1] nay,

1 Hector flees from Achilles (*Iliad* 22) as does Turnus before Aeneas (*Aeneid* 12).

he is unacquainted with the history of some great men living, who, tho' as brave as lions, ay, as tigers, have run away the Lord knows how far, and the Lord knows why, to the surprize of their friends, and the entertainment of their enemies. But if persons of such heroick disposition are a little offended at the behaviour of Adams, we assure them they shall be as much pleased with what we shall immediately relate of Joseph Andrews. The master of the pack was just arrived, or, as the sportsmen call it, *come in*, when Adams set out, as we have before mentioned. This gentleman was generally said to be a great lover of humour; but not to mince the matter, especially as we are upon this subject, he was a great *hunter of men*: indeed he had hitherto followed the sport only with dogs of his own species; for he kept two or three couple of barking curs for that use only. However, as he thought he had now found a man nimble enough, he was willing to indulge himself with other sport, and accordingly crying out, *Stole away*,[1] encouraged the hounds to pursue Mr. Adams, swearing it was the largest jack hare he ever saw; at the same time hallooing and hooping as if a conquered foe was flying before him; in which he was imitated by these two or three couple of human, or rather two-leg'd curs on horseback which we have mentioned before.

Now thou, whoever thou art, whether a muse, or by what other name soever thou chusest to be called, who presidest over biography, and hast inspired all the writers of lives in these our times: thou who didst infuse such wonderful humour into the pen of immortal Gulliver,[2] who hast carefully guided the judgment, whilst thou hast exalted the nervous manly style of thy Mallet:[3] thou who hadst no hand in that dedication, and preface, or the translations which thou wouldst willingly have struck out of the *Life of Cicero*:[4] lastly, thou who without the

---

1 A hunting phrase, meaning that the animal has left the lair ahead of its pursuers.

2 Fielding much admired the writings of Jonathan Swift, and had already imitated *Gulliver's Travels* (1726) in "The Voyages of Mr. Job Vinegar" (*The Champion*, March-October 1740).

3 David Mallett (1705-65), Scottish poet and dramatist who, like Fielding, had been opposed to Walpole.

4 T*he History of the Life of Marcus Tullius Cicero* (1741), by Conyers Middleton. Fielding had parodied the Dedication in *Shamela*. See Appendix B, pp. 443-45.

assistance of the least spice of literature, and even against his inclination, hast, in some pages of his book, forced Colley Cibber[1] to write English; do thou assist me in what I find myself unequal to. Do thou introduce on the plain, the young, the gay, the brave Joseph Andrews, whilst men shall view him with admiration and envy; tender virgins with love and anxious concern for his safety.

No sooner did Joseph Andrews perceive the distress of his friend, when first the quick-scenting dogs attacked him, than he grasped his cudgel[2] in his right hand, a cudgel which his father had of his grandfather, to whom a mighty strong man of Kent[3] had given it for a present in that day, when he broke three heads on the stage. It was a cudgel of mighty strength and wonderful art, made by one of Mr. Deard's best workmen,[4] whom no other artificer can equal; and who hath made all those sticks which the beaus have lately walked with about the Park[5] in a morning: but this was far his master-piece; on its head was engraved a nose and chin, which might have been mistaken for a pair of nut-crackers. The learned have imagined it designed to represent the Gorgon: but it was in fact copied from the face of a certain long English baronet[6] of infinite wit, humour, and gravity. He did intend to have engraved here many histories: as the first night of Captain B—'s play,[7] where you would have seen criticks in embroidery transplanted from the boxes to the pit, whose ancient inhabitants were exalted to the galleries, where they played on catcalls. He did intend to

1 See above, p. 60, n. 3.

2 The following passage parodies the description of the shield made for Achilles in the *Iliad* 18.478-613. There are a number of allusions to this work in the ensuing battle. See Appendix C, pp. 459-63.

3 William Joy (d. 1734), whose professional name was "Samson, the strong man of Kent."

4 William Deard (d. 1761), a fashionable London jeweller, toymaker, and pawnbroker.

5 The Mall in St. James's Park was a fashionable place to promenade.

6 An ironic reference to Sir Thomas Robinson (1700?-77), known as "Long Sir Thomas" because of his height. He was appointed Governor of Barbados, and was renowned for his extravagance as well as his dullness.

7 *The Modish Couple* (1732), for which Fielding provided the Epilogue, was ostensibly written by Charles Bodens. Catcalls were sounded throughout the opening performance, and the play was roundly damned.

have painted an auction-room, where Mr. Cock[1] would have appeared aloft in his pulpit, trumpeting forth the praises of a china bason; and with astonishment wondering that *Nobody bids more for that fine, that superb*—He did intend to have engraved many other things, but was forced to leave all out for want of room.

No sooner had Joseph grasped this cudgel in his hands, than lightning darted from his eyes; and the heroick youth, swift of foot,[2] ran with the utmost speed to his friend's assistance. He overtook him just as Rockwood had laid hold of the skirt of his cassock, which being torn hung to the ground. Reader, we would make a simile on this occasion, but for two reasons: the first is, it would interrupt the description, which should be *rapid* in this part; but that doth not weigh much, many precedents occurring for such an interruption: the second, and much the greater reason is, that we could find no simile adequate to our purpose: for indeed, what instance could we bring to set before our reader's eyes at once the idea of friendship, courage, youth, beauty, strength, and swiftness; all which blazed in the person of Joseph Andrews. Let those therefore that describe lions and tigers, and heroes fiercer than both, raise their poems or plays with the simile of Joseph Andrews, who is himself above the reach of any simile.

Now Rockwood had laid fast hold on the parson's skirts, and stopt his flight; which Joseph no sooner perceived, than he levelled his cudgel at his head, and laid him sprawling. Jowler and Ringwood then fell on his great-coat, and had undoubtedly brought him to the ground, had not Joseph, collecting all his force given Jowler such a rap on the back, that quitting his hold he ran howling over the plain: a harder fate remained for thee, O Ringwood. Ringwood the best hound that ever pursued a hare, who never threw his tongue but where the scent was undoubtedly true; good at *trailing*; and *sure in a highway*, no *babler*, *no over-runner*, respected by the whole pack: for, when-

---

1 Christopher Cock (d. 1748), the well-known auctioneer of Covent Garden, whom Fielding had satirized in *The Historical Register for the Year 1736* (1737).

2 A phrase commonly applied to Achilles throughout the *Iliad*.

ever he opened, they knew the game was at hand.[1] He fell by the stroke of Joseph. Thunder, and Plunder, and Wonder, and Blunder, were the next victims of his wrath, and measured their lengths on the ground. Then Fairmaid, a bitch which Mr. John Temple[2] had bred up in his house, and fed at his own table, and lately sent the squire fifty miles for a present, ran fiercely at Joseph, and bit him by the leg; no dog was ever fiercer than she, being descended from an Amazonian breed, and had worried bulls in her own country, but now waged an unequal fight; and had shared the fate of those we have mentioned before, had not Diana[3] (the reader may believe it or not, as he pleases) in that instant interposed, and in the shape of the huntsman snatched her favourite up in her arms.

The parson now faced about, and with his crab stick felled many to the earth, and scattered others, till he was attacked by Cæsar and pulled to the ground; then Joseph flew to his rescue, and with such might fell on the victor, that, O eternal blot to his name! Cæsar ran yelping away.

The battle now raged with the most dreadful violence, when lo the huntsman, a man of years and dignity, lifted his voice, and called his hounds from the fight; telling them, in a language they understood, that it was in vain to contend longer; for that Fate had decreed the victory to their enemies.

Thus far the muse hath with her usual dignity related this prodigious battle, a battle we apprehend never equalled by any poet, romance or life-writer whatever, and having brought it to a conclusion she ceased; we shall therefore proceed in our ordinary style with the continuation of this history. The squire and his companions, whom the figure of Adams and the gallantry of Joseph had at first thrown into a violent fit of laughter, and who had hitherto beheld the engagement with more delight than any chace, shooting-match, race, cock-fighting, bull or

---

1 Ringwood "threw his tongue" or "opened" (gave cry) only when the scent was "true" (fresh), and in"trailing" (following the scent) he would not "over-run" (run past) the hare's turns and dodges. Nor was he a "babler" (a barker).

2 Probably the Hon. John Temple, Esq. (1680–1752), who lived at Moor Park, Surrey, about fifty miles from Fielding's scene.

3 Diana (the Greek Artemis), goddess of the chase. Divine intervention is a commonplace of classical epic.

bear-baiting had ever given them, began now to apprehend the danger of their hounds, many of which lay sprawling in the fields. The squire therefore having first called his friends about him, as guards for safety of his person, rode manfully up to the combatants, and summoning all the terror he was master of, into his countenance, demanded with an authoritative voice of Joseph, what he meant by assaulting his dogs in that manner. Joseph answered with great intrepidity, that they had first fallen on his friend; and if they had belonged to the greatest man in the kingdom, he would have treated them in the same way; for whilst his veins contained a single drop of blood, he would not stand idle by, and see that gentleman (*pointing to Adams*) abused either by man or beast; and having so said, both he and Adams brandished their wooden weapons, and put themselves into such a posture, that the squire and his company thought proper to preponderate,[1] before they offered to revenge the cause of their four-footed allies.

At this instant Fanny, whom the apprehension of Joseph's danger had alarmed so much, that forgetting her own she had made the utmost expedition, came up. The squire and all the horsemen were so surprized with her beauty, that they immediately fixed both their eyes and thoughts solely on her, every one declaring he had never seen so charming a creature. Neither mirth nor anger engaged them a moment longer; but all sat in silent amaze. The huntsman only was free from her attraction, who was busy in cutting the ears of the dogs,[2] and endeavouring to recover them to life; in which he succeeded so well, that only two of no great note remained slaughtered on the field of action. Upon this the huntsman declared, ''twas well it was no worse; for his part he could not blame the gentleman, and wondered his master would encourage the dogs to hunt Christians; that it was the surest way to spoil them, to make them follow *vermin* instead of sticking to a hare.'

The squire being informed of the little mischief that had been done; and perhaps having more mischief of another kind in his head, accosted Mr. Adams with a more favourable aspect

1 To consider beforehand.

2 The medical practice of bleeding, as with humans.

than before: he told him he was sorry for what had happened; that he had endeavoured all he could to prevent it, the moment he was acquainted with his cloth, and greatly commended the courage of his servant; for so he imagined Joseph to be. He then invited Mr. Adams to dinner, and desired the young woman might come with him. Adams refused a long while; but the invitation was repeated with so much earnestness and courtesy, that at length he was forced to accept it. His wig and hat, and other spoils of the field, being gathered together by Joseph, (for otherwise probably they would have been forgotten;) he put himself into the best order he could; and then the horse and foot moved forward in the same pace towards the squire's house, which stood at a very little distance.

Whilst they were on the road, the lovely Fanny attracted the eyes of all; they endeavoured to outvie one another in encomiums on her beauty; which the reader will pardon my not relating, as they had not any thing new or uncommon in them: so must he likewise my not setting down the many curious jests which were made on Adams, some of them declaring that parson-hunting was the best sport in the world: others commending his standing at bay, which they said he had done as well as any badger; with such like merriment, which tho' it would ill become the dignity of this history, afforded much laughter and diversion to the squire, and his facetious companions.

CHAPTER VII

A scene of roasting[1] *very nicely adapted to the present taste and times.*

THEY arrived at the squire's house just as his dinner was ready. A little dispute arose on the account of Fanny, whom the squire who was a batchelor, was desirous to place at his own table; but she would not consent, nor would Mr. Adams permit her to be parted from Joseph: so that she was at length with him con-

1 Merciless bantering or ridiculing. Fielding denounces "roasting" in *The Champion*, 13 March 1740. See Appendix D, pp. 483-84.

signed over to the kitchin, where the servants were ordered to make him drunk; a favour which was likewise intended for Adams: which design being executed, the squire thought he should easily accomplish, what he had, when he first saw her, intended to perpetrate with Fanny.

It may not be improper, before we proceed farther to open a little the character of this gentleman,[1] and that of his friends. The master of this house then was a man of a very considerable fortune; a batchelor, as we have said, and about forty years of age: he had been educated (if we may here use that expression) in the country, and at his own home, under the care of his mother and a tutor, who had orders never to correct him nor to compel him to learn more than he liked, which it seems was very little, and that only in his childhood; for from the age of fifteen he addicted himself entirely to hunting and other rural amusements, for which his mother took care to equip him with horses, hounds, and all other necessaries: and his tutor endeavouring to ingratiate himself with his young pupil, who would, he knew, be able handsomely to provide for him, became his companion, not only at these exercises, but likewise over a bottle, which the young squire had a very early relish for. At the age of twenty, his mother began to think she had not fulfilled the duty of a parent; she therefore resolved to persuade her son, if possible, to that which she imagined would well supply all that he might have learned at a publick school or university. This is what they commonly call *travelling*; which, with the help of the tutor who was fixed on to attend him, she easily succeeded in. He made in three years the tour of Europe, as they term it, and returned home, well furnish'd with French clothes, phrases and servants, with a hearty contempt for his own country; especially what had any savour of the plain spirit and honesty of our ancestors. His mother greatly applauded herself at his return; and now being master of his own fortune, he soon procured himself a seat in Parliament, and was in the common opinion one of the finest gentlemen of his age: but what distinguished him chiefly, was a strange delight which he took in

1 John, second Duke of Montagu (1688?–1749), a notorious practical joker, may very well have provided the model here.

every thing which is ridiculous, odious, and absurd in his own species; so that he never chose a companion without one or more of these ingredients, and those who were marked by nature in the most eminent degree with them, were most his favourites: if he ever found a man who either had not or endeavoured to conceal these imperfections, he took great pleasure in inventing methods of forcing him into absurdities, which were not natural to him, or in drawing forth and exposing those that were; for which purpose he was always provided with a set of fellows whom we have before called curs; and who did indeed no great honour to the canine kind: their business was to hunt out and display everything that had any savour of the above mentioned qualities, and especially in the gravest and best characters: but if they failed in their search, they were to turn even virtue and wisdom themselves into ridicule for the diversion of their master and feeder. The gentlemen of curlike disposition, who were now at his house, and whom he had brought with him from London, were an old half-pay officer, a player, a dull poet, a quack doctor, a scraping fidler, and a lame German dancing-master.

As soon as dinner was served, while Mr. Adams was saying grace, the captain conveyed his chair from behind him; so that when he endeavoured to seat himself, he fell down on the ground; and thus compleated joke the first, to the great entertainment of the whole company. The second joke was performed by the poet, who sat next him on the other side, and took an opportunity, while poor Adams was respectfully drinking to the master of the house, to overturn a plate of soup into his breeches; which, with the many apologies he made, and the parson's gentle answers, caused much mirth in the company. Joke the third was served up by one of the waiting-men, who had been ordered to convey a quantity of gin into Mr. Adams's ale, which he declaring to be the best liquor he ever drank, but rather too rich of the malt, contributed again to their laughter. Mr. Adams, from whom we had most of this relation, could not recollect all the jests of this kind practised on him, which the inoffensive dispositon of his own heart made him slow in discovering; and indeed, had it not been for the information which we received from a servant of the family, this part of our history, which we take to be none of the least curious, must have been deplorably imperfect; tho' we must own it probable, that some more jokes were (as they call it) *cracked* during their dinner; but we have by no means been able to come at the knowledge of them. When dinner was removed, the poet began to repeat some verses, which he said were made *extempore*. The following is a copy of them, procured with the greatest difficulty.

An extempore Poem on Parson Adams.

Did ever mortal such a parson view;
His cassock old, his wig not over-new?
Well might the hounds have him for fox mistaken,
In smell more like to that, than rusty[1] bacon.*
But would it not make any mortal stare,
To see this parson taken for a hare?
Could *Phoebus* err thus grossly, even he
For a good player might have taken thee.

At which words the bard whip'd off the player's wig, and received the approbation of the company, rather perhaps for the dexterity of his hand than his head. The player, instead of retorting the jest on the poet, began to display his talents on the same subject. He repeated many scraps of wit out of plays, reflecting on the whole body of the clergy, which were received with great acclamations by all present. It was now the dancing-master's turn to exhibit his talents; he therefore addressing himself to Adams in broken English, told him, 'he was a man ver well made for de dance, and he suppose by his walk, dat he had learn of some great master. He said it was ver pretty quality in clergyman to dance;' and concluded with desiring him to dance a minuet, telling him, 'his cassock would serve for petti-

---

* All hounds that will hunt fox or other vermin, will hunt a piece of rusty bacon trailed on the ground [Fielding's note].

---

1 Rancid.

coats; and that he would himself be his partner.' At which words, without waiting for an answer, he pulled out his gloves, and the fiddler was preparing his fiddle. The company all offered the dancing-master wagers that the parson outdanced him, which he refused, saying , 'he believed so too; for he had never seen any man in his life who looked de dance so well as de gentleman:' he then stepped forwards to take Adams by the hand, which the latter hastily withdrew, and at the same time clenching his fist, advised him not to carry the jest too far, for he would not endure being put upon. The dancing-master no sooner saw the fist than he prudently retired out of it's reach, and stood aloof mimicking Adams, whose eyes were fixed on him, not guessing what he was at, but to avoid his laying hold on him, which he had once attempted. In the mean while, the captain perceiving an opportunity pinned a cracker or devil to the cassock, and then lighted it with their little smoaking candle. Adams being a stranger to this sport, and believing he had been blown up in reality, started from his chair, and jumped about the room, to the infinite joy of the beholders, who declared he was the best dancer in the universe. As soon as the devil had done tormenting him, and he had a little recovered his confusion, he returned to the table, standing up in the posture of one who intended to make a speech. They all cried out, *Hear him*, *Hear him*; and he then spoke in the following manner: 'Sir, I am sorry to see one to whom Providence hath been so bountiful in bestowing his favours, make so ill and ungrateful a return for them; for tho' you have not insulted me yourself, it is visible you have delighted in those that do it, nor have once discouraged the many rudenesses which have been shewn towards me; indeed towards yourself, if you rightly understood them; for I am your guest, and by the laws of hospitality entitled to your protection. One gentleman hath thought proper to produce some poetry upon me, of which I shall only say, that I had rather be the subject than the composer. He hath pleased to treat me with disrespect as a parson; I apprehend my order is not the object of scorn, nor that I can become so, unless by being a disgrace to it, which I hope poverty will never be called. Another gentleman indeed hath repeated some sentences, where the order itself is mentioned with contempt. He says they are taken from plays. I am sure such plays are a scandal to the government which permits them, and cursed will be the nation where they are represented. How others have treated me, I need not observe; they themselves, when they reflect, must allow the behaviour to be as improper to my years as to my cloth. You found me, sir, travelling with two of my parishioners, (I omit your hounds falling on me; for I have quite forgiven it, whether it proceeded from the wantonness or negligence of the huntsman,) my appearance might very well persuade you that your invitation was an act of charity, tho' in reality we were well provided; yes, sir, if we had had an hundred miles to travel, we had sufficient to bear our expences in a noble manner.' (At which words he produced the half guinea which was found in the basket.) 'I do not shew you this out of ostentation of riches, but to convince you I speak truth. Your seating me at your table was an honour which I did not ambitiously affect; when I was here, I endeavoured to behave towards you with the utmost respect; if I have failed, it was not with design, nor could I, certainly, so far be guilty as to deserve the insults I have suffered. If they were meant therefore either to my order or my poverty (and you see I am not very poor) the shame doth not lie at my door, and I heartily pray, that the sin may be averted from your's.' He thus finished, and received a general clap from the whole company. Then the gentleman of the house told him, 'he was sorry for what had happened; that he could not accuse him of any share in it: that the verses were, as himself had well observed, so bad, that he might easily answer them; and for the serpent,[1] it was undoubtedly a very great affront done him by the dancing-master, for which if he well thrashed him, as he deserved, (the gentleman said) he should be very much pleased to see it;' (in which probably he spoke truth.) Adams answered, 'whoever had done it, it was not his profession to punish him that way; but for the person whom he had accused, I am a witness, (says he) of his innocence, for I had my eye on him all the while. Whoever he was, God forgive

---

1 A firecracker of such a shape.

him, and bestow on him a little more sense as well as humanity.' The captain answer'd with a surly look and accent, 'that he hoped he did not mean to reflect on him; d—n him, he had as much *imanity* as another, and if any man said he had not, he would convince him of his mistake by cutting his throat.' Adams smiling, said, 'he believed he had spoke right by accident.' To which the captain returned, 'What do you mean by my speaking right? If you was not a parson, I would not take these words; but your gown protects you. If any man who wears a sword had said so much, I had pulled him by the nose before this.' Adams replied, 'if he attempted any rudeness to his person, he would not find any protection for himself in his gown;' and clenching his fist, declared he had threshed many a stouter man. The gentleman did all he could to encourage this warlike disposition in Adams, and was in hopes to have produced a battle: but he was disappointed; for the captain made no other answer than, 'It is very well you are a parson,' and so drinking off a bumper to old mother Church, ended the dispute.

Then the doctor, who had hitherto been silent, and who was the gravest, but most mischievous dog of all, in a very pompous speech highly applauded what Adams had said; and as much discommended the behaviour to him; he proceeded to encomiums on the Church and poverty; and lastly recommended forgiveness of what had past to Adams, who immediately answered, 'that every thing was forgiven;' and in the warmth of his goodness he filled a bumper of strong beer, (a liquor he preferred to wine) and drank a health to the whole company, shaking the captain and the poet heartily by the hand, and addressing himself with great respect to the doctor; who indeed had not laughed outwardly at any thing that past, as he had a perfect command of his muscles, and could laugh inwardly without betraying the least symptoms in his countenance. The doctor now began a second formal speech, in which he declaimed against all levity of conversation; and what is usually called mirth. He said, 'there were amusements fitted for persons of all ages and degrees, from the rattle to the discussing a point of philosophy, and that men discovered themselves in nothing more than in the choice of their amusements; for,' says he, 'as it must greatly raise our expectation of the future conduct in life of boys, whom in their tender years we perceive instead of taw[1] or balls, or other childish play-things, to chuse, at their leisure-hours, to exercise their genius in contentions of wit, learning, and such like; so must it inspire one with equal contempt of a man, if we should discover him playing at taw or other childish play.' Adams highly commended the doctor's opinion, and said, 'he had often wondered at some passages in ancient authors, where Scipio, Lælius, and other great men were represented to have passed many hours in amusements of the most trifling kind.'[2] The doctor reply'd, 'he had by him an old Greek manuscript where a favourite diversion of Socrates was recorded.' 'Ay,' says the parson eagerly, 'I should be most infinitely obliged to you for the favour of perusing it.' The doctor promised to send it him, and farther said, 'that he believed he could describe it. I think,' says he, 'as near as I can remember, it was this. There was a throne erected, on one side of which sat a king, and on the other a queen, with their guards and attendants ranged on both sides; to them was introduced an ambassador, which part Socrates always used to perform himself; and when he was led up to the footsteps of the throne, he addressed himself to the monarchs in some grave speech, full of virtue and goodness, and morality, and such like. After which, he was seated between the king and queen, and royally entertained. This I think was the chief part.—Perhaps I may have forgot some particulars; for it is long since I read it.' Adams said, 'it was indeed a diversion worthy the relaxation of so great a man; and thought something resembling it should be instituted among our great men, instead of cards and other idle pass-time, in which he was informed they trifled away too much of their lives.' He added, 'the Christian religion was a nobler subject for these speeches than any Socrates could have

1 Marbles.

2 Scipio Africanus Minor (c. 185-129 BC) and Caius Laelius (b. c. 186 BC), both Roman consuls and commanders, were famous for their friendship. Cicero relates that in their amusements they "used to become boys again, in an astonishing degree" (*De Oratore* 2.6.22).

invented.' The gentleman of the house approved what Mr. Adams said, and declared, 'he was resolved to perform the ceremony this very evening.' To which the doctor objected, as no one was prepared with a speech, 'unless,' said he, (turning to Adams with a gravity of countenance which would have deceived a more knowing man) 'you have a sermon about you, doctor.'—'Sir,' says Adams, 'I never travel without one, for fear what may happen.' He was easily prevailed on by his worthy friend, as he now called the doctor, to undertake the part of the ambassador; so that the gentleman sent immediate orders to have the throne erected; which was performed before they had drank two bottles: and perhaps the reader will hereafter have no great reason to admire the nimbleness of the servants. Indeed, to confess the truth, the throne was no more than this; there was a great tub of water provided, on each side of which were placed two stools raised higher than the surface of the tub, and over the whole was laid a blanket; on these stools were placed the king and queen, namely, the master of the house, and the captain. And now the ambassador was introduced, between the poet and the doctor, who having read his sermon to the great entertainment of all present, was led up to his place, and seated between their majesties. They immediately rose up, when the blanket wanting its supports at either end, gave way, and soused Adams over head and ears in the water; the captain made his escape, but unluckily the gentleman himself not being as nimble as he ought, Adams caught hold of him before he descended from his throne, and pulled him in with him, to the entire secret satisfaction of all the company. Adams after ducking the squire twice or thrice leapt out of the tub, and looked sharp for the doctor, whom he would certainly have convey'd to the same place of honour; but he had wisely withdrawn: he then searched for his crabstick, and having found that, as well as his fellow-travellers, he declared he would not stay a moment longer in such a house. He then departed, without taking leave of his host, whom he had exacted a more severe revenge on, than he intended: for as he did not use sufficient care to dry himself in time, he caught a cold by the accident, which threw him into a fever, that had like to have cost him his life.

CHAPTER VIII

Which some readers will think too short, and others too long.

ADAMS, and Joseph, who was no less enraged than his friend, at the treatment he met with, went out with their sticks in their hands; and carried off Fanny, notwithstanding the opposition of the servants, who did all, without proceeding to violence, in their power to detain them. They walked as fast as they could, not so much from any apprehension of being pursued, as that Mr. Adams might by exercise prevent any harm from the water. The gentleman who had given such orders to his servants concerning Fanny, that he did not in the least fear her getting away, no sooner heard that she was gone, than he began to rave, and immediately dispatched several with orders, either to bring her back, or never return. The poet, the player, and all but the dancing-master and doctor went on this errand.

The night was very dark, in which our friends began their journey; however they made such expedition, that they soon arrived at an inn, which was at seven miles distance. Here they unanimously consented to pass the evening, Mr. Adams being now as dry as he was before he had set out on his embassy.

This inn, which indeed we might call an ale-house, had not the words, *The New Inn*, been writ on the sign, afforded them no better provision than bread and cheese, and ale; on which, however, they made a very comfortable meal; for hunger is better than a French cook.

They had no sooner supped, than Adams returning thanks to the Almighty for his food, declared he had eat his homely commons,[1] with much greater satisfaction than his splendid dinner, and exprest great contempt for the folly of mankind, who sacrificed their hopes of heaven to the acquisition of vast wealth, since so much comfort was to be found in the humblest state and the lowest provision. 'Very true, sir,' says a grave man who sat smoaking his pipe by the fire, and who was a traveller as well as himself. 'I have often been as much surprized as you

---

1 Fare.

are, when I consider the value which mankind in general set on riches, since every day's experience shews us how little is in their power; for what indeed truly desirable can they bestow on us? Can they give beauty to the deformed, strength to the weak, or health to the infirm? Surely if they could, we should not see so many ill-favoured faces haunting the assemblies of the great, nor would such numbers of feeble wretches languish in their coaches and palaces. No, not the wealth of a kingdom can purchase any paint, to dress pale Ugliness in the bloom of that young maiden, nor any drugs to equip Disease with the vigour of that young man. Do not riches bring us sollicitude instead of rest, envy instead of affection, and danger instead of safety? Can they prolong their own possession, or lengthen his days who enjoys them? So far otherwise, that the sloth, the luxury, the care which attend them, shorten the lives of millions, and bring them with pain and misery, to an untimely grave. Where then is their value, if they can neither embellish, or strengthen our forms, sweeten or prolong our lives? Again—Can they adorn the mind more than the body? Do they not rather swell the heart with vanity, puff up the cheeks with pride, shut our ears to every call of virtue, and our bowels to every motive of compassion!' 'Give me your hand, brother,' said Adams in a rapture; 'for I suppose you are a clergyman.' 'No truly,' answered the other, (indeed he was a priest of the Church of Rome; but those who understand our laws will not wonder he was not over-ready to own it.)[1] 'Whatever you are,' cries Adams, 'you have spoken my sentiments: I believe I have preached every syllable of your speech twenty times over: for it hath always appeared to me easier for a cable rope (which by the way is the true rendering of that word we have translated *camel*) to go through the eye of a needle, than for a rich man to get into the kingdom of heaven.'[2] 'That, sir,' said the other, 'will be easily granted you by divines, and is deplorably true: but as

---

1 Laws against Roman Catholics were severe at this time though generally not enforced. Priests could be fined £200 and charged with high treason for saying mass; and Catholic laymen could not enter the professions or stand for Parliament.

2 Adams' interpretation of Matthew 19:24 is a fairly common one, though not generally accepted by biblical scholars.

the prospect of our good at a distance doth not so forcibly affect us, it might be of some service to mankind to be made thoroughly sensible, which I think they might be with very little serious attention, that even the blessings of this world, are not to be purchased with riches. A doctrine in my opinion, not only metaphysically, but if I may so say, mathematically demonstrable; and which I have been always so perfectly convinced of, that I have a contempt for nothing so much as for gold.' Adams now began a long discourse; but as most which he said occurs among many authors, who have treated this subject, I shall omit inserting it. During its continuance Joseph and Fanny retired to rest, and the host likewise left the room. When the English parson had concluded, the Romish resumed the discourse, which he continued with great bitterness and invective; and at last ended by desiring Adams to lend him eighteen pence to pay his reckoning; promising, if he never paid him, he might be assured of his prayers. The good man answered, that eighteen pence would be too little to carry him any very long journey; that he had half a guinea in his pocket, which he would divide with him. He then fell to searching his pockets, but could find no money: for indeed the company with whom he dined, had past one jest upon him which we did not then enumerate, and had picked his pocket of all that treasure which he had so ostentatiously produced.

'Bless me,' cry'd Adams, 'I have certainly lost it, I can never have spent it. Sir, as I am a Christian I had a whole half guinea in my pocket this morning, and have not now a single halfpenny of it left. Sure the Devil must have taken it from me.' 'Sir,' answered the priest smiling, 'you need make no excuses; if you are not willing to lend me the money, I am contented.' 'Sir,' cries Adams, 'if I had the greatest sum in the world; ay, if I had ten pounds about me, I would bestow it all to rescue any Christian from distress. I am more vexed at my loss on your account than my own. Was ever any thing so unlucky? because I have no money in my pocket, I shall be suspected to be no Christian.' 'I am more unlucky,' quoth the other, 'if you are as generous as you say: for really a crown would have made me happy, and conveyed me in plenty to the place I am going, which is not above twenty miles off, and where I can arrive by tomorrow night, I assure you I am not accustomed to travel pennyless. I am but just arrived in England, and we were forced by a storm in our passage to throw all we had overboard. I don't suspect but this fellow will take my word for the trifle I owe him; but I hate to appear so mean as to confess myself without a shilling to such people: for these, and indeed too many others know little difference in their estimation between a beggar and a thief.' However, he thought he should deal better with the host that evening than the next morning; he therefore resolved to set out immediately, notwithstanding the darkness; and accordingly as soon as the host returned he communicated to him the situation of his affairs; upon which the host scratching his head, answered, 'Why, I do not know, master, if it be so, and you have no money, I must trust I think, tho' I had rather always have ready money if I could; but, marry, you look like so honest a gentleman, that I don't fear your paying me, if it was twenty times as much.' The priest made no reply, but taking leave of him and Adams, as fast as he could, not without confusion, and perhaps with some distrust of Adams's sincerity, departed.

He was no sooner gone than the host fell a shaking his head, and declared if he had suspected the fellow had no money, he would not have drawn him a single drop of drink; saying, he despaired of ever seeing his face again; for that he looked like a confounded rogue. 'Rabbit[1] the fellow,' cries he, 'I thought by his talking so much about riches, that he had a hundred pounds at least in his pocket.' Adams chid him for his suspicions, which he said were not becoming a Christian; and then without reflecting on his loss, or considering how he himself should depart in the morning, he retired to a very homely bed, as his companions had before; however, health and fatigue gave them a sweeter repose than is often in the power of velvet and down to bestow.

---

1 Confound, drat.

CHAPTER IX

Containing as surprizing and bloody adventures as can be found in this, or perhaps any other authentic history.

It was almost morning when Joseph Andrews, whose eyes the thoughts of his dear Fanny had opened, as he lay fondly meditating on that lovely creature, heard a violent knocking at the door over which he lay; he presently jumped out of bed, and opening the window, was asked if there were no travellers in the house; and presently by another voice, if two men and a young woman had not taken up their lodgings there that night. Tho' he knew not the voices, he began to entertain a suspicion of the truth; for indeed he had received some information from one of the servants of the squire's house, of his design; and answered in the negative. One of the servants who knew the host well, called out to him by his name, just as he had opened another window, and asked him the same question; to which he answered in the affirmative. 'O ho!' said another; 'have we found you?' And ordered the host to come down and open his door. Fanny, who was as wakeful as Joseph, no sooner heard all this, than she leap'd from her bed, and hastily putting on her gown and petticoats, ran as fast as possible to Joseph's room, who then was almost drest; he immediately let her in, and embracing her with the most passionate tenderness, bid her fear nothing: for he would die in her defence. 'Is that a reason why I should not fear,' says she, 'when I should lose what is dearer to me than the whole world?' Joseph then kissing her hand, said he could almost thank the occasion which had extorted from her a tenderness she would never indulge him with before. He then ran and waked his bedfellow Adams, who was yet fast asleep, notwithstanding many calls from Joseph: but was no sooner made sensible of their danger than he leaped from his bed, without considering the presence of Fanny, who hastily turned her face from him , and enjoyed a double benefit from the dark, which as it would have prevented any offence to an innocence less pure, or a modesty less delicate, so it concealed even those blushes which were raised in her.

Adams had soon put on all his clothes but his breeches, which in the hurry he forgot; however, they were pretty well supplied[1] by the length of his other garments: and now the house-door being opened, the captain, the poet, the player, and three servants came in. The captain told the host, that two fellows who were in his house had run away with a young woman, and desired to know in which room she lay. The host, who presently believed the story, directed them, and instantly the captain and poet, jostling one another, ran up. The poet, who was the nimblest, entering the chamber first, searched the bed and every other part, but to no purpose; the bird was flown, as the impatient reader, who might otherwise have been in pain for her, was before advertised.[2] They then enquired where the men lay, and were approaching the chamber, when Joseph roared out in a loud voice, that he would shoot the first man who offered to attack the door. The captain enquired what fire-arms they had; to which the host answered, he believed they had none; nay, he was almost convinced of it: for he had heard one ask the other in the evening, what they should have done, if they had been overtaken when they had no arms; to which the other answered, they would have defended themselves with their sticks as long as they were able, and G— would assist a just cause. This satisfied the captain, but not the poet, who prudently retreated down stairs, saying it was his business to record great actions, and not to do them. The captain was no sooner well satisfied that there were no fire-arms, than bidding defiance to gunpowder, and swearing he loved the smell of it, he ordered the servants to follow him, and marching boldly up, immediately attempted to force the door, which the servants soon helped him to accomplish. When it was opened, they discovered the enemy drawn up three deep; Adams in the front, and Fanny in the rear. The captain told Adams, that if they would go all back to the house again, they should be civilly treated: but unless they consented, he had orders to carry the young lady with him, whom there was great reason to believe they had stolen from her parents; for notwith-

1 Compensated for.

2 Informed.

standing her disguise, her air, which she could not conceal, sufficiently discovered her birth to be infinitely superiour to theirs. Fanny bursting into tears, solemnly assured him he was mistaken; that she was a poor helpless foundling, and had no relation in the world which she knew of; and throwing herself on her knees, begged that he would not attempt to take her from her friends, who she was convinced would die before they would lose her, which Adams confirmed with words not far from amounting to an oath. The captain swore he had no leisure to talk, and bidding them thank themselves for what happened, he ordered the servants to fall on, at the same time endeavouring to pass by Adams in order to lay hold on Fanny; but the parson interrupting him, received a blow from one of them, which without considering whence it came, he returned to the captain, and gave him so dextrous a knock in that part of the stomach which is vulgarly called the pit, that he staggered some paces backwards. The captain, who was not accustomed to this kind of play, and who wisely apprehended the consequence of such another blow, two of them seeming to him equal to a thrust through the body, drew forth his hanger,[1] as Adams approached him, and was levelling a blow at his head, which would probably have silenced the preacher for ever, had not Joseph in that instant lifted up a certain huge stone pot of the chamber with one hand, which six beaus could not have lifted with both,[2] and discharged it, together with the contents, full in the captain's face. The uplifted hanger dropped from his hand, and he fell prostrate on the floor *with a lumpish noise, and his halfpence rattled in his pocket*;[3] the red liquour which his veins contained, and the white liquor which the pot contained, ran in one stream down his face and his clothes. Nor had Adams quite escaped, some of the water having in its passage shed its honours on his head, and began to trickle down the wrinkles or rather furrows of his cheeks, when one of the servants

1 Short sword.

2 In the *Aeneid* 12.896–902, Turnus seizes a stone of great size with one hand which "twice six chosen men … could with difficulty raise to their shoulders" and hurls it at Aeneas.

3 A parody of the line "He fell with a thud, and his armour clattered upon him," which appears in various forms throughout the *Iliad*.

snatching a mop out of a pail of water which had already done its duty in washing the house, pushed it in the parson's face; yet could not he bear him down; for the parson wresting the mop from the fellow with one hand, with the other brought his enemy as low as the earth, having given him a stroke over that part of the face, where, in some men of pleasure, the natural and artificial noses are conjoined.[1]

Hitherto Fortune seemed to incline the victory on the travellers side, when, according to her custom, she began to shew the fickleness of her dispostion: for now the host entering the field, or rather chamber, of battle, flew directly at Joseph, and darting his head into his stomach (for he was a stout fellow, and an expert boxer) almost staggered him; but Joseph stepping one leg back, did with his left hand so chuck him under the chin that he reeled. The youth was pursuing his blow with his right hand, when he received from one of the servants such a stroke with a cudgel on his temples, that it instantly deprived him of sense, and he measured his length on the ground.

Fanny rent the air with her cries, and Adams was coming to the assistance of Joseph: but the two serving-men and the host now fell on him, and soon subdued him, tho' he fought like a madman, and looked so black with the impressions he had received from the mop, than Don Quixotte would certainly have taken him for an inchanted Moor.[2] But now follows the most tragical part; for the captain was risen again, and seeing Joseph on the floor, and Adams secured, he instantly laid hold on Fanny, and with the assistance of the poet and player, who hearing the battle was over, were now come up, dragged her, crying and tearing her hair, from the sight of her Joseph, and with a perfect deafness to all her entreaties, carried her down stairs by violence, and fastened her on the player's horse; and the captain mounting his own, and leading that on which this poor miserable wretch was, departed without any more consid-

---

1 There are many contemporary allusions in literature to the loss of the nose through venereal disease.

2 After a drubbing at an inn, having mistaken the tavern wench for an amorous princess, Don Quixote concludes that she is "guarded by some enchanted Moor" (*Don Quixote* 1.3.3).

eration of her cries than a butcher hath of those of a lamb; for indeed his thoughts were only entertained with the degree of favour which he promised himself from the squire on the success of this adventure.

The servants who were ordered to secure Adams and Joseph as safe as possible, that the squire might receive no interruption to his design on poor Fanny, immediately by the poet's advice tied Adams to one of the bed-posts, as they did Joseph on the other side, as soon as they could bring him to himself; and then leaving them together, back to back, and desiring the host not to set them at liberty, nor go near them till he had farther orders, they departed towards their master; but happened to take a different road from that which the captain had fallen into.

CHAPTER X

A discourse between the poet and player; of no other use in this history, but to divert the reader.

BEFORE we proceed any farther in this tragedy, we shall leave Mr. Joseph and Mr. Adams to themselves, and imitate the wise conductors of the stage; who in the midst of a grave action entertain you with some excellent piece of satire or humour called a dance. Which piece indeed is therefore danced, and not spoke, as it is delivered to the audience by persons whose thinking faculty is by most people held to lie in their heels; and to whom, as well as heroes, who think with their hands, nature hath only given heads for the sake of conformity, and as they are of use in dancing, to hang their hats on.[1]

The poet addressing the player, proceeded thus: 'As I was saying' (for they had been at this discourse all the time of the engagement, above stairs) 'the reason you have no good new plays is evident; it is from your discouragement of authors. Gentlemen will not write, sir, they will not write without the

1 Between the acts of a play, whether comedy or tragedy, audiences of the period expected to be entertained by dancers.

expectation of fame or profit, or perhaps both. Plays are like trees which will not grow without nourishment; but like mushrooms, they shoot up spontaneously, as it were, in a rich soil. The muses, like vines, may be pruned, but not with a hatchet. The town, like a peevish child, knows not what it desires, and is always best pleased with a rattle. A farce-writer hath indeed some chance for success; but they have lost all taste for the sublime. Tho' I believe one reason of their depravity is the badness of the actors. If a man writes like an angel, sir, those fellows know not how to give a sentiment utterance.' 'Not so fast,' says the player, 'the modern actors are as good at least as their authors, nay, they come nearer their illustrious predecessors, and I expect a Booth on the stage again, sooner than a Shakespear or an Otway;[1] and indeed I may turn your observation against you, and with truth say, that the reason no authors are encouraged, is because we have no good new plays.' 'I have not affirmed the contrary,' said the poet, 'but I am surprized you grow so warm; you cannot imagine yourself interested[2] in this dispute, I hope you have a better opinion of my taste, than to apprehend I squinted at yourself. No, sir, if we had six such actors as you, we should soon rival the Bettertons and Sandfords[3] of former times; for, without a compliment to you, I think it impossible for any one to have excelled you in most of your parts. Nay, it is solemn truth, and I have heard many, and all great judges, express as much; and you will pardon me if I tell you, I think every time I have seen you lately, you have constantly acquired some new excellence, like a snowball. You have deceived me in my estimation of perfection, and have outdone what I thought inimitable.' 'You are as little interested,' answer'd the player, 'in what I have said of other poets; for d—n me, if there are not manly strokes, ay whole scenes, in your last tragedy, which at least equal Shakespear. There is a delicacy of

---

1 Barton Booth (1681-1733), the most famous tragic actor of his times, particularly celebrated for his portayal of Othello; Thomas Otway, best known for his two blank-verse tragedies, *The Orphan* (1680) and *Venice Preserved* (1682).

2 Concerned.

3 Thomas Betterton (1635?-1710), the greatest actor of the Restoration in both comedy and tragedy; Samuel Sandford (dates not known; second half of the seventeeth century), renowned for his stage roles as villain.

sentiment, a dignity of expression in it, which I will own many of our gentlemen did not do adequate justice to. To confess the truth, they are bad enough, and I pity an author who is present at the murder of his works.'—'Nay, it is but seldom that it can happen,' returned the poet, 'the works of most modern authors, like dead-born children, cannot be murdered. It is such wretched half-begotten, half-writ, lifeless, spiritless, low, groveling stuff, that I almost pity the actor who is oblig'd to get it by heart, which must be almost as difficult to remember as words in a language you don't understand.' 'I am sure,' said the player, 'if the sentences have little meaning when they are writ, when they are spoken they have less. I know scarce one who ever lays an emphasis right, and much less adapts his action to his character. I have seen a tender lover in an attitude of fighting with his mistress, and a brave hero suing to his enemy with his sword in his hand—I don't care to abuse my profession, but rot me if in my heart I am not inclined to the poet's side.' 'It is rather generous in you than just,' said the poet; 'and tho' I hate to speak ill of any person's production; nay I never do it, nor will—but yet to do justice to the actors, what could Booth or Betterton have made of such horrible stuff as Fenton's *Mariamne*, Frowd's *Philotas*, or Mallet's *Eurydice*,[1] or those low, dirty, last dying-speeches, which a fellow in the City or Wapping, your Dillo or Lillo,[2] what was his name, called tragedies?'—'Very well, sir,' says the player, 'and pray what do you think of such fellows as Quin and Delane, or that face-making puppy young Cibber, that ill-looked dog Macklin, or that saucy slut Mrs. Clive?[3] What work would they make with your Shakespeares, Otways

1 Elijah Fenton, *Mariamne* (1723); Philip Frowde, *Philotas* (1731); and David Mallet, *Eurydice* (1731). All three plays are tragedies.

2 George Lillo, author of *The London Merchant* (1731) and *Fatal Curiosity* (1736), two successful domestic tragedies. Fielding accepted the latter play for the Haymarket Theatre and they became close friends.

3 James Quin (1693-1766), leading actor and rival of Garrick; Dennis Delane (d. 1750), Irish tragedian; Theophilus Cibber (1703-58), like his father, a successful comedian (acted in several of Fielding's plays); Charles Macklin (1697?-1797), actor and dramatist, well-known for his performance as Shylock; and Catherine "Kitty" Clive (1711-85), celebrated comic actress and singer, to whom Fielding had dedicated his *The Intriguing Chambermaid* (1734).

and Lees?[1] How would those harmonious lines of the last come from their tongues?

> —No more; for I disdain
> All pomp when thou art by—far be the noise
> Of kings and crowns from us, whose gentle souls
> Our kinder fates have steer'd another way.
> Free as the forest birds we'll pair together,
> Without rememb'ring who our fathers were:
> Fly to the arbors, grots and flowry meads,
> There in soft murmurs interchange our souls,
> Together drink the crystal of the stream,
> Or taste the yellow fruit which autumn yields.
> And when the golden evening calls us home,
> Wing to our downy nests and sleep till morn.

Or how would this disdain of Otway,

> Who'd be that foolish, sordid thing, call'd man?'[2]

'Hold, hold, hold,' said the poet, 'do repeat that tender speech in the third act of my play which you made such a figure in.'—'I would willingly,' said the player, 'but I have forgot it.'—'Ay, you was not quite perfect enough in it when you play'd it,' cries the poet, 'or you would have had such an applause as was never given on the stage; an applause I was extremely concerned for your losing.'—'Sure,' says the player, 'if I remember, that was hiss'd more than any passage in the whole play.'—'Ay your speaking it was hiss'd,' said the poet. 'My speaking it!' said the player.—'I mean your not speaking it,' said the poet. 'You was out,[3] and then they hiss'd.'—'They hiss'd, and then I was out, if I remember,' answer'd the player; 'and I must say this for myself, that the whole audience allowed I did your part justice, so

---

1 Nathaniel Lee, a writer of heroic tragedies, including *Theodosius* (1680), from which lines are now quoted by the player.

2 In Otway's *The Orphan* (1.1.362), the line reads: "Who'd be that sordid foolish thing call'd man … ?"

3 At a loss for words.

don't lay the damnation of your play to my account.' 'I don't know what you mean by damnation,' reply'd the poet. 'Why you know it was acted but one night,' cried the player. 'No,' said the poet, 'you and the whole town know I had enemies; the pit were all my enemies, fellows that would cut my throat, if the fear of hanging did not restrain them. All taylors, sir, all taylors.'—'Why should the taylors be so angry with you?' cries the player. 'I suppose you don't employ so many in making your clothes.' 'I admit your jest,' answered the poet, 'but you remember the affair as well as myself; you know there was a party in the pit and upper-gallery, would not suffer it to be given out again; tho' much, ay infinitely, the majority, all the boxes in particular, were desirous of it; nay, most of the ladies swore they never would come to the house till it was acted again—indeed I must own their policy[1] was good, in not letting it be given out a second time; for the rascals knew if it had gone a second night, it would have run fifty: for if ever there was distress in a tragedy—I am not fond of my own performance; but if I should tell you what the best judges said of it—nor was it entirely owing to my enemies neither, that it did not succeed on the stage as well as it hath since among the polite readers; for you can't say it had justice done it by the performers.'—'I think,' answer'd the player, 'the performers did the distress of it justice: for I am sure we were in distress enough, who were pelted with oranges all the last act; we all imagined it would have been the last act of our lives.'

The poet, whose fury was now raised, had just attempted to answer, when they were interrupted, and an end put to their discourse by an accident; which, if the reader is impatient to know, he must skip over the next chapter, which is a sort of counterpart to this, and contains some of the best and gravest matters in the whole book, being a discourse between Parson Abraham Adams and Mr. Joseph Andrews.

---

1 Strategy.

CHAPTER XI

Containing the exhortations of Parson Adams to his friend in affliction; calculated for the instruction and improvement of the reader.

JOSEPH no sooner came perfectly to himself, than perceiving his mistress gone, he bewailed her loss with groans, which would have pierced any heart but those which are possessed by some people, and are made of a certain composition not unlike flint in its hardness and other properties; for you may strike fire from them which will dart through the eyes, but they can never distil one drop of water the same way. His own, poor youth, was of a softer composition; and at those words, *O my dear Fanny! O my love! shall I never, never see thee more?* his eyes overflowed with tears, which would have become any but a hero. In a word, his despair was more easy to be conceived than related.—

Mr. Adams, after many groans, sitting with his back to Joseph, began thus in a sorrowful tone: 'You cannot imagine, my good child, that I entirely blame these first agonies of your grief; for, when misfortunes attack us by surprize, it must require infinitely more learning than you are master of to resist them: but it is the business of a man and a Christian to summon Reason as quickly as he can to his aid; and she will presently teach him patience and submission. Be comforted, therefore, child, I say be comforted. It is true you have lost the prettiest, kindest, loveliest, sweetest young woman: one with whom you might have expected to have lived in happiness, virtue and innocence. By whom you might have promised yourself many little darlings, who would have been the delight of your youth, and the comfort of your age. You have not only lost her, but have reason to fear the utmost violence which lust and power can inflict upon her. Now indeed you may easily raise ideas of horror, which might drive you to despair.'—'O I shall run mad,' cries Joseph, 'O that I could but command my hands to tear my eyes out and my flesh off.'—'If you would use them to such purposes, I am glad you can't,' answer'd Adams. 'I have stated your misfortune as strong as I possibly can; but on the other side, you are to consider you are a Christian, that no accident happens to us without the Divine permission, and that it is the duty of a man, much more of a Christian, to submit. We did not make ourselves; but the same power which made us, rules over us, and we are absolutely at His disposal; He may do with us what He pleases, nor have we any right to complain. A second reason against our complaint is our ignorance; for as we know not future events, so neither can we tell to what purpose any accident tends; and that which at first threatens us with evil, may in the end produce our good. I should indeed have said our ignorance is twofold (but I have not at present time to divide properly)[1] for as we know not to what purpose any event is ultimately directed; so neither can we affirm from what cause it originally sprung. You are a man, and consequently a sinner; and this may be punishment to you for your sins; indeed in this sense it may be esteemed as a good, yea as the greatest good, which satisfies the anger of Heaven, and averts that wrath which cannot continue without our destruction. Thirdly, our impotency of relieving ourselves, demonstrates the folly and absurdity of our complaints: for whom do we resist? or against whom do we complain, but a power from whose shafts no armour can guard us, no speed can fly? A power which leaves us no hope, but in submission.'—'O sir,' cried Joseph, 'all this is very true, and very fine; and I could hear you all day, if I was not so grieved at heart as now I am.' 'Would you take physick,' says Adams, 'when you are well, and refuse it when you are sick? Is not comfort to be administred to the afflicted, and not to those who rejoice, or those who are at ease?'—'O you have not spoken one word of comfort to me yet,' returned Joseph. 'No!' cries Adams, 'what am I then doing? what can I say to comfort you?'—'O tell me,' cries Joseph, 'that Fanny will escape back to my arms, that they shall again inclose that lovely creature, with all her sweetness, all her untainted innocence about her.'—'Why perhaps you may,' cries Adams; 'but I can't promise you what's to come. You must with perfect resignation wait the event; if she be restored to you again, it is

1 That is, to make logical distinctions and order his discourse accordingly.

your duty to be thankful, and so it is if she be not: Joseph, if you are wise, and truly know your own interest, you will peaceably and quietly submit to all the dispensations of Providence; being thoroughly assured, that all the misfortunes, how great soever, which happen to the righteous, happen to them for their own good.—Nay, it is not your interest only, but your duty to abstain from immoderate grief; which if you indulge, you are not worthy the name of a Christian.'—He spoke these last words with an accent a little severer than usual; upon which Joseph begged him not to be angry, saying he mistook him, if he thought he denied it was his duty; for he had known that long ago. 'What signifies knowing your duty, if you do not perform it?' answer'd Adams. 'Your knowledge encreases your guilt—O Joseph, I never thought you had this stubbornness in your mind.' Joseph replied, 'he fancied he misunderstood him, which I assure you,' says he, 'you do, if you imagine I endeavour to grieve; upon my soul I don't.' Adams rebuked him for swearing, and then proceeded to enlarge on the folly of grief, telling him, all the wise men and philosophers, even among the heathens, had written against it, quoting several passages from Seneca,[1] and the *Consolation*,[2] which tho' it was not Cicero's, was, he said, as good almost as any of his works, and concluded all by hinting, that immoderate grief in this case might incense that power which alone could restore him his Fanny. This reason, or indeed rather the idea which it raised of the restoration of his mistress, had more effect than all which the parson had said before; and for a moment abated his agonies: but when his fears sufficiently set before his eyes the danger that poor creature was in, his grief returned again with repeated violence, nor could Adams in the least aswage it; tho' it may be doubted in his behalf, whether Socrates himself could have prevailed any better.

They remained some time in silence; and groans and sighs

1 Lucius Annaeus Seneca (c. 4 BC–AD 65), Roman dramatist and Stoic philosopher, wrote several consolatory works.

2 As only a few fragments remain of Cicero's *Consolation*, written in 45 BC shortly after the death of his daughter, Fielding is probably alluding to the spurious *Consolatio Ciceronis*, first published at Venice in 1583, and certainly known to him.

issued from them both, at length Joseph burst out into the following soliloquy:

> Yes, I will bear my sorrows like a man,
> But I must also feel them as a man.
> I cannot but remember such things were,
> And were most dear to me—[1]

Adams asked him what stuff that was he repeated?—To which he answer'd, they were some lines he had gotten by heart out of a play. —'Ay, there is nothing but heathenism to be learn'd from plays,' reply'd he—I never heard of any plays fit for a Christian to read, but *Cato* and the *Conscious Lovers*;[2] and I must own in the latter there are some things almost solemn enough for a sermon.' But we shall now leave them a little, and enquire after the subject of their conversation.

CHAPTER XII

More adventures, which we hope will as much please as surprize the reader.

NEITHER the facetious dialogue which pass'd between the poet and player, nor the grave and truly solemn discourse of Mr. Adams, will, we conceive, make the reader sufficient amends for the anxiety which he must have felt on the account of poor Fanny, whom we left in so deplorable a condition. We shall therefore now proceed to the relation of what happened to that beautiful and innocent virgin, after she fell into the wicked hands of the captain.

The man of war having convey'd his charming prize out of the inn a little before day, made the utmost expedition in his

1 This is an altered version (perhaps the influence of contemporary acting convention) of lines from *Macbeth* 4.3.221-23, where Macduff laments the murder of his family.

2 Joseph Addison's *Cato* (1713), a neo-classical tragedy, and Richard Steele's *The Conscious Lovers* (1722), a sentimental comedy, are both impeccably moral plays.

power towards the squire's house, where this delicate creature was to be offered up a sacrifice to the lust of a ravisher. He was not only deaf to all her bewailings and entreaties on the road, but accosted her ears with impurities, which, having been never before accustomed to them, she happily for herself very little understood. At last he changed this note, and attempted to soothe and mollify her, by setting forth the splendor and luxury which would be her fortune with a man who would have the inclination, and power too, to give her whatever her utmost wishes could desire; and told her he doubted not but she would soon look kinder on him, as the instrument of her happiness, and despise that pitiful fellow, whom her ignorance only could make her fond of. She answered, she knew not whom he meant, she never was fond of any pitiful fellow. 'Are you affronted, madam,' says he, 'at my calling him so? but what better can be said of one in a livery, notwithstanding your fondness for him?' She returned, that she did not understand him, that the man had been her fellow-servant, and she believed was as honest a creature as any alive; but as for fondness for men—'I warrant ye,' cries the captain, 'we shall find means to persuade you to be fond; and I advise you to yield to gentle ones; for you may be assured that it is not in your power by any struggles whatever to preserve your virginity two hours longer. It will be your interest to consent; for the squire will be much kinder to you if he enjoys you willingly than by force.'—At which words she began to call aloud for assistance (for it was now open day) but finding none, she lifted her eyes to heaven, and supplicated the Divine assistance to preserve her innocence. The captain told her, if she persisted in her vociferation, he would find a means of stopping her mouth. And now the poor wretch perceiving no hopes of succour, abandoned herself to despair, and sighing out the name of Joseph, Joseph! a river of tears ran down her lovely cheeks, and wet the handkerchief which covered her bosom. A horseman now appeared in the road, upon which the captain threatened her violently if she complained; however, the moment they approached each other, she begged him with the utmost earnestness to relieve a distressed creature, who was in the hands of a ravisher. The fellow stopt at those words; but the captain assured him it was his wife, and that he was carrying her home from her adulterer. Which so satisfied the fellow, who was an old one, (and perhaps a married one too) that he wished him a good journey, and rode on. He was no sooner past, than the captain abused her violently for breaking his commands, and threaten'd to gagg her; when two more horsemen, armed with pistols, came into the road just before them. She again sollicited their assistance; and the captain told the same story as before. Upon which one said to the other—'That's a charming wench! Jack; I wish I had been in the fellow's place whoever he is.' But the other, instead of answering him, cried out eagerly, 'Zounds, I know her:' and then turning to her said, 'Sure you are not Fanny Goodwill?'—'Indeed, indeed I am,' she cry'd—'O John, I know you now—Heaven hath sent you to my assistance, to deliver me from this wicked man, who is carrying me away for his vile purposes—O for G—'s sake rescue me from him.' A fierce dialogue immediately ensued between the captain and these two men, who being both armed with pistols, and the chariot which they attended being now arrived, the captain saw both force and stratagem were vain, and endeavoured to make his escape; in which however he could not succeed. The gentleman who rode in the chariot, ordered it to stop, and with an air of authority examined into the merits of the cause; of which being advertised by Fanny, whose credit was confirmed by the fellow who knew her, he ordered the captain, who was all bloody from his encounter at the inn, to be conveyed as a prisoner behind the chariot, and very gallantly took Fanny into it; for, to say the truth, this gentleman (who was no other than the celebrated Mr. Peter Pounce, and who preceded the Lady Booby only a few miles, by setting out earlier in the morning) was a very gallant person, and loved a pretty girl better than any thing, besides his own money, or the money of other people.

The chariot now proceeded towards the inn, which as Fanny was informed lay in their way, and where it arrived at that very time while the poet and player were disputing below stairs, and Adams and Joseph were discoursing back to back above: just at that period to which we brought them both in the two preceding chapters, the chariot stopt at the door, and in an instant Fanny leaping from it, ran up to her Joseph.—O reader, conceive if thou canst, the joy which fired the breasts of these lovers on this meeting; and, if thy own heart doth not sympathetically assist thee in this conception, I pity thee sincerely from my own: for let the hard-hearted villain know this, that there is a pleasure in a tender sensation beyond any which he is capable of tasting.

Peter being informed by Fanny of the presence of Adams, stopt to see him, and receive his homage; for, as Peter was an hypocrite, a sort of people whom Mr. Adams never saw through, the one paid that respect to his seeming goodness which the other believed to be paid to his riches; hence Mr. Adams was so much his favourite, that he once lent him four pounds thirteen shillings and sixpence, to prevent his going to goal, on no greater security than a bond and judgment,[1] which probably he would have made no use of, tho' the money had not been (as it was) paid exactly at the time.

It is not perhaps easy to describe the figure of Adams; he had risen in such a violent hurry, that he had on neither breeches nor stockings; nor had he taken from his head a red spotted handkerchief, which by night bound his wig, that was turned inside out, around his head. He had on his torn cassock, and his great-coat; but as the remainder of his cassock hung down below his great-coat; so did a small strip of white, or rather whitish linnen appear below that; to which we may add the several colours which appeared on his face, where a long piss-burnt[2] beard, served to retain the liquor of the stone pot, and that of a blacker hue which distilled from the mop.—This figure, which Fanny had delivered from his captivity, was no sooner spied by Peter, than it disordered the composed gravity of his muscles; however he advised him immediately to make himself clean, nor would accept his homage in that pickle.

The poet and player no sooner saw the captain in captivity, than they began to consider of their own safety, of which flight

1 A legal document binding a person to pay a certain sum of money to another by a specified time on forfeiture of his property and goods.

2 Brown with urine.

presented itself as the only means; they therefore both of them mounted the poet's horse, and made the most expeditious retreat in their power.

The host, who well knew Mr. Pounce and the Lady Booby's livery, was not a little surprized at this change of the scene, nor was his confusion much helped by his wife, who was now just risen, and having heard from him the account of what had past, comforted him with a decent number of fools and blockheads, asked him why he did not consult her, and told him he would never leave following the nonsensical dictates of his own numscull, till she and her family were ruined.

Joseph being informed of the captain's arrival, and seeing his Fanny now in safety, quitted her a moment, and running down stairs, went directly to him, and stripping off his coat challenged him to fight; but the captain refused, saying he did not understand boxing. He then grasped a cudgel in one hand, and catching the captain by the collar with the other, gave him a most severe drubbing, and ended with telling him, he had now had some revenge for what his dear Fanny had suffered.

When Mr. Pounce had a little regaled himself with some provision which he had in his chariot, and Mr. Adams had put on the best appearance his clothes would allow him, Pounce ordered the captain into his presence; for he said he was guilty of felony, and the next justice of peace should commit him: but the servants (whose appetite for revenge is soon satisfied) being sufficiently contented with the drubbing which Joseph had inflicted on him, and which was indeed of no very moderate kind, had suffered him to go off, which he did, threatening a severe revenge against Joseph, which I have never heard he thought proper to take.

The mistress of the house made her voluntary appearance before Mr. Pounce, and with a thousand curt'sies told him, 'she hoped his honour would pardon her husband, who was a very *nonsense* man, for the sake of his poor family; that indeed if he could be ruined alone, she should be very willing of it, *for because as why*, his worship very well knew he deserved it: but she had three poor small children, who were not capable to get their own living; and if her husband was sent to goal, they must all come to the parish;[1] for she was a poor weak woman, continually a breeding, and had no time to work for them. She therefore hoped his honour would take it into his worship's consideration, and forgive her husband this time; for she was sure he never intended any harm to man, woman, or child; and if it was not for that block-head of his own, the man in some things was well enough; for she had three children by him in less than three years, and was almost ready to cry out the fourth time.' She would have proceeded in this manner much longer, had not Peter stopt her tongue, by telling her he had nothing to say to her husband, nor her neither. So, as Adams and the rest had assured her of forgiveness, she cried and curt'sied out of the room.

Mr. Pounce was desirous that Fanny should continue her journey with him in the chariot, but she absolutely refused, saying she would ride behind Joseph, on a horse which one of Lady Booby's servants had equipped him with. But alas! when the horse appeared, it was found to be no other than that identical beast which Mr. Adams had left behind him at the inn, and which these honest fellows who knew him had redeemed. Indeed whatever horse they had provided for Joseph, they would have prevailed with him to mount none, no not even to ride before his beloved Fanny, till the parson was supplied; much less would he deprive his friend of the beast which belonged to him, and which he knew the moment he saw, tho' Adams did not: however, when he was reminded of the affair, and told that they had brought the horse with them which he left behind, he answered—*Bless me! and so I did.*

Adams was very desirous that Joseph and Fanny should mount this horse, and declared he could very easily walk home. 'If I walked alone,' says he, 'I would wage a shilling, that the *pedestrian* out-stripped the *equestrian* travellers: but as I intend to take the company of a pipe, peradventure I may be an hour later.' One of the servants whispered Joseph to take him at his word, and suffer the old put[2] to walk if he would: this proposal was answered with an angry look and a peremptory refusal by

---

1 That is, end up as dependents of the parish, under the provision of the Poor Law.
2 Duffer, clown.

Joseph, who catching Fanny up in his arms, aver'd he would rather carry her home in that manner, than take away Mr. Adams's horse, and permit him to walk on foot.

Perhaps, reader, thou hast seen a contest between two gentlemen, or two ladies quickly decided, tho' they have both asserted they would not eat such a nice morsel, and each insisted on the other's accepting it; but in reality both were very desirous to swallow it themselves. Do not therefore conclude hence, that this dispute would have come to a speedy decision: for here both parties were heartily in earnest, and it is very probable, they would have remained in the inn-yard to this day, had not the good Peter Pounce put a stop to it; for finding he had no longer hopes of satisfying his old appetite with Fanny, and being desirous of having some one to whom he might communicate his grandeur, he told the parson he would convey him home in his chariot. This favour was by Adams, with many bows and acknowledgments, accepted, tho' he afterwards said, 'he ascended the chariot rather that he might not offend, than from any desire of riding in it, for that in his heart he preferred the *pedestrian* even to the *vehicular* expedition.' All matters being now settled, the chariot in which rode Adams and Pounce moved forwards; and Joseph having borrowed a pillion from the host, Fanny had just seated herself thereon, and had laid hold on the girdle which her lover wore for that purpose, when the wise beast, who concluded that one at a time was sufficient, that two to one were odds, &c. discovered much uneasiness at this double load, and began to consider his hinder as his fore-legs, moving the direct contrary way to that which is called forwards. Nor could Joseph with all his horsemanship persuade him to advance: but without having any regard to the lovely part of the lovely girl which was on his back, he used such agitations, that had not one of the men come immediately to her assistance, she had in plain English tumbled backwards on the ground. This inconvenience was presently remedied by an exchange of horses, and then Fanny being again placed on her pillion, on a better natured, and somewhat a better fed beast, the parson's horse finding he had no longer odds to contend with, agreed to march, and the whole procession set forwards for Booby-Hall, where they arrived in a few hours without any thing remarkable happening on the road, unless it was a curious dialogue between the parson and the steward; which, to use the language of a late apologist, a pattern to all biographers, *waits for the reader in the next chapter.*[1]

CHAPTER XIII

A curious dialogue which passed between Mr. Abraham Adams and Mr. Peter Pounce, better worth reading than all the works of Colley Cibber and many others.

THE chariot had not proceeded far, before Mr. Adams observed it was a very fine day. 'Ay, and a very fine country too,' answered Pounce. 'I should think so more,' returned Adams, 'if I had not lately travelled over the downs, which I take to exceed this and all other prospects in the universe.' 'A fig for prospects,' answered Pounce, 'one acre here is worth ten there; and for my own part, I have no delight in the prospect of any land but my own.' 'Sir,' said Adams, 'you can indulge yourself with many fine prospects of that kind.' 'I thank God I have a little,' replied the other, 'with which I am content, and envy no man: I have a little, Mr. Adams, with which I do as much good as I can.' Adams answered, that riches without charity were nothing worth; for that they were only a blessing to him who made them a blessing to others. 'You and I,' said Peter, 'have different notions of charity. I own, as it is generally used, I do not like the word, nor do I think it becomes one of us gentlemen; it is a mean parsonlike quality; tho' I would not infer many parsons have it neither.' 'Sir,' said Adams, 'my definition of charity is a generous disposition to relieve the distressed.' 'There is something in that definition,' answered Peter, 'which I like well enough; it is, as you say, a disposition—and does not so much consist in the act as in the disposition to do it; but alas, Mr. Adams, who are meant by the distressed? Believe me, the distresses of mankind are mostly imaginary, and

1 At the close of chapter 4 of his *Apology*, Cibber announces that discussions on acting are "waiting in the next Chapter ..."

it would be rather folly than goodness to relieve them.' 'Sure, sir,' replied Adams, 'hunger and thirst, cold and nakedness, and other distresses which attend the poor, can never be said to be imaginary evils.' 'How can any man complain of hunger,' said Peter, 'in a country where such excellent sallads are to be gathered in almost every field? or of thirst, where every river and stream produces such delicious potations? And as for cold and nakedness, they are evils introduced by luxury and custom. A man naturally wants clothes no more than a horse or any other animal, and there are whole nations who go without them: but these are things perhaps which you, who do not know the world —' 'You will pardon me, sir,' returned Adams, 'I have read of the Gymnosophists.'[1] 'A plague of your *Jehosaphats*,' cried Peter; 'the greatest fault in our constitution is the provision made for the poor, except that perhaps made for some others.[2] Sir, I have not an estate which doth not contribute almost as much again to the poor as to the land-tax, and I do assure you I expect to come myself to the parish in the end.' To which Adams giving a dissenting smile, Peter thus proceeded: 'I fancy, Mr. Adams, you are one of those who imagine I am a lump of money; for there are many who I fancy believe that not only my pockets, but my whole clothes, are lined with bank-bills; but I assure you, you are all mistaken: I am not the man the world esteems me. If I can hold my head above water, it is all I can. I have injured myself by purchasing. I have been too liberal of my money. Indeed I fear my heir will find my affairs in a worse situation than they are reputed to be. Ah! he will have reason to wish I had loved money more, and land less. Pray, my good neighbour, where should I have that quantity of riches the world is so liberal to bestow on me? Where could I possibly, without I had stole it, acquire such a treasure?' 'Why truly,' says Adams, 'I have been always of your opinion; I have wondered as well as yourself with what confidence they could report such things of you, which have to me appeared as mere

---

1 An ancient sect of Hindu ascetics who wore little or no clothing and did not eat meat.

2 Pounce, as a substantial landowner, would be required to pay tithes to support the clergy.

impossibilities; for you know, sir, and I have often heard you say it, that your wealth is of your own acquisition, and can it be credible that in your short time you should have amassed such a heap of treasure as these people will have you worth? Indeed had you inherited an estate like Sir Thomas Booby, which had descended in your family for many generations, they might have had a colour[1] for their assertions.' 'Why, what do they say I am worth?' cries Peter with a malicious sneer. 'Sir,' answered Adams, 'I have heard some aver you are not worth less than twenty thousand pounds.' At which Peter frowned. 'Nay, sir,' said Adams, 'you ask me only the opinion of others, for my own part I have always denied it, nor did I ever believe you could possibly be worth half that sum.' 'However, Mr. Adams,' said he, squeezing him by the hand, 'I would not sell them all I am worth for double that sum; and as to what you believe, or they believe, I care not a fig, no not a fart. I am not poor because you think me so, nor because you attempt to undervalue me in the country. I know the envy of mankind very well, but I thank Heaven I am above them. It is true my wealth is of my own acquisition. I have not an estate like Sir Thomas Booby, that hath descended in my family through many generations; but I know the heirs of such estates who are forced to travel about the country like some people in torn cassocks, and might be glad to accept of a pitiful curacy for what I know. Yes, sir, as shabby fellows as yourself, whom no man of my figure, without that vice of good-nature about him, would suffer to ride in a chariot with him.' 'Sir,' said Adams, 'I value not your chariot of a rush;[2] and if I had known you had intended to affront me, I would have walked to the world's end on foot ere I would have accepted a place in it. However, sir, I will soon rid you of that inconvenience,' and so saying, he opened the chariot-door without calling to the coachman, and leapt out into the highway, forgetting to take his hat along with him; which however Mr. Pounce threw after him with great violence. Joseph and Fanny stopt to bear him company the rest of the way, which was not above a mile.

---

1 Some reason.

2 At all, one little bit.

BOOK IV

CHAPTER I

The arrival of Lady Booby and the rest at Booby-Hall.

THE coach and six, in which Lady Booby rode, overtook the other travellers as they entered the parish. She no sooner saw Joseph, than her cheeks glow'd with red, and immediately after became as totally pale. She had in her surprize almost stopt her coach; but recollected herself timely enough to prevent it. She entered the parish amidst the ringing of bells, and the acclamations of the poor, who were rejoiced to see their patroness returned after so long an absence, during which time all her rents had been drafted to London, without a shilling being spent among them, which tended not a little to their utter impoverishing; for if the court would be severely missed in such a city as London, how much more must the absence of a person of great fortune be felt in a little country village, for whose inhabitants such a family finds a constant employment and supply; and with the offalls of whose table the infirm, aged, and infant poor are abundantly fed, with a generosity which hath scarce a visible effect on their benefactor's pockets?

But if their interest inspired so publick a joy into every countenance, how much more forcibly did the affection which they bore Parson Adams operate upon all who beheld his return. They flocked about him like dutiful children round an indulgent parent, and vyed with each other in demonstrations of duty and love. The parson on his side shook every one by the hand, enquiring heartily after the healths of all that were absent, of their children and relations, and exprest a satisfaction in his face, which nothing but benevolence made happy by its objects could infuse.

Nor did Joseph and Fanny want a hearty welcome from all who saw them. In short, no three persons could be more kindly received, as indeed none ever more deserved to be universally beloved.

Adams carried his fellow-travellers home to his house, where he insisted on their partaking whatever his wife, whom with his children he found in health and joy, could provide.

Where we shall leave them, enjoying perfect happiness over a homely meal, to view scenes of greater splendour but infinitely less bliss.

Our more intelligent readers will doubtless suspect by this second appearance of Lady Booby on the stage, that all was not ended by the dismission of Joseph; and to be honest with them, they are in the right; the arrow had pierced deeper than she imagined; nor was the wound so easily to be cured. The removal of the object soon cooled her rage, but it had a different effect on her love; that departed with his person; but this remained lurking in her mind with his image. Restless, interrupted slumbers, and confused horrible dreams were her portion the first night. In the morning, Fancy painted her a more delicious scene; but to delude, not delight her: for before she could reach the promised happiness, it vanished, and left her to curse, not bless the vision.

She started from her sleep, her imagination being all on fire with the phantom, when her eyes accidentally glancing towards the spot where yesterday the real Joseph had stood, that little circumstance raised his idea[1] in the liveliest colours in her memory. Each look, each word, each gesture rushed back on her mind with charms which all his coldness could not abate. Nay, she imputed that to his youth, his folly, his awe, his religion, to every thing, but what would instantly have produced contempt, want of passion for the sex; or, that which would have roused her hatred, want of liking to her.

Reflection then hurried her farther, and told her she must see this beautiful youth no more, nay, suggested to her, that she herself had dismissed him for no other fault, than probably that of too violent an awe and respect for herself; and which she ought rather to have esteemed a merit, the effects of which were besides so easily and surely to have been removed; she then blamed, she cursed the hasty rashness of her temper; her fury was vented all on herself, and Joseph appeared innocent in her eyes. Her passion at length grew so violent that it forced her on seeking relief, and now she thought of recalling him: but

1 Image.

Pride forbad that, Pride which soon drove all softer passions from her soul, and represented to her the meanness of him she was fond of. That thought soon began to obscure his beauties; Contempt succeeded next, and then Disdain, which presently introduced her hatred of the creature who had given her so much uneasiness. These enemies of Joseph had no sooner taken possession of her mind, than they insinuated to her a thousand things in his disfavour; every thing but dislike of her person; a thought, which as it would have been intolerable to her, she checked the moment it endeavoured to arise. Revenge came now to her assistance; and she considered her dismission of him stript, and without a character,[1] with the utmost pleasure. She rioted in the several kinds of misery, which her imagination suggested to her, might be his fate; and with a smile composed of anger, mirth, and scorn, viewed him in the rags in which her fancy had drest him.

Mrs. Slipslop being summoned, attended her mistress, who had now in her own opinion totally subdued this passion. Whilst she was dressing, she asked if that fellow had been turned away according to her orders. Slipslop answered, she had told her ladyship so, (as indeed she had)—'And how did he behave?' replied the lady. 'Truly madam,' cries Slipslop, 'in such a manner that *infected* every body who saw him. The poor lad had but little wages to receive: for he constantly allowed his father and mother half his income; so that when your ladyship's livery was stript off, he had not wherewithal to buy a coat, and must have gone naked, if one of the footmen had not *incommodated* him with one; and whilst he was standing in his shirt, (and to say truth, he was an *amorous* figure) being told your ladyship would not give him a character, he sighed, and said he had done nothing willingly to offend; that for his part he should always give your ladyship a good character where-ever he went; and he pray'd God to bless you; for you was the best of ladies tho' his enemies had set you against him: I wish you had not turned him away; for I believe you have not a faithfuller servant in the house.'—'How came you then,' replied the lady,

1 A character reference, testimonial.

'to advise me to turn him away?' 'I, madam,' said Slipslop, 'I am sure you will do me the justice to say, I did all in my power to prevent it; but I saw your ladyship was angry; and it is not the business of us upper servants to *hintorfear* on those occasions.'—'And was it not you, audacious wretch,' cried the lady, 'who made me angry? Was it not your tittle-tattle, in which I believe you belyed the poor fellow, which incensed me against him? He may thank you for all that hath happened; and so may I for the loss of a good servant, and one who probably had more merit than all of you. Poor fellow! I am charmed with his goodness to his parents. Why did not you tell me of that, but suffer me to dismiss so good a creature without a character? I see the reason of your whole behaviour now as well as your complaint; you was jealous of the wenches.' 'I jealous!' said Slipslop, 'I assure you I look upon myself as his betters; I am not meat for a footman I hope.' These words threw the lady into a violent passion, and she sent Slipslop from her presence, who departed tossing her nose and crying, 'Marry come up! there are some people more jealous than I, I believe.' Her lady affected not to hear the words, tho' in reality she did, and understood them too. Now ensued a second conflict, so like the former, that it might savour of repetition to relate it minutely. It may suffice to say, that Lady Booby found good reason to doubt whether she had so absolutely conquered her passion, as she had flattered herself; and in order to accomplish it quite, took a resolution more common than wise, to retire immediately into the country. The reader hath long ago seen the arrival of Mrs. Slipslop, whom no pertness could make her mistress resolve to part with; lately, that of Mr. Pounce, her fore-runners; and lastly, that of the lady herself.

The morning after her arrival being Sunday, she went to church, to the great surprize of every body, who wondered to see her ladyship, being no very constant churchwoman, there so suddenly upon her journey. Joseph was likewise there; and I have heard it was remarked that she fixed her eyes on him much more than on the parson; but this I believe to be only a malicious rumour. When the prayers were ended Mr. Adams stood up, and with a loud voice pronounced: *I publish the banns of marriage between Joseph Andrews and Frances Goodwill, both of this parish*, &c. Whether this had any effect on Lady Booby or no, who was then in her pew, which the congregation could not see into, I could never discover; but certain it is, that in about a quarter of an hour she stood up, and directed her eyes to that part of the church where the women sat, and persisted in looking that way during the remainder of the sermon, in so scrutinizing a manner, and with so angry a countenance, that most of the women were afraid she was offended at them.[1]

The moment she returned home, she sent for Slipslop into her chamber, and told her, she wondered what that impudent fellow Joseph did in that parish? Upon which Slipslop gave her an account of her meeting Adams with him on the road, and likewise the adventure with Fanny. At the relation of which, the lady often changed her countenance; and when she had heard all, she ordered Mr. Adams into her presence, to whom she behaved as the reader will see in the next chapter.

CHAPTER II

A dialogue between Mr. Abraham Adams and the Lady Booby.

MR. ADAMS was not far off; for he was drinking her ladyship's health below in a cup of her ale. He no sooner came before her, than she began in the following manner: 'I wonder, sir, after the many great obligations you have had to this family,' (with all which the reader hath, in the course of this history, been minutely acquainted) 'that you will ungratefully show any respect to a fellow who hath been turned out of it for his misdeeds. Nor doth it, I can tell you, sir, become a man of your character, to run about the country with an idle fellow and wench. Indeed, as for the girl, I know no harm of her. Slipslop tells me she was formerly bred up in my house, and behaved as she ought, till she hankered after this fellow, and he spoiled her. Nay, she may still perhaps do very well, if he will let her alone.

---

1 In many country churches, the pews of the gentry were elevated and enclosed by curtains, and separate seating was provided for women.

You are therefore doing a monstrous thing, in endeavouring to procure a match between these two people, which will be the ruin of them both.'—'Madam,' says Adams, 'if your ladyship will but hear me speak, I protest I never heard any harm of Mr. Joseph Andrews; if I had, I should have corrected him for it: for I never have, nor will encourage the faults of those under my cure. As for the young woman, I assure your ladyship I have as good an opinion of her as your ladyship yourself, or any other can have. She is the sweetest-tempered, honestest, worthiest, young creature; indeed as to her beauty, I do not commend her on that account, tho' all men allow she is the handsomest woman, gentle or simple, that ever appeared in the parish.' 'You are very impertinent,' says she, 'to talk such fulsome stuff to me. It is mighty becoming truly in a clergyman to trouble himself about handsome women, and you are a delicate judge of beauty, no doubt. A man who hath lived all his life in such a parish as this, is a rare judge of beauty. Ridiculous! Beauty indeed,—a country wench a beauty.—I shall be sick whenever I hear beauty mentioned again.—And so this wench is to stock the parish with beauties, I hope.—But, sir, our poor is numerous enough already; I will have no more vagabonds settled here.' 'Madam,' says Adams, 'your ladyship is offended with me, I protest without any reason. This couple were desirous to consummate long ago, and I dissuaded them from it; nay, I may venture to say, I believe, I was the sole cause of their delaying it.' 'Well,' says she, 'and you did very wisely and honestly too, notwithstanding she is the greatest beauty in the parish.'—'And now, madam,' continued he, 'I only perform my office to Mr. Joseph.'—'Pray don't mister such fellows to me,' cries the lady. 'He,' said the parson, 'with the consent of Fanny, before my face, put in the banns.'—'Yes,' answered the lady, 'I suppose the slut is forward enough; Slipslop tells me how her head runs on fellows; that is one of her beauties, I suppose. But if they have put in the banns, I desire you will publish them no more without my orders.' 'Madam,' cries Adams, 'if any one puts in sufficient caution, and assigns a proper reason against them, I am willing to surcease.'—'I tell you a reason,' says she, 'he is a vagabond, and he shall not settle here, and bring a nest of beggars into the parish; it will make us but little amends that they will be beauties.' 'Madam,' answered Adams, 'with the utmost submission to your ladyship, I have been informed by Lawyer Scout, that any person who serves a year, gains a settlement[1] in the parish where he serves.' 'Lawyer Scout,' replied the lady, 'is an impudent coxcomb; I will have no Lawyer Scout interfere with me. I repeat to you again. I will have no more incumbrances brought on us; so I desire you will proceed no farther.' 'Madam,' returned Adams, 'I would obey your ladyship in every thing that is lawful; but surely the parties being poor is no reason against their marrying. G—d forbid there should be any such law. The poor have little share enough of this world already; it would be barbarous indeed to deny them the common privileges, and innocent enjoyments which nature indulges to the animal creation.' 'Since you understand yourself no better,' cries the lady, 'nor the respect due from such as you to a woman of my distinction, than to affront my ears by such loose discourse, I shall mention but one short word; it is my orders to you, that you publish these banns no more; and if you dare, I will recommend it to your master, the doctor, to discard you from his service. I will, sir, notwithstanding your poor family; and then you and the greatest beauty in the parish may go and beg together.' 'Madam,' answered Adams, 'I know not what your ladyship means by the terms *master* and *service*. I am in the service of a Master who will never discard me for doing my duty: and if the doctor (for indeed I have never been able to pay for a licence)[2] thinks proper to turn me out from my cure, G— will provide me, I hope, another. At least, my family as well as myself have hands; and He will prosper,[3] I doubt not, our endeavours to get our bread honestly with them. Whilst my conscience is pure, I shall never fear what man can do unto me.'—'I condemn my humility,' said the lady, 'for demeaning myself to converse with you so long. I shall take other

---

1 One of the ways of gaining legal settlement in a parish was to live there as a hired servant for one year.

2 In order to preach, Adams should technically have had a licence. Without it, he could be removed from his cure by either the bishop or the incumbent.

3 Make successful.

measures; for I see you are a confederate[1] with them. But the sooner you leave me, the better; and I shall give orders that my doors may no longer be open to you, I will suffer no parsons who run about the country with beauties to be entertained here.'—'Madam,' said Adams, 'I shall enter into no person's doors against their will: but I am assured, when you have enquired farther into this matter, you will applaud, not blame my proceeding; and so I humbly take my leave;' which he did with many bows, or at least many attempts at a bow.

CHAPTER III

What past between the lady and Lawyer Scout.

IN the afternoon the lady sent for Mr. Scout, whom she attacked most violently for intermeddling with her servants, which he denied, and indeed with truth; for he had only asserted accidentally, and perhaps rightly, that a year's service gained a settlement; and so far he owned he might have formerly informed the parson, and believed it was law. 'I am resolved,' said the lady, 'to have no discarded servants of mine settled here; and so, if this be your law, I shall send to another lawyer.' Scout said, 'if she sent to a hundred lawyers, not one nor all of them could alter the law. The utmost that was in the power of a lawyer, was to prevent the law's taking effect; and that he himself could do for her ladyship as well as any other: and I believe,' says he, 'madam, your ladyship not being conversant in these matters hath mistaken a difference: for I asserted only, that a man who served a year was settled. Now there is a material difference between being settled in law and settled in fact; and as I affirmed generally he was settled, and law is preferable to fact, my settlement must be understood in law, and not in fact! And suppose, madam, we admit he was settled in law, what use will they make of it, how doth that relate to fact? He is not settled in fact; and if he be not settled in fact, he is not an inhabi-

1 In league.

tant; and if he is not an inhabitant, he is not of this parish; and then undoubtedly he ought not to be published here; for Mr. Adams hath told me your ladyship's pleasure, and the reason, which is a very good one, to prevent burdening us with the poor, we have too many already; and I think we ought to have an act to hang or transport half of them. If we can prove in evidence, that he is not settled in fact, it is another matter. What I said to Mr. Adams, was on a supposition that he was settled in fact; and indeed if that was the case, I should doubt.'—'Don't tell me your *facts* and your *ifs*,' said the lady, 'I don't understand your gibberish: you take too much upon you, and are very impertinent in pretending to direct in this parish, and you shall be taught better, I assure you, you shall. But as to the wench, I am resolved she shall not settle here; I will not suffer such beauties as these to produce children for us to keep.'—'Beauties indeed! your ladyship is pleased to be merry,'—answered Scout.—'Mr. Adams described her so to me,' said the lady. '—Pray what sort of dowdy is it, Mr. Scout?'—'The ugliest creature almost I ever beheld, a poor dirty drab,[1] your ladyship never saw such a wretch.'—'Well but, dear Mr. Scout, let her be what she will,—these ugly women will bring children you know; so that we must prevent the marriage.'—'True, madam,' replied Scout, 'for the subsequent marriage co-operating with the law, will carry law into fact. When a man is married, he is settled in fact; and then he is not removeable.[2] I will see Mr. Adams, and I make no doubt of prevailing with him. His only objection is doubtless that he shall lose his fee: but that being once made easy, as it shall be, I am confident no farther objection will remain. No, no, it is impossible: but your ladyship can't discommend his unwillingness to depart from his fee. Every man ought to have a proper value for his fee. As to the matter in question, if your ladyship pleases to employ me in it, I will venture to promise you success. The laws of this land are not so vulgar, to permit a mean fellow to contend with one of

1 Slut.

2 Scout would seem to have a clear understanding of the law on this point (see Giles Jacob, *The Statute-Law Common-plac'd* [1719]), although married couples were frequently the subjects of removal actions.

your ladyship's fortune. We have one sure card, which is to carry him before Justice Frolick, who, upon hearing your ladyship's name, will commit him without any farther questions. As for the dirty slut, we shall have nothing to do with her: for if we get rid of the fellow, the ugly jade will—' 'Take what measures you please, good Mr. Scout,' answered the lady, 'but I wish you could rid the parish of both; for Slipslop tells me such stories of this wench, that I abhor the thoughts of her; and tho' you say she is such an ugly slut, yet you know, dear Mr. Scout, these forward creatures who run after men, will always find some as forward as themselves: so that, to prevent the increase of beggars, we must get rid of her.'—'Your ladyship is very much in the right,' answered Scout, 'but I am afraid the law is a little deficient in giving us any such power of prevention; however the justice will stretch it as far as he is able, to oblige your ladyship. To say truth, it is a great blessing to the country that he is in the commission; for he hath taken several poor off our hands, that the law would never lay hold on. I know some justices who make as much of committing a man to Bridewell[1] as his lordship at size would of hanging him: but it would do a man good to see his worship our justice commit a fellow to Bridewell; he takes so much pleasure in it: and when once we ha' un there, we seldom hear any more o' un. He's either starved or eat up by vermin in a month's time.'—Here the arrival of a visitor put an end to the conversation, and Mr. Scout having undertaken the cause, and promised it success, departed.

This Scout was one of those fellows, who without any knowledge of the law, or being bred to it, take upon them, in defiance of an act of Parliament,[2] to act as lawyers in the country, and are called so. They are the pests of society, and a scandal to a profession, to which indeed they do not belong; and which owes to such kind of rascallions the ill-will which weak persons

---

1 Bridewell Hospital in London, a "correctional" institution for vagrants and other minor offenders. The term, however, came to be used generally for a gaol or house of correction.

2 An act was passed in 1729 making proper qualifications compulsory for practising law. The penalty was £50 for those ignoring it.

bear towards it. With this fellow, to whom a little before she would not have condescended to have spoken, did a certain passion for Joseph, and the jealousy and disdain of poor innocent Fanny, betray the Lady Booby, into a familiar discourse, in which she inadvertently confirmed many hints, with which Slipslop, whose gallant he was, had pre-acquainted him; and whence he had taken an opportunity to assert those severe falshoods of little Fanny, which possibly the reader might not have been well able to account for, if we had not thought proper to give him this information.

CHAPTER IV

A short chapter, but very full of matter; particularly the arrival of Mr. Booby and his lady.

ALL that night and the next day, the Lady Booby past with the utmost anxiety; her mind was distracted, and her soul tossed up and down by many turbulent and opposite passions. She loved, hated, pitied, scorned, admired, despised the same person by fits, which changed in a very short interval. On Tuesday morning, which happened to be a holiday, she went to church, where, to her surprize, Mr. Adams published the banns again with as audible a voice as before. It was lucky for her, that as there was no sermon, she had an immediate opportunity of returning home, to vent her rage, which she could not have concealed from the congregation five minutes; indeed it was not then very numerous, the assembly consisting of no more than Adams, his clerk, his wife, the lady, and one of her servants. At her return she met Slipslop, who accosted her in these words:—'O meam, what doth your ladyship think? To be sure Lawyer Scout hath carried Joseph and Fanny both before the justice. All the parish are in tears, and say they will certainly be hanged: for no body knows what it is for.'—'I suppose they deserve it,' says the lady. 'What dost thou mention such wretches to me?'—'O dear madam,' answer'd Slipslop, 'is it not a pity such a *graceless* young man should die a *virulent* death? I hope the judge will take *commensuration* on his youth. As for Fanny, I don't think it signifies much what becomes of her; and if poor Joseph hath done any thing, I could venture to swear she *traduced* him to it: few men ever come to *fragrant* punishment, but by those nasty creatures who are a scandal to our *sect*.' The lady was no more pleased at this news, after a moment's reflection, than Slipslop herself: for tho' she wished Fanny far enough, she did not desire the removal of Joseph, especially with her. She was puzzled how to act, or what to say on this occasion, when a coach and six drove into the court, and a servant acquainted her with the arrival of her nephew Booby and his lady. She ordered them to be conducted into a drawing-room, whither she presently repaired, having composed her countenance as well as she could; and being a little satisfied that the wedding would by these means be at least interrupted;[1] and that she should have an opportunity to execute any resolution she might take, for which she saw herself provided with an excellent instrument in Scout.

The Lady Booby apprehended her servant had made a mistake, when he mentioned Mr. Booby's lady; for she had never heard of his marriage: but how great was her surprize, when at her entering the room, her nephew presented his wife to her, saying, 'Madam, this is that charming Pamela, of whom I am convinced you have heard so much.' The lady received her with more civility than he expected; indeed with the utmost: for she was perfectly polite, nor had any vice inconsistent with good-breeding. They past some little time in ordinary discourse, when a servant came and whispered Mr. Booby, who presently told the ladies he must desert them a little on some business of consequence; and as their discourse during his absence would afford little improvement or entertainment to the reader, we will leave them for a while to attend Mr. Booby.

---

1 That is, there would now be an interruption in the publishing of the banns leading to the marriage of Joseph and Fanny.

CHAPTER V

Containing justice business; curious precedents of depositions, and other matters necessary to be perused by all justices of the peace and their clerks.

THE young squire and his lady were no sooner alighted from their coach, than the servants began to enquire after Mr. Joseph, from whom they said their lady had not heard a word to her great surprize, since he had left Lady Booby's. Upon this they were instantly informed of what had lately happened, with which they hastily acquainted their master, who took an immediate resolution to go himself, and endeavour to restore his Pamela her brother, before she even knew she had lost him.

The justice, before whom the criminals were carried, and who lived within a short mile of the lady's house, was luckily Mr. Booby's acquaintance, by his having an estate in his neighbourhood. Ordering therefore his horses to his coach, he set out for the judgment-seat, and arriv'd when the justice had almost finished his business. He was conducted into a hall, where he was acquainted that his worship would wait on him in a moment; for he had only a man and a woman to commit to Bridewell first. As he was now convinced he had not a minute to lose, he insisted on the servants introducing him directly into the room where the justice was then executing his office, as he called it. Being brought thither, and the first compliments being past between the squire and his worship, the former asked the latter what crime those two young people had been guilty of. 'No great crime,' answered the justice. 'I have only ordered them to Bridewell for a month.' 'But what is their crime?' repeated the squire. 'Larceny, an't please your honour,' said Scout. 'Ay,' says the justice, 'a kind of felonious larcenous thing. I believe I must order them a little correction too, a little stripping and whipping.' (Poor Fanny, who had hitherto supported all with the thoughts of her Joseph's company, trembled at that sound; but indeed without reason, for none but the Devil himself would have executed such a sentence on her.) 'Still,' said the squire, 'I am ignorant of the crime, the fact I mean.' 'Why, there it is in peaper,' answered the justice, shewing him a deposition, which in the absence of his clerk he had writ himself, of which we have with great difficulty procured an authentick copy; and here it follows *verbatim et literatim*.[1]

> *The Depusition of James Scout, layer, and Thomas Trotter, Yeoman, taken befor mee, on of his Magesty's Justasses of the Piece for Zumersetshire.*

'These deponants saith, and first Thomas Trotter for himself saith, that on the   of this instant October, being sabbath-day, betwin the ours of 2 and 4 in the afternoon, he zeed Joseph Andrews and Francis Goodwill walk akross a certane felde belunging to Layer Scout, and out of the path which ledes thru the said felde, and there he zede Joseph Andrews with a nife cut one hassel-twig, of the value, as he believes, of 3 half pence, or thereabouts; and he saith, that the said Francis Goodwill was likewise walking on the grass out of the said path in the said felde, and did receive and karry in her hand the said twig, and so was cumfarting, eading and abatting to the said Joseph therein. And the said James Scout for himself says, that he verily believes the said twig to be his own proper twig, &c.'

'Jesu!' said the squire, 'would you commit two persons to Bridewell for a twig?' 'Yes,' said the lawyer, 'and with great lenity too; for if we had called it a young tree they would have been both hanged.'—'Harkee, (says the justice, taking aside the squire) I should not have been so severe on this occasion, but Lady Booby desires to get them out of the parish; so Lawyer Scout will give the constable orders to let them run away, if they please; but it seems they intend to marry together, and the lady hath no other means, as they are legally settled there, to prevent their bringing an incumbrance on her own parish.' 'Well,' said the squire, 'I will take care my aunt shall be satisfied in this point; and likewise I promise you, Joseph here shall never be any incumbrance on her. I shall be oblig'd to you therefore,

1 "Word for word and letter for letter."

if, instead of Bridewell, you will commit them to my custody.'—'O to be sure, sir, if you desire it,' answer'd the justice; and without more ado, Joseph and Fanny were delivered over to Squire Booby, whom Joseph very well knew; but little ghest how nearly he was related to him. The justice burnt his *mittimus.* The constable was sent about his business. The lawyer made no complaint for want of justice, and the prisoners, with exulting hearts, gave a thousand thanks to his honour Mr. Booby, who did not intend their obligations to him should cease here; for ordering his man to produce a cloakbag[1] which he had caused to be brought from Lady Booby's on purpose, he desired the justice that he might have Joseph with him into a room; where ordering his servant to take out a suit of his own clothes, with linnen and other necessaries, he left Joseph to dress himself, who not yet knowing the cause of all this civility, excused his accepting such a favour, as long as decently he could. Whilst Joseph was dressing, the squire repaired to the justice, whom he found talking with Fanny; for during the examination she had lopped her hat over her eyes, which were also bathed in tears, and had by that means concealed from his worship what might perhaps have rendered the arrival of Mr. Booby unnecessary, at least for herself. The justice no sooner saw her countenance cleared up, and her bright eyes shining through her tears, than he secretly cursed himself for having once thought of Bridewell for her. He would willingly have sent his own wife thither, to have had Fanny in her place. And conceiving almost at the same instant desires and schemes to accomplish them, he employed the minutes whilst the squire was absent with Joseph, in assuring her how sorry he was for having treated her so roughly before he knew her merit; and told her, that since Lady Booby was unwilling that she should settle in her parish, she was heartily welcome to his, where he promised her his protection, adding, that he would take Joseph and her into his own family, if she liked it; which assurance he confirmed with a squeeze by the hand. She thanked him very kindly, and said, 'she would acquaint Joseph with the offer,

1 Valise, portmanteau.

which he would certainly be glad to accept; for that Lady Booby was angry with them both; tho' she did not know either had done any thing to offend her: but imputed it to Madam Slipslop, who had always been her enemy.'

The squire now returned, and prevented any farther continuance of this conversation; and the justice out of a pretended respect to his guest, but in reality from an apprehension of a rival; (for he knew nothing of his marriage,) ordered Fanny into the kitchin, whither she gladly retired; nor did the squire, who declined the trouble of explaining the whole matter, oppose it.

It would be unnecessary, if I was able, which indeed I am not, to relate the conversation between these two gentlemen, which rolled, as I have been informed, entirely on the subject of horse-racing. Joseph was soon drest in the plainest dress he could find, which was a blue coat and breeches, with a gold edging, and a red waistcoat with the same; and as this suit, which was rather too large for the squire, exactly fitted him; so he became it so well, and looked so genteel, that no person would have doubted its being as well adapted to his quality as his shape; nor have suspected, as one might when my Lord —, or Sir —, or Mr. — appear in lace or embroidery, that the taylor's man wore those clothes home on his back, which he should have carried under his arm.

The squire now took leave of the justice, and calling for Fanny, made her and Joseph, against their wills, get into the coach with him, which he then ordered to drive to Lady Booby's.—It had moved a few yards only, when the squire asked Joseph, if he knew who that man was crossing the field; for, added he, 'I never saw one take such strides before.' Joseph answered eagerly, 'O sir, it is Parson Adams.'—'O la, indeed, and so it is,' said Fanny; 'poor man he is coming to do what he could for us. Well, he is the worthiest best natur'd creature.'—'Ay,' said Joseph, 'God bless him; for there is not such another in the universe.'—'The best creature living sure,' cries Fanny. 'Is he?' says the squire, 'then I am resolved to have the best creature living in my coach,' and so saying he ordered it to stop, whilst Joseph at his request hollowed to the parson, who well knowing his voice, made all the haste imaginable, and soon came up with them; he was desired by the master, who could scarce refrain from laughter at his figure, to mount into the coach, which he with many thanks refused, saying he could walk by its side, and he'd warrant he kept up with it; but he was at length over-prevailed on. The squire now acquainted Joseph with his marriage; but he might have spared himself that labour; for his servant, whilst Joseph was dressing, had performed that office before. He continued to express the vast happiness he enjoyed in his sister, and the value he had for all who belonged to her. Joseph made many bows, and exprest as many acknowledgments; and Parson Adams, who now first perceived Joseph's new apparel, burst into tears with joy, and fell to rubbing his hands and snapping his fingers, as if he had been mad.

They were now arrived at the Lady Booby's, and the squire desiring them to wait a moment in the court, walked in to his aunt, and calling her out from his wife, acquainted her with Joseph's arrival; saying, 'Madam, as I have married a virtuous and worthy woman, I am resolved to own her relations, and shew them all a proper respect; I shall think myself therefore infinitely obliged to all mine, who will do the same. It is true, her brother hath been your servant; but he is now become my brother; and I have one happiness, that neither his character, his behaviour or appearance give me any reason to be ashamed of calling him so. In short, he is now below, drest like a gentleman, in which light I intend he shall hereafter be seen; and you will oblige me beyond expression, if you will admit him to be of our party; for I know it will give great pleasure to my wife, tho' she will not mention it.'

This was a stroke of fortune beyond Lady Booby's hopes or expectation; she answered him eagerly, 'Nephew, you know how easily I am prevailed on to do any thing which Joseph Andrews desires—Phoo, I mean which you desire me, and as he is now your relation, I cannot refuse to entertain him as such.' The squire told her, he knew his obligation to her for her compliance, and going three steps, returned and told her—he had one more favour, which he believed she would easily grant, as she had accorded him the former. 'There is a young woman—' 'Nephew,' says she, 'don't let my good-nature make you desire, as is too commonly the case, to impose on me. Nor think, because I have with so much condescension agreed to suffer your brother-in-law to come to my table, that I will submit to the company of all my own servants, and all the dirty trollops in the country.' 'Madam,' answer'd the squire, 'I believe you never saw this young creature. I never beheld such sweetness and innocence joined with such beauty, and withal so genteel.' 'Upon my soul, I won't admit her,' reply'd the lady in a passion; 'the whole world shan't prevail on me, I resent even the desire as an affront, and—' The squire, who knew her inflexibility, interrupted her, by asking pardon, and promising not to mention it more. He then returned to Joseph, and she to Pamela. He took Joseph aside and told him, he would carry him to his sister; but could not prevail as yet for Fanny. Joseph begged that he might see his sister alone, and then be with his Fanny; but the squire knowing the pleasure his wife would have in her brother's company, would not admit it, telling Joseph there would be nothing in so short an absence from Fanny, whilst he was assured of her safety; adding, he hoped he could not so easily quit a sister whom he had not seen so long, and who so tenderly loved him—Joseph immediately complied; for indeed no brother could love a sister more; and recommending Fanny, who rejoiced that she was not to go before Lady Booby, to the care of Mr. Adams, he attended the squire up stairs, whilst Fanny repaired with the parson to his house, where she thought herself secure of a kind reception.

CHAPTER VI

Of which you are desired to read no more than you like.

THE meeting between Joseph and Pamela was not without tears of joy on both sides; and their embraces were full of tenderness and affection. They were however regarded with much more pleasure by the nephew than by the aunt, to whose flame they were fewel only; and this was increased by the addition of dress, which was indeed not wanted to set off the lively colours in which nature had drawn health, strength, comeliness, and youth. In the afternoon Joseph, at their request, entertained them with the account of his adventures, nor could Lady Booby conceal her dissatisfaction at those parts in which Fanny was concerned, especially when Mr. Booby launched forth into such rapturous praises of her beauty. She said, applying to her niece, that she wondered her nephew, who had pretended[1] to marry for love, should think such a subject proper to amuse his wife with: adding, that for her part, she should be jealous of a husband who spoke so warmly in praise of another woman. Pamela answer'd, indeed she thought she had cause; but it was an instance of Mr. Booby's aptness to see more beauty in women than they were mistresses of. At which words both the women fixed their eyes on two looking-glasses; and Lady Booby replied that men were in the general very ill judges of beauty; and then whilst both contemplated only their own faces, they paid a cross compliment to each other's charms. When the hour of rest approached, which the lady of the house deferred as long as decently she could, she informed Joseph (whom for the future we shall call Mr. Joseph, he having as good a title to that appellation as many others, I mean that incontested one of good clothes) that she had ordered a bed to be provided for him; he declined this favour to his utmost; for his heart had long been with his Fanny; but she insisted on his accepting it, alledging that the parish had no proper accommodation for such a person, as he was now to esteem himself. The squire and his lady both joining with her, Mr. Joseph was at last forced to give over his design of visiting Fanny that evening, who on her side as impatiently expected him till midnight, when in complacence to Mr. Adams's family, who had sat up two hours out of respect to her, she retired to bed, but not to sleep; the thoughts of her love kept her waking, and his not returning according to his promise, filled her with uneasiness; of which however she could not assign any other cause than merely that of being absent from him.

---

1 Professed.

Mr. Joseph rose early in the morning, and visited her in whom his soul delighted. She no sooner heard his voice in the parson's parlour, than she leapt from her bed, and dressing herself in a few minutes, went down to him. They past two hours with inexpressible happiness together, and then having appointed Monday, by Mr. Adams's permission, for their marriage, Mr. Joseph returned according to his promise, to breakfast at the Lady Booby's, with whose behaviour since the evening we shall now acquaint the reader.

She was no sooner retired to her chamber than she asked Slipslop what she thought of this wonderful creature her nephew had married. 'Madam?' said Slipslop, not yet sufficiently understanding what answer she was to make. 'I ask you,' answer'd the lady, 'what you think of the dowdy, my niece I think I am to call her?' Slipslop, wanting no further hint, began to pull her to pieces, and so miserably defaced her, that it would have been impossible for any one to have known the person. The lady gave her all the assistance she could, and ended with saying—'I think, Slipslop, you have done her justice; but yet, bad as she is, she is an angel compared to this Fanny.' Slipslop then fell on Fanny, whom she hack'd and hew'd in the like barbarous manner, concluding with an observation that there was always something in those low-life creatures which must eternally distinguish them from their betters. 'Really,' said the lady, 'I think there is one exception to your rule, I am certain you may ghess who I mean.'—'Not I, upon my word, madam,' said Slipslop.—'I mean a young fellow; sure you are the dullest wretch,' said the lady.—'O la, I am indeed—Yes truly, madam, he is an *accession*,' answer'd Slipslop.—'Ay, is he not, Slipslop?' returned the lady. 'Is he not so genteel that a prince might without a blush acknowledge him for his son. His behaviour is such that would not shame the best education. He borrows from his station a condescension in every thing to his superiours, yet unattended by that mean servility which is called good-behaviour in such persons. Every thing he doth hath no mark of the base motive of fear, but visibly shews some respect and gratitude, and carries with it the persuasion of love—And then for his virtues; such piety to his parents, such tender affection to his sister, such integrity in his friendship, such bravery, such goodness, that if he had been born a gentleman, his wife would have possest the most invaluable blessing.'—'To be sure, ma'am,' says Slipslop.—'But as he is,' answered the lady, 'if he had a thousand more good qualities, it must render a woman of fashion contemptible even to be suspected of thinking of him, yes I should despise myself for such a thought.' 'To be sure, ma'am,' said Slipslop. 'And why to be sure?' reply'd the lady, 'thou art always one's echo. Is he not more worthy of affection than a dirty country clown, tho' born of a family as old as the flood, or an idle worthless rake, or little puisny[1] beau of quality? And yet these we must condemn ourselves to, in order to avoid the censure of the world; to shun the contempt of others, we must ally ourselves to those we despise; we must prefer birth, title and fortune to real merit. It is a tyranny of custom, a tyranny we must comply with: for we people of fashion are the slaves of custom.'—'Marry come up!' said Slipslop, who now well knew which party to take, 'if I was a woman of your ladyship's fortune and quality, I would be a slave to no body.'—'Me,' said the lady, 'I am speaking, if a young woman of fashion who had seen nothing of the world should happen to like such a fellow.—Me indeed; I hope thou dost not imagine —' 'No, ma'am, to be sure,' cried Slipslop.—'No! what no?' cried the lady. 'Thou art always ready to answer, before thou hast heard one. So far I must allow he is a charming fellow. Me indeed! No, Slipslop, all thoughts of men are over with me.—I have lost a husband, who—but if I should reflect, I should run mad.—My future ease must depend upon forgetfulness. Slipslop, let me hear some of thy nonsense to turn my thoughts another way. What dost thou think of Mr. Andrews?' 'Why I think,' says Slipslop, 'he is the handsomest most properest man I ever saw; and if I was a lady of the greatest degree, it would be well for some folks. Your ladyship may talk of custom if you please; but I am *confidous* there is no more comparison between young Mr. Andrews, and most of the young gentlemen who come to your ladyship's house in London; a parcel of *whipper-snapper* sparks: I

---

1 Puny.

would sooner marry our old Parson Adams. Never tell me what people say, whilst I am happy in the arms of him I love. Some folks rail against other folks, because other folks have what some folks would be glad of.'—'And so,' answered the lady, 'if you was a woman of condition, you would really marry Mr. Andrews?'—'Yes, I assure your ladyship,' replied Slipslop, 'if he would have me.'—'Fool, idiot,' cries the lady, 'if he would have a woman of fashion! Is that a question?' 'No truly, madam,' said Slipslop, 'I believe it would be none, if Fanny was out of the way; and I am *confidous* if I was in your ladyship's place, and liked Mr. Joseph Andrews, she should not stay in the parish a moment. I am sure Lawyer Scout would send her packing, if your ladyship would but say the word.' This last speech of Slipslop raised a tempest in the mind of her mistress. She feared Scout had betrayed her, or rather that she had betrayed herself. After some silence and a double change of her complexion; first to pale and then to red, she thus spoke: 'I am astonished at the liberty you give your tongue. Would you insinuate, that I employed Scout against this wench, on account of the fellow?' 'La ma,am,' said Slipslop, frighted out of her wits. 'I *assassinate* such a thing!' 'I think you dare not,' answered the lady, 'I believe my conduct may defy malice itself to assert so cursed a slander. If I had ever discovered[1] any wantonness, any lightness in my behaviour: if I had followed the example of some whom thou hast I believe seen, in allowing myself indecent liberties, even with a husband: but the dear man who is gone (*here she began to sob*) was he alive again, (*then she produced tears*) could not upbraid me with any one act of tenderness or passion. No, Slipslop, all the time I cohabited with him, he never obtained even a kiss from me, without my expressing reluctance in the granting it. I am sure he himself never suspected how much I loved him.—Since his death, thou knowest, tho' it is almost six weeks (it wants but a day) ago, I have not admitted one visitor, till this fool my nephew arrived. I have confined myself quite to one party of friends.—And can such a conduct as this fear to be arraigned? To be accused not only of a passion which I have

1 Shown, revealed

always despised; but of fixing it on such an object, a creature so much beneath my notice.'—'Upon my word, ma'am,' says Slipslop, 'I do not understand your ladyship, nor know I any thing of the matter.'—'I believe indeed thou dost not understand me.—Those are delicacies which exist only in superior minds; thy coarse ideas cannot comprehend them. Thou art a low creature, of the Andrews breed, a reptile of a lower order, a weed that grows in the common garden of the creation.'—'I assure your ladyship,' says Slipslop, whose passions were almost of as high an order as her lady's, 'I have no more to do with *Common Garden*[1] than other folks. Really, your ladyship talks of servants as if they were not born of the Christian *specious*. Servants have flesh and blood as well as quality; and Mr. Andrews himself is a proof that they have as good, if not better. And for my own part, I can't perceive my *dears*[*] are coarser than other people's; and I am sure, if Mr. Andrews was a *dear* of mine, I should not be ashamed of him in company with gentlemen; for whoever hath seen him in his new clothes, must confess he looks as much like a gentleman as any body. Coarse, quotha![2] I can't bear to hear the poor young fellow run down neither; for I will say this, I never heard him say an ill word of any body in his life. I am sure his coarseness doth not lie in his heart; for he is the best-natur'd man in the world; and as for his skin, it is no coarser than other people's, I am sure. His bosom when a boy was as white as driven snow; and where it is not covered with hairs, is so still. Ifaukins![3] if I was Mrs. Andrews, with a hundred a year, I should not envy the best she who wears a head.[4] A woman that could not be happy with such a man, ought never to be so: for if he can't make a woman happy, I never yet beheld the man who could. I say again I wish I was a great lady for his sake, I believe when I had made a gentleman of him,

---

* Meaning perhaps ideas [Fielding's note].

---

1 A colloquial variant of Covent Garden, a haunt of prostitutes (or "common women").

2 Indeed.

3 In faith, by my faith. (Also efags.)

4 That is, who sports the highest fashion (of hair styles).

he'd behave so, that no body should *deprecate* what I had done; and I fancy few would venture to tell him he was no gentleman to his face, nor to mine neither.' At which words, taking up the candles, she asked her mistress, who had been some time in her bed, if she had any farther commands; who mildly answered she had none; and telling her, she was a comical creature, bid her good-night.

CHAPTER VII

Philosophical reflections, the like not to be found in any light French romance. Mr. Booby's grave advice to Joseph, and Fanny's encounter with a beau.

HABIT, my good reader, hath so vast a prevalence over the human mind, that there is scarce any thing too strange or too strong to be asserted of it. The story of the miser, who from long accustoming to cheat others, came at last to cheat himself, and with great delight and triumph, picked his own pocket of a guinea, to convey to his hoard, is not impossible or improbable. In like manner, it fares with the practisers of deceit, who from having long deceived their acquaintance, gain at last a power of deceiving themselves, and acquire that very opinion (however false) of their own abilities, excellencies and virtues, into which they have for years perhaps endeavoured to betray their neighbours. Now, reader, to apply this observation to my present purpose, thou must know, that as the passion generally called love, exercises most of the talents of the female or fair world; so in this they now and then discover a small inclination to deceit; for which thou wilt not be angry with the beautiful creatures, when thou hast considered, that at the age of seven or something earlier, miss is instructed by her mother, that master is a very monstrous kind of animal, who will, if she suffers him to come too near her, infallibly[1] eat her up, and grind her to pieces. That so far from kissing or toying with him of her own

1 Certainly, surely.

accord, she must not admit him to kiss or toy with her. And lastly, that she must never have any affection towards him; for if she should, all her friends in petticoats would esteem her a traitress, point at her, and hunt her out of their society. These impressions being first received, are farther and deeper inculcated by their school-mistresses and companions; so that by the age of ten they have contracted such a dread and abhorrence of the above named monster, that whenever they see him, they fly from him as the innocent hare doth from the greyhound. Hence to the age of fourteen or fifteen, they entertain a mighty antipathy to master; they resolve and frequently profess that they will never have any commerce with him, and entertain fond hopes of passing their lives out of his reach, of the possibility of which they have so visible an example in their good maiden aunt. But when they arrive at this period, and have now past their second climacteric,[1] when their wisdom grown riper, begins to see a little farther; and from almost daily falling in master's way, to apprehend the great difficulty of keeping out of it; and when they observe him look often at them, and sometimes very eagerly and earnestly too, (for the monster seldom takes any notice of them till at this age) they then begin to think of their danger; and as they perceive they cannot easily avoid him, the wiser part bethink themselves of providing by other means for their security. They endeavour by all the methods they can invent to render themselves so amiable in his eyes, that he may have no inclination to hurt them; in which they generally succeed so well, that his eyes, by frequent languishing, soon lessen their idea of his fierceness, and so far abate their fears, that they venture to parley with him; and when they perceive him so different from what he hath been described, all gentleness, softness, kindness, tenderness, fondness, their dreadful apprehensions vanish in a moment; and now (it being usual with the human mind to skip from one extreme to its opposite, as easily, and almost as suddenly, as a bird from one bough to another;) love instantly succeeds to fear: but as it happens to

1 According to ancient belief, the "climacteric" is a critical period in a person's life, usually thought to occur every seven years. Hence the second of these marked the beginning of pubescence.

persons, who have in their infancy been thoroughly frightned with certain no persons called ghosts, that they retain their dread of those beings, after they are convinced that there are no such things; so these young ladies, tho' they no longer apprehend devouring, cannot so entirely shake off all that hath been instilled into them; they still entertain the idea of that censure which was so strongly imprinted on their tender minds, to which the declarations of abhorrence they every day hear from their companions greatly contribute. To avoid this censure therefore, is now their only care; for which purpose they still pretend the same aversion to the monster: and the more they love him, the more ardently they counterfeit the antipathy. By the continual and constant practice of which deceit on others, they at length impose on themselves, and really believe they hate what they love. Thus indeed it happened to Lady Booby, who loved Joseph long before she knew it; and now loved him much more than she suspected. She had indeed, from the time of his sister's arrival in the quality of her niece; and from the instant she viewed him in the dress and character of a gentleman, began to conceive secretly a design which love had concealed from herself, 'till a dream betrayed it to her.

She had no sooner risen than she sent for her nephew; when he came to her, after many compliments on his choice, she told him, 'he might perceive in her condescension to admit her own servant to her table, that she looked on the family of Andrews as his relations, and indeed her's; that as he had married into such a family, it became him to endeavour by all methods to raise it as much as possible; at length she advised him to use all his art to dissuade Joseph from his intended match, which would still enlarge their relation to meanness and poverty; concluding, that by a commission in the army, or some other genteel employment, he might soon put young Mr. Andrews on the foot of a gentleman; and that being once done, his accomplishments might quickly gain him an alliance, which would not be to their discredit.'

Her nephew heartily embraced this proposal; and finding Mr. Joseph with his wife, at his return to her chamber, he immediately began thus: 'My love to my dear Pamela, brother, will extend to all her relations; nor shall I shew them less respect than if I had married into the family of a duke. I hope I have given you some early testimonies of this, and shall continue to give you daily more. You will excuse me therefore, brother, if my concern for your interest makes me mention what may be, perhaps, disagreeable to you to hear: but I must insist upon it, that if you have any value for my alliance or my friendship, you will decline any thoughts of engaging farther with a girl, who is, as you are a relation of mine, so much beneath you. I know there may be at first some difficulty in your compliance, but that will daily diminish; and you will in the end sincerely thank me for my advice. I own, indeed, the girl is handsome: but beauty alone is a poor ingredient, and will make but an uncomfortable marriage.' 'Sir,' said Joseph, 'I assure you her beauty is her least perfection; nor do I know a virtue which that young creature is not possest of.' 'As to her virtues,' answered Mr. Booby, 'you can be yet but a slender judge of them: but if she had never so many, you will find her equal in these among her superiors in birth and fortune, which now you are to esteem on a footing with yourself; at least I will take care they shall shortly be so, unless you prevent me by degrading yourself with such a match, a match I have hardly patience to think of; and which would break the hearts of your parents, who now rejoice in the expectation of seeing you make a figure in the world.' 'I know not,' replied Joseph, 'that my parents have any power over my inclinations; nor am I obliged to sacrifice my happiness to their whim or ambition: besides, I shall be very sorry to see that the unexpected advancement of my sister, should so suddenly inspire them with this wicked pride, and make them despise their equals, I am resolved on no account to quit my dear Fanny, no, tho' I could raise her as high above her present station as you have raised my sister.' 'Your sister, as well as myself,' said Booby, 'are greatly obliged to you for the comparison: but, sir, she is not worthy to be compared in beauty to my Pamela; nor hath she half her merit. And besides, sir, as you civilly throw my marriage with your sister in my teeth, I must teach you the wide difference between us; my fortune enabled me to please myself; and it would have been as overgrown a folly in me to have omitted it, as in you to do it.' 'My fortune enables me to please myself likewise,' said Joseph; 'for all my pleasure is centred in Fanny, and whilst I have health, I shall be able to support her with my labour in that station to which she was born, and with which she is content.' 'Brother,' said Pamela, 'Mr. Booby advises you as a friend; and no doubt, my papa and mamma will be of his opinion, and will have great reason to be angry with you for destroying what his goodness hath done, and throwing down our family again, after he hath raised it. It would become you better, brother, to pray for the assistance of grace against such a passion, than to indulge it.'—'Sure, sister, you are not in earnest; I am sure she is your equal at least.'—'She was my equal,' answered Pamela, 'but I am no longer Pamela Andrews, I am now this gentleman's lady, and as such am above her—I hope I shall never behave with an unbecoming pride; but at the same time I shall always endeavour to know myself, and question not the assistance of grace to that purpose.' They were now summoned to breakfast, and thus ended their discourse for the present, very little to the satisfaction of any of the parties.

Fanny was now walking in an avenue at some distance from the house, where Joseph had promised to take the first opportunity of coming to her. She had not a shilling in the world, and had subsisted ever since her return entirely on the charity of Parson Adams. A young gentleman attended by many servants, came up to her, and asked her if that was not the Lady Booby's house before him? This indeed he well knew; but had framed the question for no other reason than to make her look up and discover if her face was equal to the delicacy of her shape. He no sooner saw it, than he was struck with amazement. He stopt his horse, and swore she was the most beautiful creature he ever beheld. Then instantly alighting, and delivering his horse to his servant, he rapt out half a dozen oaths that he would kiss her; to which she at first submitted, begging he would not be rude: but he was not satisfied with the civility of a salute, nor even with the rudest attack he could make on her lips, but caught her in his arms and endeavoured to kiss her breasts, which with all her strength she resisted; and as our spark was not of the Herculean race, with some difficulty prevented. The young gentleman being soon out of breath in the struggle, quitted her, and remounting his horse called one of his servants to him, whom he ordered to stay behind with her, and make her any offers whatever, to prevail on her to return home with him in the evening; and to assure her he would take her into keeping. He then rode on with his other servants, and arrived at the lady's house, to whom he was a distant relation, and was come to pay a visit.

The trusty fellow, who was employ'd in an office he had been long accustomed to, discharged his part with all the fidelity and dexterity imaginable; but to no purpose. She was entirely deaf to his offers, and rejected them with the utmost disdain. At last the pimp, who had perhaps more warm blood about him than his master, began to sollicit for himself; he told her, tho' he was a servant, he was a man of some fortune, which he would make her mistress of—and this without any insult to her virtue, for that he would marry her. She answer'd, if his master himself, or the greatest lord in the land would marry her, she would refuse him. At last being weary with persuasions, and on fire with charms which would have almost kindled a flame in the bosom of an antient philosopher, or modern divine, he fastened his horse to the ground, and attacked her with much more force than the gentleman had exerted. Poor Fanny would not have been able to resist his rudeness any long time, but the deity who presides over chaste love sent her Joseph to her assistance. He no sooner came within sight, and perceived her struggling with a man, than like a cannon-ball, or like lightning, or any thing that is swifter, if any thing be, he ran towards her, and coming up just as the ravisher had torn her handkerchief from her breast, before his lips had touched that seat of innocence and bliss, he dealt him so lusty a blow in that part of his neck which a rope would have become with the utmost propriety, that the fellow staggered backwards, and perceiving he had to do with something rougher than the little, tender, trembling hand of Fanny, he quitted her, and turning about saw his rival, with fire flashing from his eyes, again ready to assail him; and indeed before he could well defend himself or return the first blow, he received a second, which had it fallen on that part of the stomach to which it was directed, would have been probably the last he would have had any occasion for; but the ravisher lifting up his hand, drove the blow upwards to his mouth, whence it dislodged three of his teeth; and now not conceiving any extraordinary affection for the beauty of Joseph's person, nor being extremely pleased with this method of salutation, he collected all his force, and aimed a blow at Joseph's breast, which he artfully parry'd with one fist, so that it lost its force entirely in air. And stepping one foot backward, he darted his fist so fiercely at his enemy, that had he not caught it in his hand (for he was a boxer of no inferiour fame) it must have tumbled him on the ground. And now the ravisher meditated another blow, which he aimed at that part of the breast where the heart is lodged; Joseph did not catch it as before, yet so prevented[1] its aim, that it fell directly on his nose, but with abated force. Joseph then moving both fist and foot forwards at the same time, threw his head so dextrously into the stomach of the ravisher, that he fell a lifeless lump on the field, where he lay many minutes breathless and motionless.

When Fanny saw her Joseph receive a blow in his face, and blood running in a stream from him, she began to tear her hair, and invoke all human and divine power to his assistance. She was not, however, long under this affliction, before Joseph having conquered his enemy, ran to her, and assured her he was not hurt; she then instantly fell on her knees and thanked G—, that he had made Joseph the means of her rescue, and at the same time preserved him from being injured in attempting it. She offered with her handkerchief to wipe his blood from his face; but he seeing his rival attempting to recover his legs, turned to him and asked him if he had enough; to which the other answer'd he had; for he believed he had fought with the Devil, instead of a man, and loosening his horse, said he should not have attempted the wench if he had known she had been so well provided for.

---

1 Hindered, baffled.

Fanny now begged Joseph to return with her to Parson Adams, and to promise that he would leave her no more; these were propositions so agreeable to Joseph, that had he heard them he would have given an immediate assent: but indeed his eyes were now his only sense; for you may remember, reader, that the ravisher had tore her handkerchief from Fanny's neck, by which he had discovered such a sight; that Joseph hath declared all the statues he ever beheld were so much inferiour to it in beauty, that it was more capable of converting a man into a statue, than of being imitated by the greatest master of that art. This modest creature, whom no warmth in summer could ever induce to expose her charms to the wanton sun, a modesty to which perhaps they owed their inconceivable whiteness, had stood many minutes bare-necked in the presence of Joseph, before her apprehension of his danger, and the horror of seeing his blood would suffer her once to reflect on what concerned herself; till at last, when the cause of her concern had vanished, an admiration at his silence, together with observing the fixed position of his eyes, produced an idea in the lovely maid, which brought more blood into her face than had flowed from Joseph's nostrils. The snowy hue of her bosom was likewise exchanged to vermillion at the instant when she clapped her handkerchief round her neck. Joseph saw the uneasiness she suffered, and immediately removed his eyes from an object, in surveying which he had felt the greatest delight which the organs of sight were capable of conveying to his soul. So great was his fear of offending her, and so truly did his passion for her deserve the noble name of love.

Fanny being recovered from her confusion, which was almost equalled by what Joseph had felt from observing it, again mention'd her request; this was instantly and gladly complied with, and together they crossed two or three fields, which brought them to the habitation of Mr. Adams.

CHAPTER VIII

A discourse which happened between Mr. Adams, Mrs. Adams, Joseph and Fanny; with some behaviour of Mr. Adams, which will be called by some few readers, very low, absurd, and unnatural.

THE parson and his wife had just ended a long dispute when the lovers came to the door. Indeed this young couple had been the subject of the dispute; for Mrs. Adams was one of those prudent people who never do any thing to injure their families, or perhaps one of those good mothers who would even stretch their conscience to serve their children. She had long entertained hopes of seeing her eldest daughter succeed Mrs. Slipslop, and of making her second son an exciseman by Lady Booby's interest. These were expectations she could not endure the thoughts of quitting, and was therefore very uneasy to see her husband so resolute to oppose the lady's intention in Fanny's affair. She told him, 'it behoved every man to take the first care of his family; that he had a wife and six children, the maintaining and providing for whom would be business enough for him without intermeddling in other folks affairs; that he had always preached up submission to superiours, and would do ill to give an example of the contrary behaviour in his own conduct; that if Lady Booby did wrong, she must answer for it herself, and the sin would not lie at their door; that Fanny had been a servant, and bred up in the lady's own family, and consequently she must have known more of her than they did, and it was very improbable if she had behaved herself well, that the lady would have been so bitterly her enemy; that perhaps he was too much inclined to think well of her because she was handsome, but handsome women were often no better than they should be; that G— made ugly women as well as handsome ones, and that if a woman had virtue, it signified nothing whether she had beauty or no.' For all which reasons she concluded, he should oblige the lady and stop the future publication of the banns: but all these excellent arguments had no effect on the parson, who persisted in doing his duty without regarding the consequence it might have on his worldly interest; he endeavoured to answer her as well as he could, to which she had just finished her reply, (for she had always the last word every where but at church) when Joseph and Fanny entered their kitchin, where the parson and his wife then sat at breakfast over some bacon[1] and cabbage. There was a coldness in the civility of Mrs. Adams, which persons of accurate speculation[2] might have observed, but escaped her present guests; indeed it was a good deal covered by the heartiness of Adams, who no sooner heard that Fanny had neither eat nor drank that morning, than he presented her a bone of bacon he had just been gnawing, being the only remains of his provision, and then ran nimbly to the tap, and produced a mug of small beer, which he called ale, however it was the best in his house. Joseph addressing himself to the parson, told him the discourse which had past between Squire Booby, his sister and himself, concerning Fanny: he then acquainted him with the dangers whence he had rescued her, and communicated some apprehensions on her account. He concluded, that he should never have an easy moment till Fanny was absolutely his, and begged that he might be suffered to fetch a licence, saying, he could easily borrow the money. The parson answered, that he had already given his sentiments concerning a licence, and that a very few days would make it unnecessary. 'Joseph,' says he, 'I wish this haste doth not arise rather from your impatience than your fear: but as it certainly springs from one of these causes, I will examine both. Of each of these therefore in their turn; and first, for the first of these, namely, impatience. Now, child, I must inform you, that if in your purposed marriage with this young woman, you have no intention but the indulgence of carnal appetites, you are guilty of a very heinous sin. Marriage was ordained for nobler purposes, as you will learn when you hear the service provided on that occasion read to you. Nay perhaps, if you are a good lad, I shall give you a sermon *gratis*, wherein I shall demonstrate how little regard ought to be had to the flesh on such occasions. The text will be, child, Matthew the 5th, and part of the 28th verse, *Whosoever looketh on a woman*

---

1 A term regularly applied to pork in general.
2 Perception.

so as to lust after her. The latter part I shall omit, as foreign to my purpose.[1] Indeed all such brutal lusts and affections are to be greatly subdued, if not totally eradicated, before the vessel can be said to be consecrated to honour. To marry with a view of gratifying those inclinations is a prostitution of that holy ceremony, and must entail a curse on all who so lightly undertake it. If, therefore, this haste arises from impatience, you are to correct, and not give way to it. Now as to the second head which I proposed to speak to, namely, fear. It argues a diffidence highly criminal of that power in which alone we should put our trust, seeing we may be well assured that he is able not only to defeat the designs of our enemies, but even to turn their hearts. Instead of taking therefore any unjustifiable or desperate means to rid ourselves of fear, we should resort to prayer only on these occasions, and we may be then certain of obtaining what is best for us. When any accident threatens us, we are not to despair, nor when it overtakes us, to grieve; we must submit in all things to the will of Providence, and not set our affections so much on any thing here, as not to be able to quit it without reluctance. You are a young man, and can know but little of this world; I am older, and have seen a great deal. All passions are criminal in their excess, and even love itself, if it is not subservient to our duty, may render us blind to it. Had Abraham so loved his son Isaac,[2] as to refuse the sacrifice required, is there any of us who would not condemn him? Joseph, I know your many good qualities, and value you for them: but as I am to render an account of your soul, which is committed to my cure,[3] I cannot see any fault without reminding you of it. You are too much inclined to passion, child, and have set your affections so absolutely on this young woman, that if G— required her at your hands, I fear you would reluctantly part with her. Now believe me, no Christian ought so to set his heart on any person or thing in this world, but that whenever it shall be

---

1 In omitting the latter part of Matthew 5:28, Adams has adapted the text to his own purpose: "But I say unto you, That whosoever looketh on a woman to lust after her hath committed adultery with her already in his heart."

2 God tests Abraham by commanding him to sacrifice his son Isaac (Genesis 22:1-18).

3 Spiritual charge.

required or taken from him in any manner by Divine Providence, he may be able, peaceably, quietly, and contentedly to resign it.' At which words one came hastily in and acquainted Mr. Adams that his youngest son was drowned. He stood silent a moment, and soon began to stamp about the room and deplore his loss with the bitterest agony. Joseph, who was overwhelmed with concern likewise, recovered himself sufficiently to endeavour to comfort the parson; in which attempt he used many arguments that he had at several times remember'd out of his own discourses both in private and publick, (for he was a great enemy to the passions, and preached nothing more than the conquest of them by reason and grace) but he was not at leisure now to hearken to his advice. 'Child, child,' said he, 'do not go about impossibilities. Had it been any other of my children I could have born it with patience; but my little prattler, the darling and comfort of my old age—the little wretch to be snatched out of life just at his entrance into it; the sweetest, best-temper'd boy, who never did a thing to offend me. It was but this morning I gave him his first lesson in *Quæ genus.*[1] This was the very book he learnt, poor child! it is of no further use to thee now. He would have made the best scholar, and have been an ornament to the Church—such parts and such goodness never met in one so young.' 'And the handsomest lad too,' says Mrs. Adams, recovering from a swoon in Fanny's arms.—'My poor Jacky,[2] shall I never see thee more?' cries the parson.—'Yes, surely,' says Joseph, 'and in a better place, you will meet again never to part more.'—I believe the parson did not hear these words, for he paid little regard to them, but went on lamenting whilst the tears trickled down into his bosom. At last he cry'd out, 'Where is my little darling?' and was sallying out, when to his great surprize and joy, in which I hope the reader will sympathize, he met his son in a wet condition indeed, but alive, and running towards him. The person who brought the news of his misfortune, had been a little too eager, as people sometimes are, from I believe no very good principle,

1 Part of the Eton College Latin grammar dealing with irregular nouns (*An Introduction to the Latin Tongue* [1758]).

2 Adams later calls the boy Dick.

to relate ill news; and seeing him fall into the river, instead of running to his assistance, directly ran to acquaint his father of a fate which he had concluded to be inevitable, but whence the child was relieved by the same poor pedlar who had relieved his father before from a less distress. The parson's joy was now as extravagant as his grief had been before; he kissed and embraced his son a thousand times, and danced about the room like one frantick; but as soon as he discovered the face of his old friend the pedlar, and heard the fresh obligation he had to him, what were his sensations? not those which two courtiers feel in one another's embraces; not those with which a great man receives the vile, treacherous engines[1] of his wicked purposes; not those with which a worthless younger brother wishes his elder joy of a son,[2] or a man congratulates his rival on his obtaining a mistress, a place, or an honour.—No, reader, he felt the ebullition, the overflowings of a full, honest, open heart towards the person who had conferred a real obligation, and of which if thou can'st not conceive an idea within, I will not vainly endeavour to assist thee.

When these tumults were over, the parson taking Joseph aside, proceeded thus—'No, Joseph, do not give too much way to thy passions, if thou dost expect happiness.'—The patience of Joseph, nor perhaps of Job, could bear no longer; he interrupted the parson, saying, 'it was easier to give advice than take it, nor did he perceive he could so entirely conquer himself, when he apprehended he had lost his son, or when he found him recover'd.'—'Boy,' reply'd Adams, raising his voice, 'it doth not become green heads to advise grey hairs—Thou art ignorant of the tenderness of fatherly affection; when thou art a father thou wilt be capable then only of knowing what a father can feel. No man is obliged to impossibilities, and the loss of a child is one of those great trials where our grief may be allowed to become immoderate.' 'Well, sir,' cries Joseph, 'and if I love a mistress as well as you your child, surely her loss would grieve me equally.' 'Yes, but such love is foolishness, and wrong in

1 Means.

2 The eldest son of the eldest brother, according to the right of primogeniture, inherits the family estate.

itself, and ought to be conquered,' answered Adams, 'it savours too much of the flesh.' 'Sure, sir,' says Joseph, 'it is not sinful to love my wife, no not even to doat on her to distraction!' 'Indeed but it is,' says Adams. 'Every man ought to love his wife, no doubt; we are commanded so to do; but we ought to love her with moderation and discretion.'—'I am afraid I shall be guilty of some sin, in spight of all my endeavours', says Joseph; 'for I shall love without any moderation, I am sure.'—'You talk foolishly and childlishly,' cries Adams. 'Indeed,' says Mrs. Adams, who had listened to the latter part of their conversation, 'you talk more foolishly yourself. I hope, my dear, you will never preach any such doctrine as that husbands can love their wives too well. If I knew you had such a sermon in the house, I am sure I would burn it; and I declare if I had not been convinced you had loved me as well as you could, I can answer for myself I should have hated and despised you. Marry come up! Fine doctrine indeed! A wife hath a right to insist on her husband's loving her as much as ever he can: and he is a sinful villain who doth not. Doth he not promise to love her, and to comfort her, and to cherish her, and all that? I am sure I remember it all, as well as if I had repeated it over but yesterday, and shall never forget it. Besides, I am certain you do not preach as you practise; for you have been a loving and a cherishing husband to me, that's the truth on't; and why you should endeavour to put such wicked nonsense into this young man's head, I cannot devise. Don't hearken to him, Mr. Joseph, be as good a husband as you are able, and love your wife with all your body and soul too.' Here a violent rap at the door put an end to their discourse, and produced a scene which the reader will find in the next chapter.

CHAPTER IX

A visit which the good Lady Booby and her polite friend paid to the parson.

THE Lady Booby had no sooner had an account from the gentleman of his meeting a wonderful beauty near her house, and perceived the raptures with which he spoke of her, than immediately concluding it must be Fanny, she began to meditate a design of bringing them better acquainted; and to entertain hopes that the fine clothes, presents and promises of this youth, would prevail on her to abandon Joseph: she therefore proposed to her company a walk in the fields before dinner, when she led them towards Mr. Adams's house; and as she approached it, told them, if they pleased she would divert them with one of the most ridiculous sights they had ever seen, which was an old foolish parson, who, she said laughing, kept a wife and six brats on a salary of about twenty pounds a year; adding, that there was not such another ragged family in the parish. They all readily agreed to this visit, and arrived whilst Mrs. Adams was declaiming, as in the last chapter. Beau Didapper,[1] which was the name of the young gentleman we have seen riding towards Lady Booby's, with his cane mimicked the rap of a London footman at the door. The people within; namely, Adams, his wife, and three children, Joseph, Fanny, and the pedlar, were all thrown into confusion by this knock; but Adams went directly to the door, which being opened, the Lady Booby and her company walked in, and were received by the parson with about two hundred bows; and by his wife with as many curt'sies; the latter telling the lady, 'she was ashamed to be seen in such a pickle, and that her house was in such a litter: but that if she had expected such an honour from her ladyship, she should have found her in a better manner.'[2] The parson made no apologies, tho' he was in his half-cassock and a flannel

1 The original of this character was John, Lord Hervey, Baron of Ickworth (1696-1743), an effeminate, foppish courtier (as the name implies) and a favourite of Walpole.

2 That is, in a more favourable state socially and domestically to receive her.

night-cap. He said, 'they were heartily welcome to his poor cottage,' and turning to Mr. Didapper, cried out, '*Non mea renidet in domo lacunar.*'[1] The beau answered, 'he did not understand Welch;' at which the parson stared, and made no reply.

Mr. Didapper, or Beau Didapper, was a young gentleman of about four foot five inches in height. He wore his own hair, tho' the scarcity of it might have given him sufficient excuse for a periwig. His face was thin and pale: the shape of his body and legs none of the best; for he had very narrow shoulders, and no calf; and his gait might more properly be called hopping than walking. The qualifications of his mind were well adapted to his person. We shall handle them first negatively. He was not entirely ignorant: for he could talk a little French, and sing two or three Italian songs: he had lived too much in the world to be bashful, and too much at court to be proud: he seemed not much inclined to avarice; for he was profuse in his expences: nor had he all the features of prodigality; for he never gave a shilling:—No hater of women; for he always dangled after them; yet so little subject to lust, that he had, among those who knew him best, the character of great moderation in his pleasures. No drinker of wine; nor so addicted to passion, but that a hot word or two from an adversary made him immediately cool.

Now, to give him only a dash or two on the affirmative side: 'Tho' he was born to an immense fortune, he chose, for the pitiful and dirty consideration of a place of little consequence, to depend entirely on the will of a fellow, whom they call a great-man; who treated him with the utmost disrespect, and exacted of him a plenary obedience to his commands; which he implicitly submitted to, at the expence of his conscience, his honour, and of his country; in which he had himself so very large a share.'[2] And to finish his character, 'As he was entirely well satisfied with his own person and parts, so he was very apt to ridicule and laugh at any imperfection in another.' Such was

---

1 A contraction of Horace, *Odes* 2.18.1-2: "No ivory or gilded ceiling glitters in my house."

2 Conyers Middleton's praise of Hervey, in the Dedication to his *Life of Cicero* (1741), is satirically converted here (in the quoted passage) by Fielding.

the little person or rather thing that hopped after Lady Booby into Mr. Adams's kitchin.[1]

The parson and his company retreated from the chimney-side, where they had been seated, to give room to the lady and hers. Instead of returning any of the curt'sies or extraordinary civility of Mrs. Adams, the lady turning to Mr. Booby, cried out, '*Quelle bête! Quel animal!*' And presently after discovering Fanny (for she did not need the circumstance of her standing by Joseph to assure the identity of her person) she asked the beau, 'whether he did not think her a pretty girl?'—'Begad, madam,' answered he, ''tis the very same I met.' 'I did not imagine,' replied the lady, 'you had so good a taste.' 'Because I never liked you, I warrant,' cries the beau. 'Ridiculous!' said she, 'you know you was always my aversion.' 'I would never mention aversion,' answered the beau, 'with that face*; dear Lady Booby, wash your face before you mention aversion, I beseech you.' He then laughed and turned about to coquette it with Fanny.

Mrs. Adams had been all this time begging and praying the ladies to sit down, a favour which she at last obtained. The little boy to whom the accident had happened, still keeping his place by the fire, was chid by his mother for not being more mannerly: but Lady Booby took his part, and commending his beauty, told the parson he was his very picture. She then seeing a book in his hand, asked, 'if he could read?' 'Yes,' cried Adams, 'a little Latin, madam, he is just got into *Quæ genus*.'—'A fig for *quere genius*,' answered she, 'let me hear him read a little English.'—'*Lege*, Dick, *lege*,' said Adams: but the boy made no answer, till he saw the parson knit his brows; and then cried, 'I don't understand you, father.' 'How, boy,' says Adams, 'what doth *lego* make in the imperative mood? *Legito*, doth it not?' 'Yes,' answered Dick.—'And what besides?' says the father. '*Lege*,' quoth the son, after some hesitation. 'A good boy,' says the

* Lest this should appear unnatural to some readers, we think proper to acquaint them, that it is taken verbatim from very polite conversation [Fielding's note].

1 Within the second set of quotation marks, there are several allusions to passages in Pope's *A Letter to a Noble Lord* (privately circulated in 1733) and *An Epistle to Dr. Arbuthnot* (1735). Among other things, Pope was responding to Hervey's ridicule of his physical deformity.

father: 'and now, child, what is the English of *lego*?'—To which the boy, after long puzzling, answered, he could not tell. 'How,' cries Adams in a passion,—'what hath the water washed away your learning? Why, what is Latin for the English verb *read*? Consider before you speak.'—The child considered some time, and then the parson cried twice or thrice, '*Le*—, *Le*—.'—Dick answered, '*Lego*.'—'Very well;—and then, what is the English,' says the parson, 'of the verb *lego*?'—. '*To read*,' cried Dick.—'Very well,' said the parson, 'a good boy, you can do well, if you will take pains.—I assure your ladyship he is not much above eight years old, and is out of his *Propria quæ maribus*[1] already.—Come, Dick, read to her ladyship;'—which she again desiring, in order to give the beau time and opportunity with Fanny, Dick began as in the following chapter.

CHAPTER X

The History of Two Friends, which may afford an useful lesson to all those persons, who happen to take up their residence in married families.

'LEONARD and Paul were two friends.'—'Pronounce it *Lennard*, child,' cry'd the parson.—'Pray, Mr. Adams,' says Lady Booby, 'let your son read without interruption.' Dick then proceeded. 'Lennard and Paul were two friends, who having been educated together at the same school, commenced a friendship which they preserved a long time for each other. It was so deeply fixed in both their minds, that a long absence, during which they had maintained no correspondence, did not eradicate nor lessen it: but it revived in all its force at their first meeting, which was not till after fifteen years absence, most of which time Lennard had spent in the East-Indi-es.'—'Pronounce it short *Indies*,' says Adams.—'Pray, sir, be quiet,' says the lady.—The boy repeated—'in the East-Indies, whilst Paul had served his king and country in the army. In which different

1 "Proper names belonging to the male kind" (part of the Eton College Latin grammar).

services, they had found such different success, that Lennard was now married, and retired with a fortune of thirty thousand pound; and Paul was arrived to the degree of a lieutenant of foot; and was not worth a single shilling.

'The regiment in which Paul was stationed, happened to be ordered into quarters, within a small distance from the estate which Lennard had purchased; and where he was settled. This latter, who was now become a country gentleman and a justice of peace, came to attend the quarter-sessions, in the town where his old friend was quartered, soon after his arrival. Some affair in which a soldier was concerned, occasioned Paul to attend the justices. Manhood, and time and the change of climate had so much altered Lennard, that Paul did not immediately recollect the features of his old acquaintance: but it was otherwise with Lennard. He knew Paul the moment he saw him; nor could he contain himself from quitting the bench, and running hastily to embrace him. Paul stood at first a little surprized; but had soon sufficient information from his friend, whom he no sooner remembred, than he returned his embrace with a passion which made many of the spectators laugh, and gave to some few a much higher and more agreeable sensation.

'Not to detain the reader with minute circumstances, Lennard insisted on his friend's returning with him to his house that evening; which request was complied with, and leave for a month's absence for Paul, obtained of the commanding officer.

'If it was possible for any circumstance to give any addition to the happiness which Paul proposed in this visit, he received that additional pleasure, by finding on his arrival at his friend's house, that his lady was an old acquaintance which he had formerly contracted[1] at his quarters; and who had always appeared to be of a most agreeable temper. A character she had ever maintained among her intimates, being of that number, every individual of which is called quite the best sort of woman in the world.

'But good as this lady was, she was still a woman; that is to say, an angel and not an angel—' 'You must mistake, child,' cries

---

1 Developed a relationship with.

the parson, 'for you read nonsense.' 'It is so in the book,' answered the son. Mr. Adams was then silenc'd by authority, and Dick proceeded—'For tho' her person was of that kind to which men attribute the name of angel, yet in her mind she was perfectly woman. Of which a great degree of obstinacy gave the most remarkable, and perhaps most pernicious instance.

'A day or two past after Paul's arrival before any instances of this appear'd; but it was impossible to conceal it long. Both she and her husband soon lost all apprehension from their friend's presence, and fell to their disputes with as much vigour as ever. These were still pursued with the utmost ardour and eagerness, however trifling the causes were whence they first arose. Nay, however incredible it may seem, the little consequence of the matter in debate was frequently given as a reason for the fierceness of the contention, as thus: *If you loved me, sure you would never dispute with me such a trifle as this.* The answer to which is very obvious; for the argument would hold equally on both sides, and was constantly retorted with some addition, as—*I am sure I have much more reason to say so, who am in the right.* During all these disputes, Paul always kept strict silence, and preserved an even countenance without shewing the least visible inclination to either party. One day, however, when madam had left the room in a violent fury, Lennard could not refrain from referring his cause to his friend. Was ever anything so unreasonable, says he, as this woman? What shall I do with her? I doat on her to distraction; nor have I any cause to complain of more than this obstinacy in her temper; whatever she asserts she will maintain against all the reason and conviction[1] in the world. Pray give me your advice.—First, says Paul, I will give my opinion, which is flatly that you are in the wrong; for supposing she is in the wrong, was the subject of your contention anywise material? What signified it whether you was married in a red or yellow waistcoat? for that was your dispute. Now suppose she was mistaken, as you love her you say so tenderly, and I believe she deserves it, would it not have been wiser to

1 Proof.

have yielded, tho' you certainly knew yourself in the right, than to give either her or yourself any uneasiness? For my own part, if ever I marry, I am resolved to enter into an agreement with my wife, that in all disputes (especially about trifles) that party who is most convinced they are right, shall always surrender the victory: by which means we shall both be forward to give up the cause. I own, said Lennard, my dear friend, shaking him by the hand, there is great truth and reason in what you say; and I will for the future endeavour to follow your advice. They soon after broke up the conversation, and Lennard going to his wife, asked her pardon, and told her his friend had convinced him he had been in the wrong. She immediately began a vast encomium on Paul, in which he seconded her, and both agreed he was the worthiest and wisest man upon earth. When next they met, which was at supper, tho' she had promised not to mention what her husband told her, she could not forbear casting the kindest and most affectionate looks on Paul, and asked him with the sweetest voice, whether she should help him to some potted-woodcock?—Potted partridge, my dear, you mean, says the husband. My dear, says she, I ask your friend if he will eat any potted woodcock; and I am sure I must know, who potted it. I think I should know too, who shot them, reply'd the husband, and I am convinced I have not seen a woodcock this year; however, tho' I know I am in the right I submit, and the potted partridge is potted woodcock, if you desire to have it so. It is equal to me, says she, whether it is one or the other; but you would persuade one out of one's senses; to be sure you are always in the right in your own opinion; but your friend I believe knows which he is eating. Paul answered nothing, and the dispute continued as usual the greatest part of the evening. The next morning the lady accidentally meeting Paul, and being convinced he was her friend, and of her side, accosted him thus:—I am certain, sir, you have long since wonder'd at the unreasonableness of my husband. He is indeed in other respects a good sort of man; but so positive, that no woman but one of my complying temper could possibly live with him. Why last night now, was ever any creature so unreasonable?—I am certain you must condemn him—Pray answer me, was he not in the wrong? Paul, after a short silence, spoke as follows: I am sorry, madam, that as good-manners obliges me to answer against my will, so an adherence to truth forces me to declare myself of a different opinion. To be plain and honest, you was entirely in the wrong; the cause I own not worth disputing, but the bird was undoubtedly a partridge. O sir, reply'd the lady, I cannot possibly help your taste.—Madam, returned Paul, that is very little material; for had it been otherwise, a husband might have expected submission.—Indeed! sir, says she, I assure you!—Yes, madam, cry'd he, he might from a person of your excellent understanding; and pardon me for saying such a condescension would have shewn a superiority of sense even to your husband himself.—But, dear sir, said she, why should I submit when I am in the right?—For that very reason, answer'd he, it would be the greatest instance of affection imaginable: for can any thing be a greater object of our compassion than a person we love, in the wrong? Ay, but I should endeavour, said she, to set him right. Pardon me, madam, answered Paul, I will apply to your own experience, if you ever found your arguments had that effect. The more our judgments err, the less we are willing to own it: for my own part, I have always observed the persons who maintain the worst side in any contest, are the warmest. Why, says she, I must confess there is truth in what you say, and I will endeavour to practise it. The husband then coming in, Paul departed. And Lennard approaching his wife with an air of good-humour, told her he was sorry for their foolish dispute the last night: but he was now convinced of his error. She answered smiling, she believed she owed his condescension to his complacence;[1] that she was ashamed to think a word had past on so silly an occasion, especially as she was satisfy'd she had been mistaken. A little contention followed, but with the utmost goodwill to each other, and was concluded by her asserting that Paul had thoroughly convinced her she had been in the wrong. Upon which they both united in the praises of their common friend.

'Paul now past his time with great satisfaction; these disputes

1 Desire to please.

being much less frequent as well as shorter than usual: but the Devil, or some unlucky accident in which perhaps the Devil had no hand, shortly put an end to his happiness. He was now eternally the private referee of every difference; in which after having perfectly as he thought established the doctrine of submission, he never scrupled to assure both privately that they were in the right in every argument, as before he had followed the contrary method. One day a violent litigation happened in his absence, and both parties agreed to refer it to his decision. The husband professing himself sure the decision would be in his favour, the wife answer'd, he might be mistaken; for she believed his friend was convinced how seldom she was to blame—and that if he knew all.—The husband reply'd—My dear, I have no desire of any retrospect, but I believe if you knew all too, you would not imagine my friend so entirely on your side. Nay, says she, since you provoke me, I will mention one instance. You may remember our dispute about sending Jacky to school in cold weather, which point I gave up to you from mere compassion, knowing myself to be in the right, and Paul himself told me afterwards, he thought me so. My dear, replied the husband, I will not scruple[1] your veracity; but I assure you solemnly, on my applying to him, he gave it absolutely on my side, and said he would have acted in the same manner. They then proceeded to produce numberless other instances, in all which Paul had, on vows of secrecy, given his opinion on both sides. In the conclusion, both believing each other, they fell severely on the treachery of Paul, and agreed that he had been the occasion of almost every dispute which had fallen out between them. They then became extremely loving, and so full of condescension on both sides, that they vyed with each other in censuring their own conduct, and jointly vented their indignation on Paul, whom the wife, fearing a bloody consequence, earnestly entreated her husband to suffer quietly to depart the next day, which was the time fixed for his return to quarters, and then drop his acquaintance.

1 Doubt.

'However ungenerous this behaviour in Lennard may be esteemed, his wife obtained a promise from him (tho' with difficulty) to follow her advice; but they both exprest such unusual coldness that day to Paul, that he, who was quick of apprehension, taking Lennard aside, prest him so home, that he at last discovered the secret. Paul acknowledged the truth, but told him the design with which he had done it—To which the other answered, he would have acted more friendly to have let him into the whole design; for that he might have assured himself of his secrecy. Paul reply'd, with some indignation, he had given him a sufficient proof how capable he was of concealing a secret from his wife. Lennard returned with some warmth—He had more reason to upbraid him, for that he caused most of the quarrels between them by his strange conduct, and might (if they had not discovered the affair to each other) have been the occasion of their separation. Paul then said—' But something now happened, which put a stop to Dick's reading, and of which we shall treat in the next chapter.

CHAPTER XI

In which the History is continued.

JOSEPH Andrews had borne with great uneasiness the impertinence of Beau Didapper to Fanny, who had been talking pretty freely to her, and offering her settlements; but the respect to the company had restrained him from interfering, whilst the beau confined himself to the use of his tongue only; but the said beau watching an opportunity whilst the ladies eyes were disposed another way, offered a rudeness to her with his hands; which Joseph no sooner perceived than he presented him with so sound a box on the ear, that it conveyed him several paces from where he stood. The ladies immediately skreamed out, rose from their chairs, and the beau, as soon as he recovered himself, drew his hanger, which Adams observing, snatched up the lid of a pot in his left hand, and covering himself with it as with a shield, without any weapon of offence in his other hand, stept in before Joseph, and exposed himself to the enraged beau, who threatened such perdition and destruction, that it frighted the women, who were all got in a huddle together, out of their wits; even to hear his denunciations of vengeance. Joseph was of a different complexion,[1] and begged Adams to let his rival come on; for he had a good cudgel in his hand, and did not fear him. Fanny now fainted into Mrs. Adams's arms, and the whole room was in confusion, when Mr. Booby passing by Adams, who lay snug under the pot-lid, came up to Didapper, and insisted on his sheathing the hanger, promising he should have satisfaction; which Joseph declared he would give him, and fight him at any weapon whatever. The beau now sheathed his hanger, and taking out a pocket-glass, and vowing vengeance all the time, re-adjusted his hair; the parson deposited his shield, and Joseph running to Fanny, soon brought her back to life. Lady Booby chid Joseph for his insult on Didapper; but he answered he would have attacked an army in the same cause. 'What cause?' said the lady. 'Madam,' answered Joseph, 'he was rude to that young woman.'—'What ,' says the lady, 'I suppose he would have kissed the wench; and is a gentleman to be struck for such an offer? I must tell you, Joseph, these airs do not become you.'—'Madam,' said Mr. Booby, 'I saw the whole affair, and I do not commend my brother; for I cannot perceive why he should take upon him to be this girl's champion.'—'I can commend him,' says Adams, 'he is a brave lad; and it becomes any man to be the champion of the innocent; and he must be the basest coward, who would not vindicate a woman with whom he is on the brink of marriage.'—'Sir,' says Mr. Booby, 'my brother is not a proper match for such a young woman as this.'—'No,' says Lady Booby, 'nor do you, Mr. Adams, act in your proper character, by encouraging any such doings; and I am very much surprized you should concern yourself in it. I think your wife and family your properer care.'—'Indeed, madam, your ladyship says very true,' answered Mrs. Adams, 'he talks a pack of nonsense, that the whole parish are his children. I am sure I don't understand

---

1 Disposition, temperament.

what he means by it; it would make some women suspect he had gone astray: but I acquit him of that; I can read Scripture as well as he; and I never found that the parson was obliged to provide for other folks children; and besides he is but a poor curate, and hath little enough, as your ladyship knows, for me and mine.'—'You say very well, Mrs. Adams,' quoth the Lady Booby, who had not spoke a word to her before, 'you seem to be a very sensible woman; and I assure you, your husband is acting a very foolish part, and opposing his own interest; seeing my nephew is violently set against this match: and indeed I can't blame him; it is by no means one suitable to our family.' In this manner the lady proceeded with Mrs. Adams, whilst the beau hopped about the room, shaking his head; partly from pain, and partly from anger; and Pamela was chiding Fanny for her assurance,[1] in aiming at such a match as her brother.—Poor Fanny answered only with her tears, which had long since begun to wet her handkerchief; which Joseph perceiving, took her by the arm, and wrapping it in his, carried her off, swearing he would own no relation to any one who was an enemy to her he lov'd more than all the world. He went out with Fanny under his left arm, brandishing a cudgel in his right, and neither Mr. Booby nor the beau thought proper to oppose him. Lady Booby and her company made a very short stay behind him; for the lady's bell now summoned them to dress; for which they had just time before dinner.

Adams seemed now very much dejected, which his wife perceiving, began to apply some matrimonial balsam. She told him he had reason to be concerned; for that he had probably ruined his family with his foolish tricks: but perhaps he was grieved for the loss of his two children, Joseph and Fanny. His eldest daughter went on:—'Indeed father, it is very hard to bring strangers here to eat your children's bread out of their mouths.—You have kept them ever since they came home; and for any thing I see to the contrary may keep them a month longer: are you obliged to give her meat, tho' she was never so handsome? But I don't see she is so much handsomer than

---

1 Presumption.

other people. If people were to be kept for their beauty, she would scarce fare better than her neighbours, I believe.—As for Mr. Joseph, I have nothing to say, he is a young man of honest principles, and will pay some time or other for what he hath: but for the girl,—why doth she not return to her place she ran away from? I would not give such a vagabond slut a halfpenny, tho' I had a million of money; no, tho' she was starving.' 'Indeed but I would,' cries little Dick; 'and father, rather than poor Fanny shall be starved, I will give her all this bread and cheese.'—(*offering what he held in his hand.*)—Adams smiled on the boy, and told him he rejoiced to see he was a Christian; and that if he had a halfpenny in his pocket he would have given it him; telling him, it was his duty to look upon all his neighbours as his brothers and sisters, and love them accordingly. 'Yes, papa,' says he, 'I love her better than my sisters; for she is handsomer than any of them.' 'Is she so, saucebox?' says the sister, giving him a box on the ear, which the father would probably have resented, had not Joseph, Fanny, and the pedlar, at that instant, returned together.—Adams bid his wife prepare some food for their dinner; she said, 'truly she could not, she had something else to do.' Adams rebuked her for disputing his commands, and quoted many texts of Scripture to prove, *that the husband is the head of the wife, and she is to submit and obey.*[1] The wife answered, 'it was blasphemy to talk Scripture out of church; that such things were very proper to be said in the pulpit: but that it was prophane to talk them in common discourse.' Joseph told Mr. Adams 'he was not come with any design to give him or Mrs. Adams any trouble; but to desire the favour of all their company to the George (an alehouse in the parish,) where he had bespoke a piece of bacon and greens for their dinner.' Mrs. Adams, who was a very good sort of woman, only rather too strict in œconomicks,[2] readily accepted this invitation, as did the parson himself by her example; and away they all walked together, not omitting little Dick, to whom Joseph gave a shilling, when he heard of his intended liberality to Fanny.

---

1 For example, Ephesians 5:22: "Wives, submit yourselves unto your own husbands, as unto the Lord."

2 Household management.

CHAPTER XII

Where the good-natur'd reader will see something which will give him no great pleasure.

THE pedlar had been very inquisitive from the time he had first heard that the great house in this parish belonged to the Lady Booby; and had learnt that she was the widow of Sir Thomas, and that Sir Thomas had bought Fanny, at about the age of three or four years, of a travelling woman; and now their homely but hearty meal was ended, he told Fanny, he believed he could acquaint her with her parents. The whole company, especially she herself, started at this offer of the pedlar's.—He then proceeded thus, while they all lent their strictest attention: 'Tho' I am now contented with this humble way of getting my livelihood, I was formerly a gentleman; for so all those of my profession are called. In a word, I was a drummer in an Irish regiment of foot. Whilst I was in this honourable station, I attended an officer of our regiment into England a recruiting. In our march from Bristol to Froome (for since the decay of the woollen trade, the clothing towns have furnished the army with a great number of recruits)[1] we overtook on the road a woman who seemed to be about thirty years old, or thereabouts, not very handsome; but well enough for a soldier. As we came up to her, she mended her pace, and falling into discourse with our ladies (for every man of the party, namely, a serjeant, two private men, and a drum, were provided with their woman, except myself) she continued to travel on with us. I perceiving she must fall to my lot, advanced presently to her, made love to her in our military way, and quickly succeeded to my wishes. We struck a bargain within a mile, and lived together as man and wife to her dying day.'—'I suppose,' says Adams interrupting him, 'you were married with a licence: for I don't see how you could contrive to have the banns published

1 Since the 1720s, wool centres in the West Country (such as Frome, near Bath) had been in a state of decline. The huge numbers of young men enlisting in the army, as the result of rising unemployment in the region, was a regular feature in the Opposition journals at the time of the writing of *Joseph Andrews*.

while you were marching from place to place.'—'No, sir,' said the pedlar, 'we took a licence to go to bed together, without any banns.'—'Ay, ay,' said the parson, '*ex necessitate*, a licence may be allowable enough; but surely, surely, the other is the more regular and eligible way.'—The pedlar proceeded thus, 'She returned with me to our regiment, and removed with us from quarters to quarters, till at last, whilst we lay at Galloway, she fell ill of a fever, and died. When she was on her death-bed she called me to her, and crying bitterly, declared she could not depart this world without discovering a secret to me, which she said was the only sin which sat heavy on her heart. She said she had formerly travelled in a company of gipsies, who had made a practice of stealing away children;[1] that for her own part, she had been only once guilty of the crime; which she said she lamented more than all the rest of her sins, since probably it might have occasioned the death of the parents: for, added she, it is almost impossible to describe the beauty of the young creature, which was about a year and half old when I kidnapped it. We kept her (for she was a girl) above two years in our company, when I sold her myself for three guineas to Sir Thomas Booby in Somersetshire. Now, you know whether there are any more of that name in this county.'—'Yes,' says Adams, 'there are several Boobys who are squires; but I believe no baronet now alive, besides it answers so exactly in every point there is no room for doubt; but you have forgot to tell us the parents from whom the child was stolen.'—'Their name,' answered the pedlar, 'was Andrews. They lived about thirty miles from the squire; and she told me, that I might be sure to find them out by one circumstance; for that they had a daughter of a very strange name, Paměla or Pamēla;[2] some pronounced it one way, and some the other.' Fanny, who had changed colour at the first mention of the name, now fainted away, Joseph turned pale, and poor Dicky began to roar; the parson fell on his knees and ejac-

1 The itinerant nature of most gypsy communities made them vulnerable to charges of robbery and disorder. In particular, the theft of infants by these travelling companies was widely believed and deeply feared, especially in the more rural areas.

2 Pamela is the name of a heroine in Sir Philip Sidney's *Arcadia* (1590). Although Richardson accented the first syllable, its pronunciation was the subject of considerable discussion.

ulated many thanksgivings that this discovery had been made before the dreadful sin of incest was committed; and the pedlar was struck with amazement, not being able to account for all this confusion, the cause of which was presently opened by the parson's daughter, who was the only unconcerned person; (for the mother was chaffing Fanny's temples, and taking the utmost care of her) and indeed Fanny was the only creature whom the daughter would not have pitied in her situation; wherein, tho' we compassionate her ourselves, we shall leave her for a little while, and pay a short visit to Lady Booby.

CHAPTER XIII

The history returning to the Lady Booby, gives some account of the terrible conflict in her breast between love and pride; with what happened on the present discovery.

THE lady sat down with her company to dinner: but eat nothing. As soon as her cloth was removed, she whispered Pamela, that she was taken a little ill, and desired her to entertain her husband and Beau Didapper. She then went up into her chamber, sent for Slipslop, threw herself on the bed, in the agonies of love, rage, and despair; nor could she conceal these boiling passions longer, without bursting. Slipslop now approached her bed, and asked how her ladyship did; but instead of revealing her disorder, as she intended, she entered into a long encomium on the beauty and virtues of Joseph Andrews; ending at last with expressing her concern, that so much tenderness should be thrown away on so despicable an object as Fanny. Slipslop well knowing how to humour her mistress's frenzy, proceeded to repeat, with exaggeration if possible, all her mistress had said, and concluded with a wish, that Joseph had been a gentleman, and that she could see her lady in the arms of such a husband. The lady then started from the bed, and taking a turn or two cross the room, cry'd out with a deep sigh,—*Sure he would make any woman happy.*—'Your ladyship,' says she, 'would be the happiest woman in the world with him.—A fig for custom and nonsense. What *vails* what people say? Shall I be afraid of eating sweetmeats, because people may say I have a sweet tooth? If I had a mind to marry a man, all the world should not hinder me. Your ladyship hath no parents to *tutelar* your *infections*; besides he is of your ladyship's family now, and as good a gentleman as any in the country; and why should not a woman follow her mind as well as a man? Why should not your ladyship marry the brother, as well as your nephew the sister? I am sure, if it was a *fragrant* crime I would not persuade your ladyship to it.'—'But, dear Slipslop,' answered the lady, 'if I could prevail on myself to commit such a weakness, there is that cursed Fanny in the way, whom the idiot, O how I hate and despise him—' 'She, a little ugly mynx,' cries Slipslop, 'leave her to me.—I suppose your ladyship hath heard of Joseph's *fitting* with one of Mr. Didapper's servants about her; and his master hath ordered them to carry her away by force this evening. I'll take care they shall not want assistance. I was talking with his gentleman, who was below just when your ladyship sent for me.'—'Go back,' says the Lady Booby, 'this instant; for I expect Mr. Didapper will soon be going. Do all you can; for I am resolved this wench shall not be in our family; I will endeavour to return to the company; but let me know as soon as she is carried off.' Slipslop went away, and her mistress began to arraign her own conduct in the following manner:

'What am I doing? How do I suffer this passion to creep imperceptibly upon me! How many days are past since I could have submitted to ask myself the question?—Marry a footman! Distraction! Can I afterwards bear the eyes of my acquaintance? But I can retire from them; retire with one in whom I propose more happiness than the world without him can give me! Retire—to feed continually on beauties, which my inflamed imagination sickens with eagerly gazing on; to satisfy every appetite, every desire, with their utmost wish.—Ha! and do I doat thus on a footman! I despise, I detest my passion.—Yet why? Is he not generous, gentle, kind?—Kind to whom? to the meanest wretch, a creature below my consideration. Doth he not?—Yes, he doth prefer her; curse his beauties, and the little low heart that possesses them; which can basely descend to this despicable wench, and be ungratefully deaf to all the honours I do him.—And can I then love this monster? No, I will tear his image from my bosom, tread on him, spurn him. I will have those pitiful charms which now I despise, mangled in my sight; for I will not suffer the little jade I hate to riot in the beauties I contemn. No, tho' I despise him myself; tho' I would spurn him from my feet, was he to languish at them, no other should taste the happiness I scorn. Why do I say happiness? To me it would be misery.—To sacrifice my reputation, my character, my rank in life, to the indulgence of a mean and a vile appetite.—How I detest the thought! How much more exquisite is the pleasure resulting from the reflection of virtue and prudence, than the faint relish of what flows from vice and folly! Whither did I suffer this improper, this mad passion to hurry me, only by neglecting to summon the aids of reason to my assistance? Reason, which hath now set before me my desires in their proper colours, and immediately helped me to expel them. Yes, I thank Heaven and my pride, I have now perfectly conquered this unworthy passion; and if there was no obstacle in its way, my pride would disdain any pleasures which could be the consequence of so base, so mean, so vulgar—' Slipslop returned at this instant in a violent hurry, and with the utmost eagerness, cry'd out,—'O, madam, I have strange news. Tom the footman is just come from the George; where it seems Joseph and the rest of them are a *jinketting*;[1] and he says, there is a strange man who hath discovered that Fanny and Joseph are brother and sister.'—How, Slipslop,' cries the lady in a surprize.—'I had not time, madam,' cries Slipslop, 'to enquire about *particles*, but Tom says, it is most certainly true.'

This unexpected account entirely obliterated all those admirable reflections which the supreme power of reason had so wisely made just before. In short, when despair, which had more share in producing the resolutions of hatred we have seen taken, began to retreat, the lady hesitated a moment, and then forgetting all the purport of her soliloquy, dismissed her woman again, with orders to bid Tom attend her in the par-

1 Junketing (partying).

lour, whither she now hastened to acquaint Pamela with the news. Pamela said, she could not believe it: for she had never heard that her mother had lost any child, or that she had ever had any more than Joseph and herself. The lady flew into a violent rage with her, and talked of upstarts and disowning relations, who had so lately been on a level with her. Pamela made no answer: but her husband, taking up her cause, severely reprimanded his aunt for her behaviour to his wife; he told her, if it had been earlier in the evening, she should not have staid a moment longer in her house; that he was convinced, if this young woman could be proved her sister, she would readily embrace her as such; and he himself would do the same: he then desired the fellow might be sent for, and the young woman with him; which Lady Booby immediately ordered, and thinking proper to make some apology to Pamela for what she had said, it was readily accepted, and all things reconciled.

The pedlar now attended, as did Fanny, and Joseph who would not quit her; the parson likewise was induced, not only by curiosity, of which he had no small portion, but by his duty, as he apprehended, to follow them: for he continued all the way to exhort them, who were now breaking their hearts, to offer up thanksgivings, and be joyful for so miraculous an escape.

When they arrived at Booby-Hall, they were presently called into the parlour, where the pedlar repeated the same story he had told before, and insisted on the truth of every circumstance; so that all who heard him were extremely well satisfied of the truth, except Pamela, who imagined, as she had never heard either of her parents mention such an accident, that it must be certainly false; and except the Lady Booby, who suspected the falshood of the story, from her ardent desire that it should be true; and Joseph who feared its truth, from his earnest wishes that it might prove false.

Mr. Booby now desired them all to suspend their curiosity and absolute belief or disbelief, till the next morning, when he expected old Mr. Andrews and his wife to fetch himself and Pamela home in his coach, and then they might be certain of perfectly knowing the truth or falshood of this relation; in which he said, as there were many strong circumstances to induce their credit, so he could not perceive any interest the pedlar could have in inventing it, or in endeavouring to impose such a falshood on them.

The Lady Booby, who was very little used to such company, entertained them all, *viz.* her nephew, his wife, her brother and sister, the beau, and the parson, with great good-humour at her own table. As to the pedlar, she ordered him to be made as welcome as possible, by her servants. All the company in the parlour, except the disappointed lovers, who sat sullen and silent, were full of mirth: for Mr. Booby had prevailed on Joseph to ask Mr. Didapper's pardon; with which he was perfectly satisfied. Many jokes past between the beau and the parson, chiefly on each other's dress; these afforded much diversion to the company. Pamela chid her brother Joseph for the concern which he exprest at discovering a new sister. She said, if he loved Fanny as he ought, with a pure affection, he had no reason to lament being related to her.—Upon which Adams began to discourse on Platonic love; whence he made a quick transition to the joys in the next world, and concluded with strongly asserting that there was no such thing as pleasure in this. At which Pamela and her husband smiled on one another.

This happy pair proposing to retire (for no other person gave the least symptom of desiring rest) they all repaired to several beds provided for them in the same house; nor was Adams himself suffered to go home, it being a stormy night. Fanny indeed often begged she might go home with the parson; but her stay was so strongly insisted on, that she at last, by Joseph's advice, consented.

CHAPTER XIV

Containing several curious night-adventures, in which Mr. Adams fell into many hair-breadth 'scapes, partly owing to his goodness, and partly to his inadvertency.

ABOUT an hour after they had all separated (it being now past three in the morning) Beau Didapper, whose passion for Fanny permitted him not to close his eyes, but had employed his imagination in contrivances how to satisfy his desires, at last hit on a method by which he hoped to effect it. He had ordered his servant to bring him word where Fanny lay, and had received his information; he therefore arose, put on his breeches and nightgown, and stole softly along the gallery which led to her apartment; and being come to the door, as he imagined it, he opened it with the least noise possible, and entered the chamber. A savour now invaded his nostrils which he did not expect in the room of so sweet a young creature, and which might have probably had no good effect on a cooler lover. However, he groped out the bed with difficulty; for there was not a glimpse of light, and opening the curtains, he whispered in Joseph's voice (for he was an excellent mimick) 'Fanny, my angel, I am come to inform thee that I have discovered the falshood of the story we last night heard. I am no longer thy brother, but thy lover; nor will I be delayed the enjoyment of thee one moment longer. You have sufficient assurances of my constancy not to doubt my marrying you, and it would be want of love to deny me the possession of thy charms.'—So saying, he disencumbered himself from the little clothes he had on, and leaping into bed, embraced his angel, as he conceived her, with great rapture. If he was surprized at receiving no answer, he was no less pleased to find his hug returned with equal ardour. He remained not long in this sweet confusion; for both he and his paramour presently discovered their error. Indeed it was no other than the accomplished Slipslop whom he had engaged; but tho' she immediately knew the person whom she had mistaken for Joseph, he was at a loss to guess at the representative of Fanny. He had so little seen or taken notice of this gentlewoman, that light itself would have afforded him no assistance in his conjecture. Beau Didapper no sooner had perceived his mistake, than he attempted to escape from the bed with much greater haste than he had made to it; but the watchful Slipslop prevented him. For that prudent woman being disappointed of those delicious offerings which her fancy had promised her pleasure, resolved to make an immediate sacrifice to her virtue. Indeed she wanted an opportunity to heal some wounds which her late conduct had, she feared, given her reputation; and as she had a wonderful presence of mind, she conceived the person of the unfortunate beau to be luckily thrown in her way to restore her lady's opinion of her impregnable chastity. At that instant therefore, when he offered to leap from the bed, she caught fast hold of his shirt, at the same time roaring out, 'O thou villain! who hast attacked my chastity, and I believe ruined me in my sleep; I will swear a rape against thee, I will prosecute thee with the utmost vengeance.' The beau attempted to get loose, but she held him fast, and when he struggled, she cry'd out, 'Murther! Murther! Rape! Robbery! Ruin!' At which words Parson Adams, who lay in the next chamber, wakeful and meditating on the pedlar's discovery, jumped out of bed, and without staying to put a rag of clothes on, hastened into the apartment whence the cries proceeded. He made directly to the bed in the dark, where laying hold of the beau's skin (for Slipslop had torn his shirt almost off) and finding his skin extremely soft, and hearing him in a low voice begging Slipslop to let him go, he no longer doubted but this was the young woman in danger of ravishing, and immediately falling on the bed, and laying hold on Slipslop's chin, where he found a rough beard, his belief was confirmed; he therefore rescued the beau, who presently made his escape, and then turning towards Slipslop, receiv'd such a cuff on his chops, that his wrath kindling instantly, he offered to return the favour so stoutly, that had poor Slipslop received the fist, which in the dark past by her and fell on the pillow, she would most probably have given up the ghost.—Adams missing his blow, fell directly on Slipslop, who cuffed and scratched as well as she could; nor was he behind-hand with her, in his endeavours, but happily the darkness of the night befriended her—She then cry'd she was a woman; but Adams answered she was rather the Devil, and if she was, he would grapple with him; and being again irritated by another stroke on his chops, he give her such a remembrance in the guts, that she began to roar loud enough to be heard all over the house. Adams then seizing her by the hair (for her double-clout[1] had fallen off in the scuffle) pinned her head down to the bolster, and then both called for lights together. The Lady Booby, who was as wakeful as any of her guests, had been alarmed from the beginning; and, being a woman of a bold spirit, she slipt on a nightgown, petticoat and slippers, and taking a candle, which was always burnt in her chamber, in her hand, she walked undauntedly to Slipslop's room; where she entered just at the instant as Adams had discovered, by the two mountains which Slipslop carried before her, that he was concerned with a female. He then concluded her to be a witch, and said he fancied those breasts gave suck to a legion of devils. Slipslop seeing Lady Booby enter the room, cried, *Help! or I am ravished*, with a most audible voice, and Adams perceiving the light, turned hastily and saw the lady (as she did him) just as she came to the feet of the bed, nor did her modesty, when she found the naked condition of Adams, suffer her to approach farther.—She then began to revile the parson as the wickedest of all men, and particularly railed at his impudence in chusing her house for the scene of his debaucheries, and her own woman for the object of his bestiality. Poor Adams had before discovered the countenance of his bedfellow, and now first recollecting he was naked, he was no less confounded than Lady Booby herself, and immediately whipt under the bed-clothes, whence the chaste Slipslop endeavoured in vain to shut him out. Then putting forth his head, on which, by way of ornament, he wore a flannel nightcap, he protested his innocence, and asked ten thousand pardons of Mrs. Slipslop for the blows he had struck her, vowing he had mistaken her for a witch. Lady Booby then, casting her eyes on the ground, observed something sparkle with great lustre, which, when she

1 A piece of cloth folded and worn in the manner of a kerchief.

had taken it up, appeared to be a very fine pair of diamond buttons for the sleeves. A little farther she saw lie the sleeve itself of a shirt with laced ruffles. 'Heyday!' says she, 'what is the meaning of this?'—'O, madam,' says Slipslop, 'I don't know what hath happened, I have been so terrified. Here may have been a dozen men in the room.' 'To whom belongs this laced shirt and jewels?' says the lady.—'Undoubtedly,' cries the parson, 'to the young gentleman whom I mistook for a woman on coming into the room, whence proceeded all the subsequent mistakes; for if I had suspected him for a man, I would have seized him had he been another Hercules, tho' indeed he seems rather to resemble Hylas.'[1] He then gave an account of the reason of his rising from bed, and the rest, till the lady came into the room; at which, and the figures of Slipslop and her gallant, whose heads only were visible at the opposite corners of the bed, she could not refrain from laughter, nor did Slipslop persist in accusing the parson of any motions towards a rape. The lady therefore desired him to return to his bed as soon as she was departed, and then ordering Slipslop to rise and attend in her own room, she returned herself thither. When she was gone, Adams renewed his petitions for pardon to Mrs. Slipslop, who with a most Christian temper not only forgave, but began to move with much curtesy towards him, which he taking as a hint to be gone, immediately quitted the bed, and made the best of his way towards his own; but unluckily instead of turning to the right, he turned to the left, and went to the apartment where Fanny lay, who (as the reader may remember) had not slept a wink the preceding night, and who was so hagged out[2] with what had happen'd to her in the day, that notwithstanding all thoughts of her Joseph, she was fallen into so profound a sleep, that all the noise in the adjoining room had not been able to disturb her. Adams groped out the bed, and turning the clothes down softly, a custom Mrs. Adams had long accustomed him to, crept in, and deposited his carcase on the bedpost, a place which that good woman had always assigned him.

---

1 A youth of great beauty, loved by Hercules.
2 Tired out, fatigued.

As the cat or lapdog of some lovely nymph for whom ten thousand lovers languish, lies quietly by the side of the charming maid, and ignorant of the scene of delight on which they repose, meditates the future capture of a mouse, or surprizal of a plate of bread and butter: so Adams, lay by the side of Fanny, ignorant of the paradise to which he was so near, nor could the emanation of sweets which flowed from her breath, overpower the fumes of tobacco which played in the parson's nostrils. And now sleep had not overtaken the good man, when Joseph, who had secretly appointed Fanny to come to her at the break of day, rapped softly at the chamber-door, which when he had repeated twice, Adams cry'd, *Come in, whoever you are.* Joseph thought he had mistaken the door, tho' she had given him the most exact directions; however, knowing his friend's voice, he opened it, and saw some female vestments lying on a chair. Fanny waking at the same instant, and stretching out her hand on Adams's beard, she cry'd out,—'O heavens! where am I?' 'Bless me! where am I?' said the parson. Then Fanny skreamed, Adams leapt out of bed, and Joseph stood, as the tragedians call it, like the statue of Surprize.[1] '*How came she into my room?*' cry'd Adams. '*How came you into hers?*' cry'd Joseph, in an astonishment. 'I know nothing of the matter,' answered Adams, 'but that she is a vestal[2] for me. As I am a Christian, I know not whether she is a man or woman. He is an infidel who doth not believe in witchcraft. They as surely exist now as in the days of Saul.[3] My clothes are bewitched away too, and Fanny's brought into their place.' For he still insisted he was in his own apartment; but Fanny denied it vehemently, and said his attempting to persuade Joseph of such a falshood, convinced her of his wicked designs. 'How!' said Joseph, in a rage, 'hath he offered any rudeness to you?'—She answered, she could not accuse him of any more than villainously stealing to bed to her, which she thought rudeness sufficient, and what no man would do with-

1 See above, p. 82, n. 1.

2 A chaste woman. Vestal virgins were priestesses who had charge of the sacred fire in the temple of Vesta at Rome.

3 Saul consulted the Witch of Endor to raise a spirit from the dead (I Samuel 28:7–25).

out a wicked intention. Joseph's great opinion of Adams was not easily to be staggered, and when he heard from Fanny that no harm had happened, he grew a little cooler; yet still he was confounded, and as he knew the house, and that the women's apartments were on this side Mrs. Slipslop's room, and the men's on the other, he was convinced that he was in Fanny's chamber. Assuring Adams, therefore, of this truth, he begged him to give some account how he came there. Adams then, standing in his shirt,[1] which did not offend Fanny as the curtains of the bed were drawn, related all that had happened, and when he had ended, Joseph told him, it was plain he had mistaken, by turning to the right instead of the left. 'Odso!' cries Adams, 'that's true, as sure as sixpence, you have hit on the very thing.' He then traversed the room, rubbing his hands, and begged Fanny's pardon, assuring her he did not know whether she was man or woman. That innocent creature firmly believing all he said, told him, she was no longer angry, and begged Joseph to conduct him into his own apartment, where he should stay himself, till she had put her clothes on. Joseph and Adams accordingly departed, and the latter soon was convinced of the mistake he had committed; however, whilst he was dressing himself, he often asserted he believed in the power of witchcraft notwithstanding, and did not see how a Christian could deny it.

CHAPTER XV

The arrival of Gaffar and Gammar Andrews, with another person, not much expected; and a perfect solution of the difficulties raised by the pedlar.

As soon as Fanny was drest, Joseph returned to her, and they had a long conversation together, the conclusion of which was, that if they found themselves to be really brother and sister,

1 In the previous scene, however, Adams had leaped out of bed naked and rushed into Slipslop's bedchamber upon hearing the noise.

they vowed a perpetual celibacy, and to live together all their days, and indulge a Platonick friendship for each other.

The company were all very merry at breakfast, and Joseph and Fanny rather more cheerful than the preceding night. The Lady Booby produced the diamond button, which the beau most readily owned, and alledged that he was very subject to walk in his sleep. Indeed he was far from being ashamed of his amour, and rather endeavoured to insinuate that more than was really true had past between him and the fair Slipslop.

Their tea was scarce over, when news came of the arrival of old Mr. Andrews and his wife. They were immediately introduced and kindly received by the Lady Booby, whose heart went now pit-a-pat, as did those of Joseph and Fanny. They felt perhaps little less anxiety in this interval than Œdipus himself whilst his fate was revealing.[1]

Mr. Booby first open'd the cause, by informing the old gentleman that he had a child in the company more than he knew of, and taking Fanny by the hand, told him, this was that daughter of his who had been stolen away by the gypsies in her infancy. Mr. Andrews, after expressing some astonishment, assured his honour that he had never lost a daughter by gypsies, nor ever had any other children than Joseph and Pamela. These words were a cordial to the two lovers; but had a different effect on Lady Booby. She ordered the pedlar to be called, who recounted his story as he had done before.—At the end of which, old Mrs. Andrews running to Fanny, embraced her, crying out, *She is, she is my child.* The company were all amazed at this disagreement between the man and his wife; and the blood had now forsaken the cheeks of the lovers, when the old woman turning to her husband, who was more surprized than all the rest, and having a little recovered her own spirits, delivered herself as follows. 'You may remember, my dear, when you went a serjeant to Gibraltar you left me big with child, you staid abroad you know upwards of three years. In your absence I was brought to bed, I verily believe of this daughter, whom I

1 In Sophocles' *Oedipus Rex*, the old herdsman arrives during the tragedy's climax revealing the king's true parentage and hence his incestuous relationship with his mother.

am sure I have reason to remember, for I suckled her at this very breast till the day she was stolen from me. One afternoon, when the child was about a year, or a year and half old, or thereabouts, two gipsy women came to the door, and offered to tell my fortune. One of them had a child in her lap; I shewed them my hand, and desired to know if you was ever to come home again, which I remember as well as if it was but yesterday, they faithfully promised me you should—I left the girl in the cradle, and went to draw them a cup of liquor, the best I had; when I returned with the pot (I am sure I was not absent longer than whilst I am telling it to you) the women were gone. I was afraid they had stolen something, and looked and looked, but to no purpose, and Heaven knows I had very little for them to steal. At last hearing the child cry in the cradle, I went to take it up—but *O the living!*[1] how was I surprized to find, instead of my own girl that I had put into the cradle, who was as fine a fat thriving child as you shall see in a summer's day, a poor sickly boy, that did not seem to have an hour to live. I ran out, pulling my hair off, and crying like any mad after the women, but never could hear a word of them from that day to this. When I came back, the poor infant (which is our Joseph there, as stout as he now stands) lifted up its eyes upon me so piteously, that to be sure, notwithstanding my passion, I could not find in my heart to do it any mischief. A neighbour of mine happening to come in at the same time, and hearing the case, advised me to take care of this poor child, and G— would perhaps one day restore me my own. Upon which I took the child up, and suckled it to be sure, all the world as if it had been born of my own natural body. And as true as I am alive, in a little time I loved the boy all to nothing as if it had been my own girl.—Well, as I was saying, times growing very hard, I having two children, and nothing but my own work, which was little enough, G— knows, to maintain them, was obliged to ask relief of the parish; but instead of giving it me, they removed me, by justices warrants,[2] fifteen miles to the place where I now live,

1 A milder, abbreviated version of the oath "Oh the living God!"

2 Apparently the Andrews were not legally settled in the parish, and so with his departure she was removed to the place of last legal settlement.

where I had not been long settled before you came home. Joseph (for that was the name I gave him myself—the Lord knows whether he was baptized or no, or by what name) Joseph, I say, seemed to me to be about five years old when you returned; for I believe he is two or three years older than our daughter here; (for I am thoroughly convinced she is the same) and when you saw him you said he was a chopping[1] boy, without ever minding his age; and so I seeing you did not suspect any thing of the matter, thought I might e'en as well keep it to myself, for fear you should not love him as well as I did. And all this is veritably true, and I will take my oath of it before any justice in the kingdom.'

The pedlar, who had been summoned by the order of Lady Booby, listened with the utmost attention to Gammar Andrews's story, and when she had finished, asked her if the supposititious child had no mark on its breast? To which she answered, 'Yes, he had as fine a strawberry as ever grew in a garden.' This Joseph acknowledged, and unbuttoning his coat, at the intercession of the company, shewed to them. 'Well,' says Gaffar Andrews, who was a comical sly old fellow, and very likely desired to have no more children than he could keep,[2] 'you have proved, I think, very plainly that this boy doth not belong to us; but how are you certain that the girl is ours?' The parson then brought the pedlar forward, and desired him to repeat the story which he had communicated to him the preceding day at the alehouse; which he complied with, and related what the reader, as well as Mr. Adams, hath seen before. He then confirmed, from his wife's report, all the circumstances of the exchange, and of the strawberry on Joseph's breast. At the repetition of the word *strawberry*, Adams, who had seen it without any emotion, started, and cry'd, *Bless me! something comes into my head.* But before he had time to bring any thing out, a servant called him forth. When he was gone, the pedlar assured Joseph, that his parents were persons of much greater circumstances than those he had hitherto mistaken for such; for that he had been stolen from a gentleman's house, by those whom

1 Strapping.

2 Support.

they call gypsies, and had been kept by them during a whole year, when looking on him as in a dying condition, they had exchanged him for the other healthier child, in the manner before related. He said, as to the name of his father, his wife had either never known or forgot it; but that she had acquainted him he lived about forty miles from the place where the exchange had been made, and which way, promising to spare no pains in endeavouring with him to discover the place.

But Fortune, which seldom doth good or ill, or makes men happy or miserable by halves, resolved to spare him this labour. The reader may please to recollect, that Mr. Wilson had intended a journey to the west, in which he was to pass through Mr. Adams's parish, and had promised to call on him. He was now arrived at the Lady Booby's gates for that purpose, being directed thither from the parson's house, and had sent in the servant whom we have above seen call Mr. Adams forth. This had no sooner mentioned the discovery of a stolen child, and had uttered the word *strawberry*, than Mr. Wilson, with wildness in his looks, and the utmost eagerness in his words, begged to be shewed into the room, where he entred without the least regard to any of the company but Joseph, and embracing him with a complexion all pale and trembling, desired to see the mark on his breast; the parson followed him capering, rubbing his hands, and crying out, *Hic est quem quæris, inventus est*, &c.[1] Joseph complied with the request of Mr. Wilson, who no sooner saw the mark, than abandoning himself to the most extravagant rapture of passion, he embraced Joseph, with inexpressible extasy, and cried out in tears of joy, *I have discovered my son, I have him again in my arms*. Joseph was not sufficiently apprized yet, to taste the same delight with his father, (for so in reality he was;) however, he returned some warmth to his embraces: but he no sooner perceived from his father's account, the agreement of every circumstance, of person, time, and place, than he threw himself at his feet, and embracing his

1 "Here is the one you are seeking; he is found." Adams seems to combine two biblical allusions here, one being the announcement of the angel to the two Marys that Christ was risen (Matthew 28:5-6 or perhaps John 20:15) and the other the return of the Prodigal Son (Luke 15:24).

knees, with tears begged his blessing, which was given with much affection, and received with such respect, mixed with such tenderness on both sides, that it affected all present: but none so much as Lady Booby, who left the room in an agony, which was but too much perceived, and not very charitably accounted for by some of the company.

CHAPTER XVI

Being the last.
In which this true history is brought to a happy conclusion.

FANNY was very little behind her Joseph, in the duty she exprest towards her parents; and the joy she evidenced in discovering them. Gammar Andrews kiss'd her, and said she was heartily glad to see her: but for her part she could never love any one better than Joseph. Gaffar Andrews testified no remarkable emotion, he blessed and kissed her, but complained bitterly, that he wanted his pipe, not having had a whiff that morning.

Mr. Booby, who knew nothing of his aunt's fondness, imputed her abrupt departure to her pride, and disdain of the family into which he was married; he was therefore desirous to be gone with the utmost celerity: and now, having congratulated Mr. Wilson and Joseph on the discovery, he saluted Fanny, called her sister, and introduced her as such to Pamela, who behaved with great decency on the occasion.

He now sent a message to his aunt, who returned, that she wished him a good journey; but was too disordered to see any company: he therefore prepared to set out, having invited Mr. Wilson to his house, and Pamela and Joseph both so insisted on his complying, that he at last consented, having first obtained a messenger from Mr. Booby, to acquaint his wife with the news; which, as he knew it would render her completely happy, he could not prevail on himself to delay a moment in acquainting her with.

The company were ranged in this manner. The two old people with their two daughters rode in the coach, the squire, Mr. Wilson, Joseph, Parson Adams, and the pedlar proceeded on horseback.

In their way Joseph informed his father of his intended match with Fanny; to which, tho' he expressed some reluctance at first, on the eagerness of his son's instances he consented, saying if she was so good a creature as she appeared, and he described her, he thought the disadvantages of birth and fortune might be compensated. He however insisted on the match being deferred till he had seen his mother; in which Joseph perceiving him positive, with great duty obeyed him, to the great delight of Parson Adams, who by these means saw an opportunity of fulfilling the Church forms, and marrying his parishioners without a licence.

Mr. Adams greatly exulting on this occasion, (for such ceremonies were matters of no small moment with him) accidentally gave spurs to his horse, which the generous beast disdaining, for he was high of mettle, and had been used to more expert riders than the gentleman who at present bestrode him: for whose horsemanship he had perhaps some contempt, immediately ran away full speed, and played so many antic tricks, that he tumbled the parson from his back; which Joseph perceiving, came to his relief. This accident afforded infinite merriment to the servants, and no less frighted poor Fanny, who beheld him as he past by the coach; but the mirth of the one, and terror of the other were soon determined,[1] when the parson declared he had received no damage.

The horse having freed himself from his unworthy rider, as he probably thought him, proceeded to make the best of his way: but was stopped by a gentleman and his servants, who were travelling the opposite way; and were now at a little distance from the coach. They soon met; and as one of the servants delivered Adams his horse, his master hailed him, and Adams looking up, presently recollected he was the justice of peace before whom he and Fanny had made their appearance.

---

1 Ended.

The parson presently saluted him very kindly; and the justice informed him, that he had found the fellow who attempted to swear against him and the young woman the very next day, and had committed him to Salisbury goal, where he was charged with many robberies.

Many compliments having past between the parson and the justice, the latter proceeded on his journey, and the former having with some disdain refused Joseph's offer of changing horses; and declared he was as able a horseman as any in the kingdom, re-mounted his beast; and now the company again proceeded, and happily arrived at their journey's end, Mr. Adams by good luck, rather than by good riding, escaping a second fall.

The company arriving at Mr. Booby's house, were all received by him in the most courteous, and entertained in the most splendid manner, after the custom of the old English hospitality, which is still preserved in some very few families in the remote parts of England. They all past that day with the utmost satisfaction; it being perhaps impossible to find any set of people more solidly and sincerely happy. Joseph and Fanny found means to be alone upwards of two hours, which were the shortest but the sweetest imaginable.

In the morning, Mr. Wilson proposed to his son to make a visit with him to his mother; which, notwithstanding his dutiful inclinations, and a longing desire he had to see her, a little concerned him as he must be obliged to leave his Fanny: but the goodness of Mr. Booby relieved him; for he proposed to send his own coach and six for Mrs. Wilson, whom Pamela so very earnestly invited, that Mr. Wilson at length agreed with the entreaties of Mr. Booby and Joseph, and suffered the coach to go empty for his wife.

On Saturday night the coach return'd with Mrs. Wilson, who added one more to this happy assembly. The reader may imagine much better and quicker too than I can describe, the many embraces and tears of joy which succeeded her arrival. It is sufficient to say, she was easily prevailed with to follow her husband's example, in consenting to the match.

On Sunday Mr. Adams performed the service at the squire's parish church, the curate of which very kindly exchanged duty, and rode twenty miles to the Lady Booby's parish, so to do; being particularly charged not to omit publishing the banns, being the third and last time.

At length the happy day arrived, which was to put Joseph in the possession of all his wishes. He arose and drest himself in a neat, but plain suit of Mr. Booby's, which exactly fitted him; for he refused all finery; as did Fanny likewise, who could be prevailed on by Pamela to attire herself in nothing richer than a white dimity night-gown.[1] Her shift indeed, which Pamela presented her, was of the finest kind, and had an edging of lace round the bosom; she likewise equipped her with a pair of fine white thread stockings, which were all she would accept; for she wore one of her own short round-ear'd caps, and over it a little straw hat, lined with cherry-coloured silk, and tied with a cherry-coloured ribbon. In this dress she came forth from her chamber, blushing, and breathing sweets; and was by Joseph, whose eyes sparkled fire, led to church, the whole family attending, where Mr. Adams performed the ceremony; at which nothing was so remarkable, as the extraordinary and unaffected modesty of Fanny, unless the true Christian piety of Adams, who publickly rebuked Mr. Booby and Pamela for laughing in so sacred a place, and so solemn an occasion. Our parson would have done no less to the highest prince on earth: for tho' he paid all submission and deference to his superiors in other matters, where the least spice of religion intervened, he immediately lost all respect of persons. It was his maxim, that he was a servant of the Highest, and could not, without departing from his duty, give up the least article of his honour, or of his cause, to the greatest earthly potentate. Indeed he always asserted, that Mr. Adams at church with his surplice on, and Mr. Adams without that ornament, in any other place, were two very different persons.

When the church rites were over, Joseph led his blooming bride back to Mr. Booby's (for the distance was so very little, they did not think proper to use a coach) the whole company attended them likewise on foot; and now a most magnificent

---

1 Evening dress.

entertainment was provided, at which Parson Adams demonstrated an appetite surprizing, as well as surpassing every one present. Indeed the only persons who betrayed any deficiency on this occasion, were those on whose account the feast was provided. They pampered their imaginations with the much more exquisite repast which the approach of night promised them; the thoughts of which filled both their minds, tho' with different sensations; the one all desire, while the other had her wishes tempered with fears.

At length, after a day past with the utmost merriment, corrected by the strictest decency; in which, however, Parson Adams, being well filled with ale and pudding, had given a loose to more facetiousness than was usual to him: the happy, the blest moment arrived, when Fanny retired with her mother, her mother-in-law, and her sister. She was soon undrest; for she had no jewels to deposite in their caskets, nor fine laces to fold with the nicest exactness. Undressing to her was properly discovering, not putting off ornaments: for as all her charms were the gifts of nature, she could divest herself of none. How, reader, shall I give thee an adequate idea of this lovely young creature! the bloom of roses and lillies might a little illustrate her complexion, or their smell her sweetness: but to comprehend her entirely, conceive youth, health, bloom, beauty, neatness, and innocence in her bridal-bed; conceive all these in their utmost perfection, and you may place the charming Fanny's picture before your eyes.

Joseph no sooner heard she was in bed, than he fled with the utmost eagerness to her. A minute carried him into her arms, where we shall leave this happy couple to enjoy the private rewards of their constancy; rewards so great and sweet, that I apprehend Joseph neither envied the noblest duke, nor Fanny the finest duchess that night.

The third day, Mr. Wilson and his wife, with their son and daughter returned home; where they now live together in a state of bliss scarce ever equalled. Mr. Booby hath with unprecedented generosity given Fanny a fortune of two thousand pound, which Joseph hath laid out in a little estate in the same parish with his father, which he now occupies, (his father having stock'd it for him;) and Fanny presides, with most excellent management in his dairy; where, however, she is not at present very able to bustle much, being, as Mr. Wilson informs me in his last letter, extremely big with her first child.

Mr. Booby hath presented Mr. Adams with a living of one hundred and thirty pounds a year. He at first refused it, resolving not to quit his parishioners, with whom he hath lived so long: but on recollecting he might keep a curate at this living, he hath been lately inducted into it.

The pedlar, besides several handsome presents both from Mr. Wilson and Mr. Booby, is, by the latter's interest, made an excise-man; a trust which he discharges with such justice, that he is greatly beloved in his neighbourhood.

As for the Lady Booby, she returned to London in a few days, where a young captain of dragoons, together with eternal parties at cards, soon obliterated the memory of Joseph.

Joseph remains blest with his Fanny, whom he doats on with the utmost tenderness, which is all returned on her side. The happiness of this couple is a perpetual fountain of pleasure to their fond parents; and what is particularly remarkable, he declares he will imitate them in their retirement; nor will be prevailed on by any booksellers, or their authors, to make his appearance in *High-Life*.[1]

---

1 As well as Richardson's two-volume sequel to *Pamela* (December 1741), tracing the life of its heroine "*In her Exalted Condition*," several spurious continuations also appeared, one by John Kelly entitled *Pamela's Conduct in High Life* (May 1741).

Appendix A: Social History of the Times

[The following excerpts, taken from various social histories dealing with eighteenth-century England, present different aspects of the society in which *Joseph Andrews* is set.]

1. Mobility Within the Social Scale

In London in the eighteenth century we see a society which still clung to the old safeguards and prejudices, to the restriction of workers to their place of settlement, to rigid demarcations between class and class, to the exclusiveness of trades and corporations, to a fierce hatred of foreigners. But in spite of—sometimes even because of—these restrictions there was a ceaseless movement to and fro between the metropolis, Great Britain, Ireland, and the Continent, as well as upwards and downwards in the social scale. Leslie Stephen[1] has pointed out that the eighteenth century is conspicuous for the number of men who rose from the humblest positions to distinction in science, art, and literature. And in the anonymous strata of labourers, artisans, clerks, shopkeepers and men of business, many rose from the bottom of the ladder to establish positions. The corollary to the thousands of decayed housekeepers who filled the workhouses and debtors' prisons were the thousands of people of lowly beginnings who took their places, and as the middle classes were increasing, there was more room for the movement upwards than downwards.

[Source: M. Dorothy George, *London Life in the Eighteenth Century* (1925; Harmondsworth, UK: Penguin, 1992) 308.]

2. Coinage

The coinage in the reigns of Anne and the first two Georges [1702-60] consisted of:

1 Leslie Stephen, *English Literature and Society in the Eighteenth Century* (London: Duckworth, 1904).

Gold	*Silver*	*Copper*
Five guineas	Crown	Halfpenny
Two guineas	Halfcrown	Farthing
Guinea	Shilling	
Half-guinea	Sixpence	
	Fourpence	
	Threepence	
	Twopence	
	Penny	

The copper coinage only came into regular use after Anne's death [in 1714]....

[Source: Duncan Taylor, *Fielding's England* (London: Dobson, 1966) 28.]

3. London

There is one thing which stands out clearly—the enormous importance of London. London was then far more important, commercially, industrially and socially, in relation to the rest of the country than it has ever been since. London was the only great city in England where town life was sharply cut from country life. The only place it could be compared with was Paris, and people were fond of discussing which was the larger and which the more wicked.... Out of a total of about 5½ millions [early in the century] London's share is estimated at 674,000 odd. And enormous as a town population of over half a million then was, the place impressed people as so colossal that there were sober calculators who made out that it had at least a million inhabitants....

... London, with its noisy crowded streets, lighted shop windows, its post office ... stock exchange ... and the astonishing brilliance and luxury of its shops, its legendary and fascinating wickedness, seemed to belong to a different world and a different age from the country village and the country life. The lure of London as a place where fortunes were to be made, where life was altogether on an easier, more luxurious scale was tremendous. And country people, when they came to town were so conspicuously different from Londoners, and gazed about with such open-mouthed wonder that they were an easy prey to sharpers and harpies of both sexes.

[Source: M. Dorothy George, *England in Transition: Life and Work in the Eighteenth Century* (London: Routledge, 1931) 32-33, 41-42.]

4. The Parks and Pleasure Gardens of London

English people, so foreign observers thought, loved crowds and noise and bustle. They seemed to spend little time indoors, flocking together, enjoying each other's company in a rowdy, joking way. In London they walked in their hundreds in the parks and in the pleasure gardens of which there were over sixty in addition to Ranelagh and Vauxhall. A German visitor thought the medley of people in St James's Park "astonishing," while a Frenchman described the crowds at Vauxhall as the largest he had ever seen gathered together in one place.... At Ranelagh in Chelsea, where the charge for admittance was 2s 6d "tea and coffee included"—5s on fireworks night—the grounds were equally packed. The rotunda—into which "everybody that loves eating, drinking, staring or crowding" was admitted for a shilling—was often so full that the orchestra could only just be heard above the din. At Hampstead Wells all kinds of people from fashionable ladies to Fleet Street sempstresses, from attorneys to chimney-sweeps, came to dance and to listen to the music, to promenade up and down Well Walk and to bowl and gamble on the Heath.

[Source: Christopher Hibbert, *The English: A Social History 1066-1945* (1987; London: Paladin, 1988) 363.]

5. Uproar in the Theatres

In these audiences pickpockets abounded, and prostitutes were numerous, though these generally kept to their own special parts of the house. Drunkenness and fighting were still quite common; duels took place in the aisles and on the stairs ...

Sometimes the disturbances turned into riots. There were riots in 1737 when a French company was granted a licence to perform at the Little Theatre, Haymarket; there were riots when prices were raised at Drury Lane; and there were riots when managements attempted to end the custom of allowing people into the theatres at half price after the end of the third act of the main item on the programme. Seats were torn up, curtains pulled down, sconces[1] and mirrors smashed, box partitions splintered.

[Source: Hibbert 414.]

6. Eating and Drinking Habits Among the Working Classes

... In 1725 ... [Benjamin Franklin] worked in a London printing-house—Watts', near Lincoln's Inn Fields, where nearly fifty men were employed, a large establishment for the time. He was that (in those days) very exceptional thing, a water-drinker, and after having paid his contribution in the press-room where he first worked he moved to the composing-room. Here a further contribution of 5s. was demanded and after resisting payment for two or three weeks he had to give in. Nevertheless, he established an ascendancy over the other compositors, as he induced them to alter their Chapel rules (the name at least a tradition from the days of Caxton), and many of them, he says, in the end followed his example and gave up "their muddling breakfast of beer, and bread, and cheese, finding they could with me be supplied from a neighbouring house with a large porringer of hot-water gruel sprinkled with pepper, crumbled with bread, and a bit of butter in it for the price of a pint of

1 Decorative wall brackets for candles.

beer, viz., three halfpence." Franklin calls the other workmen "great guzzlers of beer." He says,

> ... we had an alehouse boy who attended always in the house to supply the workmen. My companion at press drank every day a pint before breakfast, a pint at breakfast ... a pint between breakfast and dinner, a pint in the afternoon about 6 o'clock, and another pint when he had done his day's work ... it was necessary he supposed to drink strong beer that he might be strong to labour.

In spite of Franklin's exhortations, "he drank on ... and had 4s. or 5s. to pay out of his wages every Saturday night for that muddling liquor.... And thus these poor devils keep themselves always under"[1]....

[Source: George, *London Life* 282.]

7. Female Domestics

There was one numerous class [of immigrants] whose position was especially difficult and dangerous. These were the girls who came from the country to find places as domestic servants. Colquhoun[2] estimated in 1800 that there were seldom less than 10,000 domestic servants of both sexes out of a place in London. John Fielding[3] in 1753 speaks of the "amazing number" of women servants wanting places, though there was always a shortage of maids of all work.

> The body of servants ... that are chiefly unemployed ... are those of a higher nature such as chambermaids, etc., whose number far exceeds the places they stand candidates for, and as the chief of these come from the country,

1 *Autobiography of Benjamin Franklin* (1868; London: Cassell, 1905) 54-55.

2 Patrick Colquhoun, *A Treastise on the Police of the Metropolis*, 6th ed. (London, 1800) 634n.

3 The writer's younger half-brother and fellow magistrate (1721-80). The following passage is from a letter written in 1753 and published in the *London Chronicle* on 6 April 1758.

they are obliged when out of place to go into lodgings and there to subsist on their little savings, till they get places agreeable to their inclinations ... and this is one of the grand sources which furnish this town with prostitutes.

[Source: George, *London Life* 119.]

8. Tea, Coffee, and Chocolate

... [Tea] had first reached England, together with coffee and chocolate, towards the middle of the seventeenth century. It was then drunk, as the Chinese drink it, without milk or sugar. In the first half of the eighteenth century tea became much more popular than chocolate or coffee. It was taken with milk or cream and sugar (which by that time was no longer a rare luxury); but it was not yet firmly established as a national drink.... There was ... [some] opposition to tea on grounds of health. John Wesley was convinced that tea-drinking affected his nerves and made his hand shake. He first tried taking it weaker, with more milk and sugar, but finally gave it up altogether....

[Source: Taylor 75-76.]

9. Transportation

There was no public transport [in Fielding's time]. Most people went about London on foot. Those who were very rich had private coaches, sometimes with as many as six horses [a coach and six]—four driven by the coachman and the leading pair by a postilion, who rode on one of them. For hire there were the Thames boats, hackney coaches drawn by two horses, and sedan chairs carried by two chairmen. "Chairs," as they were called, had first become popular in Queen Anne's reign. Their charge, fixed by law, was a shilling a mile; a hackney coach had to go a mile and a half for the same fare. Chairs were convenient for short distances in crowded streets—convenient, that is to say, for the occupants; they could be a nuisance to pedestrians....

The only form of transport which took a number of passengers at the same time was the stage coach. It carried six passengers inside and several on top, at the cost to each of about threepence a mile. But the coaches did not ply for hire in town. You only took one if you wanted to leave London ...

[Source: Taylor 34-35.]

10. The Environs of London

Although eighteenth-century London was incredibly dirtier, more dilapidated and more closely-built than it afterwards became, was there no compensation in its greater compactness, the absence of straggling suburbs, the ease with which people could take country walks? This is at least doubtful. The roads round London were neither very attractive nor very safe. The land adjoining them was watered with drains and thickly sprinkled with laystalls and refuse heaps. Hogs were kept in large numbers on the outskirts and fed on the garbage of the town. A chain of smoking brick-kilns surrounded a great part of London and in the brickfields vagrants lived and slept, cooking their food at the kilns. It is true that there was an improvement as the century went on. In 1706 it was said of the highways,

> ... tho' they are mended every summer, yet everybody knows that for a mile or two about this City, the same and the ditches hard by are commonly so full of nastiness and stinking dirt, that oftentimes many persons who have occasion to go in or come out of town, are forced to stop their noses to avoid the ill-smell occasioned by it....[1]

In 1751 Corbyn Morris remarks that the roads round London had greatly improved of late. But footpads and vagrants made the roads and fields round London unsafe, except on Sundays, when numbers gave safety and the people streamed in crowds to the various tea-gardens and pleasure resorts near the town.

[Source: George, *London Life* 105.]

---

1 *Proposals for establishing a Charitable Fund in the City of London* (London, 1706).

11. Highways

... "In Summer the Roads are suffocated and smothered with Dust," wrote Robert Phillips in 1736 in his *Dissertation Concerning the Present state of the High Roads of England, especially of those near London,*

> and towards the Winter, between wet and dry, they are deep Ruts full of water with hard dry Ridges, which make it difficult for Passengers to cross by one another without overturning. And in the Winter they are all Mud, which rises, spues and squeezes into the Ditches; so that the Ditches and Roads are full of Mud and Dirt all alike.

Such descriptions are so common that it cannot be doubted that in the first half of the eighteenth century the roads of England were deplorable. It was a well-known fact, the *Gentleman's Magazine* maintained twenty years after Phillip's *Dissertation* appeared, that a "party of ladies and gentlemen would sooner travel [from London] to the south of France and back again than down to Falmouth."

[Source: Hibbert 348.]

12. Highwaymen

The ordinary dangers of the road were compounded by those threatened by highwaymen. No doubt these dangers were exaggerated by contemporaries, and have subsequently been overemphasized; yet, while we may doubt that Englishmen in the 1750s really were, as Horace Walpole said they were, forced to travel even at noon as if they were going to battle, there was no doubt that highwaymen did constitute a major hazard on the road. "I was robbed last night as I expected," the Prime Minister, Lord North, wrote with characteristic placidity and resigned acceptance in 1774. "Our loss was not great, but as the postilion did not stop immediately, one of the two highwaymen fired at him.... It was at the end of Gunnersbury Lane." The following year the Norwich coach was held up in Epping Forest; three of the seven highwaymen were shot dead before the guard was killed himself. One of the highwaymen who robbed Walpole threatened him with a pistol which exploded in his face and blackened his skin with powder and shot marks. He was left thinking that had he been sitting an inch nearer the window, the ball would have passed through his brain. In the words of one experienced traveller, highwaymen were as "common as crows."

[Source: Hibbert 349.]

13. Inns as Depots

The transport system of the country depended upon inns and alehouses. The place of the modern railway station and receiving office was taken by the inn yard. Riverside alehouses were starting places for the west country barges. The hundreds of coaches and wagons which plied between London and provincial towns had their headquarters in inns. The carriers and carters who came to London from the home counties had some public-house to which they regularly resorted, and there the simple countryman was apt to get into bad company. The numerous inns and alehouses which did this sort of business collected a crowd of hangers-on and helpers whose reputation was of the worst, many of whom were connected with the gangs of thieves who specialized in depredations on passengers' luggage and other goods....

[Source: George, *London Life* 290.]

14. The Village Inn

The easy-going way in which labouring men frequented the village inn astonished ... a Swedish visitor in 1748. It was not unusual, he says, "to see many sit the whole day at the inn. But the custom of the country that friends and neighbours come together, sit and converse, the abundance of money in this country, the ease with which a man could in every case have his food if only he was somewhat industrious seem to have conduced to this result.... It is not to be wondered at, then, if a great many labourers and others, however large the daily wages and profits they can make, can for all that scarcely collect more than what goes from hand to mouth." There was little of the penuriousness of the peasant in England.

[Source: George, *England in Transition* 28-29.]

15. Pretentions of Servants

Association with the great was supposed to confer a kind of gentility upon those who worked for them; and the more distinguished the master or mistress the more respect his footmen or maids felt was their due. A lady's-maid, in referring to a grocer in a copy of the *Carlton House Magazine*, is made to remark, "Such low people are beneath our attention, though some have the *frontery* to put themselves upon a footing with a nobleman's attendant."

> We sometimes condescend indeed to talk with them in familiar terms, as if they were our equals [she continues], and this has encouraged them to be arrogant. That enormous mass of a woman, our butcher's wife in St James's Market, accosts me with as much freedom and as little *embarrassment* as if she belonged to a family of rank as well as myself. But I always discountenance such people and convince them that I know how to support the *spear* of life to which my stars have elevated me.[1]

[Source: Hibbert 508.]

1 *Carlton House Magazine* 1 (1792) 163.

16. Settlement in a Parish

The devices used to prevent people obtaining a settlement in a parish, and so a right to relief, beggar description. One was to destroy cottages lest they should become the nest of "beggars' brats." The hustling of pregnant women out of parishes lest the expected child should gain a settlement was done with the most callous brutality. Here is an entry from the records of a Cambridgeshire parish: Seventeen and sixpence was paid to remove "Mary Pateman neear her labour and suspected alsoe to be sick of the small poc. To send her away with all convenient speed and in time." And there are worse entries than this.

Couples were forced to marry under threats of penalties under the bastardy laws so that the woman and her child should be burdens upon some other parish. Such was the marriage which Parson Woodforde recorded in his diary on November 22, 1769: "I married Tom Bunge of Amsford to Charity Andrews of Castle Cary by License this morning. The Parish of Cary made him marry her, and he came handcuffed to Church for fear of running away, and the Parish of Cary was at all the expence of bringing them to, I received of Mr. Andrew Russ the Overseer of the Parish of Cary for it .0. 10. 6."[1]

[Source: George, *England in Transition* 138-39.]

17. Justices of the Peace

Rural England was governed by the patriarchal sway of the Justices of the Peace. It lay with them to decide if a local rate should be raised for any purpose, and how it should be spent. The Justices, nominally appointed by the Crown, were really appointed by the Lord Lieutenant influenced by the opinion of the gentry of the shire....

The powers and functions of the J.P.s covered all sides of country life. They administered in quarter or petty sessions, or in the private house of a single magistrate. They were supposed

---

1 James Woodforde, *The Diary of a Country Parson: 1758-1802* (1924-31; Oxford: Oxford UP, 1978) 54. The year of this entry is, in fact, 1768.

to keep up the roads and bridges, the prisons and workhouses. They licensed the public houses. They levied a county rate when a rate was levied at all. These and a hundred other aspects of county business lay in their control. Yet they had not any proper staff, or any effective bureaucracy to carry out local administration. For that would have meant a big county rate which men were unwilling to pay; they preferred inefficient local government provided only it was cheap....

In the middle of the century, Fielding, Smollett, and other observers of the injustices of life, bitterly satirized the irresponsible power of the J.P.s and its frequent misuse in acts of tyranny and favouritism. There was a corrupt type of J.P. known as "trading justices," men of a lower order of society who got themselves made magistrates in order to turn their position to financial profit. But generally speaking, the Justices who did most of the work in rural districts were substantial squires, too rich to be corrupt or mean, proud to do hard public work for no pay, anxious to stand well with their neighbours, but often ignorant and prejudiced without meaning to be unjust, and far too much a law unto themselves.

[Source: G.M. Trevelyan, *English Social History: A Survey of Six Centuries* (1942; Harmondsworth, UK: Penguin, 1986) 367-68.]

18. Vagrancy and the Law

The vagrancy laws encouraged a perpetual travelling and their effect was probably rather to bring people to London than to remove them from it. In theory they were separate from the poor laws, or rather they were the penal side of the poor laws, but in practice the two branches were inextricably mixed. Under the poor laws, a poor person had to be removed to his place of settlement under a removal order signed by two justices, and was supposed to be delivered to the parish officers there by an overseer of the removing parish which bore the cost, often very considerable. It was therefore a constant practice when the settlement was a distant one to remove by means of a vagrant pass. By this in theory a person who had committed some act of vagrancy, such as "wandering and begging" or "sleeping abroad in the open air," after being duly punished by whipping or imprisonment in a house of correction or both, was "passed," that is, conveyed in a cart from constable to constable till he reached his parish, the expense being borne by the counties through which he passed. The vagrancy laws were so severe that they defeated their own ends and punishments were seldom inflicted except in exceptional circumstances....

[Source: George, *London Life* 155-56.]

19. Debtors and Imprisonment

Terrible as were the effects of drink in the early nineteenth century, there had been a progressive improvement in the last fifty years of the eighteenth century. Another closely connected cause of misery and ruin was imprisonment for debt. The abuses connected with this remained so glaring, and the sufferings of individuals so grievous, that the great restriction in its scope has been given little attention. "'Tis reckoned there are about 60,000 miserable debtors perishing in the prisons of England and Wales," wrote a critic of the system in 1716.[1] One naturally assumes that this is a wild exaggeration, but conceivably (and allowing for those dependent on the prisoners) it was not so very far from the truth. In 1714 it was said "the Marshalsea[2] alone generally contains seven or eight hundred prisoners ... two or three commonly perishing in one day in this miserable and wasting condition"[3] A Parliamentary Committee reported in 1719 that three hundred persons had died in the Marshalsea in less than three months.[4] Oglethorpe's committee in 1729 found the prisoners on the common side in the Marshalsea, then "upwards of 350," literally dying of starvation. They took steps to feed them, but before this, the committee report, "a day seldom passed without a death, and upon the

---

1 T. Baston, *Thoughts on Trade and a Public Spirit* (London, 1716).

2 A debtors' prison in Southwark, across the Thames from London.

3 *Piercing Cryes of the poor and miserable Prisoners for Debt* (London, 1714).

4 *Commons Journals*, 21 January 1718-19.

advancing of spring not less than eight or ten usually died every twenty-four hours." Yet by 1729 the Act of 1725 had reduced the number of prisoners for small debts.

In 1779 the total number of prisoners for debt in England and Wales, according to Howard, was 2,076, ninety-two of whom were in the Marshalsea....

...The consequences of imprisonment for debt were so devastating that the reduction in the number of prisoners is of the greatest importance. Many families were left destitute because the wage-earner was either in prison or had fled from home to escape arrest; many apprentices were thrown on the world because their masters were in the Mint (before 1724) or in the Verge,[1] beyond seas, or in a debtors' prison with no hope of release. A vindictive spirit and ruinous litigation were encouraged by the hordes of attorneys and bailiffs who had bought their offices and lived at the expense of the community. Children were brought up in the Fleet and the King's Bench[2] with disastrous results. The Deputy Warden of the Fleet said in 1814 that he believed the Fleet to be the biggest brothel in the metropolis....

[Source: George, *London Life* 297-98, 300.]

20. Capital Punishment

Throughout the century, Parliament went on adding statute after statute to the "bloody code" of English law, enlarging perpetually the long list of offences punishable by death: finally they numbered two hundred. Not only were horse and sheep stealing and coining capital crimes, but also stealing in a shop to the value of five shillings, and stealing anything privily from the person, were it only a handkerchief. But such was the illogical chaos of the law, that attempted murder was still very lightly punished, though to slit a man's nose was capital. The effect of increased legal severity in an age that was becoming more

1 Areas of sanctuary for debtors.

2 Debtors' families lived on the premises of these two prisons. King's Bench was regarded as the most desirable place for incarceration in London.

humane, was that juries often refused to convict men for minor offences that would lead them to the scaffold. Moreover it was easy for a criminal, by the help of a clever lawyer, to escape on purely technical grounds from the meshes of an antiquated and over-elaborate procedure. Out of six thieves brought to trial, five might in one way or another get off, while the unlucky one was hanged....

[Source: Trevelyan 363-64.]

21. Marriage Without Banns or Licence

... Before the Marriage Act of 1753, though against the canons, marriage was valid without banns or licence, at any hour, in any building, and without a clergyman. In 1686 and 1712 fines were imposed on such marriages, and they became a civil offence, but fines, like ecclesiastical penalties, were useless against those who had neither money, liberty nor credit to lose. Prisons and their precincts being sheltering places for illicit traffic of all kinds, these marriages flourished especially in the Rules of the Fleet prison[1] ... A trade sprang up in the tenements and alehouses in the Rules of the Fleet, and pliers or touts competed for custom.[2] [Thomas] Pennant describes Fleet Street as it was before 1753:

> ... in walking along the street in my youth ... I have often been tempted by the question, "Sir, will you be pleased to walk in and be married?" Along this most lawless space was hung up the frequent sign of a male and female hand conjoined with "Marriages performed within" written beneath. A dirty fellow invited you in. The parson was seen walking before his shop, a squalid profligate fellow clad in a tattered plaid night-gown, with a fiery face and ready to couple you for a dram of gin or a roll of tobacco....

---

1 A defined area around Fleet prison (and King's Bench prison) within which certain prisoners, especially debtors, were permitted to live on giving proper security.

2 That is, the agents of the Fleet Street parsons solicited for business.

There were endless ramifications in the evil consequences of these marriages. Entries in the Fleet Street registers could always, for a consideration, be forged, antedated, or expunged. The practice was a direct incitement to bigamy, fictitious marriage for purposes of seduction, or marriage as the result of a drunken frolic. By persuasion, force, or fraud, women were taken to the purlieus of the Fleet and there married, to be stripped of their fortune and deserted. Heirs (of either sex) were entrapped by fortune hunters. Women married insolvent debtors in order to rid themselves of their debts....

[Source: George, *London Life* 305.]

22. Women's Education

Women's education was sadly to seek. Among the lower classes it was perhaps not much worse than men's, but the daughters of the well-to-do had admittedly less education than their brothers. It was before the days of "ladies' academies," and though there were "boarding schools" for girls, they were few and indifferent. Most ladies learnt from their mothers to read, write, sew, and manage the household.... The want of education in the sex was discussed as an admitted fact, one side defending it as necessary in order to keep wives in due subjection, while the other side, led by the chief literary men of the day, ascribed the frivolity and the gambling habits of ladies of fashion to an upbringing which debarred them from more serious interests.

Nevertheless, country-house letters of the period show us wives and daughters writing as intelligent advisers of their menfolk. Such correspondents were something better than brainless playthings or household drudges. A whole class of the literature of the day, from the *Spectator* downwards, was written as much for ladies as for their fathers and brothers. And it was observed that the ladies took a part, often too eager, in the Whig and Tory feuds that divided town and country. As in rural pastimes ... Belinda of Farquhar's play ... tells her friend "I can gallop all the morning after the hunting horn and all the evening after a fiddle. In short I can do everything with my father but drink and shoot flying."[1]

[Source: Trevelyan 327-28.]

23. Dress

"Nightgowns" were what we would call dressing-gowns—worn, together with a soft, pointed cap, when you first got up, until it was time to put on more formal clothes—but some men did not bother to change out of their nightgowns before paying the first visit of the day to a coffee house.

... "Wig" is short for "periwig," from the French *perruque.* The word came into use towards the end of the seventeeth century when the wearing of wigs by gentlemen had become normal practice....

... Bewigged, in shirt, breeches and stockings, a man had only to put on a lace cravat (a cross between a scarf and a tie), a waistcoat and a coat, both reaching almost to the knees, to be fully dressed for indoors. Before going out, in Queen Anne's reign, he would put on a sword; but this practice was gradually dropped under the Hanoverians. He carried a three-cornered hat, but often did not wear it because of the size of his wig. He also carried a stout but elegant cane and wore a cloak, if the weather made it necessary. Accessories such as snuff-box, watch, handkerchief and purse were now carried in pockets, a convenience invented by tailors about 1670.

... Hooped skirts [for women] came in during Queen Anne's reign and grew wider, as the Elizabethan farthingale had done. By 1730 these skirts were six feet in diameter, making it difficult for two women to sit side by side in a coach. The hoops were of whalebone, sewn into the petticoat or into the skirt itself....

... Women were not prepared to shave off their hair and depend entirely on wigs, as men were doing, but fashionable ladies might have other hair mixed with their own, particularly in the complicated styles of Queen Anne's reign, when hair was

1 These lines are spoken by Silvia (not Belinda) in act one, scene two of *The Recruiting Officer* (1706).

piled high round a wire framework called a *commode* and topped with an elaborate lace cap.

Powdering of the hair or wig was important for both sexes and in houses of the period you can still find "powder-closets" (like small rooms or big cupboards) where ladies and gentlemen once sat in dust cloaks, sometimes holding stiff paper cones, like dunces's caps, over their faces, while their heads were powdered and perfumed ...

... Women's stockings, gartered below the knee like those of men, were of all colours, until about 1737, when white became fashionable.... The fashion was condemned as immoral, white being considered only one remove from nudity, but it persisted. Anyhow no one except the wearer saw very much of the stockings, unless by accident.

A fan was the commonest accessory, and there was a wide variety of jewellery. Like men, women wore cloaks out of doors in cold or rainy weather. These were fitted with hoods. Hats were varied....

Parasols to keep off the sun had been introduced from the East and a similar device was beginning to be used to keep off the rain. This came to be called an "umbrella" (in spite of the fact that the word comes from the Latin "umbra," meaning shade). Though used by women in our period it had not become an elegant accessory. To carry one was an admission that you could not afford a coach or a sedan chair. Men thought umbrellas effeminate. Not till about 1750 did the London merchant Jonas Hanway use one regularly in public and umbrellas were not generally accepted by men until later in the century.

[Source: Taylor 80-87.]

24. Religion

English eighteenth-century religion, both within the Establishment and among the Dissenting bodies, was of two schools, which we may call for brevity the latitudinarian and the Methodist. If either is left out of the foreground, the social landscape of that age is wrongly delineated. Each of these two complementary systems had its own function; each had the defects of its qualities, which the other made good. The latitudinarian stood for the spirit of tolerance, for lack of which Christianity had for centuries past wrought cruel havoc in the world it set out to save; the latitudinarian stood also for reasonableness in the interpretation of religious doctrines, without which they were unlikely to be received by the more scientific modern mind. Methodism, on the other hand, renewed the self-discipline and the active zeal without which religion loses its power and forgets its purpose; and this new evangelism was allied to an active philanthropy....

[Source: Trevelyan 371.]

Appendix B: Pamela *and* Shamela

SAMUEL RICHARDSON

From *Pamela: or, Virtue Rewarded*

[*Pamela* was first published anonymously in two volumes on 6 November 1740. It became an immediate "best seller," the first in the history of English fiction, running through six editions in little more than a year. In Letter I, Pamela tells her mother and father of the death of her lady and of the kindness of Mr. B., her lady's son. In her subsequent correspondence, however, there is a growing sense of uneasiness concerning the master's intentions. The following passages are from the first edition.]

LETTER X.

Dear Mother,

You and my good Father may wonder that you have not had a Letter from me in so many Weeks; but a sad, sad Scene has been the Occasion of it. For, to be sure, now it is too plain, that all your Cautions were well-grounded. O my dear Mother! I am miserable, truly miserable!—But yet, don't be frighted, I am honest!—God, of his Goodness, keep me so!

O this Angel of a Master! this fine Gentleman! this gracious Benefactor to your poor *Pamela!* who was to take care of me at the Prayer of his good dying Mother; who was so careful of me, lest I should be drawn in by Lord *Davers's* Nephew, that he would not let me go to Lady *Davers's*:[1] This very Gentleman (yes, I must call him Gentleman, tho' he has fallen from the Merit of that Title) has degraded himself to offer Freedoms to his poor Servant! He has now shew'd himself in his true Colours, and to me, nothing appears so black and so frightful.

I have not been idle; but have writ from time to time how

---

1 Mr. B.'s sister.

he, by sly mean Degrees, exposed his wicked Views: But somebody stole my Letter, and I know not what is become of it. It was a very long one. I fear he that was mean enough to do bad things, in one respect, did not stick at this; but be it as it will, all the Use he can make of it will be, that he may be asham'd of *his* Part; I not of *mine*. For he will see I was resolv'd to be honest, and glory'd in the Honesty of my poor Parents. I will tell you all, the next Opportunity; for I am watch'd, and such-like, very narrowly; and he says to Mrs. *Jervis*,[1] This Girl is always scribbling; I think she may be better employ'd. And yet I work all Hours with my Needle, upon his Linen, and the fine Linen of the Family; and am besides about flowering him a Waistcoat.—But, Oh! my Heart's broke almost; for what am I likely to have for my Reward, but Shame and Disgrace, or else ill Words, and hard Treatment! I'll tell you all soon, and hope I shall find my long Letter.

Your most afflicted Daughter.

I must *he* and *him* him now; for he has lost his Dignity with me!

LETTER XV.

Dear Mother,

I Broke off abruptly my last Letter; for I fear'd he was coming; and so it happen'd. I thrust the Letter into my Bosom, and took up my Work, which lay by me; but I had so little of the Artful, as he called it, that I look'd as confused, as if I had been doing some great Harm.

Sit still, *Pamela*, said he, and mind your Work, for all me.—You don't tell me I am welcome home after my Journey to *Lincolnshire*.[2] It would be hard, Sir, said I, if you was not always welcome to your Honour's own House.

I would have gone; but he said, Don't run away, I tell you. I

---

1 The housekeeper.

2 Mr. B. has an estate in Lincolnshire, which shortly becomes Pamela's place of confinement.

have a Word or two to say to you. Good Sirs, how my Heart went pit-a-pat! When I was a *little kind,* said he, to you in the Summer-house, and you carry'd yourself so *foolishly* upon it, as if I had intended to do you great harm, did I not tell you, you should take no Notice of what pass'd, to any Creature? And yet you have made a common Talk of the Matter, not considering either my Reputation or your own.—I made a common Talk of it, Sir, said I! I have nobody to talk to, hardly!

He interrupted me, and said *Hardly!* you little Equivocator! what do you mean by *hardly?* Let me ask you, Have you not told Mrs. *Jervis* for one? Pray your Honour, said I, all in Agitation, let me go down; for 'tis not for me to hold an Argument with your Honour. Equivocator, again! said he, and took my Hand, what do you talk of an *Argument?* Is it holding an Argument with me, to answer a plain Question? Answer me what I asked. O good, Sir, said I, let me beg you will not urge me further, for I fear I forget myself again, and be sawcy.

Answer me then, I bid you, says he, Have you told Mrs. *Jervis?* It will be sawcy in you, if you don't answer me directly to what I ask. Sir, said I, and fain would have pulled my Hand away, may be I should be for answering you by another Question, and that would not become me. What is it, says he, you would say? Speak out!

Then, Sir, said I, why should your Honour be so angry I should tell Mrs. *Jervis*, or any body else, what passed, if you intended no harm?...

He [then] by Force kissed my Neck and Lips; and said, Who ever blamed *Lucretia,*[1] but *the Ravisher* only? and I am content to take all the Blame upon me; as I have already borne too great a Share for what I have deserv'd. May I, said I, *Lucretia* like, justify myself with my Death, if I am used barbarously? O my good Girl! said he, tauntingly, you are well read, I see; and we shall make out between us, before we have done, a pretty Story in Romance, I warrant ye!

He then put his Hand in my Bosom, and the Indignation gave me double Strength, and I got loose from him, by a sud-

1 Lucretia, a legendary Roman heroine, stabbed herself after being raped by Tarquinius Sextus.

den Spring, and ran out of the Room; and the next Chamber being open, I made shift to get into it, and threw-to the Door, and the Key being on the Inside, it locked; but he follow'd me so close, he got hold of my Gown, and tore a Piece off, which hung without the Door.

I just remember I got into the Room; for I knew nothing further of the Matter till afterwards; for I fell into a Fit with my Fright and Terror, and there I lay, till he, as I suppose, looking through the Key-hole, spy'd me lying all along upon the Floor, stretch'd out at my Length; and then he call'd Mrs. *Jervis* to me, who, by his Assistance, bursting open the Door, he went away, seeing me coming to myself; and bid her say nothing of the Matter, if she was wise....

LETTER XXIV.

Dear Father and Mother,

I Shall write on, as long as I stay, tho' I should have nothing but Silliness to write; for I know you divert yourselves at Nights with what I write, because it is mine. *John*[1] tells me how much you long for my coming; but he says, he told you, he hop'd something would happen to hinder it.

I am glad you did not tell him the Occasion of my coming away; for *if* they should guess, it were better so, than to have it from you or me: Besides, I really am concern'd that my poor Master should cast such a Thought upon such a Creature as me; for besides the Disgrace, it has quite turn'd his Temper; and I begin to think he likes me, and can't help it; and yet strives to conquer it, and so finds no way but to be cross to me.

Don't think me presumptuous and conceited; for it is more my Concern than my Pride, to see such a Gentleman so demean himself, and lessen the Regard he used to have in the Eyes of all his Servants on my Account.—But I am to tell you of my new Dress to Day.

And so, when I had din'd, up Stairs I went, and lock'd myself

---

1 A footman, who would attend the carriage, etc.

into my little Room. There I trick'd myself up[1] as well as I could in my new Garb, and put on my round-ear'd ordinary Cap; but with a green Knot[2] however, and my homespun Gown and Petticoat, and plain-leather Shoes; but yet they are what they call *Spanish* Leather, and my ordinary Hose, ordinary I mean to what I have been lately used to; tho' I shall think good Yarn may do very well for every Day, when I come home. A plain Muslin Tucker[3] I put on, and my black Silk Necklace, instead of the *French* Necklace my Lady gave me; and put the Ear-rings out of my Ears; and when I was quite 'quipp'd, I took my Straw Hat in my Hand, with its two blue Strings, and look'd about me in the Glass, as proud as any thing.—To say Truth, I never lik'd myself so well in my life.

O the Pleasure of descending with Ease, Innocence and Resignation!—Indeed there is nothing like it! An humble Mind, I plainly see, cannot meet with any very shocking Disappointment, let Fortune's Wheel turn round as it will....

LETTER XXV.

My dear Parents,

O Let me take up my Complaint, and say, Never was poor Creature so unhappy, and so barbarously used, as your *Pamela!* O my dear Father and Mother, my Heart's just broke! I can neither write as I should do, nor let it alone; for to whom but to you can I vent my Griefs, and keep my poor Heart from bursting! Wicked, wicked Man!—I have no Patience left me!—But yet, don't be frighted—for,—I hope—I hope, I am honest!—But if my Head and my Heart will let me, you shall hear all.—Is there no Constable nor Headborough,[4] tho', to take me out of his House? for I am sure I can safely swear the Peace against him:[5] But, alas! he is greater than any Constable, and is a

1 Dressed up.
2 A bunch of ribbon loops, worn on the hair or in the cap.
3 A ruffle or frill, worn around the top of the bodice.
4 A parish officer similar to a petty constable.
5 That is, to swear that one is in bodily fear from another, so that he may be bound over to keep the peace.

Justice himself; such a Justice, deliver me from!—But God Almighty, I hope, in time, will right me!—For he knows the Innocence of my Heart!—

John went your way in the Morning; but I have been too much distracted to send by him; and have seen nobody but Mrs. *Jervis*, and *Rachel*, and one I hate to see: And indeed I hate now to see any body. Strange things I have to tell you, that happen'd since last Night, that good Mr. *Jonathan's* Letter,[1] and my Master's Harshness put me into such a Fluster. But I will no more *preambulate*.

I went to Mrs. *Jervis's* Chamber; and Oh! my dear Father and Mother, my wicked Master had hid himself, base Gentleman as he is! in her Closet, where she has a few Books, and Chest of Drawers, and such-like. I little suspected it; tho' I used, till this sad Night, always to look into that Closet, and another in the Room, and under the Bed, ever since the Summerhouse Trick, but never found any thing; and so I did not do it then, being fully resolv'd to be angry with Mrs. *Jervis* for what had happen'd in the Day, and so thought of nothing else.

I sat myself down on one side of the Bed, and she on the other, and we began to undress ourselves; but she on that side next the wicked Closet, that held the worst Heart in the World. So, said Mrs. *Jervis*, you won't speak to me, *Pamela!* I find you are angry with me....

Hush! said I, Mrs. *Jervis*, did you not hear something stir in the Closet? No, silly Girl, said she! your Fears are always awake!—But indeed, says I, I think I heard something rustle!—May-be, says she, the Cat may be got there: But I hear nothing.

I was hush; but she said, Pr'ythee, my good Girl, make haste to-bed. See if the Door be fast. So I did, and was thinking to look in the Closet; but hearing no more Noise, thought it needless, and so went again and sat myself down on the Bed-side, and went on undressing myself. And Mrs. *Jervis* being by this time undrest, stept into Bed, and bid me hasten, for she was sleepy.

I don't know what was the Matter; but my Heart sadly mis-

---

1 Mr. Jonathan, the butler, had sent a letter of warning to Pamela just before the following scene.

gave me; but Mr. *Jonathan's* Note was enough to make it do so, with what Mrs. *Jervis* had said. I pulled off my Stays, and my Stockens, and my Gown, all to an Under-petticoat; and then hearing a rustling again in the Closet, I said, God protect us! but before I say my Prayers, I must look into this Closet. And so was going to it slip shod,[1] when, O dreadful! out rush'd my Master, in a rich silk and silver Morning Gown.[2]

I scream'd, and run to the Bed; and Mrs. *Jervis* scream'd too; and he said, I'll do you no harm, if you forbear this Noise; but otherwise take what follows.

Instantly he came to the Bed; for I had crept into it, to Mrs. *Jervis*, with my Coat on, and my Shoes; and, taking me in his Arms, said, Mrs. *Jervis*, rise, and just step up Stairs, to keep the Maids from coming down at this Noise; I'll do no harm to this Rebel.

O, for God's sake! for Pity's sake! Mrs. *Jervis*, said I, if I am not betray'd, don't leave me; and, I beseech you, raise all the House. No, said Mrs. *Jervis*, I will not stir, my dear Lamb; I will not leave you. I wonder at you, Sir, said she, and kindly threw herself upon my Coat, clasping me round the Waist, you shall not hurt this Innocent, said she; for I will lose my Life in her Defence. Are there not, said she, enough wicked ones in the World, for your base Purpose, but you must attempt such a Lamb as this!

He was desperate angry, and threaten'd to throw her out of the Window; and to turn her out of the House the next Morning. You need not, Sir, said she; for I will not stay in it. God defend my poor *Pamela* till To-morrow, and we will both go together.—Says he, let me but expostulate a Word or two with you, *Pamela*. Pray, *Pamela*, said Mrs. *Jervis*, don't hear a Word, except he leaves the Bed, and goes to the other End of the Room. Aye, out of the Room! said I; expostulate To-morrow, if you must expostulate!

I found his Hand in my Bosom, and when my Fright let me know it, I was ready to die; and I sighed, and scream'd, and fainted away....

---

1 In slippers.

2 Dressing gown.

[After Letter XXXI, the "editor" introduces certain pertinent material, including the following letter from Pamela to Mrs. Jervis.]

"*Dear Mrs.* Jervis,

"I Have *been vilely trick'd*, and, instead of being driven by *Robin*[1] to my dear Father's, I *am* carry'd off, to where I have no Liberty to tell.[2] However, I am at present not used hardly *in the main*; and I write to beg of you to let my dear Father and Mother (whose Hearts must be well-nigh broken) know, That I am well, and that I am, and, by the Grace of God, ever will be, their dutiful and honest Daughter, as well as

"*Your obliged Friend*,
"PAMELA ANDREWS.

"I must neither send Date nor Place. But have most solemn Assurances of honourable Usage. *This is the only Time my low Estate has been troublesome to me, since it has subjected me to the Frights I have undergone. Love to your good self, and all my dear Fellow-servants. Adieu! Adieu! But pray for poor* PAMELA."...

[Following Letter XXXII, a journal form is adopted with letters interspersed.]

WEDNESDAY *Night*.

If, my dear Parents, I am not destin'd more surely than ever for Ruin, I have now more Comfort before me, than ever I yet knew. And am either nearer my Happiness or my Misery than ever I was. God protect me from the latter, if it be his blessed Will! I have now such a Scene to open to you, that I know will alarm both your Hopes and your Fears, as it does mine. And this it is.

After my Master had din'd, he took a Turn into the Stables, to look at his Stud of Horses; and, when he came in, he open'd

1 Mr. B.'s Lincolnshire coachman.
2 That is, Mr. B.'s Lincolnshire estate.

the Parlour-door, where Mrs. *Jewkes*[1] and I sat at Dinner; and, at his Entrance, we both rose up; but he said, Sit still, sit still; and let me see how you eat your Victuals, *Pamela.* O, said Mrs. *Jewkes*, very poorly, Sir, I'll assure you. No, said I, pretty well, Sir, considering. None of your *Considerings!* said he, Pretty-face, and tapp'd me on the Cheek. I blush'd, but was glad he was so good-humour'd; but I could not tell how to sit before him, nor to behave myself....

My Master took two or three Turns about the Room, musing and thoughtful, as I had never before seen him; and at last he went out, saying, I am going into the Garden ... I rose and curcheed, saying, I would attend his Honour; and he said, Do, good Girl!

Well, said Mrs. *Jewkes*, I see how things will go. O *Madam*, as she call'd me again, I am sure you are to be our Mistress! And then I know what will become of me. Ah! Mrs. *Jewkes*, said I, if I can but keep myself virtuous, 'tis the utmost of my Ambition; and, I hope, no Temptation shall make me otherwise....

So he was pleas'd to say, Well, *Pamela*, I am glad you are come of your own Accord, as I may say: Give me your Hand. I did so; and he look'd at me very steadily, and pressing my Hand all the time, at last said, I will now talk to you in a serious manner....

You know I am not a very abandon'd Profligate: I have hitherto been guilty of no very enormous or vile Actions. This of seizing you, and confining you thus, may, perhaps, be one of the worst, at least to Persons of real Innocence. Had I been utterly given up to my Passions, I should before now have gratify'd them, and not have shewn that Remorse and Compassion for you, which have repriev'd you more than once, when absolutely in my Power; and you are as inviolate a Virgin as you was when you came into my House.

But, what can I do? Consider the Pride of my Condition. I cannot endure the Thought of Marriage, even with a Person of equal or superior Degree to myself; and have declin'd several Proposals of that kind: How then, with the Distance between us, and in the World's Judgment, can I think of making you my

---

1 Mrs. Jewkes is the wicked counterpart of Mrs. Jervis.

Wife?—Yet I must have you; I cannot bear the Thoughts of any other Man supplanting me in your Affections. And the very Apprehension of that, has made me hate the Name of *Williams*,[1] and use him in a manner unworthy of my Temper....

TUESDAY *Morning*.

Getting up pretty early, I have written thus far, while Mrs. *Jewkes* lies snoring in bed, fetching-up her last Night's Disturbance. I long for her Rising, to know how my poor Master does.[2] 'Tis well for her she can sleep so purely. No Love, but for herself, will ever break her Rest, I am sure. I am deadly sore all over, as if I had been soundly beaten. Yet I did not think I could have liv'd under such Fatigue.

Mrs. *Jewkes*, as soon as she got up, went to know how my Master did, and he had had a good Night; and having drank plentifully of Sack-whey, had sweated much; so that his Fever had abated considerably. She said to him, that he must not be surprized, and she would tell him News. He asked, What? and she said, I was come. He raised himself up in his Bed; Can it be? said he:—What, already! ...

As soon as he saw me, he said, O my beloved *Pamela!* you have made me quite well. I'm concern'd to return my Acknowledgements to you in so unfit a Place and Manner; but will you give me your Hand? I did, and he kissed it with great Eagerness. Sir, said I, you do me too much Honour!—I am sorry you are ill.—I can't be ill, said he, while you are with me. I am well already.

Well, said he, and kissed my Hand again, you shall not repent this Goodness. My Heart is too full of it, to express myself as I ought. But I am sorry you have had such a fatiguing Time of it.—Life is no Life without you! If you had refused me, and yet I had hardly Hopes you would oblige me, I should have had a

---

1 Mr. Williams, the chaplain at Mr. B.'s Lincolnshire estate, befriends Pamela and becomes deeply entangled in the affair. At one point, Mr. B. arranges a marriage between him and Pamela, and then later has him imprisoned.

2 Upon learning of Mr. B.'s illness, despite his cruel treatment, Pamela returns immediately to his residence, tired and bruised by the journey.

severe Fit of it, I believe; for I was taken very oddly, and knew not what to make of myself: But now I shall be well instantly. You need not, Mrs. *Jewkes*, added he, send for the Doctor from *Stamford*, as we talked Yesterday; for this lovely Creature is my Doctor, as her Absence was my Disease....

He took my Hand, and said, One thing I will tell you, *Pamela*, because I know you will be glad to hear it, and yet not care to ask me, I have taken *Williams's* Bond for the Money; for how the poor Man had behaved, I can't tell; but he could get no Bail; and if I have no fresh Reason given me, perhaps I shall not exact the Payment; and he has been some time at Liberty; and now follows his School; but, methinks, I could wish you would not see him at present.

Sir, said I, I will not do any thing to disoblige you wilfully; and I am glad he is at Liberty, because I was the Occasion of his Misfortunes. I durst say no more, tho' I wanted to plead for the poor Gentleman; which, in Gratitude, I thought I ought, when I could do him Service. I said, I am sorry, Sir, Lady *Davers*, who loves you so well, should have incurr'd your Displeasure, and there should be any Variance between your Honour and her. I hope it was not on my Account. He took out of his Waistcoat Pocket, as he sat in his Gown, his Letter-case, and said, Here, *Pamela*, read that when you go up Stairs, and let me have your Thoughts upon it; and that will let you into the Affair. He said, he was very heavy of a sudden, and would lie down, and indulge for that Day; and if he was better in the Morning, would take an Airing in the Chariot. And so I took my Leave for the present, and went up to my Closet, and read the Letter he was pleased to put into my Hands; and which is as follows:

"*Brother,*

"I Am very uneasy at what I hear of you; and must write, whether it please you or not, my *full* Mind. I have had some People with me, desiring me to interpose with you; and they have a greater Regard for your Honour, than, I am sorry to say it, you have yourself. Could I think that a Brother of mine would so meanly run away with my late dear Mother's Waiting-maid, and keep her a Prisoner from all her Friends, and to the Disgrace of your own. But I thought, when you would not let the Wench come to me on my Mother's Death, that you meant no good.—I blush for you, I'll assure you. The Girl was an innocent, good Girl; but I suppose that's over with her now, or soon will. What can you mean by this, let me ask you? Either you will have her for a kept Mistress, or for a Wife. If the former; there are enough to be had, without ruining a poor Wench that my Mother lov'd, and who really was a very good Girl; and of *this* you may be asham'd. As to the *other*, I dare say, you don't think of it; but if you *should*, you would be utterly inexcusable. Consider, Brother, that ours is no upstart Family; but is as ancient as the best in the Kingdom; and, for several Hundreds of Years, it has never been known that the Heirs of it have disgraced themselves by unequal Matches: And you know you have been sought to by some of the first Families in the Nation, for your Alliance. It might be well enough, if you were descended of a Family of Yesterday, or but a Remove or two from the Dirt you seem so fond of. But, let me tell you, that I, and all mine, will renounce you for ever, if you can descend so meanly; and I shall be ashamed to be called your Sister. A handsome Gentleman as you are in your Person; so happy in the Gifts of your Mind, that every body courts your Company; and possess'd of such a noble and clear Estate; and very rich in Money besides, left you by the best of Fathers and Mothers, with such ancient Blood in your Veins, untainted! for *you* to throw away yourself thus, is intolerable; and it would be very wicked in you to ruin the Wench too. So that I beg you will restore her to her Parents, and give her 100 *l.* or so, to make her happy in some honest Fellow of her own Degree; and that will be doing something, and will also oblige and pacify

"*Your much grieved Sister.*

"If I have written too sharply, consider it is my Love to you, and the Shame you are bringing upon yourself; and I wish this may have the Effect upon you intended by your very loving Sister."...

WEDNESDAY.

Now, my dear Parents, I have but this *one* Day, between me and the most solemn Rite that can be perform'd. My Heart cannot yet shake off this heavy Weight. Sure I am ingrateful to God's Goodness, and the Favour of the best of Benefactors!—Yet I hope I am not!—for at times, my Mind is all Exultation, with the Prospect of what Good tomorrow's happy Solemnity may possibly, by Leave of my generous Master, put it in my Power to do. O how shall I find Words to express, as I ought, my Thankfulness, for all the Mercies before me!—...

THURSDAY, *Six o'Clock in the Morning.*

I Might as well have not gone to-bed last Night, for what Sleep I had. Mrs. *Jewkes* often was talking to me, and said several things that would have been well enough from any body else of our Sex; but the poor Woman has so little Purity of Heart, that it is all *Say* from her, and goes no further than my Ears.

I fancy my Master has not slept much neither; for I heard him up, and walking about his Chamber, ever since Break of Day. To be sure, poor Gentleman, he must have some Concern, as well as I; for here he is going to marry a poor foolish unworthy Girl, brought up on the Charity, as one may say, (at least, Bounty) of his worthy Family! And this foolish Girl must be, to all Intents and Purposes, after Twelve o'Clock this Day, as much his Wife, as if he were to marry a Dutchess!—And here he must stand the Shocks of common Reflection; The great 'Squire B. has done finely! he has marry'd his poor Servant *Wench!* will some say. The Ridicule and rude Jests of his Equals, and Companions too, he must stand: And the Disdain of his Relations, and Indignation of Lady *Davers*, his lofty Sister!—Dear good Gentleman! he will have enough to do, to be sure!—O how shall I merit all these things at his Hands! I can only do the best I can; and pray to God to reward him, and to resolve to love him with a pure Heart, and serve him with a sincere Obedience. I hope the dear Gentleman will continue to love me for this; for, alas! I have nothing else to offer! But, as

I can hardly expect so great a Blessing, if I can be secure from his Contempt, I shall not be unfortunate; and must bear his Indifference, if his rich Friends should inspire him with it, and proceed with doing my Duty with Chearfulness....

THURSDAY, *near Three o-Clock.*

... My dear Master came to me, at entering the Chapel, and took my Hand, and led me up to the Altar. Remember, my dear Girl, whisper'd he, and be chearful. I am, I will, Sir, said I; but I hardly knew what I said; and so you may believe, when I said to Mrs. *Jewkes*, Don't leave me; pray, Mrs. *Jewkes*, don't leave me; as if I had all Confidence in her, and none where it was most due. So she kept close to me. God forgive me! but I never was so absent in my Life, as at first: Even till Mr. *Williams* had gone on in the Service, so far as to the awful Words about *requiring us, as we should answer at the dreadful Day of Judgment*; and then the solemn Words, and my Master's whispering, Mind this, my Dear, made me start. Said he, still whispering, Know *you* any Impediments? I blush'd, and said, softly, None, Sir, but my great Unworthiness.

Then follow'd the sweet Words, *Wilt thou have this Woman to thy wedded Wife*, &c. and I began to take Heart a little, when my dearest Master answer'd, audibly, to this Question, *I will.* But I could only make a Curchee, when they asked me; tho', I am sure, my Heart was readier than my Speech, and answer'd to every Article of *obey*, *serve*, *love*, and *honour*....

And thus, my dearest, dear Parents, is your happy, happy, thrice happy *Pamela*, at last, marry'd; and to who?—Why, to her beloved, gracious Master! the Lord of her Wishes!—And thus the dear, once naughty Assailer of her Innocence, by a blessed Turn of Providence, is become the kind, the generous Protector and Rewarder of it. God be evermore blessed and praised! and make me not wholly unworthy of such a transcendent Honour!—And bless and reward the dear, dear good Gentleman, who has thus exalted his unworthy Servant, and given her a Place, which the greatest Ladies would think themselves happy in!...

FRIDAY *Evening.*

O How this dear, excellent Man indulges me in every thing! Every Hour he makes me happier, by his sweet Condescension, than the former. He pities my Weakness of Mind, allows for all my little Foibles, endeavours to dissipate my Fears; his Words are so pure, his Ideas so chaste, and his whole Behaviour so sweetly decent, that never, surely, was so happy a Creature as your *Pamela!* I never could have hoped such a Husband could have fallen to my Lot! And much less, that a Gentleman, who had allow'd himself in Attempts, that now I will endeavour to forget for ever, should have behav'd with so very delicate and unexceptionable a Demeanour. No light, frothy Jests drop from his Lips; no alarming Railleries; no offensive Expressions, nor insulting Airs, reproach or wound the Ears of your happy, thrice happy Daughter. In short, he says every thing that may embolden me to look up, with Pleasure, upon the generous Author of my Happiness.

At Breakfast, when I knew not how to see him, he embolden'd me by talking of *you*, my dear Parents; a Subject, he generously knew, I could talk of: And gave me Assurances, that he would make you both happy. He said, he would have me send you a Letter, to acquaint you with my Nuptials; and, as he could make Business that way, *Thomas* should carry it purposely, as to-morrow. Nor will I, said he, my dear *Pamela*, desire to see your Writings, because I told you I would not; for now will I, in every thing, religiously keep my Word with my dear Spouse (O the dear delightful Word!); and you may send all your Papers to them, from those they have, down to this happy Moment; only let me beg they will preserve them, and let me have them when they have read them, as also those I have not seen; which, however, I desire not to see till then; but then shall take it for a Favour, if you will grant it.

It will be my Pleasure, as well as my Duty, Sir, said I, to obey you in every thing. And I will write up to the Conclusion of this Day, that they may see how happy you have made me....

[Source: Samuel Richardson, *Pamela*: *or, Virtue Rewarded*, ed. T. C. Duncan Eaves and Ben D. Kimpel (New York: Houghton Mifflin, 1971).]

HENRY FIELDING

From *An Apology for the Life of Mrs. Shamela Andrews*

[*Shamela* was published on 2 April 1741, by which time three editions of *Pamela* had appeared. While Fielding never acknowledged that he had written the work, there is now little doubt about its authorship. The following passages are from the second edition, evidently somewhat revised by him before its publication on 3 November 1741.]

To Miss *Fanny*, &c.[1]

MADAM,

It will be naturally expected, that when I write the Life of *Shamela*, I should dedicate it to some young Lady, whose Wit and Beauty might be the proper Subject of a Comparison with the Heroine of my Piece. This, those, who see I have done it in prefixing your Name to my Work, will much more confirmedly expect me to do; and, indeed, your Character would enable me to run some Length into a Parallel, tho' you, nor any one else, are at all like the matchless *Shamela*.

You see, Madam, I have some Value for your Good-nature, when in a Dedication, which is properly a Panegyrick, I speak against, not for you; but I remember it is a Life which I am presenting you, and why should I expose my Veracity to any Hazard in the Front of the Work, considering what I have done in the Body. Indeed, I wish it was possible to write a Dedication, and get any thing by it, without one Word of Flattery; but since it is not, come on, and I hope to shew my Delicacy at least in the Compliments I intend to pay you.

First, then, Madam, I must tell the World, that you have tickled up and brightened many Strokes in this Work by your Pencil.

---

1 Pope's name for the effeminate Lord Hervey (see above, p.372, n. 1), to whom Conyers Middleton, only a few months before the publication of *Shamela*, had dedicated his *Life of Cicero*.

Secondly, You have intimately conversed with me, one of the greatest Wits and Scholars of my Age.

Thirdly, You keep very good Hours, and frequently spend an useful Day before others begin to enjoy it. This I will take my Oath on; for I am admitted to your Presence in a Morning before other People's Servants are up; when I have constantly found you reading in good Books; and if ever I have drawn you upon me, I have always felt you very heavy.

Fourthly, You have a Virtue which enables you to rise early and study hard, and that is, forbearing to over-eat yourself, and this in spite of all the luscious Temptations of Puddings and Custards, exciting the Brute (as Dr. *Woodward* calls it) to rebel.[1] This is a Virtue which I can greatly admire, though I much question whether I could imitate it.

Fifthly, A Circumstance greatly to your Honour, that by means of your extraordinary Merit and Beauty; you was carried into the Ball-Room at the *Bath*, by the discerning Mr. *Nash*;[2] before the Age that other young Ladies generally arrived at that Honour, and while your Mamma herself existed in her perfect Bloom. Here you was observed in Dancing to balance your Body exactly, and to weigh every Motion with the exact and equal Measure of Time and Tune; and though you sometimes made a false Step, by leaning too much to one Side; yet every body said you would one Time or other, dance perfectly well, and uprightly.

Sixthly, I cannot forbear mentioning those pretty little Sonnets, and sprightly Compositions, which though they came from you with so much Ease, might be mentioned to the Praise of a great or grave Character.

And now, Madam, I have done with you; it only remains to pay my Acknowledgments to an Author, whose Stile I have exactly followed in this Life, it being the properest for Biography. The Reader, I believe, easily guesses, I mean *Euclid's*

---

1 In *The State of Physic and of Diseases* (1718), John Woodward blames most social evils on foreign cookery.

2 Richard "Beau" Nash (1674-1762) was master of ceremonies at the fashionable health resort of Bath.

Elements; it was *Euclid* who taught me to write. It is you, Madam, who pay me for Writing. Therefore I am to both,

A most Obedient, and
obliged humble Servant,
CONNY KEYBER.[1]

* * *

An APOLOGY For the Life of Mrs. Shamela Andrews.

Parson TICKLETEXT *to Parson* OLIVER.

Rev. SIR,

Herewith I transmit you a Copy of sweet, dear, pretty *Pamela*, a little Book which this Winter hath produced; of which, I make no doubt, you have already heard mention from some of your Neighbouring Clergy; for we have made it our common Business here, not only to cry it up, but to preach it up likewise: The Pulpit, as well as the Coffee-house, hath resounded with its Praise, and it is expected shortly, that his L——p will recommend it in a —— Letter to our whole Body.[2]

And this Example, I am confident, will be imitated by all our Cloth in the Country: For besides speaking well of a Brother, in the Character of the Reverend Mr. *Williams*, the useful and truly religious Doctrine of *Grace* is every where inculcated.

This Book is the "SOUL of *Religion*, Good-Breeding, Discretion, Good-Nature, Wit, Fancy, Fine Thought, and Morality. There is an Ease, a natural Air, a dignified Simplicity, and MEASURED FULLNESS in it, that RESEMBLING LIFE, OUT-

1 There is probably a double joke here, the "author's" name alluding to both Colley Cibber and Conyers Middleton.

2 Edmund Gibson (1669-1748), Bishop of London, issued frequent pastoral letters to the clergy of his diocese.

GLOWS IT. The Author hath reconciled the *pleasing* to the *proper*; the Thought is every where exactly cloathed by the Expression; and becomes its Dress as *roundly* and as close as *Pamela* her Country Habit; or *as she doth her no Habit*, when modest Beauty seeks to hide itself, by casting off the Pride of Ornament, and displays itself without any Covering;" which it frequently doth in this admirable Work, and presents Images to the Reader, which the coldest Zealot cannot read without Emotion....

As soon as you have read this yourself five or six Times over (which may possibly happen within a Week) I desire you would give it to my little God-Daughter, as a Present from me. This being the only Education we intend henceforth to give our Daughters. And pray let your Servant-Maids read it over, or read it to them. Both your self and the neighbouring Clergy, will supply yourselves for the Pulpit from the Booksellers, as soon as the fourth Edition is published.[1] I am,

Sir,

Your most humble Servant,

Tho. TICKLETEXT.

Parson OLIVER *to Parson* TICKLETEXT.

Rev. SIR,

I received the Favour of yours with the inclosed Book, and really must own myself sorry, to see the Report I have heard of an epidemical Phrenzy now raging in Town, confirmed in the Person of my Friend.

If I had not known your Hand, I should, from the Sentiments and Stile of the Letter, have imagined it to have come from the Author of the famous Apology,[2] which was sent me last Summer; and on my reading the remarkable Paragraph of *measured Fulness, that resembling Life out-glows it*, to a young Baronet, he cry'd out, *C—ly C—b—r*[3] by G—. But I have

---

1 The first edition of *Shamela* appeared on 2 April 1741, and the fourth one of *Pamela* on 5 May.

2 The first edition of Cibber's *Apology* was published in April 1740, followed by a second a month later.

3 That is, Colley Cibber.

since observed, that this, as well as many other Expressions in your Letter, was borrowed from those remarkable Epistles, which the Author, or the Editor hath prefix'd to the second Edition which you send me of his Book....

The History of *Pamela* I was acquainted with long before I received it from you, from my Neighbourhood to the Scene of Action. Indeed I was in hopes that young Woman would have contented herself with the Good-fortune she hath attained; and rather suffered her little Arts to have been forgotten than have revived their Remembrance, and endeavoured by perverting and misrepresenting Facts to be thought to deserve what she now enjoys: for though we do not imagine her the Author of the Narrative itself, yet we must suppose the Instructions were given by her, as well as the Reward, to the Composer. Who that is, though you so earnestly require of me, I shall leave you to guess from that *Ciceronian* Eloquence, with which the Work abounds; and that excellent Knack of making every Character amiable, which he lays his hands on.

But before I send you some Papers relating to this Matter, which will set *Pamela* and some others in a very different Light, than that in which they appear in the printed Book, I must beg leave to make some few Remarks on the Book itself, and its Tendency, (admitting it to be a true Relation,) towards improving Morality, or doing any good, either to the present Age, or Posterity: which when I have done, I shall, I flatter myself, stand excused from delivering it, either into the hands of my Daughter, or my Servant-Maid.

The Instruction which it conveys to Servant-Maids, is, I think, very plainly this, To look out for their Masters as sharp as they can. The Consequences of which will be, besides Neglect of their Business, and the using all manner of Means to come at Ornaments of their Persons, that if the Master is not a Fool, they will be debauched by him; and if he is a Fool, they will marry him. Neither of which, I apprend, my good Friend, we desire should be the Case of our Sons.

And notwithstanding our Author's Professions of Modesty, which in my Youth I have heard at the Beginning of an Epilogue, I cannot agree that my Daughter should entertain herself with some of his Pictures; which I do not expect to be contemplated without Emotion, unless by one of my Age and Temper, who can see the Girl lie on her Back, with one Arm round Mrs. *Jewkes* and the other round the Squire, naked in Bed, with his Hand on her Breasts, &c. with as much Indifference as I read any other Page in the whole Novel. But surely this, and some other Descriptions, will not be put into the hands of his Daughter by any wise Man, though I believe it will be difficult for him to keep them from her; especially if the Clergy in Town have cried and preached it up as you say.

But, my Friend, the whole Narrative is such a Misrepresentation of Facts, such a Perversion of Truth, as you will, I am perswaded, agree, as soon as you have perused the Papers I now inclose to you, that I hope you or some other well-disposed Person, will communicate these Papers to the Publick, that this little Jade may not impose on the World, as she hath on her Master.

The true name of this Wench was SHAMELA, and not *Pamela*, as she stiles herself. Her Father had in his Youth the Misfortune to appear in no good Light at the *Old-Bailey*;[1] he afterwards served in the Capacity of a Drummer in one of the *Scotch* Regiments in the *Dutch* Service; where being drummed out, he came to *England*, and turned Informer against several Persons on the late Gin-Act;[2] and becoming acquainted with an Hostler at an Inn, where a *Scotch* Gentleman's Horses stood, he hath at last by his Interest obtain'd a pretty snug Place in the *Custom-house*. Her Mother sold Oranges in the Play-House; and whether she was married to her Father or no, I never could learn.

After this short Introduction, the rest of her History will appear in the following Letters, which I assure you are authentick.

---

1 The central criminal court in London.

2 In 1736, Parliament passed a bill greatly increasing the duty on gin and other strong liquors. The Act was very unpopular with the public, and informers against offenders risked mob violence.

Letter I.

SHAMELA ANDREWS *to Mrs.* HENRIETTA MARIA HONORA ANDREWS *at her Lodgings at the* FAN *and* PEPPER-BOX *in* DRURY-LANE.

Dear Mamma,

This comes to acquaint you, that I shall set out in the Waggon on *Monday*, desiring you to commodate me with a Ludgin, as near you as possible, in *Coulstin's-Court*, or *Wild-Street*, or somewhere thereabouts; pray let it be handsome, and not above two Stories high: For Parson *Williams* hath promised to visit me when he comes to Town, and I have got a good many fine Cloaths of the Old Put my Mistress's, who died a wil ago; and I beleve Mrs. *Jervis* will come along with me, for she says she would like to keep a House somewhere about *Short's-Gardens*, or towards *Queen-Street*; and if there was convenience for a *Bannio*,[1] she would like it the better; but that she will settle herself when she comes to Town.—*O! How I long to be in the Balconey at the Old House*[2]—so no more at present from

Your affectionate Daughter,

SHAMELA.

Letter II.

SHAMELA ANDREWS *to* HENRIETTA MARIA HONORA ANDREWS.

Dear Mamma,

O what News, since I writ my last! the young Squire hath been here, and as sure as a Gun he hath taken a Fancy to me; *Pamela*, says he, (for so I am called here) you was a great Favorite of your late Mistress's; yes, an't please your Honour, says I; and I believe you deserved it, says he; thank your Honour for your good Opinion, says I; and then he took me by the Hand, and I pretended to be shy: Laud, says I, Sir, I hope you

1 A "brothel" ("bath" in Italian, somewhat equivalent to the modern Turkish bath or sauna).

2 Drury Lane Theatre.

don't intend to be rude; no, says he, my Dear, and then he kissed me, 'till he took away my Breath—and I pretended to be Angry, and to get away, and then he kissed me again, and breathed very short, and looked very silly; and by Ill-Luck Mrs. *Jervis* came in, and had like to have spoiled Sport.—*How trouble-some is such Interruption!* You shall hear now soon, for I shall not come away yet, so I rest,

Your affectionate Daughter,

SHAMELA.

Letter III.

HENRIETTA MARIA HONORA ANDREWS *to* SHAMELA ANDREWS.

Dear Sham,

Your last Letter hath put me into a great hurry of Spirits, for you have a very difficult Part to act. I hope you will remember your Slip with Parson *Williams*, and not be guilty of any more such Folly. Truly, a Girl who hath once known what is what, is in the highest Degree inexcusable if she respects her *Digressions*, but a Hint of this is sufficient. When Mrs. *Jervis* thinks of coming to Town, I believe I can procure her a good House, and fit for the Business; so I am,

Your affectionate Mother,

HENRIETTA MARIA HONORA ANDREWS.

Letter IV.

SHAMELA ANDREWS *to* HENRIETTA MARIA HONORA ANDREWS.

Marry come up, good Madam, the Mother had never looked into the Oven for her Daughter, if she had not been there herself. I shall never have done if you upbraid me with having had a small One by *Arthur Williams*, when you yourself—but I say no more. *O! What fine Times when the Kettle calls the Pot!* Let me do what I will, I say my Prayers as often as another, and I read in good Books, as often as I have Leisure; and Parson *Williams* says, that will make amends.—So no more, but I rest

Your afflicted Daughter,

S——.

Letter V.

HENRIETTA MARIA HONORA ANDREWS *to* SHAMELA ANDREWS .

Dear Child,

Why will you give such way to your Passion? How could you imagine I should be such a Simpleton, as to upbraid thee with being thy Mother's own Daughter! When I advised you not to be guilty of Folly, I meant no more than that you should take care to be well paid before-hand, and not trust to Promises, which a Man seldom keeps, after he hath had his wicked Will. And seeing you have a rich Fool to deal with, your not making a good Market will be the more inexcusable; indeed, with such Gentlemen as Parson *Williams*, there is more to be said; for they have nothing to give, and are commonly otherwise the best Sort of Men. I am glad to hear you read good Books, pray continue so to do. I have inclosed you one of Mr. *Whitefield's* Sermons, and also the Dealings[1] with him, and am

Your affectionate Mother,

HENRIETTA MARIA, &C.

Letter VI.

SHAMELA ANDREWS *to* HENRIETTA MARIÀ HONORA ANDREWS.

O Madam, I have strange Things to tell you! As I was reading in that charming Book about the Dealings, in comes my Master—to be sure he is a precious One. *Pamela*, says he, what Book is that, I warrant you *Rochester's* Poems.[2]—No, forsooth, says I, as pertly as I could; why how now Saucy Chops, Bold-

---

1 In *A Short Account of God's Dealings with the Reverend Mr. George Whitefield* (1740), the Methodist preacher describes his early years and spiritual awakening. On Whitefield, see above, p.123, n. 1.

2 John Wilmot, second Earl of Rochester (1647-80), was a writer of indecent love poetry.

face, says he—Mighty pretty Words, says I, pert again.—Yes (says he) you are a d—d, impudent, stinking, cursed, confounded Jade, and I have a great Mind to kick your A—. You, kiss—says I. A-gad, says he, and so I will; with that he caught me in his Arms, and kissed me till he made my Face all over Fire. Now this served purely you know, to put upon the Fool for Anger. O! What precious Fools Men are! And so I flung from him in a mighty Rage, and pretended as how I would go out at the Door; but when I came to the End of the Room, I stood still, and my Master cryed out, Hussy, Slut, Saucebox, Boldface, come hither—Yes to be sure, says I; why don't you come, says he; what should I come for, says I; if you don't come to me, I'll come to you, says he; I shan't come to you I assure you, says I. Upon which he run up, caught me in his Arms, and flung me upon a Chair, and began to offer to touch my Under-Petticoat. Sir, says I, you had better not offer to be rude; well, says he, no more I won't then; and away he went out of the Room. I was so mad to be sure I could have cry'd.

Oh what a prodigious Vexation it is to a Woman to be made a Fool of.

Mrs. *Jervis* who had been without, harkening, now came to me. She burst into a violent Laugh the Moment she came in. Well, says she, as soon as she could speak. I have Reason to bless myself that I am an Old Woman. Ah Child! if you had known the Jolly Blades of my Age, you would not have been left in the lurch in this manner. Dear Mrs. *Jervis*, says I, don't laugh at one; and to be sure I was a little angry with her.—Come, says she, my dear Honeysuckle, I have one Game to play for you; he shall see you in Bed; he shall, my little Rosebud, he shall see those pretty, little, white, round, panting —— and offer'd to pull off my Handkerchief.—Fie, Mrs. *Jervis*, says I, you make me blush, and upon my Fackins, I believe she did: She went on thus. I know the Squire likes you, and notwithstanding the Aukwardness of his Proceeding, I am convinced hath some hot Blood in his Veins, which will not let him rest, 'till he hath communicated some of his Warmth to thee my little Angel; I heard him last Night at our Door, trying if it was open, now to-night I will take care it shall be so; I warrant that he makes the second Trial; which if he doth, he shall find us ready to receive him. I will at first counterfeit Sleep, and after a Swoon; so that he will have you naked in his Possession: and then if you are disappointed, a Plague of all young Squires, say I.—And so, Mrs. *Jervis*, says I, you would have me yield myself to him, would you; you would have me be a second Time a Fool for nothing. Thank you for that, Mrs. *Jervis*. For nothing! marry forbid, says she, you know he hath large Sums of Money, besides abundance of fine Things; and do you think, when you have inflamed him, by giving his Hand a Liberty with that charming Person; and that you know he may easily think he obtains against your Will, he will not give any thing to come at all—. This will not do, Mrs. *Jervis*, answered I. I have heard my Mamma say, (and so you know, Madam, I have) that in her Youth, Fellows have often taken away in the Morning, what they gave over Night. No, Mrs. *Jervis*, nothing under a regular taking into Keeping, a settled Settlement, for me, and all my Heirs, all my whole Lifetime, shall do the Business—or else crosslegged, is the Word, faith, with *Sham*; and then I snapt my Fingers.

Thursday Night, Twelve o'Clock.

Mrs. *Jervis* and I are just in Bed, and the Door unlocked; if my Master should come—Odsbobs! I hear him just coming in at the Door. You see I write in the present Tense, as Parson *Williams* says. Well, he is in Bed between us, we both shamming a Sleep, he steals his Hand into my Bosom, which I, as if in my Sleep, press close to me with mine, and then pretend to awake.—I no sooner see him, but I scream out to Mrs. *Jervis*, she feigns likewise but just to come to herself; we both begin, she to becall, and I to bescratch very liberally. After having made a pretty free Use of my Fingers, without any great Regard to the Parts I attack'd, I counterfeit a Swoon. Mrs. *Jervis* then cries out, O, Sir, what have you done, you have murthered poor *Pamela*: she is gone, she is gone.—

O what a Difficulty it is to keep one's Countenance, when a violent Laugh desires to burst forth.

The poor Booby frightned out of his Wits, jumped out of Bed, and, in his Shirt, sat down by my Bed-Side, pale and trembling, for the Moon shone, and I kept my Eyes wide open, and pretended to fix them in my Head. Mrs. *Jervis* apply'd Lavender Water, and Hartshorn,[1] and this, for a full half Hour; when thinking I had carried it on long enough, and being likewise unable to continue the Sport any longer, I began by Degrees to come to my self.

The Squire who had sat all this while speechless, and was almost really in that Condition, which I feigned, the Moment he saw me give Symptons of recovering my Senses, fell down on his Knees; and O *Pamela*, cryed he, can you forgive me, my injured Maid? by Heaven, I know not whether you are a Man or a Woman, unless by your swelling Breasts. Will you promise to forgive me: I forgive you! D—n you (says I) and d—n you, says he, if you come to that. I wish I had never seen your bold Face, saucy Sow, and so went out of the Room.

O what a silly Fellow is a bashful young Lover!

He was no sooner out of hearing, as we thought, than we both burst into a violent Laugh. Well, says, Mrs. *Jervis*, I never saw any thing better acted than your Part: But I wish you may not have discouraged him from any future Attempt; especially since his Passions are so cool, that you could prevent his Hands going further than your Bosom. Hang him, answer'd I, he is not quite so cold as that I assure you; our Hands, on neither side, were idle in the Scuffle, nor have left us any Doubt of each other as to that matter.

Friday Morning.

My Master sent for Mrs. *Jervis*, as soon as he was up, and bid her give an Account of the Plate and Linnen in her Care; and told her, he was resolved that both she and the little Gipsy (I'll assure him) should set out together. Mrs. *Jervis* made him a saucy Answer; which any Servant of Spirit, you know, would,

1 Fainting remedies.

tho' it should be one's Ruin; and came immediately in Tears to me, crying, she had lost her Place on my Account, and that she should be forced to take to a House, as I mentioned before; and that she hoped I would, at least, make her all the amends in my power, for her Loss on my Account, and come to her House whenever I was sent for. Never fear, says I, I'll warrant we are not so near being turned away, as you imagine; and i'cod, now it comes into my Head, I have a Fetch for him, and you shall assist me in it. But it being now late, and my Letter pretty long, no more at present from

Your Dutiful Daughter,

SHAMELA.

Letter X.

SHAMELA ANDREWS *to* HENRIETTA MARIA HONORA ANDREWS.

O Mamma! Rare News! As soon as I was up this Morning, a Letter was brought me from the Squire, of which I send you a Copy.

Squire BOOBY *to* PAMELA.

Dear Creature,

I hope you are not angry with me for the Deceit put upon you, in conveying you to *Lincolnshire*,[1] when you imagined yourself going to *London*. Indeed, my dear *Pamela*, I cannot live without you; and will very shortly come down and convince you, that my Designs are better than you imagine, and such as you may with Honour comply with. I am,

My Dear Creature,
Your doating Lover,

BOOBY.

Now, Mamma, what think you?—For my own Part, I am

1 Mr. Booby has abducted Shamela to his estate in Lincolnshire.

convinced he will marry me, and faith so he shall. O! Bless me! I shall be Mrs. *Booby*, and be Mistress of a great Estate, and have a dozen Coaches and six, and a fine House at *London*, and another at *Bath*, and Servants, and Jewels, and Plate, and go to Plays, and Opera's, and Court; and do what I will, and spend what I will. But, poor Parson *Williams*! Well; and can't I see Parson *Williams*, as well after Marriage as before: For I shall never care a Farthing for my Husband. No, I hate and despise him of all Things....

SHAMELA BOOBY *to* HENRIETTA MARIA HONORA ANDREWS.

Madam,

In my last I left off at our sitting down to Supper on our Wedding Night,* where I behaved with as much Bashfulness as the purest Virgin in the World could have done. The most difficult Task for me was to blush; however, by holding my Breath, and squeezing my Cheeks with my Handkerchief, I did pretty well. My Husband was extreamly eager and impatient to have Supper removed, after which he gave me leave to retire into my Closet for a Quarter of an Hour, which was agreeable to me; for I employed that time in writing to Mr. *Williams*, who, as I informed you in my last, is released, and presented to the Living, upon the Death of the last Parson. Well, at last I went to Bed, and my Husband soon leap'd in after me; where I shall only assure you, I acted my Part in such a manner, that no Bridegroom was ever better satisfied with his Bride's Virginity. And to confess the Truth, I might have been well enough satisfied too, if I had never been acquainted with Parson *Willams*....

P. S. The strangest Fancy hath enter'd into my Booby's Head, that can be imagined. He is resolved to have a Book made about him and me; he proposed it to Mr. *Williams*, and offered him a Reward for his Pains; but he says he never writ any thing of that kind, but will recommend my Husband, when

---

* This was the Letter which is lost.

he comes to Town, to a Parson[1] *who does that Sort of Business for Folks*, one who can make my Husband, and me, and Parson *Williams*, to be all great People; for he *can make black white*, it seems. Well, but they say my Name is to be altered, Mr. *Williams*, says the first Syllabub hath too comical a Sound, so it is to be changed into *Pamela*; I own I can't imagine what can be said; for to be sure I shan't confess any of my Secrets to them, and so I whispered Parson *Williams* about that, who answered me, I need not give my self any Trouble; for the Gentleman *who writes Lives*, never asked more than a few Names of his Customers, and that he made all the rest out of his own Head; you mistake, Child, said he, if you apprehend any Truths are to be delivered. So far on the contrary, if you had not been acquainted with the Name, you would not have known it to be your own History. I have seen a *Piece of his Performance*, where the Person, whose Life was written, could he have risen from the Dead again, would not have even suspected he had been aimed at, unless by the Title of the Book, which was superscribed with his Name. Well, all these Matters are strange to me, yet I can't help laughing to think I shall see my self in a printed Book....

Parson TICKLETEXT *to Parson* OLIVER.

Dear SIR,

I have read over the History of *Shamela*, as it appears in those authentick Copies you favour'd me with, and am very much ashamed of the Character,[2] which I was hastily prevailed on to give that Book. I am equally angry with the pert Jade herself, and with the Author of her Life: For I scarce know yet to whom I chiefly owe an Imposition, which hath been so general, that if Numbers could defend me from Shame, I should have no Reason to apprehend it.

As I have your implied Leave to publish, what you so kindly

---

1 The target may again be Conyers Middleton (see Introduction, pp. 10–11). Another possibility is the Reverend Thomas Birch, who wrote lives for Bayle's *Dictionary* (1734–41).

2 Recommendation.

sent me, I shall not wait for the Originals, as you assure me the Copies are exact, and as I am really impatient to do what I think a serviceable Act of Justice to the World.

Finding by the End of her last Letter, that the little Hussy was in Town, I made it pretty much my Business to enquire after her, but with no effect hitherto: As soon as I succeed in this Enquiry, you shall hear what Discoveries I can learn. You will pardon the Shortness of this Letter, as you shall be troubled with a much longer very soon: And believe me,

Dear Sir,
Your most faithful Servant,
THO. TICKLETEXT.

P. S. Since I writ, I have a certain Account, that Mr. *Booby* hath caught his Wife in bed with *Williams*; hath turned her off, and is prosecuting him in the spiritual Court.[1]

FINIS.

[Source: Henry Fielding, *Joseph Andrews with Shamela and Related Writings*, ed. Homer Goldberg (New York: Norton, 1987).]

1 Moral offences of the clergy were under the jurisdiction of the ecclesiastical courts.

Appendix C: Other Works of Influence by Other Writers

HOMER

From Pope's translation of the *Iliad*

[Pope's *Iliad* was published in six volumes between 1715 and 1720, with further editions appearing by the time of Fielding's writing of *Joseph Andrews*. The following excerpts are from Book XI: Agamemnon, having armed himself, leads the Grecians to battle; Hector prepares the Trojans to receive them; and Jupiter, Juno and Minerva give the signals of war.]

BOOK XI

THE Saffron Morn, with early Blushes spread,
Now rose refulgent from *Tithonus'* Bed;
With new-born Day to gladden mortal Sight,
And Gild the Courts of Heav'n with sacred Light.
When baleful *Eris*, sent by *Jove's* Command,
The Torch of Discord blazing in her Hand,
Thro' the red Skies her bloody Sign extends,
And, wrapt in Tempests, o'er the Fleet descends.
High on *Ulysses'* Bark her horrid Stand
She took, and thunder'd thro' the Seas and Land.
Ev'n *Ajax* and *Achilles* heard the Sound,
Whose Ships remote the guarded Navy bound.
Thence the black Fury thro' the *Grecian* Throng
With Horror sounds the loud *Orthian* Song:
The Navy shakes, and at the dire Alarms
Each Bosom boils, each Warrior starts to Arms.
No more they sigh, inglorious to return,
But breathe Revenge, and for the Combat burn.
The King of Men[1] his hardy Host inspires

1 Agamemnon, the king of Mycenae, leader of the Greeks against Troy.

With loud Command, with great Example fires;
Himself first rose, himself before the rest
His mighty Limbs in radiant Armour drest.
And first he cas'd his manly Legs around
In shining Greaves, with silver Buckles bound:
The beaming Cuirass next adorn'd his Breast,
The same which once king *Cinyras* possest:
(The Fame of *Greece* and her assembled Host
Had reach'd that Monarch on the *Cyprian* Coast;
'Twas then, the Friendship of the Chief to gain,
This glorious Gift he sent, nor sent in vain.)
Ten Rows of azure Steel the Work infold,
Twice ten of Tin, and twelve of ductile Gold;
Three glitt'ring Dragons to the Gorget rise,
Whose imitated Scales against the Skies
Reflected various Light, and arching bow'd,
Like colour'd Rainbows o'er show'ry Cloud:
(*Jove's* wond'rous Bow, of three celestial Dyes,
Plac'd as a Sign to Man amid the Skies.)
A radiant Baldrick, o'er his Shoulder ty'd,
Sustain'd the Sword that glitter'd at his side:
Gold was the Hilt, a silver Sheath encas'd
The shining Blade, and golden Hangers grac'd.
His Buckler's mighty Orb was next display'd,
That round the Warrior cast a dreadful Shade;
Ten Zones of Brass its ample Brims surround,
And twice ten Bosses the bright Convex crown'd;
Tremendous Gorgon frown'd upon its Field,
And circling Terrors fill'd th' expressive Shield:
Within its Concave hung a silver Thong,
On which a mimic Serpent creeps along,
His azure Length in easy Waves extends,
Till in three Heads th' embroider'd Monster ends.
Last o'er his Brows his fourfold Helm he plac'd,
With nodding Horse-hair formidably grac'd;
And in his Hands two steely Javelins wields,
That blaze to Heav'n, and lighten all the Fields.
. . . .

Near *Ilus'* Tomb, in Order rang'd around,
The *Trojan* Lines possess'd the rising Ground.
There wise *Polydamas* and *Hector* stood;
Æneas, honour'd as a guardian God;
Bold *Polybus*, *Agenor* the divine;
The Brother-Warriors of *Antenor's* Line;
With youthful *Acamas*, whose beauteous Face
And fair Proportion match'd th' etherial Race.
Great *Hector*, cover'd with his spacious Shield,
Plies all the Troops, and orders all the Field.
As the red Star now shows his sanguine Fires
Thro' the dark Clouds, and now in Night retires;
Thus thro' the Ranks appear'd the Godlike Man,
Plung'd in the Rear, or blazing in the Van;
While streamy Sparkles, restless as he flies,
Flash from his Arms as Light'ning from the Skies.
As sweating Reapers in some wealthy Field,
Rang'd in two Bands, their crooked Weapons wield,
Bear down the Furrows, till their Labours meet;
Thick fall the heapy Harvests at their Feet.
So *Greece* and *Troy* the Field of War divide,
And falling Ranks are strow'd on ev'ry side.

. . . .

Thus while the Morning-Beams increasing bright
O'er Heav'ns pure Azure spread the growing Light,
Commutual Death the Fate of War confounds,
Each adverse Battel goar'd with equal Wounds.
But now (what time in some sequester'd Vale
The weary Wood-man spreads his sparing Meal,
When his tir'd Arms refuse the Axe to rear,
And claim a Respite from the Sylvan War;
But not till half the prostrate Forests lay
Stretch'd in long Ruin, and expos'd to Day)
Then, nor till then, the *Greeks* impulsive Might
Pierc'd the black *Phalanx*, and let in the Light.
Great *Agamemnon* then the Slaughter led,
And slew *Bienor* at his People's Head:
Whose Squire *Oïleus*, with a sudden spring,

Leap'd from the Chariot to revenge his King,
But in his Front he felt a fatal Wound,
Which pierc'd his Brain, & stretch'd him on the Ground:
Atrides spoil'd, and left them on the Plain;
Vain was their Youth, their glitt'ring Armour vain:
Now soil'd with Dust, and naked to to the Sky,
Their snowy Limbs and beauteous Bodies lie.

Two Sons of Priam[1] next to Battel move,
The Product one of Marriage, one of Love;
In the same Car the Brother-Warriors ride,
This took the charge to combat, that to guide:
Far other Task! than when they wont to keep
On *Ida's* Tops, their Father's fleecy Sheep.
These on the Mountains once *Achilles* found,
And captive led, with pliant Osiers bound;
Then to their Sire for ample Sums restor'd;
But now to perish by *Atrides'* Sword:
Pierc'd in the Breast the base-born *Isus* bleeds;
Cleft thro' the Head, his Brother's Fate succeeds.
Swift to the Spoil the hasty Victor falls,
And stript, their Features to his Mind recalls.
The *Trojans* see the Youths untimely die,
But helpless tremble for themselves, and fly.
So when a Lion, ranging o'er the Lawns,
Finds, on some grassy Lare, the couching Fawns,
Their Bones he cracks, their reeking Vitals draws,
And grinds the quiv'ring Flesh with bloody Jaws;
The frighted Hind beholds, and dares not stay,
But swift thro' rustling Thickets bursts her way;
All drown'd in Sweat the panting Mother flies,
And the big Tears roll trickling from her Eyes.

. . . .

Say Muse! when *Jove* the *Trojan's* Glory crown'd,
Beneath his Arm what Heroes bit the Ground?
Assæus, *Dolops*, and *Autonous* dy'd,
Opites next was added to their side,

---

1 The old king of Troy, husband of Hecuba, who witnessed the deaths of many of his fifty sons.

Then brave *Hipponous* fam'd in many a Fight,
Opheltius, *Orus*, sunk to endless Night,
Æsymnus, *Agelaus*; all Chiefs of Name;
The rest were vulgar Deaths, unknown to Fame.
As when a western Whirlwind, charg'd with Storms,
Dispells the gather'd Clouds that *Notus* forms;
The Gust continu'd, violent, and strong,
Rolls sable Clouds in Heaps on Heaps along;
Now to the Skies the foaming Billows rears,
Now breaks the Surge, and wide the bottom bares.
Thus raging *Hector*, with resistless Hands,
O'erturns, confounds, and scatters all their Bands.
Now the last Ruin the whole Host appalls;
Now *Greece* had trembled in her wooden Walls;
But wise *Ulysses* call'd *Tydides* forth,
His Soul rekindled, and awak'd his Worth.
And stand we deedless, O eternal Shame!
Till *Hector's* Arm involve the Ships in Flame?
Haste, let us join, and combat side by side.
The Warrior thus, and thus the Friend reply'd.
No martial Toil I shun, no Danger fear;
Let *Hector* come; I wait his Fury here.
But *Jove* with Conquest crowns the *Trojan* Train;
And, *Jove* our Foe, all human Force is vain.
He sigh'd; but sighing, rais'd his vengeful Steel,
And from his Car the proud *Thymbræus* fell:
Molion, the Charioteer, pursu'd his Lord,
His Death ennobled by *Ulysses'* Sword.
There slain, they left them in eternal Night;
Then plung'd amidst the thickest Ranks of Fight.
So two wild Boars outstrip the following Hounds,
Then swift revert, and Wounds return for Wounds.
Stern *Hector's* Conquests in the middle Plain
Stood check'd a while, and *Greece* respir'd again....

[Source: Alexander Pope, trans., *The Iliad of Homer*, ed. Maynard Mack, vols. 7 and 8 of The Twickenham Edition of the Poems of Alexander Pope (London: Methuen, 1967).]

MIGUEL DE CERVANTES SAAVEDRA

From *El Ingenioso Hidalgo Don Quixote de la Mancha*

[Part I of Cervantes' *Don Quixote* was published in 1605, Part II in 1615. From that time down to the writing of *Joseph Andrews*, a half dozen or so English translations appeared, which went through numerous editions. There is some evidence to suggest that the early eighteenth-century version used here (somewhat regularized) was known to Fielding.]

PART I, BOOK 3, CHAPTER 2

What happen'd to Don Quixote in the inn which he took for a castle.

The inn-keeper, seeing Don Quixote lying quite a-thwart the ass, ask'd Sancho what ail'd him? Sancho answer'd, "'Twas nothing, only his master had got a fall from the top of a rock to the bottom, and had bruis'd his sides a little."[1] The inn-keeper had a wife, very different from the common sort of hostesses, for she was of a charitable nature, very compassionate of her neighbour's affliction; which made her immediately take care of Don Quixote, and call her daughter, (a good handsom girl,) to set her helping hand to his cure. One of the servants in the inn was an Asturian wench, a broad-fac'd, flat-headed, saddle-nos'd dowdy; blind of one eye, and t'other almost out: However, the grace of her body supply'd all other defects. She was not above three foot high from her heels to her head; and her shoulders, which somewhat loaded her, as having too much flesh upon 'em, made her look downwards oftner than she could have wish'd. This charming original likewise assisted the mistress and the daughter; and with the latter, help'd to make the knight's bed, and a sorry one it was; the room where it stood was an old gambling cock-loft, which by manifold signs seem'd to have been, in the days of yore, a repository for chopt-straw.

---

1 Both Don Quixote and Sancho had been badly beaten by some carriers whose mares were molested by Rocinante.

Somewhat further, in a corner of that garret, a carrier had his lodging; and tho' his bed was nothing but the pannels and coverings of his mules, 'twas much better than that of Don Quixote; which only consisted of four rough-hewn boards laid upon two uneven tressels, a flock-bed,[1] that, for substance, might well have pass'd for a quilt, and was full of knobs and bunches; which had they not peep'd out thro' many a hole, and shewn themselves to be of wool, might well have been taken for stones: The rest of that extraordinary bed's furniture, was a pair of sheets, which rather seem'd to be of leather than of linen cloth, and a coverlet whose every individual thread you might have told, and never have miss'd one in the tale.

In this ungracious bed was the knight laid to rest his belabour'd carcase, and presently the hostess and her daughter anointed and plaister'd him all over, while Maritornes (for this was the name of the Asturian wench) held the candle....

Now you must know, that the carrier and she had agreed to pass the night together; and she had given him her word, that as soon as all the people in the inn were in bed, she wou'd be sure to come to him, and be at his service. And 'tis said of this good-natur'd thing, that whenever she had pass'd her word in such cases, she was sure to make it good, tho' she had made the promise in the midst of a wood and without any witness at all. For she stood much upon her gentility, tho' she undervalu'd her self so far as to serve in an inn, often saying that nothing but crosses and necessity cou'd have made her stoop to it.

Don Quixote's hard, scanty, beggerly, miserable bed was the first of the four in that wretch'd apartment; next to that was Sancho's kennel; which consisted of nothing but a bed-mat and a coverlet, that rather seem'd shorn canvas than a rug. Beyond these two beds was that of the carrier, made, as we have said, of the pannels and furniture of two of the best of twelve mules which he kept, every one of 'em goodly beasts and in special good case,[2] for he was one of the richest muleteers of Arevalo, as the Moorish author of this history relates, who makes particular mention of him, as having been acquainted with him, nay,

---

1 A bed with stuffing made from coarse tufts and refuse of wool, etc.

2 Condition.

some don't stick to say he was somewhat a-kin to him. However it be, it appears that Cid Mahomet Benengeli was a very exact historian, since he takes care to give us an account of things that seem so inconsiderable and trivial. A laudable example which these historians should follow, who usually relate matters so concisely, that they seem scarce to have dipp'd in 'em, and rather to have left the most essential part of the story drown'd in the bottom of the inkhorn, either through neglect, malice, or ignorance.... But, to return to our story, you must know that after the carrier had dress'd his mules and given 'em their night's provender, he laid him down on his hard bed, expecting the most punctual Maritornes's kind visit. By this time, Sancho, duly greas'd and anointed, was crept into his sty, where he did all he could to sleep but his aching ribs did all they could to prevent him. As for the knight, whose sides were in as bad circumstances as his squire's, he lay with both his eyes open like a hare. And now was every soul in the inn gone to bed, not any light to be seen, except that of a lamp which hung in the middle of the gate-way. This general tranquillity setting Don Quixote's thoughts at work, offer'd to his imagination one of the most absurd follies that ever crept into a distemper'd brain, from the perusal of romantick whimsies. Now he fansy'd himself to be in a famous castle, (for, as we have already said, all the inns he lodg'd in, seem'd no less than castles to him) and that the inn-keeper's daughter (consequently daughter to the lord of the castle) strangely captivated with his graceful presence and galantry, had promis'd him the pleasure of her embraces, as soon as her father and mother were gone to rest. This chimera disturb'd him, as if it had been a real truth. So that he began to be mightily perplex'd, reflecting on the danger to which his honour was expos'd. But at last his virtue overcame the powerful temptation, and he firmly resolv'd not to be guilty of the least infidelity to his lady Dulcinea del Toboso; tho' queen Genever her self, with her trusty Matron Quintaniona[1] should join to decoy him into the alluring snare.

While these wild imaginations work'd in his brain, the gen-

1 Queen Guinevere's *duenna* or chaperone in Spanish accounts of Arthurian romance.

tle Maritornes was mindful of her assignation, and with soft and wary steps, barefoot and in her smock, with her hair gather'd up in a fustian coif,[1] stole into the room, and felt about for her beloved carrier's bed. But scarce had she got to the door, when Don Quixote, whose ears were on the scout, was sensible that something was coming in; and therefore having rais'd himself in his bed, sore and wrapt up in plaisters, as he was, he stretch'd out his arms to receive his fancy'd damsel, and caught hold of Maritornes by the wrist, as she was, with her arms stretch'd, groping her way to her paramour; he pull'd her to him, and made her sit down by his bed's-side, she not daring to speak a word all the while: Now, as he imagin'd her to be the lord of the castle's daughter, her smock which was of the coarsest canvas, seem'd to him of the finest Holland,[2] and the glass-beads about her wrist, precious oriental pearls; her hair that was almost as rough as a horse's mane, he took to be soft flowing threads of bright curling gold; and her breath that had a stronger hogoe[3] than stale venison, was to him a grateful compound of the most fragrant perfumes of Arabia. In short, flattering imagination transform'd her into the likeness of those romantick beauties, one of whom, as he remember'd to have read,[4] came to pay a private visit to a wounded knight, with whom she was desperately in love; and the poor gentleman's obstinate folly had so infatuated his outward sense, that his feeling and his smell could not in the least undeceive him; and he thought he had no less than a balmy Venus in his arms, while he hugg'd a fulsom bundle of deformities that would have turn'd any man's stomach but a sharp-set carrier's. Therefore clasping her still closer, with a soft and amorous whisper, "Oh! thou most lovely temptation," cry'd he, "Oh! that I now might but pay a warm acknowledgement for the mighty blessing which your extravagant goodness would lavish on me; yes, most beautiful charmer, I would give an empire to purchase your more desirable embraces: But Fortune, madam, Fortune,

---

1 A close-fitting coarse cloth cap.

2 Linen.

3 Foul smell.

4 In chivalric romances of the late Middle Ages and afterwards.

that tyrant of my life, that unrelenting enemy to the truly deserving, has maliciously hurry'd and rivetted me to this bed, where I lie so bruis'd and macerated, that tho' I were eager to gratify your desires, I should at this dear unhappy minute be doom'd to impotence: Nay to that unlucky bar, Fate has added a yet more invincible obstacle; I mean my plighted faith to the unrival'd Dulcinea del Toboso, the sole mistress of my wishes, and absolute sovereign of my heart. Oh! did not this oppose my present happiness, I could never be so dull and insensible a knight as to lose the benefit of this extraordinary favour which you have now condescended to offer me."

Poor Maritornes all this while sweated for fear and anxiety, to find her self thus lock'd in the knight's arms; and without either understanding or willing to understand his florid excuses, she did what she could to get from him, and sheer off, without speaking a word: On the other side, the carrier, whose lewd thoughts kept him awake, having heard his trusty lady when she first came in, and listen'd ever since to the knight's discourse, began to be afraid that she had made some other assignation; and so without any more ado, he crept softly to Don Quixote's bed, where he listen'd a while to hear what would be the end of all this talk, which he could not understand: But perceiving at last, by the struggling of his faithful Maritornes, that 'twas none of her fault, and that the knight strove to detain her against her will, he could by no means bear his familiarity; and therefore taking it in mighty dudgeon, he up with his fist, and hit the enamour'd knight such a swinging blow in the jaws, that his face was all over blood in a moment. And not satisfy'd with this, he got o'top of the knight and with his splay feet betrampled him as if he had been treading a hay-mow. With that the bed, whose foundations were none of the best, sunk under the additional load of the carrier, and fell with such a noise that it wak'd the inn-keeper, who presently suspected it to be one of Maritornes's nightly skirmishes; and therefore having call'd her aloud, and finding that she did not answer, he lighted a lamp and made to the place where he heard the bustle. The wench, who heard him coming, knowing him to be of a passionate nature, was fear'd out of her wits, and fled for shelter to Sancho's sty, where he lay snoreing to some tune: There she pigg'd in, and slunk under the coverlet, where she lay snug, and truss'd up as round as an egg. Presently her master came in, in a mighty heat. "Where's this damn'd whore?" cry'd he; "I dare say this is one of her pranks." By this, Sancho awak'd; and feeling that unusual lump, which almost overlaid him, he took it to be the night-mare,[1] and began to lay about him with his fists, and thump'd the wench so unmercifully, that at last flesh and blood were no longer to bear it; and forgetting the danger she was in, and her dear reputation, she paid him back his thumps as fast as her fists could lay 'em on, and soon rous'd the drousy squire out of his sluggishness, whether he would or no. Who finding himself thus pommell'd, by he did not know who, he bustled up in his nest, and catching hold of Maritornes, they began the most pleasant skirmish in the world. When the carrier perceiving by the light of the inn-keeper's lamp, the dismal condition that his dear mistress was in, presently took her part; and, leaving the knight whom he had more than sufficiently mawl'd flew at the squire, and paid him confoundedly. On the other hand, the inn-keeper, who took the wench to be the cause of all this hurly-burly, cuff'd and kick'd, and kick'd and cuff'd her over and over again: And so there was a strange multiplication of fisticuffs and drubbings. The carrier pommel'd Sancho, Sancho mawl'd the wench, the wench belabour'd the squire, and the inn-keeper thrash'd her again: And all of 'em laid on with such expedition, that you would have thought they had been afraid of losing time. But the best jest was that in the heat of the fray, the lamp went out, so that being now in the dark, they ply'd one another at a venture, they struck and tore, all went to rack, while nails and fists flew without mercy....

---

1 A female demon or spirit thought to plague sleeping people.

PART II, CHAPTER 16

What happen'd to Don Quixote with a sober gentleman of La Mancha.

... "Sir," reply'd Don Quixote, "children are the flesh and blood of their parents, and, whether good or bad, are to be cherish'd as part of our selves. 'Tis the duty of a father to train 'em up from their tenderest years in the paths of vertue, in good discipline and Christian principles, that when they advance in years they may become the staff and support of their parents' age, and the glory of their posterity. But as for forcing them to this or that study, 'tis a thing I don't so well approve. Persuasion is all, I think, that is proper in such a case; especially when they are so fortunate as to be above studying for bread, as having parents that can provide for their future subsistence, they ought in my opinion to be indulged in the pursuit of that science to which their own genius gives them the most inclination. For though the art of poetry is not so profitable as delightful, yet it is none of those that disgrace the ingenious professor.[1] Poetry, sir, in my judgment, is like a tender virgin in her bloom, beautiful and charming to amazement: All the other sciences are so many virgins, whose care it is to enrich, polish and adorn her, and as she is to make use of them all, so are they all to have from her a grateful acknowledgement. But this virgin must not be roughly handl'd, nor dragg'd along the street, nor expos'd to every market-place, and corner of great men's houses. A good poet is a kind of an alchymist, who can turn the matter he prepares into the purest gold and an inestimable treasure. But he must keep his muse within the rules of decency, and not let her prostitute her excellency in lewd satires and lampoons, nor in licentious sonnets. She must not be mercenary, though she need not give away the profits she may claim from heroick poems, deep tragedies, and pleasant and artful comedies. She is not to be attempted by buffoons, nor by

1 Practitioner.

the ignorant vulgar, whose capacity can never reach to a due sense of the treasures that are lock'd up in her. And know, sir, that when I mention the vulgar, I don't mean only the common rabble; for whoever is ignorant, be he lord or prince, is to be listed in the number of the vulgar. But whoever shall apply himself to the muses with those qualifications; which, as I said, are essential to the character of a good poet, his name shall be famous, and valu'd in all the polish'd nations of the world. And as to what you say, sir, that your son does not much esteem our modern poetry; in my opinion, he is somewhat to blame; and my reason is this: Homer never wrote in Latin, because he was a Grecian; nor did Virgil write in Greek, because Latin was the language of his country. In short, all your ancient poets wrote in their mother-tongue, and did not seek other languages to express their lofty thoughts. And thus, it wou'd be well that custom shou'd extend to every nation; there being no reason that a German poet shou'd be despised, because he writes in his own tongue; or a Castilian or Biscayner, because they write in theirs. But I suppose, your son does not mislike modern poetry, but such modern poets as have no tincture of any other language or science, that may adorn, awaken, and assist their natural impulse. Though even in this too there may be error. For, 'tis believ'd, and not without reason, that a poet is naturally a poet from his mother's womb, and that, with the talent which Heaven has infus'd into him, without the help of study or art, he may produce these compositions that verify that saying, *Est deus in nobis*, &c.[1] Not but that a natural poet, that improves himself by art, shall be much more accomplished, and have the advantage of him that has no title to poetry but by his knowledge in the art; because art cannot go beyond nature, but only adds to its perfection.... Shou'd your son write satires to lessen the reputation of any person, you wou'd do well to take him to task, and tear his defamatory rhimes; but if he studies to write such discourse in verse, to ridicule and explode vice in general, as Horace so elegantly did, then encourage him: For a poet's pen

---

1 "There is a god in us" (Ovid, *Fasti* 6.5).

is allow'd to inveigh against envy and envious men, and so against other vices, provided it aim not at particular persons. But there are poets so abandon'd to the itch of scurrility, that rather than lose a villainous jest, they'll venture being banish'd to the island of Pontus.[1] If a poet is modest in his manners, he will be so in his verses. The pen is the tongue of the mind; the thoughts that are formed in the one, and those that are traced by the other, will bear a near resemblance. And when kings and princes see the wonderful art of poetry shine in prudent, vertuous, and solid subjects, they honour, esteem, and enrich them, and even crown them with leaves of that tree,[2] which is ne'er offended by the thunderbolt, as a token that nothing shall offend those whose brows are honour'd and adorn'd with such crowns." The gentleman hearing Don Quixote express himself in this manner, was struck with so much admiration, that he began to lose the bad opinion he had conceiv'd of his understanding. As for Sancho, who did not much relish this fine talk, he took an opportunity to slink aside in the middle of it, and went to get a little milk of some shepherds that were hard by keeping their sheep....

[Source: Miguel de Cervantes Saavedra, *The Life and Atchievements of the Renown'd Don Quixote*, trans. Peter Motteux et al., rev. John Ozell, 4 vols. (1700; London, 1725).]

PAUL SCARRON

From *Le Roman comique*

[The first two parts of *Le Roman comique* were published in 1651 and 1657; the third, however, was left unfinished with Scarron's death in 1660. The fortunes of an itinerant acting troupe are recounted, along with their camp followers, which include a poet, a provincial officer and a dwarfish advocate by the name of Ragotin. As well, the principal players relate their

1 Ovid was exiled to Pontus, an ancient city bordering on the Black Sea, by the Roman Emperor Augustus.

2 The laurel tree.

romantic histories, the vicissitudes of Destiny and Star (supposedly brother and sister) being chief among them.]

PART I, CHAPTER 1

A company of strollers come to the town of Mans.

BRIGHT Phœbus had already performed above half his career;[1] and his chariot having passed the meridian, and got on the declivity of the sky, rolled on swifter than he desired. Had his horses been willing to have made use of the slopingness of the way, they might have finished the remainder of the day in less than half a quarter of an hour; but instead of pulling amain, they curveted[2] about, snuffing a briny air, which set them a-neighing, and made them sensible that they were near the sea, where their father is said to take his rest every night. To speak more like a man, and in plainer terms, it was betwixt five and six of the clock, when a cart came into the market-place of Mans....

CHAPTER 12

A combat in the night.

I AM too much a man of honour not to advertise the courteous reader, that if he be offended at all the silly trifles he has already found in this book, he will do well not to go on with the reading of it; for, upon my conscience, he must expect nothing else, although the volume should swell to the bigness of that of the Grand Cyrus:[3] and if from what he has read he doubts what will follow, perhaps I am in the same quandary as well as he. For one chapter draws on another, and I do with my book as some do with their horses, putting the bridle on their necks, and trusting to their good conduct. But perhaps I have a fixed design, and without filling my chapters with examples for imi-

---

1 Course.
2 Frisked.
3 See above, p.42, n. 1.

tation, shall instruct with delight after the same manner as a drunken man creates in us an aversion for drunkenness, and yet may sometimes divert us with his merry impertinence. Let us end this moral reflection, and return to our strollers, whom we left in the inn.… Destiny was about to begin his story, when they heard a great noise in the next chamber. Destiny stood listening a while; but the noise and squabble increasing, and somebody crying out, "Murder! help! murder!"—he with three leaps got out of the chamber at the expense of his doublet, which Cave and Angelica[1] had torn as they were going to stop him. He went into the chamber from whence the noise came, which was so dark that he could not see his own nose; and where the fisticuffs, boxes on the ears, and several confused voices of fighting men and women, together with the hollow noise of naked feet stamping on the floor, made a hideous and frightful uproar. He ran very rashly amongst the combatants, and in one moment received a cuff on one side, and a box on the ear on the other; which changed his good intention of parting those hobgoblins into a violent thirst for revenge. He began to set his hands agoing, and made a flourish with his two arms, by which many a maimed chops were belaboured, as it afterwards appeared by his bloody fists. The scuffle lasted so long that he received twenty cuffs more, which he however returned with double the number. In the heat of the fight he felt himself bit on the calf of the leg, when clapping his hands to the place, he met with something hairy, which he for that reason took to be a dog; but Cave and her daughter, who appeared at the chamber door at that interim with a candle, like the fire of St. Helmo after a storm, discovered to Destiny that he was amidst seven persons in their shirts, who having been in close conflict before, began to let one another go as soon as the light appeared.…

1 One of the actresses and her daughter.

CHAPTER 20

The shortest in this present book. Ragotin's fall off his horse, and something of the like nature which happened to Roquebrune.

WE left Ragotin planted on the pummel of a saddle, not knowing how to behave himself, and much perplexed how he should get off. I scarce believe the defunct Phæthon, of unhappy memory, was ever more troubled with his father's four fiery steeds,[1] than was at this time our little lawyer, with this one tit,[1] on which he nevetheless sat as quiet as a lamb. That it did not cost him his life, as it did Phæthon, he was beholden to Fortune, whose caprices would be a fit subject for me to expatiate on, were I not in conscience obliged to release Ragotin from the imminent danger he is in, having besides many more things to treat of concerning our strollers, during their residence in Mans. As soon as the disastrous Ragotin felt what an uneasy cushion he had under the two most fleshy parts of his body, on which he used to sit, as all other rational creatures are wont; I mean, as soon as he found how narrow his seat was, he quitted the bridle like a man of discretion, and laid hold of the horse's mane, who at the same time ran away full speed. Thereupon the carabine went off. Ragotin thought he had been shot, his horse undoubtedly believed the same, and therefore made such a foul stumble, that the little man lost his seat; insomuch, that for a time, he hung by the horse's mane, with one foot entangled by his spur in the saddle-cloth, and the other with the rest of his body, hanging dangling towards the earth in expectation of a fall, as soon as his spur should break loose; together with his sword, carabine, and bandoleer. At length his foot being disengaged, his hands let go the mane, and down he tumbled, though with more grace and skill than he had got up....

---

1 In Greek mythology, the sun god Helios granted his mortal son Phaethon his wish to drive the chariot of the sun for one day. Unable to control the horses, he was about to incinerate the earth when Zeus struck him down with a thunderbolt.

2 Little horse, nag.

PART II, CHAPTER 10

How Madame Bouvillon[1] could not resist a certain temptation; and besides, how she got a bunch[2] in her forehead.

... As soon as Destiny had done eating, the voider[3] was brought and the table cleared.

Then Madame Bouvillon clapping herself down at the feet of the bed, pulled him down by her, and her servant (letting the waiters of the inn go out first) leaving her likewise, drew the door after her, and shut it. This Madame Bouvillon perceiving, and thinking that Destiny had also observed it, said to him, "See, this foolish jade has shut the door after her."

To which he replied, "If you please, madam, I'll go open it."

"No," said she, stopping him, "let it alone; but you know," continued she, "when two persons are locked up together, as they have an opportunity to do what they please, people will judge of them as they think fit."

"It is not on such reputations as yours, madam," replied Destiny, "for people to pass rash judgments."

"However, sir," quoth Bouvillon, "one cannot have too much caution against slander."

"Well, madam," replied Destiny, "but people will not talk without grounds, and sure they can have none when they reflect upon the inequality of our conditions. Will you please therefore, madam," continued he, "that I go open the door?"

"By no means, sir," quoth she, going to bolt it, and adding withal, "for as long as people think it shut, it is better it were really so, that nobody may come in upon us without our consent."

Having said thus much, and performed the office of a friend for herself, she turned towards Destiny, giving him to understand by her large fiery cheeks, and little sparkling eyes, what sport she had a mind to be at; then she proceeded to take off

1 A lady of some wealth and position, who happened to be staying at the same inn as Destiny.

2 A lump.

3 A tray or basket for dirty dishes.

her handkerchief from her neck, and thereby discovered to her lover at least ten pounds of exuberant flesh; that is to say, near the third part of her bosom, the rest being distributed in two equal portions under her arm pits. This ill intention of hers causing her to blush, (which sometimes the most impudent will do) her neck was become as red as her face, and both together might be well taken at any distance for a scarlet riding cap. All this made Destiny to blush too, but it was with shame, when I'll give you leave to guess what might be the cause of Madame Bouvillon's blushing. Then she began to complain, that she had something troubled her in the back, and therefore moving herself about in her harness, as if she had itched, begged of Destiny to thrust his hands down her stays to scratch her. This the youth immediately obeyed her in, trembling all the while, but whilst he was employed in pleasing her behind, she diverted herself with him before, handling his sides through his waistcoat, and asking him often, If he was not ticklish? Whilst these lovers were thus pleasing each other, Ragotin came to the door, and knocking and bawling like to any madman, called out aloud to Destiny to open to him. This Destiny going to perform, drew his hand all sweaty from Bouvillon's back, but offering to go between her and the table, as the shortest cut, chanced to trip against a nail in the floor, which brought him down with his head against a bench after that violent manner, that he lay sometime for dead.

Madame Bouvillon in the meantime caught up her handkerchief, and having thrown it over her shoulders, made all the haste she could to open the door, which having done, and Ragotin pushing against it with all his force at the same time, gave the poor lady so cruel a blow on the face, that it almost flattened her nose, and also raised a bump on her forehead of the bigness of one's fist. This made her to cry out, she was dead; which, though the little rascal heard, he nevertheless made no excuse for, but leaping and bounding about the room like a madman, bawled out, "Mrs.[1] Angelica's found! Mrs. Angelica's found!" This he did the louder to provoke Destiny's

1 Mistress, regularly prefixed at this time to the name of an unmarried lady or girl.

anger, who was all this while calling for Madame Bouvillon's maid to come and help her mistress, which she nevertheless could not possibly hear, by reason of the noise which Ragotin made. At length the servant came, and brought water and a clean napkin, when between her and Destiny there was quickly some small reparation made for the damage done by the door. But however great was Destiny's impatience to know what more news Ragotin had brought, he notwithstanding would not leave Madame Bouvillon till her face was washed and anointed, and her forehead bound up with a bandage. At last he offered to be gone, but that calling Ragotin a thousand rogues for the mischief he had done on the one hand, while Ragotin drew him after him on the other to give him a farther account of his message....

[Source: Paul Scarron, *The Comical Romance, and Other Tales*, trans. Tom Brown et al., 2 vols. (1700; London, 1892).]

PIERRE CARLET DE CHAMBLAIN DE MARIVAUX

From *Le Paysan parvenu, ou les Memoirs de* M * * *

[*Le Paysan parvenu*, which was published in five parts between 1734 and 1736, relates the adventures of Jacob, a poor but handsome and enterprising young man from the country. Upon arriving in Paris, he becomes a servant in a prosperous household, soon attracting the interest of his mistress and other women of various social ranks. Written as the memoirs of the central figure, Marivaux abandoned the work at the end of the fifth part.]

PART I

... Catherine[1] was tall and gaunt, plainly dressed, and on her face wore an expression of forbidding piety, angry and blazing,

1 A cook in the home of two spinsters.

which apparently came from the heat her mind acquired from her kitchen fire and ovens, apart from the fact that the brain of a devout female, and a cook into the bargain, is naturally dry and burnt up.

I wouldn't say this about the mind of a genuinely pious woman, for there is a great deal of difference between the truly pious and those who are commonly called religious. The religious upset people and the pious uplift them. In the former it is only their lips that are religious, in the latter their hearts; the religious go to church just for the sake of going and enjoying the pleasure of being there, but the truly pious go to pray to God, and have humility, whereas the religious don't hold with it except in others. The ones are true servants of God, the others only look like it. They go through their devotions so as to be able to say, I am performing them, carry books of devotion to church so as to handle, open and look at them, retire into a corner and lurk there in order to enjoy a posture of meditation ostentatiously, work themselves up into holy transports in order to convince themselves how very distinguished their souls are if they do indeed feel any; in fact they really experience transports, born of their own conceited anxiety to experience something of the kind – for the devil, who spares nothing to deceive them, supplies plenty. Then they return from church inflated with self-satisfaction and lofty pity for ordinary souls. And then they imagine that they have acquired the right to give themselves a little rest after these holy exercises by indulging in a thousand little luxuries meant to protect their delicate health.

Such are what I call the religious, from whose religiosity the wily tempter gets all the benefit, as it is easy to see.

As for genuinely pious people, they are kind even to the wicked, who do much better out of them than out of their own kind, for the worst enemy of the wicked is somebody like them....

PART V

... The carriage stopped, we had reached the theatre,[1] and I only had time to answer such affectionate words with a smile.

"Follow me," he said, after giving a footman money to buy some tickets, and we went in. So there I was at the Comédie Française, at first in the foyer, if you please, where Count d'Orsan greeted some of his friends.

At this moment all those puffed-up feelings I mentioned, all those fumes of vanity that had gone to my head vanished into thin air.

The airs and graces of this world filled me with confusion and panic. Alas, my bearing showed that I was such a nobody, I realized I looked so clumsy and lost in the midst of this society that had something so easy and elegant about it. "What are you going to do about yourself?" I wondered.

So I shall say nothing about my demeanour because I hadn't one at all, unless you say that not having one at all is to have a kind of one. However, it simply was not in my power to give myself any other, and I don't think I could ever manage it or achieve any expression that did not look unsuitable or shamefaced. If it had been merely a case of being astonished I should not have minded my face simply showing that – it would only have been a proof that I had never been to the Comédie Française, and there would not have been much harm in that. But there was an inner embarrassment at finding myself there at all, a certain feeling of unworthiness that prevented my putting up a bold front, and this I would very much have preferred not to be seen on my face, and of course it showed all the more because I was endeavouring to conceal it.

My eyes were the trouble, for I didn't know who to look at. I dared not take the liberty of looking at the others for fear that they might read into my nervousness that I had no right to the honour of being with such grand people and was being smuggled in. I can't think of anything that expresses my

---

1 Count d'Orsan takes Jacob (now known as Monsieur de la Vallée) to the Comédie Française, famous for its repertoire of classical French drama, and frequented by fashionable Parisian society.

meaning more clearly than that term, which is not very high class.

It is also true that I had not passed through enough stages of education or advances in fortune to be able to comport myself in the midst of this society with the requisite self-assurance. I had jumped into it too fast; I had just been made a gentleman, and what was more I had not gone through the preliminary training of people of my kind, and trembled lest my appearance should show that the gentleman had been just Jacob. Some in my shoes might have been brazen enough to carry it off, I mean they might have cheeked their way through, but what is to be gained by that? Nothing. Doesn't that make it clear that a man is brazen only because he has reason to be ashamed?

"You don't look too well," said one of the gentlemen to Count d'Orsan. "I certainly don't," he answered, "but I might have been worse." Thereupon he told them about his adventure and consequently mine,[1] and in the most flattering way to me. "So you see," he concluded, "I owe to this gentleman the honour of seeing you again."

A fresh trial for La Vallée, to whom this speech drew their attention. They looked up and down my weird figure, and I think nothing could have been as silly as I was or so funny-looking. The more Count d'Orsan sang my praises the more he embarrassed me.

But I had to make some reply, in my modest silk jacket and my reach-me-down finery that I had given up being proud of since seeing many magnificent outfits all round me. But what could I say? "Oh, not at all, Sir, you can't be serious," or again: "It's only a very small thing, don't mention it; it was the only thing to do; I am your servant."

Such were my replies, accompanied by frequent jerky bobbings, which apparently appealed to these gentlemen, for not one of them failed to compliment me in order to get one for himself.

One of them whom I saw turn round to laugh put me wise to the joke and finished me off. No more bowings and scrap-

1 Earlier in the day, the Count had been rescued by La Vallée after being viciously attacked by three men.

ings, my face behaved as best it could and so did my answers. Count d'Orsan, who was a well-bred man with an honest and straightforward type of mind, went on talking without noticing what was happening to me. "Let's go to our seats," he said, and I followed him. He led me on to the stage,[1] where the number of people made me immune from such indignities, and where I sat with him like a man finding sanctuary....

[Source: Pierre Carlet de Chamblain de Marivaux, *Up from the Country, Infidelities, and The Game of Love and Chance*, trans. Leonard Tancock and David Cohen (Harmondsworth, UK: Penguin, 1980).]

1 It was the custom at that time to have rows of seats on the stage itself, which were largely patronized by the young men of fashion.

Appendix D: Other Related Writings by Fielding

From *The Champion*

[*The Champion; or, British Mercury*, edited and partly owned by Fielding, was a thrice weekly periodical which ran from 15 November 1739 to June 1741. Professedly the work of Captain Hercules Vinegar, champion and censor of Great Britain, it was at least in part an organ of the Patriots.]

THURSDAY, *March* 13, 1739-40.

... THERE is a certain diversion called roasting, which, notwithstanding it is in some vogue with the polite part of the world, I have no notion of. This term is well known to be taken from cookery, from whence those who are great adepts in the art, borrow also several others; such as putting the person to be roasted on the spit, turning him round till he is done enough, &c.

But though this, as I have said before, is thought a very delicate entertainment by some people of good taste, yet, as it is attended with great pain and torment to the poor wretch who is thus roasted alive, I have always thought it too barbarous a sacrifice to luxury. Nor have I ever more willingly given in to it, than in to those cruelties which are executed on particular animals in order to heighten their flavour; I am an utter enemy to all roasting alive, from this which is performed on one of our own species to that which is practised on a lobster.

It hath been thought, that this custom of man-roasting was originally introduced among us from some nation of cannibals: it is indeed more than probable that our savage ancestors used to eat the flesh of their enemies roasted in this manner; though this latter custom hath been so long left off, that we find no traces thereof in our annals.

A learned antiquarian of my acquaintance does not carry the original of this custom so high: he derives it only from the roasting of heretics, in use among the Roman Church, and fancies it an unextirpated remain of that barbarous execution. He brings, as a strengthener of this his opinion, the choice which we make of an odd creature, or in his own words, a heretic to the common forms of behaviour to perform it on. He is a great enemy to this practice, being as he thinks, more consistent with the principles of Jesuitism than true Christianity.

But, for my part, I imagine this term of roasting to have been given to this diversion, from the torments which the person spitted is supposed to endure in his mind, even equal to those bodily pains which he would undergo, was he to be roasted alive.

Now the pleasure which we take in such amusements as this, must arise either from a great depravity of nature, which delights in the miseries and misfortunes of mankind, or from a pride which we take in comparing the blemishes of others with our own perfections.

As for the first, my Lord Shaftesbury says, "There is an affection nearly related to inhumanity, which is a gay and frolicsome delight in what is injurious to others, a sort of wanton mischievousness and pleasure in what is destructive, a passion, which, instead of being restrained, is encouraged in children, so that it is indeed no wonder if the effects of it are very unfortunately felt in the world: for it will be hard, perhaps, for any one to give a reason, why that temper, which was used to delight in disorder, and ravage when in a nursery, should not afterwards find delight in other disturbances, and be the occasion of equal mischiefs in families among friends, and in the public."[1] I advise all parents to whip this spirit out of their children, the doing which may be truly called a wholesome severity....

SATURDAY, *March* 22, 1739-40.

... STANDING the other day, in Fleet Street, with my son the Templar,[2] and being prevented from crossing the way by what

---

1 Anthony Ashley Cooper, third Earl of Shaftesbury, *An Inquiry Concerning Virtue, or Merit* (1699) 2.2.3.

2 A barrister or other person occupying chambers in the Inner or Middle Temple, London. See above, p. 259, n. 1. Tom, Vinegar's son, was a student for five years at Lincoln's Inn.

they call a stop of coaches, I observed, with great indignation, an ill-looking fellow most cruelly lashing a pair of starved horses, who laboured to the utmost of their power to drag on a heavy burthen. And, as they were prevented from making greater haste, even had they been able, by the coaches which were before them, this gentleman must have exercised his arm thus for nothing more than his own innocent diversion, at the expense of the skins of these poor unhappy beasts.

As I look on myself to have been sent into the world as a general blessing, that I am endowed with so much strength and resolution to redress all grievances whatsoever, and to defend and protect the brute creation, as well as my own species from all manner of insult and barbarity, which, however exercised, is, after the several severe edicts I have published, no less than a most impudent opposition to my authority, I had certainly pulled the fellow from his box, and laid my little finger on him, had not my son interposed, and begged me not to raise a disturbance, by punishing him there: for that he had marked his number, and that I might find him at my leisure. Whether the fellow saw my brows knit at him, a sight very few people are able to endure, I can't tell, but he began to withhold his whipping, and suffered me to be persuaded by my son, especially as there were some ladies in his coach, whom I would by no means have ventured to frighten by such an execution.

My son Tom told me, as we pursued our walk, that he had a facetious acquaintance in the Temple, who professed the Pythagorean principles, and affirms that he believes the transmigration of souls. This gentleman, as Tom informed me, comforts himself on all such occasions with a persuasion that the beasts he sees thus abused have formerly been themselves hackney coachmen; and that the soul of the then driver will in his turn pass into the horse, and suffer the same punishment which he so barbarously inflicts on others.

But to pass by such whimsical opinions, I have often thought that the wisdom of the legislature would not have been unworthily employed in contriving some law to prevent those barbarities which we so often see practised on these domestic creatures. A boy should, in my opinion, be more severely punished for exercising cruelty on a dog or a cat, or any other animal, than for stealing a few pence or shillings, or any of those lesser crimes which our courts of justice take notice of....

THURSDAY, *March* 27, 1740.

... Good-nature is a delight in the happiness of mankind, and a concern at their misery, with a desire, as much as possible, to procure the former, and avert the latter; and this, with a constant regard to desert.

Good-nature is not that weakness which, without distinction, affects both the virtuous and the base, and equally laments the punishment of villainy, with the disappointment of merit; for as this amiable quality respects the whole, so it must give up the particular, to the good of the general.

It is not that cowardice which prevents us from repelling or resenting an injury; for it doth not divest us of humanity, and like charity, though it doth not end, may at least begin at home.

From these propositions, the truth of which will not, I believe, be denied, unless, for the sake of argument, I draw the following conclusions:

That those who include folly and cowardice, as the certain ingredients of good-nature, compound their idea of good-nature of very different simples from those who exclude them.

That as good-nature requires a distinguishing faculty, which is another word for judgment, and is perhaps the sole boundary between wisdom and folly; it is impossible for a fool, who hath no distinguishing faculty, to be good-natured.

That as good-nature, which is the chief if not only quality in the mind of man in the least tending that way, doth not forbid the avenging an injury, Christianity hath taught us something beyond what the religion of nature and philosophy could arrive at; and consequently, that it is not as old as the creation, nor is revelation useless with regard to morality, if it had taught us no more than this excellent doctrine, which, if generally followed, would make mankind much happier, as well as better than they are.

That to be averse to, and repine at the punishment of vice and villainy, is not the mark of good-nature but folly; on the contrary, to bring a real and great criminal to justice, is, perhaps, the best natured office we can perform to society, and the prosecutor, the juryman, the judge, and the hangman himself may do their duty without injuring this character; nay, the last office, if properly employed, may be in truth the best natured, as well as the highest post of honour in the kingdom....

Lastly, that as good-nature is a delight in the happiness of mankind, every good-natured man will do his utmost to contribute to the happiness of each individual; and consequently that every man who is not a villain, if he loves not the good-natured man, is guilty of ingratitude.

This is that amiable quality, which, like the sun, gilds over all our other virtues; this it is, which enables us to pass through all the offices and stations of life with real merit. This only makes the dutiful son, the affectionate brother, the tender husband, the indulgent father, the kind master, the faithful friend, and the firm patriot. This makes us gentle without fear, humble without hopes, and charitable without ostentation, and extends the power, knowledge, strength, and riches of individuals to the good of the whole....

SATURDAY, *March* 29, 1740.

... I have heard of a pamphlet, called Reasons of the Contempt of the Clergy.[1] If by the clergy, the author means the order, I hope there is no such contempt; nay, I will venture to say, there is not among sensible and sober men, the only persons whose ill opinion is to be valued, or by any argument to be removed. This contempt, therefore, must be meant of particular clergymen, and even this I should be unwilling to allow justifiable, or to assign any reason for it. Human frailty is indeed such, that it is very difficult, if not impossible, to preserve any body (especially so large a one) from some rotten members, but the utmost care is here taken on that regard. Numberless public schools are instituted for the instruction of our youth, the masters of which are preferred with proper respect to their morals

1 Either John Eachard's *The Grounds and Occasions of the Contempt of the Clergy and Religion enquired into* (1670) or John Hildrop's *The Contempt of the Clergy Considered, in a Letter to a Friend* (1739).

as well as learning. Hence the scholars are removed to one or other of two excellent universities, alike remarked for their erudition, sobriety, and good order. After which the strictest and most impartial examination must be undergone before the candidate will be admitted into holy orders, in which the young divine can afterwards expect no promotion, but from his merit, no ecclesiastical preferments being by any means whatever to be purchased; and as for the mitre, it is always inscribed (or at least of late hath been so) with these words, *Detur Magis Pio.*[1]

If, notwithstanding all this care, a few unworthy members creep in, it is certainly doing a serviceable office to the body to detect and expose them; nay, it is what the sound and uncorrupt part should not only be pleased with, but themselves endeavour to execute, especially if they are suspicious of, or offended at contempt or ridicule, which can never fall with any weight on the order itself, or on any clergyman, who is not really a scandal to it.

Though I am, as I have before said, very far from acknowledging that sensible or sober minds are tainted with any such general contempt, as hath been intimated, yet as perhaps some idle and unthinking young men may express too little respect (to use a common phrase) for the cloth, I shall here attempt to set a clergyman in a just and true light, which will, I believe, be sufficient to guard him from any danger of a treatment which such a person can never suffer, but through the ignorance of those who are guilty of it. Such ignorance I shall therefore attempt to remove, since I do not recollect any modern writings tending this way, and it may require some reflection and parts to collect a true idea of so amiable a character from nice observations on the general behaviour of the clergy....

The first I shall name is humility; a virtue of which He himself was so perfect a pattern, and which He so earnestly recommended to His disciples, that He rebuked them when they contended who should be reckoned the greatest;[2] and in another place, exhorted them "to beware of the scribes which desire to walk in long robes, and love greetings in the markets,

---

1 "Let it be given to the more pious."

2 Matthew 18:1-5; Mark 9:34-37; Luke 9:46-48; 22:24-27.

and the highest seats in the synagogues, and the chief rooms at feasts, which devour widows' houses, and for show make long prayers," &c. Luke xx. 46, 47. And St. Paul is frequent in the same advice, forbidding any to think high of himself, for which he gives them this reason, that very few wise, or mighty, or noble, in a wordly sense, were called to the ministry, but such as were reputed to be the filth of the world and the offscouring of all things.[1] Our blessed Saviour Himself, instead of introducing Himself into the world in the houses or families of what we call the great, chose to be born of the wife of a carpenter, His disciples were poor fishermen, and Paul himself no more than a tent-maker; He everywhere practised and taught contempt of wordly grandeur and honours, often inculcating in His excellent discourses that His kingdom was not of this world, nor His rewards to be bestowed in it, intending to lay the foundation of a truly noble, refined, and divine philosophy, and not of any pomp or palaces, any of the show, splendour, or luxury of the heathenish religions, for His disciples, or their successors to enjoy.

As we have not room for half the virtues of a clergyman in this paper, we shall defer the further prosecution of this subject till next Saturday; on which day, weekly, we shall endeavour to communicate something good to our readers, for the instruction of such as frequent coffee-houses on a Sunday.

SATURDAY, *April* 5, 1740.

—"*Movet tantæ pietatis imago*."[2]—VIRGIL.

THE APOLOGY FOR THE CLERGY,— *continued.*

CHAPTER II.

The next virtue which I shall mention is charity, a virtue not confined to munificence or giving alms, but that brotherly love and friendly disposition of mind which is everywhere taught in

1 Romans 12:3; I Corinthians 1:26; 4:13.

2 "May such an image of piety move you" (*Aeneid* 6.405).

Scripture. Thus the word *ἀγάπη*, which some versions render charity, is better rendered by others love, in which sense it is described by the Apostles in the 13th chapter of his first epistle to the Corinthians. "Charity suffereth long, and is kind; charity envieth not; charity vaunteth not itself, is not puffed up. Doth not behave itself unseemly, seeketh not her own, is not easily provoked, thinketh no evil. Rejoiceth not in iniquity; but rejoiceth in the truth. Beareth all things, believeth all things, hopeth all things, endureth all things."

First, then, a minister of the Gospel must forgive his enemies; "charity suffereth long, is not easily provoked, beareth all things, endureth all things." Thus Christ Himself saith, "If you do not forgive, neither will your Father in Heaven forgive your trespasses."[1] Indeed this is the characteristic of a Christian minister, and must distinguish him from the best of the heathens, who taught no such doctrine.

Secondly, "charity is kind;" or, as the Greek signifies, does good offices, behaves kindly; not confined to our wishes merely, but our actions, under which head I shall introduce liberality, a necessary qualification of any who would call himself a successor of Christ's disciples. By this virtue, which is generally called charity itself (and perhaps it is the chief part of it), is not meant the ostentatious giving a penny to a beggar in the street (an ostentation of which I do not accuse the clergy, having to my knowledge never seen one guilty of it), as if charity was change for sixpence, but the relieving the wants and sufferings of one another to the utmost of our abilities. It is to be limited by our power, I say, only....

Thirdly, "charity envieth not." This is a negative, and consequently excludes all who are tainted with it; but as this cursed disposition was in as great abhorrence among the heathens as among the Christians, I shall say no more of it than that it is a quality which cannot belong to a true disciple of Christ.

Fourthly, "it vaunteth not itself, is not puffed up, doth not behave itself unseemly." By which we may be assured that all pride is inconsistent with this quality; but as I have treated of

---

1 Matthew 6:15.

this already, under the head of its opposite virtue humility, which I placed first, as it is indeed the very introduction of Christianity, sufficiently signified, as I have there shown, by the birth of Christ, and by the election He made of His disciples, it is needless to repeat it again here.

Fifthly, "it seeketh not her own." By these words the Apostle plainly points out the forgiveness of debts, as before he hath done of injuries (for this is the plain meaning of the Greek, whatever forced construction may be put upon it)....

Sixthly, "charity thinketh no evil." It is void of suspicion, not apt to censure the actions of men, much less to represent them in an evil light to others. Hence we may judge how inconsistent that odious malignity, which is the parent of slander, is with the character of a true Christian disciple; a cursed temper of mind fitter for the devil and his angels, than for a professor of that love which was taught by Christ, and which Solomon had long before told us covered all sins.[1]

Seventhly, "rejoiceth not in iniquity." By this the Apostle doth not, I apprehend, point at that joy which sin may be supposed to give to an evil mind, in the same manner as virtue delights a good one: but rather to caution us against that feigned delight in sin, which we sometimes put on from a subserviency to great ones. By not rejoicing in iniquity is meant, not taking the wages of sinful men, nor partaking of their dainties at the expense of flattering them in their iniquity. This is a virtue, which as it becomes every Christian, so more particularly a minister of the Gospel, whose business it is to rebuke and reprove such men, not to fall in with, or flatter their vices, but,

Eighthly, "to rejoice with the truth." To rejoice in the company of good and virtuous men, without the recommendation of titles and wealth, or the assistance of dainties and fine wines. To give God thanks who hath revealed the truth to us, and to rejoice in all those who walk in it.

Ninthly, "charity believeth all things, hopeth all things." It is inclined to maintain good and kind thoughts of men. It is a stranger to all sourness and bitterness of mind, that moroseness

---

1 Proverbs 10:12.

of temper which seduces us to think evil of others; whereas, charity always turns the perspective,[1] with a friendly care to magnify all good actions, and lessen evil. It weighs all mankind in the scales of friendship, and sees them with the eyes of love.

Charity is all this, and he who falls short of any of these, falls short of charity, without which, the Apostle tells us, "That gift of prophecy, the understanding mysteries, all knowledge, all faith," nay, even martyrdom itself are nothing, profit nothing, nor will they make a man a Christian, much less a successor of Christ's disciples.[2]...

TUESDAY, *April* 15, 1740.

... No passion hath so much the ascendant in the composition of human nature as vanity: indeed, I could almost venture to affirm, that there is no ingredient so equally distributed amongst us as this, not even fear, of which my Lord Rochester asserts;[3] all men would show it if they durst; so I apprehended all men would show their vanity if they durst, and that we are not distinguished from one another by the degrees of these passions, but by the power of subduing, or rather concealing them: for good sense will always teach us, that by betraying either fear or vanity, we expose both to the attacks of our enemies.

This observation, perhaps, gave rise to an opinion that men were a sort of puppets, formed to entertain the gods by their ridiculous gestures, or, as Mr. Pope terms it, "made the standing jest of Heaven:"[4] for, as vanity is the true source of ridicule, it might possibly be imagined that so large and almost equal a proportion could be distributed among us for no other end. I have often thought that such wise men as conceal their vanity, make a large amends to themselves by feeding this passion with contemplation on the ridiculous appearance of it in others.

Vanity, or the desire of excelling, to cast it in a ridiculous

---

1 Telescope.

2 I Corinthians 13:2-3.

3 John Wilmot, Earl of Rochester, "A Satire against Reason and Mankind" (1675?), ll. 139-58. See above, p. 451, n. 2.

4 Epistle 3.4 of the *Moral Essays* (1731-35).

light (for it may be seen in one very odious, being perhaps at the bottom of most villainy, and the cause of most human miseries) may be considered as exerting itself two ways; either as it pushes us on to attempt excelling in particulars, to which we are utterly unequal, or to display excellence in qualities which are in themselves very mean and trivial. As I have before touched on the former of these, I shall at present only animadvert on the latter, or that species of vanity, which exerts itself in mean, indifferent, and sometimes vicious habits.

Hence it is, that in the country many gentlemen become excellent fox-hunters, or great adepts in horse-racing and cock-fighting; and in the town an admirable taste is discovered in dress and equipage; and that several persons of distinction are remarked for putting on their clothes well, whilst others are not a little vain in showing that, though fortune hath destined them to ride in coaches, they are nevertheless as fit to drive, or ride behind them.

Nay, there is an excellence (if I may so call it) in badness. A certain great genius hath laid down rules for the art of sinking in writing, or in other words, of writing as ill as possible, in which perfection our greatest poet hath thought fit to celebrate such as have chiefly excelled, in an epic poem;[1] nay, the numerous frequenters of Hurlothrumbo,[2] all acknowledge their pleasure arose from the exquisite badness of the performance, and many persons have exprest an impatience to read the Apology for the Life of Mr. Colley Cibber Comedian;[3] asserting, they are sure it must be the saddest stuff that ever was writ....

---

1 Pope's essay, *Martinus Scriblerus peri Bathous, or, the Art of Sinking in Poetry*, which Fielding attributed to Swift, appeared in 1728 as part of the third volume of *Miscellanies* by the Scriblerus Club. In the same year, the first version of *The Dunciad* was published, referred to here as an "epic poem."

2 Generally regarded as a satire of heroic drama, *Hurlothrumbo: or, The Super-Natural*, by Samuel Johnson of Cheshire, was hugely popular for a year or so after it opened at the Little Theatre in the Haymarket in March 1729.

3 See Introduction, p. 11.

From *An Essay on the Knowledge of the Characters of Men*

["An Essay on the Knowledge of the Characters of Men" was first published in *Miscellanies* on 7 April 1743, a three-volume collection including *A Journey from This World to the Next* and *The Life of Mr. Jonathan Wild the Great*.]

... Those who predicate[1] of man in general, that he is an animal of this or that disposition, seem to me not sufficiently to have studied human nature; for that immense variety of characters, so apparent in men even of the same climate,[2] religion, and education, which gives the poet a sufficient licence, as I apprehend, for saying that,

> "Man differs more from man, than from beast,"[3]

could hardly exist, unless the distinction had some original foundation in Nature itself. Nor is it perhaps a less proper predicament[4] of the genius of a tree, that it will flourish so many years, loves such a soil, bears such a fruit, &c., than of man in general, that he is good, bad, fierce, tame, honest, or cunning.

This original difference will, I think, alone account for that very early and strong inclination to good or evil, which distinguishes different dispositions in children, in their first infancy; in the most uninformed savages, who can have thought to have altered their nature by no rules, nor artfully acquired habits; and lastly, in persons who, from the same education, &c., might be thought to have directed Nature the same way; yet, among all these, there subsists, as I have before hinted, so manifest and extreme a difference of inclination of character, that almost obliges us, I think, to acknowledge some unacquired, original distinction, in the nature or soul of one man, from that of another....

---

1 Assert.

2 Region.

3 John Wilmot, Earl of Rochester, "A Satire against Reason and Mankind," (1675?), l. 224. See above, p, 451, n. 2.

4 Predication, assertion.

Thus while the crafty and designing part of mankind, consulting only their own separate advantage, endeavour to maintain one constant imposition on others, the whole world becomes a vast masquerade, where the greatest part appear disguised under false vizors and habits; a very few only showing their own faces, who become, by so doing, the astonishment and ridicule of all the rest.

But however cunning the disguise be which a masquerader wears; however foreign to his age, degree,[1] or circumstance, yet if closely attended to, he very rarely escapes the discovery of an accurate observer; for Nature, which unwillingly submits to the imposture, is ever endeavouring to peep forth and show herself; nor can the cardinal, the friar, or the judge, long conceal the sot, the gamester, or the rake.

In the same manner will those disguises, which are worn on the greater stage, generally vanish, or prove ineffectual to impose the assumed for the real character upon us, if we employ sufficient diligence and attention in the scrutiny. But as this discovery is of infinitely greater consequence to us; and as, perhaps, all are not equally qualified to make it, I shall venture to set down some few rules, the efficacy (I had almost said infallibility) of which, I have myself experienced. Nor need any man be ashamed of wanting or receiving instructions on this head; since that open disposition, which is the surest indication of an honest and upright heart, chiefly renders us liable to be imposed on by craft and deceit, and principally disqualifies us for this discovery....

The truth is, we almost universally mistake the symptoms which Nature kindly holds forth for us; and err as grossly as a physician would, who should conclude, that a very high pulse is a certain indication of health; but sure the faculty would rather impute such a mistake to his deplorable ignorance than conclude from it that the pulse could give a skilful and sensible observer no information of the patient's distemper.

In the same manner, I conceive the passions of men do commonly imprint sufficient marks on the countenance; and it is

---

1 Rank or class.

owing chiefly to want of skill in the observer that physiognomy is of so little use and credit in the world.

But our errors in this disquisition would be little wondered at, if it was acknowledged, that the few rules, which generally prevail on this head, are utterly false, and the very reverse of truth. And this will perhaps appear, if we condescend to the examination of some particulars. Let us begin with the instance, given us by the poet above, of austerity; which, as he shows us, was held to indicate a chastity, or severity of morals, the contrary of which, as himself shows us, is true.

Among us, this austerity, or gravity of countenance, passes for wisdom, with just the same equity of pretension. My Lord Shaftesbury tells us that gravity is of the essence of imposture.[1] I will not venture to say, that it certainly denotes folly, though I have known some of the silliest fellows in the world very eminently possessed of it. The affections which it indicates, and which we shall seldom err in suspecting to lie under it, are pride, ill-nature, and cunning. Three qualities, which when we know to be inherent in any man, we have no reason to desire any farther discovery to instruct us, to deal as little and as cautiously with him as we are able.

But though the world often pays a respect to these appearances, which they do not deserve; they rather attract admiration than love, and inspire us rather with awe than confidence. There is a countenance of a contrary kind, which hath been called a letter of recommendation;[2] which throws our arms open to receive the poison, divests us of all kind of apprehension, and disarms us of all caution: I mean that glavering[3] sneering smile, of which the greater part of mankind are extremely fond, conceiving it to be the sign of good-nature; whereas this is generally a compound of malice and fraud, and as surely indicates a bad heart, as a galloping pulse doth a fever.

---

1 Anthony Ashley Cooper, third Earl of Shaftesbury, *A Letter Concerning Enthusiasm* (1708) sec. 2.

2 Diogenes Laertius, a third-century Greek writer, states in his *Lives and Opinions of Eminent Philosophers* (5.18) that beauty is "a greater recommendation than any letter of introduction." He ascribes the saying to Aristotle.

3 Deceitful, flattering.

Men are chiefly betrayed into this deceit, by a gross, but common mistake of good-humour for good-nature. Two qualities, so far from bearing any resemblance to each other, that they are almost opposites. Good-nature is that benevolent and amiable temper of mind, which disposes us to feel the misfortunes, and enjoy the happiness of others; and, consequently, pushes us on to promote the latter, and prevent the former; and that without any abstract contemplation on the beauty of virtue, and without the allurements or terrors of religion. Now good-humour is nothing more than the triumph of the mind, when reflecting on its own happiness, and that, perhaps, from having compared it with the inferior happiness of others....

From the *Preface* to *David Simple*

[*The Adventures of David Simple: Containing An Account of his Travels Through the Cities of London and Westminster, in Search of a Real Friend* (1744), though immediately attributed to Fielding, was written by his sister Sarah (1710-68). Consequently, in a signed preface to the second edition later the same year, while admitting to "the correction of some small errors," he declined "the honour of this performance."]

... I have attempted, in my Preface to Joseph Andrews, to prove, that every work of this kind is in its nature a comic epic poem, of which Homer left us a precedent, though it be unhappily lost.[1]

The two great originals of a serious air, which we have derived from that mighty genius, differ principally in the action, which in the Iliad is entire and uniform; in the Odyssey, is rather a series of actions, all tending to produce one great end. Virgil and Milton are, I think, the only pure imitators of the former: most of the other Latin, as well as Italian, French, and English epic poets, choosing rather the history of some war, as Lucan and Sillius Italicus; or a series of adventures, as Ariosto, &c. for the subject of their poems.[2]

---

1 See Preface to *Joseph Andrews*.

2 Marcus Annaeus Lucanus and Silius Italicus were Roman epic poets of the first

In the same manner the comic writer may either fix on one action, as the authors of Le Lutrin, the Dunciad, &c.; or on a series, as Butler in verse, and Cervantes in prose have done.[1]

Of this latter kind is the book now before us, where the fable[2] consists of a series of separate adventures, detached from and independent on each other, yet all tending to one great end; so that those who should object want of unity of action here, may, if they please, or if they dare, fly back with their objection, in the face even of the Odyssey itself.

This fable hath in it these three difficult ingredients, which will be found on consideration to be always necessary to works of this kind, viz., that the main end or scope be at once amiable, ridiculous, and natural.

If it be said that some of the comic performances I have above mentioned differ in the first of these, and set before us the odious instead of the amiable; I answer, that is far from being one of their perfections; and of this the authors themselves seem so sensible, that they endeavour to deceive the reader by false glosses and colours, and by the help of irony at least to represent the aim and design of their heroes in a favourable and agreeable light.

I might further observe, that as the incidents arising from this fable, though often surprising, are every where natural (credibility not being once shocked through the whole), so there is one beauty very apparent, which hath been attributed by the greatest of critics to the greatest of poets, that every episode bears a manifest impression of the principal design, and chiefly turns on the perfection or imperfection of friendship; of which noble passion, from its highest purity to its lowest falsehoods and disguises, this little book is, in my opinion, the most exact model....

---

century, who wrote the *Pharsalia* and *Punica* respectively. The Italian writer Ludovico Ariosto, in his *Orlando Furioso* (1532), traces tales of knightly adventure in the context of the war between Charlemagne and the Saracens.

1 *Le Lutrin* (1674) by Nicholas Boileau-Despréaux; *The Dunciad* (1728; 1743) by Alexander Pope; *Hudibras* (1663; 1664; 1678) by Samuel Butler; *Don Quixote* (1605; 1615) by Miguel de Cervantes Saavedra.

2 Plot.

From the *Preface* to *Familiar Letters*

[Fielding contributed a preface and five letters (40-44) to *Familiar Letters between the Principal Characters in David Simple, and Some Others*, a work written largely by his sister Sarah and published on 10 April 1747.]

... But in reality the knowledge of human nature is not learnt by living in the hurry of the world. True genius, with the help of a little conversation, will be capable of making a vast progress in this learning; and indeed I have observed, there are none who know so little of men as those who are placed in the crowds either of business or pleasure. The truth of the assertion, that pedants in colleges have seldom any share of this knowledge, doth not arise from a defect in the college, but from a defect in the pedant, who would have spent many years at St. James's[1] to as little purpose: for daily experience may convince us, that it is possible for a blockhead to see much of the world, and know little of it.

The objection to the sex of the author hardly requires an answer: it will be chiefly advanced by those who derive their opinion of women, very unfairly, from the fine ladies of the age; whereas, if the behaviour of their counterparts, the beaus, was to denote the understanding of men, I apprehend the conclusion would be in favour of the women, without making a compliment to that sex. I can of my own knowledge, and from my own acquaintance, bear testimony to the possibility of those examples which history gives, of women eminent for the highest endowments and faculties of the mind. I shall only add an answer to the same objection, relating to David Simple, given by a lady of very high rank, whose quality is, however, less an honour to her than her understanding. "So far," said she, "from doubting David Simple to be the performance of a woman, I am well convinced it could not have been written by a man."

In the conduct of women, in that great and important business of their lives, the affair of love, there are mysteries, with

---

1 St. James's coffee-house. See above, p. 258, n. 1.

which men are perfectly unacquainted: their education being on this head in constraint of, nay, in direct opposition to truth and nature, creates such a constant struggle between nature and habit, truth and hypocrisy, as introduce often much humour into their characters; especially when drawn by sensible writers of their own sex, who are on this subject much more capable than the ablest of ours....

From *Tom Jones*

[*The History of Tom Jones*: *A Foundling* (originally entitled *The Foundling*) was published in six volumes around 3 February 1749. So keen was demand for it that three further editions were published before the end of the year.]

BOOK II, CHAPTER 1

Showing what kind of a history this is; what it is like, and what it is not like.

THOUGH we have properly enough entitled this our work, a history, and not a life; nor an apology for a life, as is more in fashion;[1] yet we intend in it rather to pursue the method of those writers who profess to disclose the revolutions of countries, than to imitate the painful and voluminous historian who, to preserve the regularity of his series, thinks himself obliged to fill up as much paper with the detail of months and years in which nothing remarkable happened, as he employs upon those notable eras when the greatest scenes have been transacted on the human stage.

Such histories as these do, in reality, very much resemble a newspaper, which consists of just the same number of words, whether there be any news in it or not. They may likewise be compared to a stage coach, which performs constantly the same course, empty as well as full. The writer, indeed, seems to think

1 In all probability Colley Cibber's autobiography is again the target. See Introduction, p. 11.

himself obliged to keep even pace with time, whose amanuensis he is ...

Now it is our purpose, in the ensuing pages, to pursue a contrary method. When any extraordinary scene presents itself (as we trust will often be the case), we shall spare no pains nor paper to open it at large to our reader; but if whole years should pass without producing anything worthy his notice, we shall not be afraid of a chasm in our history; but shall hasten on to matters of consequence, and leave such periods of time totally unobserved....

BOOK VI, CHAPTER 1

Of love.

IN our last book we have been obliged to deal pretty much with the passion of love, and in our succeeding book shall be forced to handle this subject still more largely. It may not, therefore, in this place be improper to apply ourselves to the examination of that modern doctrine by which certain philosophers, among many other wonderful discoveries, pretend to have found out that there is no such passion in the human breast....

To avoid, however, all contention, if possible, with these philosophers, if they will be called so, and to show our own disposition to accommodate matters peaceably between us, we shall here make them some concessions, which may possibly put an end to the dispute.

First, we will grant that many minds, and perhaps those of the philosophers, are entirely free from the least traces of such a passion.

Secondly, that what is commonly called love, namely, the desire of satisfying a voracious appetite with a certain quantity of delicate white human flesh, is by no means that passion for which I here contend. This is indeed more properly hunger; and as no glutton is ashamed to apply the word love to his appetite, and to say he LOVES such and such dishes, so may the lover of this kind with equal propriety say he HUNGERS after such and such women.

Thirdly, I will grant, which I believe will be a most acceptable concession, that this love for which I am an advocate, though it satisfies itself in a much more delicate manner, doth nevertheless seek its own satisfaction as much as the grossest of all our appetites.

And, lastly, that this love, when it operates towards one of a different sex, is very apt, towards its complete gratification, to call in the aid of that hunger which I have mentioned above; and which it is so far from abating, that it heightens all its delights to a degree scarce imaginable by those who have never been susceptible of any other emotions than what have proceeded from appetite alone.

In return to all these concessions, I desire of the philosophers to grant that there is in some (I believe in many) human breasts a kind and benevolent disposition which is gratified by contributing to the happiness of others. That in this gratification alone, as in friendship, in parental and filial affection, as indeed in general philanthropy, there is a great and exquisite delight. That if we will not call such disposition love, we have no name for it. That though the pleasures arising from such pure love may be heightened and sweetened by the assistance of amorous desires, yet the former can subsist alone, nor are they destroyed by the intervention of the latter. Lastly, that esteem and gratitude are the proper motives to love, as youth and beauty are to desire, and, therefore, though such desires may naturally cease, when age or sickness overtakes its object, yet these can have no effect on love, nor ever shake or remove, from a good mind, that sensation or passion which hath gratitude and esteem for its basis.

To deny the existence of a passion of which we often see manifest instances, seems to be very strange and absurd; and can indeed proceed only from that self-admonition which we have mentioned above; but how unfair is this! Doth the man who recognizes in his own heart no traces of avarice or ambition conclude, therefore, that there are no such passions in human nature? Why will we not modestly observe the same rule in judging of the good as well as the evil of others? Or why, in any case, will we, as Shakespeare phrases it, "put the world in our own person?"[1]

Predominant vanity is, I am afraid, too much concerned here. This is one instance of that adulation which we bestow on our own minds, and this almost universally. For there is scarce any man, how much soever he may despise the character of a flatterer, but will condescend in the meanest manner to flatter himself.

To those, therefore, I apply for the truth of the above observations, whose own minds can bear testimony to what I have advanced....

[Source: *The Complete Works of Henry Fielding, Esq.*, ed. William Ernest Henley, 16 vols. (1903; New York: Barnes & Noble, 1967).]

---

1 From Benedick's speech in act two, scene one of *Much Ado About Nothing* (1598?).

Appendix E: History of the Publication

1. During Fielding's lifetime, five authorized and at least two unauthorized editions of *Joseph Andrews* appeared in Great Britain. On the Continent, moreover, translations of the work were soon available in French, German, Danish, and Italian. Of the five authorized versions, which were published in London by Andrew Millar, the first four are considered authoritative in that Fielding was quite clearly involved in their revision. For the final one, however, although the title page states that the edition was "Revised and Corrected," whatever changes took place are almost certainly the work of the compositor.

The first edition of *Joseph Andrews* reached the bookstalls on 22 February 1742. Encouraged by its reception, after fairly extensive "Alterations and Additions by the Author," a second edition went to press within months. Although its authorship was an open secret, Fielding's name did not appear on the title page of the book until the third edition, which was published in early 1743. However, this edition and the fourth one of 1748, representing Fielding's final revision, indicate only limited authorial changes. Indeed in these two editions, as well as in the unauthoritative fifth one of 1751, it is apparent that a fair number of printer's errors have been introduced.

2. The following excerpt is to be found in Charles F. Partington, *The British Cyclopædia of Biography* (London, 1837) 1. 706. According to the story, the poet James Thomson introduced Fielding to the publisher Andrew Millar who, heeding his wife's recommendation, agreed to purchase the manuscript of *Joseph Andrews*. After a good dinner at a coffee-house in the Strand, the negotiations began in earnest:

> "I am a man," said Millar, "of few words, and fond of coming to the point; but really, after giving every consideration I am able to your novel, I do not think I can afford to give you more than 200 *l.* for it." "What!" exclaimed Fielding, "two hundred pounds!" "Indeed, Mr.

> Fielding," returned Millar, "indeed I am sensible of your talents; but my mind is made up." "Two hundred pounds!" continued Fielding in a tone of perfect astonishment; "*two hundred pounds* did you say?" "Upon my word, Sir, I mean no disparagement to the writer or his great merit; but my mind is made up, and I cannot give one farthing more." "Allow me to ask you," continued Fielding with undiminished surprise, "allow me, Mr. Millar, to ask you, whether you are *serious*?" "Never more so," replied Millar, "in all my life; and I hope you will candidly acquit me of every intention to injure your feelings, or depreciate your abilities, when I repeat that I positively cannot afford you more than two hundred pounds for your novel." "Then, my good Sir," said Fielding, recovering himself from this unexpected stroke of good fortune, "give me your hand; the book is yours."[1]

Although this amusing anecdote has likely been much improved in the telling, the basic facts may well be true. In any event, by early January Millar had placed the copy with the printer Henry Woodfall the elder, who was apparently instructed to run off 1,500 sets of the novel. This is quite clear from his ledger, which includes the following item:

> Feb. 15, 1741/2. History of the Adventures of Joseph Andrews, &c., 12mo., in 2 vols., No. 1500, with alterations.

Accordingly, after a week and more of advertising in the newspapers, and certain "alterations" made by Fielding in the proofs, the first edition of *Joseph Andrews* appeared on 22 February.

3. The formal assignment of the copyright for *Joseph Andrews* was postponed until 13 April, when Fielding signed over to Millar all rights and titles to three of his works: *A Full Vindica-*

---

1 This story is quoted in Martin C. Battestin with Ruthe R. Battestin, *Henry Fielding: A Life* (London: Routledge, 1989) 325. Partington mistakenly told it of *Tom Jones*.

tion of the Dutchess Dowager of Marlborough, *Miss Lucy in Town*, and *Joseph Andrews*. The document is written by the author himself in the legal jargon of the day, and witnessed by the Reverend William Young, the original of Parson Adams. On the back of it, Millar notes the sum for each piece, £5. 5*s*. being paid to Fielding for the pamphlet, £10. 10*s*. for the farce, and £183. 11*s*. for the novel. The full text of the agreement is as follows:

> Know all Men by these Presents that I Henry Fielding of the Middle Temple Esq[r] for and in Consideration of the Sum of one hundred ninety nine Pounds six Shillings of lawful Money of Great Britain to me in Hand paid by Andrew Millar of S[t] Clement[s] Danes in the Strand Bookseller, the Receipt whereof is hereby acknowledged, and of which I do acquit the said Andrew Millar his Execrs and Assigns have bargained sold delivered assigned and set over, and by these Pres[ents] do bargain sell deliver assign and set over all that my Title Right and Property in and to a certain Book printed in two Volumes known and called by the Name and Title of the History of the Adventures of Joseph Andrews and of his Friend M[r] Abraham Adams written in Imitation of the Manner of Cervantes Author of Don Quixotte, and also in and to a certain Farce called by the Name of Miss Lucy in Town a Sequel to the Virgin unmasqued, and also in and to a certain Pamphlet called a full Vindication of the Dutchess Dowager of Marlborough [&c] with all Improvements, Additions or Alterations whatsoever which now are or hereafter shall at any time be made by me or any one else by my Authority to the said Book Farce or Pamphlet, to have and to hold the said bargained Premises unto the said Andrew Millar his Exrs Admrs or Assigns to the only proper Use and Behoof of the said Andrew Millar his Exrs Admrs or Assigns for ever, and I do hereby covenant and with the said Andrew Millar his Exrs Admrs and Assigns that I the said Henry Fielding the Author of the said bargained Premises have not at any time heretofore

done committted or suffered any Act or thing whatsoever by means whereof the said bargained Premises or any Part thereof is or shall be impeached or incumbered in any wise and I the said Henry Fielding for myself my Exrs Admrs and Assigns shall warrant and defend the s[d] bargained Premises f[or] ever against all Persons whatsoever claiming under me my Exrs Admrs or Assigns. In witness whereof I have hereunto set my Hand and Seal this 13 of April 1742.

Signed sealed and delivered by the
within named Hen: Fielding the
Day and year within mentioned
in the Presence of W[m] Young Hen. Fielding
W[m] Hawkes [Seal][1]

4. *Joseph Andrews* was first published in two pocket-sized duodecimo volumes costing six shillings bound. The title page is reproduced on page 508.

1 Cited in the General Introduction to *Joseph Andrews*, ed. Martin C. Battestin (Middleton, CT: Wesleyan UP, 1967) xxx–xxxi.

THE

HISTORY

OF THE

ADVENTURES

OF

JOSEPH ANDREWS,

And of his FRIEND

Mr. *ABRAHAM ADAMS.*

Written in Imitation of

The *Manner* of CERVANTES,

Author of *Don Quixote.*

IN TWO VOLUMES.

VOL. I.

LONDON:

Printed for A. MILLAR, over-against *St. Clement's Church,* in the *Strand.*

M.DCC.XLII.

The title page above is reproduced courtesy of the Bodleian Library, Oxford University.

Appendix F: Early Reception[1]

[Although *Joseph Andrews* was an immediate success, with a second edition called for within months of the first publication, the critical response was limited and, not surprisingly, fairly mixed. The initial reaction was registered largely through personal letters, and centred on Fielding's "lowness" and truth to "nature." The character of Parson Adams was also an important issue, both in relation to the Anglican clergy and real life more generally. But by the early 1750s, in essays and reviews as well as through public and private letters, the debate had broadened to include more detailed literary discussions about such questions as the true nature of comedy in fiction and the author's claim to having created a new kind of writing.]

1. Letter from Dr. George Cheyne to Samuel Richardson, 9 March 1742.

... had Feilding's [*sic*] wretched Performance, for which I thank you. It will entertain none but Porters or Watermen....

[Source: Alan D. McKillop, ed., *Samuel Richardson: Printer and Novelist* (Durham: U of North Carolina P, 1936) 77.]

2. Letter from Thomas Gray to Richard West, April 1742.

... I have myself, upon your recommendation, been reading Joseph Andrews. The incidents are ill laid and without invention; but the characters have a great deal of nature, which always pleases even in her lowest shapes. Parson Adams is perfectly well; so is Mrs. Slipslop, and the story of Wilson; and throughout he shews himself well read in Stage-Coaches, Country Squires, Inns and Inns of Court. His reflections upon high people and low people, and misses and masters, are very

1 For a fuller account see *Henry Fielding: The Critical Heritage*, ed. Ronald Paulson and Thomas Lockwood (London: Routledge, 1969). I am much indebted to this work for various material here.

good. However the exaltedness of some minds (or rather as I shrewdly suspect their insipidity and want of feeling or observation) may make them insensible to these light things, (I mean such as characterize and paint nature) yet surely they are as weighty and much more useful than your grave discourses upon the mind, the passions, and what not....

[Source: Paget Toynbee and Leonard Whibley, eds., *The Correspondence of Thomas Gray* (Oxford: Clarendon P, 1935) 1. 191-92.]

3. Letter from Catherine Talbot to Elizabeth Carter, 1 June 1742.

... I want much to know whether you have yet condescended to read Joseph Andrews, as I am well assured the character of Mr. Adams is drawn from one in real life:[1] if the book strikes you as it did me, you will certainly come up to town next winter, that you and I may join in contriving some means of getting acquainted with him. I have known you throw away your contrivance upon people not half as well worth it ...

[Source: *A Series of Letters Between Mrs. Elizabeth Carter and Miss Catherine Talbot From the Year 1741 to 1770* (London, 1809) 1. 16.]

4. Letter from William Shenstone to Richard Graves, 1742.

... —Indeed, as to the little parody you send, it would fix your reputation with men of sense as much as (greatly more than) the whole tedious character of Parson Adams. I read it half a year ago; the week after I came to town: but made Mr. Shuckburgh[2] take it again, imagining it altogether a very mean performance.—I liked a tenth part pretty well; but, as Dryden says of Horace (unjustly), he shews his teeth without laughing:[3]

---

1 That is, the Reverend William Young (see above, p. 256, n. 3).

2 A London bookseller.

3 *A Discourse concerning the Original and Progress of Satire* (1693), *Essays of John Dryden*, ed. W.P. Ker (Oxford: Clarendon P, 1900) 2.84.

the greater part is *unnatural* and *unhumourous*. It has some advocates; but I observe, those not such as I ever esteemed tasters. Finally, what makes *you endeavour* to like it?...

[Source: Duncan Mallam, ed., *Letters of William Shenstone* (Minneapolis: U of Minnesota P, 1939) 44.]

5. Letter from "The Chevalier Ramsay" to "Monsieur de Ramsay" (probably Michael Ramsay), 1 September 1742.

... I have read the first book of "The History of Joseph Andrews," but don't believe I shall be able to finish the first volume. Dull burlesque is still more unsupportable than dull morality. Perhaps my not understanding the language of low life in an English style is the reason of my disgust; but I am afraid your Britannic wit is at as low an ebb as the French....

[Source: John Hill Burton, *Life and Correspondence of David Hume* (Edinburgh, 1846) 1. 12, n. 1.]

6. Letter from Elizabeth Carter to Catherine Talbot, 1 January 1743.

... I must thank you for the perfectly agreeable entertaiment I have met in reading Joseph Andrews, as it was your recommendation that first tempted me to enquire after it. It contains such a surprizing variety of nature, wit, morality, and good sense, as is scarcely to be met with in any one composition; and there is such a spirit of benevolence runs through the whole, as I think renders it peculiarly charming. The author has touched some particular instances of inhumanity which can only be hit in this kind of writing, and I do not remember to have seen observed any where else; these certainly cannot be represented in too detestable a light, as they are so severely felt by the persons they affect, and looked upon in too careless a manner by the rest of the world.

It must surely be a marvellous wrongheadedness and perplexity of understanding that can make any one consider this complete satire as a very immoral thing, and of the most dangerous tendency, and yet I have met with some people who treat it in the most outrageous manner....

[Source: *A Series of Letters Between Mrs. Elizabeth Carter and Miss Catherine Talbot From the Year 1741* to *1770* (London, 1809) 1. 23-24.]

7. Letter to Caleb D'Anvers in *The Craftsman*, 1 January 1743.

... I Honour the Author of that facetious Work, *The History of* JOSEPH ANDREWS, for what he saith in his Preface, by Way of Explanation of the *Ridiculous, viz. What could exceed the Absurdity of an Author, who should write the* Comedy *of* Nero, *with the* merry *Incident of ripping up his Mother's Belly?* Nor do I know any one Piece of Criticism better worth the Study (if they study at all) of those Critics, or Orators, who endeavour to divert their Audience, or Readers, with pleasant Images of the public Calamities, and arch Charactures of those Persons to whom they are thought to be owing....

[Source: Reprinted in *Gentleman's Magazine* 13 (January 1743) 25.]

8. Pierre François Guyot DesFontaines, review of *Joseph Andrews*,[1] 1743.

A work appeared in England last summer which the English rank above all the novels that have ever been written, or at least place it on the same footing as the Adventures of *Don Quixote* and Scarron's *Roman comique*.[2] It is called *The History of the adventures of Joseph Andrews* ... It is a judicious and moral novel, full of wit and amusement and yet unsullied by libertine thought or sentiment, one which exalts in virtue and is

1 Translated from French. The Abbé DesFontaines also translated *Joseph Andrews* in 1743.

2 See above, p. 240, n. 4.

infinitely moving. The complications and episodes are charming. The denouement, prepared for from the beginning, is only realized in the final chapter, and cannot be guessed earlier; so until then the uncertain reader does not know what the outcome will be of the ingenious *imbroglio*. Moreover, nothing is so simple as the plot contrivance. The style is comic throughout, except for the passages where a tender and lawful love provides the interest. Joseph Andrews is the brother of Pamela, who appears on the scene near the end of the second volume with the English nobleman who has married her; this results in the most agreeable situations. In short, I have no fear of affirming that England has never before produced such a perfect example of this kind. But even more, this is not a vain and frivolous fiction; it instructs the reader in the customs of the English which are quite unknown in France, and informs us of a hundred curious particulars worthy of the attention of the gravest person. The author is Mr. Feilding [*sic*], one of the best comic poets of England. The dialogue is also an excellent part of the book. Everywhere there are lively, unaffected, fine, even delicate strokes, always amusing and sometimes burlesque....

[Source: *Observations sur les écrits modernes* 33 (1743) 189-91.]

9. Letter from William Shenstone to Lady Henrietta Luxborough, 22 March 1749.

... I return your two first volumes of Tom Jones which I have read with some Pleasure, tho' I see no Character yet y[t] is near so striking as Mr Abraham Adams. *That* was an *original*, I think; unattempted before, & yet so natural y[t] most people seem'd to know y[e] Man....

[Source: Duncan Mallam, ed., *Letters of William Shenstone* (Minneapolis: U of Minnesota P, 1934) 138.]

10. Letter signed "T. P." to "Mr. Urban" in *Gentleman's Magazine* 19 (June 1749) 252.

... Granting what is here insinuated to be true, that is, granting that the greatest treasure of critical learning that ever was offer'd to the world is, at present, thrown by as rubbish;[1] will it be any great wonder to a man, that considers how the world is run a madding after that fool parson *Adams*, and that rake *Tom Jones*? But the time will shortly come, when these trifles shall vanish in smoak, and the best edition of *Shakespeare* shall shine forth in all its glory....

11. Letter from Samuel Richardson to Lady Dorothy Bradshaigh, November-December 1749.

... So long as the world will receive, Mr. Fielding will write. Have you ever seen a list of his performances? Nothing but a shorter life than I wish him, can hinder him from writing himself out of date. The Pamela, which he abused in his Shamela,[2] taught him how to write to please, tho' his manners are so different. Before his Joseph Andrews (hints and names taken from that story, with a lewd and ungenerous engraftment) the poor man wrote without being read, except when his Pasquins, &c. roused party attention and the legislature at the same time[3] ... But to have done, for the present, with this fashionable author....

[Source: John Carroll, ed., *Selected Letters of Samuel Richardson* (Oxford: Clarendon P, 1964): 133-34.]

---

1 The writer is referring to William Warburton's edition of Shakespeare, which was brought out in eight volumes in 1747 and had not sold well.

2 *Pamela* had been published in November 1740, *Shamela* in April 1741.

3 See Introduction, pp. 9-10.

12. From *The Student, or, The Oxford and Cambridge Monthly Miscellany*, 20 January 1750.

... I have heard the character of Mr. ADAMS the clergyman, in an ingenious work of FIELDING'S, highly condemn'd, because, it seems, he *knew not the world*; and I am sorry to find that many of our divines are of the same opinion, and for the same reason.—But how much more laudable and agreeable figure does he now make, than he wou'd have done, had he been represented as ready to impose, as he is now liable to be impos'd upon? I know not what may be the opinion of others, but to me, his innocent ignorance of this world and its ways, demonstrates him not to have been a child of it, and if so, what they, his brothers of the cloth, who are so thoroughly knowing in this point, are, who is not able to guess?...

13. Francis Coventry, from *An Essay on the New Species of Writing founded by Mr. Fielding*, 1751.

... Sometime before this new Species of Writing appear'd, the World had been pester'd with Volumes, commonly known by the Name of Romances, or Novels, Tales, &c. fill'd with any thing which the wildest Imagination could suggest. In all these Works, Probability was not required: The more extravagant the Thought, the more exquisite the Entertainment. Diamond Palaces, flying Horses, brazen Towers, &c. were here look'd upon as proper, and in Taste. In short, the most finish'd Piece of this kind, was nothing but Chaos and Incoherency. *France* first gave Birth to this strange Monster, and *England* was proud to import it among the rest of her Neighbour's Follies. A Deluge of Impossibility overflow'd the Press. Nothing was receiv'd with any kind of Applause, that did not appear under the Title of a Romance, or Novel; and Common Sense was kick'd out of Doors to make Room for marvellous Dullness.... The disease became epidemical, but there were no Hopes of a Cure, 'till Mr. *Fielding* endeavour'd to show the World, that pure Nature could furnish out as agreeable Entertainment, as those airy non-entical Forms they had long ador'd, and persuaded the

Ladies to leave this Extravagance to their *Abigails*[1] with their cast Cloaths. Amongst which Order of People, it has ever since been observ'd to be peculiarly predominant.

His Design of Reformation was noble and public-spirited, but the Task was not quite so easy to perform, since it requir'd an uncommon Genius. For to tread the old beaten Track would be to no Purpose. Lecture would lose it's Force; and Ridicule would strive in vain to remove it. For tho' it was a Folly, it was a pleasing one: And if Sense could not yield the pretty Creatures greater Pleasure, Dear Nonsense must be ador'd.

Mr. *Fielding* therefore, who sees all the little Movements by which human Nature is actuated, found it necessary to open a new Vein of Humour, and thought the only way to make them lay down *Cassandra*,[2] would be to compile Characters which really existed, equally entertaining with those Chimæras which were beyond Conception. This Thought produced *Joseph Andrews*, which soon became a formidable Rival to the *amazing* Class of Writers; since it was not a mere dry Narrative, but a lively Representative of real Life. For chrystal Palaces and winged Horses, we find homely Cots and ambling Nags; and instead of Impossibility, what we experience every Day.

[Source: Francis Coventry, *An Essay on the New Species of Writing founded by Mr. Fielding*, ed. Alan D. McKillop, Augustan Reprint Society 95 (Los Angeles: U of California, 1962).]

14. Letter from Samuel Richardson to Anne Donnellan, 22 February 1752.

... Parson Young[3] sat for Fielding's Parson Adams, a man he knew, and only made a little more absurd than he is known to be. The best story in the piece, is of himself and his first wife....

---

1 From the name of the "waiting gentlewoman" in Francis Beaumont and John Fletcher's popular play *The Scornful Lady* (c. 1613).

2 See above, p. 42, n. 1.

3 See above, p. 256, n. 3.

[Source: John Carroll, ed., *Selected Letters of Samuel Richardson* (Oxford: Clarendon P, 1964): 197.]

15. Sarah Fielding (and Jane Collier?), from Prologue to Part the Fifth of *The Cry: A New Dramatic Fable* (London, 1754) 2. 168–70.

… To travel through a whole work only to laugh at the chief companion allotted us, is an insupportable burthen. And we should imagine that the reading of that incomparable piece of humour left us by *Cervantes*, can give but little pleasure to those persons who can extract no other entertainment or emolument from it than laughing at *Don Quixote's* reveries, and sympathizing in the malicious joy of [his tormentors] … and that strong and beautiful representation of human nature, exhibited in *Don Quixote's* madness in one point, and extraordinary good sense in every other, is indeed very much thrown away on such readers as consider him only as the object of their mirth. Nor less understood is the character of parson *Adams* in *Joseph Andrews* by those persons, who, fixing their thoughts on the hounds trailing the bacon in his pocket (with some oddness in his behaviour, and peculiarities in his dress) think proper to overlook the noble simplicity of his mind, with the other innumerable beauties in his character; which, to those who can understand *the word to the wise*,[1] are placed in the most conspicuous view.

That the ridiculers of parson *Adams* are designed to be the proper objects of ridicule (and not that innocent man himself) is a truth which the author hath in many places set in the most glaring light. And lest his meaning should be perversely misunderstood, he hath fully displayed his own sentiments on that head, by writing a whole scene, in which such laughers are properly treated and their* characters truly depicted. But those

* *Joseph Andrews*, book iii. chap. 7. The characters are an old half-pay officer, a dull poet, a scraping fiddler, and a lame *German* dancing master.

1 A refrain in *The Cry*.

who think continual laughter, or rather sneering, to be one of the necessary ingredients of life, need not be at the trouble of travelling out of their depths to find objects of their merriment: they may spare themselves the pains of going abroad after food for scorn; as they may be bless'd with a plenteous harvest ever mature and fit for reaping on their own estates, without being beholden to any of their neighbours....

16. Arthur Murphy, from *Gray's Inn Journal*, 31 August 1754.

... The Dispute that subsisted among the learned for a considerable Time and is perhaps not yet determined, *viz.* Whether Ridicule is a Test of Truth, is, in my humble Opinon, extremely idle and frivolous; the Faculty of Reason, which compares our Ideas, and sustains or rejects the various Affirmations concerning them, being the sole Judge of Truth, however complicated the Means may be by which it gains its End. I have often wondered, that neither *Aristotle*, *Tully*, nor *Quintilian*, have given a just and adequate Definition of Ridicule. To say that it consist [*sic*] in raising our Laughter, at some Turpitude, is a very insufficient Account of the Matter. Mr. *Fielding*, in his Preface to his *Joseph Andrews*, has thrown some Light upon the Matter, but as he places the Source of it in Affectation, he appears to me not to have taken a comprehensive Survey of his Subject. I apprehend the Ridiculous may be formed, where there is no Affectation at the Bottom, and his Parson *Adams* I take to be an Instance of this Assertion.

The best and most accurate Definition I have ever met with of the Ridiculous is in a note of Doctor *Akenside's* to his excellent Poem *on the Pleasures of Imagination.*[1] "*That, says he, which makes Objects ridiculous is some Ground of Admiration or Esteem connected with other more general Circumstances, comparatively worthless or deformed; or it is some Circumstances of Turpitude or Deformity connected with what is in General excellent or beautiful; the inconsistent Properties existing either in the Objects themselves, or in the Apprehension of the Person to whom they relate, implying Sentiment*

1 Mark Akenside, *The Pleasures of Imagination* (1744), revised as *The Pleasures of the Imagination* (1757).

or Design, and exciting no acute or vehement Emotion of the Heart."...

The Emotions here intended are Laughter and Contempt, and these it is the Business of Comedy to excite, by making striking Exhibitions of inconsistent Circumstances, blended together in such a thwarting Assemblage, that a gay Contempt irresistably shall take Possession of us....

17. Arthur Murphy, from *Literary Magazine*, 15 February-15 March 1757.

... The primary intention of farce is, and ever ought to be, to promote laughter by scenes of pleasantry. It does not from hence follow that an author has a right to pursue every whimsical caprice that enters into his imagination, or that he is licenced to indulge himself in a frolicsome deviation from nature. Farce is to Comedy what the *caricatura* is to the just and regular designs of portrait-painting:[1] a feature may allowably be exaggerated beyond its due proportion; a cast may be given to the eye; the nose may be represented shapeless, defects may be heightened into enormities, and the drapery may be so fantastically imagined as to give a burlesque appearance to the whole form; but in the general air of the countenance and the figure, there must be still a regard to nature, and some touches of resemblance must be preserved to shew that it is not a non-existence, a mere creature of the writer's overheated imagination. The same rule will hold good with regard to the exhibition of farcical personages. Foibles may be enlarged, and even imaginary circumstances may be obtruded, in order to season the ridicule as highly as possible, and to give a kind of grotesque attitude to the portraiture. These touches of bizarre imitation sometimes occur in scenes of comedy, where exactness and truth are more in demand: and we likewise find something of this stile in picturing the manners of the comic romance, which is to comedy, what the sublime epic is to tragedy. This distinction is as old as *Aristotle*, and would in all

---

1 See Preface to *Joseph Andrews*.

probability be felt by every reader, had not the *Margites* of *Homer* unfortunately perished. For instances of farcical imitation there is no necessity of pointing out the *Bobadil* of *Johnson*, the Sir *Joseph Wittol* and *Nol Bluff* of *Congreve*,[1] together with many personages of *Shakespeare*. In the mock epic we may reasonably presume that there are many strokes of this overcharged painting in the *Don Quixote* of *Cervantes*, and in *Scarron's* comic romance. In the only writer of deserved estimation in this way among ourselves, it is not difficult to remember lineaments extended beyond their boundaries, without turning over the pages of *Joseph Andrews* and *Tom Jones* for the example; though in general it must be said of Mr. *Fielding* that the strokes of his brush are correct and reserved. If this liberty is taken in compositions of the highest comic, a farce writer may surely be allowed to "outstep the modesty of nature,"[2] in order to impress the signatures of ridicule more strongly on the mind, and thereby more powerfully to answer the primary intention of his work, which is raise a laugh.

[Source: *New Essays by Arthur Murphy*, ed. Arthur Sherbo (East Lansing: Michigan State UP, 1963) 119-20.]

18. Oliver Goldsmith, from *The Bee*, 10 November 1759.

... Instead, therefore, of romances, which praise young men of spirit, who go through a variety of adventures, and at last conclude a life of dissipation, folly, and extravagance in riches and matrimony, there should be some men of wit employed to compose books that might equally interest the passions of our youth, where such an one might be praised for having resisted allurements when young, and how he at last became lord mayor; how he was married to a lady of great sense, fortune, and beauty; to be as explicit as possible, the old story of Whittington, were his cat left out, might be more serviceable to the tender mind, than either Tom Jones, Joseph Andrews, or an

---

1 Ben Jonson, *Every Man in his Humour* (1598); William Congreve, *The Old Bachelor* (1693).

2 *Hamlet* 3.2.19.

hundred others, where frugality is the only good quality the hero is not possessed of....

[Source: *Collected Works of Oliver Goldsmith*, ed. Arthur Friedman (Oxford: Clarendon P, 1966) 1. 461.]

19. Samuel Johnson, in conversation, 6 April 1772.

... Fielding being mentioned, Johnson exclaimed, "he was a blockhead"; and upon my expressing my astonishment at so strange an assertion, he said, "What I mean by his being a blockhead is that he was a barren rascal." BOSWELL. "Will you not allow, Sir, that he draws very natural pictures of human life?" JOHNSON. "Why, Sir, it is of very low life. Richardson used to say, that had he not known who Fielding was, he should have believed he was an ostler. Sir, there is more knowledge of the heart in one letter of Richardson's, than in all 'Tom Jones.' I, indeed, never read 'Joseph Andrews.'" ERSKINE. "Surely, Sir, Richardson is very tedious." JOHNSON. "Why, Sir, if you were to read Richardson for the story, your impatience would be so much fretted that you would hang yourself. But you must read him for the sentiment, and consider the story as only giving occasion to the sentiment."—I have already given my opinion of Fielding; but I cannot refrain from repeating here my wonder at Johnson's excessive and unaccountable depreciation of one of the best writers that England has produced....

[Source: James Boswell, *The Life of Johnson*, ed. George Birbeck Hill and L. F. Powell (Oxford: Clarendon P, 1934) 2. 173-75.]

20. Letter from Hannah More to a sister, 1780.

... I never saw [Samuel] Johnson really angry with me but once; and his displeasure did him so much honour that I loved him the better for it. I alluded rather flippantly, I fear, to some witty passage in Tom Jones: he replied, "I am shocked to hear you quote from so vicious a book. I am sorry to hear you have read it: a confession which no modest lady should ever make. I scarcely know a more corrupt work." I thanked him for his correction; assured him I thought full as ill of it now as he did, and had only read it at an age when I was more subject to be caught by the wit, than able to discern the mischief. Of Joseph Andrews I declared my decided abhorrence. He went so far as to refuse to Fielding the great talents which are ascribed to him, and broke out into a noble panegyric on his competitor, Richardson; who, he said, was as superior to him in talents as in virtue; and whom he pronounced to be the greatest genius that had shed its lustre on this path of literature....

[Source: *Memoirs of the Life and Correspondence of Mrs. Hannah More* (New York, 1834) 1. 101.]

21. James Harris, from "Philological Inquiries," 1781.

... His JOSEPH ANDREWS and TOM JONES may be called *Master-pieces* in the COMIC EPOPEE, which none since have equalled, tho' multitudes have imitated; and which he was peculiarly qualified to write in the manner he did, both from his *Life*, his *Learning*, and his *Genius*.

Had his *Life* been *less irregular* (for irregular it was, and spent in a promiscuous intercourse with persons of *all* ranks) his *Pictures of Human kind* had neither been so *various*, nor so *natural*.

Had he possest less of *Literature*, he could not have infused such a spirit of *Classical Elegance*.

Had his Genius been less fertile in *Wit and Humour*, he could not have maintained that *uninterrupted Pleasantry*, which never suffers his Reader to feel fatigue....

[Source: James Harris, *Works* (London, 1781) 3. 163-64.]

22. Sir John Hawkins, from *The Works of Samuel Johnson* (London, 1787) 1. 214-15.

... At the head of these [writers of fiction] we must, for many reasons, place Henry Fielding, one of the most motley of literary characters. This man was, in his early life, a writer of comedies and farces, very few of which are now remembered; after that, a practising barrister with scarce any business; then an anti-ministerial writer, and quickly after, a creature of the duke of Newcastle, who gave him a nominal qualification of *100 l.* a year, and set him up as a trading-justice, in which disreputable station he died. He was the author of a romance, intitled "The history of Joseph Andrews," and of another, "The Foundling, or the history of Tom Jones," a book seemingly intended to sap the foundation of that morality which it is the duty of parents and all public instructors to inculcate in the minds of young people, by teaching that virtue upon principle is imposture, that generous qualities alone constitute true worth, and that a young man may love and be loved, and at the same time associate with the loosest women. His morality, in respect that it resolves virtue into good affections, in contradiction to moral obligation and a sense of duty, is that of lord Shaftesbury vulgarised, and is a system of excellent use in palliating the vices most injurious to society. He was the inventor of that cant-phrase, goodness of heart, which is every day used as a substitute for probity, and means little more than the virtue of a horse or a dog; in short, he has done more towards corrupting the rising generation than any writer we know of.

Select Bibliography

Bibliographies

Battestin, Martin C. "Fielding." *The English Novel: Select Bibliographical Guides*. Ed. A. E. Dyson. London: Oxford UP, 1974. 71-89.

——. "Henry Fielding." *The New Cambridge Bibliography of English Literature*. Ed. George Watson. Cambridge: Cambridge UP, 1971. 2: 925-48.

Hahn, H. George. *Henry Fielding: An Annotated Bibliography*. Metuchen, NJ: Scarecrow P, 1979.

Morrissey, L. J. *Henry Fielding: A Reference Guide*. Boston: G. K. Hall, 1980.

Stoler, John A., and Richard D. Fulton. *Henry Fielding: An Annotated Bibliography of Twentieth-Century Criticism, 1900-1977*. New York: Garland, 1980.

Biographies

Battestin, Martin C., with Ruthe R. Battestin. *Henry Fielding: A Life*. London: Routledge, 1989.

Cross, Wilbur L. *The History of Henry Fielding*. 3 vols. 1918. New York: Russell & Russell, 1963.

Dudden, F. Homes. *Henry Fielding: His Life, Works, and Times*. 2 vols. 1952. Hamden, CT: Archon, 1966.

Rogers, Pat. *Henry Fielding*. 1979. New York: Scribner's, 1983.

Thomas, Donald. *Henry Fielding*. London: Weidenfeld & Nicolson, 1990.

General Studies

Alter, Robert. *Fielding and the Nature of the Novel*. Cambridge: Harvard UP, 1968.

——. *Rogue's Progress: Studies in the Picaresque Novel*. Cambridge: Harvard UP, 1964.

Bartolomeo, Joseph F. *A New Species of Criticism: Eighteenth-Century Discourse on the Novel.* Newark, NJ: U of Delaware P, 1994.

Battestin, Martin C. *The Providence of Wit: Aspects of Form in Augustan Literature and the Arts.* Oxford: Clarendon P, 1974.

Bell, Ian A. *Literature and Crime in Augustan England.* London: Routledge, 1991.

Blanchard, Frederic T. *Fielding the Novelist: A Study in Historical Criticism.* New Haven: Yale UP, 1926.

Booth, Wayne C. *The Rhetoric of Fiction.* 2nd ed. Chicago: U of Chicago P, 1983.

—. *The Rhetoric of Irony.* Chicago: U of Chicago P, 1974.

—. "The Self-Conscious Narrator in Comic Fiction Before *Tristram Shandy.*" *PMLA* 67 (1952): 163-85.

Braudy, Leo. *Narrative Form in History and Fiction: Hume, Fielding, and Gibbon.* Princeton: Princeton UP, 1970.

Butt, John. *Fielding.* Rev. ed. London: Longmans, Green, 1959.

Cleary, Thomas R. *Henry Fielding, Political Writer.* Waterloo, ON: Wilfrid Laurier UP, 1984.

Coley, William B. "The Background of Fielding's Laughter." *ELH* 26 (1959): 229-52.

Copley, Stephen, ed. *Literature and the Social Order in Eighteenth-Century England.* Beckenham, UK: Croom Helm, 1984.

Digeon, Aurélien. *The Novels of Fielding.* 1925. New York: Russell & Russell, 1962. Trans. of *Les Romans de Fielding.* 1923.

Dircks, Richard J. *Henry Fielding.* Boston: Twayne, 1983.

Frank, Judith. "Literacy, Desire, and the Novel: From *Shamela* to *Joseph Andrews.*" *The Yale Journal of Criticism* 6 (1993): 157-74.

George, M. Dorothy. *England in Transition: Life and Work in the Eighteenth Century.* London: Routledge, 1931.

—. *London Life in the Eighteenth Century.* 1925. Harmondsworth, UK: Penguin, 1992.

Golden, Morris. *Fielding's Moral Psychology.* Amherst: U of Massachusetts P, 1966.

Hatfield, Glenn W. *Henry Fielding and the Language of Irony*. Chicago: U of Chicago P, 1968.

Hulme, Robert D. *Henry Fielding and the London Theatre*. Oxford: Oxford UP, 1988.

Hunter, J. Paul. *Before Novels: The Cultural Contexts of Eighteenth-Century English Fiction*. New York: Norton, 1990.

——. *Occasional Form: Henry Fielding and the Chains of Circumstance*. Baltimore: Johns Hopkins UP, 1975.

Irwin, W. R. "Satire and Comedy in the Works of Henry Fielding." *ELH* 13 (1946): 168-88.

Johnson, Maurice. *Fielding's Art of Fiction: Eleven Essays on Shamela, Joseph Andrews, Tom Jones, and Amelia*. Philadelphia: U of Pennsylvania P, 1961.

Kropf, C. R. "Educational Theory and Human Nature in Fielding's Works." *PMLA* 89 (1974): 113-19.

Lynch, James J. *Henry Fielding and the Heliodoran Novel: Romance, Epic, and Fielding's New Province of Writing*. Rutherford, NJ: Fairleigh Dickinson UP; London: Associated U Presses, 1986.

Mace, Nancy A. *Henry Fielding's Novels and the Classical Tradition*. Newark, NJ: U of Delaware P; London: Associated U Presses, 1996.

Maresca, Thomas E. *Epic to Novel*. Columbus: Ohio State UP, 1974.

McKeon, Michael. *The Origins of the English Novel, 1600-1740*. Baltimore: Johns Hopkins UP, 1987.

McKillop, Alan D. *The Early Masters of English Fiction*. Lawrence: U of Kansas P, 1956.

Paulson, Ronald, ed. *Fielding: A Collection of Critical Essays*. Englewood Cliffs, NJ: Prentice-Hall, 1962.

——. *Satire and the Novel in Eighteenth-Century England*. New Haven: Yale UP, 1967.

Paulson, Ronald, and Thomas Lockwood, eds. *Henry Fielding: The Critical Heritage*. London: Routledge; New York: Barnes & Noble, 1969.

Preston, John. *The Created Self: The Reader's Role in Eighteenth-Century Fiction*. London: Heinemann, 1970.

Rawson, C. J. *Henry Fielding: A Critical Anthology*. Harmondsworth, UK: Penguin, 1973.
—. *Henry Fielding and the Augustan Ideal Under Stress*. 1972. Atlantic Highlands, NJ: Humanities P International, 1991.
—. *Order from Confusion Sprung: Studies in Eighteenth-Century Literature from Swift to Cowper*. London: Allen and Unwin, 1985.
—. *Satire and Sentiment, 1660-1830*. Cambridge: Cambridge UP, 1994.
Richetti, John. "The Old Order and the New Novel of the Mid-Eighteenth Century: Novelists and Authority in Fielding and Smollett." *Eighteenth-Century Fiction* 2 (1990): 203-18.
Sacks, Sheldon. *Fiction and the Shape of Belief: A Study of Henry Fielding, with Glances at Swift, Johnson, and Richardson*. 1964. Chicago: U of Chicago P, 1980.
Sherbo, Arthur. *Studies in the Eighteenth-Century English Novel*. East Lansing: Michigan State UP, 1969.
Sherburn, George. "Fielding's Social Outlook." *Philological Quarterly* 35 (1956): 1-23.
Scheuermann, Mona. "Henry Fielding's Images of Women." *The Age of Johnson* 3 (1990): 231-80.
Smallwood, Angela J. *Fielding and the Woman Question: The Novels of Henry Fielding and Feminist Debate 1700-1750*. Hemel Hempstead, UK: Harvester Wheatsheaf; New York: St. Martin's P, 1989.
Spacks, Patricia M. *Desire and Truth: Functions of Plot in Eighteenth-Century Novels*. Chicago: U of Chicago P, 1990.
Thornbury, Ethel M. *Henry Fielding's Theory of the Comic Prose Epic*. 1931. New York: Russell & Russell, 1966.
Uglow, Jenny. *Henry Fielding*. Plymouth, UK: Northcote House, 1995.
Varey, Simon. *Henry Fielding*. Cambridge: Cambridge UP, 1986.
Watt, Ian. *The Rise of the Novel: Studies in Defoe, Richardson, and Fielding*. Berkeley: U of California P, 1957.
Williams, Aubrey. "Interpositions of Providence and the Design of Fielding's Novels." *South Atlantic Quarterly* 70 (1971): 265-86.

Wright, Andrew. *Henry Fielding: Mask and Feast.* 1965. Berkeley: U of California P, 1966.

Studies on Joseph Andrews

Baker, Sheridan. "Fielding's Comic Epic-in-Prose Romances Again." *Philological Quarterly* 58 (1979): 63-81.

—. "Henry Fielding's Comic Romances." *Papers of the Michigan Academy of Science, Arts, and Letters* 45 (1959): 411-19.

Bartolomeo, Joseph F. "Interpolated Tales as Allegories of Reading: *Joseph Andrews*." *Studies in the Novel* 23 (1991): 405-15.

Battersby, James. "The Importance of Putting Joseph's Fanny on the Road." *Hypotheses* 6 (1993): 2-4.

Battestin, Martin C. "Fielding's Changing Politics and *Joseph Andrews*." *Philological Quarterly* 39 (1960): 39-55.

—. "Fielding's Revisions of *Joseph Andrews*." *Studies in Bibliography* 16 (1963): 81-117.

—. "Lord Hervey's Role in *Joseph Andrews*." *Philological Quarterly* 42 (1963): 226-41.

—. *The Moral Basis of Fielding's Art: A Study of Joseph Andrews.* Middletown, CT: Wesleyan UP, 1959.

Brooks, Douglas. "The Interpolated Tales in *Joseph Andrews* Again." *Modern Philology* 65 (1968): 208-13.

—. "Richardson's *Pamela* and Fielding's *Joseph Andrews*." *Essays in Criticism* 17 (1967): 158-68.

Campbell, Jill. " 'The exact picture of his mother': Recognizing Joseph Andrews." *ELH* 55 (1988): 643-64.

Cauthen, I. B., Jr. "Fielding's Digressions in *Joseph Andrews*." *College English* 17 (1956): 379-82.

Costa, Astrid Masetti Lobo. "Up and Down Stairways: Escher, Bakhtin, and *Joseph Andrews*." *Studies in English Literature, 1500-1900* 31 (1991): 553-68.

Donovan, Robert A. "*Joseph Andrews* as Parody." *The Shaping Vision*. Ithaca: Cornell UP, 1966. 68-88.

Ehrenpreis, Irvin. "Fielding's Use of Fiction: The Autonomy of *Joseph Andrews*." *Twelve Original Essays on Great English Novels*. Ed. Charles Shapiro. Detroit: Wayne State UP, 1960. 23-41.

Evans, James E. "Fielding, *The Whole Duty of Man*, *Shamela*, and *Joseph Andrews*." *Philological Quarterly* 61 (1982): 212-19.

Frank, Judith. "The Comic Novel and the Poor: Fielding's Preface to *Joseph Andrews*." *Eighteenth-Century Studies* 27 (1993-94): 217-34.

Goldberg, Homer. *The Art of Joseph Andrews*. Chicago: U of Chicago P, 1969.

—. "Comic Prose Epic or Comic Romance: The Argument of the Preface to *Joseph Andrews*." *Philological Quarterly* 43 (1964): 193-215.

—. "The Interpolated Stories in *Joseph Andrews* or 'The History of the World in General' Satirically Revised." *Modern Philology* 63 (1966): 295-310.

Jenkins, Owen. "Richardson's *Pamela* and Fielding's 'Vile Forgeries.'" *Philological Quarterly* 44 (1965): 200-10.

Knight, Charles A. "*Joseph Andrews* and the Failure of Authority." *Eighteenth-Century Fiction* 4 (1992): 109-24.

Kropf, Carl R. "A Certain Absence: *Joseph Andrews* as Affirmation of Heterosexuality." *Studies in the Novel* 20 (1988): 16-26.

Palmer, E. T. "Fielding's *Joseph Andrews*: A Comic Epic in Prose." *English Studies* 52 (1971): 331-39.

Paulson, Ronald. "Models and Paradigms: *Joseph Andrews*, Hogarth's *Good Samaritan*, and Fénelon's *Télémaque*." *MLN* 91 (1976): 1186-1207.

Reed, Walter L. "*Joseph Andrews* and the Quixotic: The Politics of the Classic." *An Exemplary History of the Novel*. Chicago: U of Chicago P, 1981. 117-36.

Reid, B. L. "Utmost Merriment, Strictest Decency: *Joseph Andrews*." *Sewanee Review* 75 (1967): 559-84.

Schneider, Aaron. "Hearts and Minds in *Joseph Andrews* and Parson Adams and a War of Ideas." *Philological Quarterly* 66 (1987): 367-89.

Spacks, Patricia Meyer. "Some Reflections on Satire." *Genre* 1 (1968): 22-30.

Spilka, Mark. "Comic Resolution in Fielding's *Joseph Andrews*." *College English* 15 (1953): 11-19.

Stephanson, Raymond. "The Education of the Reader in Fielding's *Joseph Andrews*." *Philological Quarterly* 61 (1982): 243-58.

—. " 'Silenc'd By Authority' in *Joseph Andrews*: Power, Submission, and Mutuality in 'The History of Two Friends.' " *Studies in the Novel* 24 (1992): 1-12.

Taylor, Dick, Jr. "Joseph as Hero in *Joseph Andrews*." *Tulane Studies in English* 7 (1957): 91-109.

Weinbrot, Howard D. "Chastity and Interpolation: Two Aspects of *Joseph Andrews*." *JEGP* 69 (1970): 14-31.

Weinstein, Arnold. "The Body Beautiful: *Joseph Andrews*." *Fictions of the Self: 1550-1800*. Princeton: Princeton UP, 1981. 114-28.

Wilner, Alene Fish. "Henry Fielding and the Knowledge of Character." *Modern Language Studies* 18 (1988): 181-94.

from the publisher

A name never says it all, but the word "broadview" expresses a good deal of the philosophy behind our company. We are open to a broad range of academic approaches and political viewpoints. We pay attention to the broad impact book publishing and book printing has in the wider world; we began using recycled stock more than a decade ago, and for some years now we have used 100% recycled paper for most titles. As a Canadian-based company we naturally publish a number of titles with a Canadian emphasis, but our publishing program overall is internationally oriented and broad-ranging. Our individual titles often appeal to a broad readership too; many are of interest as much to general readers as to academics and students.

Founded in 1985, Broadview remains a fully independent company owned by its shareholders—not an imprint or subsidiary of a larger multinational.

The interior of this book is printed on 100% recycled paper.